The Victor McCain Collection

The Victor McCain Collection

Books 1-3 of
The Victor McCain Thriller Series

By

Tony Acree

Hydra
Publications

The Hand of God
Copyright © 2013 by Tony Acree
All rights reserved.

The Watchers
Copyright © 2014 by Tony Acree
All rights reserved.

Nightmare
Copyright © 2015 by Tony Acree
All rights reserved.

The Speaker
Copyright © 2015 by Tony Acree
All rights reserved.

Printed in the United States of America

ISBN: 978-1-942212-60-7
Cover by Karri Klawiter

Hydra Publications
Goshen, Kentucky 40026
www.hydrapublications.com

Dedication

This book is dedicated to all the people
who said I'd never make it as a writer.

snicker

The Hand of God

Book One

Chapter One

It was 6 P.M. when the Devil walked into my office and had a seat.

Now when I say the Devil, I'm not talking figuratively. Lord knows that having spent the last five years as a bounty hunter, I've come face to face with every form of evil that walks on this scum-ridden planet: murderers, rapists, even a couple of freakin' child molesters. So I have more than a passing acquaintance with evil, of both the male and female varieties.

But no, in this case, I'm talking in the literal sense. You know, as in Satan, Lucifer, Beelzebub, the goddamned Father of all goddamned Lies. That Devil.

You're probably wondering if he was all red, with horns, a pointed tail and pitchfork. Sorry to disappoint you, but he wasn't. He looked like any other well-dressed bastard in a snazzy suit and shoes to match. OK, he did have a red tie, but I couldn't see any tail coming out his ass. He was around six feet tall, blond hair and icy blue eyes. Guess we know where Hitler got his ideas for all that superior race crap.

And I bet you're also wondering just how the hell I knew it was the Fallen Angel himself. I guess it was the same way Moses knew that the burning bush was really God and not just a couple of his buddies lighting the damned thing on fire and then pretending to be God while hiding behind the closest rock laughing. Let's put it this way, if the Devil walks through your door one day, you won't have any doubts either. Take my word for it.

Anyway, I'd had a good week and was just getting ready to leave and lock the place up, looking forward to taking the weekend off from chasing bad guys and heading down to Molly Malone's, when the door opened and in waltzed Satan, just as pretty as you please. He pulled up a chair near my desk and sat down flashing a row of pearly whites the Kardashian family would be proud of.

"Victor, you know who I am?" he said, eyebrows all arched and superior, although it was more of a proclamation than a question.

I nodded back and calmly opened the top right drawer of my desk and grabbed my Glock 9 millimeter I keep there in case of emergencies. I figured if this didn't qualify for an emergency then nothing would.

"You know that won't do you any good," he said.

He was right. Somehow I knew that. After all, for more than a couple of millennium at a bare minimum, people have wanted to kick Satan's backside with no success. I just knew it wouldn't do me any good.

But I pulled the gun out and shot the son-of-a-bitch right between the eyes anyway. Blamo!

A perfect gun powdered entry wound appeared smack dab between his eyes. But I could see no blood and no head explosion out the back, just a big hole and an annoyed look on Satan's formerly pristine mug.

Now you would think that a guy, after being shot in the head, would exhibit some sort of adverse effects, but not this time. And folks, that's just wrong.

I asked myself, "Why did I do that?" and the only thing I could come up with was that I was trying to score some brownie points with the big guy upstairs, you know, just in case I ever made it to the Heavenly gates.

Guess I should mention that's something else that happened right when he walked in. I became a full-fledged believer in God right there on the spot. I mean, if the Devil exists, you can bet to holy high heaven that God does, too.

Funny thing was, before then? I wasn't what one would call an overly "religious" person. To be honest, I never gave it much thought as to whether God existed or not. Life was what it was and no God was going to change that. So why should I worry about it? I think the only time I ever did talk about God was at the end of the night with my buddies down at the bar and I was usually dead ass drunk.

But right then and there I became what I guess you would call, born again. I immediately promised God that I would be a three times a week church going, down on my knees praying, holier than thou living son of a gun if I could just keep on breathing awhile longer. Amen.

And you know there was another thing that happened that I was surprised about, too. I wasn't out of my boots afraid and pissing my pants right there in my chair. After all, they don't come any more frightening than old Lucifer, right? But instead of being afraid? I felt edgy, and more alive. And I knew what he wanted.

"You can't have it," I said.

"I don't want it," he shot back.

"Huh?" And here people say I'm not a great conversationalist.

"I don't want your soul," he replied. His accent sounded like he'd lived here in Louisville all his life. I thought he was going to have a deep otherworldly kind of voice, or at least a British-sounding accent like in all those horror flicks where people get possessed and then commit all kinds of stupid evil acts. Seems the Devil always has a British accent.

"I'm confused," I said, and I'm sure it showed all over my face. "I just figured--"

"That's the problem with your feeble-minded people," he said smoothing out his lapel, still with that nasty bullet hole in his head, bugging me more now than it was obviously bothering him. "Always trying to figure things out. Idiots, really. But, if you're giving your soul away, sure, I'll take it. What I want, though, is to hire you. I want you to find someone for me."

Well, I couldn't help but feel a tad uncomfortable. I figured if the Devil needed help and he was looking at me, I was in a bit of a bind. "If that's all you want, the answer is No. Not even if hell itself freezes over. By the way, has that ever happened?" I couldn't help but be curious.

He ignored the question and continued, "Oh, you'll take the job," he said with a confidence that made the hair stand up all over my freakin' body. It pissed me off.

"You can keep your 30 pieces of silver or whatever in hell else you plan on offering me," I said, "I won't do it."

Then he pulled out a sheet of paper from his inner suit pocket. "This," he said holding the paper out so I could see it, "Is a soul contract."

"You've got to be kidding me," I said. I always thought that was just some more movie made up bullshit, like in that bad Brendan Frazier movie. "But you've already mentioned you don't want my soul. So I guess lying is something that comes natural for someone in your line of work?"

"This isn't for you, my friend," he said. I didn't like that he was calling me 'friend.' "This one has already been signed: by your big brother, of all people."

Now, when my mom introduces Michael Christopher McCain as my big brother, people have a tendency to snicker. I'm six and a half feet tall and nearly three-hundred pounds and 'big bro' has to work hard to reach five foot nothing and one-hundred and forty pounds soaking wet. The only thing that makes him bigger is that he's six years older than me and is a bigger prick.

My yahoo of a brother spends most of his life trying to overcompensate for his shortcomings, with one over-the-top scheme after another. After high school, hell, you name it, he tried it: selling Amway, timeshares, cars, and even opening up his own line of car washes, but the sucker investors took the bath, not the damned cars.

Yes, sir. Vic McCain's older brother struck out more times than a blind one-armed batter hitting in a hurricane. But that all seemed to change about five years ago.

He opened this import-export business. I asked how he was planning on exporting the manure I was sure he was spreading around. Next thing you know? His warehouses are full of stuff and he's moving goods around the world—and making money hand over fist.

He went from driving a beat up old Honda to a brand spanking new Lexus 400 convertible. He even loaned me the cash to get my bounty hunting business up and running. With interest, of course.

But now, with the Devil sitting in front of me dangling this piece of paper, I knew just how Mikey boy had broken the ole' piggy bank. Step right up: One soul for sale. Attention Wal-Mart shoppers. And Satan closed the deal and was more than willing to make another purchase.

I never thought a smile could be so...evil looking. The Devil's eyes lit up like the sparkles the sun makes when it hits ripples on a mountain lake. It was in stark contrast to that bull's-eye blackened hole I tattooed on his forehead.

He spoke. "You see, in twenty-four hours your brother will die. It will be horrible, and he will suffer. Badly. I'm honestly looking forward to it. It will be bloody. There will be screaming. He'll sound like a little girl in the end, pleading for his soul."

"Oh, and I want you to know how this works," he said leaning a bit forward. "One of the conditions of his contract is that his heart must still be beating when I claim my possession. He must be aware I have taken his everlasting soul." He leaned back into the chair comfortably and continued. "I think it's more fun for me that way, really. Seeing the realization that a man has abandoned his God for a pittance of earthly glory. It just makes me... giddy."

"But let me be perfectly clear, the writhing pain and torment he will be experiencing when I rip his heart from his chest will be minuscule compared to what the rest of eternity will hold for him." He leaned forward and gave me a barracuda grin. "Let me give you just a taste of what lies ahead for your brother."

And he snapped his fingers.

In an instant, I was nailed to a wall by my hands, shoulders, stomach, knees, and feet by large barbed spikes. My arms were above my head and my legs were spread eagle to near the breaking point. Flames were dancing all over my body and I could smell the sour odor of my flesh as it burned away to expose the muscle and bone underneath. Worst of all, there was a mirror on the wall across from me and I was watching it all happen. I couldn't look away, no matter how hard I tried. My whole body just started to melt and slide downward, like a wax museum statue tossed on this year's Halloween bonfire. And I could see it all and I howled as my nervous system sent the pain from the heat crashing into my brain. My lungs were scorched as I breathed in the flames and I wished I would die. But I didn't.

The next instant I was standing up back in my office. Sweat flowed out from every pore of my body and my heart thundered inside my ears. My stomach tried hard to reverse engines with today's lunch, but I resisted. The smell of sulfur still clogged my nose and lungs as my breath was coming in great 'Please, Lord, let the air back in my body' wheezes. I fought, but finally lost the battle as I vomited into a garbage can next to my desk. I rubbed my arms as the pain lingered from my flesh being set on fire. I couldn't blink from the shock I just experienced. It may have only been seconds? It felt like forever.

The Devil looked casually down at his hands and thumbed over his well-manicured nails. "Anyway," he said, "That's what will happen, over and over for eternity, to your only brother unless you do exactly what I say."

I'm not overly close to my brother, honestly. But dear God, I can't let this happen to him. I can't.

I dropped down in my big swivel chair because, quite frankly, my legs were going all jelly doughnuts on me. I tried to get my mind around what was going on, but something didn't make any sense.

I said, "Why me? Why can't you find this guy? Hell, why can't you find anyone on God's green earth any time you want?"

"It's not *God's* green earth," he snarled, anger flashing through those ice blue eyes, "It's mine. He may hold sway in Heaven…for the moment. But not here." My eyes opened up a bit and my breathing stopped, but then he took a moment and regained his composure, so I did, too.

"Besides," he said, "It's not a man that I need: it's a woman. And finding her is not something I can just 'do'. Not even the so-called Almighty can just tap the shoulder of anyone He needs. People, with their damned free will, have to be found. And I don't want to waste my time. You mortals and your vanity in thinking that He and I both keep track of your every waking moment disgust me."

I couldn't help myself after that comment, so I said, "If anyone would know about vanity, I'm betting that would be you. After all, isn't that what got your sorry butt kicked to the basement to begin with? Thinking you were better than God? From what I've heard, you got yours handed to you in a sling." I was beginning to recover from my near hell experience and I would be damned, so to speak, if I was going to let him lecture me about good and evil. I mean, come on.

He stood slowly and reached inside his jacket. I tensed, ready for just about anything. I didn't know if he was going to strike me down with a bolt of lightning or throw sickness dust on me to make me suffer. All he did, though, was pull out another sheet of paper and drop it on the desk. I wondered how this paper was going to kill me.

He said, "This is who I want, her name and last known address. Bring her to me, here, in twenty-four hours. If you do as I ask, I will tear up your brother's contract and his immortal soul will be returned to him. If you don't? Your brother will die and his soul will forever burn in hell."

"Why?" I said. "What do you want this woman for?"

"The reasons are my own. Just have her by six tomorrow evening." Opening the door, he turned back. "Make sure she's alive, Victor. If she comes to me otherwise…"

He let the thought trail off. "I get the picture, butt-head."

The Devil looked at me and flashed those politician teeth. "I like your spirit, Vic," he said, and then he laughed, just like he always does in the movies, as he strolled out the door.

Chapter Two

For a moment, I just sat there, my mind numb with the implications of taking on a job for Satan. And more importantly, I thought about what it meant for my brother if I didn't.

I snatched up the phone and dialed my brother's cell. I just knew he was going to answer and I'd find out I was having one hell of a bad daydream brought on by a stressful job and way too many quarter pounders with cheese.

But when Mikey Boy answered the phone, it became clear all this was way too real.

"Oh Jesus Christ, Vic, I'm screwed!" he yelled into the phone. He sounded out of breath and as if he was running like his life depended on it. Bingo, Mikey Boy.

"Mikey, where are you? What's happening?"

Mikey let out a scream. It sounded like he fell, his cell phone bouncing across the ground. There was a moment of silence that had me gritting my teeth, picturing all manner of very bad things that could be happening to him when Satan picked up my bro's phone and said, "You're wasting time, Victor. Don't you have better things to do right now?"

The line went dead. I just hope my brother didn't go dead with it. I slammed the receiver back down in frustration.

There had to be a way out of this, though for the life of me, I couldn't see what it was. All I could do, for now, was find the girl. That, at least, would give me some options. If I could find out why Satan wanted her, I might find the leverage I could use to free my brother and not hand over the girl. Helping Satan had to be bad for the world in general, the girl in particular. Somehow I had the feeling this wasn't going to be a stroll through the park.

Ninety percent of all bail jumpers are caught by bounty hunters, not cops, as we have advantages the cops don't. In most states, I don't need a warrant to bust your door down and drag your sorry ass to jail. I don't need an extradition hearing to take you across state lines. I just need the trunk of my car. When a felon signs on with a bail bondsman, he signs away any rights he might otherwise have expected.

But what the cops and I both need, in most cases, is time. It can take weeks, even months to catch some wayward criminal. I had twenty-four hours. And just what would be the chances of me catching her sitting at home, watching Oprah, just waiting for the bounty hunter of her dreams, to come waltzing through her door to whisk her away to a future life with the king of all evil, Satan? About as much chance as I have of getting a date with Sandra Bullock: El-Zippo, her mistake with Jessie James notwithstanding.

The information on the girl was typed on standard computer paper in regular black ink. The fact it wasn't done in blood was somehow disappointing.

The note was short and to the point: Miranda Olivia Chernenko, 540 South Third Street, Apartment 2A. That was it, a name and address. Thanks a whole heap there Satan, ole' buddy.

I fired up my computer and started a skip trace on Ms. Miranda. As I did, my mind wandered down a path foreign to any previous thinking I'd ever done. I mean, Christ, the Devil doesn't just sashay on in and tell you he needs you to do work for him…not unless there was something biblical associated with the request.

Biblical. Listen to me. I was thinking Molly Malone's for dinner not more than 30 minutes ago. Now the word biblical was consuming my thoughts. I laughed at myself for that one. Biblical. Bible. God. What did I know of God? As far as I knew, life was just a frickin' biological journey of birth, growth, and death, with a little sex in the middle there to pass the time and give a person a sense of belonging. If you were lucky, lots of sex. If you were really, really lucky, you died while having sex.

But now, it was different. Heaven was in the picture. Heaven…God…Jesus, what have I gotten myself into? Before the Devil showed up, life eternal meant nothing to me. Now, life eternal was looming over me like the executioner's ax.

I'd never really pictured myself as the strumming harps kind of guy. I wanted to live, and then die. Go out with the knowledge that that was it. That I'd done everything I could do. Now it was over. But Nooooooo. Now, there were the harps, pearly gates, sitting on clouds, strumming endlessly. I wondered if there was sex in heaven. I wondered a lot of things.

I snapped out of it as the computer beeped letting me know it was ready. I ran Miranda Olivia Chernenko through all the major databases: criminal check, social security, motor vehicle, Nexus-Lexus, etc. Nothing. Go figure. I Googled her and came up bupkis. As far as cyberspace was concerned, she didn't exist. And if you don't exist there, what type of life are you leading, anyways?

The street address, 540 South Third St. Apt. 2A, was down in Old Louisville, near the University of Louisville. I decided that trying to dig up anything else on her here was wasting time. Devil or no, my brother was in trouble and it looked like I was the only one in the world who could help. I grabbed my gun and my keys and walked over to the door the Devil had walked through a short time before.

I paused. If I turned the knob and walked through the door, would there be Hell or a hallway on the other side? Seemed to me there was a better than average chance I just died from a heart attack, with the Devil playing a cruel joke. He could be there in Hell laughing at me right now, which, I suppose, he was doing regardless.

Walking through the door would be like walking through the portal to the rest of my sorry existence. I decided, actually very quickly, it didn't make one goddamned bit of difference one way or the other. I've never been much on second guessing or worrying about things I'd no control over.

I grabbed the knob, turned it, and walked out into the hallway of the same building in which I'd been working for the last several years. No flames, no flickering shadows, no evilness… just the hard wood floors and taupe wall paint. "If this is Hell, it's bland," I said to myself as I flipped the light off in the hallway and walked out into the damp early evening air.

Chapter Three

Sitting in my car, waiting at the light in front of the Burger King, I looked at the address on the Devil's typed piece of paper. The only option available to me meant heading to her place. If she wasn't just sitting around waiting for the Devil to find her, I would toss the place and see what I could dig up. I mean, after all, how much trouble could I get myself into? I had the frickin' Devil as a client. What? Did I think the Louisville police force would be a big deal if they showed up? "I'm so sorry, officer, about the breaking and entering. But, I'm going to Hell soon. So I thought, why not?"

I shook my head, the light turned green. I turned and floored up the entrance ramp onto I-64. I made the fifteen miles to Spaghetti Junction in twelve minutes. Now there's a piece of highway that Satan must have had a hand in developing. I slowed a bit to make the off ramp onto I-65, but the tires of my red '69 Chevelle squealed constantly around the turn anyway. Two exits later I made my way into the part of town known as Old Louisville. Here the houses are beautifully maintained Victorian mansions from the late 1800s. The yards are small and usually bordered by black wrought iron fences with little spearheads on each one. Dickens would have fit right at home.

Today, many of these old brick homes are sectioned into duplexes or quad apartments for University students to inhabit. This was the case for number 540. I parked on the street staying just out of the glow of one of the many street lamps and locked my gun in the glove box. If I got busted while in the apartment, no use adding armed robbery to the charge. I walked up the 5 concrete steps to the large covered porch.

The white columns supporting the roof were adorned with hanging baskets of bleeding hearts and ivy, and the oval leaded glass on the front door seemed to sag in its black painted heavy wood frame. I turned the slightly tarnished brass knob and walked into the lighted foyer. So much for security.

There was a door on each side of the main entryway on the first level, 1A and 1B. There was a single antique glass lamp hanging from a decorative chain in the center of the twelve-foot ceiling. It illuminated the curved wooden banister and wooden steps going up, and then turned to continue on to the second floor. I looked at the paper again. 2A. I went up.

The upper foyer was identical to the lower, except it had a large double hung window with stained glass in the place of the front door and a soft single bulb light overhead. There were two apartments. I rapped softly on apartment 2A's door. I didn't expect anything, but wanted to alleviate any suspicions from the residents of 2B in case they heard my arrival.

When no one came to the door, I reached into my jacket pocket, pulled out my trusty set of lock picks, and made short work of the skeleton-keyed bolt. I was lucky. You always see guys busting these locks on TV in less time than it takes to get a beer from the fridge during a commercial, but they can be a pain in the ass sometimes.

I quickly and quietly opened the door half-way, and slid in. I shut it behind me, holding the knob in my hand so as not to make a click with the latch. Then I let the knob loose slowly, relocked the door, flipped a light switch on, and turned to look at the apartment.

Her place was very nice and not typical of the starving college students that cycled through this area every four years. Ethan Allen furniture filled the room, arranged in a manner that would make the finest of those wacko cable show interior decorators envious. A large brick fireplace crouched on the far wall, with an Oriental rug under the coffee table. Bistro lights over the breakfast bar marked the physical border between the gourmet kitchen and living room. The place smelled of fine leather. The place screamed money. One large window, the blinds partially drawn, looked out over a small side yard between this house and the next. But no girl.

I shut the blinds the rest of the way and went straight to the bedroom. Here it became clear this was a chick's place. No bachelor's pad in history was this neat. Her bedroom had the same quality of furniture I'd found in the living room: four poster bed, matching dresser and armoire. A computer desk was placed along one wall, a brand spanking new Dell (complete with twenty-one inch flat screen) parked on top. The annoying little Windows icon bounced around the PC gleefully in obvious screen saver mode. I stuck my head into the bathroom, just to make sure she wasn't hiding out in the shower. But again, no luck. I stood for a moment, looking around. Odd. I found no pictures or wall hangings anywhere in the room. I glanced back out into the main room. Same thing. Nada. Since when did any babe not have 'things' hanging on the walls? There were no pictures anywhere in the apartment. So, I still didn't have a clue what Ms. Chernenko looked like.

I tossed the room, emptying every dresser drawer, her armoire, and the one small closet. I didn't bother being neat about it, just throwing the stuff on the floor. I didn't have nearly enough time to be Mr. Clean. If I found her, I'd apologize. When I finished, I still found nothing giving me the least little bit of info on my mark, other than she dresses well, uses Channel No. 5 perfume, and is a neat freak. Won't she be happy when she gets home?

I moved to the PC, taking a seat in the small swivel chair, my ass feeling like it was going to sink right through it any moment. I moved the mouse and her desktop came to life. I just thanked God she didn't password protect her stuff. People will never learn.

I clicked on the icon and jumped straight to her email. This chick needed a spam filter in the worst sort of way. One email did jump out from the rest of the garbage littering her Inbox. It was dated today at 1 P.M., from someone using the name TheDevilMadeMeDoIt, with a subject title of *8 P.M. Tonight*. Bingo.

I double-clicked the email and the rest of it appeared. It read:.

I am willing to meet you. Tonight, 8 P.M., at The Down and Dirty Bar on Bardstown Road. How will I recognize you? This will be the only time I am willing to do this. If you are not there, don't contact me again.

That was it, short and sweet. No signed name. I closed the email and clicked on her Sent items. She sent a response at 1:06 P.M. indicating she would be there with her hair tied back in a red scarf and wait at the bar, so that he would know who she was.

I checked her machine for any other information. Her My Documents and My Pictures folder was as empty as a Hobo's soup pan. This woman truly had no life.

Something started to bother me. I glanced around the bedroom. Everything was showroom new, with not a nick, scratch, or dent of any kind. Even the PC was new.

I walked back out to the living room. All brand-spanking new. You could have been standing on a showroom floor, with the only thing missing being the price tags. Even the garbage can in the kitchen was empty. Something just didn't feel right.

It was then that my train of thought was derailed by a sound coming from the front door. Holy crap: someone was trying to pick the lock!

I flipped off the lights, plunging the room into near darkness. I took pleasure as whoever it was picking the lock took much longer than I did to break in. Finally, the lock made a soft click, followed by a moment of silence. I rested a finger on the door and could feel someone slowly turn the knob and open it.

I couldn't help but think this girl was turning out to be way too popular. I positioned myself behind the door. As it opened I knew immediately I was in trouble.

The hallway light no longer offered up its reassuring glow outside the door, having either been unscrewed or busted out, which left little doubt as to the intentions of the new folks.

My eyes, now adjusted to the darkness, allowed me to see three fairly large individuals move into the room. I had no doubt how I would handle this situation. They were in the apartment illegally, clearly up to no good. The mere fact I'd done exactly the same thing was beside the point. These guys were interfering with my objectives and that meant I needed to find out what they were doing here and why. If I'd brought my gun with me this would already be over, but I hadn't.

I got the feeling that just asking, "Hey fellas, just what the Sam hell you think you're doing?" wasn't going to work. Physicality was needed. When I was young, my father taught me that the person who fought fair when he was out numbered or when his or her life was on the line, was the chump that was going to get their ever lovin' ass kicked. Fighting by Marquis de Queensberry rules is for idealistic dreamers with good medical insurance.

I took one large step to the left, putting me right behind the three intruders. When fighting more than one guy there are several things to consider. Surprise is number one and I had it. They should have looked behind the door, but the dumb asses didn't. So they were sure as Hell going to be surprised when I lowered the boom on them. Second, you don't want a long-term fight. Hit them hard, fast and continuously and put as many of them on the ground as quickly as possible. Don't hold back. And lastly, you need to stay off the ground yourself. Once you go down, when outnumbered, you're staying down. So you need to choose a plan putting them on the ground while you remain King of the Mountain.

There may be no quicker way of taking a guy down from behind, short of using lethal force, than a kidney punch. The pain is intense, like being kicked in the balls. Hit them hard enough and the person is guaranteed to collapse and may fall into shock. It's possible to even kill someone with a kidney punch. Boxing outlaws the punch for a reason.

I hit the guy directly in front of me, rotated at the hips and shot my right arm out from my waist with enough force to take out a baby bull, hitting him in his lower back, on the right. He collapsed, screaming in pain, and dropped something to the ground he was holding in his hands. I shoved him into the guy on the left, taking them to the ground. As they fell, I saw a flash and heard a hiss as Taser darts flew by my head, hitting into the wall behind me.

Jesus, I hate those things. There are as much as fifty-thousand volts in one shot and just the thought of that much Ben Franklin juice coursing through my veins made me shiver. And it made me hesitate a fraction of a second, giving the one guy left standing his chance and he took it, connecting with a left cross to my jaw. I turned with the punch, reducing the blow, but it still stung like a nest of hornets had landed on my cheek. It staggered me back a step and I tripped over the other two guys, crashing down on top of Miss Chernenko's new coffee table, splintering it into firewood. So much for no scratches or dents in the furniture.

I rolled over and kicked out hard with both legs just as he bore down on top of me. He reversed directions, flying hard up and over the love seat, taking out a lamp for good measure.

I started to get to my feet. The guy I kidney punched was still down, while the other guy frantically searched for the missing item on the floor. He saw me rising and dove into me, taking me back off my feet, and believe me, that's no easy trick.

We thrashed about on the floor and he ended up on top of me, smelling of too much garlic and more than a touch of Kentucky bourbon. I shifted my weight, preparing to flip him, when I felt cold steel pressing against my throat.

"Brother, make one more move and I'll slice you cleaner than a Thanksgiving turkey." He remained on top of me, with only my right arm free, but I let my body relax. One, because he had a knife to my throat. Second, because even though I couldn't see his face, I knew who it was. That voice was all J.B.

James Allan Booker, J.B. to his friends and associates, is the second best bounty hunter in the area, right behind me, of course. A black man in his middle forties, J.B. has been around the block a few times. Growing up in the projects in Louisville's West End, his youth was spent dodging gangs, the law, and whoever else might want a piece of his hide.

Tough neighborhoods and tough situations were nothing to J.B. He was a survivor. After doing a stint as an MP in Uncle Sam's Army, he moved back to Louisville. Looking for work, a bondsman gave him a job hunting down jumpers. He was good at it and found out he liked it.

If there was a knock on J.B.'s resume, it was that his returned jumpers came back a little more banged up than most others. But who was going to complain about a bail skipper getting a few more bruises on the return trip.

"J.B., is that you, ole' buddy ole' pal?" I said in my most friendly how the hell are ya kind of tone.

"Well I'll be damned, Victor McCain." I could hear the surprise in his voice. "You really shouldn't have jumped me and my boys like that."

"My mistake, J.B. Let me buy you a beer and make it up to you."

"Uh-uh, Vic. You ain't movin' till you tell me just what you're doin' here. You must be after the same bitch we are, ain't you? Don't lie to me now."

The warning in his voice wasn't lost on me as his knife continued to press down on my neck, just this side of drawing blood. "Look, J.B., it's important I find the girl. I don't want any trouble with you and yours. Let's just chalk this up to stupid ass fate and let bygones be bygones. You find her first, I'll be there to shake your hand and call you the better bounty hunter. If I find her first…"

"Sorry Vic. Man offered me a lot of green to bring this piece of ass to him straight away. No ways I'm going to give you a chance to mess that up." He paused, and then continued, "I tell you what. Make you a deal. You work for me on this one and I'll split the money with ya. Say, seventy-five twenty-five."

Christ, guess this wasn't going to go well after all. "Let me ask you something, J.B. If our positions were reversed, would you agree to a deal like that? And why shouldn't it be fifty-fifty?" I was stalling, grasping at anything to keep him talking.

Laughing, he said, "Guess not. And no fifty-fifty. I have men to pay and mouths to feed. So if you don't take the offer, too bad. Tell me Vic, I'm guessing the blonde prick that hired me set you after the woman, too. But he wouldn't tell me what the bitch had done to piss him off. You have any ideas?"

All very civil with a knife to my throat. While I didn't think J.B. would slit my throat under normal circumstances, this situation was far from normal. Had Satan offered him a deal like mine? Or was it just pure unadulterated greed that had J.B. a quick motion away from sending me to the other side. Either way, I couldn't afford to wait and see how he would handle the situation.

I could hear the other two guys starting to stir, so time was up. "J.B., the Devil only knows why. But I need you to put your knife down and let me up. Can you do that for me?"

"Sorry, Vic. The Man offered me a ton of cash and I can't pass that up. I just have to figure out what to do with you until that happens. I don't want to cause you any permanent harm, but if you get in my way on this one, someone's going to get hurt and it sure as hell won't be me."

I said, "Thought you were going to say something like that. So let me apologize in advance. I hope you're still able to have a few more kids when this is over."

Unfortunately for J.B., my free hand now held what he'd been searching for: the other guy's Taser. Finding it lying just underneath the couch, I pressed it to J.B.'s crotch. Not hesitating, I pulled the trigger, his balls taking fifty-thousand volts straight up. His body began to spasm and I hurled myself up, throwing him off, with the knife dragging across my skin and drawing blood, but doing no real damage. As for J.B., I don't think he was going to feel much like doing the horizontal bop any time soon.

One of the other guys was just getting to his feet, but I beat him to it. I bull-rushed him, crushing him into the wall, and then dashed out the door. I went down the stairs, stumbling as much as walking, and rubbed my sore jaw where the guy had popped me. Nothing like getting the night off to a great start.

Chapter Four

The clock on the dash flashed 7:34 as I floored the Chevelle, pissed as all get out. I mean, it's bad enough my brother sells his soul to the Devil and I have to bail him out. Add the fact the only hope I have of finding his key to salvation is a woman I don't know, have no description of, and that my only chance of finding her is if she shows up at the Down and Dirty, and if she wears a red scarf and if, if, if.

But for Satan to also sick Booker and his gang onto this woman really ticked me off. I have to work in the same community as these guys. And let's face it, you Taser a guy in the nuts and he isn't likely to keep you on his frickin' Christmas card list. No sir, J.B. was going to want a piece of me and sooner rather than later. Count on it. Nothing like complications.

And why would Satan do that? Besides just being a mean son of a bitch. Did he think I couldn't get the job done? Was he hoping Booker would beat me to the girl and he could then keep my brother's soul as well? Hell, for all I know he was hoping the Beatles would get back together, John and George being dead notwithstanding.

All and all, I guess it really didn't matter much. I still had to find her and try and help my brother. And that's what really pissed me off more than anything. After tossing her place, I knew little more about her now than I did when I started.

I thought about the person she planned to meet, with an email name like Devil Made Me Do It sure sounded like Satan's kind of guy. I wondered if she was planning to sell her soul and this guy was some kind of soul wholesaler? Christ, this sucked.

By my watch, I would be at the Double D in fifteen minutes, and J.B. no more than 30 minutes behind me, at best, if he found the same email—probably less with his extra help and driving like a bat out of hell to catch me. I could only hope that Ms. Chernenko would be there early.

A short time later, I pulled into the parking lot. The place was just a square concrete slab, one story building. No lights illuminated either the parking lot or the building itself, with the exception of the purple neon sign mounted above the door proclaiming the name of the place, though both D's bounced between flickering and out. Who the hell thinks of these dumb-ass bar names, anyway?

Only three cars were parked in the lot: a '72 Monte Carlo with what looked like a gajillion miles on it, a late model Ford Taurus, and a black 2011 Mercedes SLS AMG. The Mercedes stood out like a pimple on a Victoria's Secret super model's face.

I parked the Chevelle next to the Mercedes and got out. I lit a cigarette and took a long drag. People keep telling me that one day they're going to kill me and I've thought about quitting. But tonight, it really didn't seem like black lung disease would be what I would die from. Not the way this day was going. I walked slowly to the door with the cigarette anchored in the corner of my mouth, pushed it open and stepped inside your standard bar.

Round wooden tables filled the center of a large single-room with booths slung along one side of the place. A casual glance told me only four people were there. A man and woman occupied one booth, and they didn't seem to give a rat's patootie about my entrance as they were deep in conversation.

The man was skinny, on the verge of emaciated, and wore a brown mesh baseball cap with a picture of a wrecking truck on the front advertising 'Mike's Towing.' The woman had ratty mid-length hair, no figure to speak of, and nearly as skinny as the man. Both were smoking Marlboro's as fast as they could get them lit, if the overflowing ashtray between them was any clue. Maybe they weren't aware of the city's no smoking ordinance. They were a striking couple and I guessed 'Monte Carlo and Taurus' as I dropped my cig to the floor, grinding it out with the heel of my boot.

There was a jukebox glowing in the corner with its yellow and purple neon bubble trim fighting to be seen through the smoke filled air. Motley Crue was playing, not loud enough to be annoying, but annoying anyway. Next to that, on the far wall, were two shut doors side-by-side with small black signs on them. One of the signs said "Men", the other "omen." There was a gap in the bar next to the 'omen's' room where the bartender could get through, and an opening in the wall beyond leading to a dimly lit back room.

Between the alcohol and the inside edge of the bar, standing there partially turned to the door and to the small portable TV that was mounted in front of the mirror amidst the bottle bleachers, was the bartender. A heavy set, unshaven man, his hairy arms protruded like limbs of a tree from the black t-shirt covering his barrel-chested body. I could just make out a faded Marine Corps tattoo on his left bicep, half-hidden by his shirt. The man bobbed and weaved slightly, sliding his head left then right, his fists clenching and then elevating slightly, while watching a boxing match on the TV.

On the outside edge of the bar, unevenly spaced along its length, were wooden low-back bar stools, all empty, save one. She sat facing the mirror but looking down, a long finger tracing the lip of an empty shot glass. Dressed for a night on the town in a black, mid-thigh evening dress, she slid a glance my way as I approached the bar, then went back to her shot glass. My eyes were drawn to legs any professional dancer would kill for. A red scarf held long blond hair pulled back into a ponytail. Bingo.

They say the path to Hell is paved with good intentions. I had to wonder if I was taking the first of my steps down that path. And then it hit me. I had no earthly idea what I should do next. With a regular perp that I have a legit reason for going after, I would just walk over, handcuff 'em, and drag their sorry ass out. But I didn't have that authority this time. If I forcefully carried her out of here it would be kidnapping. And while the Marlboro twins might not give me any trouble, the guy tending bar looked more than capable of slowing me down until the cops got here, if he got lucky.

I needed to try and come up with a reason to get her out of the bar and fast. J.B. would be here soon. So I needed something that would motivate the lovely Miranda on to her feet and out the door. What I needed was a good pick up line.

I thought of some of the bad pick up lines my brother used when we go bar hopping. Things like, "Excuse me. Do you want to screw or should I just apologize?" Or, "Hey baby, wanna go halves on a bastard?" Good old Mikey boy. He isn't a loser for nothing. I could always go literal and say, "Hey darlin', come with me tonight and I'll show you a Devil of a good time." To hell with it, winging it's always better anyway.

I'm a good enough looking guy. My last girlfriend said I look a little like Chris Hemsworth, the guy who played Thor in the recent comic book movie. Wearing my beat up Wrangler jeans, black T-shirt with the Bad Samaritan on the front, bomber jacket and boots, I think I'm better looking than he is, but he's richer and has the babes. Guess it's a wash.

Walking to the bar, I slid onto the barstool next to her, got the barkeeps attention and ordered a Miller. On the bar in front of her was a thin black case with gold hinges on the back and matching gold clasps on the front. It was about the size of a pool stick case, but a little longer. This was a bit confusing, since I didn't see any pool tables in this joint. And from her email, I couldn't for the life of me guess why she would be packing around her own stick.

I glanced into the mirror and our eyes met. Green eyes looked back into my baby blues. Mr. Happy started a full salute and I spent a moment trying to get my woody to understand this wasn't going to be his night.

I turned towards her and before I could say anything she said, "I'm not interested."

"I'm sorry, what was that?"

"I'm not interested," she said again.

"Interested in what?"

Her brow furrowed and she said, "In, well, you know."

"No," I said, pausing. "I don't."

She didn't have an accent I could place. Sounded like she might be from the east coast, but it wasn't thick. Her voice was on the soft side and just this side of a purr, carrying an almost sexual quality. This I knew was Mr. Happy's wishful thinking.

The bartender sat the beer in front of me and pointed to her glass. She shook her head No. He gave me a sympathetic look, and then went back to the TV and his boxing match.

She said, "Never mind."

"Oh. You thought I wanted to pick you up, take you back to my place and spend the rest of the night in bed. Sorry, I'd love to, but something tells me you're a terrific lover, and it intimidates me a little. I'd probably have performance anxiety, then things would get awkward and next thing you know it's all over town. So, no, you're safe on that account." I took a swig of my beer.

While she didn't exactly break out in a belly laugh, she did at least smile. She stole another glance at the mirror, watching the door. "He must be a real studley, the guy you're waiting on."

"One, who says I'm waiting on anyone? And two, if I was, who says it's a guy?"

"Well, you keep watching the door. Plus, women who look like you don't end up in dives like this by choice. Ergo, you're meeting someone. And, as far as you waiting for a woman? That would be wrong on so many different levels from this red-blooded-American-male's point of view. So you just can't be playing for the other team." I stuck my hand out. "I'm Vic."

"Ergo?" She smiled, taking my hand, her grip firm, her skin soft. My heart beat about a hundred times faster at her touch. "Miranda." And I now knew I had the right woman. I felt like a man who hit the lottery jackpot. I honestly didn't think I would find her this quickly.

I considered my next line when two things happened at almost the same time: Miranda slipped off her bar stool, wrapped her arms around my neck and kissed me deeper than any woman ever kissed me before. One hand slid up my neck and into my hair. Being the calm, cool and collected professional I am, I went with it. Like this kind of thing happened to me all the time, I returned the kiss with the same passion, my own hands moving to the small of her back, pulling her tightly against me.

The second thing that happened, just fractions before the kiss, was the door to the bar opened and a man, a Billy Idol wannabe with spiked blond hair and Elvis Presley sneer, stuck his head inside. Acne scars covered his face and it appeared he hadn't had a passing encounter with a shower in some time.

Miranda turned us so her back was to the door, watching him through nearly closed eyes using the mirror. The twerp leered at us for a moment, checked out the Marlboro couple and went back outside, closing the door.

The moment the door closed, Miranda broke off the kiss, picked up her case and a coat lying on the next bar stool, then headed for the far end of the bar into the back room, me one step behind her. If there were any questions about why she kissed me, there wasn't any longer.

The bartender said, "Hey! You can't go back there!" He grabbed for Miranda, but she ducked and eluded his grasp. When I pushed him out of the way, he took a step back and launched a roundhouse right hand that started back somewhere in Illinois.

He quickly learned the biggest difference between shadow boxing and real boxing. Shadows don't hit back. I stepped into the punch, taking the blow on my left shoulder and fired off two quick right hooks to his midsection, followed by a left cross to his chin and then, "Down goes Frazier! Down goes Frazier!"

By the time I got to the back room, Miranda was already out the door.

Chapter Five

Opening the door, I exited the Double D into a short parking lot for deliveries, lit by a powerful floodlight. One side was a dead end, with a dumpster taking up most of the space. A retaining wall followed the length of the alley. The only other thing in sight was a Harley Davidson Fat Boy motorcycle that I guessed belonged to the bartender, and Miranda, peeking around the far corner of the building.

The door closed behind me and I heard a loud snick as the bolt caught. Miranda turned and quickly ran back towards me. "I have to get back inside! Now!" she said, panic in her voice.

"No can do, sister," I said, trying the door knob. "It's locked. What's the problem?"

"The problem is I'll be dead soon if I don't get out of this alley!"

Running past, she began to climb up on the dumpster as the blond twerp came around the corner, sauntering our way. Looking at her, I said, "What? You're worried about this blond reject from the Lollipop Guild?"

Evidently I pissed Blondie off because he picked up the motorcycle and threw it at my head. At. My. Head.

I've spent a lot of time hanging with and tracking down members of the Hell's Angels and happen to know A Fat Boy weighs north of six-hundred pounds. Blondie couldn't have weighed more than a buck fifty, yet the bike flew by me like a Randy Johnson fastball. I ducked just in time and Miranda jumped off the dumpster, as the bike hit the top of it, leaving a huge dent in it and the bike. No doubt the bartender was having a really bad day—though he didn't know it yet.

"Dude, you have to lay off the steroids. It's leading to anger issues. Let me guess," I asked, "Too late for an apology and a group hug?"

Guess so. Growling like some rabid dog, he charged me. This threw me for a loop as most men run away from me, not towards me. Then again, I've never had anyone throw a bike at me, either. As he was crashing into me, I hit him hard with a two-handed blow to the back of his head, trying to end things right then and there. No dice. Lifting me off my feet and slamming me into a dumpster, he knocked the wind out of my sails. Jesus

Christ, the shot I gave him would have crippled most men. Yet, all he did was start to laugh.

He said, "Tough bastard, you are. But 'ole Eamon is tougher, don't you think?"

It was all I could do not to start gagging from the stench of his breath as it smelled like he'd been eating road kill for dinner. "First off," I said, "Talking about yourself in the third person points to some severe psychological issues. Second, man, you could use some Tic-Tacs."

I leaned back, then drove forward and struck him in the nose with a fierce headbutt. I heard his nose crunch and break, a smushed lump in the middle of his acne craters. He started giggling and tried headbutting me back, but I shifted my head at the last moment and he struck the side of the dumpster, leaving another huge dent.

I think he would have killed my ass right then and there, but Miranda tried running past him.-Blondie lunged at her, grabbing hold of her hair. A blonde wig came off in his hands as she spun away from him, revealing short red hair the color of a setting sun. In one fluid motion, she opened her case, and instead of a pool stick, her hand emerged holding a long, thin sword, its razor edge glinting in the spill of light from the backdoor bulb.

She made a slashing cut towards his hand, making Blondie jump back. Tossing the wig aside, he began approaching her cautiously, forgetting all about me. "Now Samantha, you want to be careful with that thing, girl. A child such as yourself ought not to be playing with a man's toy." He started dancing a little jig as he talked, trying to cut her off from the open end of the alley, but she continued circling, holding the sword in front of her, keeping him from blocking her escape.

"You took what wasn't yours to take," he chortled. "So they sent old Eamon to bring you back, they did. But they didn't say how or in what condition, don't you know. So if you don't put that pig sticker away, when I do take it from you, well, then I'm going to use it on you a few times, then have me fun with you. Show you what a real man is like."

"Eamon, I swear to God, you pull out your shortcomings and I'll slice it off and shove it down your throat." There was fear on her face, but the sword in her hands remained steady. She kept backing away from him, but he maintained the same pace.

Samantha? I know I'd had my helmet pummeled pretty hard, but what the hell? Guess Miranda wasn't her real name. At the moment, though, her name didn't make any difference. What mattered was that Blondie now had his back to me. Pushing my way to my feet, my back screamed in protest. Sometimes it just doesn't pay to get out of bed.

The Hand of God

I don't care what type of freak of nature you are, if you turn your back to me during a fight, I'm going to make you pay. Running a couple of steps I hurled myself in a flying tackle, hitting Blondie square in the back, jack-knifing him right in the middle, with me taking him off his feet. This resulted in his head being thrown backwards. Miranda stepped smoothly to the side, and swung the sword across in a deadly arc. Blondie's scream was cut off as his head went flying from his neck.

Chapter Six

When you separate a man's head from his shoulders, it's messy. The carotid artery will spray a jet of blood rhythmically as the heart continues to pump out the last few beats of life. The body will spasm, while the head drips a bloody trail wherever it lands. It's amazing what you can learn from watching the History Channel.

So imagine my surprise, when, instead of landing on a decapitated body, I found myself landing on a body turning to blackened stone. Bright red veins ran up and down his torso, like embers from a dying fire and the smell of sulfur filled the air. Crashing to the ground, the body disintegrated into a cloud of yellow ash, and his head rolled to a stop next to the retaining wall. Blondie's mouth was open in a frozen scream that would now never end. Kind of a reverse Venus De Milo.

Jumping up and backing away, I dusted off the coating of ash from my bomber jacket, I was beginning to feel like someone had just dropped me in the Twilight Zone. Miranda, or Samantha, or whoever the hell she was, started putting her sword back into its case.

Walking hurriedly up to me, she leaned in and kissed me on the cheek. "I can't thank you enough and I know you have questions, but I really have to go."

She turned and started to head out of the alley, with me following, the feeling of her lips lingering on my cheek. "Hey, wait up. You have to tell me what the hell just happened back here. I mean, this is beyond freaky. You can't just bail on me like this."

She kept walking, talking over her shoulder. "I don't have time. Believe me, the best thing you can do is get out of here and forget you ever met me."

She was going around the corner, when I pulled her back. Shrugging out of my grip, anger flashed in her eyes. She started to say something, until she noticed me put a finger to my lips and make a hush sound. I pointed to J.B. and his two goons, who were just going in the Double D's front door. They'd gotten here much quicker than I expected and J.B. looked ready to tear somebody's head off. Lucky me.

I said, "The guy you just off'd was sitting with those three in the

Escalade parked over there by my car and they were having an in-depth conversation. My guess is it had to be about you."

I told the lie so smoothly. As a bounty hunter, you often have to lie your way into and out of situations. It's part of the job and I usually never give it a second thought. Truth be told, most times its fun. I have a very creative imagination. But when I told this one, I could feel my stomach turn into knots as I could feel my soul sliding further down the slippery slope to Hell.

Waiting until they went inside, she took off running over to her Mercedes, but she wasn't going anywhere. Someone had slashed the tires on her car. I guess Blondie left her a nice 'screw you' parting gift. The other cars in the lot, including mine, were untouched. She started looking around wildly, her face etched in desperation.

Opening the passenger door to my car, I said, "Get in, I'll get you out of here." She looked at me and then at the bar, considering what waited for her inside. "Look lady, you need help and I can provide it. You want to wait for those three to come back out?"

She hesitated a moment longer and then decided to finally hop in my car. I did a quick reverse out of the parking lot, threw the shifter in drive, and slammed the pedal down, tearing out of the parking lot. I made several quick turns, keeping an eye on the rear view mirror. I saw no sign of J.B. or anyone else. My passenger was eyeballing her side mirror intently, watching for the same signs of pursuit. When there was none, she started to relax a bit, but continued to keep a tight grip on her sword case.

"You're pretty good with that thing," I said, nodding to the case.

"My father insisted I study martial arts, starting when I was very young. I had learned how to use a sword after getting my black belt."

"Strike one up for Dad. So, where to?"

She was still watching her mirror. "If you don't mind, just drive for a bit while I think about it."

I did as she asked, taking us on a path over towards I-65, changing directions occasionally. "Care to explain what just happened back there?"

Leaning her head against the window and closing her eyes, she said, "You wouldn't believe me if I told you."

"Lady, I just had a Smurf throw a motorcycle at my head, after which you go all Highlander on his ass and then he turns to stone? Considering my night so far, you might be surprised at what I'd believe. So try me." Glancing at her I could feel my heart catching. I'm guessing there have been wars fought over women who were not half so beautiful. And here I was, in less than twenty-four hours, supposed to hand her over to the Devil.

Opening her eyes she sat staring at me for a long moment, as if sizing me up and trying to decide whether to trust me or not. I waited. Finally, she took a deep breath, and said, "O.K. If you really want to know, the guy back there was a vampire."

I'm not sure what I expected, but this was nowhere near the top of the list. "You mean like Twilight or True Blood? That type of vampire?"

"No. Nothing like them at all. That's all Hollywood made up bullshit." She stopped, struggling with what she should, or shouldn't say next. "Let me ask you something. Do you believe in Heaven and Hell? God and the Devil?"

Before this morning, I thought, I could not have cared less. Now, they were both all too real. I said, "As a recovering Catholic, yeah, I guess I do. It's not like I've spent much time thinking about it, but sure. I believe in both. Why do you ask?"

"Here's the deal, O.K.?. When someone is evil, and I mean really, truly evil, after they die, sometimes Satan will offer them a second chance at life on Earth if they'll come back here and do his bidding. But if they die a second time, then their punishment is beyond horrific. Or if they don't do exactly what he asks them to do, they can be punished here, before they are called back to Hell. When they come back here, they don't age. They don't sleep."

"And the only way to kill them is to cut off their heads? Seriously?" I asked.

She shook her head. "That's just the most permanent way. You can burn them and turn them into human bonfires. Or you can bury them deep in the ground or in cement. They aren't dead when you do that, but they're out of the picture. If you chop an arm off, they just keep coming. But cut off their head and they're toast."

She said, more to herself than to me, "I don't believe this. I really, don't believe this. They've sent a goddamned vampire after me?"

She pulled her knees up to her chest, wrapping her arms around them and clung to her sword case. Her dress slipped down her thighs...but I tried not to notice "Look it, I know I sound nuts. But what I'm telling you is the truth. But there's more. And if I die, what I know dies with me. I have to tell someone."

I said, "Lay it on me."

She said, "Alright. Eamon was born in the early 1800's in Ireland. During the Great Famine, he would murder people for their food and that's one of the less offensive things he would do. Children disappeared near any town he lived in. When he couldn't find food to steal, he would eat people.

After he died, he got another chance and has been one of Satan's top foot soldiers. Or used to be. Now he's back in Hell where he belongs."

"He said you took something and they want it back. What'd you steal and who is 'they'?"

"The 'what' isn't important." She sat for a long time, gazing out the window, considering her reply. Then said, "The who is the Church of the Light Reclaimed."

"Never heard of them. Who the hell are they?"

"Devil worshippers." She glanced my way, waiting for a reaction, but I continued to drive. "Satan thinks of himself as the Angel of Light, hence the name. He's seeking what he thinks is his rightful place in Heaven, over God. And they're looking for me, and want me bad enough to send a vampire after me." She shivered, and not from the cold.

And not to mention at least two bounty hunters and who the hell else knows what. "Is that why you know so much about vampires, because you're a member?"

She said, "No. Well, I guess you could say that. My father told me about them. And he should know. He's Lucifer's pope."

My jaw dropped, but before I could ask anything else, her hand slid into a coat pocket and took out a cell phone and she started to make a phone call. I could hear a man's voice begin talking as the call went to voicemail. She said, "David, there've been complications. You have to call me back, please." Ending the call, she put her phone away.

"Is David the guy you were waiting for at the bar?"

"No. David's a reporter. He's involved in all this and helped me set up the meeting I was supposed to have tonight, but the guy never showed and I got Eamon instead."

"Who were you supposed to meet?"

"Just a guy David thought could help stop whatever the Church has planned. I'd never met the guy before."

"The vamp called you Samantha. I'm guessing Miranda's not your real name, is it?"

Letting out a another long sigh, she said, "No. It's not. I guess since my cover's blown, what difference does it make? My real name is Samantha." Laying a hand on my arm, she said, "Look, you've been really great helping me like this. But if you're anywhere near me when they catch me, they'll kill you. Once I get a hold of David and make a plan B, you can drop me off at a car rental place and I'll get out of your hair."

The Devil had offered me a deal: find the girl and save my brother's soul. Now I had her and all I had to do was take her to my office and wait until 6 P.M. tomorrow and hand her over. Job complete. I'd gotten lucky. Another five minutes later and Eamon would have taken her and my brother would have been damned for all time. But now that she sat in the seat next to me, I was torn. Not because she was drop dead gorgeous, although that never hurt. It's because I was now just as worried about my own soul as I was my brother's. Would doing this job for Satan see me end up in Hell? Driving, I sat and kept racking my brain for a way out, but couldn't remember any of my classes with Sister Margaret covering this situation. The only thing I did have was a little more time. So I decided playing it out a while longer and seeing what happened would be the best I could do.

I said, "They can try and kill me, but doing it will be a different matter. For what it's worth, seems you need someone to watch your back. I'm good at doing that. Besides, you're a hell of a kisser. Promise me another one when this is over and I'll help you out." I flashed her my best aw shucks grin.

Letting out a short bark of a laugh, she asked, "What do you mean you're good at it? You make a habit of rescuing damsels in distress?"

"Sort of. I work as a bouncer. Before that, a couple of tours with Special Forces in Iraq and Afghanistan. Watching your buddies back is the only way to stay alive. Helping you will be like old times, except you're a hell of a lot cuter than the guys in my unit. So I know how to handle myself in tough situations. Ask Eamon."

While I never worked as a bouncer, I served the time in the Middle East. One day I was just out of range of an exploding IED that unfortunately took the lives of my three closest friends in Iraq. Another day I shot a boy who raised a gun my direction while shouting at me in a language I couldn't understand. The wars, especially the one in Afghanistan, are Hell on Earth. Riding with Samantha I could feel my heartbeat quickening, like it did every time I thought about being over there.

Samantha brought me back to the here and now. "I seem to remember I was the one that cut off his head," she said.

"True, you're the one that turned him into a pigeon stand, but I'm the one that gave you the opportunity. Like I said, you need someone to watch your back. At least things around you aren't boring, and I miss the action. So what do you say?"

She thought about it. "O.K. You're right. I do need the help. I can't do this alone. I can pay you. Name your price."

I waved her off and smiled. "The kiss is payment enough for now," I said. "Let's see how things are in twenty-four hours. Who knows what the future holds?" I was beginning to feel only Heaven knew.

Chapter Seven

"So what next," I asked.

Biting her bottom lip, she thought for a moment and said, "It would sure help if David would call me back."

"If he won't, then let's go to him. Do you know where he lives?"

"Yes. He's renting a small home in Butchertown that backs up to Eastern Cemetery. He told the owners he wanted to write a book about the area."

"Vampires, devil worshipers, cemeteries? What's up with you people?"

She gave me the directions along with a Spock eyebrow raise and we headed that way.

"O.K. How about giving me the low-down on how this reporter fits in? Who does he write for and what's his angle in all of this?"

"The guy's a freelancer for several different Christian magazines and newspapers. About two months ago, he had gotten wind of something the Church was planning called the Exodus Project. He has a source, but all the source could tell him was the Project involved doing something that would hurt Christian schools in the South, while at the same time starting a religious war between Christians and Muslims, and that it would be going down here in Louisville. So he started looking for a way to get inside the Church for more information."

"And he found you. How exactly? Craig's List for Satanists?"

Shrugging one beautiful shoulder she said, "Close enough. I spend a lot of time reading blogs, including some about the Church. He posted on several of them. Over the course of a couple of weeks we struck up a conversation. He had dropped a few hints about the Exodus Project in some emails and it got me curious, so I started nosing around. David and I met a couple of times over the last few weeks."

"How does digging around in Church business square with you being a cheerleader for Satan?" I found myself watching her, her face moving in and out of shadows created by passing street lights and I could feel my heart shifting, my soul slipping.

Shaking her head she said, "I'm hardly a cheerleader. As a matter of fact, I'm an atheist. Or, at least I was. The only reason I'm a member of the Church is because my dad is one. To me, God and the Devil have always been like Santa Claus or the Easter Bunny: figments of the imagination. When I found out my dad worshiped the Devil, I just thought he was weird, you know? Then again, I thought people who believed in God were weird. So when he asked me to help with Church stuff I did. But since I've been poking around, I've discovered some things that have had me questioning everything I thought I knew. Now I do think Satan exists, but I'm not sure God does."

"How can you have one without the other? Yin, Yang, all that bullshit? If the Devil exists then, ergo, God does, too, does he not?"

"Not when one of them is dead," she said. "Look around you: wars, murders, rape, abuse. And what has God done to stop it? Not a damn thing. You see the Devil's fingerprints everywhere. But how about God? Ever since they nailed his Son up on a couple of wooden ties, there's been nothing for at least two-thousand years."

Thinking about what she was saying, it didn't ring true for me. The Devil isn't all powerful and if God was dead, he sure as hell would be the one calling all the shots. And in our brief meeting, Satan seemed pissed as all get out at God. But it's not like I could tell Samantha the truth.

"Well, like I said, I'm a recovering Catholic, but I still believe in the Big Man upstairs. So do you think your dad knows that the church sent a vamp after you?" I asked.

"Nothing happens in that church that he doesn't know about." She rubbed her eyes with the heel of her hands as she tried to stop the tears from falling.

"Wow. That's harsh." I thought about my own dad, who had to track me down on some of my wild nights when I was a teenager out on the town. My mother would be worried sick. To think a father would send something like Eamon after his own daughter made him one royal son of a bitch.

We had a few more minutes until we reached David's house. "If you don't mind my asking, can you tell me more about the Church and about this Exodus Project? What kind of things have you found out?"

Being so direct and pushing her was a gamble. But I could tell she felt betrayed by her father. And I needed to know as much about what was going on as possible if I was to save my brother. The gamble paid off. Whether from desperation, stress, or a sense of betrayal, after a moment's hesitation, the dam broke.

"I had nosed around my dad's office and one thing I found out is that the Church has an enemies list. The file's a list of people or organizations that the Church feel are a threat and what actions to take against them.

"There's also a complete background on several "fixers" the Church uses. Eamon is one, or was. I'd met him once or twice and dad had told me about him being a vampire and all, but I just laughed it off. I mean, come on? The first time I read the file, I thought it was somebody's idea of a joke. Vampires? I mean, get real. Then I did a search on the names of the people they supposedly sent him after and they all turned up either dead or missing.

"Dad also told me about ways to slow vampires down or kill them, in case they get out of control. That's why I was carrying around my sword. I didn't think they'd really send one after me, but I thought I should be ready just in case. The Church punished one vampire by burying her in cement under a new baseball stadium. Vampires don't need to breathe or eat, so she will be there for an eternity. And she evidently hated sports. They learned not to bury them in dirt because they'll eventually dig their way out."

"Sucks to be her," I said. This conversation made me start to understand how Alice must have felt when she dropped down the rabbit hole. I prodded her to continue. "What were you able to learn about this Exodus Project itself?"

"Unfortunately, not much. I just know that whatever it is, it will happen soon. My dad may be a big muckety-muck, but I'm not. People started noticing I was asking a lot of questions. So I cooled it for a bit. Then one night I came back to my place and could tell it had been searched. There was nothing for them to find because I'd been careful, but still. It both scared me to death and pissed me off. So I took off."

Took off with something the Church and Satan wanted very badly, I thought. I could sense I was getting closer to the truth of the matter. I needed to find out what she stole. Perhaps I could use what she'd taken as leverage for my brother's soul without actually serving her up on a silver platter.

We were now in the eastern part of Louisville, near Beargrass Creek. The area is called Butchertown because back in the day, the creek had been lined up one side and down the other with slaughterhouses and butcher shops. They would throw the scraps and what not into the creek and just let it take all the crap to the Ohio River. I can only imagine the smell of the place on a hot August day.

Butchertown is home to two cemeteries, Eastern Cemetery and right next door to that, Cave Hill Cemetery. Cave Hill is Louisville's crown jewel of cemeteries with many of the city's dignitaries buried in and around the hills. It's wonderfully maintained and surrounded by a brick wall with razor wire on top to keep out unwanted visitors. People take tours of Cave Hill Cemetery. It's on the National Register of Historic Places. It's beautiful and peaceful. I even have relatives buried there.

Eastern Cemetery is nothing like Cave Hill. Home to many of the city's past prominent black leaders, it's also home to one of the city's darkest secrets. It was discovered that since the 1920's, the people who were running the cemetery had been burying multiple corpses in the same graves. Not only that, but they were mixing the cremated remains of different people into the same boxes. I would hate to find out my Great Aunt Edna was buried with somebody else's Uncle Hubert.

The cemetery has been largely abandoned since the late 80's when it was learned they had buried nearly forty-eight thousand people in sixteen-thousand graves. Tombstones were desecrated, records were lost. Word around town is some guy decided on his own to mow the grass there because no one else would. It breaks my heart to think of all the loved ones that were not buried with the respect they had earned in life.

We turned onto David's street and pulling to the curb. I stopped. "Which house is it?" I asked.

"The last one at the end, on the right."

I spent a few moments getting a feel for the neighborhood. The cool air made for a pleasant night. Most of the houses up and down the street had cars in the driveway or parked in front. Putting the car back in drive, I drove slowly down the street and watched for anything out of place, but didn't see anything. When we got to David's house, there were lights on in the back and a car in the driveway.

"Looks like someone's home. Is that his car?"

"Yeah, the green Hyundai."

I kept on going and then turned at the end of the street, circling the block. "Call him back."

Pulling out her phone, she did so. After a moment, she looked at me and shook her head. No answer. "He knew my meeting was tonight and told me to call as soon as it was over. I don't know why he's not answering. Why aren't we stopping?"

My years of busting perps had my Spidey senses tingling at full blast. Phoenix Hill Tavern was across the street from the entrance to Eastern Cemetery. Easing into the lot, I took the time and backed into a space.

I parked the car and sat back in my seat, I said, "Let me ask you a few things first, starting with how many people knew about your meeting at the Down and Dirty?"

We could hear the music pounding from inside the tavern, people having fun letting their hair down on a Friday night. While across the street, the cemetery waited quietly, with a clientele that had left the party a long time ago.

She took a deep breath. "Just David, me, and the guy I was meeting." She paused. "Which means I have a problem."

I thought about it. It was unlikely that Eamon found out about her meeting the same way I did, as I couldn't picture the vamp locking the door behind him when he left. And even if he was working with J.B., I doubt he could get there that quickly. Which left one other option.

"Yep. Sure seems like someone might have sold you out. Sounds like David has a vested interest in what you're doing, so that makes me think your date tonight set you up."

She waved the comment off dismissively. "No. He wouldn't. And that's the real problem. Have you ever heard of the Hand of God?"

"Sorry, I can't say that I have. Then again, if it isn't on the side of a beer bottle, I might not have anyway. Enlighten me."

"David told me about this guy that does God's dirty work here on Earth. The Hand of God is…special. Kind of like God's James Bond with a license to kill."

She continued, "People tend to forget that in the Old Testament, God had no problems punishing the wicked with extreme violence. Noah's flood, the nuking of Sodom and Gomorrah, closing the Red Sea on Pharaoh's army. Piss God off and the penalties could be steep. This guy deals out the same type of punishment, just quieter and on a smaller scale."

My kind of guy. More than once I wish I had the power to dish out the ultimate punishment on some douche bag. The thing stopping me is I don't like bars I can't walk out of, and prison is not a place I want to end up in.

"And that's who you were meeting?" I asked.

"Yes. So there is zero chance that the Hand of God would be working with the Church of the Light Reclaimed. Her eyes filled with concern and not a little fear. "I have a bad feeling about all this, Vic. I worked for weeks to set that meeting up. For him not to have shown is beyond bad. And for David not to answer his phone is even worse."

She didn't have to say more. I said, "O.K. That brings us back to how they found out where you were going to be. It may be David had no choice in giving you up, which is why I didn't pull into his driveway. Here's what you and I are going to do. His house backs up to the cemetery. So let's you and I take a little stroll and approach his house from the rear and see what we can see."

Nodding, she got out carrying her case. I walked around to her side of the car. I glanced around to make sure we were more or less alone and then unlocked the glove box, took out my gun and slipped the holster clip on my belt, making sure it was covered by my jacket.

"You need to use that thing much as a bouncer?" she asked.

"You can't imagine how many drunken boozers I toss out on an average night that wait in the parking lot to get a piece of me when I leave. I show them this and they back off. It's why I'm off tonight. I got into it with a few guys and my boss suggested I take the rest of the night off and cool it a bit."

Liar, Liar, pants on fire, kept running through my mind, with the image of my body melting from my bones coming along for the ride. I have a great poker face, but in this case I didn't need it. Samantha either believed my line of bull shit or she simply didn't care, with bigger worries on her mind, as she never blinked at the explanation. As for me, I knew damn well if anyone else threw something large at me, I was going to blow them away, whether it stopped them or not.

Chapter Eight

Crossing the street and heading into the cemetery, we left Phoenix Hill Tavern behind. A large, bright full moon, kind enough to light our path, meant there was no need for a flashlight, even though I keep one in a zipped pocket inside my jacket along with the lock picks and a few other tools of the trade, like a small can of mace.

We walked down a long path between rows of headstones, many of them knocked to the ground or with the tops of some of the more ornate ones vandalized. The grass had not been mowed in some time and it was like I could feel the outrage of those laid to rest at Eastern Cemetery. Guess the volunteer mower had given up the ghost as well.

It only took about five minutes to reach the back of Dave's rental property. Finding a hole in the chain link fence, we were soon standing in the deeper shadows of an oak tree and spent the next several minutes watching the house. The rear of the house featured a screened-in back porch. We could see a light on in a back room that Samantha said was the kitchen. But the only window had the shade drawn, the blind glowing yellow in the night.

We quietly made our way across the backyard and onto the porch, opening the screen door slowly. We could hear voices inside the house and we moved over to the window. There was a small sliver of space between the shade and the sill, and I took a quick look inside.

There were three men in the kitchen and I could pick out David right away. Not because one looked more like a reporter than the other two. It was because I knew he was most likely the one with his torso and arms duct taped to a kitchen chair, with a dish towel in his mouth and two fingers missing from his left hand, dripping a steady stream of blood. Well, the fingers weren't really missing; they were lying on the kitchen floor, where the dweeb with the garden shears let them fall after cutting them off his hand.

The man with the shears was tall and young, with scruffy hair and a beard with several days growth. He was dressed in a James Taylor T-shirt and jeans and looked like the kind of guy you would find playing guitar in a coffee house--as long as you could look past the whole bloody garden shears cutting fingers off part. He also had a 9 millimeter stuck in the back waistband of his pants.

The other man looked like George Clooney, with movie star good looks and a deep tan, a comfortable six feet tall. He was dressed in what looked like a very expensive suit and was clearly the man in charge. He leaned back against the kitchen counter, his hands clasped loosely in front of him.

I pointed to Samantha to take a look, but to keep quiet when she did so. She nodded she understood, then eased to where she could look through the window. Her eyes went wide and her hands flew to cover her mouth as she stifled a scream.

After a moment she regained her composure and placing her mouth next to my ear, she said, "The man in the suit is Preston Deveraux. He works for my dad. He's another one of the Church fixers. The other is a low-life scumbag named Kevin Hall. He does odd jobs at the church headquarters."

I was struggling to concentrate on what she was telling me, with my body paying more attention to the feel of her breath in my ear and the way her hand rested on my neck.

Swallowing hard before putting my mouth next to her ear, I asked, "Is either one of them a vampire?"

She shook her head no. That was good news, at least. I like it when things I shoot will stay on the ground instead of getting back up and trying to kick my ass. I was glancing back through the gap when Deveraux opened his trap and started talking.

"All right, Mr. Mangus. We're going to try this again. When we run out of fingers I'll have my associate pull down your pants and start cutting off other things. He's going to take the rag out of your mouth and you're going to answer my questions. Do you understand me?"

David raised his head, with effort, and nodded. He appeared to be around fifty or sixty years old, with a round face and closely cropped gray hair. He was breathing hard, his face covered in sweat.

Deveraux asked, "What's the Exodus Project?"

Hall removed the dish towel and David said, his voice strained, "It's a....it's a planned attack on Christian schools using a computer virus," he stammered. Tears streaked his bloodied face and his body shook in pain.

I could feel my anger rising and pulled my gun from its holster. Samantha watched me do this, opened her case and then took out her sword. When I raised an eyebrow, she whispered, "It works on regular people just as well as vampires." She got no argument from me. Any port in a storm and any weapon in a dogfight.

"And who told you about the Exodus Project, Mr. Mangus? And

remember, I know the answers to most of these questions already. One more lie and the night will be over for you. And then I'll leave here, drive to your daughter Linda's house in Atlanta and see what she knows."

He looked up in panic at the mention of his daughter.

"That's right, Mr. Mangus. We know quite a bit about you. Cooperate with me now and we'll leave you as you are. You won't be able to play the piano anymore, but at least you'll be alive."

Fat chance on that one, David. I could see in his eyes that he felt the same, but still, he answered. "Leave my...leave my daughter alone," he stuttered. "I'll tell you what you want to know." He paused for a moment, in significant pain, but continued. "Rebecca Thomas contacted me with information on Exodus. She said the Church of the Light Reclaimed was planning an attack on Christian schools in the South with a computer virus. That's all she knew. And that's all I know. I swear!"

I looked at Samantha and mouthed the name Rebecca Thomas and she mouthed back no clue.

Kevin Hall was whistling a tune and after a moment I realized it was *Sunshine on My Shoulders*. Never thought anyone could make John Denver sound creepy, but ole' Kevin pulled it off.

Deveraux asked, "One last question, Mr. Mangus. You contacted someone in the Church. Who was it?"

David swallowed hard a couple of times, then said in a near whisper, "Samantha. Samantha Tyler." He dropped his head to his chest and started to sob.

Samantha, eyes closed, slowly shook her head back and forth. .

Deveraux moved in front of David. He bent over and lifted up his chin, so that he and David were looking eye to eye. "Where is she now, Mr. Mangus?"

David stared back and said, "I, I have no clue. Really. I don't know."

Preston Deveraux stood up straight and took a couple of steps back. He looked at Kevin, then nodded at David. I knew what that meant. Moving to the door and trying the knob, I found it was unlocked, so I opened it and stepped into the kitchen, Samantha right behind me, sword raised.

"I'm right here, you son of a bitch!" she shouted.

I pointed my gun at the two men, while using my free hand to hold Samantha back. I knew she wanted nothing more than to run both of them through, and I had no problem with her doing so. But I didn't want her between me and the two men when the shit hit the fan.

If Preston Deveraux was surprised at our entrance, you would never have known it. He looked like someone just walked in and asked him what time it was. A half-smile creased his face as he nonchalantly leaned back on the counter. He raised his hands out to his side, showing he was unarmed. Kevin, on the other hand, jumped and started to reach for his gun.

I said, in my best Danny Glover voice, "I don't want to kill you, and you don't want to be dead, but if your hand moves another inch, that's what's going to happen."

Kevin said, "Mr. Deveraux, I think I can take him." Licking his lips, he moved a fraction more towards his gun. Deveraux just looked at him with a blank stare, watching, but saying nothing.

I felt like I was in a Clint Eastwood western. And I knew how this was going to end. And then it did. Kevin made a quick move for his weapon, but he wasn't nearly as fast as he thought he was. Before he could even get a grip on his 9, I had, for the second time in just the last few hours, shot a man. This time, things happened the way they were supposed to.

The bullet struck Kevin fractions of an inch above the bridge of his nose, throwing him back against the counter, then his lifeless body collapsed to the floor. Blood and brain matter made a weird looking pattern on David's tiled kitchen backsplash. As his head exploded. I wasn't sure, but I could swear I could see a butterfly. David, for his part, just kept saying, "Oh my God, oh my God" over and over and thrashing around on his kitchen chair. The only move Deveraux made was to cross his legs at the ankles, while keeping his hands out to his sides.

Smiling at me, he said, "You just can't find good help these days. Stupid is as stupid does." Turning his attention to Samantha, he said, "How are you, beautiful?"

"Fuck you, Preston." Moving over to David, she tried calming him down. Searching around the kitchen and finding a knife on the counter, she started cutting him free of the duct tape.

I knew I should be feeling some level of guilt at what I'd just done, but I didn't. In truth, I didn't feel anything at all. During my years in the sandpits of the Middle East, I killed dozens of men. And back then all I could muster was a mental shrug of the shoulders. This, for me, was no different. I've laid in bed many nights wondering if my moral compass pointed to nowhere. In this case, I'd warned him. So, he got what he deserved. But deep down inside, my lack of remorse bothered me a hell of a lot more than the killing.

"We've been looking for you, Samantha. Your father is very worried about you," Deveraux said.

"I'll just bet he is." The sarcasm in her voice was obvious.

"Why don't you introduce me to your new friend?" He looked at me and said, "And you are?"

"No one of consequence," I replied. I made sure to keep my gun leveled right at his chest. Over the years I've become a good judge of who is and isn't dangerous. Deveraux struck me as more dangerous than a bed of Eastern Kentucky rattlers.

"Kevin would surely disagree with you. But no matter. Let me make you an offer. You help me return Samantha to her father and we will pay you a finder's fee."

"A finder's fee? Sorry friend, while you may be a looker, I prefer the redhead, thank you very much. You know what I mean? I think you do." I gave it my best Elvis drawl, but Deveraux wasn't overly impressed.

Samantha, after cutting David away from his chair, began wrapping his hand in a clean towel. Looking at me she said, "We have to get David to a hospital, like now."

I said, "Let's call the cops. They can handle things from here. I have you and David as witnesses for the shooting. So let them take over."

"We can't. No cops. We have to get David medical treatment, but no cops. No way." She said this with a strong shake of her head.

"Why the hell not? You want to put pressure on the Church, and this will sure as hell do that."

Deveraux spoke up, "She doesn't want the cops because she doesn't want them to find out what she's done. Isn't that right, Samantha?"

Looking back and forth between the two of them, I asked, "And what is it you're claiming she did?"

Deveraux smiled. "Not much. Only a little matter of the theft of thirty million dollars."

Chapter Nine

Samantha kept her gaze locked on me as I thought about someone stealing thirty million dollars. I could now understand why Satan, the Church and a billion other people might be looking for her if it was true she'd stolen the money. And since I have always been nothing if not direct, I asked her.

I gave a low whistle. "So, did you steal it?"

"Yes." Walking over to a cabinet and staying clear of Deveraux, she got out a bowl and used another clean wash towel to pick up David's fingers, putting them in the bowl. She then got ice out of the fridge and covered the fingers with the cubes.

I couldn't even fathom what having that much money would be like. Not to mention what it would take to have the balls to steal that much money. You take a couple of thousand and maybe not much happens. You steal thirty million and you can bet your sweet ass the ones you stole it from would be hunting you night and day.

Helping David to his feet and then picking up her sword, Samantha stood facing me and waited.

I smiled and said, "You go, girl. Thirty million? Sweet."

Deveraux cleared his throat and said, "Let me up my offer, since you hold the gun. Turn Samantha over to me, help us recover the money, and we will pay you a million dollars. What do you say?"

This guy was starting to royally piss me off. "You know what Preston? May I call you Preston?"

"By all means."

"Preston, I don't know what pisses me off more. That you think I could be bought or that you think I'm that damn stupid. I mean, after all, as you pointed out, I have the gun. Why would I settle for a million from you when I got thirty million standing right there?"

I could see Samantha tensing, so I continued, "But it doesn't matter. I don't need your money or hers. I've never been much of a materialistic kind of guy. The little lady needs help, and I'm giving it to her. Besides, my daddy told me never trust a man with a spray on tan."

All pretense of being friendly disappeared as he said, "Then you're a dead man, you and the reporter both."

"Yeah, yeah, yeah, blah, blah, blah. Have a seat." I waved him over to the chair David had been sitting in and told him to put his hands behind his back. Keeping my gun on him the whole time, I had Samantha duct tape his hands to the chair, then his chest.

I had to give it to the guy. He looked like a man sitting down to have a cup of coffee at Starbucks without a care in the world. He said, "There are forces at work here of which you have no clue. Powers beyond your comprehension, which will all turn their attention to you, once we have Samantha back."

"Yeah? You mean like vampires?"

Deveraux lost his poker face, for just a moment, as an expression of surprise flew across his features, before it returned to casual indifference.

I said, "You must mean Eamon. I met him earlier this evening. You won't get another chance to see him until you get to Hell. But when you do ask him how things are working out for him, since he's dead. Again."

"My, my. It seems I may have underestimated you. Killing a vampire? Bravo."

"Technically, Samantha killed him. But I wore him down for her first before she used her razor and then--" I made a slashing motion across my throat.

Samantha rolled her eyes, and said, "Jeez. What a crock. I had him right where I wanted him, you were just getting in my way."

"Keep on dreaming, sister." David was starting to sway on his feet, so I holstered my gun and took him by the elbow. "Let's get you to a hospital because, man, you don't look too good."

"You should kill me now," said Deveraux. "Leaving me alive is a mistake you can't afford to make. I'll hunt you down and peel the skin from your body and then feed it to you if you leave me alive." The really scary thing is, I could tell he meant it. Both the part about me killing him and the part about hunting me down.

I said, "I don't think you're quite getting the hang of this whole the-tables-are-turned thing. You're supposed to be begging for us not to kill you. The part about peeling my skin thing was good. I would keep pulling the T.V. bad guy card, maybe throw in how I'm going to regret this, that I'll regret the day I was born. Things like that."

He said, "I've been promised a special place by my Lord, the Angel of Light, by his side when he ascends to Heaven. Kill me now and I'll take Eamon's place. Either way, alive or dead, I'll be rewarded. Kill me now and I'll be even more powerful."

I laughed. "Obi-Wan Kenobi you are not."

I started David towards the front of the house, with Samantha returning to the porch and picking up her case, then grabbing the bowl full of fingers.

Deveraux was smiling again. "See you soon, Samantha. Enjoy your freedom and the money while you can. You won't have either for long."

I asked David for his car keys and he pointed to the counter. I picked them up and headed to the front door. I was reaching for the doorknob when I heard car doors open and then shut in the driveway.

"Speaking of tables turning," said Deveraux, "that would be the cavalry."

Four men, dressed in coveralls, were standing next to a white panel van. When they started towards the front door, we made a beeline for the back door.

Deveraux said, "One last chance, friend, to-"

He never finished the sentence because I picked up a wooden cutting board from David's kitchen counter and whacked him hard upside the head, stunning him.

"Jesus, but that man was getting on my nerves." Neither David nor Samantha complained about my method of silencing Deveraux, with both the former Satanist and the Christian keeping quiet.

We made our way out the back door, quickly through the yard to the hole in the fence, and into the cemetery. David was moaning softly under his breath, and I couldn't blame him. There could be no doubt the brutality of the evening would stay with him for the rest of his life.

I asked him, "We heard you mention the name of your source, Rebecca Thomas. Who is she, because you need to call and warn her. After we drop you off at the hospital, we can go pick her up."

I could just make out a couple strolling down the main drag of the cemetery, stopping before they reached us to suck face. Couples sometimes used the cemetery for a little privacy when things got too hot for Phoenix Hill, despite the creepiness factor. Some chicks just dig cemeteries.

Using his good hand, he searched for and then found a cell phone in his pants pocket and flipped it open. Typing in a number he said, "The Church has a computer guru named Lincoln Townsend. Rebecca is both Townsend's maid and mistress. He mentioned the Exodus Project to her during pillow talk. He likes to get high after they have sex and he let something slip one night while high as a kite. It scared the living bejesus out of her. She had read some columns I'd written and contacted me." Hitting the send button, he raised the phone to his ear.

I asked, "Why not go to the police? Did she steal thirty million, too?"

"She was afraid no one would believe her."

David frowned at the couple as we walked by them, their make out session getting more intense, the two of them moaning in pleasure. I just shook my head. The man was wearing a London Fog style overcoat and a fashion sharp fedora hat. The woman had her hands under the man's coat and I resisted the urge to yell out, "Hand check."

In hindsight, it would have been a good idea. As we passed them, the couple broke their embrace, and the woman spun and jammed an ice pick she was holding under her partner's coat, in at the base of David's skull, up and into his brain.

Stiffening, he collapsed like a rag doll, dropping the phone onto the gravel path. He went from being tortured, with seemingly no hope of being saved, to his rescue like a gift from God, only to have his life snuffed out in an instant—and not even knowing how or why. Life can be such a bitch. A cynic would wonder if Samantha was right and God was dead when things like this happen.

Catching the move out of the corner of my eye, I spun around just as the man pulled out his own ice pick and attempted to stab me in my neck. I did a contortion move any yoga instructor would be proud of, seized the man's wrist with my right hand, pulling him forward and then slightly past me. I drove my left hand through the man's elbow, shattering it, with the arm bending nearly back upon itself.

He howled in pain, dropping the ice pick. I started to turn back towards the woman, who had pulled her weapon out of David's gray matter, but I knew I would not be fast enough to stop her from using me like a human pincushion.

Thankfully all that martial arts training Samantha endured paid off as she spun in a circle kick, taking out the woman's legs and then smashing her elbow into the woman's nose as she fell to the ground. Samantha stomped the hand holding the ice pick with the pointed end of her four inch heels and the woman screamed.

I have to give the man an A for effort, as he tried grabbing me with his free hand. But considering he was of average height and weight, and down to one good arm, he found out that trying to go after me was a very poor decision on his part. I blocked his hand to the side, took a step closer and picking him up by the neck and crotch, lifted him off the ground and slammed him down onto the closest headstone. I heard his back break and I let him slide off the headstone and onto the ground. His bad guy days were now over, unless he planned to terrorize the world from a wheelchair.

I turned to find Samantha kicking the holy hell out of the female side of the Ice Pick Lovers. The woman tried to curl up into a fetal position, this time moaning with pain, instead of pleasure, with each kick. I wrapped my arms around her and lifted her away, as she thrashed trying to get out of my grip to keep punishing the fallen woman. It took a few minutes, but she got herself under control and I sat her back onto her feet, letting her go.

I looked at Phoenix Hill, which was about a hundred yards off, and could see no indication that anyone noticed what had transpired in Eastern Cemetery. Life went on at the tavern, with the death and destruction taking place just a short way into the darkness going unnoticed.

I stepped over David, who was now, I had to guess, strumming the harps and floating on the clouds in Heaven, and picked up his phone. "Hello? Miss Thomas, are you there?"

A very frightened woman asked, "Who is this, what's happening? Where's David?"

"Listen, my name is Victor and I'm a friend of David's. I don't have time to explain, but you're in serious danger. The Church knows who you are and that you're David's source. They'll be sending people your way as soon as they find out where you live, if they haven't already. You have to get out of there and I mean now."

There was a very long pause and I thought she'd hung up.

"Hello? Hello?"

She finally answered me. "How do I know you're not with the Church and just trying to flush me into the open? And tell me what's happened to David?"

"I'm sorry. David's dead. The Church got to him. And there's no way for me to convince you that we're not with the Church. But if you don't listen to me, they'll find you and kill you. He was forced to tell them who his source was before he died, and he named you. So you need to get to a safe place where the Church can't get to you. If you need protection, tell me where you're at, or where we can meet you, and I'll make sure you're safe."

"I don't have a way to leave," she wailed. "I loaned my sister my car for the night!"

"Then go to a neighbor or somewhere near your house that's a public place."

"You don't understand, I live out in the middle of nowhere. I have a small cottage on a farm where I used to work. What am I going to do?"

"O.K. I'll come get you. I'm a big guy wearing a black bomber jacket and I'll be driving a red Chevelle. I'll have a friend with me, and she has red hair. If you see any other car or any other people come to your door, then head somewhere out onto the farm and call us. We called a cell phone, right?"

"Yes. But please hurry." She gave me directions to the farm which was about twenty minutes from us.

"We're on our way." I ended the call.

Samantha knelt in the gravel, stroking David's hair as his eyes stared up at nothing. Tears streamed down Samantha's face. "What do we do with David?" The surrounding tombstones remained silent so I answered.

"Not a damn thing." I looked back towards David's house and I could see movement in the shadows. It would seem Satan's cavalry had figured out how we had made our escape. "I'm sorry Samantha, but if we don't get to Rebecca's first, she's a goner. So we have to get moving and fast."

Samantha looked at me pleadingly. "We can't just leave him here, Vic, we can't."

"We can and we are." I took her by an arm and hauled her to her feet. "His soul has taken the escalator up to Heaven. His body means nothing to him anymore. Now come on, let's go."

She nodded and wiped her eyes with the sleeve of her coat. Then she kicked the Ice Pick Lover one more time for good measure and we took off.

Chapter Ten

As we got closer to exiting the cemetery, I could see my Chevelle in the parking lot with Winston Reynolds leaning against the back bumper, watching the front door to Phoenix Hill.

Winston was one of J.B.'s two helpers. A former linebacker for the University of Louisville football team, he worked out hard to maintain his physique. A black man in his early twenties, he was considered J.B.'s protégé because of his reputation as a smart and quick learner. He's also one of the guys I saw walking into the Double D with J.B. How the hell they tracked us here I had no idea and no time to figure out.

I whispered to Samantha, "Recognize him? That's one of the guys who was after you back at the bar. The other two must be inside looking for us. Wait here on the sidewalk and let me take care of this."

She did as I asked. Their Cadillac Escalade was parked a few spots down from mine, so I strolled over to it, took out my pocket knife, and slowly used it to let the air out of the SUV's back right tire.

Winston continued to watch the front door with his arms crossed, looking bored. I walked around the Escalade, and around Winston's blind side.

I asked, "Hey buddy, got a light?"

He turned his head to look in my direction and I hit him hard, right in the jaw, knocking him off my car, then pressed my attack, hitting him a couple of more times. There were several people in the parking lot and they came over to watch us go at each other.

I have to give Winston credit. He put up a good fight, but my sucker punch gave me the advantage as I'd rung his bell and his reflexes and timing were slow. In short order he was on the ground, not moving.

I ran to the Chevelle, got in, fired her up and pulled out of the lot, stopping long enough to throw the door open for Samantha to jump in, then tore off as soon as she had her door shut. I could see the men in the coveralls jogging towards the cemetery entrance as we zoomed by. I flipped them off with a smile as we accelerated into the night.

Samantha turned in her seat to watch them as we drove away. The men waited a couple of heartbeats, one of them talking on a phone, and then they ran back the way they had come.

"I don't understand. How could those guys at the bar find us so quickly?" she asked.

"I have no earthly idea." And I didn't. "If they're working with Eamon, then the Church must have had them drive over to David's house. But why on Earth they were checking for us in the tavern, I have no clue. Who the hell knows? Problem is, they now know what I'm driving, and we sure as hell can't go back and get your car."

I now had to wonder if the lie I told her was closer to the truth than I realized. It was possible that Satan had put J.B. in touch with Deveraux and that's how they found us, but I didn't think so. Maybe they had sent out word they were looking for my car and someone called and told them it was parked at Phoenix Hill Tavern and that was how they tracked us down, but right then I didn't have time to worry about it.

I took several random turns, but like earlier, could see no pursuit. Not yet, at least.

Samantha put her head back on the head rest and then clenched her fists. Her entire body shook as she fought back tears. "Those goddamned sons of bitches. Before they kill me, I'll make them pay for what they did to David. I swear it."

"First, we're not going to let them kill you. Second, that's why you stole the money, wasn't it? Not to get rich, but to hurt the Church. You wanted to hit them where it hurts, by taking off with their cash."

She nodded. "I couldn't find out exactly what the Exodus Project was, but by what little I could find out from my dad, I could tell it was going to cost the Church a lot of money. I figured if I drained the accounts, they wouldn't be able to go through with the plan, no matter what it is. It was the only way I could think of to slow them down."

"Couldn't they just get more money?"

"No. They're not like a regular church, with a lot of different donors. They don't have as many people to get money from, so losing this much money really puts a hurt on their plans. They can replace the money eventually, but not right away. I helped my dad with the books. He didn't trust anyone else. I knew in which accounts the money was being held and what his passwords were to access them."

I realized that was why Satan wanted her found. He wanted to keep the Exodus Project on schedule, and to do that, they had to find Samantha and the money. Now I had to figure out how to make that information work for me, to save my brother. For the first time all night, I had hope I could free my brother's soul without having to turn over Samantha.

"You also knew it would make you a target. Risky move."

"Yeah, but I thought that my father being who he was would protect me, you know? And so far it has, but look what's happening to the people around me. David's dead now because of what I did. They almost killed you as well."

I shook my head. "David was a big boy and knew what he was getting involved in. He came to you, after all. But you poke a hornets' nest with a stick; there's a good chance you'll get stung. I'm sure he never thought he would pay with his life, but at least he knew where his ticket is punched to end up now that his life is over. As for me, it'll take more than a pointed stick to take me out."

Samantha stopped shaking and took a couple of deep breaths. "I'll say it again, God is dead. If people like David are working to save Christian school kids, how could God let something like this happen to him? Tortured? Murdered? No way, Vic. God's dead."

I would have loved to have argued for the home team, but what could I say? That this was just a test for people like her and me? A woman that didn't believe in either God or Satan until recently? A man like me, who just a couple of hours ago was a casual believer who really couldn't have cared less?

Frankly, I had no clue why God let things like this happen. My parish priest taught us that there wasn't always a reason why things happened. Earthquakes, floods, hurricanes and the like were part of life. No one knows when they'll be called home. Or to the basement, for that matter. It makes the free will that men and women have even more important.

We all have a choice whether we believe in God or not, and you don't want to get caught with your shorts around your ankles when your time to go before the Almighty comes around.

But I knew I couldn't convince her, right at this moment, one way or the other. So I let the question go and changed the subject. "What I don't get is all this is over a computer virus? Just how in God's name is this supposed to start a religious war? This makes no sense to me. I mean, I've had a virus before on my computer and wanted to kill the guy who designed it, but I wouldn't actually kill him. Maybe rough him up a little if I actually caught him, but a religious war?"

"No clue," she said. "Then again Muslims got really ticked when that newspaper guy drew a cartoon of Mohammed and they wanted to kill him for it. Remember that? But the information we have says the attacks will come against Christian schools, not Muslim schools. All I do know is I want to make them pay. And I plan on starting with my father.

"When this crap is over, I plan on holding a press conference. He and the Church do everything in the dark and I'll drag them into the media spotlight and that will ruin them. My father lives in Philadelphia, where he is considered to be a 'Pillar of the Community.' Wait until they find out he has a hand in murdering people and planning attacks on school kids. This time Cy Tyler will be on every news channel and on the cover of every magazine in the country, if not the world, but for a different reason. That's the way you hurt my father and the Church."

"Cy Tyler? You mean Congressman Cy Tyler, the right wing conservative nut job who wants to outlaw nearly anything that's fun in this country and is the darling of the Christian Right? You're telling me that he's a Satanist?

"One and the same, and not just any Satanist, but *the* Satanist."

"Huh. Well, if you do that, your life will never be the same. Until the day they put you in the ground, you'll be known as "That Girl." Can you imagine what it would've been like being Hitler's daughter? You'll get to find out if you shove your dad and the Church into the light."

"So what? You think I should just keep my mouth shut? You want to just let them get away with it? Is that it? Give me a break." She did not try to hide her contempt.

"Hell no. I just think you should consider doing it differently, is all. Just because you sucked at trying to create a new identity for yourself the first time doesn't mean you shouldn't try it again. I know people that can help with that kind of thing. And once you have a new identity, leak things to the media and the powers that be. You can do just as much damage to the Church by lobbing bombs from the shadows, but avoid standing in front of a group of microphones. It gives you a chance at a normal life. You do it your way, and you're hosed."

She didn't say yes and she didn't say no. As a matter of fact, for the rest of the drive, she didn't say anything. As much as my life had been turned upside down, I could only imagine what she was going through. It's one thing to know your father was leading a double life. But to then find out he's an out and out royal bastard is even worse.

We drove the twenty miles out of Louisville into the countryside. Rebecca's cottage was off Covered Bridge Road, a long, winding road taking us farther and farther from civilization. I knew the area because as a kid I used to go to a Boy Scout camp not far from the farm she was living on. There used to be an actual covered bridge, but it was replaced some years ago by a new, wider, modern concrete bridge which screamed progress if not atmosphere. Not only that, there was a rumor devil worshippers used to hold meetings in a field just down from the bridge. Groups of kids would camp out on the hill overlooking the field, watching for them, but they never actually saw them. I would have bet everything I owned devil worshippers, in any great numbers, didn't exist. And it seems I would have lost the bet.

We found the driveway turn off with some difficulty, having gone past it once and backtracking, before finally seeing it, tucked under overhanging oak trees. The farm itself straddled a long ridge, with a beautiful view of the Louisville skyline lit up in the distance. Old growth trees surrounded the property, with many of them having lost their leaves now that we were in the first week of November.

The cottage was situated about a half mile from the main house, down a dirt road with two tire track ruts along its length. We pulled to the end of the drive, parked and got out. The home was small, but well maintained, with neatly trimmed hedges in front and a rose garden off to one side. A creek ran through the back of the property.

I could see a curtain move as we approached the door, then drop back into place. I knocked and the door opened a fraction, showing an attractive woman who appeared to be in her mid-thirties.

"Miss Thomas?" I asked.

She looked past us to see if she could see anyone else. When she didn't, she asked, "I still don't know if I should trust you."

"Look, Miss Thomas, if I wanted to do you harm, I would have kicked the door in and this would be over. This is Samantha. She was working with David. Did he tell you about her?"

"Not by name. He told me he had someone on the inside he was working with, but not who it was."

She opened the door and motioned for us to come in.

I said, "We don't have much time. We have to get out of here, like pronto. They've killed David and have tried to kill me as well. These people are vicious. Let's get moving."

"I'm packing a bag. It'll only take me a few more minutes."

She headed back to a small bedroom and we followed. I asked, "So tell us how this got started. David said you were involved with some computer geek?"

She had a suitcase open on the bed and had been throwing clothes and a few other personal items in it. She opened a drawer and added to the pile. "Yes. I clean houses to make extra money. I started working for Lincoln a few months back. He's a nice enough guy and, well, you know, one thing led to another and we ended up in bed. He likes to get high after sex and one night after a few joints he starts bragging about this thing he was involved in."

"The Exodus Project," Samantha said.

"That's right. Starts telling me they wouldn't have a chance of pulling it off without him and that when the shit goes down, it would be worldwide news. And all because he figured out how to make it happen. Said the Christians in this country would, and I quote, "Want revenge on every Muslim on the planet."

She finished packing and closed the suitcase. She said, "That's all I know. But the look in his eyes scared me. So I decided I needed to tell someone. My mother loves reading David's columns and since he's an investigative reporter, I contacted him."

She teared up. "You said they killed him. How exactly?" she asked.

Samantha looked at me and I gave a slight nod. She gave Rebecca a brief account of what happened at David's house and in the cemetery, while glossing over some of the gorier parts.

I lifted the suitcase. "Come on, ladies, let's skedaddle. It's after ten o'clock and time's a wastin'."

We made it outside the cottage into the unseasonably warm fall night, but stopped when we heard a sound. It was a car and it was headed up the driveway.

Chapter Eleven

There was no way we'd be able to get into my car and past the one coming up the driveway. I asked Rebecca which way to the mansion from here and she pointed off to the left of the cottage to a path that disappeared into the woods. We ran in that direction and had just made it into the darkness under low-hanging branches when a Cadillac Escalade pulled up behind my car, blocking it.

I stopped Samantha and Rebecca a short ways down the path and the three of us watched from behind a large oak tree as J.B. and another guy got out of the Cadillac. I could see Winston behind the wheel, holding an ice pack up to his jaw.

Both men moved forward with guns out as they checked my car and moved to the door of the cottage. I held my own down at my side, the safety off.

Samantha asked, "He has to be working for Deveraux if they're already here."

I thought if that was true, how were they already at Phoenix Hill Tavern when we took off from David's house. They weren't looking for us in the cemetery, trying to cut us off. They were inside the tavern. Hell, Winston wasn't even looking towards David's house. Then it hit me. They weren't tracking Samantha, they were tracking me. They must have put a GPS device somewhere on my car. I swore under my breath. I should have thought of a tracker when they showed up at Phoenix Hill, and I didn't. I was slipping and it could get us killed.

J.B. stayed outside while the hired goon checked the house. It didn't take long. He came back out and said something to J.B. who then looked around at the surrounding woods. He then said something to Winston who headed back down the drive, probably to the mansion.

J.B. started turning around in a slow circle and shouted into the darkness surrounding him, "Alright, Vic. I know you're out there somewhere. You win. I won't hold the taser to the family jewels against you. Heck, if I'd been in your position, I might have done the same thing. You and I can work something out on the girl. That fifty-fifty deal you made me would work. But this is a onetime offer, Vic. My boys and I are getting a little tired of putting up with your shit."

Samantha grabbed me by the arm and whispered, "You know him?" I could hear the hurt in her voice, could feel the way her nails dug into my bomber jacket.

At that moment I was really glad she left her sword in the car. It was near pitch black under the oak tree, but I didn't have to see her eyes to feel the look she was giving me.

"Look, it's complicated. When we get out of this, I'll explain. I'm not giving you up. You have my word on that."

She said, "You're pathetic. Like your word is worth anything. I really thought you were on my side." Feeling betrayed, she let go of my arm with a shove and moved away a few feet from me. The rebuke in the move cut me to the quick, though I didn't blame her. The tactical advantage the space gave her as a black belt wasn't lost on me either. At the moment, though, I had bigger problems.

Rebecca remained silent, but I could only imagine what she was thinking. I whispered to her, "We need to hide out somewhere. Where can we can go to besides the mansion?"

"There's an old barn a couple of fields over. I've walked there many times. I think I can get us there in the dark."

J.B. yelled out, "Tick-tock-tick-tock, Vic."

I told Rebecca to lead the way and whispered for Samantha to follow her. She hesitated for a moment, but then started off and I fell in behind her. At one point there was a break in the trees and we could pick our way by the moonlight. I watched as Samantha slipped off her heels, and enjoyed the sway of her hips as she picked up the pace to catch up to Rebecca.

We hadn't gone very far when we heard yet someone else coming up the driveway. We were still close enough to see through the mesh of leaves as a van pulled up and parked behind the Caddy. The four men we had seen outside David's house, still dressed in coveralls, got out, each one holding some sort of small machine gun.

J.B. asked, "Who the hell are you guys?" He and his hired help still had their guns in their hands, but held them out to the side.

The driver of the van asked, "Where's the girl?"

"What girl?" J.B. decided to play dumb. Turned out to be a bad move. The driver shot J.B.'s henchman with a short burst from the machine gun, the bullets causing him to dance backwards a few steps, and then he went down hard, collapsing into the shrubs.

The gunman leveled his gun at J.B. and said, "Let me ask this one more time, where's the girl?" This time J.B. didn't hesitate.

"We followed her here, but she wasn't inside. She has to be here someplace. We think she's with a bounty hunter named Victor McCain. That's his car. I know him. He's a real pain in the ass, but good at what he does, a professional. Let me find them for you. I can talk to Vic and get him to hand over the girl and save you a lot of trouble."

The driver considered this for a moment, then asked "What about the other girl?"

"What other girl? Who the hell you talking about, man? Don't shoot me, man, I don't have a clue who you're talking about."

The driver motioned for two of the other guys to search the house. I didn't need to hear any more and motioned Rebecca to keep going.

Samantha said, her voice low, "You lying son of a bitch. I trusted you."

"And you still can," I shot back. "Give me a chance to explain when there is less of a chance of getting our asses shot off, will you?"

She gave it a rest as we followed Rebecca off the path, and moving as quietly as we could, to the barn. We were about ten minutes into our walk when we once again heard the short bark of a machine gun. Looks like they didn't feel they needed J.B anymore. I felt myself grow angry. J.B. was a good guy and didn't deserve to be shot like some rabid dog. There was going to be hell to pay when this was finished. Literally. Samantha wasn't the only one who now wanted retribution.

It wasn't long before we could see flashlights back on the path headed towards the mansion. It wouldn't take them long to figure we weren't there either and for them to broaden their search. I had to wonder what Winston was doing right at this moment. If he had any sense, he would have bolted at the first sounds of automatic gunfire. Three flashlights meant they most likely left one guy back with the cars, so circling back there would be risky.

The barn looked several decades old, with planks missing here and there, and smelled of hay. The front doors were open so we went inside. I took out my iPhone and from the phone's soft glow, I could see the barn was filled mostly with square bales of hay. Nowadays most people used round bale, so this was something of a surprise.

I walked over to a missing slat and watched the trail leading back to the cottage. I couldn't see anyone. Samantha rounded on me and asked, "Who hired you? Deveraux had no clue who you were, neither did Kevin, so it wasn't them. So who hired you? My father?"

I told Rebecca to keep an eye out while I searched the barn. "No. It wasn't your father. It was someone above his pay grade." I felt my jaw clenching in irritation and forced myself to relax. It wasn't her fault I was in this mess. Her only confidant had been murdered, her father had sent a minion from Hell to find her and then she finds out I wasn't what I claimed I was.

"Oh come off it, Vic. No one's above my father when it comes to the Church. Deveraux offered you a million. How much did you sell me out for, Vic? Or is that even your real name?"

I found empty canning jars on a work bench near the front door, as well as an old red five gallon container sitting on top of a broken down lawnmower. I unscrewed the cap and took a sniff. Gasoline. I looked around and found a dusty blanket on the ground and brought it with the can over to the bench, shaking the dirt out of the blanket.

"Unlike you, Vic is my real name. I told you, my situation is complicated. And you're wrong. There is someone above your father."

I don't know why I felt the need to explain to her and get her to understand. One thing I've learned as a bounty hunter is not to get attached to who you had caught. Everyone has a sad story. Some would beg, some would even plead for you to let them go. Some offered money, or drugs, or sex. Keeping a distance between you and the perp made things easier. Point is, I had her in my custody and if I did get her out of here safely, I was planning on turning her over to Satan, so best to keep my distance.

Or was I going to turn her over? The more the night went on, I became less sure of exactly what I was going to do with her. Would trading her for my brother's soul be the right thing to do? In the abstract, from my point of view, yes it was. I trade her for my brother. If she believed in God, with any luck, He would protect her, at least in the afterlife, if not this one. My brother was screwed if I didn't bring her in. There was only one person in the world that could save my brother, and I was it. Yet deep down inside, I felt a need for her to understand why I was doing what I was doing.

"Oh, give me a break. I had a reason for changing my name and you know it. How complicated could it be for you, Vic? You've seen what these people are like. You're in bed with them so how are you any different?"

I used the glow of my phone to see by, as I ripped the blanket into thin strips. I didn't reply to her, concentrating on what I was doing. Samantha walked to me and leaning back on the bench said, "Damn it Vic, answer me." When I said nothing, she continued, "Tell me this, at least. How much did it take to buy you?"

For several seconds I didn't reply. I laid the blanket strips onto the bench, and then held onto the edge of the bench myself as I bowed my head.

"My brother's soul."

I could hear Samantha's sharp intake of breath. I couldn't look at her or Rebecca. "The Devil came to me and told me if I found you and brought you to him, that he would release my brother from a soul contract he signed."

She crossed her arms across her chest. "Right. You expect me to believe that you had a face to face with the Devil? Do I *look* like an idiot?"

I felt very tired. I went back to my work, unscrewing the gas cap and filling two jars with gasoline. I soaked two blanket strips in gasoline as well and then dropped one end of the strips into the jars and put the screw lids back on top, making two quick Molotov cocktails.

"So asks the woman who earlier this evening told me about vampires. Look, at this point, whether you believe me or not, doesn't really matter. But your dad prays to him. Eamon was back on Earth because of him, and I've met the prick. And if I really was anxious to hand you over, I've had several chances to do so and haven't. You should be asking yourself why not?"

She furrowed her brow and I could tell she was doing just that: thinking about why I hadn't turned her over to Deveraux. I took a couple of the hay bales, ripped them apart and spread them across the barn's dirt floor. Then I poured the rest of the gasoline onto the hay.

Looking alarmed, Rebecca asked, "What the hell are you doing?"

"Backup plan. Always have a backup plan. Tell us everything you told David about the Exodus Project?"

"I told you most of it. Lincoln was bragging that he had solved some big technical problem they were having with the computers and the computer virus. He told me about how they were going to hit Christian schools and start a religious war with Muslims.

"I was with him again last night. He left his computer laptop on while he went to take a shower. I checked his computer and it had some file up and I took a picture of the documents he had open. They were all technical mumbo-jumbo to me. So I took pictures of them with my phone and then texted them to David."

"Do you still have them on your phone?"

She nodded yes. "Send them to me."

Pointing to Samantha, she asked, "Why? If you were hired to find her, why do you care?"

"Just do it, please." I shoved my hands in my pockets, suddenly exhausted. "I'll say it again, it's complicated. If you two don't want my help, fine by me. But if you do, you need to start letting me help you."

I gave her my cell number and I took her place watching for the bad guys while she texted the photos to me.

Samantha walked up beside me and stood there looking out into the night for a bit, content to listen to the night sounds before she said anything. I could tell she was thinking hard as she began biting her bottom lip again.

"You said I should be asking myself why you didn't turn me over to Deveraux. Well, I have and I can't come up with anything. Rebecca's right, why even help me at all?"

I said nothing.

"I mean, if you really did promise Satan you'd find me for him, why didn't you just hand me over right away when you had the chance?"

I said nothing. My phone beeped as the photos from Rebecca found their way to my account.

She laid a hand on my arm, gently this time. "Talk to me, Vic. I'm just trying to understand what's going on."

"I'll tell you later."

She reached up and took my chin in her hand, turning my face towards her. I could see her eyes in the starlight falling through the gap in the barn wall, eyes mixed with fear and concern. "Why won't you tell me now?"

I pointed off into the darkness. "Because they're coming."

Chapter Twelve

The flashlights were headed in our direction. Guess someone at the mansion had told them about the barn.

Frightened, Rebecca asked, "Why don't we make a run for it?"

"We won't get very far. I have a flashlight app on my phone, but we can only move so fast and Samantha isn't exactly wearing hiking boots." She did look damn good though, in her black evening dress with her coat unzipped, her feet bare. I gave myself a mental slap to get back to business.

"They have better flashlights and are better equipped. I think it's time to even the odds some." I looked at Samantha. "Just a wild guess, you're using a throw away cell phone, right?

"Yes, why?" She got her phone out of her coat pocket.

"Anyone else have that number besides David?" There wasn't much time before the bad guys made their appearance.

"No. He got the phone for me. I only used it to call him and vice versa."

"Good, then you won't miss it. Give your number to Rebecca so she can call you on it right now. I'd use David's phone, but it doesn't have a speakerphone option."

She did so and Rebecca, nervous and fumble-fingered, took two attempts to dial the number. I took the phone and pressed the speakerphone button, went over to the stacked bales of hay, pulled one out and placed the phone down behind it.

Then I walked over and picked up the two Molotov cocktails. "Leave the connection open. I want the two of you to go a little ways into the woods, but stay where you can still see the light from my phone. When I flash you twice, here's what I want you to do."

I told them and then led them out to the edge of the woods. "If you two bolt on me, all three of us are as good as dead. Or at least Rebecca and I are." I looked at Samantha. "You'll get to live, at least for a little while. Until they get their money back, at any rate. And before they do that, I'll come back and haunt you from beyond the grave."

Samantha asked, "How do I know I can trust you, Vic?" She looked me straight in the eyes. No sarcasm, no anger. Just a simple question.

"You don't. But believe me when I say, right now, the only thing between you and a date with the Devil: is me."

I smiled and said, "But if they kill me, feel free to run like hell." I turned and walked back to the barn. There was an old tractor parked next to it on the side closest to the woods, and I kneeled down behind it. I looked through some missing slats to the other side and could see the coverall crew was almost to the barn. I sheltered my iPhone in my bomber jacket and turned on the flashlight app, which uses the phone's camera flash as a bright flashlight. I stuck my hand through the gap in the barn wall and showed the light around the inside of the barn briefly, then turned the app off.

Just as I hoped, the three men who were approaching saw the light and broke into a quick jog towards the barn. I waited a moment and faced my phone in the direction of the women and clicked my phone on and off twice, with the more gentle glow of the startup screen facing towards them.

From inside the barn I heard Rebecca say, "Here they come, hide!" Followed by Samantha saying, "Be quiet or you'll give us away."

The men approached the front of the barn and two men came in as one of them shouted, "We know you're in here. Come out now and we won't hurt you. You have our word."

The other one said, "Do you smell that? Smells like gasoline."

"We're coming out," shouted Samantha. "Please don't shoot!"

The men moved a little further into the barn and that was enough for me. I took my Bic lighter out of my pocket, struck it and set the blanket strip on fire and tossed the Molotov cocktail through the gap in the slats, hitting the ancient lawnmower on the front grill, shattering the glass.

The gasoline ignited in a ball of fire and the small explosion set the gasoline soaked hay into an instant blaze. The old barn went up instantly in flames. The men screamed as they were engulfed by the fire. I lit the other Molotov cocktail and threw it between them and the door.

The men ran from the barn with their clothing on fire. They dropped their guns as they fell on the ground, rolling, in an attempt to put out the flames that engulfed them. Two down, one more to go. I pulled out my own gun and turned the corner of the barn, searching for the third man.

From behind me, I heard, "Drop the weapon and turn around." Looks like he found me. He must have run to the back of the barn and circled behind me when the fire started.

I did as he asked. I dropped my gun and turned around slowly to find myself looking down the short barrel of his machine gun. I wish I could say my life flashed before my eyes, but it didn't. The one thought that went through my mind was...figures. I can't tell you how many nights I lay in my bunk in Afghanistan wondering if I would die the next day and how. Would I get taken out by an IED, or would a sniper get me? I envisioned a million different ways to die.

After I got home from the war, I had dreams about how I'd be busting down some door and a perp or his girlfriend would shoot me. But I never dreamed this would be the way I'd go out. As I said: figures.

"Hey, did you bring any marshmallows? Or maybe hot dogs?" I asked. "As long as we have this fire going, we might as well take advantage of it." I sniffed the air as the smell of burning flesh was carried on the otherwise pleasant night breeze. "Smells like crispy critters. Guess two rats went up with the fire."

I gave him my best what the hell grin. He wasn't impressed. "You must be the bounty hunter. For what you did to Frank and Willy, I should make you suffer like they did. But tell me where the women are and I'll kill you quickly. You're a dead man either way. But how you die is up to you."

Like hell he would. I knew telling him I didn't know wasn't a good answer, as it hadn't done much for J.B.'s sidekick. I also knew I couldn't tell him where the girls were either. Before I could come up with another snide remark, a man stepped out from behind the tractor, put the muzzle of his gun against the back of the man's head and said, "I will give you one chance to lower your gun or I will blow your head off." Politely said, but with an unmistaken authority.

The gunman looked to be Latino. He was of average height, but broad in the shoulders, somewhere north of thirty years old, wearing a dark jacket, washed out jeans and worn leather boots. His hair was cropped very close to his skull and in the flickering light from the fire, I couldn't help but notice the tattoos that ran down his neck and beneath the collar of his shirt. Gang tattoos. Mexican gang tattoos.

The gun hand was steady and never wavered. The barn fire was picking up steam and the heat was growing intense, along with the situation.

The man holding his gun on me dropped his weapon. My savior took him by the collar of his coveralls and, keeping the gun pressed to his head, led him away from the now raging inferno and towards the woods. He nodded for me to follow. When I bent down to pick up my gun he said, "Take it easy my friend, use only the fingers and grab by the barrel."

Since he was the man with the plan, I did as he said. His accent was definitely from south of the border, but his English was better than some Kentuckians. He moved with an easy grace, like one of the pros on Dancing with the Stars. Once we were by the woods, he forced the man in coveralls to his knees, looked at me and said, "Throw the gun."

I did so. And I did so slowly. He watched me carefully, like a panther watching a rabbit he has trapped between his paws.

"Señoritas, please join us." He waited a moment. "I know you are here, I watched you walking in the trees. I will not hurt you, I promise."

After a moment Samantha and Rebecca came out from hiding, Rebecca still holding her suitcase. They approached to within a few feet, but no closer. They looked at me and then back to the man holding the gun. Neither came to stand by me. Probably a smart move on their part.

"So you are Victor McCain, the bounty hunter?" he asked me, while never taking his gun from Deveraux's man.

"That's right. But call me Vic. All my friends do, especially those holding a gun."

"A bounty hunter who looks for women?"

Not a man into witty banter. "Just one of them, the mouthy redhead. Her name's Samantha. We came out to try and save the other one from the Church of the Light Reclaimed. Her name's Rebecca."

He looked at Samantha. "So, this man was looking for you, but you come to help this other señorita?"

Ever have one of those moments, when you know you're whole life may depend on the answer, but you have no clue why? This seemed to be that kind of moment. The man's attitude remained casual, but there seemed to be more to what he was asking than simple curiosity. It was as if my life depended on her answer.

Samantha looked at me for what seemed a long time. "Yeah," she said. "We came here together. He saved my life earlier tonight. He also tried to help save the life of a friend of mine, though he died anyway, but it wasn't Victor's fault. And he was doing what he could to save us again when you showed up."

Samantha didn't mention that I deceived her from the beginning and that she wasn't aware I was a bounty hunter until *after* J.B. arrived. And that I was doing as much to save my ass as I was theirs when he showed up. This conversation took place while the barn fire roared, baking the side of my face.

"Who's your jefe, Victor McCain? Who do you work for?" the man asked.

Once again, I knew the answer was important, without really knowing why. I also knew lying to this man, whoever he was, would be a really bad move.

"I was hired by Satan, to track down Miranda Chernenko, who, it turns out, is really Samantha Tyler."

He pursed his lips and nodded. If he thought I was nuts for saying I'd been hired by Satan, he kept it to himself. "And, you do this willingly?"

"No," I said. "I took the job because my brother sold his soul to the Devil and I was told if I found her and took her to him, he would tear up the soul contract and release his soul back to him."

"Tough deal, ah?" the man said. "So, Victor, why help the woman? Your job was to turn her in to the Dark One." Both Samantha and Rebecca had asked me the same question and I hadn't answered them. Mainly because I wasn't sure what the answer would be. I knew this man would not settle for an 'I'll tell you later.'

"I've been looking for a different way out. One that would save my brother, but not require me to hand her over."

"And you find the way?" Samantha watched me intently, as I considered my answer.

I sighed. "No. I haven't. I'm still working on it."

The man in coveralls, kneeling in the soft grass of the field, said, "Don't kill me, please don't kill me."

The man pushed forward with the barrel of the gun against the kneeling man's head and said, "Shhhh. Your final day is coming amigo, but now we are discussing Victor. Take your time to pray to God and the Saints so they may forgive your sins."

He continued, "If you don't find a better way, would you still save your brother instead of her?"

I could easily say no, that I'd changed my mind, that I would never do such a thing now. But I knew that was a lie. And while I never had a problem lying to people to get the information I wanted, I told him the truth. "I don't know. I'm still working on that one, too."

I thought this would anger the man, and that I would find myself kneeling in the mud, asking for him not to punch my ticket. But life is full of surprises. "I like your answer, Victor. I respect an honest man in situations like this."

"You keep using my name, but I don't know yours."

He smiled, revealing several teeth capped in gold. "My name is Dominic Montoya."

"Jesus," Samantha said, "It's the Hand of God."

Chapter Thirteen

So God's trigger man on Earth is a tattooed Mexican cartel gang banger. You might as well have told me my great Uncle Rupert, the one that hates kids and loves his Irish Whiskey, is really Santa Claus. I could see the shock on Samantha's face, and the awe on Rebecca's face. Guess the man had a reputation.

Samantha said, "You were supposed to meet me at the Down and Dirty tonight, but you never showed." Her tone made her statement an accusation. To a man holding a gun, no less. Tough girl.

"I was busy with another thing. I got there late but you were gone fast. I heard the men in the Cadillac talking about you and Victor. They say they had a tracker on Victor's auto and when they follow for you, I follow them. I was curious why they want you bad. Then I was in the parking lot at Phoenix Hill when you left the cementerio. Victor, very nice plan. Very nice."

I shook my head. "Not really. I sucker punched him. Not one of my proudest moments."

He shrugged his shoulders. "We do what we has to do" He continued, "When the men left to follow for you, I did the same and lucky you, it seems. Which brings us to this man," he said, gesturing with his free hand to the man kneeling before him. "I know he kill two men this evening" He pushed the man's head lightly with his gun. "What is your name?"

The man's crying had stopped. He said in a very soft voice, "Dutch. Dutch Simpson."

"Who is your jefe?" Montoya's words were simply said, but they carried an undertone of authority.

"I work for Preston Deveraux. He works for the Church of the Light Reclaimed."

"And what were your instructions for tonight?"

"Go fuck yourself. Let's get this over with."

"As you wish." The Hand of God motioned for the two women to turn around. Rebecca did so and hid her face in trembling hands. Samantha continued to watch Montoya, her face showing no emotion, as he prepared to execute the man before him. I guessed she wanted to see some payback for what happened to David. But I couldn't believe what I was seeing.

"Wait," I said, "You don't have to do this. Why don't we just turn him over to the
cops. That's what our legal system is for. Let them take care of this douche bag."

"Sorry, but I deliver an Old Testament justice. I answer to no earthly jurisdiction."

And with that he pulled the trigger. Simpson toppled face first into the short green grass of the pasture, while some of his blood and brains sprayed onto my boots. I felt anger at his death. I have no problem killing people when there is no other choice. Hell, I'd just killed two men by burning them to death and shot another man to death earlier in the evening. But I killed them because that was my only option if I wanted to keep breathing. Montoya did have a choice and there were other options besides blowing the man's head off. Simpson may have been evil, but he was defenseless and no threat to us. We could have tied him up and hauled his ass off to the cops.

And now I had to wonder if I was next. I found out soon enough as The Hand of God focused his attention back on me.

Montoya said, "Step out from the gun and go with the women."

I released the breath I'd been holding and did as he asked and stood by Samantha. He picked up my gun, slid out the clip and ejected the round I had hot in the chamber. He put the extra round back in the magazine and then tossed me my gun and clip. "For now, put the clip in your coat pocket and the gun back in its holster. If I see you looking for them without my permit, I will kill you."

Of this I had no doubts. "Should I say thank you, or what?"

"You should say thank you, God" He looked at the barn fire and said, "Vamonos. Soon someone will see the flames and call it in. We go before authorities arrive."

The man had a point and we started back to the cottage at a brisk walk, leaving the raging fire behind. Considering the amount of dead bodies, it would pay to be anywhere but here when the cops arrived.

Montoya asked, "What was your deal with el Diablo? Tell me specifically what you promised to do and when."

I told him the arrangements Satan and I had made. "Then there is time to decide what you do. When Luci makes a deal, he must adhere to the agreement, down to the last letter. You have put your own soul at risk by agree to work for Luci. If you do this thing, then your soul will also be lost.

Your brother cannot be saved. Once he agree to sell his soul he was lost to you and to God."

"I thought God allowed anyone to ask forgiveness for his sins and to enter Heaven if he or she truly means it. And why do you call him Luci?"

He smiled. "Luci is what I call the evil one as I will not honor him with any other name. As for forgiveness, your brother made a deal with the devil, Victor. Even if you deliver Samantha to Luci and he tears up your brother's soul contract, your brother will still go to Hell. Luci will find a way to trick you or him. You must accept this fact. God gives us the freedom to choose our path in life and death and your brother has chosen the path to Hell. He knew this when he sold his soul."

To hell with that, I thought. There had to be a way to save my brother and I would find it. I kept this to myself, however, as I had no desire to join Simpson in the great beyond. As we neared the cottage, I said to Montoya, "There was a fourth man. They must have left him waiting at the cottage."

Montoya said, "He is not a problem."

"What, you killed him, too?"

In the pale moon's light, I could see Montoya's jaw muscles clench. "I do not answer you, comprende? Thank you God put me here to save you tonight like the women. I do what I do on God's behalf, not yours or another's."

"What ever happened to turn the other cheek? Love thy neighbor? Do unto others as you would have them do unto you?" I could feel myself growing more angry and I wasn't sure why. My frustration level was shooting through the roof and I was having a real problem putting a lid on my emotions.

There could be little doubt things were spinning out of my control. With the Hand of God on the scene, I didn't know what this would mean for my brother. A new dynamic had been introduced and I would have to find a way to adapt. Making decisions when you are anything other than level-headed is a short path to disaster.

When we reached the cottage, Montoya asked the women to wait by the door as he motioned me to follow him to the back of the van. He opened the door and inside there were six bodies. David's body was there as well as that of the two Ice Pick Lovers, Kevin, J.B., and his hired hand. Guess the Church didn't suffer failure when it comes to their assassins. "God's love means nothing to men who would do something like this. Do you recognize any of these unfortunates?" he asked.

I told him who each corpse was and then told him how David died.

He crossed himself and said a short prayer for the dead. Montoya said, "I sad that the reporter is dead. He was a very, very good man. He was the one that contact me first, through an intermediary, and asked me to meet with Miss Tyler."

"So what now?" I asked. This simple question could very well decide not only my brother's fate, but mine.

"What are you going to do with Rebecca? She cannot stay here," Montoya said.

"I have no real plans other than to get her away from here and someplace the Church won't find her."

"Very well, I know a place I can take her where she be safe, for now at least." We closed the doors on the back of the van.

"And Samantha?" I asked.

"That will be up to her." He motioned for me to return to the women, who were speaking in low tones as we approached. Montoya said to them, "Here is the plan. Rebecca, I will take you away from the guys that are looking for you. Don't you have a car here, eh?"

"No," she said, "I was going to ride with Victor and Samantha."

"You can go with me. My car is just down the street. And you, Samantha, who would you like to go with?"

I was surprised at the question, assuming she would ride with the Hand of God. She said, "I'll ride with Vic. Someone has to keep him out of trouble." She took a few steps until she was standing close to me and I felt a surge run through my body as if an electrical charge had jumped from her body to mine. I don't know why she was staying with me, but I didn't care.

"OK. You two follow me. After I see to it that Rebecca is good, the three of us will find a place to speak."

I jabbed my thumb at the van. "What should we do about this?"

"There is no time. Someone will find them soon enough. The Lord's will be done."

I said to Rebecca, "Call your sister and tell her not to come anywhere near this place."

"I will." She gave Samantha and me quick hugs. "Thank you. I'd be dead if it wasn't for the two of you." We said our goodbyes and she and Montoya quickly headed down the drive.

Before Samantha and I got in the Chevelle, I ran my hand under the edge of the car and found the GPS device, a Spark Nano, stuck to the underside of the back bumper. I shook my head again and said, "I should have guessed this right off." I turned it off and put it in my jacket pocket.

We got in the car and I did a quick turn around and scooted by the van with its cargo of the dead. Won't the cops be happy when they find this little dust up? She asked me what was in the back of the van and I told her. Then I said, "I'm more than a little surprised that you would get back in the car with me, you know, considering."

"I have faith in you, Vic. From what I've seen tonight, I don't think you're the kind of guy that would just hand me over like that. Besides, I have way too many sins of my own to go car hopping with the Hand of God." She let out a small laugh, but then turned more serious. "Let's just do our best to convince him to do something about the Exodus Project."

I found it ironic that a woman like Samantha, who believed God was dead was talking about faith, and more to the point, faith in me. She knew how important she was to me when it came to saving my brother's soul and knew I still had not decided on if I would make the trade.

Yet here she was, slouched in her seat, feet up on the dashboard, riding into the night with me. While she looked exhausted from the evening's events, she, at the same time, looked more relaxed. Perhaps having the Hand of God on the scene gave her more hope. It had done just the opposite for me. His pronouncement that there was no way to save my brother's soul had me worried.

We soon caught up to Montoya and Thomas as they were getting into a green Jeep Wrangler. He pulled out and we fell in behind him. We hit Covered Bridge Road and headed back towards the city. It wasn't long before a fire truck and two police cars raced past us going in the direction of the farm. The shit was getting ready to hit the fan and I, for one, felt happy I wouldn't be there when it did.

Chapter Fourteen

We made our way back into the city. Montoya pulled into a gas station on Market Street. We pulled up next to him and the zip flap on his window was down. He said, "Wait here. I'll be back in about fifteen minutes."

Rebecca gave us a shy wave and with that, he pulled back out and was gone. I slid my phone out of my pocket and said, "Let's see what documents Rebecca sent me." I thumbed over to my text messages and downloaded the images. I leaned to the middle of the car so that Samantha could look as well. Once again I caught the hint of her perfume, this time mixed with a whiff of smoke from the barn fire.

I swallowed hard and briefly closed my eyes, resisting the urge to move even closer to her. I'd been hired to find this woman and had done so. But here I was wanting to take her into my arms, and world be damned when it came to the consequences. My body was having a fight with my brain and my brain was starting to lose the fight. And if that happened, I might just lose both my soul and that of my brother's.

I had to wonder if she was feeling the same thing, as she was leaning in closer than she needed in order to view my phone screen. I had to snap out of it! I was starting to think like a love-sick high school kid.

Lucky for me, the pictures finished their download. The first few images were a little blurry, but appeared to be some parts order list. It looked to be all computer equipment type-stuff and in large quantities: motherboards, computer cases, and the like, with five hundred of each. So they were going to build five hundred machines? And then what?

The last two images were of a flier. It was for an academic tournament to be held on December 20th called *God's Vision Academic Challenge*. Parochial schools from around the region would be competing on the same day using something called God's Vision 2012 software to compete and earn prizes for the schools. The second page touted the fact that the software and the computers would be donated by some outfit called Inspiration Global Software. Guess we now knew where the five hundred computers were going to end up.

"Have you ever heard of Inspiration Global Software?" I asked. She shook her head no. I switched over to the browser on my phone and Googled the company. There was a place holder website listing their address in St. Matthews, an eastern suburb of Louisville. They had a phone number as well, but when I called I got a recording asking me to call back during business hours.

The only other information on the site said they were a company that designed educational software for parochial schools and that more information would be available soon. There was one link, and that was to a page that listed the same information as the flier.

If they were planning a computer attack, this appeared to be how they would go about it. Donate the computers with the computer virus built into the software. And they were going to use this to start a religious war? How the hell they planned on doing that was anybody's guess. I'd known some people to get really ticked off over a computer virus, but mad enough to start a war? Maybe enough to slug a geek, but not enough to go to war.

Montoya pulled back up next to us, Rebecca no longer in the car. He offered up no explanation as to where he'd taken her and we didn't ask. He suggested we hit the Dizzy Whizz burger joint, which was fine with me. I'd spent my last meal in Louisville there before shipping off for basic training at Fort Leonard Wood, Missouri by catching a Greyhound Bus a few blocks over. Besides, nothing like a little grease after offing a few guys.

We followed him over to the diner and I thought about the evening on the drive over. No matter what happened before my 6 P.M. deadline, life forever changed with my killing of three men and one former man. My fingerprints were going to show up at two crime scenes. And since my prints were on file with the state as part of the licensing process to become a bounty hunter, they would be looking for me—sooner rather than later.

I dialed my brother's number again, but it went straight to voicemail. Samantha asked, "Are you and your brother close?"

"Not overly. But he and my mother are. And if he died, my mom would be crushed. If she ever found out he sold his soul, I can't imagine what it would do to her."

"How about your dad? Is he still in the picture?"

"Nah. He died of a heart attack. Worked his ass off to save enough money to put us through college, but Mikey flunked out and I ended up leaving right after I graduated from college to join the Army to kick some Al Qaeda backside."

We pulled in at the Dizzy Whizz next to Montoya and the three of us went inside. After ordering, we took a table near the back. We had to make quite the scene. Between my size, Montoya's gang tats and the beauty of Samantha, we were a strange mix. She brought her case inside with her and sat next to me. Perhaps she planned on using it to cut her burger in half. She did a good enough job on Eamon. I doubted a knock down drag out would take place at the Dizzy Whizz, but guess it's better to be prepared than not.

Sitting this close to Samantha was messing with my thought process. There had to be a pheromone reaction going on between us, at least on my end.

Dominic Montoya broke my reverie and asked, "So, now that you and me get to have our sit down Miss Tyler, what I can do for you?"

Samantha gave him the quick rundown on what she knew about what the Church had in motion with the Exodus Project and her stealing the thirty million dollars to slow them down. I added my input on the documents that Rebecca had texted to me. We also told him about what happened at David's house and Deveraux's part in our little drama. Montoya chomped down on a couple of fries while he listened to us without interrupting.

"This weekend is critical for the Church. I overheard my father say they would shell out millions for something that's going to take place here in Louisville. It's why I took off from Philadelphia a couple weeks ago with the money and came here. David and I were trying to figure out what. Now you know what we know."

When we finished he said, "I do not see what I can do for you. This is not the type of thing I get into it. And like you, I do not see how the Satanists plan on causing a religious war with a computer virus. If they plan a physical attack on children, it will be more different. But with what you tell me tonight, I do not think I can be of service to you."

Samantha leaned forward and said, "It has to be something big, though. There have been messages going back and forth between my father and people involved. They've been really jazzed over this thing. Plus, I know for a fact they have a lot of money wrapped up in this attack. You have to help us." There was desperation in her voice and exasperation on her face.

Montoya was unperturbed. He took a bite of his burger and said around the mouthful, "Keep digging, I will give you the number to my cell. It is only good this weekend. If you come up with something, then call me. I am in town one, maybe two days. Without more information, I cannot help you as I am here on other business. If I hear something, I will be in touch."

"So, what, that's it? You're just blowing us off?" She threw her hands up in the air. "I don't believe this. David lost his life over this," she said. "The Church is going to great lengths to silence anyone who knows anything at all about the Exodus Project. There has to be something you can do?"

"I did. I save your lives. I know you are upset. But I get ask to help in many things and many ways, and I only have so much time to give. Believe me, my friend, when I tell you there are problems more dangerous than computer virus. As I say, find me more on the threat and I will consider lending more aid. Until then, I cannot."

I said, "What about Deveraux? You know he's responsible for several murders. Aren't you going to dole out some Old Testament justice to him like you did Simpson?"

"At some point, I may have to deal with Deveraux the same way I did Simpson, but that is not my focus. If I kill everyone who committed murder in this world, I never sleep. As I say, I have something much more important that I work on. Give me more and then we see."

I was really ticked. I had a timeline to save my brother and, coincidentally, the Church was running on the same timeline. I don't like coincidences. It frustrated me to have a resource like the Hand of God in town, and for him not to help at such a critical point just blows. With his help, I could perhaps save my brother and protect Samantha. But, without him? It seemed an impossible task. What if my handing over Samantha brought about the holy war the Church had planned? The pressure to figure out this Rubik cube of a problem was mounting.

Montoya said, "One more question, Victor. Why you?"

My blood pressure shot up and I could feel my face flush red at the question. "Perhaps it's because I'm damn good at what I do. Did you stop to think about that? Samantha slid a hand over top of mine and gave it a squeeze.

He said, "Please forgive me, but you do not understand me. I'm not suggesting you are not good at your job. But if Luci had Miss Tyler's address, why involve you at all? Why not have members of the Church go to her address? Luci is a creature as old as Heaven itself. If he chose you, he did so for more reasons than the obvious. It is something you have to think about."

I cooled off as I realized he was right. I took a moment, considering what he said. "It could be as simple as he knew I would do what it takes to help my brother."

"Maybe," he said.

He ate the rest of his burger and fries and then asked Samantha, "You now have a choice to make before I go. If you want, you can go with me, and I do for you as I do for Miss Thomas. I will see to it you are a safe from harm, at least for now. There will be nothing Victor can do about it. Or

I can keep him here until you find your own way from this diner. Or you can continue to work with the bounty hunter. The choice is yours."

His hand was resting in his coat pocket, the same one where he stashed his gun. I kept my hands resting on the table top, in plain sight, and concentrated on not making any sudden movements.

"That's O.K. I know a big part of the Exodus Project happens this weekend, and if I'm in hiding, I won't be able to help stop it. And if you won't step up and do something about it, then I guess that leaves me." She looked at me. "I don't think Victor has it in him to turn me over to Satan. At least he's offered to help me and I plan on holding him to that commitment."

"How can you be so sure about a man you just met?" asked the Hand of God.

She gave a dazzling, but weary smile and said, "I have faith Mr. Montoya. I have faith. Maybe not in God, but I do in Victor. And I have a big shiny sword."

Honestly, I thought she was nuts. Lord knows I didn't have faith I wouldn't turn her over in exchange for my brother. In fact, I was rather conflicted about the whole thing. Blood is thicker than most anything else and I was on a mission to find a way to save Mikey. What if turning over Samantha was my only option to save him? I still had no clue what I would do. If I was in her shoes, I would want to run as far away from me as possible.

Montoya said, "The choice is yours, my friend. But let me say this to you, Victor. If you hand over Miss Tyler to Luci, I will make it a point to hunt you down myself. Comprende? You have my word."

I would normally have had any one of a dozen smart ass replies, like I always do when someone threatens me. Not this time. Not with this man. I said, "If I do that, then the Hand of God won't have to hunt me down, you'll find me in my office waiting."

He took out a pen and, on a napkin, wrote down his cell number and passed it over to me. "So be it. Good luck to you and may God protect you." And with that The Hand of God got up and left the building, thank you very much.

Chapter Fifteen

Samantha took a long swig of her Diet Coke and said, "Well, that sucked." She sat back in the booth deflated and stared out the window, watching the cars go by outside. I had to agree with her. She and David had worked to put together a meeting with the man they thought would ride in and save the day, the Hand of God no less. But instead, here she was stuck with a man who was only there so that in less than twenty-four hours, he could trade her in for someone else's damaged soul.

When you consider her main confidant had been tortured and brutally murdered, her cover blown, and the Hand of God brushed her off, then my day didn't look so bad. Of course, the night was still young.

She turned back to me and said, "So it's you and me, Vic. The Hand of God is out. How 'bout you? Still willing to help?"

"Sure, why not. I don't have anything planned until six tomorrow night. Until then, I'm free."

This got me another eye roll, which women seem to be really good at when I'm around. I was trying to lighten the mood, but she seemed almost blasé about the possibility that I might trade her in. I know I didn't feel that way, with my stomach in knots just thinking about it.

I said, "What do you want to do next?"

"Well, let's take another look at those documents on your phone Rebecca sent you. Do you know anything about computers?"

I got my iPhone back out and said, "Not much. I know how to turn them on and use the Google Machine part. And I know how to look for deleted items and search through email folders. That's how I found you, by the way. You didn't delete the email of your meeting tonight. Nice apartment."

She hit me hard on the shoulder. "You broke into my apartment and went through my computer?"

"Yep. And all your drawers. I was in a hurry, so I had to just dump the stuff on the floor. Things aren't quite as neat as you left them." This got me an eyebrow raise. "I did keep my eyes mostly closed while dumping out your underwear drawer." The eyebrow went higher. "I did try and help out, though. I put a whuppin' on J.B. and his boys when they broke in right after I did. Oh. And we sort of broke some furniture during the fight. Sorry about that, Chief."

"Anything else?" she asked, giving me the kind of stare my mom would use when she and I both knew I'd been caught breaking house rules.

"No, that's pretty much it. For future reference, I'd make sure and delete any email you don't want others to read. Just saying."

She shook her head and shifted her eyes back to the parts list again, embarrassed. "It's not like I've ever tried to disappear before. I'm kind of new at this."

I said, "Not bad for a first effort. And let's face it, they did send a pro like me to find you. So you didn't have much of a chance anyway. You've been spending the thirty million, haven't you? Everything in your apartment is brand new. And the Mercedes. It threw me off at first. That and the fact you had no pictures on the walls."

"Yeah, I spent some of the money. But the rest is hidden. I plan on donating it to different charities, as soon as I can figure out how to do it so it doesn't come back on me. The Church will never get their money back." She pointed to the phone and said, "This is all gibberish to me."

"Hang on. We're making this too hard on ourselves. I know somebody who's good at this computer crap."

I tapped over to my contacts and pulled up the number for Kurt Pervis. I use Kurt when I need some minor hacking or research done and I don't have the time or expertise to do it myself. In his mid-twenties, Kurt worked for the local cable company doing tech support during the day. A borderline genius, he never managed to make it in the corporate "tech world" because of his reputation for not playing well with others and having the social skills of a ten year old. On the phone, one on one, he's fine. But in social situations, such as dealing with co-workers? Not too good. He typically spends eight hours a day at work wearing a headset and talking to strangers. And during his break? He reads, keeping to himself.

I hit send on the number and after a few rings he said, "What the hell do you want, Vic. It's late on a Friday night and I have three women over here. You're interrupting my groove, man."

"Yeah, right. Put the blow up dolls down for a minute. I got something I want you to look at. I'll text you the images. It's some kind of parts list for building computers. I want you to tell me what kind they're building and anything else you can tell me about them.

"Aw man. I'm really busy. Can't this wait until tomorrow?"

"No way, Kurt. This is a priority job. I have to make some decisions on what I do next based on what you tell me. Don't make me come over there in person. If you do, I'll take a straight pin and pop all your women."

"Yeah, yeah, cut the crap, Vic. I'll do it. No need to yank my chain, man. Text away."

I cut off the call, tapped into my texts from Rebecca and sent the images to Kurt. I added a note asking him to dig into Inspiration Global Software. Kurt had a knack for sifting through digital records to find what others would hope you never noticed. I once joked about him being a part of the hacker group Anonymous and he nearly coughed up a lung, so I wondered how close I got to the truth.

The Dizzy Whizz was getting ready to close so I said to Samantha, "While we're waiting on Kurt to call back, we might as well drive over to Inspiration Global Software and snoop around."

She agreed and we headed out into the night. It was now almost 11 P.M. and the night was cooling off quickly. I opened the door for Samantha and she thanked me as she got in. We could've been just another couple out on a date. Any other time I would have been thrilled to have a woman like her in my car at this time of night.

But not this night, not this girl. Instead of taking home a beautiful babe, I was killing time until I had to decide what I'd do when it came time to trade her in. I pulled out of the parking lot laying down more rubber than I should have, as my frustration showed in my driving.

Inspirational Global Software was located in the heart of St. Matthews, a bustling commercial district made up of shops and old neighborhoods in far eastern metro Louisville. The office was part of an open plan walking mall, with an anchor store being Molly Malone's Irish Pub, my waterhole of choice. The office was tucked into the back of the complex between one shop selling musical equipment and one selling sports gear. Molly's was the only thing open this time of night and they were packed.

I said, "After we take a look, you should let me buy you a drink. Molly's is known for a great selection of beer and Lord knows I could use one right about now."

"First you wanted to kidnap me, now you want to get me liquored up? Maybe I'm not that kind of girl, Vic."

"God, I sure hope you are." I pulled around the complex and parked a couple of blocks down the street. We sat for a moment looking around. It was quiet on this end, well away from Molly Malone's. I couldn't see any security cameras, but I had to operate under the assumption they were there. "Let's go take a look, but keep your head down in case there are cameras."

We got out of the car and I offered her my arm. "We can pretend we're a couple out for a stroll."

With one hand she took my arm. With the other she held her sword case and we walked around to the front of the building. We peered into the front window. I could see a counter with a sliding glass window for a receptionist as well as a door off to the left of the counter. There were two armchairs and that was about it. The walls were a soft powdered blue with a couple of outdoor prints hung here and there.

People were milling about on the mezzanine outside Molly Malone's at the far end of the walk. So, there were too many people watching for me to take a run at the front door. And the back door didn't have a keyhole. It must be secured from the inside. I'd just have to wait till later when people moved inside to get out of the cool night air, to attempt to get inside the front door.

I turned my back to the crowd, slipped the gun and magazine from my pockets, slid the magazine into the gun, and put the gun back into the holster. I said, "I'm guessing the Hand of God doesn't mind me putting myself back together. After all, you have your sword. I'm feeling kind of naked without it—especially since things seem to happen around you. Do you have a problem with it?"

"I don't. Like I told Montoya, I don't think you'll hand me over. So I would rather you be armed and ready than not."

I offered my arm again and we strolled down towards Molly's. "You do realize you're nuts. You only met me a few hours ago, you know nothing about me and yet you think you know whether or not I would trade you to Satan for a family member? While I'm glad you feel that way, are you always this trusting? I still don't know what I'm going to do, yet you think you do? Considering who you're up against, that kind of trust might just get you killed at some point."

She squeezed my arm and gave me a reassuring smile. "You won't do it, Vic. I know you won't."

We walked in and I asked the hostess for my regular table away from the crowd. From my spot I could see both front entrances and the hallway to the backdoor. A DJ was playing some decent rock-n-roll and people were out dancing. There's a huge difference between the Double D and Molly's. For one, you felt like at Molly's you wouldn't catch something that might kill you just by sitting down.

A waitress came to our table and I ordered a Guinness and Samantha had a scotch, neat. We sat in silence until after the waitress brought us our drinks and left.

She twirled her glass around on the table for a moment, watching the amber liquid swirl. She said, "You know, I can't get the image of David being murdered out of my mind. Up until now, this night has seemed so surreal, like it was happening to someone else." She looked at me with those stunning green eyes, pulling me in. Turning serious, she continued, "Let me ask you something, when you killed that man at David's house, and then those two men in the barn, it didn't seem to really bother you. Why not?"

"Truth is, it doesn't. When I was fighting in the Middle East, I was part of a unit that spent most of our time hunting down high value Taliban and Al Qaeda targets. I had no problems with it because of what they did on 9-11. They earned it. Just like the guys I killed tonight. They earned it and I had no choice. They would have killed me for sure, and probably Rebecca, and maybe even you eventually. The one that did bother me was Simpson. He couldn't hurt us. So killing him was pointless. There were other ways to handle him. I know Montoya says it's Old Testament justice, but that was cold-blooded murder. Pure and simple."

Surprisingly accepting, she replied, "Eye for an eye, Vic. He murdered two men tonight, and God only knows how many others. I didn't have a problem with it." I wondered if she really meant it when she downed the shot of scotch in one gulp. "I want to thank you, though. If you hadn't pulled me off that woman I would have kicked her to death. In that moment I wanted nothing more than for her to suffer and die. I'm not sure I could have lived with myself if I'd done that."

Before I could respond, she stood up and slipped off her coat. "Come on, let's dance. With all the death tonight, I want to feel alive." I could now admire her figure fully as her black dress hung nicely in all the right places and the only word that kept going through my mind was "wow". I took my coat off, wreaking of smoke and sulfur, and untucked my dirty shirt to cover my gun.

I followed her out to the dance floor and you could just see all the men in the room turning to watch her dance. The DJ was just finishing up a song I didn't know when we hit the center of the room. Then he jumped right into *Bad, Bad, Leroy Brown.*

Samantha laughed and said, "It's almost like they know you."

"Hell, woman, I think they're singing about you."

And for a few minutes, we lost ourselves in the dancing. No Satan, no Mikey Boy, no death and no lies. I took her hand and spun her around. The Lord works in mysterious ways. Earlier in the day, if you would have told me I'd end the evening at Molly Malone's dancing with a beautiful redhead, I'd have said it would be the perfect evening.

Dancing with Samantha was close. Maybe it was what we'd been through already tonight and the couple of near death experiences. Maybe it was just good old-fashioned chemical attraction, but there was energy to our dancing and I could just feel the intensity rolling off of her. I never wanted a woman more than I wanted her, right then and there.

Yet I couldn't help thinking about an Elvis song: *Hard Headed Woman*. The song was written about temptation, from Eve offering Adam an apple to Samson and Delilah, to Jezebel. I took the job from Satan to save my brother. And here I was dancing and lusting after the one thing that could buy his freedom from Hell. Was this my temptation, my garden of Gethsemane, where Jesus said the spirit is willing, but the flesh is weak? Sister Margaret might be proud of how much I remembered, after all. Elvis, too.

The song ended and most of the people started to head back to their tables. We stood there for a moment, close to each other, when the next song started, *Just the Two of Us* by Bill Withers. I hesitated for just a moment, not sure what to do, when she took a half step forward, put her hands on my chest and moved them up and around my neck.

Like at the Down and Dirty, she made the first move. And like then, I went with it. I slid my hands around to her back and pulled her close, enjoying the feel of her body through the dress. Her body pressed against mine and we moved together. The rest of the room disappeared. She put her head on my shoulder and I leaned my cheek up against her head and breathed deeply, taking her in. For one more song I didn't worry about anything beyond holding her close. I had no idea how many more happy moments I would have. So I put thoughts of my brother and everyone else out of mind and just enjoyed the feel of her against me.

When the song ended she gazed up at me and said, "I don't want to die."

Chapter Sixteen

After the slow dance, we went back to our table and ordered a couple more drinks. I said, "Tell me more about you. Brothers, sisters? Is your mom a member of the Church?"

"Well, I'm an only child and my mother died when I was six years old. She had cancer and it ate her up pretty quick. That's what made my dad listen to Satan in the first place. Dad said Satan came to him one night in a dream and pointed out how God had never answered his prayers, but he would. He explained to him that the Bible was just the victor writing the history and God no longer cared about Man, because if he did care, he would save people like my mother. Satan presented himself as the Angel of Light that would restore man's faith in a divine being. This made the choice for my dad an easy one, from his point of view.

Satan promised to make him rich and famous, and he did. My dad is one of the most famous politicians in the country. The most powerful men and women in the world seek him out and ask his advice. So when it comes down to it, Satan had answered my dad's prayers and kept his promises and God didn't, which is why I think God is dead."

I shook my head. "At least now I can tell you that when the Devil made me the offer to help my brother, I got the impression that God still had him by the short hairs. So if the Devil's reaction is any indication, I think God is still alive. Don't ask me why God didn't save your mother. Probably for the same reason he didn't save my father from the heart attack that killed him, or answer my brother's prayers to become wealthy and famous." I took a moment to down my beer and wave to the waitress for another one for me and a shot for Samantha.

"And I have no clue what that reason is. The problem your dad has, though, is that he did the same thing my brother did. He traded his soul for wealth and power. Those things don't last. A rich man and a poor man take the same things into the great beyond: their souls. The Devil gave me a glimpse of what's in store for my brother. And if the same thing awaits your dad, heaven help him."

This time Samantha sipped her scotch. "Heaven can't save my

father. Even if I wanted to save him, he wouldn't listen. He never listens. Dad tells everyone else what to do. You never tell him what to do. After mom died, he shut everybody out."

"Bummer. Even you?"

"Especially me. I was raised by nannies and boarding schools for most of my life. Dad was always out on the campaign trail or traveling to other countries on fact finding trips. Look, I know I make it sound like my dad is an awful person, but he's not. After mom died, he was, I don't know, bitter I guess. When we're together, he's loving enough, in his own way. I know I do love him. That's why I'm trying to stop the Exodus Project. I'm trying to save dad from himself. In a way, I'm trying to save my dad, like you're trying to save your brother.

I didn't bring up the obvious: that her father must have a screw loose if he planned to attack kids and start a holy war. But she was right that our intentions were very much alike and had brought us to this point together. Before I could say anything else my phone rang and Kurt's picture flashed on my screen. I leaned across the table so Samantha could hear, too, and answered it. "What'cha got, brother from another mother?"

Kurt said, "Dude, are you out at a bar? I can hear the music playing. You're out partying while you have me working? That sucks."

"Man, I'm working a case, stopping busting my balls and let me know what you got."

"Fine, whatever. First things first. Seems they have the parts to make five hundred really good computers. Eight gigs of RAM, one terabyte hard drives, top of the line graphics cards, the works. There is one weird thing, though. Each computer has three fans, one over the chip, one blowing out the back, and one blowing air out the top. Pretty standard in some of these higher end computers. But near one of the fans, the front one, they're installing an aerosol canister. It must be some kind of new scent thing. Never heard of it, but I'm curious to see how they tie it in. Be kind of cool if you're playing a game and you could smell the place you're at as well as see it."

I said, "Since the last game I played was Asteroids, I don't think it would help me much."

"Dude, you're so old school. Like *really* old school."

"What else?"

"That's pretty much it on the computers. I've made progress on the company but it's tougher. They're really trying hard to hide the real owners of this thing by using shell and holding companies. The trail has lead me to a holding company in London, but there are more layers for me to get through."

"London, Kentucky?"

"No, dipshit, London, England. But it doesn't stop there. I need to hack into a few more databases and I'll have more information for you later. But definitely pointing to not American owned."

"Huh. Thanks Kurt. Keep digging. This helps out a lot."

"No sweat, Vic. But man you're going to owe me another one, if you know what I mean."

Samantha looked at me questioningly. I winked at her and said to Kurt, "Look man, I set you up the last time and you crashed and burned."

"Dude, she wasn't my kind of woman. It wasn't my fault we didn't work out."

Samantha stifled a laugh. "She was too your kind of woman. She was breathing and had a pulse. And yes, it was your fault it didn't work out. You took her to Wendy's for dinner. Sharon is used to eating at places where they come to your table to take your order, not the other way around. Not exactly a great dinner choice."

"Hey. I had coupons. Still, you'll owe me."

"I'll do what I can, Kurt. The rest is up to you," and hung up.

Samantha asked, "Where did he really take her?"

"To Wendy's. As the man said, he had coupons."

She laughed some more and said, "O.K. I've told you about my family. How about yours? Tell me about your brother."

I told her about Mikey Boy and our upbringing in a blue collar Catholic neighborhood here in Louisville. I talked about my dad, who worked at the Ford plant for nearly forty years before passing away.

"I went to the University of Kentucky and got a degree in history. While I was there, I joined ROTC. After I graduated, I did my four year hitch and liked it, so I re-upped and spent another tour playing in the sand and helping to hunt down Al Qaeda and Taliban wackos. When I got out, I became a bounty hunter. I put what I learned overseas to use back here on this side of the pond."

We spent the rest of the time talking about old boyfriends and girlfriends, the fact that neither of us could seem to keep a relationship going and that we could both agree that lima beans suck. I think we were both just doing our best to put off what we had to do next, but it was time to get moving. The waitress came by, but Samantha and I passed on any more imbibing. I asked her for the check and after she left I said, "I think we need to get inside Inspirational Global Software and see what they're up to."

"Can you get us in?"

"Yes, but we may not have much time once we're inside. If an alarm goes off, or we hear a panel beeping, we get the hell out of Dodge. We don't want to risk getting picked up by the cops. If they've found the van at Rebecca's, then they'll have found David and sooner or later, they're going to fingerprint Dave's house and our fingerprints are going to turn up. Mine are on file with the state as part of my license."

She said, "Mine aren't on file anywhere, but I agree. Now's not the time to be stuck in a holding cell someplace."

The waitress came back and I paid the bill. I helped Samantha put her coat on and then shrugged into mine and we went back out into the night. We walked back past the software company's front door. I stopped and looked at the lock. I told Samantha to keep a watch out and took a set of keys from my inside pocket. I searched around and found what I needed a few doors up at a small flower shop. I picked up a small decorative rock and went back to the front door.

"Since this is a brand of lock I know, I have a bump key that may work."

"What's a bump key?" She leaned up against the wall, blocking the view of anyone watching from down towards Molly's.

"It's a trick I learned from an A.T.F. buddy of mine. Every lock has keys with cuts and grooves to make the tumblers move out of the way to let the cylinder turn. A bump key is a key that is filed down so that the ridges are very short. This allows the key to be inserted all the way in." I sorted out a key and put it in the lock. "Then you pull the key out one notch, apply just a small amount of pressure and hit the key with something hard." I held up the rock. "This bumps the tumblers like billiard balls and allows you to turn the cylinder. If you're lucky." I struck the key with the rock and turned the key. With a click the cylinder turned and the door unlocked.

"Wow. Impressive. Is this how you got into my apartment?"

"Nah. I just picked yours. But let this be a lesson for you, buy better locks."

We entered the office and I closed the door behind us. We stood there for just a minute listening for a beeping from an alarm system, but didn't hear any. We looked around for a security panel and didn't find one. I asked Samantha to watch for cops as I went to the inner door and turned the knob. It opened and I stepped through, once again listening for the sound of an alarm system, but heard nothing nor saw a keypad. I told her to lock the door and join me.

We both moved to the interior office and I flipped on a light switch. There was a counter behind the receptionist's window which held a telephone, a can with a couple of pens and pencils and one of those three hundred and sixty-five day desk calendars, with a different quote from George W. Bush on each page. No one had turned a page since the middle of October and the quote said, *"I'll be long gone before some smart person ever figures out what happened inside this Oval Office."* George W. Bush, Washington, D.C., May 12, 2008. No shit there Sherlock.

The room had two desks, each with a swivel chair and a computer station. There were two doors in the room with one opening to a bathroom and the other to an empty back room with the rear exit. I moved behind one desk, Samantha to the other. A framed photo of two cute kids eating cotton candy sat on the desk, along with a few papers on top stacked neatly. A quick shuffle showed them to be letters thanking Inspirational Global Software for the upcoming donation of the computers and software and several personal notes on how they were looking forward to using the software to teach their children more about the Bible. There were dozens of such letters.

I moved the mouse on my computer and the screen came alive, but asked for a password. No dice. I looked over at Samantha and the computer on her desk showed the same thing. I shrugged my shoulders and started opening drawers. Inside one of them I found a long cardboard box with what I at first thought were business cards, but turned out to be peel-off stickers. They were in some kind of Arabic language that I had no clue how to read.

I showed one to Samantha and asked, "Any chance you read Arabic?"

"No chance. You were the one stuck over there. Didn't you pick up anything?"

"I never talked to them, I just killed them." The only other thing I found in the other drawers was office supplies.

I said, "Looks like to me this is just a front. They must want a physical address in case anyone gets curious and checks them out. My desk has more on it than these two do combined."

"I have to agree. Mine is exactly the same, minus the stickers. I wonder what they say?"

"Sounds like another job for Kurt. Won't he be thrilled." I took a photo of the sticker with my phone and texted it to Kurt, asking for a translation. I got a quick text back saying he wasn't my personal slave, followed by another one that said he was on it.

I sat and thought for a second. "There's something we're missing. I mean, think about it. They have five hundred computers. Let's say they each cost a grand. That would be five hundred thousand. Let's say it costs a hundred each to ship. That's another fifty grand, so a total of about five hundred and fifty thousand dollars. What are they planning on spending millions of dollars on this weekend?"

She started to give me her thoughts but I never heard what she said as a man opened the inner office door, stepped through with his gun raised and shot me in the chest.

Chapter Seventeen

When I picked History to major in at U of K my mother thought I'd end up teaching. Then I joined R.O.T.C. and though it meant I would have to do a four year stint, she never really worried, figuring me for an administrative job. When I was chosen to become a member of a unit which went behind enemy lines, she was terrified; convinced I would die over there. It made things worse because I was never allowed to talk about what I did in service for my country.

When I came home she broke down in tears of joy, like many mothers of returning sons and daughters whose children came back safely. My mom just knew I'd finally get my teacher's certificate and then my master's and become a professor. But me, I craved that adrenaline. If the Army could have promised me other missions where I wouldn't have to spend the next dozen years playing in sand dunes, I might have stayed in and continued the good fight. But they couldn't. And I got tired of finding sand and dirt in places where the sun don't shine.

When I told my mom I decided to become a bounty hunter, she started crying all over again. I made every promise in the book I'd do what I could to stay safe. That included my sworn promise to always wear a bulletproof vest every day I worked. I had mine on that morning and hadn't had a chance to take it off.

Which turned out to be a good thing. I was reaching for my gun when the force of the shot struck me in the chest, knocking me backwards out of the chair and half-way across the floor. It was like somebody took a sledgehammer and pounded me with it. All the air rushed from my lungs, and I fought to stay focused.

Muscle memory reflexes took over and saved my life. Despite the crushing pain, I managed to pull out my gun from its holster. From what seemed like far away, I could hear Samantha yelling at me. As a man moved towards the desk and me, I took aim, and shot him in the ankle. He screamed and collapsed as his ankle disintegrated. The moment he hit the ground, I shot him in the head. It occurred to me, if he'd only shot me like I'd just shot him, I would finally have the answer to the question of which direction I would be heading on that big elevator in the sky.

Samantha crawled to me and ran her hands over my chest, tearing at my shirt, looking for a bullet wound as I struggled, but failed, to get up. She found the vest and said, "I thought I felt one of these while we were dancing. My God Vic, are you alright?"

"Yes," I lied. "Now let me up."

I rose to the level of the desk, my gun hand outstretched as another man stuck his head in the doorway, saw me and ducked back. I shoved Samantha towards the back room and moved to follow her just as the man's hand appeared around the corner and let loose a few rounds in the direction of the desk, luckily striking it and not me. I fired two shots through the wall next to the door and was rewarded with a grunt followed by the sound of a body hitting the floor. Dry wall makes a pretty poor defense against a nine millimeter round.

My chest hurt like hell as I followed Samantha into the back room, closing the door and turning the doorknob lock. It wouldn't slow them down if they decided to kick the door in, but it would give me some warning. The room we were in was about fifteen by fifteen feet and there was not a single stick of furniture in the room. From behind me Samantha said, "I'll check the back door."

I shouted, "No!" But she already had the door open. When she did another man gripped the door from the outside and pulled it further open while taking Samantha by the throat. She swung the sword case up, smashing it into his wrist. He let go of her with that hand, only to snatch her with the other as a second man appeared at the back door and took a shot in my direction. I couldn't shoot back without taking a chance of hitting her, yet I couldn't get closer to help without getting myself shot.

The two of them took hold of Samantha and pulled her kicking and screaming outside. I ran to the closing door and was about to push it open when round after round of gunfire hit it, with one round grazing my arm as it went by. Now my chest had company in the agony department. More rounds were fired from the inside of the office and I retreated to the far corner and hit the ground to avoid being caught in the crossfire as the room exploded with flying plaster.

The shooting stopped and in the ensuing quiet in the room, I could finally hear what the shooters must have heard: sirens. Someone had called the boys in blue. I ran to the back door and opened it just in time to see a black Lincoln Town car go tearing out of the parking lot, taking Samantha with it.

There would be no time to get back and circle the building and to my car before the cops arrived. Sons of bitches. I stuck a finger through the bullet hole in the sleeve of my jacket and probed the wound, but there wasn't that much blood. I took off running across the parking lot and made my way through a series of side streets, putting as much distance between the office and me as I could while furiously thinking what to do about what just happened.

I had to find Samantha again, and soon. And not just for my brother's sake. If they did to her what they did to David-- I let the thought stop there, as it was enough to make me want to throw up. I took a moment to catch my breath and was hit by a new emotion: pure hate.

Many times in my life I've been angry, even severely pissed off. But this was beyond that. I wanted to find them and kill the lot of them: Deveraux, her dad, the guys who kidnapped her, all of them. My phone rang and I yanked it out of my pocket. It was Kurt. I answered with a growl, "What?"

"Dude, we're in deep shit. What the hell have you got me into, Vic?"

I took several deep breaths and tried to calm down. "Where are you Kurt? Like, right at this moment." I could hear background noise and could tell he was in his car.

"Damn it, Vic? Are you hearing me, man? Things have gone to Hell in a hand basket. We need to talk and you need to make things right."

"Kurt, calm the fuck down and answer my question. Where are you?"

"Jesus man, alright. Sorry. I'm just a little wigged out, you know? I'm in the Highlands. I was at that all night cyber café when--"

I cut him off and said, "Pick me up at the corner of Browns Lane and Wetherford. You got it?"

"You mean now? Why don't I just meet you at your place?"

"I'm not at home, Kurt. Just do what I ask please. O.K.?"

"Sure, Vic. Alright. I'm on my way. Geesh. Don't get your panties in a wad."

I leaned against a large maple tree and dry washed my face with my hands. It was now about 1:30 A.M. and the fatigue was starting to catch up with me. Going to Molly Malone's may have been a mistake.

The pain in my chest and arm brought me back to the here and now. I had allowed myself to relax once I had Samantha. And while I hadn't had that much to drink at Molly's, it added to the relaxation and I'd made some poor choices. I should have left Samantha on lookout in case someone had shown up. I should have done more to protect her and instead I only added to the body count while allowing her to be taken.

I did my best to calm down and think while waiting for Kurt. It took him about ten minutes to get there. He pulled up in a blue Toyota Sienna minivan. Most bachelors drive a muscle car. Or at least a nice sedan. Not our boy Kurt. He said he bought it from a friend who offered it to him dirt cheap. When I tried to explain chicks don't dig minivans unless they have kids, he just blew me off. Right now, I didn't care. I came around to the driver's side and he rolled his window down.

"Where's your car?" he asked.

"Scoot over. I'm driving." I opened the car door and he just looked at me. "Kurt, move to the passenger seat, please." I'm not sure what my face looked like, but his reply died on his lips. He unbuckled his seat and scrambled over to the other seat.

I got in and adjusted his seat some. Kurt wasn't what you'd expect when you hear that he's a computer geek who has trouble getting dates and can't keep a girlfriend. At six feet tall, lean swimmer's build, sandy brown hair and chocolate brown eyes, his male-model good looks made every woman notice him when he walked into a room.

His problem was when he opened his mouth. Women, unfortunately, noticed that, too. He had a knack for saying the wrong things at the wrong time. Invariably, when Kurt was alone with a member of the opposite sex, he'd freeze up.

Good thing tonight he and I were not going date hopping, though we were after women. Or at least, one woman. "Jesus Vic, what's happened? No, wait. Let me tell you what happened with me first."

"Hold up, Kurt. You have your laptop with you, right?" The man never went anywhere without it.

"Yes, but that's part of what I need to tell you--"

I cut him off again and said, "In a minute. Get it out and find me the address for Winston Reynolds. Young guy, around twenty-three or twenty-four years old."

He reached around his seat and got his backpack, then pulled out a net book with a satellite connection. In just a couple of minutes he had the machine fired up and an address for Winston. "Why are you looking for him?"

"He has something I need." I knew the part of town Winston lived in and headed that way. "Now, Kurt, what's got a bug up your ass?

"Dude, let me tell you. To dig deeper into Inspirational Global Software, I needed to hack into a few databases. I don't like to do that at home, so I went to Bytes Me, that all night cyber cafe on Frankfort Avenue. Anyways, I was there and I hacked into a business database in London for corporate filings. That led me to other companies and other databases. I ended up in one in Saudi Arabia.

That's when I got to the end of the line on who really owns Inspirational Global Software. A man named Fazil Al Haqar. And Vic, this is a very, very bad man. He's on the terrorist watch list. He's Al Qaeda's point man when it comes to chemical and biological weapons. Our government wants him in the worst sort of way."

Turns out Kurt didn't have to tell me who Haqar was. I'd heard of him. He was one of the men we tried to track down when I was with my unit in Afghanistan. We had a list, kind of like the deck of cards used for Saddam Hussein and his henchmen. Haqar was a high value target we never could find. We thought he was killed by a drone strike in Helmand Province, but we missed him.

Kurt continued, "And then I ran O.C.R. software on that image you sent me, the one in Arabic. Once I did that, I used Arabic translation software and was then able to read the damn thing. It said, "Blessed be to Allah. The infidels in the West now know what it is like to lose innocents. Let this be a warning. Stay out of Muslim countries. Leave the Middle East and never return."

"Vic, the company is owned by a terrorist. And that's not what's got me scared shitless. The program I use to do my hacks has built-in sniffer alarms. They started going off while I was trying to run down more info on Haqar. I panicked and shut down my connection before they could find me. Or so I thought. I left the café and drove over to the Thornton's across the street. While I was gassing up, several cars came flying up to Bytes and a bunch of men got out wearing suit and ties. They just wreaked Feebs. Jesus Vic, they were there less than ten minutes after I'd gotten out of my chair. What the hell have you got me mixed up in?"

Hell, Kurt. I was on a trip to Hell and it seemed I was taking him along for the ride.

Chapter Eighteen

I gave him the condensed version, leaving out Satan, vampires and devil worshipers. Which meant I told him that I'd been hired to find a girl and that in doing so I'd uncovered a plot to attack Christian schools with a computer virus. I told him the bad guys had gotten wind of the investigation and had captured Samantha and that I planned on getting her back. While not quite the truth, it was not quite a lie. If he asked me about the other stuff, I'd tell him. For right now it was better that he not know what could definitely kill him.

The longer I talked, the paler Kurt got. When I finished, Kurt said, "Holy shit, Vic. I'm happy to help, but you're into really heavy stuff man. Have you, uh, hurt anybody tonight?"

I shot him a look that made him raise his hands in surrender and take the question back. He put Winston's address into his GPS and a few minutes later we were there. Winston lived in a ranch house located in a nice older neighborhood on the city's Southside. I parked in the street a few houses down and told Kurt to sit tight.

There were several street lights to see by as I walked up the driveway. I didn't see the Cadillac, but there was a Ford Mustang in the driveway. It was now almost 2 A.M. and the neighborhood was quiet. I stepped up onto the porch and rang the doorbell a couple of times.

It took a bit, but I could hear someone coming to the door. The porch light came on and I could see someone look through the peephole. There was a pause, but the door opened. Winston looked at me with one hand on the door knob and one behind his back. I held both my hands open at my sides, showing him I didn't have a weapon.

The side of his face showed a mark where I'd slugged him. One didn't have to be a psychic to know he wanted nothing more than to beat me down like I had him.

"They're dead, aren't they?" He asked this in a monotone. Like I said, he was smart, and he knew the answer to his question, but he had to ask it nonetheless.

"Yes. Both of them. That's why I'm here. I need your help."

He shook his head very slowly. "J.B. always said you had balls. But you're something else, Vic. I think the best thing you can do is take your sorry ass off my property and get the hell out of here."

"No can do, Winston. I need help and you're the only one that can do it. You want to let me in so we can talk about it or do you want to keep this up on your porch?"

He looked up and down the street, taking his time. "I ain't letting you in this house. No chance in hell. You got something else to say, then say it."

"Fair enough. The men that killed J.B. and the other guy, what was his name?"

"Ian. Ian Adams. Good kid."

"I'm sure. The men that killed the two of them also tried to kill me. Several times tonight, as a matter of fact. They're the men that hired both J.B and me to find the girl. They followed us there and even though J.B. told him the girl was close, they shot him and Ian like rabid dogs. They didn't deserve that. They now have the girl. I plan on getting her back and make them pay for what they did to J.B. and Ian."

"Shit man. You want the bounty that bad? It ain't worth it."

"It's not about the money. They set J.B. and me up against each other and planned on killing us instead of paying up. These are very bad men, Winston. I've since found out they plan on attacking kids and I won't let them get away with it."

The news about attacking kids made him stop and think. I didn't tell him that it would be with a computer virus, but then again, I didn't care. I just needed his help. "What do you want me to do?"

"You guys used a Spark Nano GPS device to find us. I found it before we left the farm under my back bumper. Just before they took the girl, I slipped the tracker into her coat pocket. I need the remote you used to follow us to now find her. It would be great if you joined in and helped me with the payback, but at the very least, I need to know how to follow that GPS tracker."

My brother always told me you gotta have a backup plan. When I helped Samantha on with her coat at Molly Malone's I dropped the tracker into her pocket. I felt like a real douche bag doing it, but I had no idea if she would change her mind and bolt on me. I had to hedge my bets. Turns out it was the right thing to do.

"Man beats the crap out of me then asks me for help. Why should I?"

I took a step closer to him and growled, "Because the sons of bitches must pay. For J.B, for Ian, for the girl and for others they've killed tonight. And, so help me God, they will. You can pretend this doesn't affect you, but it does. They took something from you tonight and you need to take it back."

Winston didn't back down when I invaded his personal space. "Maybe it's time to go to the cops on this. It's gone from bad to royally fucked up. Let them wind things down. If she's been kidnapped, they can even bring in the Feds."

No doubt Winston was right. Hell, it was the same advice I gave to Samantha earlier in the evening. Bringing in the cops now would be the smart thing to do. Things were spiraling out of control. But the moment I did that, I would be on the hook trying to explain why I'd killed four men tonight. Self-defense might work. Might not. But either way, my brother was dead. I had climbed out on a very thin limb that could break under me at any time, but I couldn't stop.

"I'm a bounty hunter. I don't go to the cops for help. Besides, just how would you explain what you and J.B. were doing? Or me, for that matter. We didn't have a warrant to track down Samantha. That's kidnapping. I had my reasons for taking the job. They have something on my brother and I've been trying to get him off the hook. I know J.B. was a good guy, so what did they offer him to take the job?"

"A million dollars. I told him it wasn't worth it, but he took the job anyway. J.B. has his kids in private school. Bills have been piling up. He needed the extra cash. So we took the job. Cost him his life. Like I said, wasn't worth it."

"If he hadn't sent you over to the mansion, you'd be dead right now," I said. "And I'd be avenging your death along with theirs. You don't want to go with me, fine. Just tell me how to find her and I'll get out of your hair."

He looked at me for awhile longer, thinking. Finally he said, "Wait here." He closed the door and was gone for a couple of minutes. When the door opened again, he had a dark red University of Louisville jacket on.

"The info on the tracker is in J.B.'s Caddy, so I'll come with you. Besides, someone has to keep you from getting your ass shot off," he said. "But I'm doing this for J.B. and Ian. When this is over, I'm going to kick your behind for cold cocking me."

"You're going to try and kick my behind. Won't be any different when it's a fair fight. But thank you. I mean it. Thanks."

I offered him my hand and he took it. I led the way back to the van and opened the passenger door. I said, "Kurt, Winston. Winston, Kurt." I nodded with my head and said to Kurt, "Now get in the back seat."

"Come on, dude. It's my car. If I don't get to drive, at least I get to ride shotgun."

"Fine, you tell Rosa Parks here to ride in the back of the bus." I went to the driver side while Winston didn't say anything, just stood there. Kurt said, "Right. My bad. Sorry."

Kurt grabbed his computer, got out and opened the sliding side door and got in. Winston hopped into the passenger seat and I asked him, "Where to?"

"J.B.'s Caddy is at my uncle's house in his garage. I told him I needed to stash it for a bit." He gave me directions. "Now tell me what the hell is going on."

I did so and, like I did for Kurt, I left out the part about the Devil and my brother's soul contract, just telling him that they had him and planned on killing him if I didn't help out. I gave him a run down about what took place at the farm, how J.B. and Ian were killed, and how I took out two of the four guys.

"There's another player in this, however. Samantha, that's the girl's real name, and the reporter, had scheduled a meeting with a man they thought would take on the bad guys for them. Lucky for us, he was outside the Double D when you guys were there, heard you discussing the job and followed you, first to Phoenix Hill, then to the farm. He took out the other two of their men, including the one that shot J.B and Ian. He might be able to help us if we can find out where she is."

Winston listened to the whole thing without interrupting. When I was finished, he asked the same question we all did when this started. Why did they want her? I didn't see telling him would hurt and it might even keep him involved. "She stole thirty million from them. She knew they needed the money for the Exodus Project. She figured no money, no project. The way they've been after her, seems she was right."

"That's a boatload of cash," Winston said. "But it sounds like this is like stealing from the Mafia. They can't go to the cops to get their money back, but they don't mind killing people if they have to. Shit, sends a message. Fuck with us and you pay with your life. We do this, Vic, they're going to be coming after us hard."

"You got a problem with that?" I asked.

"Nah. You do our kind of work, they always be people wanting payback. Let them try."

"That's the way I feel. Up to now, they've been driving the bus. Now, it's time for some of their own medicine. Payback's a bitch."

Kurt said, "Uh, guys? I'm really not into hell-bent Satanists wanting to come after me. Anyway, we can keep me out of this whole payback's a bitch part?"

I said, "Come on, Kurt. The chicks love bad boys. Think of what this will do to your reputation."

He said, "I'm thinking more about what it will do to my lifespan. But while you two have been getting all buddy-buddy, I've been thinking about a different approach with this Inspirational Global Software side of things. I found a Catholic school outside Atlanta and hacked into their systems. First, I cracked open their web servers. Luckily they've got one of those rolling message ads on their main page so I modified it to look for an inbound request from the IGS domain. It will load up a nasty little bug I concocted on any user's machine coming to the page from the Inspirational Global Software network.

"Next, I got into their email server and uploaded a script that will allow me to send mail from the school President's account and will reroute any incoming email from IGS to a fake email account I setup on another service. With all that in place, I fired off an email to IGS from the school president saying how he heard about the contest from another school and how interested he was in what they were doing and to please consider them for the program. I then included a link to the page containing the bug. Once loaded, that baby will route any traffic from that computer back to me—via a very circuitous route, of course. With any luck I'll be in the Inspirational Global Software network in no time."

I looked at Winston and asked, "Did you get any of that?"

Winston said, "Yeah. They click on the link and they're fucked."

I laughed and said, "Any help would be appreciated, Kurt." I couldn't blame him for worrying about his own ass. If the Church found out he's involved, I had no doubt just what action they'd take, based on tonight's events.

We made it to Winston's uncle's house. He owned a couple of acres in a more rural part of the county. Winston called ahead to let him know we'd be headed to the garage and that he might take a few other things while we were there. I didn't ask what "things," as I would find out soon enough.

The garage turned out to be as big as the barn on the farm where Rebecca lived. Winston had me back up through the wide double doors then he hopped out and opened them and motioned me back, guiding me into the barn, parking next to the Caddy. He closed the doors and Kurt and I got out of the van. Winston motioned us to follow him to a door towards the back of the garage.

He took out a key ring, selected the right one and unlocked the door. He opened it and turned on an inside light. We went down about a dozen steps, revealing what could only be Rambo's wet dream. One side of the room was lined with display shelves with several rows of automatic weapons, side arms and even a crossbow. The other side had boxes of ammo, grenades and several other boxes of weapons.

"Who the hell is this guy?" I asked. I walked over and looked at one of the shelves and found flash bang and concussion grenades. "How did he get all this stuff?"

"My uncle is convinced one day the Chinese are going to invade the United States and try and take all our guns away. Or the Federal government is going to outlaw all guns and come and take all our guns away. Or take your pick. Someone is always coming to take his guns, and he plans on making his last stand from here. He has friends in the militia movements and picks up what he needs from them."

I whistled while turning around looking at all the firepower in this one room. If the world ever started to come to an end, I wanted to come make my stand with Winston's uncle.

"What can we take?" I asked, picking up a couple of each of the types of grenades.

"He said we can help ourselves and bring back the guns when we're done with them. I told him we'd pay to replace anything we use and can't bring back, so, help yourself. It's your bank account funding this trip."

Great. If I managed to save Samantha, save my brother, save myself, and live to see another day, I would have to hit her up for an expense account. I pocketed grenades and then checked out my choices of sub-machine guns.

I had a choice of several versions of the MP5, a 9mm sub-machine gun used by Navy Seals and one we used in Afghanistan, so I was familiar with it. It has a closed bolt action which means little kick. I settled on an MP5K with a Gemtech suppressor and a couple of boxes of the Remington 9mm Luger subsonic ammo. This time the Church wouldn't have the edge in firepower. And as quiet as this baby would be, they wouldn't hear it coming either.

Winston loaded up in a similar fashion and we took the gear, along with a duffle bag to put the stuff in, and loaded it into the back of the van. He then went over to the Caddy and pulled out a net book, powered it up and opened a document. "We use the Spark Nano. All you need is the sign on name and password. J.B. kept the info in this Word doc. The sign on name is JBRocks and the password is KissMyAss."

Kurt snickered at the password and opened up his own laptop, went to the BrickHouse Security site, and typed in the login and password. A moment later, a map appeared on the screen with a blue dot showing where the tracker had stopped.

Deveraux and the Church had been playing by their rules. Time they learned a lesson. Rules change.

Chapter Nineteen

The BrickHouse security site showed a Google Earth view of where the tracker was at any given moment, and with any luck, where Samantha was currently located. The map showed a house, with several outbuildings, surrounded by nothing but pasture. Kurt clicked on the blue icon and it popped up an address. He then used routing software to pinpoint where it was in relation to us.

"Looks like it's just outside of La Grange, out Highway 53. We can be there in about a half hour. And there's a gravel farm road that runs behind the property. You might be able to approach it from that direction."

Now we were doing things that I was good at. We had a target, knew where they were and it was time to storm the castle, rescue the damsel in distress and make the bad guys pay. I looked at my watch and saw it was just after three in the morning. I looked at Winston and asked, "Are you ready for this?"

"Yea, just let me get a few more things out of the Caddy. He went to the rear of the Cadillac and brought back a smaller duffel. He said, "Three pairs of night goggles, three flashlights and a few other things that might come in handy."

"Sweet. Let's go kick some ass."

I got back behind the wheel and started the van while Winston opened the doors of the garage, then shut them behind us after I pulled out. Kurt was typing away on his laptop from the back, yawning the whole time. Winston hopped back into the van and I put the address of the target into the Garmin and we hit the road.

In my rear view mirror, I could see a porch light turn on and an elderly black man, step out onto the porch. He was dressed in pajamas, but had a gun belt around his waist with a couple of hand guns on each side. He watched us pull out and then headed towards his garage.

Kurt said, "I've looked up the address we're headed to and it's owned by one of the shell companies that owns IGS. So it's definitely part of the Church's network. I can tell you they're current on their taxes and utility bills, but not much else."

I asked, "Can you tell if the bad guys made any other stops on the way?"

Kurt hit a few keystrokes and said, "They made one stop, a house in the Cherokee Park area. One sec' and I'll tell you who owns it." A few moments later he said, "It's owned by Lincoln Townsend."

I nodded. "The computer guy. He's the Church's version of you."

"Not a chance he's as cool as me. Let me see what I can find on the dude."

I was really starting to feel my ass drag from the lack of sleep. I whipped into a gas station and got coffee for Winston and me, heavy on the cream and sugar, and a Diet Dr. Pepper for Mr. Watching-His-Girlish-Figure in the back. The man lived on Diet D.P. I also grabbed some bottled waters and snack bars for later, as well as several energy drinks in case we needed them.

The three of us were quiet as we rode into the countryside. We took I-71 north until we reached La Grange, slipped off the exit and made our way up the hill and through town. La Grange started as a railroad town, with the buildings along main street hailing from the early twentieth century. Today, most were antique shops, specialty stores, restaurants, an art gallery and even a publishing house. But at this hour the town was ghostly quiet.

We crossed the tracks and passed through the other side of town and into rural farmland, with a light fog forming in the cool November air. Kurt had his Garmin set to use a British voice and she happily told us we were point two miles from our destination.

Kurt said, "The farm road will be coming up on the right."

I said, "Let's continue past the place and turn around where the highway dead ends into Highway 42. You and Winston keep an eye out as we go by, though it's not like you're going to see anything in the dark."

And I was right. The house sat far enough back off the road that no lights were visible. This was probably the point. We made it to the end of the highway and turned around at the T. As we approached the gravel road, I killed the lights and made the turn. I rolled down my window, Winston did the same, and we drove slowly, listening to the country night sounds. I stopped when Kurt said we were about even with the farmhouse, which was still a good three quarters of a mile away across open fields, did a quick three point turn in the narrow road and stopped the van.

I had him turn off the dome light and the three of us got out. We left the doors ajar and the van's sliding side door open—just in case we needed to make a quick dive and drive getaway. There was a thin strip of trees at the edge of the road between us and the property, with a three line barbed wire fence.

I said to Kurt, "Get behind the wheel, leave the windows down, but the motor off. I'll call or text you to let you know we are headed back to the van. Don't be a hero. If you think Winston and I aren't coming back, take off. Call the cops. Tell them everything you know. But wait as long as you can, do you understand?"

"Got it, man. No worries on the whole hero thing. I like you. And Winston seems O.K. But, dude, I'm kind of against the whole dying part."

I slapped him on the back, which sent him staggering a couple of steps. "Just be ready to haul ass when we get back here."

Winston and I went to the rear of the van and opened the back door. We opened the two duffle bags and started taking out what we'd need for the raid. Winston took out a pair of thermal night vision goggles, handing me one. I put the goggle harness on my head, adjusted it for my larger head, and flipped them up.

He then took out two Bluetooth earpieces which we synced with our phones. Next we turned our phones on vibrate and dimmed the screens. Finally, we took out the MP5Ks and attached the suppressors. I handed him an extra clip, picked up one of my own and loaded the ammo, while he did the same. He asked, "How do you want to play this?"

"Let's approach them from two sides. Since you're younger and in better shape, I'll let you hoof it around to the far side of the house. If you see anyone on guard duty, let me know, and I'll do the same. I'll call you and we can leave the call open."

He said, "No problem, ole' man."

"If there's no one out watching, then we'll move in closer and assess."

I handed him a flash bang. "We try to hit them, front and back, at the same time. But don't be squeamish if someone points a gun in your direction. Take them out. These guys won't hesitate to blow your ass away."

Winston said, "You don't have to worry about that with me. Let's get this party started."

I handed him a couple of snack bars and a bottled of water. "We may have to watch for a bit, so just in case."

He took the snacks and water, stuffed them in his coat pockets, slung the gun strap over his shoulder, put on his night vision goggles, grabbed a fence post, hopped over and was off at a steady jog. I did a quick fist bump with Kurt and off I went into the dark night, right behind Winston.

I saw Winston swing out wide so as to not risk being seen from the house. Clouds were beginning to move in and the moon kept popping in and out from its hiding place. As long as the bad guys weren't looking out with night vision or thermal goggles of their own, we were pretty safe from detection.

There were several small hills between me and the house, and as I eased up on one, I could clearly see the house in the thermal image. I lay flat on my stomach and scanned the surrounding area. There were two out buildings. One was a small shed. The other appeared to be a detached garage. I could see the back of the house and there was one back porch light on illuminating a small area. I watched for several minutes, but saw no movement. I looked off to my right and could just make out Winston moving to the other side of the house.

I took out a snack bar and devoured it, then washed it down with some water. The quick buzz from the coffee was starting to wear off, so I pulled an energy drink from my pocket and downed that as well, all the while, watching the house.

Winston said softly in my ear piece, "There's a man walking the perimeter of the house. He has no night eyes and is smoking a cigarette. He will be coming into your line of vision shortly." And right on cue, he came around the house to where I could see him. His cigarette glowed brighter as seen by my goggles. I pushed them up as he walked into the light and stopped to look around.

The man was ruining any night vision he might have had by standing in the light. Rookie. He was wearing the coveralls that I was now beginning to think of as their uniforms. He had an M16 slung over around his neck and cradled it in front of him. After a moment, he started back on his rounds and I alerted Winston.

There were several lights on in the house, but the curtains were drawn and I couldn't see anything. Winston said, "I see a black Lincoln Town car in the driveway. Has to be your guys."

I agreed. "When he circles past you again, move in closer to the house. I'm going to take care of him on this side. We're not waiting any longer."

"Roger that," Winston replied.

I couldn't wait longer even if I'd wanted to. I kept thinking of what these guys might be doing to Samantha and I could feel the anger rising inside me like a tidal wave threatening to sweep all other thoughts away. I pulled the goggles back down, moved even closer and lay back down in the grass and waited. Sure enough, the man once again stopped in the circle of light. I pushed the goggles back on my head, and steadied the guns site center mass on my target. I took in a breath, let it out slowly and squeezed the trigger.

There was a soft pfpt from my gun, followed by the man being thrown backwards, then hitting the ground. I was up and running before he even landed. I pulled the goggles back down and said to Winston, "One down, move in."

I got up and sprinted towards the man I'd just killed. I gave Montoya grief for killing Simpson, yet I'd just killed a man without giving it a single thought. I had no clue if the man had ever hurt anyone or was just a hired hand. And I didn't care. He was in the way and I needed him removed, so I shot him. End of story. What was my lack of caring doing to my own soul? I told myself I was doing it for the right reasons, that I was fighting on the side of the righteous. But I had my doubts.

For the moment, I pushed all such thoughts aside, and when I reached the man I grabbed him by the shoulders and dragged him around the house and into the deeper shadows. He looked young, maybe early twenties. He should have been out painting the town instead of lying dead in someone else's yard. Definitely sucked to be him. I pulled the M16's strap up and over his head, then put it over mine, pushing it so it hung down my back. I ran my hands over his coveralls, feeling for anything else that might come in handy or help us, but found nothing.

Winston said, "I'm by the front door. Let me know when you're ready."

I was about to respond when the back door opened and someone called out, "Yo, Janssen."

I moved to the corner of the house and flattened against the wall, holding my gun against my chest. The voice said, "Janssen! Answer me for Christ's sake."

The man was moving towards me and I could see his shadow, thrown by the bulbs light, stretching my direction and moving closer. Just as he reached the corner I stepped forward and put the muzzle of my MP5 against his forehead and said, "You so much as sneeze and I'll clear out your sinuses permanently, got it?"

The man nodded and I motioned him towards the darkness of the deeper shadows at the side of the house. I said to Winston, "I have one of them hostage. Hold tight while I ask this guy a few questions.

"Roger."

I turned the man around and put my gun to the base of his skull. I said, "Answer my questions softly and quickly. Do you have the redhead girl inside?"

"Yes. She's there. Aw, shit man, you killed Janssen?"

"Without even blinking. And I'll do the same to you if you piss me off. How many men left inside?"

"Three more. Two guys in the living room watching TV, one with the girl in the bedroom."

I could feel my face flush. "If you guys have hurt her, so help me God, I'll rip all of you to pieces. What, you guys taking turns?"

The man said "No man, it's not like that. She's tied to the bed, but we haven't touched her. I swear to God, no one's done anything to her."

"If I get in there and find out you lied, shooting you is the best you can hope for."

"I'm not lying, man, she's out. The only thing we did was give her something to make her sleep. She was fighting too much and we needed her to calm down. So Bautista made her take a couple of sleeping pills. That's it, I swear it."

"Who's Bautista? And is Deveraux here?"

The man licked his lips. He said, "Bautista is in charge here at the house. And no, Deveraux isn't here yet. He'll be here first thing in the morning."

"Is the front door locked?"

"No. Not with all of us here. Besides, we could see someone coming up the drive from quite a ways off. Or so we thought."

I asked the guy for the floor plan inside and found out the others were watching TV in the front room, where the front door is located and the bedroom where they were keeping Samantha was down off the kitchen.

I relayed that info to Winston and said, "I'm going to take this guy in through the back door. I'll toss a flash bang where they're watching the boob tube and you come through and take them down. I'll head to the bedroom and get Samantha. Ready?"

"Lead the way, old man. Hope you don't have to stop and take a leak along the way."

"You need to learn to respect your elders."

I grabbed the Church guy by the scruff of the neck and walked him to the backdoor. "If you don't want to end up like Janssen, then do exactly what I tell you. I have no problems shooting a man in the back. What's your name?"

"Troy."

"O.K. Troy. Whether you live or die will be decided in the next couple of minutes. It's up to you."

I told him to open the back door and we walked into a mudroom that was just off the kitchen. I could hear a TV in another room and I had Troy stop while I took out the flash bang. I pulled the pin and then prodded him with my gun to move forward. The kitchen had an opening straight ahead and a hallway that ran to my right with several doors on the left side, one to the right and one straight ahead.

I tapped Troy on the shoulder and pointed down the hall, and mouthed which one. He mouthed end of the hall, I pointed him towards the front room and just before he reached it I shoved him forward into the room and tossed in the flash bang.

There was a brief second and then a thundering boom, accompanied by a flash of bright light, hence the flash bang name. It was strong enough that plaster fell from the ceiling. The front door crashed open as I took off down the hallway.

I was half-way down the hall when the door on the right opened and a man came hurrying out still zipping up his pants. To say he was surprised to see me is something of an understatement. He was almost as tall as me, but so skinny that if he turned sideways I wouldn't have been able to see him.

I give the guy credit. He took a swing and landed a left to my chin. Too bad for him he did nothing more than hurt his hand. I grabbed him by the neck and drove his face into the wall, making a nice face print in the dry wall and breaking the guy's nose, as blood came gushing out. I was about to toss him out of the way when the door at the end of the hallway opened, with a guy standing behind it holding a handgun.

I tossed Slim down the hallway as the other guy opened fire, hitting Slim several times and spinning him around. I let loose a short burst with the MP5 and the shooter went down. I'd now killed as many men in one night as I had in any single night fighting for my country.

I made it to the bedroom and glanced quickly inside. Samantha was tied to the headboard of a queen sized bed, sound asleep despite the loud action going on in the house. She was still wearing her black dress, but her shoes were missing. Her coat was tossed on the floor next to the bed and her sword case was open with the sword still inside, sitting on a chest of drawers. I cleared the room by checking a bathroom and a closet, then went back to check on Winston.

He had Troy and an older Hispanic man handcuffed with plastic ties, hands behind their backs, lying on their stomachs. Both still looked dazed.

Winston said, "Hope you don't mind, but I didn't just go off and shoot these two."

"No worries, I only shoot them when I have to." But I was lying. I wished he had just shot them. I wanted them all dead. That was the thought rolling through my brain and banging to get out. Kill them all. I said, "See what you can get out of these two, I'll be right back."

In the kitchen I found a knife and went back to the bedroom and cut Samantha loose. I paused just a moment to watch her lying there, sleeping peacefully, and several what ifs passed through my mind, about what life with a woman like her would be like. I took a deep breath and pushed such thoughts aside. I shook her for a bit and she started to wake up. I said, "Come on, Samantha, we've got to get moving." The ropes had chafed her skin where she must have fought being restrained. I lifted her up into a sitting position and her eyes fluttered open. She said, "Victor? You're here? How did you find me?"

"Magic. Now let's get you up and out of here. Come on."

With my help she got out of bed and I picked up her coat and slipped it on her shoulders. I looked for her shoes but came up empty. I closed her sword case and brought it with us. She stopped to look at the man lying in a growing pool of blood on the bedroom's hardwood floors. She said not a word, but stepped around him and then over Slim. I put my arm around her waist as we made our way down the hallway to the living room, and she leaned her head against my shoulder then slipped her arm around my waist. I felt a surge of relief go through me now that I had her back.

We had stormed the castle and rescued the damsel in distress. Now we just had to get her out and someplace safe. Question now was would this fairy tale have a happy ending?

Chapter Twenty

Winston said, "So this is the girl everyone wants? I can see why." He smiled and continued, "I've been talking to these two while you were in the back. They had someone watching the office you broke into, just in case you showed up. They were keeping tabs on several different places she might have known about."

"And Deveraux, when is he supposed to get here?"

"Sometime in the morning, but they weren't given a specific time."

I walked over and crouched down next to the man I assumed was Bautista. "Tell me about the Exodus Project."

He said, "I don't know nothin' about that. It's not in my job description."

I rolled him over onto his back, pulled out my 9, forced his mouth open and shoved the gun's muzzle into his mouth. "See, I think you know more than you're saying. So I'm going to ask you again and if you can't tell me about the Exodus Project, I'm going to air out the back of your head and see what Troy can tell me. So let's try this again. Tell me what you know about the Exodus Project."

I took the gun out of his mouth and pressed the muzzle against his forehead. Bautista said, "O.K. Listen, all I know is bits and pieces. They don't share things with the hired help. But I overheard Mr. Deveraux talking about this guy that's flying in today. And that's why they need the girl. They owe him money and I guess she took off with it. So they have to get her to tell them where the money's at. I swear to God that's all I know."

"Why is it you Satanists all swear to God when you get your nuts in a vice? Why not swear by the Lord of the Light Reclaimed?"

"Sir, do not jest about the Lord of Light. He's real. You don't want to invoke his name so lightly."

I stood up and said, "I've met him. I wasn't impressed with Luci. That's what all his BFF's call him."

Samantha was leaning against the door jamb listening to the conversation and yawning hard enough to make me want to take a nap right there. I took out my other energy drink and handed it to her. "See if this peps you up at all."

She took the drink and downed it while I walked over to a lamp, yanked out the cord and walked over to Bautista and tied up his ankles. Winston did the same to Troy with a telephone line. He asked, "What do you want to do with these two?"

"Leave 'em. Let Deveraux deal with them."

Troy, a panicked look on his face, said, "Take us with you. You can't leave us like this, he'll kill us!"

"True that," I said. "But you should have read the small print when you signed up."

I asked Samantha, "Did either of these guys hurt you?"

She said, "Not much. They weren't exactly gentle when they tied me down, but I'm O.K."

Good for the continued health of Bautista and Troy because I'm not sure what I would have done if she had said they had. I went and looked out the window into the night for a moment. I had to get control of this runaway anger I was feeling coursing through my body. Maybe I was just overly tired, on top of everything else going on. I pride myself on being calm, cool and collected in any situation, but I could feel that calm slipping away and I was struggling to get it back.

I turned to Winston and Samantha. "As much as I would like to stay and wait for Deveraux to show up, there's no telling what kind of help he'll bring with him. So we'd better get out of here."

We went out the front door and I shot the tires of the Lincoln. Winston and I led Samantha back across the fields towards the van. I called Kurt to let him know we were on our way back.

We were halfway across the field when I heard a sound that gave me goose bumps all over my body. It was the howl of a dog, but unlike any I'd ever heard before. I instantly knew how Sherlock Holmes must have felt standing on the moor and hearing the Hound of the Baskervilles.

Samantha said, "My God. They have a Hellhound here. Run!"

The three of us took off at a dead sprint, running as if our lives depended on it. Winston, younger and faster than either Samantha or I, slowed down to keep pace with us. Admirable, but not a good idea. I said, "Don't hold back. Take off and get over the fence, and help Samantha when she gets there."

"Done deal. Don't slow down, old man. I'd hate to have to avenge you, too." And with that, the former All Big East linebacker took off.

I said to Samantha, "How do you kill one of these things? Do I have to chop its head off, too?" The Hellhound howled again and it was definitely headed our way and gaining.

"No, but they're harder to kill than a regular dog, if my father's stories are true."

Great. "Keep going and don't stop." And doing just the opposite, I stopped, turned and waited. I opened her sword case and took out the sword, then stuck it in the soft ground should I need it and tossed the case on the ground.

Samantha stopped and asked, "What the hell are you doing? Come on!"

I turned to look at her just in time to see her eyes go wide. I glanced back to see a dog racing across the field towards us, though calling this a dog is like calling a lion a cat. The thing was huge, larger than a Great Dane and as stocky as a baby bull. Its fur was a midnight black, with eyes that glowed a sickly yellow color, which made it easy to follow as it closed upon the two of us.

"Samantha, if you don't make it to the van I'll be very pissed at you. So would you please run now?"

She let out a tortured moan and then took off. At least there was one woman in the world that did as I asked. I had to wonder if I would get a chance to get used to it.

I reached into my pocket and took out the last flash bang grenade. I wanted to make sure the thing focused on me and not the fleeing woman, so I started whistling and saying, "Here doggy, doggy. Come here, boy. Good doggy."

When the Hellhound was about a hundred yards away, I took careful aim and let him have it with the MP5. The first round or two hit it and it slowed fractionally, then started to weave slightly, making it harder to hit. Damn thing was smart. I hit it a few more times as it got closer, but I couldn't see that I was doing much damage.

I pulled the pin and let the clip go on the flash bang when the thing was only twenty or so yards away. I threw the grenade and said, "Fetch!" The Hellhound growled and caught the flash bang in its mouth and bit down hard. The grenade went off, the blast taking off part of the hound's jaw. An incredibly scary sound came from its throat, somewhere between a howl and a growl. I yelled back at the top of my lungs. Despite losing half its jaw, as it reached me it leaped for my throat.

In one motion I grabbed the sword, fell to my knees and as the Hellhound sailed over me by inches, I rammed the sword deep into its chest. I held on to the sword, with both hands, ripping it from chest to groin. Blood splattered me and burned where it touched bare skin.

The Hellhound collapsed to the ground when it landed, wrenching the sword from my grasp. I emptied the rest of my clip into its head for good measure and the beast stayed down.

I approached the thing cautiously, not wanting to leave Samantha's sword behind. No telling when we might run across another vampire. Other than a few leg twitches, the life had fled the body. I pulled the sword out, the blade blackened, snatched up her case, and jogged after Samantha and Winston.

We needed to skedaddle as someone had to have let the Hellhound loose and I wanted to be long gone before anything else showed up.

As I neared the fence, I saw Winston in the van's side door, weapon aimed back my way. He lowered it when he saw it was me, hopped out and got in the passenger seat. I got in the van, slammed the door shut and Kurt took off down the road.

Samantha wrapped me in a fierce hug, and then kissed me. Unlike the kiss at the Double D, this one set my body on fire. Right then, I'd have walked through Hell wearing a gasoline suit to kick Satan's ass, if she had asked me to. When the kiss ended, she rested her forehead against mine and said, "I knew you would come for me. When they took me, I was terrified they would do to me what they'd done to David. The one thing that helped was I knew you would find me. And you did."

"Sons of bitches needed to pay. And I plan on seeing to it they keep paying."

Kurt hit the highway, switched on the lights, turned left and accelerated back towards La Grange. He asked, "Where to now?"

"Head back to the interstate and into Louisville. I'll think about it as we get closer to town."

I made the introductions and brought Samantha and Kurt up-to-date on what we'd learned from the Church's men. I asked, "Did they say anything to you while they had you?"

"Nothing important. They just told me that Deveraux would be there in a few hours and that I'd better cooperate with him. They made me take a couple of sleeping pills and I was so tired to begin with, I was out before I knew it."

As we approached a rest area, I had Kurt pull in so that we could change places driving—just in case we ran into more surprises. Kurt drove like my grandmother and his idea of evasive driving was never leaving home. I said, "What we need is some rest. Winston, why don't we drop you off at home? Kurt can run Samantha and me back to my car, and then we can cut you lose, too, Kurt. After we get some rest, we can figure out what our next move will be."

When we got to Winston's house, I got out and walked him to his door. "Thanks Winston. J.B. would've been very proud of you tonight."

He nodded and said, "Yeah. I think so, too. Look, Vic, you be careful. You seem to be falling hard for this girl. Don't let it screw with your brain, man. If you can use my help in whatever your brother's into, give me a shout. I'll do what I can. You can keep my uncle's stuff until this is over. Call me later and let me know what's going on."

I said I would and went back to the van. I drove back to my car, and stopped a few blocks down the street to check things out. I told Kurt and Samantha to wait while I went back to get my car.

No one seemed to be around, but I gave the car a quick search, looking for any new GPS tracking devices. Convinced the car was clean, I fired it up, drove back and picked up Samantha and the gear. I rolled down my window and said to Kurt as he got back behind the wheel of the van, "You did great tonight, Kurt. We wouldn't have Samantha back without your help. Go home and get some rest. I'll call you later."

"I have just one question for you, Vic. Does she have a sister?"

"Get the hell out of here. And watch your ass."

We both pulled out and took off. I made a quick stop at the 24-hour Wal-Mart so Samantha could pick up shoes, jeans and a couple of tops and I could buy a T-shirt and change of underwear. I hated to see the black evening dress go and the view that went with it, but I had to think she could wear a burlap sack and look great. I then headed to a low rent motel on the south-side of town. We went inside, paid for a room in the back and within ten minutes had the gear inside and the curtains drawn. I used one of the room's chairs and propped it under the doorknob for good measure.

I told Samantha I was going to take a shower. I smelled like sulfur, and was covered in an assortment of blood, both my own and others. I sat a gun on the nightstand and told her if anything or anyone tried to come through the door, blow it the hell away. I went into the bathroom, stripped down, turned the water on scalding hot, and stepped into the shower. I was bone tired and the adrenaline rush had long since passed.

I leaned my head against the shower wall and tried to think of what we needed to do next. I had to stop charging like the proverbial bull in a china shop and start planning ahead.

I heard the bathroom door open, then the shower curtain slide back and Samantha joined me. It was clear it was her body that made the dress look good and not the other way around. For one of the few times in my life, I was speechless. Our eyes met and hers were full of playfulness. She took the soap from my hand and started slowly lathering my chest as we kissed. My hands slid down her back and around her bottom. The touch of her skin felt electric when her breasts pressed against me. When her hands moved down my stomach and then lower, I took the soap from her hand and set it back on the soap rack.

I turned her around and she put her hands on the wall as I entered her. While we made love, she leaned back against me and ran her fingers in my wet hair as I kissed her neck and shoulders. I'd never wanted a woman more than I did Samantha and from her response, I could tell she felt the same for me.

When we finished, the tiny motel bathroom now felt like a sauna. We took turns drying each other off. She gently stroked the bruise on my chest and the wound on my arm where I'd been shot earlier. She kissed both spots and while I'm not sure they felt any better, I know I damn well didn't care.

We made our way back into the other room, pulled back the bedding and fell into bed together. We made love again, this time in a slow, tender way that was a total contrast to how the rest of the evening had gone. When we finished, she laid her head on my chest and I played with her still damp hair.

She said, "For the first time tonight, I feel safe."

"We should be safe, for a while at least. Why don't you get some rest?"

Whether it was the sleeping pills she'd taken earlier, or just sheer exhaustion, in just a few minutes, she slipped into a deep sleep.

I was awake for quite some time, listening to her breathing, feeling her warm body against mine, thanking God she was still alive. It would be sunrise before long and I had decisions to make.

Chapter Twenty-One

I must have fallen asleep because I was jolted awake by the ringing of my iPhone. I use the old fashioned telephone ring because it's loud. When my eyes opened, I found Samantha sitting on the side of the bed, the blanket pulled around her hips, holding the Spark Nano tracker in her hands. She was staring at it while idly turning it over and over.

I picked up my phone from the nightstand, and seeing the call was from Kurt, answered it, while watching Samantha who kept her back to me.

"Morning. This better be good, Kurt."

"They clicked on the link. You know what that means.

"Yep. They're fucked. What you got?"

"Not on the phone. Meet me for breakfast. Bob Evans over off Hurstbourne Lane. You're buying, big guy."

"You got it, but give me an hour, will you?"

"See you then."

I ended the call and put the phone down. Samantha looked perfect in the muted sunlight coming through the drab curtains of our motel room. I rolled over and trailed my fingers down the curve of her back and caressing the side of her hip.

She said, "I wondered how you found me. I didn't think about it much last night. But this morning, I was curious. And I thought about how the other bounty hunter had tracked us by putting a GPS device on your car. So I checked my coat and found it. When did you put it there?"

"When we left Molly's, when I helped you on with your coat."

She finally looked at me and I saw disappointment. "You didn't trust me, did you?"

"It wasn't a matter of if I did or didn't. It was a matter of I couldn't afford to take the chance you'd bolt. If you took off on me, I would be out of options," Vic said.

"You mean about your brother."

"Yes, that's what I mean. Turns out it's a good thing I did. I don't know if I would have found you otherwise out there in the middle of nowhere."

She nodded. "I know. So I'm saved by a betrayal." She held up her hand to stop me from speaking. "Don't get me wrong. I'm glad you found me. It's just..." She tossed the Spark Nano onto the nightstand and gave me a small sad smile. "It doesn't matter. Thank you."

She leaned down and kissed me and I took her into my arms and we spent the next half hour making love before getting out of bed and getting dressed.

I could tell even during our lovemaking that things had changed. I knew she was upset with me and I couldn't blame her. Yet if I hadn't done what I did, there's no telling what Deveraux might be doing to her right at this very moment. Damned if you do, damned if you don't. And that pretty much summed up the choices I was facing.

I kept asking myself, if you do bad things for a good reason, how are you judged when your eternal soul is on the line? I had killed several men the night previous, so what kind of balance did my scale hold? I had seen the Hand of God kill a man. I presume he had authority to act in God's name. But what about me? If fighting the Church of the Light Reclaimed meant killing people, would I be forgiven?

By the time we left the motel and made it to Bob Evans, we arrived only a few minutes late, arriving a little after 9 A.M., and found Kurt waiting on a bench outside the restaurant, with his laptop on in his lap, typing away. He didn't even see us walk up. I tapped him on the shoulder. "If you keep that up you're going to get that hand disease."

"Carpal tunnel? Even if I do, they make great speech-to-text programs. Let's go in, I'm starving." Captain Literal once again failed to get it.

We were seated at a table in a corner and made small talk until the waitress took our orders. Kurt could barely hold back his excitement. When the waitress left, he said, "Someone clicked on at 6:48 A.M. and that gave me access. I automatically made an image of the hard drive and while that was being done, I had a look around. You said they were expecting someone in town today, right?"

"Yeah. That's why they needed Samantha. Whoever it is, they're paying them the big bucks. Did you find out who?"

"You betcha. I got onto their email server and there were several emails of interest, including an itinerary for someone named Raakel Korhonen. She's flying in this morning at eleven to Louisville International on a charter flight from Helsinki, Finland."

Samantha asked, "Were you able to find out who she is?"

"Well, that's not as easy as you might think. Both her first and last names are some of the more popular names in Scandinavia. It's like being called Jane Smith here. I did some checking and there are several possibilities. I was high on one that works for a company called Virasynth because I thought it might be a computer company, but it turns out it's not. Wrong kind of bug. So I moved on to the next one who looks the most promising. She works at the Ministry of Defense. I think--"

I said, "Wait. What do you mean wrong kind of bug?"

"She doesn't work for a computer company. Virasynth works with infectious diseases, trying to find things like a vaccine for bird flu, protection against anthrax, that kind of thing."

And then it hit me. It wasn't a computer virus they were buying, but a virus IN the computers. Kurt continued on with his list, but I was no longer listening, as I was thinking about how many people, especially children, they could kill if they unleashed a virus at all those different schools.

"Stop," I said, cutting him off. "I think you were right the first time. Don't you guys see? The one question we've been asking, over and over, is how you start a religious war with a computer virus. The answer is: you don't. But you could if you used a real virus. A highly contagious virus. Those canisters that you said were being built into the computers, the ones that were right next to the computer fans, what if those canisters held a virus set to be blown into the room at a certain time? Like during an academic competition when all those children and their teachers would be gathered around them?"

"Holy shit," Kurt said. "And those stickers you had me translate. That would explain Fazil Al Haqar's involvement. If those computers really did have a virus in them, eventually they'll track back to who owns ISG, just like I did. If each computer had one of those stickers placed inside all holy hell would break loose."

Samantha said, "And that would also explain why they need all that cash. I'd have to think a bio-weapon on the black market would bring tens of millions of dollars."

We stopped talking as our waitress brought us our food. Samantha and Kurt had seemed to lose their appetite, but I dug in. There's nothing like biscuits and milk gravy to get a bounty hunter ready to kick some ass. I said, "Eat up. It could be a long day and you always take nourishment where you can get it."

Samantha said, "So they really are planning to kill children. And my dad is a part of this? A part of mass murder? What am I going to do?" Her eyes teared up, so I took her hand and squeezed.

Trying to reassure her, I said, "We're going to stop it, that's what.

Samantha, you slowed them down by taking the money. I'd like to think that if we just keep you out of sight for the next few days and they can't pay, then what's-her-name will just go home. But there can be no doubt that if she doesn't hand over the virus willingly, they'll find another way to make her, so we can't rely on that to happen."

Kurt said, "Dude, perhaps we should call Homeland Security and let them know about this. I mean, they have to be onto something, right? When I hacked back and came across Fazil's name, they were on my ass within minutes. Let's just tip them off and let them handle it."

Samantha threw up her hands in exasperation. "And tell them what, exactly?" Samantha asked. "That a group of evil Satanists plan on attacking kids with a killer virus? Released by a computer, no less? Come on, Kurt. Say that out loud and listen to how it sounds. And what's our proof? No way. Not a chance. Then there's Vic to think about."

I shoveled more biscuits and gravy into my mouth. "How so?"

Samantha said, "Look it, if we tell them the whole story and they really do investigate, then how are you going to explain the trail of bodies you've left behind? *I* know they were in self-defense, *you* know they were in self-defense, but will they believe it?"

"Well, I would rather avoid going to jail for the rest of my life. So we take care of this ourselves. I'd rather do that anyways. The Church made this personal when they killed J.B and Ian and then shot me in the chest."

With sudden realization, Kurt asked, "Wait. We're dealing with Satanists? The bad guys are devil worshipers? Jesus Christ."

I said, "We may all want to stop taking the Lord's name in vain, considering we need all the help we can get."

Samantha said, "They'll never let you rest, now that they know who you are. The Church never forgets."

"Then I'll make sure to give them something to remember." I asked Kurt, "Does this virus chick have a photo we can look at?"

"Sure. One sec'." After a moment of typing, he turned his laptop around. Raakel Korhonen's bio page on the Virasynth website showed an attractive middle-aged woman with long blonde hair and an easy smile. Definitely not your prototypical terrorist. Then again, greed knows no particular look.

Her company bio said she got her Bachelor's at Oxford and her PhD at New York University in bio-genomics. The bio listed a ton of awards and accreditations and she had been working at Virasynth for just over ten years. Sounded like the lady knew her stuff. Which meant if the virus is as deadly as she is good, then there were a lot of children in real danger.

I said, "One person we can call is the Hand of God. Now that there's an actual physical attack on someone, maybe we can get him to jump in."

"Uh, you guys have been leaving out a few things. Just who is this Hand of God person?" asked Kurt.

"Picture someone like me, but working directly for God. On His orders. Kind of God's bounty hunter."

He looked back and forth between us. "You can't really be serious. God's bounty hunter? Satanists? Dude, you're punking me, right?"

When I shook my head "No" he put his head in his hands and I thought for sure he was going to cry, but he pulled himself together and asked, "Is there anything else you've been holding back?"

And I thought what the hell. If he was going to help and risk his life, he should know it all. So I told my story again, this time not leaving anything out. I wasn't sure he could get any paler, but I was wrong. He excused himself and ran to the bathroom.

Samantha said, "Cute guy, but he's not exactly 'hero material'. Are you sure you want him involved in this? I like him. And I owe him for helping to save my life. Things could get really bad for him if they learn who he is."

"That's why I told him the whole truth. But I need him. Look what we've already learned with his help. He'll be O.K. once he stops throwing up."

"Does he do that a lot?"

"Usually only around pretty women. I'm surprised you haven't caused him to have dry heaves."

While Kurt was in the bathroom I got up and went to pay the bill. They joined me at the register and we went outside. I said, "We need to know about that flight. I know a guy with the T.S.A. Let me call him and see what he can tell us."

I found his number and rang him up. Lucky for us, he was at work. I told him what I needed to know and he promised he'd get back to me in just a couple of minutes.

I hung up and the three of us sat on the bench outside the restaurant enjoying a glorious morning. There was a nip in the air, but the sky was pure blue with just a couple of wisps of cloud. It was mornings like this that always renewed my faith in God.

My phone rang and I answered, "That was quick. What'cha got for me?"

Satan replied, "A long and painful death, followed by an eternity of torment. Good morning, Victor."

Chapter Twenty-Two

"Well, if it isn't Luci. Don't count your tortures before they happen there, big guy. You don't have me yet."

"You would be better served by showing more respect. One day soon I will rule in Heaven. And even if I don't, at the rate you're sending people to spend eternity with me, you won't be far behind them. Either way, eventually you'll be mine and I will remember your insolence."

Samantha's eyes went wide when she heard me use the Hand of God's pet name for Lucifer. I angled the phone so she could listen as well. When Kurt looked at us she mouthed the word "Satan" and Kurt about had a conniption, lowering his head to his knees and wrapping his arms around his legs.

"And perhaps I might just be the one to find a way to kick your sorry ass. What do you want, Luci? You're spoiling a great morning that the Lord hath made. Amen, glory hallelujah."

"Where's the girl? We had a deal. You bring her to me and I free your brother's soul."

"It wasn't really a deal. You made me an offer: find the girl in exchange for my brother's soul. You also gave me 'til six P.M. It's not six yet, so you'll just have to wait, won't you?"

"Where is she?" I could tell by the sound of his voice he would definitely have a special place in Hell just for me if he could ever get his hands on my soul.

"Disney World. She's probably on Space Mountain right this very minute."

This got me another roll of the eyes from Samantha.

"Bring her to me now and not only will I free your brother's soul, but I will make you a king among men."

"Tempting as your offer is, I have to decline. Selling his soul to you didn't work out too well for Mikey. I'm afraid you'll just have to wait." My phone beeped and I said, "Hey Luci, I'd love to chat, but I've got a call coming in. I think it's a telemarketer and I'd rather talk to them than you."

"Don't you dare--" I did and hung up on him and answered the other call. It was my friend from the T.S.A. "The private charter is an hour behind schedule and will land around noon. They're coming in at the Louisville Express Charter hangar, right off Grade Lane. You can see the hangar they'll arrive at from the end of the ramp. I'll let you know when they're here, cleared Customs, and what car they pick her up in." He paused. "Vic, is there anything we need to know about this woman?"

"No," I lied. "I hope she's going to lead me to a guy I'm looking for. As far as I know she's just a science geek. But the people she's meeting with, one of them has a guy working for them that is on the run. I follow her, I get my guy."

I thanked him and disconnected the call. Kurt said, "You get phone calls from Satan? I think I'm going to puke."

"Yeah, but it's not like we're B.F.F.s. Or at least I sure as hell hope we're not. O.K. according to my contact, they have a car arranged to meet her at the plane. He'll let us know when they pick her up, what the car looks like, and then we can follow her to her destination and decide what to do next."

Kurt asked, "Speaking of what to do next, have you decided what you're going to do about your brother? Or her? Dude, you only have eight hours to make a decision. Have you decided?"

Samantha and I sat looking at each other, with Bob Evan's customers coming and going. I searched her face for what she might be thinking, but this woman had one hell of a poker face.

I took a deep breath and though I was talking to Kurt, I looked Samantha in the eyes and said, "Yeah. I guess I have. I'll have to find another way to save my brother. Turning Samantha over would mean a lot of people could be hurt, especially if the Church gets their money back. Besides, she's only tried to help things. If I turned her over to Luci, I don't know if I could live with that. I'll just have to think of something else."

Her stoic demeanor broke and I could see relief pass across her features. Samantha asked, "How much do you trust Kurt?" Kurt began to sputter and she leaned over and kissed him on the cheek. He went from sputtering to deadly still.

I said, "You can trust him. He wouldn't be here if you couldn't. Why?"

She said to Kurt, "If I give you my account numbers and passwords, can you hide the money somewhere else?"

Kurt stuttered out a, "Sure." She spent the next few minutes dictating to him account numbers and passwords for accounts at several different banks. He asked, "I'll let you know where I've parked it once it's all moved."

"No. I don't want to know. If they catch me, I can't tell them what I don't know."

He said, "True. That means I'll be the only one who knows. So..." He trailed off and his face took on a green tinge.

I said, "Kurt, they don't know who you are. Samantha only knows your first name. To find you, they'll have to go through me, and they won't be able to do that."

"Look, Vic, you're the baddest dude I know, but everyone has a breaking point...even you."

"Alright. Let's do this. You find places to move the money and when it comes time to enter passwords, I'll do that part, so that they would have to have both of us to get the money. Perhaps I can use the cash as leverage to get my brother loose while keeping Samantha out of it."

"O.K. But man, you have to make sure they don't find out about me. He looked around, suspiciously. "I don't want to do it here, though. We need to go someplace a bit more private."

We went to the nearest library where Kurt and I spent time hiding thirty million dollars. I could tell Kurt was nervous by the way he had to keep backspacing while typing, something he never did. Samantha sat where she couldn't see what we were doing, flipping through a Rolling Stone Magazine.

I had Kurt put just under ten grand into his own account. When we were finished I said, "With only you knowing the account numbers and me the passwords, they're screwed. I think it's time you take a vacation, Kurt. Someplace far from here. If I need your talents for anything else, I can call you and you can do work for me remotely. Your time as a field operative is over. You said you've been wanting to take some time off, so here's your chance. Thanks man, you did great work last night."

"You watch your ass, Vic. There are plenty of people trying to get a piece of it." We said our goodbye's and Kurt even managed to give Samantha a hug without getting sick.

As she watched Kurt drive off she asked, "So. What next?"

"Time to get the Hand of God involved. If killing children isn't going to do it, nothing will. Then we find out where the virus chick is going."

I dialed the number Montoya gave me and he answered on the third ring. I said, "Remember me?"

"Si, señor," replied the Hand of God. "I trust Miss Tyler is alive and well?"

"She is, and we've got the low-down on what we think the Church is up to. They're going to kill kids and lots of them." I then spent the next few minutes lining out what I knew about Korhonen and what we suspected she and the Church had planned.

"It is God's will you have been brought into this, Victor. Our paths now cross. I am in Louisville looking for a man who holds a high position for the Church of the Light Reclaimed, one who is involved in the Church's attack plans on every level, but who has remained…Como se dice? Elusive. He goes by the name Belial, but I have not been able to find out his real name. He is supposed to be at a meeting here. If she is in town, then perhaps she will be meeting with this man. Do you know where she is going?"

"Not yet, but I will. Her plane lands at noon. Care to join us?"

"Sí. Where can I meet you?"

"There's a gas station right when you get off of the exit for Grade Lane off of I-65. We'll meet you there at 11:30." He agreed and hung up.

Samantha's T-shirt had writing on the front that said 'Unless your name is Google, stop acting like you know everything.' So not only is she drop dead gorgeous, she also has a sense of humor.

She said, "We finally get his help, but only after David is murdered and others are killed. If God has a plan, it sure is one screwed-up plan."

I called Winston and gave him a rundown on what we learned and he agreed to meet us at the station. Finally, we were getting a handle on what Lucifer and the Church planned to do. If we could stop the virus before my six P.M. deadline, I could try and negotiate with the Devil on a soul buy-back plan and free Mikey from Hell.

We got to the station and found Winston waiting in his blue Jeep Grand Cherokee. I pulled up next to him and rolled down my window so we could chat. He looked none the worse for wear following our overnight raid. We made small talk until Montoya walked up to Samantha's side of the Chevelle and tapped on the window. Where he came from I have no clue, as there was no other car in the parking lot. The dude sure had a habit of just popping up out of nowhere.

Samantha rolled down her window and Montoya leaned in. He said, "If I may make a suggestion. Why doesn't la señorita ride with your friend and you and me ride together."

Samantha looked at me and after I nodded, she shrugged and got out of the car with Montoya taking her place. After Samantha climbed in with Winston, Montoya said, "They'll have to pass by here to get to the interstate. Why don't you have your friend wait a few blocks up? When they leave, we can alternate chase cars, so not to bring suspicion."

His suggestion made great sense. I also got the feeling he was trying to get me alone or perhaps away from Samantha. Either way, as we needed his help, I told Winston to do as he said and we would call him when the Swedish chick was headed his direction.

I could see concern on Samantha's face, but gave her my best smile and she and Winston pulled off. I said, "O.K. Now that you have me alone, what did you want to talk to me about?"

"I learned you let the Church take Miss Tyler away from you. It is good to see you got her back."

"I didn't let them *take* her, they just did. And yes, I got her back. Just how did you know this?"

"I have my own sources inside the Church. They are very upset you kill one of their young Hellhounds."

"Holy crap. Young? You're telling me that thing was a small one?"

"Sí, they can grow to be quite large. You have kill a vampire and a Hellhound. Maravilloso! But you are also killing men at an alarming rate." He shook a finger at me and said, "You must be careful, amigo. You are breaking one of God's commandments and doing so with little regard to how it affects your own soul. In your mind, I am sure the killings are justified and perhaps they have been. Don't cross the line to where you are doing things to save your brother and that lead you on a path away from God's grace."

I could feel myself getting hot under the collar. Here the Hand of God was lecturing *me* about the exact same thing he does and it made me feel like a little kid being dressed down by a disapproving parent. "You don't seem to have a problem with it. How come you get a free pass with killing people? Tell me that, Oh-Wise-One."

"I do not have a problem with it as my soul was lost a long time ago. I kill now, but only those deserved of God's wrath. There was a time that was not the case. I work now to make amends for the terrible things I have done."

I nodded at his gang tattoos. "You were a member of a Mexican drug cartel. You're talking about things you did for them?"

He looked out the front window at the planes taking off and landing from Louisville International. "Sí, señor, I kill my first man at the age of diez, ahh, ten. I work first as mule, delivering drugs. Then a man tried to steal the drugs from me rather than pay the money he owed. I knew what the man I worked for would do to me if I came back without the money. The man who took the drugs laughed at my face and turned to walk away. I pulled out a gun and shot him in the back. Many time I shot this man, to send a message to anyone else who would try and do the same thing."

"I feel nothing following his death. No anger, no sorrow, no remorse, nada. My employer found out. Soon I no longer delivered drugs. I delivered 'messages.' By the time I was sixteen, I'd kill dozens of men, even women. Soon I became the cartel's top assassin. I killed whomever they told me to kill and for a handsome dinero."

Listening to him talk I felt like I was in another place. The words he used, a mixture of Spanish and English, and the cadence, took me back to trips I had made to Mexico. His voice was rich and easy, the kind of voice to make women swoon. Around us people went about their business, with no clue what was going on around them. Montoya told his story without shame. Just told it as if it happened to someone else.

He continued, "Then, one day they had a new 'message' to send to a man who'd stolen money from them. The man had tres chicas bonitas—three lovely daughters, all under the age of twelve. They sent me to kill his children, but to leave the father alive.

"One night when I knew he was gone, I broke into the house and went into the bedroom of the first child. She was ten years old. When I closed the door behind me, there she was, sitting up in bed waiting for me. She said God told her I was coming and that she wanted to pray for me and asked if that would be O.K. I nodded. She closed her eyes and then prayed for me and her sisters. When she finished, she said 'muchas gracias'."

Montoya swallowed hard. "I killed so many, but no one had ever pray for me or accepted fate as this child. For the first time in my life, I couldn't do it. I stood there unable to speak, unable to move. She opened her eyes and looked at me and said, "You have a choice. You don't have to do this anymore." And then I cried, something I had not done since I was a small boy. I cried and could not stop. It took many minutes for me to get control of myself. When I did, I awoke the mother, gathered up the children and then hid them with someone I trusted.

I then went back to the compound of the man that I worked for and killed him and the men with him. Los mate a todos. *All of them.* I spared the women and children of his family, but killed everyone else. I left Mexico. I wandered for many months, and then found my way to Brazil. There I stopped at a small church. I'd never listened to a Catholic Mass, but I did that day. When it was over, I entered the confessional and unburdened my soul to a small town priest. He heard my confession without interruption or condemnation. When I finished, he blessed me and said there was a way out for me, a way to try and make good on the evil I had visited upon the world.

"He put me in touch with a man that would forever change my life. Since then I have been the Hand of God, doing what is asked of me and removing some of the truly evil people and things that are among us. So when I tell you I know how easy it is to lose your soul, I know what I am talking about. I kill as easily as you breathe. I was born with a talent to kill other men and before I was renewed, I did so, with no thought of God."

He paused for a moment, and then continued. "You have been walking a fine line, Victor, and it can be easy to fall on the wrong side. I know you want to save your brother, but I will tell you again: he cannot be saved. He made his choice. If you turn this woman over to Luci, not only will you be sealing your fate, but you will *not* save your brother. I do not even know if my own soul can be saved. I just do, today, what I should have been doing all along: and that is serving God."

I was floored by his story. I could feel my eyes filling with tears forming while he talked. This man had led a life I could barely comprehend. I knew what he was telling me was the truth about my soul, yet I also knew I would still do everything I could to save my brother, short of handing over Samantha. I'd always been able to solve problems and I felt I could solve this one, too. I had always wanted to be the hero. Now I had to wonder if I would end up losing my soul like Montoya.

My phone rang and my T.S.A. contact told me the plane would land in ten minutes and the plane's guests would be picked up by a white Mercedes limo. I thanked him and hung up. I then called Winston to pass on the info.

Montoya and I sat in silence, each lost in our own thoughts, until the plane, which looked to be some type of Gulfstream, landed. The limo drove out onto the tarmac, the driver got out of the car, and stood waiting by the back passenger door. A few minutes later, the plane's door was dropped. Customs cleared the crew and passengers. Then Raakel Korhonen got out with two other men who followed and seemed demure in her presence. She wore a black pant suit, her blonde hair tied back. She walked as if she owned the world. If the Church paid off, she would certainly own a larger part of the planet. The men were dressed in well-tailored suits and each carried a briefcase.

The driver opened the door for the three of them and they got inside. After closing the door, the driver and one of the pilots transferred luggage from the plane to the car. There were several small suitcases and I wondered if the killer virus was possibly hidden in one of them.

Twenty minutes after arrival, the limo finally pulled out and I called Winston to let him know they were on the move. The limo made the turn to go toward I-65 and I fell in line several cars back. I felt like Ahab following his white whale, but at least the car would be easy to follow.

We passed Winston and Samantha, who were waiting in a McDonald's parking lot and they joined the wagon train. The limo took the ramp to head towards the southern part of Louisville, with us right behind them.

I asked Montoya if he recognized any of the people and he said he didn't. Neither of the two men looked to be Church maniacal leader material. But the guy he was after may have been in the car already.

The limo got off on the Gene Snyder Freeway and headed into a more rural part of the county. Winston and I alternated who would stay with the limo, with one or the other of us passing them and getting off an exit and then switching lead, always keeping several cars between us.

The limo left the interstate and entered an area of multi-acre estates. We had to drop further back as there was very little traffic on the road and we were a quarter of a mile or so back when the limo put on a turn signal and drove down a tree lined driveway.

I pulled over and stopped by a low stone wall that encircled the property. I reached into the back seat for a pair of binoculars and watched as the limo stopped in a circular driveway. The driver hopped out and opened the back door.

Miss Korhonen's exit from the car was not nearly as nice as her entrance. The well-coiffed scientist had been replaced by a terrified woman. The two men, who had acted with such deference when they arrived, were anything but that now. One of the men, built like a well-rounded shrub, hauled her out of the limo by her ponytail, kicking and screaming. The other man, who looked like he belonged on the cover of a Harlequin romance novel, grabbed a hold of both her legs as they carried her to the front door of the house, which was out of my field of vision. The driver got back into the car and started back up the driveway. I gave Montoya a blow by blow account and asked what he suggested we do.

"Have your amigo in the Jeep follow the limo and let us know where it ends up. As they did not remove the luggage, if she has the virus with her, then it will be with the car. Have him call immediately if anyone else gets out of the car. You and I will visit the residents of this house and introduce ourselves."

I drove on past the driveway to the house, calling Winston and telling him to head back the other way and wait for the limo to pass and then to follow it and report where it stopped. I was more than a little pissed we wouldn't have time to pick up Samantha. She would be safer with Winston than she would be with us, at any rate. But not having her with me bothered me. I tried to put her out of my mind for a moment, as for the second time in less than a day I would be storming the castle to rescue a damsel. Or to kill her.

Chapter Twenty-Three

Montoya said, "Pull up to the driveway and park. We'll be polite and knock. If you see either of the men, leave them to me."

"No problem, Kemosabe." He gave me a confused look, but I waved him off.

The house, a two story Williamsburg-style home with blue siding and white trim, was gorgeous. We walked to the front door and Montoya reached under his jacket and pulled out a gun with a short suppressor already attached. I pulled out my Glock and held the gun down by my leg. He looked through the glass panes on either side of the door. Seeing no one, he turned the knob and found the door unlocked, so he opened it.

We stepped into a front foyer opening into a combination sitting room and dining room. Antique furniture gave the room a very warm, inviting look. Yet, once we were both inside with the door shut, the house felt…wrong.

I know no other way to describe it. The house looked Norman Rockwellian, but gave off the vibes of Norman Bates. A grandfather clock located on a far wall made the only sound I could hear, with a steady swish of its pendulum.

A hallway ran off to either side of the front door. Across the room I could see an entrance that revealed part of a kitchen on one side and some kind of TV room on the other. Montoya pointed for me to go right, while he went left. I walked stealthily down the hallway and found a large master bedroom with a walk-in-closet full of women's clothes and shoes. There were pictures on the nightstand of children playing on a swing set.

In the master bathroom hung a beautiful painted mural over the Jacuzzi tub. I walked over and took a closer look. It was an outdoor scene with a young woman sitting under an oak tree watching a boy flying a kite. I was stepping away when I thought I saw the woman sitting under the tree turn and look in my direction, which freaked the holy hell out of me.

I rubbed my eyes and leaned over the tub. She had been staring at the boy, but now she definitely was looking straight at me with the kind of smile that would make a sailor blush. She had deep blue eyes with long chestnut hair that fell loosely around her shoulders and seemed to sway in the wind. I tried to look away but couldn't, my eyes drawn to hers. And then I could hear her whispering to me. I couldn't quite make out the words so I strained harder, concentrating on the meaning of what she was saying. She was telling me we would spend eternity together, over and over. The rest of the world faded away and it was just the two of us. My breathing picked up and my heart started to race. The leaves on the tree in the painting stirred with an imaginary and ominous breeze. Sweat trickled down my face and my knees buckled. I kneeled down beside the tub and laid my gun down on the bathroom floor. Mesmerized, I kept my eyes on the woman in the painting.

The words in my head grew louder, as she told me she would never let me go. My heart was beating so fast I thought it would jump out of my chest. Her grin took on a more ghoulish look as I could feel my body ready to explode into a million pieces, with my body responding in a way it would if there had been ten Victoria Secret supermodels in the room, all vying for my attention.

Then the thought of Samantha broke through the tempest and a shot of anger burst through me. I didn't want this paint-by-numbers witch, but the beautiful woman with the sharp pointy sword. The painted woman's face suddenly changed, showing her own displeasure, as she felt the grip on my mind weaken. I embraced the anger and became royally pissed. Then I bit down hard on my cheek, the pain intense, and was finally able to break eye contact with the sinister painting.

I heard a gasp coming from behind me and dove to the side just as one of the men who brought in Korhonen, the one that looked like the romance novel cover boy, swung a large meat cleaver where my head had just been, striking the tub. He'd removed the suit jacket, rolled up his shirt sleeves and now had on an apron, covered in blood.

I snatched up my gun as I rolled on my back and shot him several times in the stomach, driving him across the bathroom, his own blood mixing with that of what I could only assume was the late Raakel Korhonen, as he fell back onto the porcelain throne. Without looking directly at her, I picked up the cleaver and buried it deeply into the cursed mural, splitting the painted lady in half. I thought it best not to look too closely to see if her expression had changed. Take that, bitch.

I moved on through a connecting hallway to the TV room and could see a straight shot to the kitchen. Montoya was on his knees looking at something on the wall in front of him. The stocky bad guy was standing right behind him holding his own butcher knife. I raised my gun and let off a single shot, taking off the top of his head and sending him down.

I made my way to Montoya, my eyes moving around the house, as the feeling of wrongness had just ramped up another level. Montoya's face was bathed in sweat, just like mine had been, as he fought the pull of a large painting framed on the wall in the kitchen. I shot the damn thing without looking at it until it fell off the wall and Montoya lowered his head to the ground, taking in huge gulps of air. After a moment, he looked at me and then to the dead man behind him.

He said, "Muchas Gracias." I offered him a hand up. He stood still for a moment getting his breathing under control, then went and examined the man lying on the kitchen floor. He had found no wallet or any other ID. "No help here."

I nodded my chin at the dead guy and said, "This makes us even. You saved me at the barn, now I saved your ass here. We're all square."

He said, "This is not a competition. While I thank you for your help, my life belongs to God, not you. Your being here is God's will. This painting, however, is not. I have heard of such things. They are called blood paintings. Blood from victims is mixed with the paint and the paintings are created during dark ceremonies from those who follow Luci. Do not look at anything you see on the walls."

"Too late. I had my own 'come to Da Vinci moment' in the bedroom." I told him what happened and that the other guy was also dead. "So the house is working like a Venus Fly Trap. I'm guessing Korhonen has come to the end of the line, if the blood on their aprons is any indication."

He walked over to a double door just off the kitchen and opened them. There were carpeted steps leading down to what must be the basement. He flicked on the light switch, illuminating the stairs, but they disappeared into a pool of darkness about half-way down. The whispering in my mind cranked back up and I could tell from the way his eyes narrowed, he heard it, too. The words were an invitation to descend the steps, of peaceful sleep and burdens relieved.

I asked, "Do we go down there?" I watched as the darkness swirled around the bottom of the steps, like a shark circling a bloodied swimmer in the ocean.

He shook his head. "No, vamonos. There is no one else here and the woman is dead. I will make sure that those who need to know are aware of this place" Good thing, because down those steps is one place I didn't want to go.

We left the house and walked back into the sunshine. The whispering in my head stopped when we crossed the threshold of the doorway. I took a deep breath and exhaled slowly. This looked like the All-American Home. I remember reading *The Amityville Horror* when I was a kid, a story about a haunted house. I never believed in that kind of stuff, but it was fun reading books about it. Living it, though, was a whole different matter.

We got back into my car and I started the engine. I pulled out my cell and called Winston, but it went directly to voicemail. It didn't even ring. I waited a moment, then dialed again with the same result.

I put the car in drive and headed back the way we'd come. "I got a bad feeling about this. I never should have let her go with him."

Montoya said, "You worry too much. Perhaps they are just in a place where there is no signal. It has happened to me since coming here to your town. He will call when he can."

Was it possible Montoya was right and Winston was just in a no service zone? I thought about it and didn't think so, not with how the last night had gone. The other problem was I also had no way to track Samantha's movements. After she found the Spark Nano in her coat at the motel, she had thrown it into a trash can as we left, and I didn't try and stop her. Now with time ticking down to the six P.M. deadline, I'd lost control of the one thing everyone wanted. What I wanted.

Inside, I was fuming. And as much as I hated to admit it, I was scared. When I first found Samantha at Double D, I gained a measure of control over the situation. I had some maneuvering room, at least until my brother's deadline. Now I was back where I started. Ground Zero.

But there was more to it than simply losing options where my brother was concerned. My feelings for Samantha were stronger than even I believed possible, considering we'd known each other less than a single day. She managed to touch something inside of me, grabbing hold and not letting go. Wild thought after wild thought passed through my brain, as I dreamed all manner of terrible scenarios.

What if Winston had decided to collect on the million dollar bounty offered to J.B.? He claimed to believe it wasn't worth it. And he'd had no problems when we split up for the night. But perhaps the temptation of having her all to himself proved more than he could pass up. If he had, I'd kill him.

Or what if the limo driver made them during the drive back to town and called in backup? The Church would risk nothing to get Samantha and the money back. They would kill Winston without blinking and Samantha wouldn't be long for this world, especially when they found out she no longer had the money.

My thoughts must have been showing on my face. Montoya said, "Breathe deeply, my friend. You've been under a lot of stress. If you grip the steering wheel any tighter, you will break it off and kill us both. Vamonos to the city."

I nodded and was silent as I drove. It was now just past one thirty in the afternoon. I had less than five hours before my brother died and hopped that express elevator going down. I called Winston's cell again with the same results.

We got to the part of Louisville known as Lively Shively, a swath of heavy commercial development along Dixie Highway in south Louisville, and I pulled over and into the parking lot of a McDonald's. I'd been thinking of how to find Samantha and Winston. I took out my phone and dialed Kurt. He answered and I asked, "If I give you Winston's cell phone number, can you find out where he is?"

"Dude, if his phone is on, and if he's in a service area, I can get you close. But not, like, in his pocket. Why? Have you lost him, too?"

I gave him the short version and Kurt said, "Damn, Vic. Not good. Hang tight and I'll get back to you in a bit."

I put the phone on my dash and gripped the wheel tight with both hands. Montoya sat in the passenger seat, with the breeze drifting through his open window, waiting like a coiled spring. I thought about Samantha, how she said she didn't want to die and how with me she felt safe. I could feel the anger boiling over. Anger at possibly losing her. Anger at my brother for selling his soul. Anger at the world in general.

I seethed while waiting for Kurt to call back. When the phone finally rang, I snatched it off the dash and said, "Tell me."

"Dude, they're at a rest area right off I-65, the one just past the exit for Shepherdsville. The signal isn't moving. Get your ass on the way and I'll let you know if he starts moving."

I floored it heading out of McD's and before long I was flying down the interstate and made it to the rest area in a time Dale Earnhardt Jr. would've been proud of. There were only two cars in the front lot. I was about to pull in when Montoya pointed towards the back lot where Winston's Jeep was parked sideways, taking up two parking spots. I pulled up and parked in front of his Jeep and Montoya and I got out.

No one else was parked in the back lot and as I came up to the driver's door, it was clear no one was inside. I could see blood on the seat and opened the door. His cell phone had fallen down onto the floor board.

Montoya approached the passenger side and said, "Victor. Come, look."

I walked to his side of the car and saw on the ground next to Montoya's feet a severed arm. It was dressed in what looked like the sleeve of black coveralls and appeared to have been cut with a very sharp instrument. Samantha had at least been fighting when she was taken. The question now was if she'd been taken alive. Blood soaked the ground, but there was no way to tell if any of it was hers.

The anger that had been building inside me, stopped and hardened. With it came a certainty and calm. They had her and I planned on getting her back, no matter what it took. No matter whom it hurt.

Montoya said, "I am sorry, Victor. We have lost her, perhaps for good, as well as your friend driving her."

"Not yet we haven't. I know someone who might know where they are." I called Kurt and said, "We found Winston's Jeep. They're not here. I think the Church has them again. You said last night that they made a stop at their geek's home. I need his address."

Kurt gave it to me and asked, "What're you going to do?"

"Time to deliver them all to Hell."

Chapter Twenty-Four

Lincoln Townsend's Cherokee Park neighborhood bordered the park itself, with his backyard looking out onto the golf course. The curving street, lined with old oaks and maples, featured a mix of home styles. Townsend lived in a three-story Victorian home, with a well-manicured front lawn and a flower bed surrounding the front. Not the kind of place I would have expected from a geek Satanist.

Montoya and I parked down the street watching the house. We had moved the guns from Winston's Jeep to my trunk, then Montoya drove it and we dropped it off at a nearby shopping mall. We left the severed arm in the rest area parking lot.

We could see a white van parked in the back. Never a good thing with these guys, as vans tended to mean dead bodies. I had to force myself to sit still and analyze the situation. My desire was to drive up, kick the door down and start shooting whoever got in my way. But if Samantha and Winston happened to be inside, rushing in could get them killed. After our last midnight rescue, you could bet your ass they wouldn't be as easy to take down this time. And if he had a pet Hellhound, then things could get even more interesting.

Montoya once again sat silently, observing the scene, seemingly unfazed by the latest developments. I know he had no emotional ties to either Samantha or Winston, but he could show some genuine concern, at least. Inside I was boiling, though on the outside, I was projecting as much calm as the Hand of God. For better or worse, I was at peace with whatever came next. The Church and Lucifer started this war and I was damn sure going to end it. If that meant taking out most of the Church in the process, then I was O.K. with that, despite Montoya's warning about my soul being in danger.

We'd been watching for about twenty minutes, when the van pulled down the driveway and away from us. The only person visible was the driver. Time to make a decision: follow the van, or see whether Townsend was home. Montoya looked at me and I decided the time had come to make a house call.

I reached into the backseat for a small gym bag. I unzipped and took out a hat with the local electric company logo on the front, a clipboard and pen. I used this ruse a lot to gain entry to a home.

I said, "I'll walk to the door and try to get in. The moment you see me make it inside, come on in and join the party."

"Be careful, Victor. And remember what I have said about your soul. You do not want to end up in Hell with your brother."

I just nodded and got out of the car. I walked down the sidewalk in front of the house and paused to look at my clipboard and then at the surrounding houses, just in case anyone was watching me.

I then walked up the driveway, keeping my eyes focused on the clipboard, the brim of my hat hiding my eyes. I made it to the front door without anyone shooting at me, or a Hellhound bounding out to chew my legs off and considered that progress.

I rang the doorbell and started whistling and tapping my pen against the clipboard. After all, no one would ever begin great mayhem while whistling a happy song. I found myself whistling *Sympathy for the Devil* by the Rolling Stones, when the door opened. A man about thirty years old, medium height and wearing Buddy Holly glasses said, "Yes? What can I do for you?"

I squinted at the clipboard and asked, "Are you Mr. Townsend, 1614 Cherokee Trail?"

"Yes. That's me. What's up?" He had a 'no' cares in the world demeanor about him. Much different than Kurt, who seemed like his body had been made for someone else. Lincoln knew who he was and loved it.

I said, "We've been having a problem with the meters out your way and I'm doing a quick check of them in your neighborhood. But I have a couple of questions first, if you don't mind.

"Fire away. Although I have to tell you, my bills have been in line, so I don't think there's any problem with mine."

I took a casual glance around and didn't see anyone else. I pointed to the top page on my clipboard. "Is this your full address and phone number?"

When he bent closer to look at the page, I head butted him hard in his left temple. My mother claimed she used to drop me on my head often, which is why it was so hard. You would have thought I'd found a power switch and turned it off the way he fell to the ground. I stepped into the house and closed the door, pulling my gun. There were steps going up and a hallway leading away from the door towards the back of the house, with a room on either side. A quick glance into both side rooms showed they were empty. I knelt and checked Townsend for a weapon, finding only a cell phone, which I pocketed.

I stood, taking Townsend by the collar of his shirt and dragged him down the hallway. I stopped and listened at the foot of the stairs, but didn't hear anything. I continued down the hallway and made it halfway when a man stepped into it from the backroom. Seeing me, he reached for a gun he had in his waistband, but way too slowly as I shot him several times in the chest. The blood oozing through the shirt told me that he didn't have on a vest.

I heard the front door open behind me, and Montoya stepped in and then closed it again. He took in the situation quickly and held up a hand for me to stop. I did and he moved past me further down the hallway with his own gun out. When he got to the end of the hall, he quickly looked around the corner to his left, and was greeted with gunfire hitting the wood next to his head. He waited a moment and then turned the corner, gun raised, and fired.

I followed him, dropped Townsend for a moment and cleared the kitchen. I glanced into the living room and saw two men Montoya had shot dead. The two men in coveralls had conveniently fallen onto a large piece of plastic spread out to protect Townsend's light-colored carpet from dripping blood. Winston's blood. They had him tied to a chair in the middle of the room. His face showed bruising from where they'd been working him over. One eye was nearly completely swollen shut. And his shoulder was bleeding from what looked like a gunshot wound.

He looked at me with his good eye and said, "Damn, Vic. Your timing is for shit. I had them right where I wanted them. If you'd given me another couple of minutes, I would have kicked their asses."

"Yeah. I can see how you were putting a hurt on them." I holstered my gun, untied him, and then helped him over to a really expensive looking sofa, which he promptly started bleeding all over. The wound on his shoulder was bad, but didn't look life-threatening.

Townsend was starting to come around so I picked him up and tied him into the same chair Winston had occupied. For a second time in less than twenty-four hours, I'd replaced a Church victim with a Church member.

Montoya came back from checking out the rest of the house. "She's not here."

Winston said, "Nah, man. They dropped her off somewhere else, then brought me here. They had me tied up on the floor and I couldn't see where it was exactly. I could see the tops of some warehouses, but not much else."

"I bet he knows," I said pointing at Townsend. "What information were they trying to get out of you?"

"Just what we knew and how we knew it. They have a real hard on about finding you, though. Deveraux wants you bad. I guess you must have messed that pretty boy up but good from what these guys were saying. He plans on doing much worse to you if he catches you."

I looked at Montoya and asked, "You know about Deveraux. I still don't know why you haven't taken him out."

Montoya said, "I want the man above him. Belial. I have been hoping he will lead me to this man. So far he has not. He will face judgment before God soon enough."

I asked Winston, "Can your shoulder handle a few more minutes while I get some information out of this guy?"

"It's all good, man. I'm just kicking back and taking it easy." He said this with a smile, but I could tell he was hurting like hell.

I walked over to Townsend and lifted his chin and said, "Lincoln. Look at me. Do you know who I am, you son of a bitch?"

He did and I could see fear in his eyes. He looked at the dead men on the floor around him, at Winston sitting on his couch bleeding, and the Hand of God leaning against the far wall. He would get no help from those two.

"Yep. Times have changed, Linc'. And if you don't answer my questions fully and honestly, then you'll be joining the others bleeding out on your carpet. Do you understand?"

He nodded yes and I slapped him on the side of the head. "I'm sorry. I couldn't hear you."

He winced with pain and tried to curl up into as much of a ball as the ropes tying him to the chair would allow. "Yes. Please don't hit me."

"Where is she?"

"I don't know. I swear. I don't know."

I pulled my gun out and placed it between his eyes. "Not an answer that's going to help you stay alive, Linc'. Let's try this again. Where is she?"

"I can't tell you. They'll kill me if I do. I can't die. I can't go to..." He stopped and stared at me with pleading eyes.

"Go to Hell? Yeah. I know about how you work for Satan. I've met him. And you're right. He'll be royally pissed when you get there. But that's where you'll be in just a few minutes if you don't answer my questions."

He swallowed hard, took a deep breath and said, "I won't tell you."

"Have it your way." I moved the gun from his forehead and put it against his left knee and pulled the trigger. The sound was deafening in the enclosed space. Lincoln started to scream the moment his knee exploded in a cloud of bone, ligaments, tendons and blood. He pounded his other leg on the floor and rocked the chair as intense pain flooded his brain. At least the plastic was keeping it off his precious carpet.

Montoya came off the wall and took me by the arm and said, "Victor, you cannot do this, my friend. This is torture and it will blacken your soul. You cannot do this to him. If he will not answer you, then so be it."

I shook him off and rounded on him. "I don't give a rat's ass right now. They'll kill her once they find out she no longer has the money. This is my best and maybe only hope of finding her. And don't forget, they plan on killing children. Don't you care about that?"

"Of course I do. You know this. But we will find another way to stop them. Not torture, that's evil."

"Back off, man. I don't want to throw down with you, but I will if I have to. God gives us free will to make our own choices, right? Well, this is MY choice. So back the hell off."

We both had our guns out, both of us holding them casually at our sides, both knowing the other would kill, if needed. I stared into his eyes, watching for any sign he had decided I'd gone too far and needed to be taken out. He seemed to be looking into my eyes just as intently. After a few tense moments, he nodded his head slightly and stepped back, sliding his gun back under his jacket and holding his hands loosely at his sides.

I turned my attention back to Lincoln and, using my gun, pushed his head back so he could look at me. "That's just a taste of what the next few minutes will be like. I don't have time to fuck around with you, so let's cut to the chase, shall we?" I lowered my gun and pressed it against his crotch. "I'm only going to shoot you one more time. I'm going to turn you into a eunuch with my next shot and let you bleed out slowly, tied to this chair. You're going to tell me what I want to know or you're going to Hell in the most painful way I can think of."

"Wait. I'll tell you. Please." He sobbed for a few minutes. "They took her to a warehouse where they're working on the Exodus Project. I have the address in my laptop. It's upstairs in my bedroom."

Montoya said, "I see one on a small desk. I will go get it."

He left and I continued the grilling. "I'm going to ask you other questions, some of which I know the answer to, some I don't. The moment you lie to me, I pull the trigger and we walk out of here." I pressed harder with the gun to make my point. "So you guys plan on releasing a virus during the academic challenge in December, using the aerosol canisters in the computers you're donating, right?"

His eyes widened. "Yes, but how do you know that?"

"Never mind how. How did Korhonen get the viruses into the

country? Between Homeland Security, the T.S.A., C.I.A, we have safeguards against that kind of thing. How'd you guys pull it off?"

"The virus was hidden inside the plane itself, inside fake soft drink cans in the plane's refrigerator. We have an inside guy with Customs in the Helsinki Airport and he cleared them to be loaded. When the plane refueled here before the flight back, we had a crew come on and clean the plane, taking the cans off with them. Then they took them to the warehouse, where another group was waiting to transfer the virus to the aerosol cans."

"What type of virus? Anthrax? Bubonic Plague?"

"A genetically engineered version of bird flu. Her company has been testing different combinations to see how easily the virus can make the transition to humans from animals and then a vaccine for it when it does."

Montoya walked back into the room with the laptop. He sat in another chair, placed the computer in his lap, opened it up and powered it on. Lincoln's eyes were starting to get a glassy look as shock set in, so I slapped him across the face, refocusing his attention back on me.

"And I'm guessing they created one that can. They must have found a way around the protein receptor problem."

"Yes. You know about virus transmissibility?"

"I read a lot, so I'm smarter than your average bear. How contagious and what's the projected mortality rate?"

"Highly and over eighty percent mortality rate. When this is released into the schools, the kids and anyone who comes in contact with it will come down with the virus and most of them will die."

"Jesus. Why? How can you be a part of this? Killing kids? Man, that's beyond evil."

Tears streamed down his face. "Because I don't have any choice. I sold my soul when I was a teenager. I agreed to do whatever I was asked to do by the Church. If I don't, I go straight to Hell. The Lord of Light has promised me a high seat when he claims his rightful seat on the throne of Heaven. I do what they ask, and I'm rich here and in the afterlife."

"What you don't seem to realize is just how royally fucked you really are. How does Fazil Al Haqar figure into this? You guys hook up with one of the world's top terrorists to kill babies?"

Townsend actually smiled, and then snickered, despite his pain. "That was my idea."

And then I knew. "He's not involved, is he? You're just going to pin it on him. That's what the labels were for, so that people would blame Muslims. You must've set up the documents for the shell companies that own Inspirational Global Software. You knew the powers that be would track down the whole thing and then pin it on Muslim extremists for the attacks. Satan then has the two major religions at war with each other. It will be total chaos."

Townsend nodded and said, "Muslims and Christians will be killing each other in the name of God. Just like they have been for hundreds of years. Fanatics of each religion will want to kill each other even more and people on the fence about God will tune out and forget about Him all together. A win-win for the Lord of Light."

"Dude, you are so hosed. Satan has lied to you from the start. All you've bought is a one way ticket to Hell. Out of curiosity, why's it called the Exodus Project?"

Townsend was starting to go pale from the blood loss and he'd begun to sweat. But his eyes were on fire. "It's payback for what God and Moses did to the Egyptians. Exodus Chapter 11, verse 5: *And all the firstborn in the land of Egypt shall die, from the firstborn of Pharaoh that sitteth upon his throne, even unto the firstborn of the maidservant that is behind the mill; and all the firstborn of beasts.* God started this fight. We're just bringing payback. The Lord of Light plans to kill as many Christian children as possible."

Montoya said, "His laptop is password protected. What's the password?"

Townsend told him a string of numbers. Montoya entered them and a moment later I heard the Windows sound. Townsend mumbled, "Look in my Outlook Contact folder under Warehouse."

Continuing my interrogation I asked, "Who do you work for? Who's your boss?"

"Preston Deveraux. I take orders from Preston."

"Who's his boss?"

Townsend licked his lips and looked to the side. "I don't know." I pressed the gun painfully into his crotch, making the man squeal. "I swear I don't know. They call him Belial, but I don't know his real name. All I know is he owns the warehouse the operation is going down in. I've never met him and that's all I know."

"And a man with your talents never looked up who the owner is? I find that hard to believe."

He said, "Don't you get it? They find out I've been looking into things like that and I'm as good as dead. When they tell you not to do something, you damn well better not do it. And trying to find out Belial's real name would be suicide. He's one of the most feared individuals on the planet."

Montoya said, "We find the owner of the warehouse and we find out who is the boss pulling the strings for the Church of the Light Reclaimed." He started typing keys and a minute later he said, "The address is 1624 Cane Run Road. Perhaps you can have your amigo find out who owns this building?"

I felt as though my whole world had collapsed in on me. I staggered back a couple of steps until I hit the edge of a coffee table and sat down.

Winston asked, "What the hell's wrong with you, man?"

"I know who owns the warehouse."

Chapter Twenty-Five

I can remember the day Mikey called me to show off his new purchase down at Louisville River Port. The building, brand spanking new and over five hundred thousand square feet, was equipped with every modern convenience. One day he gave me a tour and he sounded like a proud papa of a favorite child when talking about the place, showing me the ultra-modern control room which ran the nearly totally automated warehouse. Put in a code and the product you wanted was brought to the front of the building by automated bots on wheels. They could monitor security from the same room, along with a top of the line fire suppression system.

The building's loading docks, with access to the river, allowed product to be shipped up and down the Ohio River. It's close to major interstates for trucking within the US, Canada and Mexico. UPS's Worldport Facility, their largest automated sorting hub on the planet, is close by allowing domestic and international shipments to be delivered quickly. The place helped to give Mikey a leg up on other people in the same business and it cost him millions of dollars to get it up and running, but it was worth it.

I remembered the address because he said 1624 was the year that Louis XIII of France appointed Cardinal Richelieu the chief minister of the Royal Council and only a dweeb like Mikey would know such a thing.

Montoya said, "It's tu hermano. Your brother is Belial." His hand drifted under his jacket and stayed there as he watched me. "Belial is a name used by one of the four princes of Hell. For your hermano to have earned this name, he must be very high in Luci's eyes and truly diablo, Victor."

"Then this makes no sense. If my brother is Belial, then why would Satan end his life? Wouldn't he want him to stay alive as long as possible? It *can't* be my brother." I put my face right in front of Townsend's and said, "Maybe they forced him to let them use his warehouse, just like they forced you to do the shit you do for them. But there is no way my brother is this Belial-character. How do you know Belial owns the warehouse?"

"A couple of weeks ago, I heard Preston talking to Congressman Tyler on the phone. He told the Congressman that Belial had set up a clean room at his warehouse to handle the transfer of the virus into the individual canisters. Belial owns the warehouse."

"Your brother is one of the baddest Mofos on the planet, and you didn't know?" asked Winston.

"It's not like we pal around together, or anything. He's always been the black sheep of the family. But no, man, I had no clue."

Montoya stood up and tossed the laptop to the ground and once again pulled his gun and pointed it at me. "You must realize now, there is no doubt your hermano cannot be saved. Why Satan has decided to call in his contract now I don't know, nor do I care. I am under orders to find and send Belial to Hell, and I will do so. Please put your pistola down."

I walked over to him, raised his gun hand and put the barrel in the middle of my forehead. "No. I won't. If you're going to shoot me, then do it. I'm going to the warehouse to free Samantha. Then I'm going to find my brother and get to the bottom of this. All you have is this loser's word that my brother is Belial. For all you know, he's making this up just to screw with me. You heard what Winston said. They want me bad. Maybe this is part of their plan, to sic you on my brother and on me."

Townsend nearly choked in panic. "It's not. I swear it. I don't know who you are or who your brother is. All I know is Belial owns the warehouse. Please. I swear I'm not playing games here."

I stared at Montoya a moment longer, and then went back to Townsend. At least the Hand of God didn't shoot me in the back when I turned around. "Have you ever been to the warehouse?"

"Yes. I helped set up the computers there."

"Then you met Michael McCain while you were there?"

"I have no clue who you're talking about. None of the computer guys were named Michael."

I pressed my gun into his groin and said, "I told you if you lied to me I would shoot you and let you die."

He screamed, "I'm not lying! I'm telling the truth!" And I could tell he meant it.

"So you have a security key to get into the building, right?"

"Yes. It's in my wallet. It's white, with a series of numbers along the edge. My wallet is on the kitchen counter."

I went to the kitchen and returned with the key card. Montoya still had his gun out, but at least it wasn't pointed right at me. I went back to Townsend, unbuckled his belt and pulled it out of his pant loops, then wrapped it around his leg and cinched it tight, using it as a tourniquet.

I said, "It's your lucky day. You get to live a while longer." I said to Winston and Montoya, "They have an underground parking garage, but you need a security card to get in and they have a camera recording everyone that passes through the gate. If we just drive up to the door, we've got no chance in hell of getting in. With dipshit here, we can."

Montoya stepped in front of Townsend and asked, "How many men can we expect to find there? Where is this 'clean room'?"

Townsend grimaced, and said, "I have no clue how many men will be there. I wasn't involved in the planning of the actual transfer of the virus. I'm guessing not many. I mean, they think no one knows where and what they're doing. Plus, they didn't want workers there the day they did this. So, the warehouse guys have the day off. They think the building is going through a software upgrade on the systems, so the robots won't work. There won't be many people at the warehouse. The clean room is on the third floor in the back corner."

"Why take Samantha there, but bring Winston here?"

"Belial wanted her there." Townsend pointed at Winston and said, "This guy they didn't care about, but they wanted to learn what he knows. Since you guys knew about the safe house in the country, they decided to interrogate him at my place where we could count on privacy. Or so we thought. But the girl, he wanted her with him."

Montoya said, "That means if your hermano needs Miss Tyler to win freedom from his contract, he now has her and no longer needs your help. He will no doubt turn her over to Satan. If we don't find and free her, she is as good as dead."

I said, "Then let's get moving. We can drop Winston off at University Hospital."

Winston said, "Uh-huh. No way, man. I'm coming with you. I owe these bastards. And you're not leaving me behind."

"Dude, you've been leaking blood for hours. I don't think that's a wise move."

He said, in a very bad British accent, "It's only a flesh wound." He stood, somewhat unsteadily. "Besides, I know the address and if you drop me off at University, I'll just get a cab and show up anyway. So you might as well take me with you."

I offered my hand and he took it. I said, "J.B. made the right choice when he picked you to be his right hand. You're one tough son-of-a-bitch."

Montoya and I helped Townsend out to his car, a brand spanking new Lexus LX SUV. It still had that new car smell and darkly tinted windows. We put Townsend in the back, and Winston kept a gun pressed to his side. We moved all our gear and weapons into the Lexus. Then I got behind the wheel and Montoya in the passenger seat, and we were off.

As I pulled down the driveway and into the street, I asked Winston, "So what happened with the limo?"

"Ambushed, man. The limo driver pulled around back at the rest area and parked. I pulled into a spot in the front, on the far end, and watched. The guy got out of the limo and then walked into the woods. He was gone for like ten minutes, so we figured he wasn't coming back. We drove around to take a look inside the limo. Just as I put my car into park and Samantha opened up her door, these guys come charging out of the woods, guns raised. I didn't even have time to get my gun out before one of them shot me. Lucky for me, it just grazed my chest, but it bled like hell. So I played up being hurt, hoping they would let their guard down and I could make a move, but no such luck.

You should have seen your girl. They went to grab her and she had that sword out of its box and took one guy's arm off and stabbed two more before they tased her and took her down. That's one woman who I'm going to stay on her good side. That's one fierce lady. They threw us in the back of the limo, dropped her off, then brought me here."

I said, "She's something else, that's for sure." I looked at Townsend in the rear view mirror and asked, "Will your key card get us into the control room?"

Through gritted teeth he replied, "Yes. I have master access to the entire building. My card will get you into any part of the building you want." After a moment, he said, "Listen, guys, let's work out a deal here. I know things about the Church of the Light Reclaimed that you guys can use. Get me to a hospital and I'll tell you anything you want. Work with me here."

Montoya said, "I don't think you comprende the gravity of your situation. You are not going to a hospital. And you will tell us what you know as it is the only thing keeping you alive. When we are finished at the warehouse and I have killed Belial, then we shall see what I will do with you."

Montoya kept talking about killing my brother and I didn't know whether I'd be able to do anything to stop him, short of putting a bullet into the head of the Hand of God. I refused to believe my brother could be Belial. Mikey could be many things, but I didn't think killer would be one of them. Especially not killing kids. I just couldn't find a way to reconcile the man Montoya knew with my brother.

But what if Montoya and Townsend were right? My brain pounded trying to manage it all, and I had to push the thoughts away. First things first. Find and save Samantha. Then deal with my brother.

We arrived at Louisville River Port and I pulled in and parked behind a warehouse down the docks from my brother's place. I turned in my seat and said to Townsend, "Here's what we're going to do. We're going to put you behind the wheel to drive the rest of the way. The three of us will be here in the back. If you do anything to alert them, I'll blow a hole big enough to put my fist through. Once we get into the parking garage, we will leave you in the car. Do what we tell you and you get to keep breathing. If not, then it's cancel Christmas for you. You got it?"

He nodded yes and we helped him hobble to the front driver's seat, with Montoya and I squeezing in the back seat with Winston. I got a bullet proof vest out of the back and handed it to Winston, who gingerly stripped off his shirt, put on the vest and then put his shirt back on. I asked Montoya if he wanted one, but he declined.

I asked, "Is that because you're protected by God?"

He gave me a smile more suited to a barracuda and replied, "No, because any man that gets close enough to take a shot at me will already be dead."

O.K. then. I glanced out my window, the heavy tint turning the late fall sunshine into a twilight gloom. With any luck, the tinted glass would keep anyone from seeing us as we entered the garage. I rubbed the barrel of my gun along the side of Townsend's cheek and said, "I don't need much excuse to kill you, Lincoln. Not much at all. And the Hand of God here needs even less. Winston would kill you just for fun. So don't try to be a hero. Just do what we tell you."

With a whimper Townsend put the Lexus in drive and pulled around to the entrance of my brother's warehouse. His face was covered in sweat and he kept licking his lips. I said, "Try and relax Lincoln. Take a few deep breaths and let's get this over with." I handed him his key card.

The building, three stories tall, with loading docks and lifts that allow access to all three levels, backed up to the Ohio River. The wind had picked up and made whitecaps on the river, pushing against its never-ending flow to the Mississippi River and eventually the Gulf of Mexico. The building itself used steel framing and a rough hewn rock exterior.

Townsend pulled up to the card reader at the ramp leading to the underground parking garage for employees, slipped in his security card and the machine spat it back, with the metal grate raising to let us enter. He pulled his car down the ramp and we could see there was only a handful of cars parked in the garage, one of which was my brother's Lexus convertible. I had Townsend back in next to his car and turn the engine off, which he did with difficulty, considering the pain in his knee.

Winston opened up his door and got out, with Montoya sliding out after him, guns out and watching for trouble as I grabbed Townsend by the collar of his shirt and drug him roughly into the back seat while he offered up groans of pain. Using a couple of plastic wrist cuffs I secured him to the child car seat rings, then used some duct tape from my duffel bag, ripped off a piece and covered his mouth.

I said, "If I see you out of this car before we come back for you, I'll shoot you. No second chances with me, Lincoln. Nod if you understand."

He did so and I got out and went to the back of the Lexus and loaded up. I slung the straps of an MP5 over my shoulder, picked up the carry bag with the grenades, extra gun clips, a can of black spray paint and a few other goodies. I handed out com links and each of us slipped them onto our left ear and did a mic test. As ready as we'd ever be, I said, "This is going to take crackerjack timing, Wang."

Winston laughed and Montoya, who obviously had never seen *Big Trouble in Little China,* asked, "Who are you calling Wang?"

"Never mind. Just remember, it's all in the reflexes. Come on, let's get this done." And with that I walked into battle with Winston and the Hand of God.

Chapter Twenty-Six

We made it to the elevators with no problem. I looked around and found a brick by a large dumpster. I pushed the elevator button, but instead of taking them, I let the door open then set the brick by the door, keeping it open and we took the stairs. I didn't want to end up like Jack and Wang in *Big Trouble*, trapped in an elevator and sent to the Hell of the upside down sinners, or wherever the hell they were sent to die was. I took point, followed by the Hand of God with Winston bringing up the rear, and we entered the stairwell.

Just before we reached the first level, I said, "The control room is on the second floor. They may already know we're coming." As I pointed to the security camera in the upper corner of the stairwell, I blew the camera a kiss, took out the can of spray paint and coated the lens.

"As far as I remember, the cameras are video only, no audio. At least they won't be able to see what we prepare. You guys heard Townsend, the clean room is on the third floor, in the rear. We need to get to and take the control room before we head that direction. Once we do, Winston you'll set up there and be our eyes and the cavalry, should the shit really hit the fan."

Montoya asked, "There are executive offices in this building, no?"

"Yes. They're on the second floor, down a hallway from the elevators and across from the control room." Any idiot would know why he asked me that question: the most likely place for my brother to be would be in his office. His office included a large reception area, a conference room with video conferencing equipment and a spacious main office with a sixty inch flat screen TV. My brother had it all and it could end up being his tomb.

We headed up to the next level, so far with no resistance. "Just do me a favor, will you? Before you put a bullet in my brother's brain, let me at least talk to him. You wouldn't be here if it wasn't for my help. You owe me that much."

Montoya considered this and said, "I will do what I can. But if I have no choice, I will not hesitate." And I knew that was as much as a consideration as I was likely to get out of the former cartel hitman. I used the spray paint to cover the second floor stairwell camera.

I said, "I'll open the door a crack and see what's what. Winston, get a concussion grenade ready. If we need to use it, I'll get the door open, you toss and we hit the door hot. Then shoot anything that moves. Any questions?" Neither man said anything.

I took a deep calming breath. I could feel the adrenalin kick in, my heart begin to race, and all my senses become hyper alert. I was now fully prepared for whatever was to come next.

When I first arrived in Iraq, our unit spent time going from district to district clearing out some of the buildings where people still loyal to the old Saddam regime were holed up. It felt just like this. Knowing you were going to kick the door in and might find someone on the other side that wanted you dead—just as much as you wanted to kill them. It made me feel more alive than anything else in the world that I'd ever experienced.

From an earlier visit, I knew the stairwell and bank of elevators opened in the middle of the floor, with a good sized waiting area with a hallway running off to the right that lead to Mikey's office and the control room. To the left, there was a hallway to more conference rooms and the johns. Straight ahead, double glass doors opened up onto the warehouse floor.

The stairwell landing was large enough to allow the three of us to stand to the side of the door that opened towards us. I turned the handle, and pulled the door open a crack, only to be greeted with a hail of gunfire.

I let the door fall shut and thanked God my brother used steel frames and stone walls for this building. The solid metal door pounded with a staccato sound as bullets pounded the other side. I made sure Winston was ready with the concussion grenade. When both men nodded they were ready, I once again turned the handle and this time threw the door wide open.

Winston popped the clip and tossed the MK3 concussion grenade into the waiting room. Designed to be used in enemy bunkers to cause a maximum amount of damage, the grenade roared with the added sound of exploding glass. We hit the room hard, me diving to the left, Winston to the right. The door closed and my brain registered that Montoya had not come through the door behind us. Son of a bitch.

The grenade had done its job, with four men lying on the ground, two of them dead, the other two badly wounded. The glass walls of the reception area had been blown to pieces and dust filled the air. I pointed for Winston to head down towards the control room. I went to the wounded men and took their weapons, while keeping an eye on the warehouse floor, as I scanned for more attackers. I had a clear view down the center aisle to the far end of the building. There were four neat rows of shelving, nearly thirty feet high, packed with all types of products. I knew this floor to be packed with electronics headed overseas, as my brother's clients were mostly international companies.

I could see Winston glance into Mikey's office and evidently he didn't see anyone as he crossed the hall and put his back against the wall, then looked into the control room. He straightened up and held up two fingers: two people in the control room. I pressed my com button and, speaking softly, described my brother and asked him to nod his head if he saw him. He indicated No. I pressed the com button once again and asked for the Hand of God to respond. He didn't. I backed up to the stairwell door and opened it for a quick look up and down the stairs. No Montoya. The Hand of God had decided to do something on his own.

I jogged down the hallway and joined Winston. I told him to watch the hallway while I cleared the executive office. I did so quickly and found it empty. I did find a cup of Starbucks coffee, a venti caramel macchiato, still warm. I made fun of him for drinking these flavored metro-sexual type coffees instead of the real thing. So Mikey WAS here, and just a short time ago. I had to find him before Montoya did, or his ass was grass.

I went back to the hallway and glanced into the control room. A man and a woman, both in security guard uniforms, were hiding behind a counter lined with monitors and computer screens where the warehouse manager could move any piece of product in the warehouse by typing in the coordinates of where the items were stored and entering in a dock location. The robots would retrieve and deliver the stuff and never complain about the workload or the overtime.

I approached the door with my gun raised, Winston covered my rear. I used Townsend's keycard, and the lock lights went from red to green. I opened the door and said, "Stand up where I can see you. Do it now with your hands up and slowly, please."

They did so and I got a good look at both. The guy's eyes kept twitching, while sweat stained the armpits of his white shirt. I've seen cats on a hot tin roof that were not as nervous than this guy. The woman looked at him and said, "For Christ's sake, Ron, grow a pair, will you?" She looked at us and said, "The cops are on their way. You guys will be in deep shit if you don't leave now."

I remembered her from when Mikey gave me the grand tour. It took a moment, but I remembered her name. "Good try, Gloria. I know Mikey wouldn't let you call the cops with what he has going on here today. You didn't call anyone. Now back up."

She squinted at me and then said, "You're Mr. McCain's brother.

What the hell do you think you're doing? He's your own brother for Christ's sake. I mean, you come in here blowing things up and killing people. What the hell is wrong with you?"

"You may find this hard to believe, but I'm trying to save his life. And you guys started shooting first. We just took exception. Now where is he?"

Her eyes shifted to the bank of security monitors and then back to me and she said, "I don't have a clue."

"Next time we play poker, Gloria, I hope you join us. But, have it your way." Winston and I used more plastic cuffs to secure the two guards, sitting them on the floor where we could see them. Winston took a seat behind the control panel and took a moment learning how to move from camera to camera as we searched the building for Mikey, the Hand of God, and anyone else.

I asked the woman, "Where's the view of the clean room? I don't see it coming up on the camera rotation."

She shook her head and said, "Because there ain't one. They never did put one in there. The boss don't want no camera in that room. Said there's no need for one there."

I walked over and squatted in front of Ron and used the gun sight on the end of my gun to lift his head by his nose. "Ron, how do we view the clean room? If you tell me there isn't a way, then I'm going to turn your head into something you'd only see in a Picasso painting, capisce?"

Without hesitation, he said, "You can't get to it by going through the rotation. You have to select camera view at the bottom and then type in 69. We're not supposed to look at that room. That's for Mr. McCain only."

Gloria said, "You're such a piece of shit, Ron. You know that?"

"Fuck you. You want to die for these bastards, then go ahead. They ain't paying me enough to go down for them." Gloria just shook her head and then scooted a few feet away from him until I told her to stop.

Winston pulled up the box and entered in 69 and a view of the clean room appeared, if a limited one. We could only see about half the room, which included the door. There were two long tables with all sorts of medical equipment on them. On a section of a counter were dozens of soft drink cans with the tops cut off. On the counter opposite I could see a large quantity of small metallic canisters, which were the ones that would presumably be installed into the computers.

I could see two people moving in and out of the view of the camera. They were in what I always thought of as medical space suits, with full body coverage. Over the span of the several minutes I watched, they moved into view carrying a couple of new canisters then walked back out of view. Mikey must have set the camera up so that you could see who came and went, but not the work being done. At the door, there were two men in coveralls with machine guns cradled in their arms. Whether to protect the people moving the virus or to make sure they didn't leave, I had no idea.

With only Winston to help me, this just became a hell of a lot harder. It was no picnic with only three guys. But the Hand of God is worth a dozen other guys in a fight like this one. And now he'd gone rogue on me. I took a moment to think. My brother had to be here somewhere in the building. If he wasn't in his office, then the next likely place would be the clean room keeping tabs on what they were doing. But if he was there, then he was in the part I couldn't see.

I still couldn't believe my brother was Belial. Mikey lived with a chip on his shoulder, always looking for any sign someone was making fun of him because of his size and always ready to strike out when he thought they were. When we were kids, he had a reputation as a guy you couldn't trust further than you could throw him. But not someone capable of killing hundreds, if not thousands, of people. Could my brother really be capable of mass murder?

I didn't think so, but I admitted to myself I was now having serious second thoughts. There could be little doubt the Exodus Project was going down in his warehouse and nothing happened in this building that Mikey didn't know about. Everything pointed to Mikey being Belial, I just couldn't believe it. Or wouldn't. Winston said, "O.K. I've figured out the cameras. I can keep a view on you as you head up to the clean room. Are you sure you don't want me to go with you?"

"I think we have a better chance with you keeping an eye on things. You let me know what's ahead of me and what may be coming up behind me. It's better than being blind."

And just as I said that, the camera showing the third floor hallway outside the elevators went static, as someone took out the camera. My money was on Montoya and that he was now on the third floor after my brother. "I'd better get moving. If I go down, call the cops and get the hell out of here. You got it?"

"Got it. Be safe, man. Good luck with your brother. I hope it ain't true, you know, this Belial stuff."

"You and me both. It goes without saying, you see either Montoya or Mikey, shout it out." I shouldered the weapons bag and went out the door. Time to go hunting.

Chapter Twenty-Seven

I hit the stairwell and jogged up the steps to the third floor, took a deep breath and opened the door. There were also four rows of shelving on this floor, but with a more wide open floor plan. There were no fancy office suites up on this level, just large warehouse space. I had a clear view down the center aisle where several of the robot forklifts were parked.

The clean room was in the upper left hand corner so I stepped out and moved that direction. I hadn't taken more than two steps when Winston warned me to take cover, just as someone took a shot at me from the far end. I dove behind the closest rack and risked a look around the corner. I could see the man, his gun held at the ready, watching for me. The moment he saw me, he took yet another shot, hitting a box on the rack above my head.

Hitting any target from nearly a hundred yards away is tough. A moving one even more so. I ducked back down behind my rack and considered my options. The shelving here rose twenty feet. I slung my gun around my back and grabbed the middle support beam and began to climb. I made it to the top and eased my way between boxes of cell phone batteries and smart phone cases.

There was a small gap all the way down the racks, and I moved quietly down the length of the aisle. Winston said in my ear, "I have a different camera angle up on your level. There's a bogey with an automatic in the center aisle, headed towards the elevator. I saw you come out of the stairs, but lost you."

I clicked the com once to let him know I heard. I came to a spot where I could see between a crate of gardening tools and a box of lawn furniture. The Church dweeb had almost reached my spot, moving slowly, gun up in the ready position, scanning for me, but not looking up. When he reached me, I grabbed the edge of the lawn furniture box, which said it weighed one-hundred and fifty pounds, and toppled it over the side. He glanced up at the noise and the box hit him smack dab in the face and took him to the ground, where his legs spasmed a couple times and then stopped.

Winston said, "Damn, Vic that looked like the Roadrunner dropping an anvil on Wile E. Coyote." He then started humming *Another One Bites the Dust* by Queen as I slowly walked the rest of the way down the aisle from the top of the rack.

Winston said, "I can see the rest of the floor. At the end of the main aisle, take a left and there's a door. It has to be the clean room. I don't see anyone else."

I'd almost made it to the end of my row when I caught movement from the corner of my eye on the rack two over from me, along the left hand wall. I ducked down and l glanced around the corner of a row of blue plastic containers filled with kerosene. Kerosene is still heavily used in places like Africa for everything from lamp oil to cooking stoves and Mikey made a killing shipping the stuff all over the continent.

I watched for several more minutes, letting my breathing and heart rates slow, and extending my senses. I had no doubt there was somebody else up here besides me. The only real question was: who. Montoya? My brother? Another Church goon? After several more minutes passed, I decided I couldn't wait any longer. I clambered over the side and made my way quickly down the racks and onto the floor.

I pressed my back against the racks and looked up, seeing nothing but kerosene. I moved over to the far wall, trying to find movement, but still saw nothing. I pressed my com link and said, "There's someone else in the racks. See if you can find them. I'm going for the clean room."

"Roger that."

I moved to the clean room door and inserted and then removed the keycard. But the security light remained red. I tried again with the same results. I asked Winston to ask the guards if they could override the security from the control room. After a moment he told me, "Negatory, good buddy."

I found an intercom button next to the card reader and pushed it. After a moment a man's voice said, "There's no way in here. If you don't put down your weapon and step away from the door, we will call the authorities."

A camera was mounted right over the door. I looked into it and pushed the button and said, "I'm here to speak to Michael McCain, not some flunky. Put him on."

"I'm sorry sir, but there is no one here by that name. This is your last chance to leave before we call the cops."

"Look, tell Mikey his brother is outside the door and to get his ass out here."

I waited a few more moments and started to push the button again when a shot rang out and a man dropped from the corner of the far rack, with a bullet hole in the top of his head. I pressed my com button and said,

"Winston, far rack, up top.

"I don't see him, man. The camera on that angle is out. Has to be Montoya." I agreed with him and was just happy he wasn't shooting at me.

I looked at the tall stacks of kerosene and my mind flashed back to the barn going up at the farm and decided, fuck'em. I pressed my com and said, "Let me know if the guards inside the clean room make a move to come out. I'm going to turn the heat up on them."

I shouldered my gun and went to the stacks of kerosene, dragged several of the five gallon containers over to the clean room door and emptied them on the wall and the floor. I knew the guys inside would be watching me so I smiled at the camera while I poured. I did this several more times when I heard Winston in my ear tell me the guards were preparing to open the door. I shifted my gun to the ready position and waited, temporarily in a Mexican standoff. I pressed the intercom button and said, "I'll give you guys one more chance to put down your guns and come out. I know you've been watching me and I just poured enough kerosene out here to burn down half of Louisville. So it's now or never." I pulled my lighter out of my pocket. "You try and rush me and all of you die. You stay in there and you die. Lay down your weapons and come out and you at least get to live. You can't win. Give it up."

Winston said, "I don't know what you just said to those dudes. But the scientists inside are freaking out and waving their arms. The guys with the guns just pointed them at the scientists and they have their hands frozen in the air. This is better than watching Law and Order, man."

There was a brief pause and Winston said, "Hey, you said your brother is a little dude, right? Does he have black hair and a Vandyke beard?"

"Yeah, why? Do you see him?"

"I do. He, Samantha and some pretty boy with a banged up face are walking through the second floor warehouse, headed towards the elevators. Mike and the other guy are packing those machine pistols. What do you want me to do?"

"On the left side of the console, you'll see buttons that control their alarm and fire suppression systems. Turn them off then get over there and see if you can slow them down. Cut the leg ties on the two guards so they can get out. I'll be right there."

I wished I could give the people in the clean room more time. But I'd given them their chance and they didn't take it. I thought about the two men who burned to death at the farm. I thought about how Satan had nailed me to a wall and melted my body down to the bone. I searched for something deep inside me that said I gave a shit. I didn't find it.

I stepped back away from the pool of liquid, ripped off the corner of a box on the closest shelf, took out my lighter and set the end of it on fire. The door to the clean room started to open as I tossed the burning paper onto the floor.

The kerosene went up with a whoosh and in a blink the area was engulfed in flames and screams started from the clean room. It wouldn't be long before the rest of the kerosene went up, taking the clean room and warehouse with it. There were times when I wondered if my whole life would turn out to be about fire and damnation, I just never figured it would be, literally, about fire and damnation.

I ran for the door as the room behind me exploded and the other containers of kerosene blew up. I don't know how many people were in the room turning computers into death machines, but they were all about to pay the ultimate price and I could not have cared less. The Exodus Project was now toast, so at least something good would come from the death and mayhem.

I hit the door to the stairs running and could hear gunfire on the floor below me. I took the steps two at a time and hit my com button to let Winston know I was coming through the door.

Winston was at the corner of the waiting area, his machine gun raised, ready to fire. He said, "They split up when I fired a warning shot. Your brother went left, Samantha and the other dude right."

I shouted, "Mikey. It's Vic. I'm coming out to the floor. Don't shoot my ass."

I moved past the four now dead guards, past the broken glass and to the warehouse floor just in time to see Mikey running back my direction. "Vic! Help me! He's going to kill me!"

Mikey threw down his gun and ran towards me. Dominic Montoya, the Hand of God, turned the corner of a row of shelving, and was closing fast on Mikey. I managed to put myself between Mikey and Montoya. "Dominic," I pleaded. "I asked you to let me talk to my brother. Don't shoot."

"I'm sorry, my friend. There is nothing to talk about. There should be no doubt in your mind he is Belial and the man behind the Exodus project, among other diablos you know nothing about. His life is forfeit. Please. Step aside. I do not wish to kill you, but I will if you do not remove."

Mikey said, "I don't know who this nut job is, but I've never heard of this Belial person. Come on, Vic. You KNOW me. We have the girl. I can get my soul back. I swear to God, Vic, I'm a changed man. I'll become a monk. I'll do whatever you ask. Just don't let him kill me. I'm your brother, for Christ's sake. This guy's a liar. You can take him, Vic. You're better than he is."

Winston took a step out and trained his gun on Montoya. "You want me to take him out, Vic? He can't get both of us."

"No. No one's going to shoot anybody. The killing has to stop here."

Mikey dropped to his knees behind me, his arms going around my waist, his eyes wide in terror, as Montoya continued to advance and Mikey could see an eternity in Hell coming his way. I wanted to believe him, but I knew deep in my soul he was lying. But it didn't matter. I couldn't let my brother be shot like a rabid dog.

"Dominic, you have my word. I'll turn him over to the cops. I'll take him there myself. He'll be dealt with. Come on man, you don't have to do this. The Bible is about redemption. Don't do this. I'm begging you. He can change."

I might as well have been pleading with the statue of David for all the good it did me. Montoya said, "I am sorry, Victor. If you will not move, then you shall join your hermano in Hell. Adios, Victor."

A shot rang out.

But, it did not strike me or Mikey. The Hand of God was thrown back as he was shot by Deveraux high in the chest. Winston whirled, ready to shoot Deveraux, but the man had Samantha in front of him, his arm around her neck. Her eyes drooped and her mouth hung slightly open, a small trickle of blood flowing from her temple where he must have struck her. Winston moved back and took cover at the corner of the entrance.

Montoya lay on the ground, his arms and legs moving slowly as he died. As soon as Mikey saw him hit the ground, he stood up and slapped me on the back, and said with a wide smirk, "Thanks, Vic. I couldn't have done it without you."

I turned on him. "You little prick. What've you done? That's the Hand of God. You can't kill him."

"Au contraire, little brother. I believe I just did. Nice shot, Deveraux." He walked over to where Montoya lay and kicked him in the ribs. I felt my brain explode and I took one large step, picked my brother up and threw him against the wall and grabbed him by the throat.

"So help me God I'll beat you to death with my own hands."

Half- choking, Mikey said, "Deveraux, if my brother does not let me go in the next five seconds, shoot the bitch in the head and then him, if you please."

"With pleasure, Belial." Deveraux put the barrel of his 9 in Samantha's ear and started to count out loud.

Tony Acree

Winston said to Deveraux, "You pull that trigger and you're a dead man."

Deveraux just continued counting and on the count of four, I let Mikey go and stepped back, my chest heaving. I asked, "So you *are* Belial. Why? Why are you doing this? Killing kids? My God, Mikey, your soul. Don't you know what you're doing to your soul?"

"Your God, not mine. I've made my choice. A war's coming and I want to be on the winning team. The Lord of Light picked ME to be one of the Kings of Earth when he reclaims his place in Heaven."

I felt confused. "But, you said you wanted your soul back, that you would be a changed man. You said you wanted to save your soul. That's why you wanted Samantha, so you could get your soul back."

"I wanted her back because I wanted the money back. You can't run an operation like mine without a good cash flow, Vic. Now that I have her, I'll get my money and be back in business."

Smoke started pouring from the vents high up on the wall, a billowing black smoke. I said, "I hate to break it to you, brother, but your Exodus Project is going up in smoke as we speak. Thanks for putting a rack of kerosene right next to the clean room."

I could see anger flash across his face, but then a smile returned. "Oh well. You know me. I always have a plan B. And a C and a D. You've only set me back, not shut me down."

"Satan says you'll be dead by tomorrow. You won't get a chance to do anything else. You're a dead man walking," I said.

He shook his head and said, "That's so yesterday. I've signed a new contract, Vic. I just had to deliver the death of the Hand of God. And thanks to you, I just did. I'm now first among the four kings of Hell. And I couldn't have done it without you."

He walked up to me and all sense of brotherly love vanished. "I have let you live today because of the love I bear our mother. But if you come after me or the girl, I'll have Deveraux shoot you on sight. Do you understand me?"

"Perfectly. But there's one little problem. She doesn't have the money anymore. I do."

Mikey's eyes narrowed, and then he looked up at the smoke pouring out of the vents. "Maybe you're bluffing, maybe you're not. But I don't have time to sort it out right now. I'll find out from her if you're telling the truth."

I said, "So help me God, if you hurt her—"

"Oh, please. How much has God helped you, Vic? How much does he help any of us? Was God ever there for me growing up? How many of my prayers did God answer? None, that's how many. Not a one. The Lord of Light has given me all I asked for and more."

He walked over to Deveraux and Samantha, stroking her face. "Lucky for her, the Lord of Light has uses for her father. So if she, or you, gives us what we want, she'll live. But we'll be going now. Hug mom for me the next time you see her, won't you? Now step over there, please," he said motioning to the far side of the warehouse, "So I can be sure you won't try something stupid."

I nodded to Winston and we both moved to the far wall as Mikey, Samantha and Deveraux headed toward the steps. After they were gone, we ran to Montoya as the warehouse continued to fill with smoke and breathing became harder.

I bent down to check his wound, but it was clear he didn't have a chance, as blood soaked his shirt. His eyes opened as I knelt over him. Tears filled my eyes and I said, "I'm so, so sorry. I didn't mean for any of this to happen. Please forgive me.

He smiled weakly and said, "There is no need to ask forgiveness from me. You were trying to save your hermano. Only ask for God's forgiveness." He swallowed and said, "Your soul may be lost to you, my friend. There is still a chance you can save it. Go to the Derby Mission on Preston. Ask for Brother Joshua. Tell him what happened." He grabbed my coat and pulled me close. "Tell him I'm sorry. Tell him..." And with those final words, the Hand of God died.

Chapter Twenty-Eight

Winston shook my shoulder and said, "Man, we've got to get out of here. Let's go." I nodded, stood and we both took off for the stairs, and raced to the parking garage. We got to Townsend's Lexus and jumped in. I looked into the back seat, where Townsend lay, his throat slit from ear to ear. Mikey's car was gone and Townsend must have seen them coming and gotten their attention. Too bad for him. I had Winston drag his body out and onto the garage floor.

I threw the Lexus into drive and tore out of the garage. I could hear the sirens approaching the building and took off in the other direction, weaving our way behind other warehouses. In the rear view mirror I could see the whole building was engulfed in flames. The Exodus Project was now up in smoke. We drove slowly out the far side of Louisville Riverport and could see an army of fire engines and police cars now surrounding the building.

Winston whistled low and said, "Man, would you look at that? Your brother just took a huge beating."

I shook my head. "Knowing him, he'll make a fortune on the insurance." We quickly put the inferno behind us and for several miles neither of us said a thing. Then Winston said, "Do you really have the money?"

"Yeah, I was telling the truth. She doesn't have it anymore." I told him how she'd passed the money to Kurt and me. "My brother knows if he hurts her, he won't get a dime from me. My only hope is that as soon as they find out, they contact me to make a deal and I can trade the money for her."

"Are you sure that's a wise move? These are some evil Mofos. You give them the money back and no telling what they have planned next."

"I don't give a rat's ass. I just want to get her away from them and the money is the only bargaining chip I have."

We didn't say anything else until we made it back to Townsend's house to pick up my car. We transferred all the gear and then wiped down the Lexus and the house, and took off. I drove him to the shopping mall to retrieve his Jeep. I pulled up behind it and put the car in park. I offered him my hand and he took it.

"When they call you, you're going to need someone to watch your back. Call me and I'm there," he said.

"Count on it. Thanks Winston. If there is ever anything you need, all you have to do is ask." He nodded, got into his Jeep, fired it up and drove away.

I did the same and headed back into town. In less than twenty-four hours, my whole life had come crashing down around me. The world as I'd known it had been a lie. I went from a raging agnostic to sure that not only did Satan exist, but so did God. I went from having a brother who was merely a pain in the ass to one who very well may be the most evil man on the planet. And I'd gone from a man who had no desire to settle down, to a man who had fallen in love with the woman of his dreams, only to lose her.

I pulled up to the curb near the Derby Mission, a converted former elementary school, that served three meals a day to the homeless in the area and provided temporary housing to many of them as well. It was nearing the dinner hour and several men and a few women hung around outside, smoking and talking, in the late afternoon sunshine.

I got out, locked the Chevelle, and went inside. The cafeteria was already hopping, with the aroma of soup and warm bread filling the air. I asked a man standing in line where I might find Brother Joshua and he pointed to an elderly black man handing out soup bowls at the far end of the line.

He was of average height, with sprinkles of white around the edges of his short cropped dark hair. His arms looked muscular under his blue button down shirt. As I approached, I noticed his eyes. As he spoke to each man, his eyes bathed them with empathy and compassion and the men and women responded in kind. Each person he spoke to continued on to their table with a smile on their face, despite their circumstances. I found myself smiling as well, despite the crap I'd been through over the last twenty-four hours. That was, until he looked at me.

His gaze hit me like a hammer, the compassion gone, replaced by a searing intensity that stripped me down to my soul and found it lacking. He said something to a volunteer nearby and nodded for me to follow him to a back room. I did so, but with trepidation. I knew I was about to be judged and I was, for the first time since I'd been a very young child, afraid.

The room, a small office, sparse on furniture or decoration, seemed to close in on me as he sat behind a battered desk. There was a chair opposite the desk, but I remained standing. He watched me for a moment, then stated, in a bass voice I would have expected on a much larger man, "Dominic

Montoya is dead."

"Yes. He was shot and killed an hour or so ago."

"You're Victor McCain?" His eyes continued to bore into me as I told him I was.

"Tell me what happened. Start from the beginning."

And so I did. Starting with the visit from Lucifer through to the death of the Hand of God and the escape of my brother with Samantha. I told him of the men and at least one woman I'd killed. I told him how it was my fault Montoya had been shot. I had confessed my sins many times to our parish priest and afterwards I'd always felt better, as my burdens were lifted and I could go back out and sin again in good faith. But this time, as I finished, tears were streaming down my face and I knew my sins had not been lifted, but instead fell upon me like the proverbial ton of bricks.

I asked, in a quiet voice, "My soul. Is my soul lost?" I trembled standing there, as I knew the answer, but wanted to hear it from this man.

"You have allowed an evil to continue to work its will on mankind and you did so knowing your brother to be Belial. Your pride has handed the forces of Satan a great victory today."

"But I stopped the Exodus Project. Surely that counts for something?" I hated the pleading tone in my voice. I was Victor McCain, bounty hunter. I hunted the most dangerous men humanity could throw at me. I always believed in myself. Now I doubted. Now I was afraid.

"Once the project came to light, it was as good as dead. You could have stopped them in any one of a number of ways. Simply calling the police would have ended any chance they had of success. No. It does not count for something. You had choices and you made them. And where your soul is concerned, you made the wrong ones."

I bowed my head and wept. I knew deep inside he was right. I had killed over and over in the past day and had felt not the least bit of remorse for what I'd done. Shouldn't I have at least felt something?

"There is, however, a way out for you." I slowly looked up and into eyes that seemed far older than the man sitting in front of me.

I said, "Become the new Hand of God. You're going to offer me the same deal you offered Montoya."

He nodded. "I am. The Hand of God spoke of you to me. He said if something should happen to him that you might be a good choice to replace him."

"I have a question." I hesitated for a moment, then asked, "Did he do enough, when Montoya died, did he go to Heaven?"

"I don't know the answer to that question. It isn't for me to absolve him. He now has faced the ultimate justice. His prior life was filled with evil. He had a large slate to wipe clean. For most people who live and die, asking forgiveness is enough. For a handful of others, it is not. I pray he has found peace."

"Samantha said she believed God is dead. I *know* this can't be true, but after the last twenty-four hours, I'm not as sure. How do you convince people with the type of evil that is loose in the world that He's not?"

"I don't know the answer to that question. But then again, it's not my job to have all the answers. My role is to help people live with the questions."

"And if I accept and become the new Hand of God, can I save my soul?"

"I can quote you hundreds of different Bible verses that could come close to explaining your situation, but the truth is, your situation is unique. I do know you cannot if you don't. But understand, once you accept, there is no going back. This isn't a job you retire from. This is a job you die from. You will not die an old man while sleeping in your bed during your golden years. Your death will come sooner, rather than later, and you will most likely die violently. It's your choice. But if you choose to serve as the Hand of God, once you start down that path, there is no other."

I laughed without humor and said, "Like I have a choice."

"There is always a choice. Now you must make yours. Will you be the next Hand of God?"

I took a long cleansing breath and said, "Yes. I just hope I can do justice to the man I'm replacing." Shaking my head, "So what now? How does this work? You tell me what I'm doing, is that it? So, you're what, like Nick Fury?"

"I don't rock an eye patch and you're not Captain America. But yes, I give you your assignments. No freelancing. You don't go after anyone unless I clear it first. You're not a vigilante. You will be doing God's will. From this moment forward, you belong to God and it will be He that passes judgment on you, and may God protect you."

"Fair enough. O.K. then, what's my first job?"

"To complete the job Dominic Montoya was sent to do: find and kill your brother."

A chill settled deep inside me. And I had one thought: this job was going to be a real downer.

The Watchers

Book Two

CHAPTER ONE

Ruth Anne closed her eyes and took deep steady breaths, trying to slow her heart rate and not think about the mountain of rock pressing down on her. She'd never gone spelunking before, and after today, she never would again.

She reopened her eyes. Thanks to the light on her helmet, she could see the reason she agreed to come at all: the hunky figure of Jason Mueller snaking further down "the wormhole." That's what Jason called this part of the cave, a long very narrow tunnel through solid rock. They were both students at the University of Kentucky, he in pre-med, she still stuck on undecided while a member of the cheerleading squad. Her friends teased her she was after an MRS degree, and they weren't far off.

Jason was from one of Lexington's oldest and richest families and she had her eye on him for the entire semester. When he invited her to go cave diving, she all too quickly said yes, forgetting how much she hated being in tight spaces and was even more terrified of bugs. The thought of spiders climbing all over her kept her up at night. However, Jason was into extreme sports and she was into him. She didn't dare say no once he asked her to join him on this underground expedition, for fear she might not get a second chance to go out with him.

So here she was, a billion miles underground, on her stomach, crawling through a space where the gap left only inches to spare in any direction. He promised, since this was her first time, that they would go to an "easy" cave for her first dive and brought her to a farm his family owned down near Mammoth Cave National Park in Edmonson County, Kentucky. Jason believed their cave had to hook up at some point with Mammoth Cave, and was convinced he could find that connection given enough time.

He told her Mammoth Cave was nearly four hundred miles long, the longest in the world, blah, blah, blah. She couldn't care less. She just liked his curly black hair, blue eyes and the way he looked in his faded jeans. Wearing a red, black and blue-checkered flannel shirt, he looked like a lumberjack dreamboat.

And up until about an hour ago, their trek through the cave was the easy trip he promised with fewer bugs than expected, thank God, and no bats.

But after going through one very tight squeeze, Jason came to a complete stop. Looking up, Jason noticed an opening about six feet off the ground where a large boulder, matching the size of the hole, now rested at their feet.

"That's new," Jason said. "I'll bet those tremors earlier this year must have shaken that boulder loose and caused a breakdown. Let's take a look."

Jumping, he grabbed the edge of the ledge. Pulling himself up, he first glanced around and then climbed the rest of the way and disappeared from view. Ruth Anne nearly had a panic attack as she looked around at nothing but rock and a darkness that seemed to close in around her. She started calling for Jason, but he soon stuck his head out of the hole, his face lit up with excitement.

"You *have* to see this," he said. "Here, take my hand and I'll pull you up."

Every part of her being told her not to do it, but then she looked into those smiling blue eyes, jumped, grabbed his hands and climbed up beside him.

She crawled onto the ledge and could see another tunnel disappearing downward, further than the light of her helmet could reach. She was about to say something when she froze and goose bumps popped out all over her body. She could swear she heard what sounded like someone whispering. It was just barely audible and she closed her eyes and strained to make out the words. But it stopped and all she heard was Jason. "Think about it," he said. "No one in the history of the planet has ever seen what we're about to see. This passage goes out quite a bit, then there's a flattener and I came to get you before exploring that part. Is this awesome, or what?"

She voted for the "or what" and tried talking him into getting more people before exploring this new part of the cave, but he said he wanted to be the first one to see this area and to share it only with her. If she wanted to wait for him, well, that was up to her and she could stay here and he'd return later. She considered her limited options and decided splitting up and staying behind was a bad plan, so she reluctantly agreed to further explore the new area with him. She thought about mentioning the whispering and her growing sense of unease, but was worried he might think she was some nut job. There was no way in hell he was leaving her in the dark by herself.

She breathed in the musty cave air and continued crawling on her stomach after Jason and thought to herself, maybe he isn't worth it. After a bit, the opening widened, but the ceiling remained low. She bumped her head several times as she tried to scratch her nose.

Jason stopped. "Do you see that?" he asked.

"See what?" She inched closer to him, trying to look past him, but saw nothing.

"Turn your helmet light off for just a moment. I think I see some kind of glow up ahead."

"You *can't* be serious?"

"Just do it. It'll only be for a minute."

Ruth Anne hesitated, then reached up and begrudgingly turned off her helmet lamp. Jason did the same and for a terrifying moment, the darkness was total. She reached out and put her hand on his boot, but then she could see what caught his attention. Up ahead there was a soft red glow.

"Oh, Jesus. Do you think there's lava up there?" she asked.

"Don't be silly. There's no volcanic activity in this part of the country."

"Yeah, but what about the earthquakes. Maybe they did something and now lava is bubbling to the surface."

He switched his light on again and she did the same. "Think about it, Ruth Anne. If it were lava, it would be getting warmer. And it's not."

He was right. It was snowing when they entered the cave and it was down to about twenty-five degrees outside. Yet once in the cave the temperature stayed constant, in the mid-fifties, and it didn't feel any different the closer they got to the light.

He continued, "And we would smell sulfur. The smell would drive us out of here, but I don't smell any. Do you?"

No, not that she was aware of. They moved slowly on, towards the source of the mysterious light. They crawled another hundred feet or so where the ceiling rose to about sitting height and the bottom dropped off to a small ledge. Jason glanced over the side and said, "There's what looks like a fissure and the glow is coming down from one end. Hang on a sec'."

He swung his legs over the side and dropped down, then raised his arms up ready to catch her. Ruth Anne, backing away slightly said, "Look, Jason, let's go back. I'm getting a bad feeling about this. I mean, what if you step into a sinkhole or something like that, and get hurt? We're down here all alone and no one knows where we are."

He dropped his hands to his sides and didn't look happy. "Fine," he said. "How about this? I'll walk up the fissure a bit to see if I can tell where the glow is coming from. Then we'll head back and get a group in here to explore this new section more thoroughly. O.K?"

Ruth Anne looked down the cave fissure towards the glowing red light, her sense of unease growing. She nodded yes and said, "Be careful. And stay where I can see you. Please?"

"You got it." Jason moved quickly down the path and just to the end of her light's reach when he stopped and seemed to look off to his right, where the passageway made a sharp right turn. He shouted to her, "Just another minute," he paused. "I think I see something." He took another step and disappeared from view.

"Jason! Wait!" Ruth Anne shouted. But he didn't. She wrung her hands while counting the seconds, waiting for him to return. She could still see the glow from his helmet lamp and was watching it intently when it blinked out. The other end of the fissure was now barely illuminated by her own lamp and the same peculiar soft red glow.

She screamed his name several times, but there was no answer. A low moan escaped her body as she looked over her shoulder at the barely visible path that led them here. Her body began to shake uncontrollably and panic seeped into her bones. She wasn't sure she could remember the way they came into the cave without Jason leading the way. Frozen with fear, she was too afraid to go after Jason and too terrified to try to leave alone.

After several paralyzing moments, she knew she couldn't stay where she was. The terror of being lost forever in the cave trumped her fear of going after Jason. She jumped down and followed his footsteps, carefully.

When she reached the end of the fissure, the path made a hard right turn. She slowly peeked around the corner and could tell the red glow was stronger just up ahead. She inched forward, checking the ground for sinkholes or drop offs, but the path looked solid. Like Jason, she thought she could see something. As she moved closer and strained her eyes for a better look, she came to an abrupt stop, her mind instantly in shock beyond understanding by what she now saw.

There, in front of her, was a tall old man sitting on a stone block. She assumed he was old because his hair flowed down nearly to his waist and was as white as the snow falling outside the cave. Not only that, but the man was huge. As a cheerleader for the basketball and football teams, she spent a lot of time around some big men, but this guy was as tall or taller than any of them.

Jason must be right, she thought. The cave on his family's farm must hook up to Mammoth Cave, and that's how he got here, from another entrance. There's *no way* he could fit through the "wormhole" as we did.

The red glow was emanating from somewhere in front of and below the man, as if he sat around a fire pit. The man turned his head and she could see he was eating something. Noticing her, he stood and began taking long strides towards her. He was wearing a long robe, like you see people in the Middle East wear, but without the headdress. Her shock intensified when she noticed shackles around his wrists, with short lengths of chain dangling from them. Was he an escaped prisoner?

As he approached her, she saw he was chewing on something. Her terror exploded when she realized he was holding the end of a human arm. He casually raised it to his mouth, tore off another bite, and then wiped his mouth with his hand. Blood dripped from his fingers. The arm still contained bloody shreds of Jason's checkered shirt.

The man smiled and Ruth Anne began to scream.

CHAPTER TWO

When I was a kid, I always wanted to grow up to be a ninja. I got bit by the bug watching *Teenage Mutant Ninja Turtles*. I'd sit and watch that show for hours via the magic of a stack of well-worn videotapes. I figured, hell, if a turtle could be a ninja then I could, too. My brother Mikey and I would practice by running around the neighborhood, sneaking up on people and letting them have it with Nerf Swords, slashing and then dashing away.

However, life was kinda funny. I kept growing, and before long being ninja-stealthy was out. You don't see too many six and half-foot tall ninja fighters. I was still light on my feet, but hiding in shadows wasn't going to happen. Unless it's one big ass shadow. I can still remember working on ninja moves in the backyard and my mother yelling out, "Victor Riley McCain, stop that before you break something . . . or someone!"

As an adult, I guess I got as close as I could to being one by joining Special Forces and then later becoming a bounty hunter. I still sneak up on bad guys and like to wear black—comes with the territory. I outgrew the black ninja outfit; I don't carry a cool pretend sword and prefer my Glock. You hit a bail jumper with a rubber sword and you're in for an ass kicking.

These thoughts were running through my mind as I looked through the peephole of the door in my room at the Jefferson Hotel in Richmond, Virginia. The Jefferson was one of the nation's finest four-star hotels. It burned to the ground, was rebuilt, closed, and then reopened again. A dozen U.S. presidents have stayed here. At one point, they even had live alligators in the marble pools in the lobby. No, really. The history nut in me would have loved to explore every nook and cranny of the grand old building, but not this trip.

I was here to kill a man. A few months ago, the thought of murdering anyone in cold blood . . . it never would have entered my mind. My job as a bounty hunter was to bust the men and women who murdered people, then cut and run when they made bail. Oh, how things changed.

A few months ago, I didn't know God and Satan were real—I mean, deep down, really believed they were real. I didn't know my only brother was one of Satan's top lieutenants and plotted mass murder on an unfathomable scale. I hadn't met, fallen in love with and then lost the most beautiful woman on the planet, Samantha, kidnapped by my scum-ball brother. I also didn't know about the Hand of God, God's own bounty hunter, named Dominic Montoya. And when Montoya was killed, Lord knows I never expected to take his place as the Hand of God.

Yet here I was, trying to finish the job Montoya died trying to complete to track down and kill my own flesh and blood, Mikey. For nearly three months, I searched for him and Samantha. The douche bag even sent me a Christmas card. I showed up at mom's house for the holidays on the chance he might too, but no dice.

A tip led me here to the Jefferson and to a man staying in the Governor's Suite who might have information on where Mikey was lying low. I managed to book the room across the hallway. With the dinner hour now over I stood watching for my mark to return to his room.

As I waited, I had time to think about God. If you asked ten people to define God, you would likely receive ten different answers. For example, the priest in the parish where I grew up said that, "God is everything you see and knows everything you think." Pat Robertson thinks God is a man with a long white beard and a Republican. The nuns in my childhood Catholic school were convinced God was a woman because a man could never get things so perfect.

My friend Bob believes God is no different from Santa Claus or the Easter Bunny: a fictional character made up to help us deal with the fact that when we die and become ashes to ashes and dust to dust, there's nothing more. And that terrifies us. Therefore, we created a fictional character to help us sleep at night.

I, on the other hand, knew God was real. True, I'd never met the guy, or deity, or whatever the hell you wanted to call him. But I had met the Ying to his Yang: Satan. The S.O.B. strolled into my office and changed my life forever. Hell, he caused me to lose my very soul. So, yeah, I was sure there was a God and now I was worried I would never make it upstairs when I died to meet Him.

Samantha Tyler, the woman Satan asked me to track down for him, was convinced there was a Devil, but emphatically believed God was dead and that's why the world hadn't heard a peep out of him (or her, thank you very much Sister Margaret) in nearly two thousand years. He just went poof in the night and left us all hanging here at the mercy of Satan and his minions.

During my brief conversation with the fallen angel, I could tell he thought God was still up there, large and in charge. If God was dead, his arch nemesis hadn't gotten the memo. Satan was doing all he could to regain his place in Heaven and replace the Lord Almighty. Fat chance, Satan ol' buddy. Every fiber in my body told me God was real and still sitting high upon his throne.

My contemplations were interrupted when I saw three men, all dressed in suits, and a young girl walk into view and stop at the door across from mine. The men were laughing and smiling, but the girl kept her eyes down and didn't join in the fun. One of the men took out a key card, opened the door and let the other three in the room. Turning and closing the door, he took up a guard position outside the room.

I gave them a few minutes before I made my move, wanting the hired gun outside the room to relax. When I could see him starting to look bored, I opened my door. When you're as tall as I am, sometimes it's hard to blend in, so I do the exact opposite. I was dressed in a nondescript green sweat suit, a workout bag slung over one shoulder, and carried a basketball. When you're a head taller than anyone else is in the room, give them the illusion of what they're seeing: in this case, a cool dude basketball player. I dyed my black hair blonde and donned huge Ray-Ban aviator sunglasses. I had ear buds in each ear and rap music turned up to ear-splitting level. The things I do for my craft.

While shutting my door I bobbed my head to the music, nodded to the man, and started down the hallway. I began to twirl the basketball on my finger. Passing him, I almost dropped the ball, and then batted it into the air, high above the other man's head. As planned, natural human reaction took over. From the time we're little kids we're taught if there's a ball in the air, then catch it. And that's just what he did. He reached up with both hands to grab the ball, which meant his hands were nowhere near the gun I could tell he kept under his suit jacket.

He tilted his head up while he watched the flight of the ball. I shot my hand up and with the hard edge of my knuckles punched him hard in the throat. I could feel his windpipe collapse and his eyes bulged. The basketball dropped and bounced down the hallway.

His hands flew to his throat and I grabbed his gun from its holster and placed it into my bag. He tried hard to take a breath, but his crushed windpipe prevented even a smidgen of air to pass through. He gripped the front of my sweat suit, his eyes pleading. I opened up his jacket and took the room key from the inside pocket. Spinning him around in front of the door, I reached back into my bag and took hold of my gun, complete with suppressor already attached, and slid the key card into the door lock. All told less than fifteen seconds from start to finish. My luck held as there was no one in the hallway.

With a snick, the door unlocked and I opened it. The Governor's Suite featured multiple rooms. The door opened into a sitting room with a couch, several chairs and a flat screen TV on the wall. The door to the bedroom was closed and the other bodyguard was sitting on the couch watching an NBA game with the sound down low.

He looked up as we came in and shock froze him in place for a split second. It was all I needed. I pushed the door guard on top of him, shut the door, took two quick strides, and placed my gun against his forehead. I made a shushing motion with my free hand. He nodded he understood and rolled the other man off of him, who continued to make wheezing noises, his face turning red from lack of oxygen.

I removed his gun and dropped it into my bag, and took out plastic cuffs. I mouthed for him to lie down and face the back of the couch. He complied and I quickly cuffed his hands and legs in a hogtie position. I then took duct tape out of my bag, tore off a strip and placed it over his mouth.

The guy I hit in the throat was already passed out so I left him alone and moved to the bedroom door, and listened. I could hear music playing and a man moaning. I opened the door and stepped inside the darkened bedroom.

From the TV's glow, I saw the man was on top of the girl, who was barely a teenager, at best. Rage flared up inside me and it was all I could do not to pull him off and beat him to death with my bare hands. Instead, I strode over to the bed, grabbed a fist full of hair, and yanked him backwards and off the girl.

Yelling in pain, he turned and came off the bed ready to fight until he saw me. Or, more to the point, my gun. Coming up short, he took a step back and put his hands in the air.

I looked at the girl. "Take your clothes, go into the bathroom and get dressed," I said. "Don't come out until I tell you to. Do it now."

Without a word, she gathered up her things and quietly went to the bathroom and shut the door. The man said, "You are *so* dead. You have no clue—." He stopped suddenly when I closed the distance, struck him hard in the gut and then pushed him back onto the bed. The man was middle-aged with what was once a fairly good build, but now soft around the edges, and graying hair at his temples.

For the next few minutes, I watched with satisfaction as the naked man rolled back and forth on the bed in pain. "Do you have any clue who I am?" he finally managed to say through clenched teeth.

"You're Tommy Spenoza, a member of the Spenoza crime family out of Philly. Yeah. I know who you are. You're a frickin' pedophile, Tommy.

Your own family ratted you out. Guess you thought taking your child victims out of Philly would keep the family off your back. Well, here I am. They didn't even ask for money to spill the beans on you."

Tommy cussed a blue streak and then asked, "So. They sent you here to whack me, is that it?"

"Your family didn't send me. They just told me where to find you. What I want from you is information. Where's Belial and where have they taken Samantha Tyler?"

At the mention of the name Belial, Tommy went pale. "I don't know who you're talking about."

I shrugged and shot the pillow right by his head. The gun made a loud pfpfpt sound, despite the silencer, and the pillow jumped. Tommy made a strangled cry and tried to get off the bed but I leveled the gun at his nose and he stayed still.

"See Tommy, if you got nothin' for me, you're useless. The only thing keeping you breathing is you might have something I want. If you don't . . ." I let the thought trail off shrugging a shoulder.

"Okay, okay. I get it. Yeah, sure. I know this Belial-guy. He's a customer."

"And just what is he buying from you? You're in the construction business, right?"

"Yeah. Mostly." Tommy started to relax as he was now in more familiar territory. I was starting to get more than a little weirded out interrogating a naked mob guy, but no one said this job would be normal. "He wants to buy equipment from me. Heavy equipment."

"What does he plan to do with the so-called equipment?"

He flashed me a shark tooth grin and said, "No clue. Don't know, don't care. In my business you don't ask those kinds of questions." He paused for a moment, laid back on his elbows, completely unselfconscious, despite all Mother Nature gave him in plain view. "You know," he continued, "you got by my guys out there pretty easy and then got the drop on me. That took guts and balls the size of fuckin' Texas, you know what I mean? I can use a guy like you. I don't know what you're being paid now, but I can pay you more. You know my family. You know it's true. What do ya say?"

I ignored the offer. "When was the last time you talked to him?"

"I haven't heard from him in over a month. He placed his order and I filled it. We're not exactly texting buddies, ya know what I mean?" He laughed as if he had just told the funniest joke in the world. Moron.

I moved closer to him and asked, "Where's Samantha Tyler?" I maintained a calm demeanor, but inside my stomach was roiling waiting for an answer.

"Like I know? I know who she is, sure. But it's not as if I'm her appointment secretary. If you want to know where she is ask her dad, the Congressman."

I felt my heart sink, but it was a shot in the dark. "I only have one more question. The safe here in your room, what's the password?" I knew all the top rooms in the Jefferson had their own wall safe in the closet.

He spread his hands out and said, "Never use it. I mean, come on, who's going to steal from me? Am I right? Besides, you don't look like the thief type."

"You know, when you're right, you're right. I'm not the thief type. I'm the Hand of God. Do you think they have a special place in Hell for child molesters, Tommy? Well, you're going to find out."

Tommy's eyes widened and he raised both hands and started to say something, but he never finished. I shot him twice, once in the heart and once between the eyes. I stood there for a moment and watched the life ebb from his body. I wish I felt something, some twinge of regret at having taken another man's life. But I didn't. All my years spent overseas fighting for Uncle Sam, killing Al Qaeda and Taliban scumbags, nada. And the men I killed during the mini war with my brother, the same. And even if I was the kind to have doubts about killing a man? I don't think I would in this case. Tommy Spenoza had been trafficking in child sex slaves for years on the east coast and his death would put a real dent in the sexual predator pipeline. He deserved to die, which I guess is the point of why I was here in the first place. I put the gun back in my bag, went, and knocked softly on the bathroom door.

The girl, now dressed, opened the door, looked up at me and asked, "Is he dead?"

"Yes. He is. He can never hurt you again."

I don't know what I thought her reaction would be. Joy. Relief. Fear. Something. But she showed no more reaction than I had at Tommy's death. She looked me in the eyes and I saw nothing. She asked, "Are you going to kill me now?"

I crouched down and sat on my heels, which put us at nearly eye level. "No. I'm not. What I can do is take you to a place where you will never be hurt again. Where the people will give you a different life than you have here. Interested?"

She gave a tiny nod, but I'm not sure she believed me. "You said you're the Hand of God. What's that?"

"I'm kind of like God's bounty hunter. I track down evil people and stop them from hurting other people. People like Tommy."

"So you stop them by killing them?" She said this with a small voice, her eyes large in the bathroom lights.

I nodded. "When I have to. Guys like Tommy never change and sometimes I have no choice but to take them out. I don't like it or enjoy it, but in his case it had to be done so he wouldn't hurt any other kids."

Her brow furrowed as she thought about what I said. She gave another small nod of her own then said, "He lied to you, you know. When you asked about Belial?" She stood there, not moving. She seemed to be barely breathing.

"So you were listening to us? What part was the lie?"

"When he said he hadn't talked to Belial. He was on the phone in the car talking to some guy and he used that name. And it wasn't about any type of equipment. Mr. Spenoza has something the other guy wants and I could tell Mr. Spenoza was really scared. He told the guy he wanted more money 'cause of all the trouble he'd been through to find whatever it is he got for the guy. Then the other man started yelling and Mr. Spenoza began sweating while the other man talked."

"What's your name?" I felt such heartache for this child because that's what she really was. If she had any type of childhood, it had been ripped from her. Her eyes were not those of a young teenager, but of a woman seeing the end of the world.

She gave a shrug of her shoulders. "They call me Mary." She paused for a second and then continued, "He lied about the safe, too. He put some things in there. He used his credit card to lock it. Bragged about his American Express card. Like I cared." The last comment was the first time she said something that sounded like a real teenager.

"Do you think what the guy wants is in the safe?" She shook her head yes. "Thanks, Mary. Wait another second and then we'll get out of here."

I went and searched the room and found Tommy's wallet and cell phone in the nightstand drawer. I took out his AmEx card, went into the closet, and opened the safe. I took out a stack of papers and a small brown box with intricate writing on the sides in a language I didn't know and what looked like stars on the top. I opened the box and found a sheet of parchment, yellowed and in a protective sleeve. It was in the same language as the box. I put it back and closed the lid.

I popped the battery out of the cell phone, to keep people from tracking it, and then dumped the haul into my bag. Later I would go through the call list on Tommy's Blackberry and find the one my brother used. I might be able to use it to track him down. I zipped up the bag and went back to the girl.

She remained exactly where I left her. "Like I said earlier, I can take you away from this life to a place safe—unless there's some place else you'd rather go."

She shook her head no. "I don't have any place else. My parents sold me for meth a few years ago. Then I was sold to Tommy. Now that he's dead, I got no one."

I wanted to go back and shoot Tommy a few more times. I said, "You have my word, your life will be different from now on. I know people who will take you in and treat you like one of their own daughters." I offered her my hand. "Let's go. Don't look at Tommy and stay near me."

She stared at me a moment, then dropped her eyes to my hand. Taking a small step, she slipped her hand in mine and I blocked her view of the bed as we walked past and into the other room. I held my finger and motioned for her to stop as I knelt down by the man handcuffed on the couch. I slipped a knife out of my bag, cut the restraints, and put them back in my bag. He sat up stiffly on the couch. I ripped the tape off his mouth and he grimaced when it tore skin from his lips.

"Here's what's going to happen," I said. "You're going to call the Spenoza family and tell them Tommy got hit by three men who said they were there to get revenge for their sister who Tommy raped. You're going to tell them the men wore masks, so you couldn't see what they looked like. You're not going to mention anything about me. Not what I look like, how tall I am, or how pretty I am. I have a source in both the family and the police department. If anything ever leaks out about me then I'm gonna know. And when that happens, you and anyone you love or care about, they're dead."

I pointed to the bodyguard on the floor next to us, eyes open and unseeing in death.

"Understand?"

"Yeah," shaking his head. "Got it. I don't want no trouble." He swallowed hard a couple of times and I could see the fear racing across his features and smell it rolling off him.

"You're gonna sit here for an hour and then call the family and get them out here to clean up this mess. Let them know the brothers said they would leak info about Tommy and his predilection for young children to the press. The Philadelphia Inquirer would have a field day." I nodded towards the door. "We're leaving now."

I didn't mean a single word I said about hunting down his family or any of the rest of it, but he believed it anyway, and that's all that mattered. The man sat ramrod straight and made no move to stop us. Out in the hallway I bent down and picked up my basketball, took Mary by the hand and left the hotel through the back exit. An hour later, after making a few phone calls, I dropped Mary off at a church on the outskirts of Richmond who promised to take care of her. Then I was in my red '69 Chevelle barreling down I-64 on my way to Louisville. One-step closer to a family reunion with Mikey.

CHAPTER THREE

I have an app on my smart phone, which allows me to listen to police radios from different cities. As I made my way west I listened for any mention of problems at The Jefferson Hotel on the Richmond Police scanner, but fortunately there was no activity mentioned there. After a couple of hours, I turned it off. It started to snow, but I continued to drive through the night. My thoughts turned first to my brother and the fact that I was going to have to kill him.

When I agreed to be the Hand of God and to hunt down and kill my brother, it didn't sink in right away. The closer I got to actually punching his ticket, I wasn't sure how I felt about it all. There was no doubt my brother planned to murder hundreds, if not thousands, of children. I kept replaying the last time I saw him, hiding behind me begging me to protect him from Dominic Montoya. I thought that he was innocent. Then he started laughing and kicking Montoya as he lay dying. My brother deserved to die for his sins and it seemed I was going to be the instrument of his death.

I thought about Samantha, too, and my knuckles turned white on the steering wheel. I imagined all the unspeakable things the thugs with the Church of Light Reclaimed, soldiers for Satan, might be doing to her . . . if she was even still alive. I held out hope that her father, Congressman Cyrus Tyler, who was also the highest-ranking member of the Church, could keep her breathing. Heaven help all of them if she was not.

These thoughts rolled around in my brain until I pulled in at the back of the Derby Mission around 5 a.m. You'd think being the Hand of God might grant me nicer digs, but it didn't. It did give me a safe place to sleep at night and that was enough. I parked the car, grabbed my bag, and entered through the back door. Heading towards my room, I glanced into Brother Joshua's office and was not surprised to see him working away at his desk.

A black man somewhere north of forty years old with just the first tinges of gray in his hair, he ran both the mission and me. I don't know exactly how to describe our relationship. Boss? Scheduler? Profit of Doom? I was God's hit man and he was the man who told me who to take out. I knew, without a shred of doubt, those orders were coming from a higher power. It didn't stop me from wondering, however, how that sounds and what I would do if ever caught by the police and forced to try to explain why I did what I did.

"Yes, Officer. I kill people for God. Really. I do. And a guy who runs a homeless mission tells me whom to kill. I'm serious." An insanity plea would be easy.

But according to Brother Joshua—or just J, as I liked to call him— one of the perks of being the Hand of God was I never had to worry about being arrested by the fuzz. It's one of the two freebies that come with the job. The other one was I was safe from harm as long as I was in a Church, which is why I moved from my nice town home to a fifteen by fifteen foot room in the back of the Derby Mission. Thanks to there being a church sanctuary on the property, the forces of evil can't touch me here. That's it. Once I step off church property, no magical protection, no aura of invulnerability. I can be shot and killed just like any other man. Just ask my predecessor about that one.

Walking into his office, I shut the door and plopped into one of the two chairs facing his desk. He took off his reading glasses and put them on top of his head. Placing his elbows on his desk, he folded his hands, rested his chin on top of them, and waited. I gave him a complete rundown on Tommy Spenoza. Then I reached into my bag and passed him the box.

"Ever seen anything like this?" I asked.

He studied the box, turning it this way and that, and then opened it and took out the sheet of parchment. "The language on the box and the parchment appears to be some type of Semitic language, which I don't read." When I shot him a what-the-hell look, he further explained. "This is a group of languages from around the Horn of Africa. I'll get someone to translate it for us. As for the stars, if there is a religious meaning, it could be any one of several things: it could represent the children of Israel, angels, princes and rulers on Earth. We'll know more when we get the translation."

"Makes you wonder why Mikey-boy is hot to trot to get his hands on this" I said. "After what he tried to pull with the bird flu virus, I'd hate to think what he has up his sleeve next. Robbing his bank account has to have put a real hitch in his giddy up, but it will only slow him down for so long. I also have Tommy's phone and since Mikey called him, I have a number I can use to try to track him, though I doubt he's using anything but a burner phone. But you never know." I used the same myself. If the bad guys were looking for me as much as I was looking for them, no need to help them along.

"I'll get Kurt working on the numbers in Tommy's phone." Kurt Pervis, major hacker and computer geek, played a large role in helping me shut down the plot by the Church of the Light Reclaimed to kill children during an academic tournament by having donated computers release a virulent form of the bird flu. When it was over, he and I hid the thirty million dollars Samantha had stolen from Mikey and the Church. They wanted that money back.

And when we took on the Church back in November, Samantha, Winston and I left fingerprints in spots where there was no shortage of dead bodies. It was only a matter of time before the cops matched our fingerprints with those on file with the state when we obtained our bounty hunter licenses. No problem. Kurt and his hacker buddies broke into the state databases where my prints were on file and changed them so when my prints were run, they didn't pop up on the grid. Somehow, they got into the Department of Defense records and did the same thing. I didn't ask how. I was just thankful they did. They did the same thing for Winston. Samantha's prints were not on file anywhere, so no worries on her account. Kurt was now taking it easy in Hawaii, soaking in the sun and doing odd jobs for me.

Joshua said, "I'm not sure involving him the way you do is a good idea. You are after some of the most dangerous people, and things, on the planet. It's just a matter of time before they turn their attention on him. And from what you've told me, he is ill-equipped to protect himself."

"Look, J, I don't use him in the field. He helped me a few months back and stuck his neck out to help bring down the Church's plans. But now all he does is computer work for me. He's keeping his head down and I'm keeping him away from the dangerous stuff. He's back to being just a Geek. When I need muscle help I call on Winston. I told you about him."

"The former football player turned bounty hunter. Yes, you did. While I don't like you including him either, at least he can take care of himself." Changing the subject, he continued, "I thought you should know the girl you brought to us in Richmond will be taken in by foster parents who specialize in child abuse victims. She will be well taken care of. You must have made quite an impression," he paused, "seems she asked them if she could be placed with you."

I felt my eyes tearing up. I managed to say, "I couldn't take care of a puppy. She's better off with a good family." I ran my hands through my hair. "I sure do hope the kid makes it. J, you should have seen her eyes. The poor kid had no joy in her."

"Well, thanks to you, now she at least has a chance. Why don't you get some sleep and we can talk in the morning about what's next." He pulled his glasses back down on his nose and continued with mission business. Looking at him you would have no clue we were discussing death and destruction just minutes earlier.

With some effort, I picked my sorry ass out of the chair and made my way down the hallway, beyond the maintenance and storage rooms, to my monkish room. I was bone-tired and didn't even take my clothes or shoes off, just dropped my bag onto the ground, my phone onto the small nightstand, and collapsed on a bed barely big enough to handle my large frame. I reached up and turned off the light.

It seemed I barely closed my eyes and spread my arms out when the phone rang. Picking it up, I glanced at the caller ID and answered it.

"Kurt, you're a dead man calling me this early in the morning. Dead. Man."

"Dude. It's morning here, but the middle of the afternoon back in the Bluegrass. Wake up. I found her."

CHAPTER FOUR

I sat bolt upright in bed, all weariness driven from my body.

"Tell me," I growled.

I nearly crushed the phone in my hand waiting for the details. I'd been searching for Samantha ever since Mikey and his lapdog, Preston Deveraux, took her from his warehouse by gunpoint. I'd gotten close several times, but no dice.

"It's like this. My boys and me, we've been hammering at the Church in cyberspace, attacking them every place we can get a toehold. Then we came up with the idea to go after the guys who work for her old man, the Congressman. We love the challenge of going after government targets. That's where the real thrill in hacking is. Playing cat and mouse with Feds is a real high for a lot of them," he said unable to hide the enthusiasm in his voice.

"Anyways, we got into the email accounts and computers of several of the aides who work for that jack-ass and it paid off. One guy, a staffer named Ozzy Wheadon, sent an email to the Congressman complaining his daughter was bored and to send down a female staffer to keep her company. So, we backtracked the IP address and it came from the Naples, Florida area. We did more checking and ran everyone on his staff for property in Naples. Wheadon's family owns a vacation home in Naples. Dude, Samantha *has* to be down there."

He waited for me to respond. "When was the Email sent?" I said.

"Today. Dude, get your ass down there. We found her." I could hear the triumph in his voice as he read off an address. I turned my light on and wrote it down.

"Kurt, I won't ever forget this. I mean it. Ever. Even if it doesn't pan out. Ya hear me?"

"I do, Dude. Now make me proud. Go get her. Do you want me to fly back and get in on this?" For Kurt just to offer, for him, was huge. Danger was not his middle name. But I knew if I asked, he would be on the next plane.

"No, Kurt. But you still da man. I'll call ya as soon as we make it down there." I clicked the phone off and started to make my plans.

~*~

Kurt hung up the phone and grinned from ear to ear. Making the big guy happy and to do it by putting him on the trail of finding the lovely Samantha? Priceless. Kurt sat in a beach chair on Hanalei Beach on the island of Kauai in Hawaii. Wearing a wide-brimmed straw hat and a dab of sunscreen on his nose, Kurt looked the part of a surfer bum, with a well-toned body, reaching an easy six feet tall and light-brown hair he wore just the other side of long. His smile and chocolate brown eyes beat those of any male model, and the women loved him. The problem started when he tried to love them back.

Women paraded by him on the beach in an effort to gain his attention. Some walked back and forth more than once, but Kurt concentrated on his laptop. He was slowly trying to work up the nerve to talk to one of them. Whenever a beautiful woman talked to him, he froze up and started to hyperventilate. Sometimes he even broke out in hives. He couldn't remember a time when he didn't react this way. But that was the "old" Kurt.

He spent his time in Hawaii watching videos and listening to hypnosis tapes until he fell asleep at night. And during the day he looked for the right opportunity to try out his new self-confidence. After nearly three months in Hawaii, he hadn't quite found it yet. The "new" Kurt was a work in progress.

Of course he *had* been busy, he told himself. As part of a loose collection of hackers, he had organized a systematic and relentless attack against the Church of the Light Reclaimed and with those they did business. They made it nearly impossible for the Church to conduct business and considering they were a bunch of Satanists? They deserved it. His buddies had a hard time believing they were really Satan-lovers, but they didn't really care. And when he sicked them on Cyrus Tyler, they had a field day. Now their hard work could pay off with the rescue of Samantha. Sweet.

He was congratulating himself again when he realized a woman was staring at him, a wicked smile on her face. She was around five and a half feet tall with sandy blonde hair which fell about her shoulders, and the figure of a dancer. She looked to be somewhere near his own age of mid-twenties, but it was always hard for him to tell. Her bikini was white and extremely small, with a beach towel over one shoulder and carrying a small bag. He swallowed hard, cleared his throat, and said, "Hello." Just as the videos told him, he was keeping it simple. He took slow, even breaths and kept a smile on his face, even if inside his whole body was screaming at him to get up and run.

She walked over and spread the towel next to his chair, then slowly sat down, stretching out long legs and crossing them at the ankles. He concentrated on keeping his eyes on her face and tried not to stare at her chest, which was ample and barely covered. She tipped her head back, letting her hair cascade down over her shoulders, catching the sunlight. She then turned her head to face him and their eyes locked.

She asked, "Why would a man bring a laptop to one of the most beautiful beaches on the planet? You're watching porn, aren't you?"

Kurt blushed a deep red and slammed the lid of his laptop shut.

"No! I would never—I mean, you can't really think I—I was just—"

She laughed and placed a hand on his arm. "Take it easy champ; I was just messin' with ya. But seriously, when you're here your eyes should be on the beach and the babes. Well, at least this babe, anyways."

Kurt took another deep steadying breath and actually felt O.K. After all, she was coming on to him, which meant she had to think he was at least a decent-looking guy. And she did have a laugh he enjoyed hearing.

"You know? When you're right, you're right." He put the laptop to the side and turned his full attention to the girl. "You sound like you're from my part of the world. Where are you from?"

She took a pair of sunglasses out of her bag, slipped them on and laid back on her towel, basking in the sun. He couldn't imagine a more beautiful woman. He thought about Vic and Samantha and wondered if he just met his own "Samantha."

"I was born in Tennessee, but now I live in Lexington, Kentucky," she replied. "How about you?"

"No way. Seriously? I live in Louisville, born and raised. Go figure. I travel a million miles from home to meet a girl from just down the road."

"That's really weird. I hope you're not a dirty Cardinal bird-loving kind of guy. What brings you to Hawaii? I was supposed to be here with a girlfriend, but she got sick the day before the trip and couldn't come. She wanted me to wait, but there was no way in hell I was spending February in Kentucky. So I flew on out. You with the wife and kids? Girlfriend? Boyfriend?" She said with a slight smile on her lips.

"Uh. No," he stammered. "I'm single. Heterosexually single. I'm not into guys. Not that there's anything wrong with that. And I'm not really into sports, so I don't really care for either the Cardinals or the Cats. As for why I'm here, I'm out here on business and that's why I had the laptop with me. I design computer software and figured I might as well do it on the beach than in my hotel room."

He had perfected the lie enough he could tell it without stumbling. He longed to be able to tell someone about the whole battle with Satan-thing, but who would believe him? Heck, he could barely believe it.

"Sounds interesting," she said in a tone of voice, which sounded anything but. For the first time in the conversation, the old doubts started to creep in again and Kurt clammed up. He stared out at the ocean and berated himself for coming off so boring. I mean, the way she asked the question, she had to be a Kentucky fan and he could have played along. But no, he missed a chance to keep the conversation going. And bragging about being a software designer? Most chicks don't dig geeks. Smooth move there, Ex-lax.

He was on the verge of a major sulk when she said, "Most men have already asked me out by this part of the conversation. What's the matter? Not pretty enough?" Her lips scrunched into a child-like pout.

"No way," he said. "I don't know how you can even think that. You're gorgeous. Beyond gorgeous. You're goddess like. I mean, it's not possible for a woman to be prettier than you are. Just look at you. Da Vinci would rather paint you than the Mona Lisa, I'm sure of it. When God made woman, he had to have made Eve to look like you. You're so pretty—"

She interrupted, "Excuse me?"

"Yes?" Kurt swallowed hard a few times, waiting to hear what she would say next.

She turned and looked at him. "Shut up and just ask me out. Will you please?"

"Um. Sure." Kurt cleared his throat. "Would you like to have dinner with me tonight?"

"I'd love to have dinner with you. Now why don't you tell me your name?"

He stuck his hand out and said, "Kurt. Nice to meet you. And your name is?"

She took his hand in hers and Kurt felt a jolt go through his body at her touch. He could feel the softness of her hand and the strength of her grip and found himself falling instantly in love. She pulled her sunglasses down to the end of her nose and he felt like he was falling into the depths of her gray eyes.

"Ruth Anne. And believe me, Kurt, the pleasure's all mine."

CHAPTER FIVE

After hanging up with Kurt, I thumbed through my contact list, punched up the number for Winston Reynolds, and hit dial. After a moment he answered with a, "Your dime, your time."

"Winston, we have a lead on Samantha. A good one. Looks like she's in Naples, Florida. I'm going down to get her and I'm leaving today. I need your help."

"Alright, I'm in, but I need you to give me an hour or two. I have something to take care of here and then I'm good to go."

"You got it. Meet me at the mission around six, I'll fill you in and then we can hit the road."

"Works for me. Don't forget to bring your bottle of Metamucil."

Everyone thinks he's a comic. I'm cruising through my early thirties and Winston was still traveling through his mid-twenties.

"Kiss my ass. At least I don't have to ask my mother if I can stay out late. Besides, you may have youth on me, but I'm much better looking. See you tonight." We hung up.

I dragged out my laptop, fired up the ol'-Google Machine, and typed in the address Kurt provided me. I studied the Google Maps info on the house we were going to stake out. I then found a pen and notepad and started taking notes on exactly how I planned to rain Hell down on the people holding Samantha.

~*~

Winston hung up the phone and sipped his coffee. He took another glance around the room at the people in the diner. His eyes brushed past the young man in the corner reading The Courier-Journal who was pretending not to watch him. But Winston knew better. He picked up the tail earlier in the day after working out at Hwang's Martial Arts. Drinking some water after his session, he was looking out the second story window when he noticed the guy sitting in a silver Honda Accord watching the building. He paid no real attention, since people frequently waited for others attending martial arts classes or visited other stores in the small strip mall all the time.

But he saw the guy again when he came out of Kroger after he stopped to pick up a few things. Same guy. Same Honda, sitting and watching. To make sure he wasn't being paranoid, he drove to the Oxmoor Mall, parked and walked inside, stopping at several stores to window shop and check for the tail. Sure enough, there he was down the concourse, also window shopping and trying not to look obvious. Major fail. Winston now paid a lot more attention to his surroundings following his hook up with Victor McCain.

Life had changed since his former boss and mentor, bounty hunter J.B. Booker was murdered by the Church of the Light Reclaimed. They offered J.B. a million dollars to find and capture Samantha Tyler. During their search, they crossed paths with Vic several times and he always seemed to be just ahead of them. After the Church murdered J.B. and another of his helpers, Winston joined up with Victor for good old-fashioned revenge. In the day that followed, he saw and did things he never imagined doing, but damn, it felt good.

Since then, he helped Victor take out some very bad men as they tried to slow down the Church and find and kill his brother. He shook his head thinking about it because that's just messed up. Winston had four brothers and two sisters and didn't think he could kill any of them, even if God ordered it. But there could be no doubt Michael McCain was one evil mofo and needed to be stopped. But by his own brother? Man, that stunk.

Now he wondered who sent this guy to follow him. Not that it mattered. Truth be told, he got a charge out of it. A former All Big East linebacker for the Louisville Cardinals, he hooked up with J.B. because he loved the rush of taking guys down and sending them to jail. Now they were taking it one-step further by sending them to Hell. True, Vic did all the killings and Winston was there to watch his back and help with tracking people down, but he felt he was doing God's work. And he was smart enough to know sooner, rather than later, the bad guys would come knocking on his door.

And now, it seemed, they were here. He came into the diner for some pecan pie, coffee and to see what the tail would do. The man entered a few minutes after Winston, picking up a paper on his way to a booth. He sat down and ordered coffee. A young black man, skinny and dressed like a member of the chess team, he wore gold John Lennon-style glasses. When Winston left Kroger earlier, he drove by the man's car and noticed a Bellarmine University sticker on it. He definitely looked the college-prep type.

Winston stared out the window of the diner, at the people shopping in the mall and in the reflection he could see his own black face looking back at him. In his mid-twenties, he managed to keep his playing weight and physique, at six foot two inches tall and around two-hundred and thirty pounds. Drafted by the New York Jets, he hung around for a couple of years on the practice squad, but only played in three NFL games before being cut. He just wasn't fast enough.

He returned to Louisville to work out and to try and get another shot at the NFL, but he fell into the life of a bounty hunter instead and loved it. It gave his life purpose and helped keep his community safer by getting some truly bad men off the streets. After throwing in his lot with Vic, even more so. When Vic asked Winston to keep helping him, and he agreed, Vic told him everything: about Satan, what it meant to be the Hand of God, and how he was doing this to earn back his own lost soul. He also explained how the danger would only ramp up as the Church started to fight back against the Can-O' Whup-Ass Victor was going to open on them. He didn't want Winston to have any illusions. Amazingly to Winston, he believed him. Vic offered to pay him from the thirty million stolen from the Church of the Light Reclaimed, so money wasn't an issue. Winston asked for a couple of days to think about it. Helping a man commit murder, no matter the reason, was not something you do without some heavy-duty thinking. And Vic said they would be hunting people for the express purpose of killing them.

The first thing he did was visit his favorite Great Aunt Julia. A large woman with an even larger heart, she never missed a Sunday singing with her church choir and quoted the Bible as easily as another would tell you the name of their children. He attended every church service with her when in town and had his own deep devotion to God. He didn't tell her all of it, but enough so she could tell him whether or not he was nuts.

"Child, the Lord has been delivering punishment to the wicked ever since Eve took a bite out the apple. The Lord is leading you down the path He wants you to follow. So do what your heart tells you is right," she said.

His heart told him to help Victor with that Can-O' Whup-Ass and they were doing quite a job. In three months they removed four men who held high positions with the Church—just not the two men highest on their list: Mikey and a real piece of work named Preston Deveraux. If they really could free Samantha then they may be that much closer to punching their tickets.

Winston tipped his cup back, downing the last of his coffee. It was time to deliver a message to whoever it was following him. Gathering up his trash and tossing it into the garbage, he left through the side door of the diner and down towards the sign pointing to the restrooms. He didn't bother to check to see if the man was following him, but as soon as he turned the corner towards the restrooms, he took off at a full sprint.

As a teenager when he was a "Maller" working for a toy store which closed years ago, he remembered the hallway emptied out by the storage areas, with a supply closet directly across from the men's room. Turning the knob and finding the door unlocked, Winston shook his head. Some things never change. Opening the door he quickly ducked inside, the smell of damp mops and bleach unmistakable, his mind flashed back to more nights than he cared to remember mopping the toy store floor.

Leaving the door open the barest of cracks, he watched as the young man eased slowly past the door, glancing at the men's room. He stopped at a pair of water fountains between the men's and women's doors, and waited.

When Winston didn't come out after five minutes, the man reached into his pocket and pulled out a cell phone. He tapped in a number and after a moment said, "It's Chazaqiel. Tell Samyaza I may have lost him. I'll contact you when I know more." He ended the call and put it back in his pocket. He looked up and down the hallway, pushed the door to the men's room open and stepped inside.

Once the door closed, Winston left the supply room and followed the man, stopping the door before it closed completely, coming in quietly behind him. He caught Mr. Bellarmine straightening up after glancing under the stalls to see if Winston was hiding inside.

Moving behind him, Winston reached out to tap the young man on the shoulder, but before he could say a word, the man attacked, launching his right elbow straight back, aiming to smash Winston's nose. Instinct took over and Winston pivoted, blocking the strike with his right forearm, while at the same time snaking his left arm up and under the other man's, grabbing his neck in a half-nelson. At that point, it became an issue of mass, as Winston used his greater body weight to lift the lighter man off his feet and slammed his face down onto the long sink counter. He heard the man's nose break and a fountain of blood streaked across the countertop and mirror. His glasses went flying into the sink basin causing the automatic water dispenser to turn on with the movement.

Winston lifted the man back up, kicked open the door to one of the stalls and threw him inside and on top of a toilet. Mr. Bellarmine immediately tried to get up, but as he straightened his leg, Winston kicked out and slammed his foot into the man's right knee, driving his kneecap backwards, shattering it. He followed that kick with another to the man's chest, slamming him into the corner of the stall. The man grimaced in pain, but didn't move and said nothing.

"Tell whoever sent you, this is what will happen to anyone else I see following me around. So back the hell off," Winston said.

With that he left the men's room, walked quickly out of the Oxmoor Mall and to the main parking lot to his car.

Winston began to drive away when he noticed a commotion at the entrance. Mr. Bellarmine, blood still dripping down his face, stumbled through the door with his knee still bent backwards. People pointed and stared as the man passed them, his clothes soaked with blood. He had to be in an enormous amount of pain and looked like something out of *The Walking Dead,* but he kept limping down the pavement towards Winston.

He stopped when their eyes met. There was no expression on Mr. Bellarmine's face as he just watched which sent a shiver down Winston's spine. No way the man should've been able to follow him with a knee so completely destroyed. Yet there he stood, glaring at him and Winston knew just what was on his mind: vengeance.

CHAPTER SIX

I met Winston at the door to the mission and led him to J's office. I told him to have a seat while I went into the kitchen and asked the main man to join us for a few minutes. J always helped to prep the mission meals and then serve them. A real man of the people. I stood in the kitchen door and finally caught his attention. I nodded, pointing back down the hallway, he excused himself and followed me to his office.

After making the introductions, I gave the boss man the scoop on my conversation with Kurt, my plans to head south and if the information was correct, to rescue Samantha.

"You know it won't be as easy as it was the last time you did this, when you and Winston hit the house out in the country. Those guards weren't top notch and they didn't expect you to find them." Brother Joshua said. "This time they'll be watching, and may even be hoping you'll make a rescue attempt in order to get a shot at taking you out."

I shook my head. "You could be right, but I don't care. If I'd done more to protect her in the first place, she wouldn't be trapped with those scumbags suffering who knows what. I feel responsible for the fact they have her at all. The only real question I have for you is, will you sanction the trip or am I going rogue? These are bad men, J. I don't have to tell you that. I have to go down and try to pry her loose from the Church."

I knew to go down there kicking ass and taking names, without permission, would be breaking the agreement I made when I became the Hand of God. I agreed to only go after targets approved by J. I tried to keep my face a smooth mask of "I don't give a rat's ass." But inside I was turning into knots. Winston sat next to me, his hands folded in his lap, and kept silent.

J watched me for a few minutes before he spoke. I don't know if he was just running through his options or mind melding with the Big Guy upstairs. Eventually he said, "You can go, but try not to kill anyone while you're down there if you can help it. You assume they will all be Church thugs, but you don't really know."

"And if I can't rescue her without killing the lot of them?"

"The Lord's will be done."

"You know what, J? Sometimes the Lord's will is a pain in the ass." This got a snicker out of Winston, which earned him the evil eye from J. But Winston just stared back. I got what I needed, so I stood up and left without another word. Winston was right behind me. We made our way to my room and I motioned for Winston to take the only chair, a battered old leather swivel chair parked in front of a small desk.

"So, are you good to go?" I asked.

He nodded back and he filled me in on his adventure at the Mall.

"This black on black crime is really getting out of hand," I said.

"Says you. Whitey been beating on 'my people' for centuries, down in the hood, we're just playing catch up."

"Hood, my ass. Your mother and father are both doctors and you grew up in the East End. Hell, your dad is a member of Valhalla Country Club and on the PGA's Board of Directors. Your hood is all ascots and beamers."

"True that. But have you ever seen an Izod wearing black man when his Mercedes won't start? Brutal, man. Just brutal."

"I take it you got the license plate number of the guy following you?"

"Yeah. I got it. When he made the call he said his name was Chaz-something and he called some dude and dropped the name Sam Yaza. You ever heard of any Satanist with that name?"

"Nadda. Doesn't ring a bell."

He gave me the license number and I called a cop buddy of mine named Rusty to get the lowdown on this Chaz-guy. Rusty put me on hold for a few minutes and when he came back on the line the tone of his voice told me I had stepped in it. "Uh, Vic? Why do you want information on this particular car?"

"It's a car that's been seen around the home of a jumper I'm looking for and I thought if I could get a line on the owner, I might be able to track down my guy. There's a chance they might be bunking together. Why? What's up with this guy?"

"The car is owned by an African American male, twenty-one years old, named Mal McGeorge. Here's the thing: he was just admitted to University Hospital. Seems someone beat the ever-lovin' crap out of him down at the Oxmoor Mall. He then collapsed outside one of the entrances and when the EMTs arrived on the scene, he had no clue where he was and was screaming repeatedly about someone being in his head. Vic, the guy clawed his own eyes out of their sockets. What's the name of the guy you're looking for? Perhaps this guy is the one who assaulted Mr. McGeorge."

"Holy shit, Rusty, that's messed up. But come on, man, if I tell you and you get to him first, then I don't collect a paycheck. How about this? I'll check things out and if I find out my perp had anything to do with the attack, I'll call you personally. You know I'll play it straight."

He read off an address on Louisville's East Side. "Fair enough, Vic. You've kept your word in the past, but you'd best keep me in the loop on this one. Be careful now, ya hear?"

"Bingo, Ringo." I hung up and relayed the information to Winston.

"Might be a good thing you and I are headed south for a few days. No clue if they'll be able to link you to what happened, but being out of town for a while can't hurt. We can work on our tans."

He looked at the dark ebony of his skin, then back at me and shrugged. "Whatever works for you, man. Should we go back and tell J about all of this? If it's the Church, it's probably something he should know. And I'm telling you, when he walked out as I was leaving, he wasn't screaming and yelling. The man's shit was ice cold. I've taken down some real bad mofos and I'm telling you, Vic, none of them gave me the willies like this dude."

"Not just No, but *hell* no. We can tell him when we get back. I can't take a chance he'll want me to investigate this before we get Samantha. Once we have her, you and I can figure out who was following you and why. He sure doesn't sound like the kind of guy the Church has been using. But then again, I have no clue what it takes to be a card-carrying Satanist. Let's get our stuff into the car and hit the road. I'll fill you in on the way down. At least it'll be warmer down there. You sure you didn't have another tail following you over here?"

Winston gave me a dead fish stare as I threw on my coat and grabbed my gear. "The only tail following me I left barely standing at the mall. We're good," he said.

"Don't get your panties in a wad, I was just asking. Let's hit the road."

We made our way outside and over to a brand new Ford Flex I purchased a month earlier. After buying it, I dropped it off at Winston's uncle's house so he could make a few "modifications." A member of a local militia group, his uncle believed the government would one day come and take his guns away. He and some friends built an underground bunker with enough guns and ammo to hold off a good-sized rogue nation and knew a thing or two about hiding stuff you don't want the authorities to find. He took my Ford and built a hidden compartment to hold all my man toys—you know, the ones for which I never bothered to get permits: a couple of MPK5s, flash and concussion grenades and all the fixins' any hell-bent bounty hunter would need. Dark blue, it matched my University of Kentucky sensibilities while driving my University of Louisville sidekick nuts.

"I still can't believe you bought a soccer mom car," Winston said. "Man, next thing you know, your drinks will have little umbrellas sticking out of them, you'll be getting pedicures, and your eyebrows buzzed."

"Nothing wrong with the occasional pedi. Besides, this car blends in better than some of the others I looked at."

"It would if you were half your size and a woman. Might as well put a gorilla in a tux," Winston said with a laugh.

Winston grabbed a getaway bag from his car and we were off. The temp hovered just above zero with the wind chill factor. Where we were headed, down in Naples, it was clocking in at a balmy seventy-five degrees. I was always a fall-winter kind of guy, but even I was looking forward to spring. At least weather wouldn't be a factor when we took on the people holding Samantha hostage. The clock on the dash read almost straight up seven o'clock. It would take the better part of fifteen hours to make it to Naples with the two of us taking turns behind the wheel.

"Look in my bag on the seat behind you," I said. "You'll find a manila folder with satellite printouts of the home we're interested in." While he pulled out the folder, I continued, "The home sits off away from other houses and has several acres of land. There's a stone privacy fence around a large portion of the property with nothing but a well-manicured yard between the house and the fence. The only shots of the house are overhead, so I can't tell how tall the fence is, but with no trees or any other places of concealment, it'll be hard to sneak up on them if they have sentries posted. We did get lucky, however, in that I searched for rental properties in the area and there's one a couple of houses down. I called the realtor handling the rental and managed to wrangle a month lease. So, we can take a day or two and case the situation."

"How much did that set you back? My folks have rented down there for winter trips and it ain't cheap."

"It's twelve grand a month, with an option for a second month. But we won't need it, 'cause I'm going to want to move quickly. There's no telling how long our intel will be good. For all we know, they move her every couple of days, but I doubt it. If she's been down there long enough to be bored, then I'm guessing she's been there awhile."

"Sounds good to me." He lowered his seat back to the full reclining position. "If I'm going to drive later, then I'm taking a nap now. Besides, I always like to take a nap after a good butt kicking."

And true to his word I heard light snoring noises before driving another ten miles down the road. Winston could sleep anywhere, anytime. I guess an honest man's pillow is his peace of mind. Me? I spent most nights lying in bed for hours and willing sleep to come with no luck.

I spent most of that time thinking of Samantha when I wasn't thinking about Mikey. I also had nightmares, dreaming about the death of Dominic Montoya, the former Hand of God. He lost his life because I refused to see what was right in front of my eyes. Montoya came to town looking for a man known only as Belial and in the end, everything pointed in Mikey's direction. But I just couldn't believe it and it cost Montoya his life, Samantha her freedom, and me my soul. Now I would spend the rest of my life—however long it would be—trying to fix all the damage I caused.

I merged onto I-65, eased the Flex up to a few miles over the limit, and hit the cruise control. I settled back into my seat and tried to relax as the miles melted away. If Kurt's info turned out to be right, then I would soon see Samantha again, one way or another.

CHAPTER SEVEN

Since Kurt's idea of a great meal started and ended with a trip to Wendy's, he asked the concierge where he should take Ruth Anne for dinner and he suggested the Hanalei Dolphin, a combination restaurant, fish market and sushi bar. While just the thought of eating raw fish made his stomach do more flips than a cook at a pancake-eating contest, he called Ruth Anne and asked if it was O.K. with her. She said it sounded great and he made plans to pick her up around seven. She rented a villa just down the beach from his hotel and said she'd be ready at the appointed time.

It took him nearly an hour to decide what to wear, changing clothes about a dozen times, before choosing khaki shorts, a blue and white Hawaiian shirt and hiking sandals. Kurt stood and looked at his reflection in the mirror, and practiced his relaxation breathing but he still broke out in a light sweat. When the time came to call a cab, he almost dialed Ruth Anne back and canceled. He picked up and then lowered the phone several times before finally finding the courage in himself, saying aloud, "Screw it," and made the call.

Strolling out of the hotel lobby he found the cab waiting. He gave him the address and a few minutes later, they pulled into Ruth Anne's driveway. He told the cabbie to wait while he went to the door. Before pressing the doorbell, he leaned his head against the doorframe, asked God for the strength to get through the night, and prayed he would not break out in hives.

Please, Lord, he thought, no hives.

Following a few more deep breaths, he straightened and pressed the doorbell. He glanced over his shoulder to see the cabbie giving him two thumbs up. Kurt smiled weakly and turned back as the door opened.

When it did, his breathing stopped. He just plain forgot to breathe. Wearing a silk red evening dress, which barely made mid-thigh and her hair tied back in a ponytail, she appeared more a vision than reality. She carried a small red purse and nothing else. Doing a quick twirl with her dress rising and then falling, she said, "You like?"

When he didn't respond, she asked, "Kurt? Earth to Kurt? Come in please?"

He gave himself a mental slap and replied, "Hell yes. Wow. I mean, um, you look amazing."

He glanced down at his own clothes.

"Aw man, I feel really under-dressed. You must be embarrassed to go out with me looking like this. I can run back to the hotel and change. Give me a few minutes."

Before he could turn to leave she wrapped her arms around his neck and kissed him deeply. She broke the kiss off and purred, "You look delicious and no you won't go change. I'm starving, so let's go have dinner."

She slipped her arm into his, lead him, dazed, and stunned, to the cab. He had never been kissed like *that* before and he felt light-headed from the experience.

He hardly spoke a word all the way to the restaurant as Ruth Anne talked about the rest of her day shopping and then swimming in the pool behind her villa. Kurt sat staring at her, watching the way her mouth moved, the way she breathed.

She stopped in mid-sentence and asked, "You planning on joining in the conversation, Big Boy?"

"No. I mean, yes. I'm sorry," Kurt said. "I love watching you talk. I could spend the whole night doing nothing but watching you."

"Well, I do need you to do your part. This is a date, after all."

Kurt got a reprieve as the cab pulled up in front of the restaurant. He paid the cabbie a generous tip and as they got out, the cabbie winked at him. Kurt smiled back, giving the cabbie two thumbs up and then escorted Ruth Anne inside. Soon they were seated at their table. They made small talk until after they gave the waiter their order and when he left, she said, "O.K. It's your turn. Tell me about this software you're working on."

Kurt swallowed hard. "There's not much to tell. I help design and test website security software. Most big companies are attacked daily by hackers and my job is to try and keep them out."

He knew he couldn't tell her about what he was really doing, trying to take down the Church of the Light Reclaimed, but it wasn't a complete lie. He had been working on security software, at the request of the cable company he worked for in Louisville, after hackers tried to bring their network down and Kurt suggested ways they could prevent such an attack. That all ended when he high-tailed it out of town and continued to help Victor put the big hurt on Satan and his followers.

"And you chose to do this programming from a beach in Hawaii?" she sounded skeptical.

"I can do the work from anywhere on the planet I can get an Internet connection, so why not on a beach in Hawaii?" he replied. He could feel the first itch start on his arms and he excused himself to make a quick trip to the men's room.

She touched him on the hand as he rose and said, "Hurry back, handsome."

Once again, he felt a bolt of electricity go through his body as her fingers trailed across the back of his hand. It took every ounce of willpower not to run to the bathroom. Inside the men's room, he reached into his pocket and took out the Benadryl he carried in case of emergencies and downed the two pills with a handful of water from the bathroom sink. He stared at the man looking back at him in the mirror.

"Keep it simple, Kurt," he said aloud to himself. "She digs you. All you have to do is keep it simple."

With restored self-confidence, he headed back to the table.

~*~

Ruth Anne watched him until he disappeared into the men's room, then opened her purse, took out a small flip phone, typed in a number and hit dial. After a few rings a man's voice said, "Were you able to make the exchange?"

She said, "No, I wasn't. He must be a true believer. He's not a very complex person, so I don't think there is any room for doubt for one such as he. He either believes or doesn't. I will have to get the information we need from him another way. It would be better if you let me do it my way. I promise you, he will tell us what we need to know."

"We still have time. The Spear is busy elsewhere and he is blind to our purpose. But if you move too fast he might be alerted, so be careful how you proceed. We don't want the Spear to learn of what we are doing until the time is right. Then it will be too late for him to stop us. You have the temptation of the flesh available to you. Use it. It has forever worked," the man said to her.

Her grip tightened on the phone. "I grow weary of this game. We must move more quickly," she said.

"You will do as I tell you to do." The connection ended and Ruth Anne put her phone away just as Kurt returned to the table. Inside she was seething, but she put a smile on her face.

"Feel better?" she asked.

~*~

"Much," Kurt said. "Who was on the phone?"

"Disgruntled ex-boyfriend," she said. The look on his face must have shown the fear he felt inside. "Don't worry. He's out of the picture and thousands of miles away. I'm footloose and fancy free. I'm all yours."

It shouldn't be a surprise she has an ex, Kurt thought to himself. Look at her. No way she wouldn't have one. And she was right. She was with him, not the other guy. He even managed to add some to the conversation over dinner, once the Benadryl kicked in and saved him from head to toe hives. She ate sushi while he enjoyed the Dolphin Salad. She offered him a bite of her sushi, but he didn't think he could eat food when he could tell what it had been while still alive. He had no problem eating meat, but his burgers looked nothing like a cow, so no worries. Now if they started making beef patties in the shape of a cow? He shuddered at the thought.

When they finished dinner, they took a cab back to her villa. She slipped her hand into his and lead him down to the beach as the sun glided slowly below the horizon. As they walked, hand-in-hand, the moon rose, full and bright. Then she dropped his hand and slid hers around his waist. After hesitating for a moment, he did the same and inside started congratulating himself on the "new Kurt" when the fragile self-confidence came crashing down in flames.

She came to a stop and turned him to face her, the ocean waves crashing behind them. Her hands finger-walked up his chest, snaked behind his head and pulled it down so she could kiss him. When the kiss ended she said, "I want you to spend the night with me, at my place. What do you say?"

The panic attack hit him hard and his body went rigid. The old Monopoly saying passed his thoughts: "Go Directly to Jail. Do Not Pass Go." He tried to talk, but found it hard to breathe. He would have taken off at a dead run, but his body refused to take any orders from his brain.

Ruth Anne's face went from playful to concerned. "Kurt? Talk to me. Are you O.K?"

He racked his brain, trying to come up with an excuse she would believe. How could he have not considered this possibility? Well, because it never happened before, he berated himself. He looked up and down the beach, hoping for inspiration. Finally he blurted, "Because I have a conference call. Later tonight. In my room."

Stepping back and crossing her arms, she asked, "A conference call? It's the middle of the night back in the states. You mean to tell me you have a business call this time of night? You're so full of shit."

She turned and started walking back to her villa. He trailed behind her hitting his forehead with the heel of his hand, saying over and over in his mind, idiot, idiot, idiot. A conference call? He bit his lip thinking as she continued to walk away. Then with a stroke of inspiration, "Yes. We have to do the tests in the middle of the night, after the call centers shut down. We can't test the systems during business hours. It has to be in the middle of the night."

She stopped and turned to look at him and raised her eyebrows. "You swear?" she said not completely convinced.

He swallowed hard and replied, "I swear."

It was all he could do not to cross his fingers and pray his explanation sounded plausible.

She closed the distance between them, smiled and leaned in for a kiss. When he bent down to kiss her, she hit him hard in the arm and, boy, did it hurt. He clutched his arm and rubbed the spot where she tagged him. Wow. She was stronger than she looked!

"You should have told me about this meeting, Kurt. "

Kurt started mumbling an apology, but she cut him short.

"Learn something right now, Kurt. You're going to find out I'm not like most women. Now call your cab and I'll think about whether I want to see you tomorrow or not."

She left him standing at the end of the walkway as she stormed up to her front door, stepped inside, and slammed it behind her. He called for a cab and while he waited, he rubbed his arm where she slugged him and thought she's right. She's not like most women.

CHAPTER EIGHT

We were royally screwed. That's the conclusion I came to after two days of surveillance of the house owned by Wheadon's family in the Port Royal section of Naples. Using high-powered binoculars from the front room of our rental, we kept an around-the-clock eye on the comings and goings at Casa de Wheadon. The stone fence stood about seven feet tall with a solid iron gate at the end of the drive, surrounding the classic Spanish-style home you see a lot of here in Naples. The home sat right on the water with about two hundred feet of beach and two boat docks. The house featured balconies in both the front and back, and a wide veranda and pool in the back as well. Palm trees dotted the property, but offered no concealment.

A small security force prowled the grounds, both day and night, and they were good. Never falling into a pattern, they mixed up their routines. And there were dogs, Dobermans, both on leashes and running loose. The dogs never made a sound. Experience had taught me when dogs don't bark it's because they're saving their energy to rip you a new one. Landscape lighting popped on with the approaching darkness and left little to no shadows to hide anything larger than a grapefruit.

As night dropped around us and the sun disappeared from view, Winston and I surveyed the scene from a rented Hydra Sports 3400 CC fishing boat, with a couple poles in the water and the anchor dropped. The boat cost me a small fortune to rent, but what the hell. I was spending money stolen from devil worshipers. So what did I care?

We turned the boat in such a way to keep an eye on the target while we contemplated a water assault. Thankfully, Winston knew his way around a boat because my expertise began and ended with, "They float you're good. They sink, you're not."

Swimming was something I did when I had no other choice. If a boat turned over twenty feet from shore, I can make it; thirty was a tossup; and fifty feet was a drag the river, I'm not coming up. I love the water, but I preferred to stay on top of it. For about the millionth time that afternoon, I pulled my life vest into a more comfortable position. I spent half a day going from store to store in Naples before I found one big enough to fit me.

I lowered the binocs, rubbed my eyes and then stared off to the horizon, the Gulf of Mexico stretching out seemingly forever, while the boat gently rocked with the evening tide. I let my mind go over all the possibilities and came to the same conclusion: we were hosed. I couldn't come up with a single possible way to get in and out in one piece. A two-man assault was doomed to fail. Subterfuge wouldn't work either, as any delivery to the house was stopped at the front gate and the cars thoroughly searched. There are American embassies in backwater third world countries easier to slip into than this house.

We'd been watching from the boat for most of the early evening and going in from the water would be as suicidal as a frontal assault. We would need to cover several hundred feet of sand before we even made it to the property itself, and we'd be exposed the entire way.

I kept hoping we would catch a glimpse either of Samantha, walking the grounds or out on a balcony, but no luck. If she was inside they were keeping her on a short leash.

I said to Winston, "Storming the castle and trying to rescue the princess will only end up with you and me in body bags. We'll have to try something different."

Winston cranked his reel slowly, pulling in the line one last time and hoping for another hit. He caught and released several white trout. Me? I caught a sunburn.

He said, "I know a few guys I could probably get down here to help out. All you have to do is say the word and I'll make a few calls."

"Nah. We need a small army and there's no way to pull it off with any type of stealth. The amount of firepower we'd have to unleash would bring the cops down on us before we could even get in the front door."

"So, what. We just giving up?"

"Hell no. We're still getting her out. We'll just have to get them to bring her to us."

"And how do you figure to do that? Call up and ask?"

I sat there for a moment thinking. "Actually, not a bad idea. Let's get this boat back to its slip and I'll fill you in."

Winston and I stowed the fishing gear, raised the anchor and fired up the Hydra Sport. Cranking the wheel and opening the throttle, he guided us to shore, easing the boat in next to the dock while I jumped out and tied her off.

We got our stuff and hiked back to the Ford, rolling down the windows, and then cruised slowly by Samantha's gilded cage to our own rental. I went upstairs to take the first watch of our long distance surveillance, while Winston ordered up pizza from a local popular restaurant with the best reputation in town.

Once the pizza arrived, he brought it upstairs along with a couple of Millers. He popped the tops and handed me one. We clinked the bottles together and sat in the darkness of the room, watching for something, anything, to happen down at Wheadon's place.

"So, what bright idea do you have to get them to bring Samantha out?"

I flipped open the top to the pizza box and slid out a large slice of pepperoni, taking a huge bite and said around a mouthful of pie, "What they are relying on is no one knows where she is. They think they have her hidden away where no one can find her. So what if someone goes up, rings the bell, and asks for Samantha? And if the people doing the ringing are cops?"

He pulled out his own piece of pizza and replied, "What? You and I dressing up like cops? Man, they'll be all over us in a heartbeat. You're kind of hard to hide, even dressed in blue."

"No. Not us. Real cops. We make an anonymous call saying a woman named Samantha has been kidnapped and is being held at the house. Then one of two things happens: the cops show up and demand either they produce her and the cops take her with them, or the bad guys demand the cops come back with a warrant, and when the cops are gone, they move her. If the first happens, then we show up at the precinct and whisk her away. If they do the second, we make our move and take them out. What do ya think?"

"Sounds like a plan to me. Better than sitting around on our asses all day doing nothing. The longer we stay here, the more you sulk."

"Kiss my ass. We're going to need a few things before we make our move. Does your uncle have any contacts down here?"

"Unc has friends everywhere. What do you need?"

I told him and his eyes went wide.

"Damn, Vic. You sure about this?"

"Hell and brimstone, Winston. Hell and brimstone. Think he knows someone who can help us out?"

"Let me call him." Winston pulled out his burner cell and called his uncle. After a few minutes he hung up. "He says he might know a guy. He'll pass along the request and have him call us. I told him to use your number."

We sat in silence for about an hour, taking turns watching the house, when the phone in my pocket rang. I pulled it out and the caller ID showed the name was blocked.

I answered and a man asked, "You the Hand?"

"That's right. And you are?"

"No names. Tomorrow morning at 8 a.m. I want you to stop and have breakfast at the Third Street Cafe in Naples. You know the place?"

"No, but I'm guessing it's on Third Street. I'll find it. How will I know who you are?"

"You won't. Order some breakfast, then sit outside at the table in front. Leave your friend at home. I see anyone else but you, and you won't live to regret it." And the call went dead.

Well, wasn't he a bundle of sunshine. I looked at Winston and said, "It's on. I have a meeting tomorrow morning. You, however, aren't invited. I need you to keep an eye on the house, anyways."

"I sure hope you know what you're doing. If this goes sideways? Wow."

All I could do was nod. Story of my life.

CHAPTER NINE

The Third Street Cafe, as you can guess, was on Third Street, next to a 7 Eleven. I showed up just before eight and ordered a western omelet, hash browns and white bread toast. I chatted up with the cook and found out he moved to Naples from the Upper Peninsula of Michigan, where he toiled as a five star chef at several of the resorts there. Finally tired of the harsh winter weather, when the opportunity arose, he packed up and moved to the sun and sand of Naples.

Compared to prices at other restaurants in town, this one practically gave their food away. I watched as the cook finished preparing my breakfast, sliding the omelet and hash browns onto a plate with bacon and two slices of toast, and then set the plate on the counter. I snagged a cup of coffee, carried the food to a table outside, and dug in. And damn, if it wasn't the best breakfast I'd eaten in ages.

As I shoveled the last bite of omelet into my mouth, a man strolled up and slid into a seat on the other side of the table. About six feet tall, the man wasn't any wider than a blade of grass. His clothes seemed to hang on his body rather than fit it and when he placed his hands on the table, one on top of the other, his fingers were just as thin and very long. Eyes the color of a muddy stream stared back at my baby blues.

"Can I buy you breakfast?" I asked.

"We're not staying," he replied. And as if to put action to his words, a white van pulled up to the curb and the side door opened. The man stood up and got in the passenger seat. I rose, gathered my trash, and dropped it in the can by the 7 Eleven.

"I guess I'm not following you then, huh?" I said.

"Nope." He gestured to the open door. "Get in, or not. Up to you. But we're leaving in ten seconds."

I shrugged my shoulders and got in, sliding the door closed. I had no idea where we were going, but it didn't really matter. I was the one who asked for the meeting and considering what I wanted from them, I knew the only way it would happen is if I played by their rules.

There were two other men in the van, a driver wearing a ball cap he pulled down low on his head, and next to me a very large man who looked like a grizzled Viking warrior with hair down to his shoulders and a beard reaching half-way down his chest. But truth be told, I didn't pay much attention to his looks. I focused more on the 357 Magnum he held, pushing it against my side.

"Look, if you don't want to be my B.F.F., fine," I said. "But you don't really need to use the gun, do we fellas?"

The Viking wannabe only smiled and pushed the gun harder into my side, while the others sat in silence. I settled in and went with the "Lord's will be done" attitude. We made our way out of Naples proper, heading north on Highway 41 until we were a bit outside of Cape Coral. The van turned into a commercial district and after a few blocks pulled into a parking lot and through an open garage door. After coming to a stop in the garage, the door closed behind us and we were shut off from the outside world.

The man from the cafe got out, opened the side door and stepped aside, nodding for me to get out. I stretched, loosening up the body for whatever came next.

"Time to move, asshole," the Viking said.

"And here I thought you and I had really connected on the ride over. Guess I'm losing my touch."

He shoved me with the gun and when he pulled it back, I shot my hand out, snatched his wrist, turning it up and back, forcing him to drop the gun. I got to it before he did and raising the gun, pushed the barrel against his forehead. His eyes blinked and I could tell he was holding his breath.

The driver never even moved his head, staring straight ahead. Tall n skinny stood by the side of the van, watching. I smiled at the now defenseless wild man and stepped out of the van. I reversed the gun, holding it by the barrel and handed it to the skinny guy who made first contact with me.

"I don't mind the cloak and dagger stuff," I said. "Your house, your rules. But don't think I'm some rookie you can intimidate. Not going to happen."

The wild man rolled out of the van and said, "Give me back my gun, Paulie, and I'll beat this son of a bitch to a pulp. Let's see how tough he is then."

Paulie said, "Shut up." He half-smiled and put the gun in the waistband of his slacks, while the other man stewed.

I glanced around the garage as Paulie walked to a nearby door. Large enough for several cars, workbenches lined two of the walls and were filled with various-type tools. I was good with guns and weapons of destruction, but I was hopeless with most everyday handyman tools. In fact, I can break down an MP5 quicker than most people can tie their shoes. But use a belt sander? Forget about it.

He opened the door and motioned for me to step through. I did so and walked into an office with furniture pushed against the wall and plastic covering gray shag carpet. I took a few steps and stopped. Looking down at the plastic I gestured towards the floor and asked, "You guys planning on doin' some painting?"

"With your brains depending on how the next few minutes go," Paulie said.

Before I could come up with a witty comeback, a door on the other side of the room swung open and a man somewhere in his late fifties or early sixties, stepped into the room. He wore a long-sleeved shirt, jeans, work boots, and a wary look on a deeply tanned face lined with age. He stopped a few feet in front of me and hooked his thumbs into his front pockets.

I offered him my hand and said, "Vic McCain. The pleasure's mine."

He didn't take my hand and replied, "Understand somethin.' You only made it this far because an old friend of mine asked me to meet with you. What you're a gonna do next is strip down to the suit the good Lord gave you when you came screaming into this world. Do it now, please."

"I hate to break it to you, but you're not really my type. When I strip down for someone other than my doctor, I want it to be a 'her' and a lot younger than you are."

"Listen funny boy, I ain't going to ask ya but one more time. Strip."

I glanced over my shoulder and Paulie now held the 357 down by his side with a lopsided grin on his face.

I reminded myself: their house, their rules. I unbuttoned my shirt.

"I'm packing, belt holster, so don't you guys go getting overly excited."

I dropped the shirt and held my hands out from my body as Paulie took my gun. I then lost the shoes and pants, and stood there in my briefs.

The old man said, "Them, too, hot shot. Don't worry. We ain't interested in lookin' at your pecker."

I slid down my boxer briefs and dropped them onto the pile of clothes.

"O.K. Now what?"

"This way."

He turned and went back through the same door he entered a few minutes earlier. I followed him into a large room filled with different types of air conditioning units, one wall taken up with what I could only assume were parts to fix them. More plastic covered the section of the floor where they told me to stop, and I wiggled my toes feeling the cold concrete underneath. I had a brief vision of me lying on the ground, a bullet hole in my head. I told myself to think more positive. If they wanted me dead, they'd have shot me already.

The door behind us closed and I stood there, the old man in front of me and Paulie behind me. The old man once again hooked his thumbs in his front pockets and just stared at me. I have to admit, I now had an idea how Tommy Spenoza felt lying naked on the bed while I held my gun pointed at him. It was unnerving. And in this case, I guess that was the point. But I could guess another reason.

"You worried I might be wearing a wire?" I said.

"Crossed my mind. Stand still a minute while Paulie checks your hair."

I did as he asked while Paulie ran fingers through my hair, still blonde from my trip to Richmond and running a bit long. He found nothing and stepped back.

A minute later the Viking opened the door and said, "His stuff's clear." He sounded disappointed and left the room, closing the door behind him.

"Alright," the old man said. "Time to get down to business. You want a bomb. What're you planning on blowing to smithereens, Mr. Hand?"

"The name's Vic, and that falls under none of your damned business. The reason I need an I.E.D is my own. Besides, the less we know about each other, the better. Don't you think?"

I asked Winston's uncle to find me someone in his network who could supply me with an improvised explosive device. I didn't know how I'd use it. Not yet, anyways, but a few ideas kept bubbling to the top.

"Ain't nothin' improvised about my work. Everything I do is planned out to the millionth degree. I ain't used to providing things to strangers on short notice, but I go way back with our mutual friend and I kinda of owe him. So I'm going to give you what you ask for. But be warned. If you use it to kill children, I'll kill you. You attack a school or church, I'll kill you. The man who called me said you were a righteous man. I don't really give a shit. But you do any of the things I mentioned and you won't be able to ever sleep a peaceful night again. Do we understand each other?"

"We do. I would never do those things. I know you have no way to believe me, but it won't be an issue."

The man nodded and removed a small black remote control out of his back pocket.

"Here's a remote detonator. Place the bomb where you want it, flip up the switch guard and then press down. You can be up to a mile away."

I took the remote and said, "That simple?"

"Yep. That simple. Blowing things up ain't all that complicated. Get the right ingredients, put them together and there ya go. Who to blow up, that's different."

I nodded. "When do I get the bomb?"

"We put it in the back of your car. It's in a box wrapped with brown packing paper. Be careful and make sure you don't hit any big pot holes on the way home." He smiled then, but the smile didn't reach his eyes.

"Already in my car? What if I hadn't checked out? Why go to the trouble?" I asked.

"You were getting the bomb either way, Mr. Hand. The only question was if it would be you using the remote or me. You'd best be on your way. Get dressed and then Paulie will give you a lift to your car."

I've stared down a lot of big bad nasties in my lifetime, but the thought of me driving off into the sunset with a bomb I didn't know about in my car gave me the heebie jeebies. I went into the other room and got dressed. Paulie handed me my gun and I clipped it onto my belt and then followed him to the van.

The same man did the driving, but the Viking-dude didn't make the return trip. Paulie once again rode in the front and I hopped in the back. We drove in silence through town. When we reached the cafe, Paulie turned in the seat and said, "Good luck. I think he liked you."

Getting out, I slid the door closed behind me, stepped up to his window, and asked, "How could you tell?"

"Because he didn't kill you."

He gave me another lopsided grin and a short wave and the van pulled away.

I walked over to my Ford and raised the lift gate. I found a small package under a blue blanket wrapped neatly in brown paper. I gently dropped the blanket over the bomb and a wild thought raced through my head: what if I hadn't passed the old man's test? I only had his word the remote he'd given me was *the* remote. I glanced around the parking lot, but didn't see anyone paying any attention to me.

Screw it. Like I said, Lord's will be done.

I shut the lift gate, but very softly. Then climbed behind the wheel. A plan began pinging around the recesses of my mind and it was past time to try it out and get moving. At least now I would get their attention. Boom goes the dynamite.

CHAPTER TEN

It took me another day and a half to get things ready. I didn't want to use my Ford in the main operation, so Winston and I visited several used car dealerships until I found a Chevy S-10 with more mileage than a fifty-year old hooker with rust in several places and a couple of dents, but I didn't care. It ran fine for what I planned to use it for. I didn't need a looker.

Winston drove the Ford home while I took the Chevy for a spin out of town to a salvage yard where I bought a used tire. My final stop took me to Wal-Mart to buy another prepaid cell phone.

I could feel the excitement level building inside me. Before the day ended, if we were lucky, I'd have Samantha free and in my arms. I thought about the last time I saw her at Mikey's warehouse. She stood dazed with blood trickling down her temple from where Mikey's hired pit bull, Preston Deveraux, had slugged her.

We were together for less than a full day, yet her affect on me was life altering. I was never a love-at-first-sight kind of guy. I thought it was a load of crap. But with Samantha and me? The attraction was immediate and, well, I'm pretty sure, mutual. My daydreams were haunted by my inability to save her. My sleepless nights lingered with the memories of the two of us in bed.

Finally, I now had a chance to get Samantha back. At the rental house, Winston and I split up the firepower between the Ford and the Chevy and moved the bomb from the Ford to the truck.

"Ready to get moving?" I asked.

"You got it. Let's do this."

I nodded and pulled out the new prepaid cell phone. I'd already looked up the number of the Naples Police Department. I typed it in and hit dial.

A dispatcher answered and said, "Naples Police, what is the nature of your emergency?"

I added a high whine to my voice and said, "I was in a house doing some work today and there's a woman there who said she's been kidnapped and they were holding her against her will. You have to help her."

"What is your name, sir? And what is the address where the woman is being held?"

I gave her the address. "I can't give you my name. They'll kill me. Help her, please! She's tall and has red hair. I think her name is Samantha. Please, you have to help her!" I disconnected the call. Now all we could do was wait.

Watching with the binoculars, ten minutes after my call, two blue and whites rolled up to the house. An officer got out and pushed the call button at the front gate and I watched as the officer carried on a one-sided conversation. Then the gate swung back, the officer returned to his car, and the two police cars drove up the driveway pulling into the circle turn-around in front of the house. Four officers exited the vehicles and then started up the front steps, hands on the butt of their guns.

Before they made it to the top of the steps a bare-chested man wearing swim trunks opened the door and walked outside to greet the officers with a cheery wave. He was of average height with dark brown haircut short, sporting a news anchor quality smile. He appeared to be in his early twenties. The officers said something to the man and a look of confusion appeared on his face. He raised up a hand as if asking the officers to wait, while he turned over his shoulder and shouted back into the house.

The officers waited. A minute or so later, Samantha walked out the front door wearing a bikini top and shorts. My heart quickened. There she was. Picture the most beautiful woman in the world. Now that you have, realize that woman you pictured can't compete with the natural beauty of Samantha. Her auburn hair had grown since I last saw her. And in the Florida sun she was a bit more tanned.

Then my stomach dropped as she stepped up next to the man and slipped her arm around his waist, with him doing the same, in what looked to be a very familiar gesture. Winston moved the binocs an inch or so and glanced at me, but I kept my eyes on her.

On the day we met, we only talked about life in general for a few minutes at Molly Malone's before we hit Inspirational Global Software. Never once did she mention a boyfriend or being in a relationship. Not that she owed me anything, but watching her now with her arm around some yahoo hit me harder than a kick to the family jewels.

The officers talked for a while longer and then both Samantha and the man looked at each other and shrugged. After a few more minutes of talking, the officers waved goodbye, got back in their cars, and left.

Samantha and the man remained arm and arm as they watched the cops leave. When they drove out the front gate, Samantha dropped the smile and walked back inside. The man shouted something after her, and while I couldn't hear what was being said, I felt a surge of relief flood through me. The man raised his arm and looked down at his side where Samantha had dug her nails deeply enough into the skin to draw blood. He clenched his fists as he went inside and slammed the door. Two lovebirds they were not.

Winston said, "I don't think she's none too happy with Studley. Think she'll be O.K.? He looked mad enough to make her pay for what she did."

"She'll have to be. At least we know she's there. I'm going to go get into position. If they do decide to make a move, I want to be ready. You keep an eye on them and if all hell breaks loose, call me."

"Will do. You sure about this, man? You set that thing off, there's no telling what will happen."

"It's the best I can come up with under the circumstances."

The plan was simple. Per my request, the bomb made by the militia guys came in on the small side. My goal was to disable any car they were in, not blow them to kingdom come. I would be in the Chevy in a line of trees just down from the bomb and Winston would be following in the Ford. When the bomb went off, I'd hit them from the front and Winston from the rear.

If they stayed put and didn't move her, then I'd come up with something else. I had no clue what, but I'd find something to get her out of the house. And if Studley did hurt her, then he wouldn't be long for this world.

I packed a cooler with food and a couple of water bottles, hauled them out to the truck, and took off.

I drove a couple hundred yards up the street and backed into a stand of red maples. I knew from the road I'd be hard to see. I turned the truck off and pulled out the bomb remote, setting it on the dashboard. I reached across the seat and rolled down the passenger side window and then did the same with mine. I then pulled the duffle bag closer and zipped it open, double-checking the contents. I removed a tear gas canister and put it next to me on the seat. As ready as I'd ever be, I leaned my head back to wait.

The late afternoon sun finally gave way to nightfall and the heat of the day changed to a comfortable chill. I did something I rarely did: I thought about God.

To say I was never a Bible thumper was an understatement. To be honest I could not have cared less about God. Even after the last few months, after becoming the Hand of God, I still avoided thinking about the afterlife, but for different reasons than before. Now I cared a great deal. It was knowing I could end up in Hell with Mikey that terrified me on many levels.

I wondered if all that I now did would tip the scales back into a trip upstairs instead of the express elevator down.

My predecessor as the Hand, Dominic Montoya, had been a former Mexican drug cartel hit man, having killed dozens upon dozens of people before becoming God's bounty hunter. When he died I couldn't help but wonder if he'd done enough to take the stairway to Heaven.

Listening to the night sounds I tried to come to peace with my difficult situation. For the time being, I became resigned to my current circumstances and put thoughts of the afterlife in a back corner of my mind and shut the door. All I could do was try and do my best with whatever came next and let the rest take care of itself. I prayed it would be enough.

~*~

The wait ended just before 11 p.m. Winston called and said, "Yo, Vic. They just pulled two SUVs around to the front of the house. Hang on a sec." After a minute, he continued, "They just loaded Samantha into the back of the first car along with the pretty boy we saw earlier. One driver. Four hired guns into the second one." Another pause. "And they're off. How you want to do this? We planned on one car, not two."

"I'll use the bomb to take out the guns and improvise on the first car. Get in behind them and be ready."

"Roger that. I'll give you a shout when we hit the straight stretch. "

It was time to place the bomb. The main drag out of the area where Samantha was being kept had a long stretch of road bordering a canal where there were few homes and little traffic. I made sure I was alone, eased my way onto the road, then pulled into the middle of the straightaway and stopped the truck. I got out and grabbed the old tire and dropped it in the grass at the edge of the road.

I then opened the passenger door and gently removed my gifted bomb from the floorboard and set it inside the tire. I walked a few yards away, looked and could barely see the tire. The bomb wasn't visible at all.

I jogged back to the truck, hopped in and quickly reversed course, backing in underneath the trees, but staying close enough to see the cars coming for a good distance. I picked up the bomb remote, flipped off the trigger guard, and waited. I geared up mentally for destruction and mayhem, something I was very good at creating.

My phone rang. "Here we go. They just hit the straight away." Winston said.

"Roger that," I replied.

I could see the headlights of the two SUVs. Lucky for me the two cars were several car lengths apart. I cracked a few knuckles on the steering wheel and shifted my neck from side to side to loosen up.

I knew I only had one chance to get this right. Blow it too soon and I risked stopping Samantha's car or missing them entirely, while leaving the gunmen free to attack. Blow it too late and I risked missing both cars. I failed to ask the militia guys how long a lag time between pushing the button and the explosion, but I guess I was about to find out.

Samantha's ride passed the tire and I counted one, two and pushed the button. The bomb went up with a huge explosion in the night. *Damn!* If they made me a small bomb, I'd hate to see what a big one would do. The explosion roared like a huge shotgun blast and the second car was blown onto its side and sent rolling across the road. The rear end of the first car, despite being a dozen yards from the blast, was pushed into a skid. The driver hit the brakes, trying to get the large SUV under control.

I floored the truck, shooting out of the trees, on an interception course. The first car gunned the engine and took off, as the driver kept the pedal to the metal, trying to dart by me. He came up short and at the last moment cut the wheel as my truck crashed into his front left wheel. The collision sent a shock through my arms and I struggled to hold onto the steering wheel and maintain control of the truck. I could only pray Samantha had on her seatbelt. The old Chevy weighed in at just over two tons, the SUV about a thousand pounds more. But as a battering ram, the truck served its purpose well enough.

With the impact, the two vehicles left the road, our bumpers locked together as we flew side by side through a small chain link fence. I slammed my foot down on the brake, but it wasn't enough to prevent us from soaring down an embankment and into the canal.

I stiff-armed the steering wheel as the truck and SUV smashed into the water, the impact tearing the two cars apart. My truck started listing to the left, and water poured in my open driver side window. I grabbed the duffle bag, zipped it closed and then shimmied my large body through the window as the water rushed in around me. I looked like a bear trying to slide through a doggie door. I gripped the top of the truck and pulled myself up and out, momentarily worried the truck would roll and trap me on the bottom.

I kicked away hard from the truck and hauled the heavy duffle bag behind me when the truck plunged completely under the surface of the water. The water must've been fairly deep, as my feet didn't touch bottom. I struggled upward and finally broke the surface, sucking in the fresh Florida air. I took several strokes to the shore and threw my duffle bag onto the bank.

Panic hit me when I turned and watched the SUV sink below the surface of the water with no sign of Samantha or anyone else making it out of the car. What if the electric door locks or windows didn't work? What if they were all unconscious from the impact?

Swimming over, I dove and followed the swirling whirlpool down with the SUV settling onto the bottom of the canal. I couldn't see anything in the dark muddy water and only found it when I banged my hand on the rear of the car. I felt my way to the back doors of the vehicle which landed nose down, the weight of the engine causing it to sink quicker than the rear compartment.

Most deaths from car submersions happen because people panic. The water pressure makes opening the doors impossible unless the inside of the SUV floods completely, but I found a back door and pulled on the handle to check. Nada. I felt a thump as someone started to kick out the door's window. On the second kick the window exploded outwards. I took hold of the edge of the remaining pieces, pulled hard, and dislodged them from the doorframe, slicing my hand in the process.

With my lungs screaming in protest I once again made my way to the surface. I popped up and took a deep breath. Winston was out of the Ford and standing at the edge of the canal, the car's headlights bathing the surface of the water in light.

"Samantha's still down there," I shouted.

He kicked off his shoes and dove in. As he did so, I heard another splash, this one from the other side of the canal, but I couldn't see anything.

I took a deep breath and prepared to follow Winston down when Studley came splashing to the surface about two feet away from me. We locked eyes and the weirdest sensation hit me, a sense of wrongness. If you asked me to explain why I wouldn't be able to, other than to say looking at him made my skin crawl.

I would worry about him later, I thought. I took another deep breath and dove down after Samantha. But Studley had other ideas and snagged my ankle to stop my descent. He yanked up hard, but my momentum dragged him under water with me.

I kicked out blindly with my other foot, doing my best to break his hold. I connected and he loosened his grip on my ankle, only to try to grab the other one and then tried to pull himself up my leg to get behind me.

I twisted in the water in time to circle my arm around his neck as he reached my waist, and then punched him in the face, over and over. He returned the favor, wrapping one arm around my waist, all the while hitting me with his other hand, using my mid-section for a punching bag. The water slowed our blows, but one landed solidly in my solar plexus, causing me to exhale the breath I was holding.

My focus changed from beating the ever-loving shit out of Studley, to needing to break his grip in order to find the surface. My lungs burned. In desperation I dug my thumb deep into his left eye, pushing as hard as I could as the amount of oxygen in my bloodstream decreased and carbon dioxide skyrocketed. Once the carbon levels reached a critical point I knew I would not be able to stop my lungs from trying to drink in every ounce of water in the canal, leading to a quick and painful death.

Finally, Studley yelled in garbled pain, losing his own breath and the grip on my waist. I pushed him away, kicking and straining for the surface, my head banging with one hell of a headache. It was only seconds that I was under water, but it seemed an eternity before my face broke into the cool night air and I opened my mouth and gasped for breath. A moment later Studley surfaced, doing the same about ten feet away from me. He glared in my direction with his one good eye, his left one already swelling shut, my other punches seriously ruining his pretty boy looks.

He snarled at me and spoke in a language I never heard before, but I didn't have to know the language to understand his meaning. He wanted to kill me and that was O.K. I planned on killing him first.

Before I could close the distance and find out which of us would be right, I felt a large object slap me in the side, and instinctively reached out with my hand, feeling something rough and bumpy go swimming by me.

Studley screamed incoherently at me, took one long stroke in my direction, but that was as far as he got. The alligator, which sideswiped me, burst out of the water and lunged forward catching Studley right where his neck joined his shoulder. His scream of defiance changed to one of utter terror. The gator turned over into a death spiral, taking Studley under, his screams dying as he did. Sucked to be him.

I heard a commotion behind me and saw Winston carrying Samantha out of the water. I swam to the edge of the canal and dragged myself onto the bank as Winston gently laid Samantha on the ground.

I moved to her side, gasping from the effort. Winston put his ear to her chest. His eyes squeezed shut for the briefest of moments and then they opened and he looked at me.

"Ah, man," he said, shaking his head. "I'm sorry. She's gone."

CHAPTER ELEVEN

All my anger and rage exploded inside me, I looked heavenward and howled at God. Samantha claimed God was dead, but I knew he was all too real and he continued to punish me for coming up short in the faith department. How much was enough? How much blood did God need from me?

I'd done everything He asked of me since becoming the Hand of God. I'd given up any semblance of my former life to live like a freakin' monk. My only friends were the two men who helped me hunt down and kill people. All I wanted was to see Samantha free from the clutches of the same people God wanted me to put down. And what was my reward? The death of the one woman I can say I ever loved. I picked her up and held her to my chest, too angry to cry. I brushed wet hair from her face, the face of an angel.

Winston stood and picked up the duffel. "Man, we have to get out of here. That bomb will bring the cops down on us and we've already spent more time here than we should've."

I knew he was right, but I just didn't give a damn. I just sat on the edge of the canal bank, and held Samantha. Winston threw the duffle in the trunk and opened the back door.

"You want to give up and let the shit roll over you? Fine. But not here. Get up and put her in the car. Let's go."

He put one hand under my arm and helped lift me to my feet, and I then picked up Samantha and gently carried her to the car. As I laid her on the back seat, her head rolled sideways and a little water trickled out of her mouth. I shook myself from my pity party and realized there was still a chance.

I dove inside and Winston threw the Ford in gear and we took off away from our rental and back towards Naples. I lowered the seat completely flat and stretched Samantha out with her head tilted back. I then checked her mouth to make sure there were no obstructions and started CPR. So help me God, if she dies because I didn't start CPR in time, because I was too busy blaming God for something I'd done? I wasn't sure what I would do.

Winston took the first right into a residential section of town just as the sirens could be heard rushing towards us. Another quick left and then a right took us away from the bomb scene and out of Naples.

I laced the fingers of my hands and began chest presses, all the time talking to Samantha. "Listen to me. You listening? Wake your ass up. You die on me now and you won't believe how pissed I'll be. You hear me? Come back to me. Wake up, dammit!"

Winston watched from the rearview mirror as I continued to press. Tears streamed silently down my cheeks. I'm not sure how long I did this, but between one press and the next, she began to cough out enough water to fill a swimming pool. I rolled her on her side. She continued to vomit up water and anything else in her stomach. She started to choke and then breathe in deep, ragged breaths. But dear Lord, breathe she did.

"Hot damn. She's back!" Winston shouted, and beat the dashboard with his fist.

I picked her up and held her close. Tears dropped down on her still damp face. I closed my eyes and said a quick prayer of thanks to God. I didn't know how long it would take for God to pound his message into my brain. But this time I felt blessed, as her fingers clutched my shirt, weakly at first, and then with more strength.

Finally, she opened her beautiful green eyes and stared up at me. How I missed getting lost in those eyes. Her breathing evened out and after a moment she closed her eyes again and fell asleep.

I wanted to shake her awake, with so many questions bouncing around in my head like a pinball machine. There were so many things I wanted to tell her. But I let her drift off. I could feel her heart beating against mine and, for now, I felt almost normal. She was safe.

Winston and I planned our exit from Naples in advance. He drove on through the early morning hours, staying on the back roads for about an hour. Then he caught Interstate 75 and headed north. When we hit Gainesville, Winston pulled up hotels on the GPS and decided on a hideaway motel off the beaten path. He found the place, parked, and then went inside to pay for two rooms.

I was looking out the front window waiting for his return when I felt someone watching me and looked down to find Samantha awake. I stroked her hair and a hint of a smile turned up the corners of her mouth.

She sat up and coughed a couple of times, then wrapped her arms around my neck and kissed me. If it were possible for my heart to jump through my chest, it would have at that very moment. After a minute she broke off the kiss, leaned back, smiled at me, and then hit me with a hard left to the chin.

"You goddamned son-of-a-bitch. You let them take me? How could you?"

I rubbed my chin. "I seem to remember a man had a gun to your head. What was I supposed to do? Let him put a bullet in your brain?" I replied.

I pictured our reunion many ways, and while I never thought it would be like running towards each other in a field of clover, I never expected this kind of reaction.

"A bullet to the brain would have been better than letting them kill Montoya and take me. Do you have any idea what the last three months have been like for me?"

"Oh. I'm sure. Sure looked like you and Studley were having a *terrible* time, arm and arm, when the police showed up, weren't you?"

I knew this wasn't true, but my anger was starting to boil over and I couldn't control myself.

"Don't even start with that, Vic. You don't know what you're talking about. Let me tell you something—"

She stopped when Winston opened the door and looked in the car at both of us.

"Uhh," he hesitated. "I only got two rooms. Do I need to go and get another?"

I said, "No," the same time Samantha said, "Yes."

"*No*," I repeated. "We'll be fine. We have some catching up to do. Don't we sweetheart?"

She glowered back at me, but didn't say anything. I got out of the car and retrieved a travel bag containing a change of clothes, along with the soggy duffle.

"You sure you guys are O.K.?" Winston whispered. "What did you say to her that pissed her off so much?"

"Not a frickin' thing. All I did was kiss the girl." There were times trying to figure out a woman was like trying to understand quantum mechanics, where particles can do different things all at the same time. It's just not meant to be.

He tossed me a room key, laughed and said, "You're in number eleven down on the left. I'm next door. Feel free to knock if you need a place to sleep." He headed to his room.

Samantha got out of the car and I reached inside and hit the door locks. Then she followed me to our room. I held the door open for her and flipped on the lights. She went straight to the bathroom and slammed the door shut.

I closed and locked the door and tossed the duffle on the floor. After a moment I heard the shower start and my mind went back to the last time the two of us were in a hotel room. That time I'd taken a shower and Samantha joined me, and we got to know each other in a very intimate way. I got the feeling if I tried to join her this time I could lose parts of me I value a great deal, if you catch my drift.

I removed my soggy clothes, grabbed a spare towel and dried off. I flopped down onto the queen-sized bed. I was on the verge of falling asleep when the bathroom door opened and Samantha stepped out wearing one towel around her hair and one around her body. She padded across the room and sat on the edge of the bed next to me.

"You never should have let them shoot Dominic," she said in a small voice, staring at the floor, the sadness of recalled memories coloring her words.

"Yes. I know." I sighed.

"And your brother? He's evil. You know that, too, right?"

"To my eternal ruin. Yes, I know." I wanted to reach out to her, to touch her, but I knew now was not the time.

She finally looked at me, her hands clasped tightly in her lap. "If you'd stepped aside, Mike would be dead and maybe Dominic would still be alive. Why didn't you?"

"Because I thought I could save him. I knew it was true, that he was Belial. But I still thought I could save him. If it had been your dad Montoya was sent to kill, would you have let him shoot him down?"

She looked away again. She was silent for a long time, but I waited.

"I don't know," she said finally. "I really don't. I just wish it had turned out different."

"So do I. But it didn't." I thought about that afternoon in Mikey's warehouse, Montoya being shot by Deveraux and how my brother kicked him when he fell. I pushed the memory away. "What happened to you over the last three months?"

Tears slowly rolled down her cheeks. I put out a hand and rubbed her arm. In one quick motion she turned and lay down beside me, putting her head on my chest, and began to cry.

"I . . . I don't want to talk about it," she stammered. "Not now. I need some time. O.K.?"

"Sure. No worries." I held her until the crying stopped.

I thought she might have fallen to sleep when she said, speaking into my chest, "They told me if I tried to leave, they'd kill you . . . that they knew where you were. And all it would take is a phone call, and you'd be dead. I went to sleep every night wondering if they had already killed you and just didn't tell me."

I let out a short laugh. "I told you. I'm a lot harder to kill than you think. I'm fine."

She raised her head and turned to look at me. "So was Dominic. But he's dead." She laid her head back down. "What will the world do now with no Hand of God."

"Well, about that. Turns out when one Hand of God dies another takes his place. Kind of like how they replace James Bond in the movies. Another guy steps into the part."

"Steps into a death sentence, you mean. Taking that job is suicidal. I wonder how long it will take them to find his replacement."

"Not long at all. They found Montoya's replacement pretty quick." I paused, then continued, "I'm the new Hand of God."

She sat up as if jolted by electric shock. "What? You can't! You can't be the Hand of God. It will kill you!"

"Samantha, I didn't really have a choice. When I let Mikey kill Montoya and then escape, I became one of the damned. When I die, I'm headed straight to Hell to keep Mikey company. I was offered a chance to redeem my soul by taking over for Dominic. I need to make things right."

"What? God talked to you? God told you that you were going to Hell? This is insane!" She started to tear up all over again.

I told her about Dominic Montoya's dying words, my meeting with Brother Joshua and about what I was doing as the Hand of God for the last three months.

"I've been trying to find both you and Mikey."

"So when you find your brother, you have to kill him? I told you before God is dead. Vic, let someone else do this. What's God done for you? For me? You don't *have* to do this. You and I can take off, if you still have the money I gave you. We can hide anywhere in the world. Let God and Satan fight it out themselves. We've given enough."

Now it was my turn to shake my head.

"I can't. God is very real. Deep down, you know that. I need to do this to get myself straight. It doesn't mean we can't still be together. But first I have to take care of Mikey. I don't know what happens after that, but you said it yourself, I'm responsible for him being on the loose. And in my gut, I know Mikey is planning something else. He told me as much, so I have to stop him. What if Mikey decides to kill another group of kids. Do you think I could live with myself knowing the only reason he's alive is me?"

She slid off the bed and looked into my travel bag and pulled out a T-shirt. She took off both towels and put the shirt on.

"It's just not right," she said, lying back down beside me.

I didn't say anything in reply and after a couple of minutes, she said, "Do you mind just holding me tonight? I know you want more, but for tonight, all I want is to sleep."

"Sure."

She was right. I did want much more. But I could sense she'd been through the ringer over the last three months and with the night's rescue, what she needed most was to rest and recover. We both got under the covers and though it took awhile, she finally fell asleep.

I lay there, feeling the warmth of Samantha's body next to mine and smelled the motel shampoo scent in her hair. I thought about life, in general, and then about the future. I had two major goals. One goal I accomplished by freeing Samantha from Satan and his minions. But Mikey remained elusive. I knew I was closing in on him, but he managed to stay one-step ahead of me.

When the Church discovered Samantha was no longer their hostage, it was going to be a major blow to them. With any luck, it might force them to stick their heads out of the holes they're hiding in. When they do that? I'll be ready to bash them in again.

CHAPTER TWELVE

Bill watched through the heavy falling snow as the ghost walked deeper into the woods. He tipped back the last of his Budweiser and tossed the can into the corner of the deer blind with the other empties. He felt a long belch coming and let her rip. I mean, who was around to complain but the snow and the ghost.

He blinked his eyes several times and looked out again at the ghost. It took a moment for him to remember he didn't believe in those damned things. But there it was, a white shape moving quietly, sometimes disappearing from view and then reappearing as it moved in and out of the trees. Huh. Don't that beat all.

Then he remembered he brought a pair of binoculars with him, along with the twelve pack of Bud. He wouldn't be here at all if it weren't for his whiney-ass girlfriend. When he told her he wanted to go and check out his deer blind and see if it needed any repairs, she said he loved it more than he did her. And if he loved it so much then maybe he should move out of her place and into the goddamned blind.

With two beers already making their way through his system, he told her, "Fine, I will."

So he gathered up his gear, his guns and his pride, and stormed out of the house, slamming the door behind him. All he ever heard was, "Nag, nag, nag."

On the way out of town he stopped by the Party Mart drive-thru and ordered up the twelve pack and a couple of cans of Skol. He drank another beer on the way and made a pit stop at a Thornton's gas station to take a piss and change into his hunting coveralls and hat—the one with the big gray UK emblem on the front. Good thing, because out here in the blind it was colder than a witch's titties. But hell, it kept the beer cold.

He pawed through his hunting bag and found the binoculars and after a few tries, got them focused in on the ghost.

I'll be damned, he thought to himself. It weren't no ghost, but a girl. And one damn good lookin' one, too. If the way she filled out her winter coat was any indication.

Tony Acree

He nearly had a heart attack and almost dropped the glasses when the girl stopped and looked right in his direction. With her nearly a hundred yards out, there was no way she could really see him. But here she was staring right back at him. Long, wavy black hair spilled out from inside the hood of her coat and framed one of the most beautiful faces he'd ever seen. And Lord Almighty, but her breasts pushed the fabric of her coat out in a way which made a carnal desire blossom despite the beer.

He licked his lips a couple of times and then his brain finally caught up to what his eyes had been showing him as the girl started moving again: she was dragging a body behind her. Under each arm she gripped the legs of some guy who was either unconscious or stone cold dead. He offered no resistance and his arms trailed out behind him. Bill laughed a bit at that one. Stone cold. Damn if it wasn't.

He fought past the beer fog and decided dragging some poor fool through the woods, in the snow, was beyond peculiar and needed checking out.

He hung the binoculars around his neck and picked up his Dakota 76 Safari rifle he always hunted with. Even though it wasn't deer season it didn't mean he might not shoot one out here on the farm. Then he climbed slowly out of the deer blind, making sure to place each boot carefully on the next rung of the wooden ladder. Last thing he needed to do was stumble and fall and break his frickin' neck. He wouldn't give his girlfriend the pleasure.

Once on the ground, he took a moment to orient himself and headed in the direction where he last saw the girl. At ground level it became harder to see through the snow, but he finally caught sight of her and picked up the pace.

The voice of Elmer Fudd ran through his mind. "Be vewy quiet, I'm hunting wabbits," and he began to laugh so hard he nearly stumbled. When he straightened up, he could no longer see the girl.

He looked around through the falling curtain of snow, but no dice. He couldn't see her anywhere. He shrugged his shoulders and kept going forward, and after a moment found her trail. He started following it while thinking about who she might be. The owners of the farm lived in Lexington and paid him to keep the place up, but they hadn't been out in a few weeks. The old man and his wife only came out when the weather turned nice. They had a boy who visited more often to go traipsing through a cave on the back part of the property, but there wasn't much to do when the weather got cold. He didn't think the man being dragged was the boy, but he'd know soon enough. If the guy was hurt and needed help, she was headed in the wrong direction. The farmhouse was the other way. There weren't nothin' this way but more woods and the cave.

His thoughts were interrupted when he nearly stepped onto the man's head where he was left under the snow-covered branches of an ancient oak. Man, hell. Boy more like it. If the boy were out of his teens, he'd stop drinking for a year. Then again, maybe not. That'd be a long time without a brewsky. He knelt down, resting the gun against the trunk of the tree, and felt the side of the poor guy's neck, just like they do in all them TV doctor shows. He didn't feel nothin', so he slapped his cheeks a couple of times, but still nothin'. Huh.

He glanced around and could see the tracks stop just beyond where she let go of his legs and two things struck Bill at about the same time. The first was a thought. If you are followin' someone and the tracks stop under a tree, then maybe they climbed it. He looked up and the second thing hit him was the girl as she dropped out of the tree and he took two boots right to the kisser, and they went down together in a heap. He tried to reach for his gun as blood burst from his busted lip, staining the pristine white snow with a streak of bright red blood, but the girl was all over him.

The girl straddled him, and any other time he'd be thrilled to have a woman this hot on top of his chest. But not this one. She began to hit him in the face, over and over. Bill raised his arms to try and protect himself, but God Almighty, this girl pounded the hell out of him. He could feel himself losing consciousness.

The last thing he thought before darkness overtook him was something some actress said a long time ago: there are no good girls gone wrong, just bad girls found out.

Seems he found one of those bad girls and then his world went black.

CHAPTER THIRTEEN

Samantha slept fitfully, often moaning in her sleep. If I slept at all it was only in brief spurts. When the sun managed to slip through the curtains early the next morning, I called over to Winston and asked him to find some place to pick up clothes for Samantha along with some breakfast for the three of us.

I got up, hit the shower and shaved. When I came out she was sitting on the bed watching the coverage of the bombing. She was still wearing my T-shirt. I plopped down next to her to see what the newsies were saying about my late night raid.

The local Gainesville TV stations were covering the event non-stop, as were all the major cable news shows. According to the reports, of the four guys in the first SUV, which took the brunt of the blast, two had to be hospitalized overnight. The other two were treated and released. It was also reported they were part of a private home security force and were heavily armed at the time of the attack.

The people in the second SUV which plunged into the canal, they were not so lucky. The driver drowned, never even getting his seatbelt unhooked. As for Studley, the gator did a real number on him. They never showed the body, but reports indicated the head remained attached to the body, but only barely.

We watched transfixed as the station played a video of the gator charging out of the water directly at the police and rescue crew, only to be gunned down before it could reach any of the people involved. Normally gators shied away from that many people, but this one had a hard-on for anything walking on two legs. I shuddered at the thought of the thing slapping me in the side on the way by. Close call. They said the names of the two dead men were being withheld until notification of next of kin.

According to a spokesman for the security firm, there was no one else missing and they could not speculate as to the motive for the attack. Guess the Church and Mikey didn't want the world at large to know Samantha had been in one of the cars. I had hoped as much.

There was no news on what happened to the driver of the Chevy. The police were still searching the canal, but so far they found no body. There was much speculation the driver had escaped the scene. You bet your ass, he had.

There was also much discussion on why the bombing occurred. The radical right blamed Al Qaeda and the President for not being tough on terror. Local experts speculated it was part of an on-going turf war between drug cartels in the southern Florida area. Then a call came in from a radical militia group claiming responsibility for the bombing, saying they did it as a blow against those who would take away their rights to bear arms.

The phone call was part of the deal I made with the bomb makers. For whatever reason, they disliked the rival militia group and wanted the Feds taking a harder look in their direction. The bomb was built in such a way as to point to them directly. I didn't care, since it muddied the water for investigators, which could only be a good thing for us.

"The guy I had the knock down drag out with in the water, the one the gator got, what was his name?" I asked.

"John." She quick glanced up at me, then back at the TV, engrossed with the news coverage. "That's what most people called him. And he was from Kentucky. You know him?"

"Nope. Never seen him before."

She turned the sound down on the TV and continued, "But like your brother, he had another name he used for some of the phone calls he got. He called himself Baraquiel." She shuddered. "He only showed up on the scene a few weeks ago, but he was a really bad guy. Really bad. I'm glad he's dead."

I watched as she sat, hands clasped together so tightly her knuckles turned white. I asked, "What did he do to you?"

She only shook her head No. I got off the bed and knelt before her, taking her hands in mine. "I'm here for you. Did he hurt you?" I could feel the anger bubbling to the surface, but the man was dead. The fact I couldn't find him and pound him some more disappointed me to no end.

"Vic, I said I didn't want to talk about it. O.K.? Please?" A single tear tracked its way down her cheek and so I dropped it. For now.

"Tell me about Mikey. What happened after you left the warehouse?"

"There's not much to tell. For the first few weeks they kept me drugged up. I wasn't exactly compliant and they wanted to control me easier. Once they were satisfied I no longer had the money, they eased up on the drugs and moved me around a lot. They told me if I tried to escape, they'd kill you. They showed me several pictures taken of you in different places."

"Really?" This surprised me. I would have thought they'd kill me in a heartbeat if they had a chance. The fact they hadn't kinda surprised me. I wondered if Mikey was showing brotherly love in leaving me be, but somehow I doubted it.

"Did you overhear anything which might point to what Mikey and the Church is planning next?"

"Sorry. Not a clue. They never talked about those kinds of things when I was around. And I wasn't allowed anywhere near a phone or computer or I'd have gotten in touch with you. I did see my dad once."

"He came to see me the first week we were in Florida," she said softly. "When I asked him about the Exodus Project, he laughed and told me to stay out of his business. Then he talked as if nothing had happened."

"He didn't deny it?" She shook her head in a small no. I thought about her father, one of the most powerful men in the country, hell, the world. And when his daughter took off with thirty million dollars of the Church's money, he sent one of Satan's twelve undead minions, a vampire named Eamon, after her.

My heart ached for Samantha. When she found out her father was a Satanist, she didn't think much of it at the time. She didn't believe in God or Satan. But then she found out not only was Satan real, but her father conspired to kill thousands of schoolchildren in his name? Can you imagine finding out you're Hitler's daughter? Same kind of thing. Then the son-of-a-bitch sent Eamon, a vampire, to track her down. Eamon was a serial killing child murderer back in the time of the great potato famine in Ireland. After his death, Satan gave him an opportunity to come back to Earth for a second chance at being a monster.

Samantha, with a little help from me, sent Eamon back to Hell where he belonged. But just the thought that her dad sent such a creature after her was devastating.

I stood, bent and kissed the top of her head. She wrapped her arms around my waist, pulled me close and cried. When the tears stopped, I kissed her again and began to pace the room. Then I got my phone out and used the Google Machine to try to find out more about Baraquiel. It took me several tries at different spellings and found nothing of interest. Then I hit the right spelling and my blood froze.

Winston knocked on the door and I let him in. He put bags of clothes and a sack of Krispy Kremes on the bed and I closed the door behind him. He turned to me smiling, but it faded when he saw the look on my face.

"What?"

"We have to get back to Louisville. *Now.* I think I know what Mikey is planning."

CHAPTER FOURTEEN

Bill woke up and his face wailed in agony. He gingerly reached up and ran his fingers over puffy skin. It felt like he was hit in the face with a baseball bat—not once, but about a hundred times. Damn if he didn't need a drink.

Then he breathed in and nearly gagged from the odor which assaulted his senses. One summer, in his younger days, he picked up road kill for the county. Wherever he was now it smelled like the bed of his truck after a hot summer day of picking up dead dogs, possums and raccoons. That's what it smelled like to him.

He managed to open one eye, while the other refused to cooperate and was completely swollen shut. He lay on his back and above him he could see a rocky ceiling bathed in a soft red glow. After a moment, he realized he must be in the cave Jason spent time exploring. How the Sam Hill had he gotten in here? And who turned on a red lamp? God, he needed more than one drink.

He slowly turned his head to the side, his neck protesting, and saw two people talking. One was one heck of a pretty girl. Black hair, angel face, and great ass. Man, what a body. Then the memory came rushing back of her on top of him beating the ever-loving daylights out of him and her hotness dialed back a few notches. She was talking to a tall, skinny dude with long white hair.

They both turned to look at him and for the first time in a very long time, Bill felt fear. Glancing away from them, he trembled, but it only surged inside of him when he saw the source of the smell: body parts and rotting flesh were scattered throughout the cave. He could make out several skeletons and what appeared to be teeth marks in the flesh.

The two of them walked over and stared down at him. "You said you wanted someone older and he is that," the woman said.

The man responded, "It is needed to command respect. People pay more attention if they think you have the experience of years. You are sure he's available?"

"Yes. He's yours." She said this with a smile that chilled Bill to his very soul.

He tried sitting up, but was overcome with dizziness and he collapsed back. "If you so much as lay a finger on me, I'll kick yer ass, Old Timer."

The man laughed and the sound was . . . beautiful. It reminded him of when his mom and dad took him to see *A Christmas Carol* at Actor's Theatre when he was a child, and the laugh of the Ghost of Christmas Past. Bountiful and joyful. And for the briefest moment his fear subsided and he was in awe.

Then the laughter stopped and the feeling left him and the stench once again assaulted his nose. The man knelt before him and said, "You are injured. I'm sorry my friend felt the need to do such things to you. Please, let me put you at ease."

The old man placed a hand on either side of his face, gently, and spoke in a language Bill had never heard before. It was lyrical and soothing. Miraculously, the pain and swelling in his body receded. He could fully open both eyes now and he stared up into the eyes of the old man. They were dark black and he could swear he saw stars falling in them. The fear was replaced by a calm which warmed his whole body.

Bill smiled up into his eyes and the man smiled back and everything was right with the world. But then, in an instant, it wasn't. He could feel the man's hands pressing tighter against his skull and in a rush, another being entered his mind.

Bill thrashed on the ground as his body fought the alien presence, but the "other" crushed his will and shoved what remained of him into the deepest recesses of his mind, cornered and cowering.

And this was no man. As the being took control, he sensed a presence as old as creation, with a power he could barely comprehend. As their minds blended together, he felt what the "other" felt: hunger, pain and anger. Anger so deep there was no bottom.

"Who *are* you?" Bill asked.

The presence responded, "I am Samyaza, captain of the Watchers and you have been chosen to help free my brothers. Once that is accomplished and we once again walk upon the Earth, we will take what is rightfully ours. As it was before, so shall it be again."

The woman smiled and nodded, repeating, "As it was before, so shall it be again."

And Bill knew he was powerless to stop them.

CHAPTER FIFTEEN

It took the rest of the day for us to drive back to Louisville. Arriving at the mission around nine p.m. road-weary, the three of us trudged down the hallway to Brother Joshua's office. We found him staring out the window at the night with the box I'd taken from Tommy sitting on top of his desk.

I knocked on the door and the three of us filed into his office. He turned around and said to us, "I see you were successful in freeing Ms. Tyler." Bowing his head slightly, he continued, "Welcome to the Derby Mission."

She crossed her arms and stared at him for a moment. "So you're the one who pretends to talk to God and will be the one to get Victor killed. How many men have you sent to their deaths?" So much for a pleasant greeting.

J moved to his desk and sat down, placing his hands on the desk, one on top of the other. If he was upset at Samantha's accusation, he didn't show it.

"Ms. Tyler, what we do, the Hand of God and I, we do to make the world a better place. Everyone dies. Everyone. The only question is what happens after we die. Victor, and those who came before him, all make a choice. None are forced into God's service. From the time of Adam, men and women have the freedom to choose their fate. Victor has chosen his."

Samantha snorted. "Like he had a choice. You tell him he will burn in Hell if he doesn't and what's he supposed to do?" I gently placed a hand on her arm, but she shrugged it off. "How do you even sleep at night?"

"I sleep perfectly fine, I assure you." He changed the subject. "Now that you are free, Ms. Tyler, what are you plans?"

She looked at me and I responded, "I was hoping she could stay here for a bit, until we can figure that out."

He pursed his lips. "Fine. We can provide you a room for a time. But you must work while here, Ms. Tyler. Also, you must sleep in your own room. We do not allow cohabitation here at the mission." He followed this with a pointed look in my direction.

"I understand." After a brief pause, she added, "Thank you." From our conversation the night before, I knew just saying thank you was hard for her.

Brother Joshua picked up the phone on his desk, punched a couple of numbers and asked, "Could you come here, please."

A few moments later, a young lady with short curly blonde hair and an easy smile stuck her head in the door. "Yes?"

"Samantha Tyler, this is Lisa Crain. Ms. Crain will you show Ms. Tyler to a room in the women's dorm, please? And make sure she has what she needs when it comes to personal items. Then work with her to find a volunteer schedule she is comfortable with."

"Sure. No biggie." She stuck out a hand and Samantha took it. "Come on, I'll give you the grand tour. It will take all of five minutes." she chuckled.

Samantha left without a word and Winston and I took a seat.

"We have a problem." I said.

I filled him in on what happened in Florida, then had Winston tell him about what went down at the Mall.

"Does the name Baraquiel mean anything to you?"

"It does." He tapped the box in front of him. "You should have told me about Winston and what happened. If you had we could have moved sooner on this. The name you overheard, Winston, was not Sam Yaza, but Samyaza."

"By sooner, you mean instead of freeing Samantha, right?" I replied.

"You must remember, Victor, as I told Ms. Tyler, you agreed to be the Hand of God and all that it entails. Once you made the decision, then God chooses your course of action. Not you. Withholding such information can have dire consequences."

He was right. I made the choice freely. But Samantha was also right in that I didn't have much of a choice. Serve or go to Hell. I wasn't bitter over the decision. Mikey wouldn't be walking around wreaking havoc if it wasn't for me. But it didn't mean I had to like it.

"I didn't think it was overly important at the time. We've known the Church would eventually try and come back at us, and I planned to tell you as soon as we got back. Now we're back. Now we've told you. As for this Baraquiel character? I looked him up and it doesn't look good, if he's the real deal. And let me guess, this Samyaza guy and Baraquiel are connected?"

He nodded. "Yes. Do you know anything about the Watchers?"

I didn't, but Winston did.

"They're fallen angels, right?" Winston asked.

"Yes. Back in the early days of Man, God sent two hundred angels to watch over the affairs of men. But they began to lust after human women.

After a time, they slept with women of their choosing and their offspring were the Nephilim. Great giants who preyed upon the Earth. The Watchers began to give men knowledge in mass that they were supposed to learn gradually: how to make better weapons, the art of mining, among others."

I knew it was just my imagination, but it seemed to get darker outside J's window and the light in the room dimmed as he continued to speak.

"Then God decided to punish the Watchers and rid the world of their seed. So he sent the Great Flood to drown the Nephilim. First, he sent an angel to warn Noah and his family in order to preserve the human race. They were the only ones free of the Nephilim genes. Then God sent the rain to end their existence. Once the Nephilim were destroyed, the archangel Raphael and others chained and bound the Watchers in the valleys of the Earth, to be kept there until Judgment Day."

"Wait," I said, "I've heard of them. They're called the Grigori. Right?"

"Yes. That is another name which has been used for the Fallen, angels who rebelled against God and were punished."

"So you're saying they've managed to slip free of their chains and are loose again? How's that possible?"

"Both yes and no. No, their physical bodies are still chained. If the Watchers had managed to free themselves, in whole, you would know, for they would be a plague upon the face of the Earth. So no, their physical bodies remain chained."

Winston said, "I get the feeling there is a really bad 'but' coming next."

Brother Joshua nodded, "Are you familiar with demonic possession?"

Once again, Winston's knowledge of the Bible was much better than mine. He said, "Then Jesus asked him, 'What is your name?' 'My name is Legion,' he replied. Then Jesus cast the demons out into a bunch of pigs which ran into a lake and drowned."

"Very good. You know, Victor, spending time with Winston could have a positive effect on you."

"You can both kiss my ass. So you're telling me they're out possessing people? Why now? How's that possible? And what does that box have to do with all of this?"

"I believe they are," Joshua said. "As for why now? My guess is they've been found by someone. Most demonic possession takes place via touch. For the Watchers to possess someone, they need to be in physical contact with that person. Their powers would be limited, as they can only do so much while in someone else's body, but they would still be formidable—if only because of the knowledge they possess."

"And the box? How is the box and Mikey connected?" I asked.

"If a person knew where the Watchers were being imprisoned and knew the right words to say, they could free them from their chains. This box holds a document almost as old as the written word. It's a vision of a follower of Lucifer, and it contains portions of the proper words needed to unleash the Watchers. The language is ancient Ge'ez, a South Semitic language which originated in Ethiopia. It seems your brother means to release the Watchers and set them loose on the planet once again."

Winston let out a low whistle. "And once free, they will again produce children. The Nephilim will walk the Earth. And with God's promise to never flood the planet again, there is nothing to stop them."

Holy crap. Giants? I remembered watching old B-movies with rampaging Cyclops pillaging the countryside. Seeing them in person was not something I wanted to deal with.

"Well, if that happens, wouldn't God just send Raphael and a few of his best buds to bust their asses back into whatever dungeon they were put into in the first place?"

Brother Joshua shook his head no.

"I'm afraid not. The fate of Man is now in their own hands. If the Watchers are to be stopped, it will fall to *you* to do so."

Great. All I need to do is kill a bunch of giant-making divine beings who've been chained up for thousands of years, who could end life as we know it. No problem. I could probably get it done before breakfast in the morning. Yeah, right.

"What do we do next?"

"Find your brother. In the meantime, I'll make a few phone calls. You may need help with this one."

Ya think? I thought to myself.

"You know what? This job needs a better benefits package. Especially since there are no retirement perks."

"You're wrong. In your case, it's the best retirement plan you could ask for. Your soul."

Then Heaven help us.

CHAPTER SIXTEEN

I woke up the next morning, showered, threw on a T-shirt which said, I Hope Your Life is As Good as You Portray On Facebook, my old Wranglers and boots and shuffled out with the down trodden who came in every morning to eat breakfast at the Derby Mission. Thanks to the snow, the place was packed with many of Louisville's homeless trying to find a safe, warm place to ride out the bad weather.

I was surprised to find Samantha standing next to Lisa in the serving line, spooning out scrambled eggs onto the plates of the young and old filing into the cafeteria.

When I stopped in front of her she offered a small smile and gave me a larger portion than the others. Lisa winked at me and added several pieces of bacon. An old geezer right behind me looked at the amount she spooned out for him and then at my plate and said, "I want what he's got, if you don't mind."

"You've only been here one day and already causing chaos in the food line." I said to Samantha.

She stuck her tongue out at me. I grabbed a cup of coffee and moved to a table in the far corner of the cafeteria away from everyone else. I noticed most of the people who came into the Derby Mission were not thrilled to be in my company. Perhaps they were intimidated by my size or the weird vibes they sensed from me. Maybe they simply didn't like my aftershave. I don't know. It worked to my advantage this morning.

After a few minutes, Samantha excused herself from kitchen duties and sat down across from me. She held a cup of orange juice in her hands, twirling the cup around in circles, but rarely took a drink.

I kept spooning in mouthfuls of eggs and bacon, and let her get to where she needed to be. After a moment, she sighed deeply. "I never said thank you for rescuing me. Again. You seem to be making a habit of that. Thank you."

She reached out a hand, tentatively, and covered one of mine.

"No worries," I said. "I just figured you like presenting me with a challenge."

"Hardly. Look, I know this has been hard on you as well. And I'm sorry for the way I've acted since you freed me. The last three months have been really tough."

"Ready to talk about it?"

"No. But I will be. Thanks for not pushing me. We do need to make some decisions, though. Like where I'm going to go?"

"If it's all the same to you, I'd like you to stay here for a bit. It's not exactly the Hilton. But with Brother Joshua, you'll be safe here."

She lowered her voice, "Speaking of Joshua, what do you know about him?"

"Truthfully? Not a lot. He's not the kind of person to talk about himself. Mostly he tells me who needs killing and I make it happen," I paused. "But one thing I do know, and I don't know how I know this, he is one man you don't want to mess with—kind of like when Lucifer walked into my office. I knew he was the Devil, no doubt about it. And when it comes to Joshua, kind of the same thing. I just know if you stay here, you'll be safe. Once I get this whole Mikey-thing taken care of, then we can talk about what to do next."

She nodded and glanced back at the line which was getting longer by the moment. "I guess I better get back to it. At least here I'm doing something worthwhile."

She squeezed my hand and then stood up, but before she left she asked, "Vic, will you do something for me?"

"Sure, gorgeous. Name it."

"Be very careful when it comes to Joshua. Please? For me?"

"Sure. No problem. But I think you're just upset at him over the whole Hand of God-thing."

She gave me a half-shrug and went back to the serving line. I watched her go, relieved she was safe, but worried about her nonetheless. I could understand why she wouldn't necessarily trust Brother Joshua, but I never picked up on anything I should be worried about—other than he kept sending me on extremely dangerous situations against foes who would like nothing better than to send me to the other side. But that came with the territory and I accepted it, more or less. There was always someone wanting to take me down.

Which raised an interesting question. I finished up my breakfast and asked Lisa if she'd seen Brother Joshua this morning. He almost never missed his time in the serving line.

"Oh. He was here in the cafeteria for a bit, but had to leave. I think he has a visitor and is in his office."

I thanked her and went in search of our fearless leader, and she was right. He was both in his office and not alone. A very large man wearing an orange workout shirt and black shorts, downing a Gatorade, was visiting with Joshua in his office.

Muscles rippled as he raised the bottle and drained the rest of the purple liquid, then heaved the empty bottle into the trashcan on the side of J's desk. His raven black hair, long and wavy, reached past his shoulders. I knocked on the doorframe and J waved me in.

"Victor McCain." I stuck out my hand and introduced myself.

He took it with a firm grip and said, "Andrew Colton. It's a pleasure, finally, to meet the Hand of God."

I looked at J and raised an eyebrow.

"I told you that you needed help. I've asked Father Colton to assist you in dealing with the Watchers. If they are, indeed, possessing people, and it seems likely, then you may need to have exorcisms performed. Father Colton is the best. I told him who you are and what you are facing."

"Father Colton, you're a priest? Father Brick, more like it." I said with admiration. "Wow. Let me guess: you're a member of the ball-busting clerical order?"

He laughed. "I'm not, though I am from a parish not too far from Venice Beach, California. I caught the red eye as soon as Joshua called. I've found when dealing with demonic spirits, it pays to be in shape. Things can occasionally get . . . a little physical. And if we really are dealing with the Watchers, then I have no doubt it will get extremely violent when we try and cast them out."

"Huh. I guess just putting a bullet in the body of the person they're using wouldn't be a good thing for the possess-e."

He turned serious. "No, it wouldn't. The only thing the host body has done wrong is not have a strong faith in God. Most are decent human beings who happen to be 'available' for the taking because they have lost faith in God. If you kill them to kill the demon, then there's not much chance for them to accept the Lord God Almighty before they die."

"Yeah. I get that. But as a last resort, it will kill the bad guy, right?" I asked.

"Matthew Chapter 12, verse 45, 'When an impure spirit comes out of a person, it goes through arid places seeking rest and does not find it.' They can be forced out by the death of the host or through an exorcism. If they leave voluntarily, they must have another host to transfer to for this to happen."

"Huh. Another question. You have to be touched to be possessed, is that right?"

"In most cases, no," Colton replied. "A person can be possessed simply by having lost faith in God. Demons look for empty vessels to fill. A soul filled with the light of our God Almighty, cannot be possessed. So I, for instance, could never be possessed."

I scratched at the stubble on my chin. "You're saying the Watchers are different?"

"Yes, the Watchers are not most cases. Because of how they are imprisoned, they would have to be near enough to be touched. I know it doesn't make much sense, but it's often like that in the world of demonic possession."

"All I really care about is if we track them down, do you think you can kick their asses out of the bodies they're in?"

With a smile as broad as it was confident, "If I can't, no one can. But yes, if you can keep them still long enough, I should be able to cast them into oblivion."

"Sounds good to me."

I turned to Brother Joshua and asked, "I want to get your opinion on something I thought of while eating breakfast. Samantha told me one way they kept her in line was by showing her pictures of me in different situations, telling me they could take me out any time they wanted to. Which begs the question, why didn't they?"

"Perhaps there is a reason why they chose to keep tabs on you instead of killing you," Brother Joshua replied. "When the Hand of God dies," he continued, "we never know who the next one will be. Your brother knows who the current Hand of God is. And as long as you're alive, that remains the case. If you die, he will not know where the next threat is coming from."

I nodded. This made sense. "Then I need to start mixing things up. How many people do you think we're going to be dealing with? How many of these Watchers are there?"

Joshua replied, "There are two hundred total, with twelve captains and one leader, Samyaza. So at the most, two hundred, although the total is likely much less than that."

"*Holy shit!* Two hundred? There could be that many fallen angels running around? Why does that not sound good?"

I've never lacked for confidence, but I mean, come on, two hundred of them? I started to think of what Samantha said about the Hand of God being a death sentence.

"Actually, I believe that total is already down to one hundred and ninety nine," Father Colton replied. "Brother Joshua filled me in on what happened in Florida. Like most Americans I've seen the video of the alligator charging out of the water, trying to take a hunk out of the rescuers on shore. I believe when the alligator bit into the young man, the fallen angel Baraquiel transferred to the alligator and then attempted to make contact with someone on shore. But they shot and killed the alligator before he could pull it off. With the alligator's death, he would be cast out into the arid wasteland." He stood up. "But take heart," he continued, "they probably haven't all made it to the surface, yet. So have faith, my friend."

Yeah, as if that made me feel any better.

"Faith I have," I replied. "Lives I have but one." I stood up as well. "Time to get to work."

"What do you suggest we do first?" Colton asked.

"Well, if the person has to be touched to be possessed, I suggest we start with the man Winston took out at the Mall, Mal McGeorge. If we can talk to him, then perhaps we can find out when the fallen angel took control of his body."

"Great," Colton said. "Let me get changed and we can head out," and he left the room.

"He's good, huh?" I said to Brother Joshua.

"The best. You will need him before this is done. Move as quickly as you can, Victor, for you can rest-assured the Fallen are doing so."

I let out a bone weary sigh and responded, "Aye, aye, Captain. Your wish is my command. Time to kick some fallen angel butt."

J shook his head as I walked out of his office. I got that a lot.

CHAPTER SEVENTEEN

Father Colton joined me, dressed in a traditional priest's frock. He still looked like a brick. On the way to McGeorge's house, he said, "I'm glad we're doing this. It's important I see this young man."

"Why's that?" I asked, as I drove down slush covered side roads. The snow had finally stopped. Nearly seven inches of snow had fallen while I was in Florida, a-typical for the Louisville area. I was already missing the warmth and sunshine of Naples.

"Once a demon is forced to leave a person's body, as I said, they must wander in an arid wasteland for a time. But eventually, they find their way back to the body they were in before—if that person hasn't had a change of heart when it comes to God. And when they come back, they can bring friends with them. Other demons they meet while wandering. It's not a good thing."

"I would think not."

We remained silent, lost in our own thoughts until I found the right house. I parked in the street and we walked up a freshly shoveled drive to a small but well kept home. I knocked on the door and after a minute a woman answered. She was what my mother would call "plump" and looked as if she'd been run through the ringer.

When she saw the two of us, she eyed us suspiciously and asked with hesitation, "Can I help you?"

"Mrs. McGreorge?" When she said yes, I continued, "My name is Victor McCain and this is Father Colton. I understand the police haven't caught the person who attacked your son and I would like to help. It's what I do for a living and I want to make sure the person who did this to your son is brought to justice."

"And you're, what, a private investigator?" While she hadn't closed the door yet, she still had not invited us in. "And you brought a priest, why?"

"Not exactly. I'm a bounty hunter. And I'm very good at what I do. And this would be at no cost to you. I just want to help. As for Father Colton, I heard what your son told the police about there being someone in his head. Father Colton is good at counseling people who feel they've been possessed by someone or something. He came with me in case he could offer your son help. How is he?"

With some reluctance, she opened the door and allowed us in. "Come in. My name is Evelyn. Let me get my husband." She motioned for us to sit in the family room and then she walked down the hallway and to another room. A door opened and she shouted, "Robert. We have visitors."

She closed the door and a conversation ensued in low tones. Footsteps came back in our direction and both Colton and I stood. Robert McGeorge, middle-aged and fit, came into the room, his wife right behind him.

He didn't waste any time. "My wife says you're a bounty hunter, that right?"

"Yes sir, I am. And I'd like to help. I think the person who did this to your son is mixed up with people I'm tracking. I'd like to see to it they pay for what they did to your son."

"What people?" I watched as he clenched and unclenched his hands several times.

"I can't tell you that. At least not yet. But I promise you, Mr. McGeorge, I will find them."

"If you know something, we could tell the police and they can make you tell who you're after," she said.

Robert McGeorge shushed his wife, raising a hand. "You look like you can deal out some punishment. You give me your word you will find whoever did this and hold them responsible for hurting our boy?"

"With a priest as my witness, you have my word."

I could make the promise because I was looking for the person who did this to their son, in a roundabout way. Winston would not have put the beat down on the kid if he weren't possessed by a fallen angel. And when I found Mr. Bad Wings, I did plan on putting the hurt on him.

He nodded. "Good. What do you want from us?"

"I'd like to speak to your son. I want to ask him some questions, if that's alright."

Robert dry washed his face with his hand a couple of times. "If you can get him to talk to you. Mr. McCain, they really messed up my boy. We keep him sedated. He keeps wailing about voices in his head. He says they're gone, but he's afraid they'll come back."

Colton and I shared a look and I thought to myself, you bet your ass they'll be back.

The priest walked to Mr. McGeorge, putting his hand on his arm and said, "I believe I can bring peace to your son, so that he will rest easy. I would also like to help."

Robert, choked with emotion, said, "We would appreciate anything you can do. Please. Help my boy."

Evelyn led them up a flight of stairs and down a hallway to a darkened bedroom. Heavy curtains were pulled across the window to keep the morning light from intruding. Mal McGeorge was lying in bed, bandages covered where his eyes should be. He was sleeping but not soundly, and he mumbled as he dozed.

Father Colton whispered to me and Mrs. McGeorge, "Please give me a few minutes to speak with Mal. I will come get you when he and I have had a chance to talk."

Evelyn looked at me questioningly. I nodded and we walked down the hallway a bit. Colton closed the door.

"You plan on hurting the people who did this, don't you?" Evelyn asked.

"I only use violence when I have no other choice. But I don't plan on being gentle. The people behind this are as evil as it gets, Mrs. McGeorge. I plan on putting a stop to them."

"Call me Evelyn, please."

She didn't say another word as we waited. About five minutes later, Colton opened the door and motioned for us to come in.

Mal was sitting up in bed, propped up by several pillows. The curtains were open and light flooded the bedroom. He had his face turned towards the light, even though he couldn't see it. A silver cross now hung from a chain around his neck and he was rubbing it, back and forth, with his thumb.

When his mom saw this, her hands flew to her mouth and then she rushed to her son's side. "Mal, where did you get that cross?"

He turned towards the sound of his mother's voice, opened up his arms, and hugged his mother. "The Father gave it to me, mom. He said I can keep it."

She looked at Father Colton and mouthed, "Thank you."

Father Colton smiled and said, "It's my pleasure. Victor, I think Mal is ready to talk to you now. Mrs. McGeorge, why don't you and I let them talk while I speak to you and your husband."

He led her out and pulled the door shut behind him. I sat on the edge of his bed

"Did Father Colton tell you why we were here?" I asked him.

Mal replied, "He did. He explained what happened to me and how I can keep it from happening again. He said there could be others who are going through what I went through." In a weak voice he continued, "How do you think I can I help?"

"When the demon took control of you, do you remember where you were? We're trying to get a line on who the first one was."

Mal thought for a minute. "I . . . I was at a coffee shop down near campus. It's a place where students go to hang out, chill, get some work done, ya know? Place called DJ's Perky Brew."

I nodded, then realized he couldn't see it and said, "I do know. So tell me about what happened?"

"Well, I was studying for a big statistics test I have coming up and I saw a girl I went to high school with at Ballard, Ruth Anne Gardner. I waved hello and she came to my table and sat down." He paused at the memory. "We talked for a bit and then she put her hand on top of mine."

He stopped again and I watched his Adam's apple race up and down his throat a few times. He rubbed the cross a bit faster.

"They can't hurt you anymore, Mal. You're O.K," I reassured him.

"I know, I know. It's just . . . when she put her hand on mine, I felt this charge shoot through my body and then he was just—there. In my head. I tried to fight back, but, man, he was like nothing I've ever even dreamed of."

"Did he tell you his name?"

"Yes. Chazaqiel. He kept telling me how blessed I was." He paused again. "Look at me, man. Do I look blessed to you?" He turned his face towards the window and the light.

"It might not seem like it, but yes, you are. You have a mom and dad who love you. You're still alive and the demon has left your body and if you listen to Father Colton, it can never return. Considering how it's turned out for at least one other person, you're ahead of the game."

He said, "I don't even want to know." After a moment he continued, "Can you stop them? The demons?"

"That's my job. Kicking ass and takin' names. Father Colton will be helping me. Along with a couple of others."

"Father Colton is cool. Good luck, Vic," his voice trailed off. "I think I'd like to be alone now, if you don't mind, and think about things."

"No worries, man. You heal up. It gets better from here on out."

He didn't reply, just kept facing the window. I made my way downstairs and found Evelyn and Robert speaking in the family room with Father Colton.

Evelyn said, "Rob and I have tried to get Mal to church, but he always blew us off. We made him go on Sundays when he was a kid, but when he started college he never went. Said he didn't really care much for God." She looked right at Colton, "But now. Maybe there's hope. He's not looked that peaceful since he came home. Thank you. Oh Lord Jesus, thank you."

Robert said, "And I thank you, too. But what I really want is for you to keep your word. And when you have, you let me know, you hear?"

"I do. I won't stop until I have. When I give my word, I keep it."

"Be sure you do." He shook both our hands and we left.

When we were back in the car, Colton asked, "Learn anything useful?"

I spun the wheel on my Ford and goosed it at the end of the street, sliding back and forth in the snow and slush as I made the turn.

"Yes. I did. I have a name. Let's get back to the mission so I can check it out. When you were with McGeorge, you weren't in the room with him very long. Did you have enough time to do your hocus pocus thing?"

Father Colton laughed. "No need for an exorcism. The demon left the body voluntarily. All I had to do was sever the connection so the demon won't be able to come back. Then it was simply a matter of convincing Mal of the existence of God. He was very open to my words of counsel."

"I bet. Do you think he's safe, then?"

"From demon possession? Yes. But he will have a long road back to being whole. What he experienced is rare and leaves a lasting impression. I gave him the name of a local priest he can talk to if he starts to doubt. But he won't. So what's next for us?"

"Time to go hunting."

CHAPTER EIGHTEEN

Winston kept his strides short as he made his third trip around the Louisville Water Company Reservoir in Crescent Hill. On most nice days the place was packed from dawn until dusk with walkers and runners, enjoying the serene view of the water and historic design of the gatehouse. The gatehouse was built in 1879, back when even water treatment plants were made to look beautiful, like a quaint old stone church. The path around the water basin was conveniently marked so people could keep track of their miles and there were plenty of benches to relax on after their exercise was over. It was an awesome place to work out.

But today, with the temperature barely reaching twenty degrees and several inches of newly fallen snow on the stone pathway, he was the only one brave enough to venture out to the reservoir. Back when he played for the Cardinals, his teammates would start to bitch and moan when the weather turned cold, but not Winston.

Being outside when every breath sent a shock to the system made him feel more alive than working out on a hot summer day ever could. And today, he needed the peace and quiet of a good workout. Despite the cold, he only wore sweats and a hooded shirt as he put in his miles.

Earlier he received a call from Vic telling him how it went with Mal McGeorge and what they learned from him. By all accounts Mal was a good guy and it bothered Winston more than he wanted to admit about what he'd done to the young man. Granted, if he hadn't kicked his ass, the Watcher would have continued to control McGeorge. But that was small consolation considering the physical damage Winston inflicted.

He let his anger at being followed get the better of him, he admitted to himself. He should have handled the confrontation differently. He shrugged off the thought and decided live and learn. There was nothing he could do to rewind time and try a different solution. So be it.

He picked up the pace of his jog. While on the backside, a man walked up the snow-covered steps of the reservoir, looked around and then stopped. He rested his hands on the black iron railing and gazed down into his reflection in the water. The man was dressed in jeans and a heavy winter coat, so it was doubtful he was there to work out. But many came to the reservoir for the view, so his presence was no big deal.

Winston rounded the corner and began to make his way down towards the man. The stranger turned around, leaned against the rail and put his hands in his pockets. He appeared to be a little over six feet tall and solid. Even from this distance, Winston could see the steam from his breath rising into the still morning air.

When he was almost even with him, their eyes met and Winston gave a short nod and the man nodded back. There was a slight smile on the man's lips, but not his eyes. Winston realized he'd seen the same dead fish stare before on Mal McGeorge at the Mall.

If this thought were even a fraction of a second later, he'd be dead. But as soon as it registered, he was spinning in defense and the knife meant for his back struck a glancing blow, tearing his hoody and slicing open skin across his rib cage. Winston grunted with pain, but continued the spin, his foot slamming into the side of the man's head in a circle kick, knocking the stranger sideways.

The man recovered and began tossing the knife back and forth between his hands circling Winston. "A little different this time, huh boy? This time, I picked a body to match yours. I'm going to enjoy killing you."

"Chazy-Q, I figured it had to be you."

Winston could feel blood dripping down his side, but he pushed the thought and the pain away and concentrated on the Watcher.

"Your weak ass couldn't carry my piss bucket. You should've stayed buried in your hole because I'm going to send you out of this body, too. And when I do, you got nobody to return to. We done took care of that. You're going wandering. I know that section of the Bible and I bet your ass you do, too. No water, forever thirsty, never finding rest. You have so much to look forward to."

After what he'd done to Mal McGeorge, Winston didn't want to hurt this man, but looking at the hatred on the other guy's face, and the knife in his hand, he wasn't sure he could avoid it.

When Chazaqiel made his move, Winston had to admit, he was fast. Very fast. But not fast enough. The Watcher stabbed quick and low, aiming to gut Winston. Instead of dancing back and away from the attack, Winston pivoted and stepped forward, wrapping the man's knife arm with his and lifting up, while pressing downward on the man's shoulder in a quick motion, dislocating the arm from its socket.

The man dropped the knife and swung hard with the other hand, firing several quick jabs, pounding Winston's wound. Winston, grunting with pain, reversed his motion, hooked the man and tossed him off his hip, sending the man crashing into the fence. Winston stumbled and fell into the snow, but quickly regained his feet.

Winston kicked the knife into the water and held his side, the pain intensifying. He decided trying to stop the man without severely hurting or even killing him wasn't an option. Winston glanced around to see if anyone else was at the reservoir, but the weather had kept all sane people inside their homes. He was on his own.

The man bounced up, his right arm hanging to his side. Winston retreated a few steps.

"Looks like you're taking the same ass whipping you took at the mall. Here I thought you angels were supposed to be kind of tough badass types. You've lost your touch."

The man snarled and in one quick motion, slammed his shoulder into the side of the fence, popping it back into joint.

Damn, that had to hurt, Winston thought.

The man/fallen angel growled and then charged Winston again and over the next five minutes the two traded blows, turning the snow under foot into dirty bloody slush. As the fight continued with neither of them gaining an advantage, Winston had to admit to himself, he was losing.

The longer the fight continued, the more weak he felt due the blood loss from the knife wound. The other man didn't seem nearly as tired as he should have been. Perhaps having a fallen angel deep inside you had its benefits after all. He knew that if he didn't end this now, it would be the end of him. While Winston had no doubts as to where he was going after his mortal coil gave up the ghost, he was in no rush to get there.

Backing up a step, he slipped on the slush and fell to one knee. Seeing an opening, the fallen angel once again charged. But the slip was a perfectly timed ruse and Winston was ready for him. Years and years of football training paid off. From the time he was a little kid he was taught in order to take a man down you first must get low, get under the other man's defenses, and then come up hard. And that's exactly what he did. As Chazaqiel began to come down with a hard right, Winston shot forward underneath the blow, one arm going under the other man's crotch, the other around his waist. He lifted him high off the ground and then flung him backwards onto the rod iron fence.

As the man ricocheted off the fence, with all the power he had left in him, Winston grabbed the man's head in both hands and slammed it straight down onto one of the iron spikes.

The man's eyes bulged and his mouth opened into a silent scream.

Winston let go of him and allowed the man to slide to the ground. His eyes found Winston's and the anger he'd seen in them earlier was replaced with sheer horror.

Winston sagged to his knees, breathing as if he'd just run a marathon, and began to pray. The man reached out weakly and Winston took his hand. The man/fallen angel tried to speak, but blood poured from his mouth.

Winston continued to pray for the man's soul, if not the angel's, and a moment later felt the man's hand relax in his grip and he knew he was gone. Winston felt tears fill his own eyes, for the life stripped from this man, as he was nothing more than a victim. He had no idea if the man believed enough to make it to Heaven, and the doubt gnawed at him.

Winston reached into his pocket, slowly pulled out his cell phone and dialed 911. He told them he was attacked while running at the reservoir and to please send police and an ambulance. The dispatch operator was asking for more information when he ended the call and then dialed Victor. He gave Vic a quick rundown on what happened and then told him he would call him later and hung up before he, too, could ask a lot of questions.

He looked again at the lifeless man and the grim scene surrounding him. He knew what he'd done would forever damn the man he killed, but he had little choice. The security cameras around the reservoir, no doubt, recorded the whole attack.

He turned off his phone and, with a shaking hand, put it back into his pocket. He looked around the reservoir a final time before slipping into unconsciousness on the bloodstained snow.

CHAPTER NINETEEN

"Winston? Winston?" the phone disconnected right when Father Colton and I pulled back into the Derby Mission.

"Problems?" Father Colton asked.

I muttered a profanity under my breath and threw the phone onto the dash.

"Yeah. Seems we're down both a fallen angel and a bounty hunter." I relayed what Winston told me. "He said he's been knifed, but didn't think it was too bad. He called an ambulance. When they arrive, they'll probably take him to University Hospital, downtown. I better get down there."

Colton laid his hand on my arm and said, "Why don't you let me go. You won't be of any use sitting in a hospital. You need to stay focused on the investigation. That means tracking down Ruth Anne Gardner. Winston will understand."

He was right and I knew it. It still pissed me off. "We shoulda been more careful. We knew they were following him before and we should have expected they would again."

We got out of the car and made our way inside. "Stop beating yourself up over it. He's a big boy. Joshua told me about him and what a help he's been to you. Look, I'll go tell Joshua what happened and then head down to the hospital. You go do what you need to do."

I ran a hand through my hair, which I was sure was starting to thin out as often as I pulled it these days.

"Yeah, yeah. Thanks. You're right. Call me as soon as you know something about Winston, O.K?" I gave him my number and we parted ways.

I went to my room, turned on my computer and ran "Gardner, Ruth" through my databases and found one the right age enrolled at the University of Kentucky. At least her school choice was on the side of the righteous. I found a listing for a previous address over off Crossmore Lane, not too far from Ballard High School where both she and Mal McGeorge attended high school.

I wrote down the address and headed back out into the late morning cold. As I made my way to the east side of town, I plopped in an old Bonnie

Raitt CD and mulled my options. I considered the connection between Mikey and the Watchers. If my body was chained in some deep dark valley and I found my way to the surface, then I'd want to find someone to set me free.

This made me wonder about Tommy Spenoza. He shipped out construction equipment to Mikey. To dig them out? Possibly. The Watchers could end up being a backdoor way of finding Mikey if they were working together. The fact my brother was trying to track down things like the box with the parchment with the incantations to set them free, then you'd think they were in cahoots. There was always the outside chance Mikey wanted the stuff to try and keep them from not getting free, but who was I kidding?

Mikey and his slave master, Lucifer, wanted chaos in the world and releasing a group of two hundred pissed off fallen angels would certainly be enough to put the world into a tailspin. And I needed to make sure it didn't happen.

My mind drifted to Samantha and what our future would be like. But again, I was kidding myself. What type of future could the two of us have? As long as we were together, she was a target, like Winston. As the Hand of God, I'd never be able to reach old age with grandkids bouncing on my knee. At least I couldn't see how that would ever take place. Dominic Montoya, the Hand before me, died in his mid-thirties—early forties, at the latest—and he was one of the best contract killers on the planet. All his skills were not enough to keep him alive to become an AARP member.

Which begged the question: what did I want from Samantha? I loved her, wanted a future with her, all of that was certain. That I would never have one with her? That was nearly as certain, too. With an effort I snapped out of my minor funk. Time to concentrate on what was going on in the here-and-now, I reminded myself, and let the future take care of itself.

Gardner's home was a one-story brick ranch with an older model Toyota Camry in a driveway still covered in snow. There were no tracks in or out. So, whoever owned the car hadn't left in the last day or two.

I parked in the street and made my way to the door, ringing the bell and rubbing my hands to keep them warm. I hated to wear gloves because, in my line work, you never knew when you needed to pull your gun out and shoot the hell out of something. With my luck? The fabric would catch in the trigger and I'd never get a shot off.

I was about to ring the bell again when I felt the icy cold of a snowball explode on the side of my head. I turned towards the direction of the attack with my hand instinctively going under my coat to the butt of my gun, only to see a kid at the corner of the house laughing his ass off.

"Oh, man, I got you good." The kid was about twelve years old, dressed in snow pants, a coat, and a double-eared green knit cap with black snowflakes all over it which he pulled down tightly over his ears. In his other hand he held another snowball.

"Don't you dare throw that thing at me." I warned him.

And then he did. The kid had a pretty good arm and the snowball was heading straight for my face. But in one motion I snagged the snowball out of the air and hurled it back in his direction, hitting him in the right leg.

"Ow! Not fair!" he yelled, and started making a couple more of them. I did the same, scooping up snow from the porch. I spent the next couple of minutes reliving my childhood with the kid, trading shots back and forth. Most of them missed wildly, but it was fun.

Then I realized the front door was open. On the other side of a storm door an attractive woman somewhere north of fifty, dressed in pajamas and a robe, stood there watching me.

I raised my hand at the kid and said, "Enough, enough. Adult alert." I nodded towards the front door and the kid waved and took off again for the backyard.

I brushed snow and ice from my hair and coat and asked, "Mrs. Gardner?"

"Ex-Mrs. Gardner. It's Huffman now. What do you need?"

"My name is Victor McCain and I wanted to talk to you about Ruth Anne."

A hand went to the top of her robe and squeezed it shut.

"Have you found her? Do you work with Mr. Clifford?"

"May I come in? It's bloody cold out here."

She unlocked the door and opened it, standing back to let me in. "I'm sorry. Come in, please."

The air carried the scent of fresh baked cookies. She lead me into the living room where I took a seat on a sectional couch and she opted for a wingback chair across from me.

"No, ma'am. I don't know Mr. Clifford. Who is he?" I said.

"A private investigator I hired to find Ruth Anne. Why are you looking for my daughter?" She rested her hands in her lap, and kept rubbing one thumb with the other.

"One of her friends was attacked and I'm trying to find the ones responsible. I think she may know the people involved. So I was hoping to ask her some questions. Do you know where she is?"

"Not exactly. She dropped out of school and took off. I know she really didn't like college, but this isn't like her." She paused and then asked, "I'm sorry. But do you have some form of ID?"

I got my billfold out of my back pocket and took out my bounty hunters license. She studied it for a moment and then handed it back.

"What's the name of her friend?"

"Mal McGeorge. They went to school together at Ballard."

"I saw the report about what happened to him on the news. Can you wait here a minute?"

I said I would and she left the room. She returned a short time later with a sheaf of papers in her hand.

"Ruth Anne and I always talk every couple of days. When several days passed and she didn't answer, I called and talked to some of her friends at U.K. and they said they hadn't seen her for days. So I filed a missing persons report. The police in Lexington looked into it and had a video of her taking money out of her checking account at an ATM machine. The fact she looked normal, not under any duress, suggested to them she'd just taken off."

"Has she ever done this before?"

"Never. She's not the world's greatest student, but she gets by. That's why I hired the private investigator." She handed me the papers. "Looks like she's not the only one. A number of college kids in Lexington and here in Louisville have all gone missing. It's like they all dropped off the face of the Earth."

I started reading the report.

"How many of them did she know?"

"At least ten. But the news isn't all-good. Did you hear about that bombing down in Florida?"

I kept a neutral look on my face and said, "Yeah. I've heard a bit about it. Why?"

"The guy killed by the alligator, the one that ended up in the canal? His name was John Gabriel. He was one of the missing students. Mr. Clifford says his parents had no idea where he'd gone, and then he turns up dead. It's horrible."

"Aw, man. That's really unfortunate. Did they ever learn why he was down there?"

"I don't know. But I've contacted the parents of several of the other missing kids and they're like me. All good kids who've dropped out of school and out of sight and we have no idea why." Her voice cracked and she pulled a tissue from a pocket and began dabbing her eyes.

I knew why, lady. They were infected with the seed of a fallen angel. And ten of them. When I learned about Mal McGeorge and Ruth Anne, I had hoped they would be the only ones, but I should have known better.

"Where does Clifford think Ruth Anne is now?"

"That's just it. He tracked her movements to Hawaii. He flew out there a few days ago and I haven't heard from him since. Neither has his office. All of our calls go straight to voicemail. Mr. Clifford was worried they were mixed up with some kind of cult. Do you think she's in danger?"

Holy crap. Hawaii? I could see the helplessness and fear on her face and I wish I could have put her mind at ease, but I couldn't. Because now I was worried. Kurt was in Hawaii. They'd sent someone after Winston, put one with Samantha, no doubt waiting on me. And one in Hawaii? That couldn't be a coincidence.

"I don't know. But I intend to find out. Do you have a way to make me a copy of this report?"

"Yes. I'll be right back."

She gathered up the papers and left the room. As soon as she was gone I got out my phone and called Kurt. It rang several times and then went to voicemail. I left a message for him to call me. Right away.

Kurt wanted to spend his time lying low in paradise. Now it seemed Hell had come calling.

CHAPTER TWENTY

Kurt sat in the dining room of the hotel, moping. Ruth Anne was still mad at him and refused to see him for the last couple of days. She said she would call him if and when she wanted to see him and he would just have to wait by the phone. And so far his phone refused to ring.

He was on his second helping of pancakes when the call from Victor came in, but he let it go to voicemail. He didn't have the heart to talk to him. All he wanted to do was drown his sorrows in blueberry pancakes and maple syrup. The bad guys of the world would just have to wait.

He was debating on whether to add an order of biscuits and gravy, knowing he would have to run a lot of extra miles just to break even with the calorie count, when Ruth Anne scooted onto the seat next to him in the booth, bumping his hip so he would scoot over and give her room.

"Miss me?"

She wore a blue sundress with her hair pulled back into a ponytail and it was as if the sun had returned from a month's absence.

"Miss you? You have no idea how much. I mean, I called you every day and you just ignored me. I figured you'd met someone else, or gone back to the mainland or, hell, I don't know what. But miss you? It was like someone had removed all the music from the world. Like all my food lost its taste. Like—"

"Uh, Kurt?" she interrupted him.

He stopped. "Yes?" He looked into her eyes and for a moment he had the weirdest sensation of watching stars fall, but it passed. "Yes, Ruth Anne?"

"Shut up, will you? I want you to take me out on the island shopping. Then we're going back to my place and I'm going to fix you dinner. And you are not, I repeat, *not* allowed to leave. You're spending the night. Can you handle that?"

He swallowed hard a couple of times and realized he could. It was time to make the final jump into a real relationship. He got his phone out saying, "Let me just make a couple of phone calls. A buddy just called and I should—"

Once again she interrupted him as she snatched his phone out of his hand and dropped it into her purse.

"Not a chance, Big Boy. I can't have you called into an emergency software meeting, now can I?" She smiled coyly.

"But it will only take a minute, I'm sure."

She began to pout. "Kurt, it's like this. Today you're either mine, or you're not. If you want your phone back, then fine. You can have it. But I'm out of here. Today I want you to disconnect from everything else. Today is all about us. Can you do that? For me?"

Kurt thought about it and decided she was right. He did need a day all to himself. Free from the Church of the Light Reclaimed. Free from thoughts of Satan. Free from Vic, Winston and free from all the stress their life had become. Free to let his hair down and have fun.

"I can. Sounds great. You know what? Keep the phone the rest of the day. I don't need it. Where do you want to go first?"

"I think we'll wander a bit and see what we come up with. I promise you, Kurt. This will be a night you will never forget."

~*~

Huffman came back and handed me a copy of the P.I.'s report. I took a card from my inside coat pocket and handed it to her.

"Here's my card. My cell number is listed at the bottom. If you hear from Ruth Anne, I'd appreciate you calling to let me know. If I find out anything, I'll do the same."

We both stood. She offered her hand and said, "Mr. McCain, I don't know how to thank you or pay you for that matter. All the extra cash I had to my name I spent on Mr. Clifford."

"It's Victor. And don't worry about it. I'm doing this pro bono. Something's going on and I plan on getting to the bottom of it." Like banishing several fallen angels to the abyss, but somehow I got the feeling honesty would not be the best policy right at this very moment.

"Please, it's Rose Mary. Is it alright if I have Mr. Clifford contact you? When I hear back from him?"

"By all means, please do. Was that your son I was trading shots with outside?"

She smiled and said, "Yes. His name is Timothy. He and Ruth Anne are almost ten years apart. I haven't told him what's going on with his sister because I know he'd worry. He should enjoy just being a kid." The smile vanished. "Victor, please do what you can to bring my baby back to me."

I assured her I would and headed back to the car. I called Kurt again, but with the same results. I began to get a bad feeling about what was going on way out west, but couldn't do much about it at the moment.

Thanks to the work of the private dick, I had a lot more information to digest. Since it was lunchtime I decided to drop by Molly Malone's, an Irish pub, for a bite to eat. I parked across the street in the PNC parking lot and walked to the corner. When the pedestrian crosswalk sign turned in my favor, a black limousine pulled up next to me and a burly bald-headed man in a black suit and tie got out of the front seat, went to the back door and opened it.

"Get in," he said.

"I bet the chicks really dig that type of intro, Big Guy, but you're not my type. It doesn't really do anything for me."

He pulled back the edge of his suit jacket so I could see the gun he was wearing in a shoulder holster. I laughed and pulled back my coat.

"Mine's bigger, and in this case, size really does matter."

I think he was getting ready to actually find out the truth of that statement when a man leaned across the back seat and said, "That's alright, Brad. Mr. McCain, all I really want to do is talk. You have my word. Brad is ex-Marine and thinks in a very straightforward manner."

I glanced into the car. "I'll be damned, Congressman Tyler. What a surprise. As far as your handyman goes, what else would you expect from a jarhead? Tell me, what brings you to the great Commonwealth of Kentucky?"

My tone was light, but my senses were on high alert. I was standing in a very exposed position talking with one of the most dangerous men on the planet, Satan's Pope, no less. The chances of me getting into a car with this man were about the same as me being named a Victoria's Secret lingerie model.

"I think you know why I'm here. Please, get in. You have my word you won't be harmed."

Cyrus Tyler looked great for a sixty year old. His face showed nary a wrinkle and his hair, while going gray on the sides, was still a dark brown. Granted, his smile would look better on a great white shark, with about as much warmth, but his voice held the timber of a professional baritone.

His brand of politics would make the most extreme Tea Party candidates look timid: a far right-wing nut job who thinks homosexuals should be shot, Liberals should be jailed, and anyone who doesn't think the way he does should buy a ticket on the next boat back to wherever in the hell they came from. As the current majority leader in the House of Representatives, many think he's in line to be the next Speaker of the House.

I looked over to Molly Malone's inviting front door and said, "I tell you what. I was just about to have lunch across the street. Why don't you find a place to park your chariot and join me. Leave the jarhead at the door, though. He might scare any women and children inside."

Brad flexed his neck muscles, but like the good pit bull he was, stayed in place until his master told him to move.

I didn't wait for an answer but crossed the street, using my well-developed peripheral vision to try and watch every place at once. I pushed my way inside and breathed a bit easier when the door closed behind me with no one putting a bullet in my brain. Yay me.

I moved to my regular table where I could watch all the entrances at once and waited. After a few minutes Congressman Tyler strode into the restaurant as if he owned the place walked over to my table and joined me. The former marine stayed outside. I wondered if he was housebroken.

A waitress walked up to us with two menus and handed one to Tyler and offered me one, but I waved it off. She stared at the congressman.

"You look familiar. Are you from around here?" she said.

He smiled at her and replied, "I get that a lot, but no, I'm not from around here. I'm here on business and decided to stop and have lunch with a friend."

I bristled inside at the thought of this man calling me "friend," but kept a calm exterior.

"Janice, I'll have the usual, please." She nodded and made a note on her pad.

Tyler handed the menu back to her and responded, "I'll have whatever he's having. Thank you."

She smiled and went to place the order. If he was curious as to what the "usual" was he didn't ask.

"So, where is she?" he said.

I knew who "she" was but said, "I'm sorry, could you be a bit more specific?" He gave me his best steely glare which I'm sure intimidated most of the people he dealt with on a daily basis. But I'm not one of those folks. I stared back, trying not to blink. After a minute or two, I couldn't help it and blinked anyway. Damn. I hated losing the staring game in grade school. Still did. Before one of us could break the silence, Janice stopped back by the table, and dropped off a couple of Guinness Dark Lagers.

He waited for her to leave again and finally said, "Let me explain something to you, Victor. I love my daughter very much and when someone steals her from me, it upsets me. Greatly."

I nodded. "I can only imagine. But she's, what, twenty-four years old? I believe she's old enough to make her own decisions. And being kidnapped and stuck in whatever basement daddy wants to hide her in is not what she wants." I didn't mention she hadn't exactly been thrilled with me either the night of her rescue, but why bring up the bad stuff.

Sitting and talking to the man was beyond surreal. If Samantha and I ever tied the knot, he would be my father-in-law. A father-in-law from Hell, almost literally. I honestly believed if I lived long enough, at one point, I would be asked to hunt down this man and drive a dagger through his heart. Love makes for strange family arrangements.

"Let me explain the situation to you more clearly. When my wife died, many years ago, the only thing left in my life was Samantha."

I laughed. "Well, that and a deep hatred for God. After all, you did sell your soul to the guy who finished a distant second."

He ignored my barb. "I kept her close, perhaps too close. She was too involved in what I was doing with the Church. I thought she would feel the same way I did, but I guess not. When she ran a few months back, I panicked. I knew there were people who would hurt her, just to get at me, and I did everything I could to find her and bring her back home, where she'd be safe."

I pursed my lips. "She ran because she discovered her father was one mean son of a bitch who planned to murder thousands of innocent children. And you wanted to protect her? So let me get this straight. To protect her, you sent a vampire to hunt her down? Eamon? That's your idea of safe?"

"Eamon had a way of getting things done. He would do what it took to find her, no matter the cost. I was desperate. So yes, I asked him to help find my daughter. She'd taken something that didn't belong to her and there were some of my associates who wanted her dead. I would not allow it."

"You sure have a strange way of showing fatherly love, you know that?" We took another break as Janice brought over two bowls of shepherd's pie. The bowls were piping hot with steam curling into the air and the smell beyond good.

"Hot shepherd's pie on a cold day is good for the soul," I said. "And Lord knows yours needs all the help it can get."

Tyler continued to ignore my barbs and took up the previous conversation.

"And you think she will be safe with you? You're a dead man walking and I want my daughter nowhere near you when this blows up in your face. As hard as it may be for you to believe, I do love my daughter. If she stays with you, she will die."

I picked up a spoon, lifted a large helping of the stew to my lips, blew on it and began to eat my lunch. Tyler did the same and for a moment we ate without saying anything. I was stalling because I knew he was only saying the same thing which kept me up at night. In one nightmare, Samantha and I were lying in bed, asleep, when I awoke to find Eamon sitting on the edge of the bed, blood dripping from the vampire's mouth from where he ripped out a side of Samantha's neck. When I woke up the next morning, the sheets were wet from sweating through them during the night. The fact her father was an evil bastard didn't make him wrong on this score. I picked up my napkin and wiped my lips.

"Perhaps you're right. But the choice is not yours or mine. It's hers. And unlike you, I'm letting her decide on her own. Who knows? In the end she may tell both of us to kiss her ass and disappear."

Tyler downed a large portion of his Guinness and then set the glass on the table, staring into what remained of the dark liquid as if it held the answers to all of life's problems. He nodded to himself and then looked me in the eyes.

"One day, I'm going to kill you and I won't make it quick. It will be as long and painful as I can. I will make you scream for mercy which will never come, and you will realize the same thing I did a long time ago and that is God doesn't give a damn about you, me or anyone else. But until such time, please make sure she's safe. I couldn't bear it if she was to die. She is so much like her mother. Headstrong, beautiful, and in the end, I fear she will be the death of me. She means everything to me."

No, I thought, I'll be the death of you. But I could tell he meant what he was saying about Samantha. He really did love his daughter.

"You have my word, I'd give my life to save hers. As long as I draw breath, I will keep her safe."

He stood, tossing his napkin down, and offered me his hand.

"Thank you. I know you will." I looked at the hand for a long moment, but then took it. He reached into the breast pocket of his coat for his wallet and took out a fifty and dropped it on the table. Without another word he turned and walked out the door.

When Janice came back I ordered another Guinness and pulled the report out of my coat pocket. I placed it on the table and took a few more sips of my beer, thinking about Samantha, her father, and how we were all really royally screwed. In the end, either her father or I would die. Maybe even both of us. And if we weren't careful, Samantha could end up being collateral damage.

CHAPTER TWENTY-ONE

Kurt was having the best day of his life. After breakfast, he and Ruth Anne spent the first part of the day shopping. They picked up a few knick knacks, then stopped by a grocery store to buy steaks and vegetables for the two of them to grill later that night. Dropping the food off at her place, they headed back to the beach. For the first time in his life, Kurt spent the day with a beautiful woman and was happy.

True, he did have some apprehension when it came to how the evening would end, but he put it out of his mind and worked on trying to enjoy the moment. He never even needed the Benadryl in his pocket. He got a big kick out of other people watching the two of them strolling down the beach, hand in hand.

They made one fine looking couple. Kurt spent most of the time daydreaming about what life would be like if they got married. Surely they would have the best-looking children on the planet. Well, if they looked like their mother. And if they got his brains, then the sky would be the limit for any offspring. Mom's good lucks and dad's brains? There would be no stopping them.

When it came time for dinner, they went back to her place. He got the grill started and threw on the steaks while she prepared the veggies. They'd picked up a Shafer Vineyards red wine to go with the steaks. It cost him sixty dollars and he nearly choked over the price, since his idea of an expensive drink was buying a sixty-four ounce bottle of Diet Dr. Pepper, but she insisted so he plopped down his card. Nothing but the best for his girl.

They ate dinner on the patio, with the mid-eighties high for the day having cooled into the mid-seventies. A soft breeze blew in from the ocean. Kurt uncorked the wine, poured two glasses, and raised his in a toast.

"To the two of us. May every day forward be as much fun as today."

She clinked her glass to his and they both drank. He decided it was time to ask the questions he'd been avoiding all day.

"So, where have you been the last couple of days? I was beginning to think you headed back home."

She took a long sip of wine and replied, "I was here, but I had my own business to take care of. There were things going on back home that needed tending to."

Kurt's frowned. "What type of . . . things?" He cut up his steak and took a bite. It was grilled to perfection but could have used a little steak sauce. She slapped him with a spoon when he suggested it earlier saying it would ruin a good steak.

"Well, you know, school-type stuff. When you drop out of college and take off for Hawaii, sometimes mothers aren't happy about it. So I had to spend time filling out forms for school, so I'd have incompletes, then move some money around. That type of thing."

"And that took three days?" He found it hard to believe there was that much paperwork in the world.

She raised an eyebrow and gave him a wicked smile. "No. It didn't. I was also punishing you for leaving me alone the other night. Do you realize how long it took me to get off that night all by myself?"

Kurt choked and nearly snorted wine out of his nose when she said this, which made her giggle.

"Sorry. It was just, well, I had that call, you know, and I didn't know you wanted me to stay, I mean, that night, so I wasn't prepared for it and, well, I had to work, and—"

She kicked him hard under the table. "Will you stop it? I was only teaching you a lesson. I'm not the kind of girl you leave hanging. So tonight you're mine. All mine."

They made small talk the rest of dinner and then carried their plates inside, washed them off and put them in the dishwasher. Kurt felt downright domesticated as he and Ruth Anne worked side-by-side. When the kitchen chores were finished, he walked into the TV area, plopped on the couch and turned on the big screen.

She walked over, took the remote from his hand and turned it off. "Oh no you don't. No TV. Get your ass in the bedroom, mister."

Kurt smiled weakly, got up and followed her like a submissive puppy down the hall to her bedroom. His palms began to sweat and he brushed them against his shorts to dry them off. He contemplated taking the Benadryl, but the medication sometimes made him sleepy and he thought that would be a very bad thing to happen.

"I'm going to go into the bathroom and freshen up," she said. "Take your shirt off and make yourself comfortable." She gave him a long, slow kiss and then turned and disappeared into the bathroom, closing the door behind her.

Kurt gulped a couple of times and did as she asked, taking his shirt off and sitting on the bed for a bit, then lying down. He tried to look natural, crossing and uncrossing his legs, and then his arms. Then he flopped to his side and watched the bathroom door. Then he sat up again. He finally lay back down with his head on the pillow and stared up at the ceiling and silently repeated all the self-help techniques he learned.

He licked his lips and thought about what he was about to do. He was still a virgin, but knew enough to know how things worked. He'd heard his guy friends talk about how to please a woman often enough. He was in the middle of planning what he should do first when the bathroom door opened and all thoughts flew from his mind.

Wearing a light blue teddy which showed off her curvy tanned body to full effect, she sauntered over to the bed and climbed slowly over to him. She gave him another kiss, and ran her hand down his bare chest and to his crotch.

He nearly jumped out of the bed at her touch and he tried to sit up, but she pushed him forcefully back down and then straddled him. She kissed him all over his chest, then up to his neck. At first, he ran his hands stiffly up and down her back, occasionally patting her shoulder. But when she reached his neck, thousands of years of evolutionary genetics took over and his body began to respond.

She kissed him and slid her hands up his arms, stretching them above his head, while her hair fell across his face. This must be what Heaven was like, Kurt thought. Her fingers entwined with his as she raised them to rest against the headboard made of metal and painted white in the shape of tree limbs covered in ivy.

She took his right hand, then the left, and wrapped his fingers around the bars of the headboard, and kissed her way up his arms, pressing her breasts against his face. He closed his eyes and enjoyed her kisses. Returning the favor, he started to kiss her chest when he felt something cold around one wrist and then the other, and heard a loud snick when the handcuffs closed.

His eyes flew open with surprise as she sat up, still straddling him. "There. Now you can't leave."

He licked his lips a couple of times and said, "Ruth Anne. I'm not going to leave. Honest. Let me out of these things."

"Not a chance. I've been trying to get you into my bed and now that I have you, I'm not taking any chances." She smiled down at him, but Kurt felt more like a trapped rabbit.

All of a sudden he heard a noise coming from her purse on the nightstand and realized it was his phone with the Vic McCain ringtone. He used the song *Bounty Hunter* by Molly Hatchet.

Ruth Anne raised an eyebrow, reached into her bag and pulled out his phone. She slid the bar to answer it, put it on speaker and placed the phone next to his head. He could hear Victor asking, "Kurt? Where've you been? I've been trying to reach you all day."

Kurt swallowed a couple more times before answering. "Uh. Hey Vic, I'm kind of tied up at the moment. Can I call you back later?"

"What the hell's going on? You pick up a couple more blow up dolls?"

"Very funny. Actually, I've been on a date, if you must know. I've been busy. I do have a life, you know."

"Kurt, your date. What's her name? It's not Ruth Anne, is it? Kurt, you could be in danger—"

Ruth Anne hit the end button and tossed the phone onto the nightstand.

"Well, he got that part right. Guess the jig is up, eh Kurt?"

Panicking, Kurt pulled hard on the cuffs, but they weren't budging and neither was the headboard.

Ruth Anne rolled off of him and the bed, and stood up. She walked over to a chair in the corner, picked up a T-shirt and pulled it on.

"Look, Ruth Anne. I thought you and I were a couple? You don't have to do this. Let me go. Please? I promise I won't take off."

She laughed, "Fat chance." Raising her voice, she shouted, "You might as well come out. The Spear knows about me."

Kurt heard a door open down the hall and footsteps approaching the bedroom. When the man entered the room, Kurt closed his eyes and groaned. He tried to keep his heart from galloping out of his chest, but it was no use. He knew he was in really big trouble.

"Long time no see, Kurt. How the hell are you?" Michael Christopher "Mikey" McCain said.

Kurt knew how he was: dead.

CHAPTER TWENTY-TWO

I stared at the phone and thought about what Kurt hanging up on me meant. I could tell our conversation was on speaker and Kurt wasn't known for using that function on his phone, paranoid about other people listening in on his business. My guess was someone was listening in on our conversation.

I sat back and rested my head against the hospital waiting room wall. Father Colton called earlier to tell me Winston would soon be released. I drove down to University Hospital to relieve him so he could get some rest and to wait for Winston.

Now I needed to add Kurt to my worry list. With a fallen angel in the big islands, and Kurt with a girlfriend, I couldn't help but feel he was in some serious trouble. I promised to protect him from the dangerous side of my work. It seemed I wasn't able to keep my end of the deal.

I didn't have long to wait before Winston walked out to join me. He looked good, if a little stiff. We shook hands and I led the way back to the Ford. Once we were both inside I turned the heat on full blast.

"Let's hear it," I said as we took off. "Tell me, how did a wimpy fallen angel get the drop on you?"

He spent a few minutes telling me exactly what happened at the reservoir, up until the time he passed out.

"I woke up in the recovery room with two Louisville Metro detectives wanting to talk to me. I told them what I told you, minus the whole fallen angel part. They'd already looked at the security camera footage from the main building camera. And since it went down pretty much as I indicated, there wasn't much they could shake out of me. They kept asking why the guy attacked me, that I must have known him. Were we involved in a drug deal gone bad, regular old shit."

"Did they know the guy's name by the time they came to see you?"

I kept an eye on the rear view mirror as I drove a random path through the early morning Louisville streets. If someone was following us, they were going to have a very difficult time doing it. We were virtually the only car on the road at this time of night following a heavy snow.

He shook his head in the affirmative. "Linville Pierce. Worked out at the G.E. plant, but hadn't shown up for work in a few days. Wife hadn't seen him either. Wouldn't answer his cell phone, completely dropped off the grid. Guess he's been hunting me."

"Yep. Damn. Sure does suck for him, doesn't it?"

"Man, in the worst way. The dude had two kids. And now he'll be remembered for trying to murder a man, and for no reason. Cops said they'll look into it more, but I think I'm in the clear. Video don't lie." After a brief pause, he said, "Vic, I did everything I could not to hurt the guy, but I didn't have a choice. I guess the knife wound was worse than I thought. It was either him or me." Winston just stared out the window at the passing streetlights, shaking his head back and forth. "This stuff is really messed up."

"It is and it was you or him," I agreed. "You did what you had to do. Believe me, I feel the same way. That guy in Florida would have drowned my ass if I hadn't taken him on. True, the gator killed him before I could, but I promise you, if the gator didn't? I would have. And there's more." I told him what I learned about Ruth Anne Gardner and the other missing college students and how Ruth Anne was reportedly in Hawaii. "I'm betting Ruth Anne is the date and Kurt's in real trouble."

"Well, at least there's now only one hundred and ninety-eight of them left. That settles it then. Let's go by my place so I can pack a few things. Then you can drop me off at the airport."

"Like hell. You're in no shape to fly to Hawaii."

I watched Winston as he tried to get comfortable in the passenger seat, an occasional grimace crossing his features. I got the feeling the knife wound bothered him a lot more than he was letting on to me.

"Shut up, old man. I'm fine. At least fine enough. Let's face it you can't go. There's too much going on here. Besides, I'll have the plane ride to the coast and then across the ocean to rest up. By the time I get there I'll be O.K. We can't leave Kurt hanging out there by himself. You and I both know he's got no chance against a mugger with a banana in his pocket, let alone a Watcher."

Despite how frustrating the truth was, he was right. I couldn't leave here. And Kurt would definitely need help. Kurt was a geek who wouldn't even watch a scary movie without the lights on and the doors locked.

"Besides," Winston continued, "at least this time I know what I'm up against. They won't catch me again like they did today. Payback's a bitch. If I can track them down and subdue her, then your new buddy should be able to find me a guy on the islands who can perform an exorcism."

"O.K. I'll ask him to be ready. You won't be able to take any of our toys with you, so you will have to improvise. You sure you feel up to it?"

"Damn straight. And don't worry about me. I'll work it out. The hard part will be finding them."

"Thanks, Winston. I appreciate all you've done to help me. I mean it." I stuck out my fist and he bumped it. It paid to have friends who are bad asses in their own right. I finally made it to his place and kept watch outside while he got a few things, then dropped him off at Louisville International Airport in order to catch an American Airlines flight to Hawaii. I handed him a printout of Ruth Anne's driver's license, so he would have an idea of who he was looking for.

After he waved goodbye and entered the airport, I put the car in drive and once again made a random path through the city. But I didn't go back to the Derby Mission. Instead I ended up at the Red Roof Inn over off of Hurstbourne Lane. I wanted to keep off the bad guy radar for another day, in case they were watching the mission. Studying the report I narrowed down another possible fallen angel possession, who, if his credit card charges were any indication, was still in Louisville. I planned to drive out to his parent's place in the morning, with Father Colton in tow, to see if I could track him down.

I had a pretty good idea who pointed the Watchers in our direction. I knew Mikey had to be behind this. The sooner I snapped his ever-lovin' neck, the better the planet, as a whole, would be.

~*~

I managed to get a few hours sleep, and not much more, before my phone alarm went off with the sunrise. I took a quick hot shower, grabbed some coffee and a couple of Egg McMuffins at McD's, and then made my way into town to pick up Father Colton.

He got into the car, tossing a bag into the backseat, and I handed him a copy of Clifford's report, opened to the fourth page. "There's a photo of the guy we're looking for. His name is Charlie Sutton. He's a student at the Speed School at the University of Louisville. He went missing about the same time Mal McGeorge did. I called out and spoke to his parents yesterday afternoon, but they were reluctant to talk to me over the phone. I got the impression they might know where their son was hiding out, so I thought we might as well pay them a visit in person and impress upon them the gravity of the situation. At least with the two of us we can do good-cop-bad-cop."

"Do I get to be the bad cop?" Colton asked with a grin.

"Do I get to wear a priest's smock?" I responded back. "No? Then no, you get to be the good guy."

The Sutton's lived on a family farm in southwest Oldham County and it took us the better part of a half hour to get there. After checking several mailboxes we found the right one next to a long gravel road leading between a grove of trees.

Father Colton pointed to the sky and asked, "Are those vultures?" I looked up to where he pointed and there were dozens and dozens of them flying in a huge circle off to our right.

"Yes, but we call them buzzards. Same difference." I couldn't recall ever seeing that many in the air at once and it bothered me. They also usually waited until the day warmed up to take to the skies. But on this winter day, it was as warm as it was going to get and perhaps they somehow knew it.

We passed several tobacco barns on the way to the main house and pulled up in front of a two-story clapboard house in need of a paint job. There were a couple of trucks parked under a carport. As we got out of the car, I noticed the buzzards were flying over a part of the farm a short walk away.

The driveway was shoveled clear of snow. We went up to the front door and I knocked loudly. No answer. I peered through the front window and could see the living room and into the kitchen. A couple of straight-backed chairs were toppled onto their sides and dishes were scattered across the floor. I reached under my coat and pulled my gun out of its holster.

"Father, here's what you're going to do. You're going to go back to the car." I handed him my keys. "I want you to start it up, turn it around and point it in the other direction. I'm going to take a look around. If I find something you need to see, I'll either come get you or call you on your cell. But if you don't see or hear from me in fifteen minutes I want you to get the hell out of here and call the cops. You got it?"

"Wouldn't it be better if I watched your back?" He looked around the farm, trying to see every place at once.

I reached into my weapons bag, pulled out another 9 millimeter and handed it to him.

"What am I supposed to do with this?" He held onto the grip with two fingers, dangling the gun.

"If you're going to watch my back, you're going to shoot whatever moves when I tell you to. Can you do that?"

He handed the gun back to me and replied, "I can't. I'm sorry. But I can do other things."

"Thanks, but no. I don't want to have to watch out for you as well." He started to get all pissed off when I raised my hand and said, "Look. I'm not challenging your manhood. But I do this for a living. You don't. And I need you alive if we have a demon to kick out of its new home. You copy?"

He blew air out and took another look around. "Copy. I understand, I'm sorry."

"Don't sweat it. Now get moving. I'm going to check out the house."

Father Colton stomped off in the snow to the car and did as I asked, getting the car started and turned it around. I went to the front door and tried the knob. It was unlocked and I opened the door slowly, pushing it open wide with my foot and then I ducked my head in for a quick look.

When no one attacked, I stepped inside and stood listening, my back pressed against the wall. The house felt empty, no sound of movement, and no running water. A house with someone inside gives off a different vibe. I kept my gun out and ready as I eased into the kitchen. The place was a wreck, with broken dishes and the morning breakfast spilled over onto the floor. The table, made of white Formica, reminded me of my parents kitchen table when I was growing up. Blood, however, covered it and someone had used a finger to write a message:

I'M WAITING!

I knew it was a finger because it was still on the table, positioned above a smeared dot, making the tall portion of a macabre exclamation point. But there was no body, just a finger.

I quickly cleared the rest of the house, both upstairs and down, but found nothing. I stepped back outside and to the car, lifted the rear door, grabbed my weapons bag, and slung it over my shoulder. I slammed the car door shut, then walked up to the driver's side window. Colton rolled it down and asked, "Nothing?"

"No bodies. But there's a lot of blood in the kitchen. And a message that I think is for me. Makes me wonder what the buzzards are after. I want you to pull down the drive a bit and away from the house in case someone is hiding in one of the outbuildings or in a field watching us. Keep your eyes and ears open."

He nodded, closed the window and pulled off. On the other side of the carport a trail led off towards the woods. I could make out the occasional footprint and a distinct trail of someone dragging something behind them. The footprint was good-sized with the tread of a work boot. I followed the trail across a field towards the buzzards who were just beyond a grove of trees.

The blood and the finger left little doubt that at least one of the Suttons, if not both, were dead. And I had a good idea who the killer was. I bet the prodigal son returned, carrying extra baggage rolling around inside his mind.

I ducked under the branches of several pine trees and stepped up to the edge of a clearing and stopped to take in Hell on earth. The clearing was about fifty yards wide and spread around the entire area were body parts. The vultures on the ground closely numbered the hundred in the air. Featherless, black heads bobbed up and down as they pulled and ripped the flesh off of bone. More than a dozen bodies were scattered around the clearing.

And sitting in the middle of the nightmare feast was Charlie Sutton. He sat on a plastic tarp soaked in blood, sitting in a yoga meditation position. He wore black jeans and a blue hoody with the hood pulled up and over his head, shadowing his eyes. I could see tan leather where the blood didn't cover his boots. On the ground in front of him rested a very large machete. The Butcher of Crestwood. I once again had that sense of wrongness I experienced when I was up-close-and-personal to Studley down in Florida. Guess these guys gave off weird vibes.

"Well, Charlie. Looks like you've been busy. Get bored with school?"

He smiled. "We both know you're not talking to Charlie, don't we, Spear of Uriel?"

"Spear? Dude. I don't know where you got that name. I'm the Hand of God. Maybe you called the person who had my job that name in your day, but times have changed. Didn't you get the memo?"

"Chained in the darkness for millennia after millennia? No. I'm afraid not. But I'm making up for lost time. How do you like my work?" He gestured with one hand to the horror he'd wrought.

"That you can only get buzzards to hang out with you is no surprise to me. So, which one are you? Whose ass am I going to kick?"

"My name is Arkas." He stood in one fluid motion, picking up the machete as he did so, then bowed. "The Spears were forever sure of themselves. Most to their ruin. You are the one about to learn something new."

"What? From you? Dude, do you know just how many fashion fads have come and gone since you were buried in your shit hole?" I gestured to the bodies scattered around. "I'm guessing two of these were the Suttons. Who are the rest?"

"Some of the parents were getting to be . . . a problem. You were starting to get close and the word was spreading. So I had my host's parents invite them to the farm for a strategy meeting. Clever, huh? Seems a private detective has been involved as well. We had ten show up. One even brought her son."

I felt my heart tear apart as I looked quickly around the field and then saw a knit cap, green with two black snowflakes and two earflaps, the same as Rose Mary's son, sitting on the ground not far away from where I stood. I yanked my gun from its holster and squeezed the grip so hard it's a wonder it didn't crush in my hand.

"You know, when I guessed you were here, I planned on just subduing you so I could have you cast out of the body you're in. Now, I'm going to find out how I can make an angel suffer before we do that. So help me, God, I will find a way to make you pay. Making the kid kill his own parents? And murdering a twelve year old boy? What type of sick fuck are you?"

"You ask such questions of me? When God chose you and your kind over *me* and *my* kind? You are no more than the cattle of the field to the divine. All those years watching over you, sharing our knowledge with the sons of men, and for what? So we could watch our own children murdered? Drowned, every last one of them. Then locked away for an eternity? You will begin to know just how we felt when we had our children ripped from us. When we are once again free, we will repopulate the Earth with our seed and replace the inferior race that is man." He once again gestured around him. "I consider this a good start."

It took every effort I could muster to stop from shooting the son of a bitch where he stood. I promised to return Ruth Anne to her mother. That wasn't going to happen—if Rose Mary was one of the victims of the massacre which surrounded me.

Charlie Sutton was another lost soul whose only crime was being in the wrong place at the wrong time. He deserved a chance—even if the demon inside him did not. I'd seen my share of horrific scenes during my time serving Uncle Sam, but never anything like this kind of butchery.

I breathed deeply, despite the smell of death heavy in the air, and let it out slowly. "You should've had some of your buddies come and help you out. It's just you and me and I'm about to shove that machete up your metaphorical ass."

Spreading both arms out to his side, he said, "Just you and me? For shame, Spear of Uriel, I have many friends here. They have thanked me for providing this marvelous meal."

"What? The buzzards? You are insane. No wonder they had to bury your ass deep in some frickin' hole."

I started to move towards him, my gun ready, waiting for the trap. I knew this had to be a trap. No one sits in the middle of a field and waits to get their ass kicked. He wanted me out here, unless he thought he and his weapon of choice were enough to take me down.

I took two steps when the buzzards on the ground, all at once, turned and looked in my direction: every last one of them, in unison. Then the ones flying overhead began to fly lower. I stopped in my tracks.

"Ah," said Arkas. "Are you starting to comprehend? Each of the divine have their own special knowledge, our own expertise. Mine is the ability to speak and work with animals. And I've told them about you and what we will do here today. And how they will feast when your carcass joins the others."

With that he threw his hands skyward and every buzzard still on the ground shot instantly into the air to a height of about thirty fee and then dove straight at me.

Holy crap. I fired off a couple of rounds, with several birds falling to the ground, but there were hundreds of them and I didn't have nearly enough ammunition. Soon I was lost in a flurry of claws and beaks ripping at my head and hands. I covered my face with my arm, thankful my bomber jacket was thick, but they were shredding it like tissue paper. Blood began to flow down my face as one beak ripped a gash across my forehead and attacked my exposed hands.

I lost track of Arkas, so I tried to move backwards and almost tripped and fell, stumbling over someone's leg. Nothing else, just the leg. I could feel the first tendrils of panic stir inside me, but I shoved the feeling aside.

I said to myself, think damn it, think.

The buzzards were trying to get at my legs. I kicked out at them and managed to clip Arkas who had moved within striking distance, knocking him back just as the machete sliced down mere inches from my head.

Think, think, think. Then it hit me. I reached into my bag, feeling urgently around and found what I was looking for: a tear gas canister. I'd never removed it from my duffle after the Florida trip.

Back during my time in Basic Training with Special Forces, a sergeant challenged a couple of us, those who he thought were the most badass guys in the unit, to a competition. Late one night the four of us met the sergeant in the tear gas training room with the sergeant the only one wearing a mask. The first three out had to clean all the latrines in our building for a solid week with a toothbrush. The last one got a weekend pass —one of the most treasured rewards you could earn during basic training. I held my breath for as long as I could. In the end it was just me and one other guy. When I could tell I was about to lose the last of my air, I slapped the other guy on both sides of his face. He let out his remaining air in a rush, and then ran out. I stayed a while longer after my own air had left me to prove I was as tough as I thought I was.

I did the same thing here, took a deep breath, and then popped the top on the canister. An ugly brown smoke spewed out of the can as I began to wave it around my head and the birds scattered. They may eat carrion for a living, but they didn't like the smell of toxic smoke. My eyes began to sting, but I kept them open and resisted the urge to rub them. Good thing as I saw Arkas swing in an overhand arc with his machete. I raised my weapons bag, blocking the blow, then shoved him backwards and pointed the can directly into his face. Arkas started rubbing his eyes and when he did, I kicked him hard in the balls, putting everything I had behind it. Arkas doubled over, dropping the machete, then breathed in deep and began to retch. I'm not sure how tear gas would affect an angel, but it for damn sure affected a human body.

I hit him hard in the temple, and he crumpled to the ground, knocked out. I tossed the can of tear gas far away, trying really hard not to rub my eyes. All the buzzards had flown the coop. I reached into the bag, took out plastic cuffs and secured Arkas. Then I took out a roll of duct tape and put a large piece across his mouth. No more Dr. Doolittle for you, asshole.

I used a towel inside my bag to wipe away the blood from my forehead, then tied it around my head to keep the blood out of my eyes, watching to see if the buzzards would return, but they didn't. I slung my bag over my shoulder, picked up the unconscious Mr. Sutton and started back towards the farm. At the tree line, I stopped, dropped Sutton on the ground and said a prayer for the dead.

My heart ached for Rose Mary and her son. I should have felt the same way for all of them, but their deaths didn't affect me like the death of the little boy which really hit me hard. Arkas began to come around and I grabbed a fistful of hair, turning his eyes to meet mine.

"Remember how I told you I was going to make you pay? If I could find a way to torture you before we cast you out, without hurting the boy, I'd do it. I don't care if it's not the Christian thing to do. You are evil incarnate and I wish I could do more than cast you into Hell. But that will have to do. Your freedom is almost over."

He tried screaming things at me as I dragged him through the snow to the car, but the damn duct tape over his mouth kept me from hearing what he had to say. Ain't that just a bitch.

CHAPTER TWENTY-THREE

I called Father Colton and he met me at the door to the house carrying his bag of tricks. I stopped in front of him, dragging the fallen angel behind me. Arkas thrashed around and continued to scream, despite the tape covering his mouth. I'm not sure, but I think he called me a bad name. I grabbed him under the arms, lifting him up. Colton grabbed his legs and we carried him kicking into the house and plopped him onto a big four-poster bed in a back bedroom.

"Hold him down for a minute while I get ready," Father Colton said.

I was more than happy to help, using my weight to keep Sutton from moving around. I put my lips next to his ear and said, "You don't know how badly I want to choke you, over and over, until you're almost dead, then bring you back to life and do it all over again. But that only punishes the kid. Just think, in a few minutes you'll be spending the rest of eternity wandering through the desert until Judgment Day when you'll be cast into Hell with that other fallen angel, Lucifer. Guess you guys can start a club. And Sutton, if you can hear me in there? We're going to free you, son. Hang on a bit longer."

Arkas continued his muffled screams and it took every ounce of restraint I had not to pinch his nose and end it, right then and there. Finally, Colton said, "I'm ready. Let me get these restraints on him."

Colton took hold of one of Sutton's ankles and buckled the leather restraint. He then tied it off to one of the poster bed's large posts. He did the same thing with the other ankle.

He moved to the head of the bed and said, "Now comes the harder part. I need you to uncuff him and keep him still while I get these arm cuffs on."

"Screw that," I said. "Hold him down for a minute."

Father Colton relieved me, leaning hard on Sutton while I went back to my bag and took out a taser. I walked over to Sutton, flipped the dart cap off, revealing the bare contacts, then pressed it against his side and pressed the button.

Sutton bucked from all the juice, then was still. I quickly rolled him over, took out a knife and cut the cuffs while Colton buckled on the leather wrist restraints to the bed, securing him to the headboard.

With Arkas now immobilized, Colton went back to his bag and pulled a towel which he wrapped around his neck, then took out several items he sat on the nightstand next to the bed: a Bible, a funny looking shaker, and a large metal cross.

"Your version of a weapons bag?" I asked.

"Yes, my Jesus bag. Don't leave home without it."

"What's with the baby rattle?"

He picked up the shaker made out of ceramic and colorfully decorated. "Filled with holy water. O.K. Here's what happens next. I want you to take the tape off of his mouth and then I want you to stand over by the door. No matter what you hear, you must not respond to what the demon says. Do you understand?"

"No sweat. Would you rather me leave the room?"

"Actually, no. If he manages to break free of the bed, you'll come in real handy. But you must stay quiet. The demon will try and get you involved, to break my concentration."

"Dude, I've been trash-talked by the best of them. I'm good. You ready?"

He nodded and I walked over to Sutton, who was starting to come around. I ripped the tape from his mouth. "Ready for your one-way to ticket to oblivion, asshole?"

Sutton was about to respond when Colton picked up the cross and the Bible, and the reaction by Arkas/Sutton was immediate, as he pushed the length of his restraints, trying to move off the bed.

Colton started with a prayer, "Father, who art in Heaven, hallowed be thy name, thy kingdom come, thy will be done, on Earth as it is in Heaven."

As he continued, Arkas yanked and pulled at his restraints, rocking the bed and howling with rage. His eyes, wild and large, searched the room and found me.

He said, "Free me, Spear of Uriel, and I will make sure your loved ones survive the purge. I can make that happen. Free me!"

I responded with a wink and then scratched my nose with my middle finger. I knew it was a childish insult, but since I couldn't talk, what was a guy to do?

Colton began reading from different parts of scripture, then picked up the holy water shaker and began to rain holy water down upon the body of Charlie Sutton. Sutton's body arched off the bed so hard I was sure the restraints wouldn't hold him, but they did. Veins popped out on Sutton's neck, and he continued to shake back and forth.

Colton kept his voice in a slow measured cadence. In response, Arkas growled, low and harsh, then spit a goober the size of a quarter into Colton's face. The priest, never missing a beat, used the towel to wipe the spittle off of his chin. He began to call the demon by name. "Here me, Arkas. In the name of our Lord and Savior, Jesus Christ, I call upon you to leave this vessel."   "Never," screamed the demon. "He is mine. I will not leave."

"You will leave, in the name of the Father, the Son and the Holy Ghost." Colton emphasized his words with more shaking from the holy water shaker, moving up and down the boy's body.

The demon once again howled, and then looked straight at me.

"Do you want to know what we did to your woman, Spear of Uriel? Did she share with you the way she screamed with pleasure when my brother took her? The way she begged him to take her again and again? Baraquiel said he'd never had a woman who begged him not to leave her bed the way the red-haired bitch did each night when he finished with her."

I leaned off the wall in a flash of anger, my breathing coming in large heaves. The demon smiled and said, "That's right, Spear of Uriel, she begged him on hands and knees and pleasured him in all ways. Others will get their chance with her and we will pass her around from brother to brother before we kill her. You have my word this will happen."

Father Colton never looked at me, never said a word to me, only continued to admonish the demon to leave Sutton's body, but he did speak louder. I wanted so badly to pound on this warped piece of crap. I ground my teeth in frustration, my fists balled, and fought for control. Did the other fallen angel really do those things to Samantha?

Is that why she didn't want to talk about what happened to her down in Florida? Because she'd been raped by Baraquiel? I knew something awful happened down there. How much of what Arkas was spewing was the truth? Some of it? All of it? None of it?

I took another step. I had visions of strangling the truth out of the demon while banging his head against the headboard. Or maybe I could smash the truth out him.

Instead, I closed my eyes and calmed myself. What I wanted was what Arkas hoped I would do. He wanted me to interrupt the exorcism, as he fought desperately not to be kicked into his own form of Hell.

I reopened my eyes, gave the demon my best smile, and slowly shook my finger back and forth. Then I went back to my wall and continued to lean against it making sure it stayed in place.

Arkas howled and his thrusting became even more violent. That is, until Colton, his voice rising, issued a final command for him to leave.

"In the name of the Father, the Son and the Holy Ghost, leave this vessel!" Then he pressed the cross down upon Sutton's head. The demon's howl turned into a shriek and then the sound faded, as Sutton's body collapsed onto the bed.

Sutton, covered in sweat, closed his eyes and then reopened them. He looked around the bedroom, at Colton, and then to me and the most pitiful wail I ever heard from any man escaped his lips and he began to sob. Father Colton placed his hand upon the young man's shoulder and said, "You have been freed of the demon. He has been cast out. You are now free."

"Oh, God," he cried. "He made me kill my parents. I, I, I . . . cut them to pieces. I—killed others. Oh my God, what have I done?"

Colton motioned to me and we removed the leather restraints. Charlie curled up into a fetal position, hugging his knees and sobbed. Colton sat down beside the young man and then lifted him up into his strong arms, and held him, the whole time speaking in a low, hushed tone.

I walked out into the front room and called Brother Joshua.

"Down to one hundred and ninety-seven," I said. "But it was a close call." I filled him in on the events at the farm and then asked, "J, there's a lot of dead bodies out here. Several families have lost parents. How do you want to handle this? This kid is going to be blamed for being a mass murderer and spend his life either in prison or in an insane asylum. I hate to just turn him over to the cops."

"Bring him with you. What happens will be up to him. We all make choices, Victor, and his choice not to be one with God left him open to the attack."

"Give me a freakin' break. The kid had no chance. You know what, J, I'm all for the whole 'you make your bed you lie in it' point of view, but I'll be damned if just letting this kid hang himself is the right thing to do. This holier than thou attitude is really starting to piss me off."

Never in my interaction with Brother Joshua did I let my anger come out. I knew I crossed a line, but I really didn't care. Maybe what the demon said about Samantha clouded my judgment. Maybe it was the fact no one was there to protect a little boy and his mother. Sometimes I wondered what the hell was the point of what I was doing.

"As I said," Brother Joshua responded. "The choice is up to him. It's all about free will and choices, Victor. Have Father Colton do what he can there and then return to the mission, with the boy if he will join us or without him if he will not. There's no way we can avoid calling in the police on this one. Once you've brought them here, I want you to return to the farm and call the police. You can tell them the truth: that you were investigating the disappearance of several local college students and stumbled upon the scene."

I leaned my head against the wall and prayed for God to give me strength.

"Yeah. O.K. Fine."

I severed the connection. I closed my eyes, listening to the wailing which continued in the other room. I couldn't even imagine being forced to kill your own parents against your will. I thought about Mikey, but realized the situation was totally different. Mikey deserved the wrath of God to be rained down around him. This poor family was decimated for no other reason than a young man didn't make the right choices when it came to faith.

Father Colton came out and put his hand on my shoulder. The wailing in the other room had subsided.

"You able to put him at peace that quickly?" I asked.

He shook his head, a somber look on his face.

"No, I wasn't. That's the result of a heavy sedative I gave him. He's not out yet, but will be soon."

"For the best, all things considered. Father Joshua says we need to ask him if he'd like to come back to the mission. His choice."

"My choice and the answer is 'yes.' The man is broken and is in no shape to face the world on his own, especially considering what is to come next."

"Yeah. Mass murderer is going to be a hard tag to live with. I'm hoping there's something Joshua can do about it. But we will see."

"Victor," Father Colton said slowly, " about what Arkas said in there, you do understand that lying is what they do. He was just trying to get a reaction from you. You showed incredible restraint. I'm sorry I had to put you through all of that. Most likely what he said is not true."

I didn't say anything for a moment, but then replied, "She'll tell me in due time if it did. Something happened down there, but I'm not sure what, and I'm not sure how hard I should push her. I'm trying to give her the space she needs. But it's tough, ya know?"

"I do. For now, let's get Mr. Sutton to the mission and go from there. What are you going to do about what happened out there?"

"No choice. I'll have to call the cops and tell them as much as I can. There are too many dead people involved. I'm worried about what happens if the police corner one of these Watchers. They're like an infection. Being able to move from person to person is a real issue."

We went back to Charlie Sutton and helped the drowsy man to the back seat of my car, laying him gently down on the seat. "How long before the Watcher can try and return back to Charlie?"

"There's no set time, but it won't be soon. I have time to try and increase his faith. But his mind is broken, Vic. What he was forced to do? I'm not sure anyone can recover from such horror. I will do what I can."

And that's all any of us can do, I thought. Soldier on, do the right thing and hope it's enough. I was starting to have my doubts.

CHAPTER TWENTY-FOUR

Kurt was having a really bad dream. Like one of the worst ever. It started out great, he and Ruth Anne were in bed, she was wearing the kind of teddy he only saw in magazines, but never in person. Then she was all over him, pressing her breasts against his face. Pure heaven. But then the nightmare started when she handcuffed him to the headboard and got worse when Mikey McCain walked in. What a buzz kill.

He dreamed Ruth Anne and Mikey had an argument. They wanted something from him, but he couldn't remember what. Oh. That's right. Where Vic had hidden the money. Vic never told him, he explained to them. But Mikey wanted to cut off parts of his body until he told and that scared him. Kurt liked his body parts right where they were.

But Ruth Anne said Mikey told her she could do it her way, and Kurt was all for Ruth Anne's way, especially if it involved teddies and breasts. But it didn't. She reached into her purse and pulled out a large syringe and stuck him in the neck and he fell asleep.

Now he could hear her calling his name and he needed to wake up. He moved his neck back and forth a bit and then finally opened his eyes, but it was still dark. He went to sit up, but banged his head on something hard after moving only a few inches. He tried to raise his arms but they hit the hard thing, too. Slowly he felt around and then shot wide-awake as he realized he was in a wooden box. No, he thought. Not a box. A coffin.

Panic seized him and he began to pound on top of the box, screaming to be let out. He pushed up with all his might, but the lid didn't budge. He continued to scream until a small hole opened above his face. He stared straight up through a small cylinder at Ruth Anne's beautiful eyes.

"Ruth Anne. Let me out. Please," he begged. "I'll do anything. Get me out of here."

A frown creased Ruth Anne's brow. "Anything? You'll do anything?" she said.

"Yes. I swear it. This isn't funny. You have to let me out. Please," he pleaded.

She smiled. "So will you tell me where you and your friend hid the money? You'll do that for me, Kurt?" Kurt closed his eyes and didn't say anything. "Kurt," she continued. "You said you'd do anything, didn't you mean it?" Her smile was gone, and so was Kurt's hope.

"I don't know where the money is. He never told me." He knew they would never believe him. The night before was coming back with clarity and they didn't believe him then either.

Ruth Anne's face was replaced by that of Mikey.

"*Bullshit*, Kurt," Mikey said, trying to maintain his temper. "My brother doesn't have the brains to hide that much money. Nor the skill, but *you* do. And he trusts you. Come on, man, tell us where the two of you hid the money and we'll have you out of there in a jif."

"Go screw yourself, Mikey. I don't know and wouldn't tell you if I did." Kurt tried to keep up a strong front, but inside he was terrified. He felt a chill in his soul, as he knew he would never leave this box in the ground.

"Have it your way, Kurt. But you *will* tell us. This woman is quite talented. I wish you all the best. I'll make sure and tell Vic you said hello the next time I talk to him."

And with that, Mikey was gone and Ruth Anne was back. "Here's what I'm going to do, Kurt. I'm going to give you a while to think about it, then I'll be back."

Her face disappeared and she placed some type of cover over the cylinder and his whole world went black. Kurt started to scream again for someone to let him out, pounding on the top of the coffin. The lid was removed and Ruth Anne returned.

"Kurt, listen to me very carefully. If you don't stop screaming, then I'm going to bring the water hose over here and fill the box to the brim. Do you understand me? Shh. Now," she said, putting the lid back on.

This time Kurt stayed quiet and tried to think about how to get out of this situation. He took stock of his condition. He was shirtless, but still had on his shorts. He felt around but found his pockets were empty, so nothing there. He remembered the warning call from Vic the night before and wondered if the big guy guessed he was in trouble and what he'd do about it if he did.

For a moment Kurt started to hyperventilate and it was several minutes before he got his breathing under control. He used what space he had to feel around the seams of his makeshift prison, but could find no finger grips or gaps.

He laid there for what seemed like hours when the lid was once again removed and Ruth Anne appeared.

"Ready to talk, Kurt?" Her voice was pleasant, like it had been during their date.

"It was all a lie, wasn't it? You never liked me, did you?" Kurt asked.

Ruth Anne snorted, "Not even a little. I'd tell you I'm sorry, but I'm not. Like every other man on the planet, you think with the wrong head. You might as well go ahead and tell me what I want to know, Kurt. You're going to anyway."

"Kiss my ass, bitch." He tried to sound defiant, but the words came out in a defeated tone.

"Kurt, Kurt, Kurt. You sound like the private detective my mother sent out here to find me. He's in a box a few feet to your right. He said he wouldn't talk either. But in the end, he told me everything I wanted to know, right up until the very end. You wanted to know what I was doing the last few days. Well, that was it. I was having fun. Now it's your turn. The only question is how long it takes with you, Kurt."

Kurt whimpered softly and this made Ruth Anne laugh. She replaced the lid and left him alone with his thoughts. Kurt wished he'd done more with his life. Found a nice girl, settled down. He thought Ruth Anne would be that girl, but it was all a bag of lies.

And here Vic was looking for Mikey only to have him show up in Hawaii. He wondered how they found him. He'd done a great job covering his tracks. At least he thought so.

Finally, the lid was removed, the face of his tormenter returned.

"Time to talk, Kurt. I've waited as long as I can to let you do this on your own. Will you talk to me now?"

"Not a chance. I won't turn traitor. Do your worst." He was proud he said the words. But he knew he didn't mean it. He didn't want her worst. He didn't even want slightly bad.

"Good," she said, and sounded downright pleased with Kurt. "I was sure you wouldn't put up a fight. Michael McCain said you'd fold before the first hour was up. I'm very proud of you, Kurt. So let's get started, shall we?"

Kurt watched through the cylinder as she leaned out of view, then returned holding something which she dropped down the pipe and quickly replaced the lid. His brain roared out a word just before the object hit him in the face: snake. He turned his head and screamed as the snake landed on his cheek and then squirmed down his chest. Kurt trapped it against his stomach and could feel the thing wrap around his wrist, then felt its mouth close down on his hand, striking him over and over. Continuing to scream, Kurt grabbed the head of the snake in one hand, the body in the other, and pulled with all the adrenaline his body had left. He felt a small pop, as skin, scales, and cartilage ripped and the head tore loose.

He laid there in the dark, crying, and threw the lifeless body of the snake down by his feet. He went back to pounding on the lid, screaming for Ruth Anne to let him out. He continued to pound until he could no longer lift his arms. Exhausted, he gave up, closed his eyes and tried to sleep. Fat chance.

His eyes were still closed when Ruth Anne said, "Come on Kurt, be a real man. That was just a baby rat snake. I have others. I tell you what. I'll let you choose what I drop down next." His eyes opened to see a slice of clouds in a beautiful blue sky as Ruth Anne continued just out of site. "Let's see. I have a couple of scorpions, several rattlesnakes, and my personal favorite, several gallons of red fire ants."

Her face once again filled his vision and he wanted nothing more than to reach up through the opening and strangle her. But the pipe was several feet long and she was just out of reach.

"I had to order more of those. I didn't like the P.I. so I chose for him, filled his box with fire ants then sealed the lid shut so they couldn't get out. He screamed for hours. But I like you, so I'll let you choose. Unless you don't tell me what I need to know. If you don't, I might just dump them all down there with you. Wouldn't that be fun?" she was practically giddy. "So, Kurt, where did you and Victor McCain hide the money?"

"If I tell you, will you let me out of here?" Kurt asked.

"Count on it. You give me what I want and I'll have you dug up, then I'll make sure they let you go."

Kurt knew it was all a lie, but what else could he do? He always had visions of riding into battle, saving the day, and being the hero. But trapped in a box, underground, with a dead snake and likely more on the way, he wasn't sure he had it in him. There was one more thing he could try.

"Vic and I hid the money in two different offshore accounts. I will need my laptop to tell you which ones and the account numbers. Spring me and I'll get the computer and print out what you need."

"How about this," Ruth Anne decided, "I'll go get your computer, bring it back here and you can walk me through where the information is stored. Then I'll let you out."

"You promise?" Kurt put as much hope into his voice as he could.

"Absolutely. Now where will I find your computer?"

"Look in the second drawer of my dresser, beneath my underwear and socks. And be careful with it. That thing cost me a fortune."

"You got it. Take a little rest, Kurt. I'll be back later. Oh, and Kurt?"

"Yes?" He didn't like the tone in her voice.

"If the computer isn't there, or you're lying to me, then I will be very angry with you. You won't like me when I'm angry."

"Don't worry. I'm playing it straight up."

"Don't go anywhere, ya here?" She put the lid back in place, her laughter as black as the darkness.

CHAPTER TWENTY-FIVE

After dropping off Charlie and Father Colton, I drove back to the farmhouse and called Rusty. "Hey, Rusty. Remember when I said I'd call you if my efforts turned into anything? Well, they have, and I'm not sure you're going to like it."

An hour later, the farm was crawling with cops and forensics teams. Rusty, a state trooper not too far from retirement, stood next to me as we watched a coroner head towards the clearing with even more body bags. Rusty's face, pinched and pale, watched them for a moment, then turned back to me.

"You know, Vic, I've been doing this nearly thirty years and I've never seen anything like this. And you have no idea who's responsible?"

"Like I told you, finding missing teens wasn't really my focus. I found out about them as much by accident as anything else. When Ms. Huffman asked me to look into it, I said why not? I'd only been on the trail for a day when I found this."

"You say you spoke to Mr. and Mrs. Sutton?"

"Yes, yesterday afternoon. From the way they talked, I thought for sure they had an idea where Charlie, their son, was hiding out. So I came out here earlier in the day to try and shake some information from them. I knocked and when I didn't get an answer, I looked in the window and saw the chairs overturned. When I saw the blood and the note, I had a bad feeling about all them buzzards flying around and went to take a look."

Rusty glanced at my head and hands, and the condition of my jacket, and said, "Never known vultures to attack a human. Throw up on them maybe, but never attack. Why do you think they did that?"

"Rusty, I honestly have no clue." Of course I did, but I didn't think my friend wanted to hear about fallen angels who talk to buzzards. "I just walked out there and when I moved towards the tarp they attacked."

"And you just happened to have tear gas on you?" His frown told me he was buying that part.

"I had my bag with me. I always keep tear gas in there in case I have to break up an unruly group of family members when I make a bust. Nonlethal force. Seems to work on birds as well as people. Good thing for me."

He grunted agreement and nodded back towards my car. The two of us walked together in that direction, away from the other investigators.

"Sorry you got roped into all of this, Vic. The report the private investigator produced will be a big help. And we found the parents cars in the two barns."

He checked his list.

"I have one last question for you. That message on the kitchen table. Do you think that was meant for you?"

"I doubt it, Rusty. The only person who knew I was looking into this was me. Well, and I guess Ms. Huffman. My guess is it was meant for someone else, but I don't have a clue who."

He watched my face closely, but I'm one of the better liars on the planet and after a moment he let it go.

"So, what, you think this is some kind of cult? These are not the type of teens to be gang bangers."

"That would be my guess. It's all very strange. But now the problem belongs to you guys. Good luck with that."

He gave a laugh devoid of humor and said, "Gee, thanks. We'll be in touch."

With that he strode back towards the house and the nightmare that waited beyond. I pulled out my phone and tried calling Kurt for, like, the tenth time with similar results: voicemail.

It was approaching five o'clock and Winston should have arrived in Hawaii, so I called him next. On the second ring, he answered.

"First Florida, then Hawaii. I'm really getting used to working for you. How about next you get me a gig in Europe. I've always wanted to see London."

"If we live long enough, I'll see what I can do. What's your status?" I fired up the Ford and headed out and soon left the Stephen King scene behind, even if I carried the images with me.

"Got booked into a room down the hall from Kurt. I'm going to start the search right away. I have the print out you gave me of the girl and pictures of Kurt he messaged out a few weeks ago."

Kurt had gone to his first luau and sent us pictures of him wearing about a dozen leis and doing his best not to look scared sitting there while hula dancers did their thing.

"Hit me up as soon as you know something, alright?"

"You got it boss man. I'll find him and bring him home. Count on it."

284

I told him about the farm and the successful exorcism of the fallen angel. He asked, "What's your next plan? Just in case you get hit by a bus and I have to take over for you?"

"I should only be so lucky. I think we need to stop chasing the tail and find the front of the dog. For the fallen angels to possess someone, they have to be close enough to touch them. If they'd been buried deep enough and they didn't make it to the surface, then someone found a way down to them. Add in the fact all the people possessed, so far, are from this area, then I think the Watchers were buried somewhere nearby. I'm going to try and find out where. Find the source and maybe I'll find the rest of them."

"You're gonna need a small army if you do find them. These are some badass mofos. Make sure and wait until I get back before you hit them. I'll find Kurt and high tail it back. Be careful."

Winston hung up and I tossed the phone on the seat next to me. Don't worry, I said to myself, I will.

I sure hope I wasn't sending Winston into even more danger than he was in here. I pounded the wheel in frustration because I couldn't be in two places at once to help Kurt and to take care of things with the case here. Instead of riding the wave, I'd spent the last few days being swept under. I needed to talk to Charlie to see if he could add to what I'd learned from Mal McGeorge. Then J and I would talk, too. He and I were going to have a "come to Jesus" talk. Time to get back on top.

~*~

Winston resisted the urge to constantly scratch at the bandage on his side. He lied to Vic. Despite sleeping like the dead on the two plane rides to Hawaii, he woke up feeling weak. Thank God there was a Starbucks in the airport because he needed a caffeine jolt. But there wasn't much else he could do but get to it and find Kurt, and soon.

He first went and talked to the clerks at the front desk to ask if they'd seen Kurt. It took some convincing to prove the two of them were really friends. But after a few minutes they checked and confirmed that, aside from the cleaning crew, Kurt's door had not been opened since yesterday morning. Since Kurt had been staying there for the last three months the staff knew him pretty well. One of the desk clerks remembered seeing him eating breakfast with a pretty blonde woman the morning before. Winston showed her Ruth Anne's photo and she said that Ruth Anne was the girl he was with, but she didn't see them leave. Both of the desk clerks said Ruth Anne, however, was definitely not staying at the hotel. He gave them his card and asked that they call him if Kurt came back or they saw the girl again.

Winston thanked them and then walked down towards the beach. Now he knew Kurt was in deep trouble, having hooked up with a fallen angel. If they got wind Vic was closing in on them in Kentucky, having spoken to Ruth Anne's mom, they may have made a move on Kurt. But to what end, Winston had no clue.

There were several different kiosks just before you hit the sand and Winston repeated the inquiries. A newsstand guy named Melvin said Kurt and Ruth Anne were at his stand the day before, early in the afternoon, and he saw them sitting down by the water. He remembered because the girl was super hot, but neither one passed his stand today. Again, he would've remembered. Hot, hot, hot.

Winston thanked him and decided to walk down the beach and talk to the people there to see if anyone else knew Ruth Anne and where she might be staying. He was walking and talking to people along the beach for about forty-five minutes when his phone rang. His caller ID showed a Hawaiian area code.

The person on the line said, "Hi. This is Susan Harover. You left us your card here at the hotel in case we saw Kurt or the girl come back."

Winston turned and began jogging back up the beach, but stopped almost immediately due to the pain it caused in his side. "Is he back?"

"He's not, but she is. She just walked through the lobby and took the elevator up."

"Thanks. I'm on my way there now."

"Would you like us to detain her?" The clerk sounded excited.

"No. Don't try it. She may be very dangerous and I don't want any of you to get hurt. Just keep an eye out."

He hung up and tried to pick up the pace, but fatigue quickly overtook him. He thought about the offer to have her detained, but as deadly as these fallen angels were turning out to be, he didn't want to put innocent people at risk. Not only that, but if she found out someone was here after her, she could just hop to another body and then he'd have no clue what the person he was searching for looked like.

He finally made the turn up the beach to the front of the hotel when his phone rang again.

"Tell me," he said.

"She just walked out the front door carrying a laptop. You better hurry." Susan replied.

Winston arrived in time to see a blonde matching his picture hop into a cab and pull away. Instead of trying to catch up with her, he slowed down, walked over to the parking lot, unlocked the door to his rental car and got in.

He pulled out his phone and opened a particular app, plugged in the car charger and went in the general direction the cabbie had taken. He could feel the anticipation building inside because now he knew he had her.

CHAPTER TWENTY-SIX

Kurt heard the cover being removed and opened his eyes. He wasn't sure how much time had passed between Ruth Anne's departure and return, but it wasn't long enough to suit him. He'd tried in vain to once again push up on the lid of the coffin box he was buried in, but didn't have the strength to move that much dirt. Hell, he didn't think even Vic could muscle that much earth out of the way.

Resigned to his fate he considered his next course of action, a plan which might save him or might not. Then he spent a few moments praying. Before long he knew he'd have the answer to whether there really is a Heaven and a Hell.

"O.K. I have the laptop and it's powered on. What's your sign on password?" Ruth Anne said.

Kurt gave her a long string of numbers and he heard keys tapping. Then she said, "Crap. That's not right. Give them to me again. This time, Kurt, it better be right or there'll be consequences. You hear me?"

"Yeah, yeah, don't get your thong in a knot. I can't help it if you can't type."

But inside Kurt felt pretty damn good about himself, as his preparations months earlier were about to pay off.

~*~

Winston drove slowly up and down the residential streets not far from the beach. The cab went by him a few minutes earlier and he knew he was close. Then the app, open on his phone, beeped.

Yes! Winston said to himself.

He picked up the phone and looked closely at a map with a little blue dot a few streets over from where he now was, a spot right on the ocean. Someone tried accessing Kurt's laptop and put in the wrong password, which then sent a signal to the app on his and Victor's phones, showing exactly where the laptop was and, with any luck, right where Kurt was being held.

"Hang on buddy, I'm on my way." he said aloud.

His phone rang and the caller ID showed Vic's name. He pushed the answer button and before he could even say hello, Vic said, "You see it?"

"Yeah, man. I see it. I'm about two minutes away. Now let me do my job and stop botherin' me."

Winston hung up and watched the blue dot as he turned down Kauai Palm Lane, with the blue dot on the app matching up when he rode by number 116. A "for rent" sign rested against the house. A fence surrounded the back of the property, with the front facing the ocean with a gorgeous view. There was no one in sight and the curtains on the front window were pulled shut.

Winston drove down a few houses and found a public parking spot for those wanting access to the beach. He pulled into a spot, got out and locked the car. He wasn't sure what he would do once he reached the house, but he'd come up with something. He was always good that way. Being a linebacker meant you needed to react to what the offense did. There were times you could blitz and force the issue, but most times it was observe and react. Time to do some observing and then some kick ass reacting.

~*~

"I'm in," Ruth Anne said. "Now what?"

Kurt knew they now reached the tricky part.

"Vic and I put the money in two offshore accounts. The information is in two encrypted files. You can't just open them up and read them."

The truths was, these two accounts didn't have much money in them at all. They were there in case someone stole his laptop and then managed to break his encryption. The real account numbers were stored someplace else and numbered five in total.

"Not a very trusting soul are you, Kurt?" He could hear the snicker in her voice.

"Well, duh. Looks like I had it right, didn't I? What type of idiot do you think I am?" Kurt had no illusions as to what would happen once Ruth Anne and Mikey got into the accounts. Whatever the P.I. got he was surely to get even worse. He could only hope the signal the laptop sent out would alert Vic or Winston and for them to figure out he was in trouble and send the police to where ever he was being held. He programmed his own app and had them download it to their phones.

"So asks the man buried in a box. Do you really want me to answer that question? How do I un-encrypt them? Come on, Kurt. I'm on a deadline here."

No, he thought, I'm the one on a deadline, emphasis on dead.

"On my desktop you'll find a program called Wham. Click on it, then open the files and it will un-encrypt them. I designed the software myself. It's pretty neat. It uses several different algorithms which I don't even think the N.S.A. could crack. You see, first I—"

"Uh, Kurt, shut the hell up, will you please? Please be quiet until I get these files open."

"Whatever. Sure. It's not like I'm going anywhere." She leaned over the pipe and started at him until he shut up. A few minutes passed.

"Got them," she said. "O.K. I see a listing for two accounts with links. One moment." There was a pause. "Got the first one up. Putting in the account number. Now, what's the password?"

"I don't have it."

Her face returned with lightning speed.

"What do you mean you *don't* have it? You set the accounts up, so don't hold out on me, Kurt. You can't imagine the ways I can make you suffer."

"Honest. I don't have'm. Never did. It's a failsafe built into the system. I set up the accounts and Vic puts in the passwords. The only way you can access the accounts is to have both of us in the same place at the same time."

For the first time since he was put underground he was smiling.

"Take that, bitch. No money for you or Mikey. Oh, and those account numbers change every day. The only way you will ever get that money is if you manage to capture Victor McCain, the Hand of God, and then make him talk. You are so royally fucked. Good luck with that." He crossed his arms, feeling smug.

"How do we reset the passwords? There has to be a way to recover them in case you forget them." Unconvinced, Ruth Anne continued to re-enter the data on the computer.

"There is. You have to show up at the banks in person, present the proper I.D. and they re-set it there. But again, with it being a dual account, both Vic and I have to be there. Kill me before you have the passwords from Vic, and no money. You have to keep me alive if you want a chance at the money."

She sat up out of view and he heard the laptop slam shut.

"It's me," she said a moment later. "No. I don't have the money. He —" There was a pause in her phone conversation. "Will you . . . will you shut up for a moment and stop screaming and I'll tell you. We have to have the Spear of Uriel as well to access the money. The idiot has the account numbers and the Spear the passwords."

Idiot. Obviously he wasn't an idiot. No idiot could ever design a program like Wham. That takes brains.

"Tell Mikey I said he'll be dead before he can ever get a word out of Vic," he shouted.

"Fine. I agree. I'll take care of things here then catch the next flight back."

He heard her get up and leave and the brief burst of satisfaction he felt from screwing them over fled his body and was replaced by a gnawing fear of what was coming next. He prayed for snakes. At least a rattlesnake bite would be quick. Or so he hoped. Fire ants were his biggest fear. Thinking of all those things crawling over him, stinging him thousands of times, made him start to shake.

Finally, she was back.

"As much as I'd like to send some of my pets down to visit, I don't have the time to enjoy it. So it has to be done another way." She sighed. "Goodbye, Kurt. You're a lousy kisser, by the way."

"Hey—" he started to protest, but stopped as a burst of water hit him in the face and he had to turn his head sideways to avoid the torrent of water pouring into the casket.

Oh my God, he thought, she's going to drown me.

He pounded on the lid of his coffin and scooted a few inches up, allowing him to get his nose away from the stream of water. He screamed over and over, but the water rose quickly in the confined space.

Winston eased into the carport and moved up next to what he assumed was a door into the kitchen. He started to turn the doorknob when he heard a loud slam from the backyard. He let go of the door handle and instead went to a gate in the fence, and listened intently. He heard a one-sided conversation by a woman he assumed was Ruth Anne discussing bank accounts.

"I'll take care of things." she said.

Winston looked around the carport for a weapon, settling on a shovel as his best bet. He lifted the latch to the gate. Thankfully, it wasn't locked. He cracked it open and saw a woman in the middle of the yard holding a water hose stuck into a pipe in the ground. One hand rested on her hip and she looked bored.

Despite the pain, Winston took off at a dead sprint.

"Excuse me!" he said.

The woman turned, her eyes wide with surprise as the flat of the shovel connected to the side of her head, sending her tumbling. Winston reached down and yanked the hose out of the pipe. Ruth Anne struggled to her feet and tried to run towards the house, but Winston was on top of her before she made it two strides and slammed the shovel into her legs, sending her to the ground. Before she could stand up, he struck her again in the head with the shovel. When she fell to the ground this time she didn't get up.

He pulled her into the house by her feet, watching to make sure she didn't pop back up like Jason in the *Friday the 13th* movies. He ripped the phone cord out of the wall on the counter and tied up her hands. He did the same thing with the phone line in another room and tied her feet. Then he carried her outside and dropped her next to the pipe in the ground. He looked down and could see the tip of a nose poking up and into the pipe.

"Kurt, if you can hear me. It's Winston. I'm going to dig you out," he yelled.

While keeping one eye on Ruth Anne, Winston used the shovel for the purpose it was designed for and began to dig.

~*~

Kurt's arms were starting to get tired. He propped up his body to keep his head above the level of the water and breathed in the air he needed so desperately. Strangely, he began to smell a difference in the air with the aroma of dirt drifting down to him. Taking a deep breath he turned his head sideways and put his ear to the pipe, and listened. Through water-clogged ears, he heard the sweetest sound he ever heard in his life: the smooth baritone of Winston singing a Gospel hymn, accompanied by the sound of a shovel striking the ground and the occasional grunt from digging in the dirt. If he weren't under water he would have cried.

From time to time, Kurt pushed up on the lid, and after one huge heave the lid moved upward a few inches, then a few more, and suddenly he sat up as the lid lifted into the air and was thrown to the side. Standing at the edge of the muddy hole and casket which had entombed him was his friend Winston Reynolds, shirt off, covered in dirt, sweat, and blood streaming from a bandage on his side.

Winston smiled, offered his hand and pulled Kurt up and out of his graveyard-style dungeon. Both men, weak and tired, hugged each other and began to laugh.

Kurt stopped laughing when he turned and saw Ruth Anne on the ground, bound and glaring at him. The side of her head was covered in a growing bruise, her hair matted with dried blood and mud. He went and knelt beside her almost too tired to hold his head up, but there was something he needed to say to her.

You're a liar," he said. "I'm a great kisser."

CHAPTER TWENTY-SEVEN

I sat back in my car and nearly wept after Winston called to give me the word that Kurt was safe, if a bit wrinkled, from being submerged in water for several hours. Hearing they caught Ruth Anne and she was still alive was another plus. I pushed my way into the mission and headed to Father Colton's room and found him inside lying on his bunk reading an autobiography. He put the book aside when I came into the room. I told him about Ruth Anne.

"I'll call a friend I have on the big island," he said. "It will take some time for him to get there, but he'll be able to help. Your friend is O.K.?"

"Yes, he is. Thank you. Look, I need to talk to Charlie. Where is he?"

Colton motioned me to follow him and led me to the room next to his. He knocked and then opened the door. Another priest sat in a chair reading his Bible, while Charlie lay on his bunk facing the wall, the mission's version of a suicide watch. Colton motioned the other priest out and he left with Colton taking the now vacated seat.

"Charlie, my name is Victor McCain, we, uh, met earlier today."

He turned over and looked at me. "You're the guy he was waiting for. The demon in my head. He did what he did just to get you to come to him."

While it wasn't exactly an accusation, it wasn't said without meaning. I couldn't even begin to think what type of thoughts were going through this kid's head.

"Yes. I'm afraid so. It's my job to stop them and, well, they are ramping up the pressure. I'm so very sorry for what happened to your parents. But you understand, there was nothing you could do to stop it?"

He laughed, but without humor.

"And you think that makes me feel any better? It was my hand that held the machete, Mr. McCain. I did it and I couldn't stop it. I murdered my parents, and all those other people—as surely as the monster did."

I wasn't about to spend the rest of the night debating right and wrong with the kid. I had more pressing concerns.

"I need to ask you some questions. I'm trying to figure out where they're coming from, where they're buried. They're here somewhere in

Kentucky and someone has found the spot they were put in back in the day. Is there anything you can tell me which might give me a lead on where I can find where their bodies are buried?"

Charlie contemplated. "Maybe. It's not like we shared thoughts or anything. But we met with another one of the possessed people the day before I went home. He told Arkas that plans were under way to begin the dig. Arkas said the sooner they were freed from the cave the better. But he never said what cave or where."

"That's at least a start. Did he say anything else? Anything which might help us?"

"Not really, other than they really want you dead."

With that, Charlie flipped back over on his side again. Father Colton motioned for me to leave and he stayed behind. I closed the door and left.

I called Winston back. "Colton will have a guy headed your way, but it may be a bit. Rest up. I gave him the address and your cell number. Don't let her get away."

"I won't. But there's something else you need to know," his tone serious. "Mikey was here. In Hawaii."

"Is he still there?" I stopped where I was, stunned by the news, and waited for the answer.

"Nah, man. He flew out last night. The chick has no idea where he flew to. They didn't really get along, know what I mean? Your brother and the Watchers may be working together, but it's not one big happy family."

"Hell, he's been my brother for my entire life and I've never really gotten along with him. So yeah, I do. Keep me posted, alright?"

"Will do. Kurt and I will take shifts until the priest arrives." And with that he hung up.

I continued down to Brother Joshua's office, but before I stepped inside, I heard Samantha's voice and stopped to listen for a moment.

"You can't honestly tell me you believe the world was created in seven days and seven nights. You and I both know that's not possible," she said.

Brother Joshua responded, "With God, all things are possible. Does it really matter how long it took to create the universe and all that is in it? Isn't the creation itself wonder enough?"

Samantha barked a short laugh. "I'm not the one selling the book as gospel. You guys do that. Why not just tell the truth and let people decide for themselves?"

"The truth is told in the Bible, yet you refuse to believe it. Victor, won't you join us?"

How he did that I have no idea. I rolled into the office to see Samantha sitting in one of the chairs across from J, her legs folded beneath her. Yet again my heart soared when she looked at me and offered a small smile. But then her eyes changed to concern as she flew out of the chair and came to me.

"What the hell happened to you?"

She ran her fingers across the cuts on my hands, then up to my face and forehead.

"Are you O.K?"

"Yeah. Some birds went all Alfred Hitchcock on my ass, but I survived."

I gave her a quick rundown, and then turned my attention to Brother Joshua. "We found Ruth Anne in Hawaii. Kurt and Winston have her tied up in a villa she's renting. I already talked to Father Colton and he'll have a priest over there to perform an exorcism. So one more fallen angel kicked to the curb."

"That's great news."

"It is. I have a few questions of my own, if you don't mind." When J nodded for me to continue, I said, "Riddle me this, oh Wise One. How is it Satan gets a free hand, these days, but not a peep from God? J, that scene at the farm, it was . . . it was . . . a little boy was murdered there, J. If Satan can answer the prayers of Mikey and Samantha's father, why in the world would God not stop something like what happened out there?"

"There are several things wrong with your premise. Starting with Michael and Cyrus Tyler. I would suggest to you they did not have prayers answered. They made a trade, their soul for material wealth. God does not offer things in trade. If you believe in him, when you die you will find peace for an eternity in Heaven. It's a simple proposition, but with profound consequences both for those of faith and those without. God does answer prayers, just not in the way of Lucifer. I think when the final accounting is rendered, Michael and Cyrus will not feel they had their prayers answered when they are spending eternity in Hell."

"Fine," I said. "I won't debate the point. How about these fallen angels? He sent them to their prison in the first place. He was their jailer. If they were truly that evil and deserved their punishment, then why doesn't He take the steps to put them back in their place?"

"He is. Through you." Brother Joshua said. "God does what he does through the people of faith. You are doing God's work. And through you the threat will be stopped."

"While innocent people are murdered? He was only a boy, J. What did he ever do to deserve what happened to him?" I said, slamming my fist down on his desk. I stepped back a few feet and ran both hands through my hair, trying to get control of my temper.

"We've had this discussion. He did nothing to deserve it. The race of man makes their choices. Not all of them well. You must continue to have faith."

I shook my head and paced the room.

"It's not right. It's not." I began to wonder if my frustration was at God or at my inability to keep a young boy alive. It felt like I was running a race, going backward while everyone else was sprinting ahead.

"Read the book of Revelations, Victor. Things will be getting much worse before the end comes."

I threw my hands up in the air.

"Then what's the point of it all?"

Samantha watched the two of us, staying quiet, but she stared down Brother Joshua, waiting to hear the answer.

"Because it is what good people do and will continue to do until the end. Stopping Arkas means he will not be murdering other children. You must continue to fight those who are truly evil until your end comes."

"Which will come much sooner, thanks to you," Samantha said.

He shook his head no. "Victor made his choices. And his choices have consequences. He is paying for his sins and atoning for the wrongs he created."

Brother Joshua was right. I was responsible for my own actions. No one else. I thought I could save Mikey when all evidence told me I could not. It was my pride doing the talking. I was about to say something more when the feeling of wrongness hit me like a ton of bricks.

J closed his eyes and then snapped them open and called my name, but my gun was already in my hands.

"Get down behind the chair and stay there." I told Samantha.

I flipped the light switch off, sending the room into darkness. I heard Samantha get up and move as I requested. I glanced into the hallway. Light from a street lamp outside streamed through a window about twenty feet from me and I saw a shadow outside dart quickly from one side to the other.

"I thought we were safe here because of the Chapel?" I said quietly.

From right next to me, Brother Joshua replied, "You are safe in any house of God, as the Hand of God. Others are not as fortunate."

I cursed under my breath. "When I head out, you close and lock the door behind me." With my eyes now adjusted to the darkness I could pick out his form standing next to me. "Keep her safe, J. If you don't, it won't be pretty."

Moving into the hallway, I didn't hang around to see if he was ticked at my threat, and quickly made my way towards the front door. I knew it was near midnight and most of the homeless in the shelter were in bed. I didn't have to worry about bumping into one of them inside the mission. I eased up to the window and glanced outside. Standing across the street under the streetlamp stood one of the missing college students. I racked my brain and finally came up with the name to match the face. Kyle Beaumont.

He stood there with his arms stretched out to his sides, palms up, watching the mission, obviously making no attempt to hide. I made my way to the door, cracked it open enough to slip outside, with my gun raised to the ready.

He looked at me and then screamed, "Uriel. It is I, Shamsiel. Do you not remember me?"

"Hey, dickwad, I'm not Uriel. When are you guys going to get my name right? And no, I don't know you."

I heard the door open behind me and glanced over my shoulder. Brother Joshua stepped outside.

"He's not talking to you." Brother Joshua replied.

"Get back inside. Now." I hissed. But he ignored me and stepped towards the fallen angel. I snagged his sleeve and tried to pull him back, but he gently took hold of my hand and removed it from his arm.

"I'm in no danger, Hand of God. You may relax."

What the holy hell? Relax? After the last few days I'd been through and he wanted *me* to relax? Screw that. I watched as the body of Kyle Beaumont fell to his knees, his hands now reaching out to J, and tears streamed down his face. For my part, I pointed my gun directly at a spot between his eyes and got ready to blow him away if he so much as sneezed.

"Uriel, please forgive me. I have come to you to beg forgiveness for my sins."

Brother Joshua and I crossed the street together and I scanned the area trying to find other threats, but none appeared. Joshua went to Kyle and took his hands in his.

"I am sorry, old friend, but you are asking that which is beyond my power to grant." Brother Joshua answered.

My head snapped around to Joshua. "Old friend. Wait. You know this guy? How is that . . ." I stopped and I could almost feel my jaw hitting the pavement. "Uriel. You're Uriel, the archangel?"

"Much like the fallen, I, at times, manifest myself with Brother Joshua. Unlike what Shamsiel has done, however, I am accepted willingly."

Tony Acree

Returning his gaze to Shamsiel, he continued, "There was a time when Shamsiel helped me with different tasks. But he strayed, as did the other of the Watchers, and is sentenced to prison until Judgment Day."

"You spoke on our behalf before God," Shamsiel said. "You could do so again. I am pleading with you, Uriel. Go before God and ask for our forgiveness."

The face of Kyle Beaumont shone with a desperation one rarely sees. And looking into his eyes, I could see they were raven black with stars falling in them. I rubbed my own eyes and looked again, but the sensation of falling stars remained.

Brother Joshua placed his hands gently on either side of Kyle's head, then bent and kissed him on the forehead. Kyle closed his eyes and wept. Then J straightened, placing his hands on top of Kyle's head and said, "You have been judged, Shamsiel. You and your brothers sealed your fate the moment you turned from God. I command you, leave this body, and return no more!"

When Father Colton performed his exorcism, he worked at it for several minutes. I guess when you're an archangel you pack a bigger punch. Kyle's body arched back, his hands once again thrown out to his side and a high-pitched wail escaped his body, forcing me to cover my ears with both hands. The moment quickly passed, however, and Kyle slumped to the ground, his eyes rolling back in his head. Joshua knelt beside the young man and brushed his fingers gently across his forehead. As he did this, he muttered something softly. Kyle's eyes first closed, then opened again to reveal the black of the fallen angel now replaced by a much more normal green of the man he was before.

Joshua offered Kyle a hand and pulled him to his feet.

"I know you will have many questions, but for now may I offer you a place of rest?" Brother Joshua said to Kyle.

The boy nodded a very sleepy yes and J led us back across the street and into the mission. He asked me to wait while he took Kyle down to the room next to Charlie's. A few minutes later he came out and closed the door, and then stood in front of me.

"He will sleep soundly for the rest of the night. I will talk with him in the morning."

"That's how you know where to send me. Uriel is one of the angels allowed in the presence of God. You get your orders directly from the Big Man, right?" I may not know my Bible overly well, but I do know some of the more kick butt angels and Uriel stands near the top of the list. Knowing I was standing in his presence was more than a bit intimidating.

"The process is not exactly as you state, but close enough. When needed, Brother Joshua calls my name and I come. Most of the time you are dealing with him, but I come when needed."

"And tonight, you were needed. Back in the office, was Samantha arguing with Joshua or you?"

Brother Joshua smiled and walking by me. "Does it matter?"

"He said you argued for them before God. Is that true?"

"It is as Shamsiel said. I did argue for God to spare them, but He did not. I mourn for my brethren, but even for us, choices have consequences. Lucifer and the Watchers pay an eternal price for their defiance of God."

"And there is no chance God would change his mind?" I thought hard, trying to wrap my brain around the concept of redemption and salvation, or damnation and eternity.

"None. The judgment against the Watchers is final and there will be no reprieve."

"You know where they are, don't you? You could tell me where they're buried and allow me to end this, couldn't you?"

"I am sorry, Victor. It is not allowed. This is for you to deal with. I have faith you will do so."

"You know that's bullshit as far as I'm concerned. You guys upstairs play these games and we are nothing but pawns. God could end this in an instant, but he won't."

Once again, if Uriel was perturbed at my insolence, he let it slide.

"Things are the way they are and it's up to you and your fellow man to find your way until the end."

I slapped the wall hard with my hand in frustration, but reigned in my temper. After all, I watched as Uriel kicked a fallen angel out of a body the way I knocked a piece of lint off my shoulder.

"They keep calling me the Spear of Uriel. What's up with that?"

"From the time of the first Hand it has been my job to help them find their way in life. You are the Hand of God, but the divine have forever called them the Spear, as I use you to hunt down the most evil of your fellow man, then eliminate them. One of my jobs is to send people to Hell. You are the instrument I use."

"Great. I'm the Black and Decker tool of choice for God's handyman."

We walked together into his office and he flipped on the lights. Samantha came to me and took one of my hands in hers. "Everything O.K.?"

"Yeah. For the moment. Seems the Watchers are down another man."

I turned my attention to J. "I learned they were found in a cave.

There are a lot of caves in these parts, starting with the mother of all caves, Mammoth Cave. Charlie says Arkas and another one of the fallen talked about digging out a cave. That must be why Mikey needed the construction equipment. I think that rules out a place like Mammoth Cave. Not exactly the kind of place you can do major digging without raising suspicion. I'll go back and talk to people to see if I can find out who may know anything about a cave."

Pointing at Samantha and me, he said, "Fine. I think it's time the two of you get some rest. In separate rooms, please."

We left him alone and walked out into the hallway together.

"Still worried about Brother Joshua?" I asked.

Once again she gave me the half shoulder shrug. "I don't like the fact he's the one responsible for choosing your assignments. I mean, you have no idea what his motivations are."

I debated how much to tell her about what I just learned, but decided now was not the time.

"Well, his motivations really don't matter much to me," I said. "The people I've killed have all deserved it. I appreciate your concern, but I'm really O.K. with my situation. I think Montoya was as well."

She leaned in and kissed me. "Doesn't mean I have to like it."

I watched her turn and go inside. I made it to my own room, stripped down, climbed into bed, and thought about the investigation. I always had a sense of when an investigation was coming to an end. I felt that about this one. I was close enough to the fallen and to Mikey that I could feel it.

It was a surprise to me that Mikey was in Hawaii. But it also meant he came out in the open. And to coordinate things with the Watchers this meant he must be somewhere very close. As exhaustion and sleep overtook me my mind began to wander and I thought of the many times Mikey and I were young and actually enjoyed being together. Like the time . . . I let the thought trail off.

Damn. I was now wide-awake. Mikey was back in Kentucky and I knew exactly where he was.

CHAPTER TWENTY-EIGHT

Michael McCain was pissed. He pushed the Bluetooth button on the steering wheel to end the phone call from Hawaii and then grabbed the wheel so hard he wanted to break the damn thing off in his hands. The fallen angel bitch failed. Not only was Kurt Pervis still breathing, but he was saved at the last minute by Winston Reynolds. And they arranged for yet another exorcism, sending one more of the fallen to wander in the arid abyss. He should have cut on Kurt the first night they had him instead of letting the fallen angel play with him. Note to self: tell the fallen angels to fuck off the next time they get in his way.

This meant he was no closer than he was to the thirty million dollars stolen by Samantha Tyler, and a golden opportunity was wasted. If he were allowed to handle it his way they'd have the money. One royal screw up after another, all because people wouldn't let him do his job. Cyrus Tyler would regret the day he kept his daughter alive. Wait and see. The whole Florida operation blown. He snickered at that one and gave his brother credit. Never even considered he'd use a bomb to break her free. Good one, Vic. Let it not be said the McCain brothers weren't resourceful.

He pulled up to the security gate at the front of his driveway, punched in his code and watched it swing open. He could see the snow on the drive remained unbroken since the last snowfall. With Victor and others looking for his ass it helped to be cautious. He made sure no one was following him.

He pulled up to the old cabin he was refurbishing with all the creature comforts of home, got out of his car, hit the fob key on his keychain, and locked it. Bone tired, after all the travel he'd done in the last few days, he couldn't wait to get into bed.

He unlocked the front door, stopped to turn off and then re-arm the house alarm. He tried to change his dark mood by whistling a bluesy *Feeling Good* song he heard on the radio. Before he hit the sack, however, he needed to check on a few business items. He went to his study first, stopped at the wet bar and poured a double of Jameson Irish Whiskey, neat. Ice was for sissies. He sipped the whiskey and moved to his desk, but nearly jumped out of his skin when he heard a familiar voice.

"What, not going to pour me one?" Vic said.

~*~

"Come on, Mikey. I know you're a better host than that."

Mikey almost dropped his glass, but recovered and sat heavily into a leather swivel chair which was big enough to fit my large backside and two of his. Mikey took a long pull on the whiskey, and wiped his mouth with the back of his hand, setting the glass down on the large antique desk made of gorgeous cherry wood.

"Jesus, Vic. You scared the ever lovin' hell out of me."

His hand dropped low and out of site as I stood from a corner chair I was sitting in and walked towards his desk.

"You know, Mikey, I don't think that's possible. If I've learned anything over the last few months, is you have enough Hell in you to go around."

I didn't make it more than a couple of steps when Mikey raised his hands, pointing the business end of a Glock 19 at me.

"That's far enough, little brother. Take one more step and I will keep my promise I made to you back at the warehouse and shoot you where you stand." He stood and moved around his desk. "On your knees, if you please."

I did as he asked, slowly going first on one knee, then the other, laughing, and Mikey didn't like it. "What's so damned funny, eh brother? I'm the one with the gun and you're the one on your knees."

"I'm laughing because even on my knees I'm still almost taller than you are."

I kept laughing and he struck out, hitting me in the side of the face, the gun ripping a line across my cheek. I could feel the blood running down my face, but I ignored it. Between the damn buzzards and Mikey, my face was taking a beating.

"So here we are. The mighty Victor McCain on his knees. I've always been better than you, Vic. Always. There's nothing you don't want I can't take. I am curious. How did you figure out where I was hiding?"

"When dad died and mom had to sell this place, you threw a fit. It's one of the few places you seemed to actually care about. I thought back to that time when we came out here with dad, just the three of us, on a guy's weekend. Hunting, fishing, we all had a blast. Then a few years ago, I heard the old place had been purchased by some corporation who planned to use it for business retreats. It sounded like something you'd come up with so I did a property search first thing this morning. Then called up Kurt and had him track down the owners of the corporation. Low and behold, your name came up. So I figured you would run to the one place you loved. And here you are."

"Guess I shouldn't have used the same alarm code either, huh? Dad's birthday is one of the few things I can remember. Well, good job on hunting me down. But you should've shot me when I came through the door. Gun still in its holster?"

I slowly lifted the flap of my coat and showed him he was right, then let the coat flap fall back into place. "You're not going to shoot me, Mikey. You don't have it in you."

"Oh, really? Hmm. We'll see about that. Tell me, Vic, there were no car tracks. Did you really walk all the way into here from across the mountain?"

He tried hard to keep his eyes on me, but he couldn't help glancing around to make sure I didn't have someone else with me.

"Yep. I parked down at old man Hobart's place inside his barn. It really isn't that hard of a walk. Well, it isn't for real men. For pussies like you who don't even like to get their shoes wet, you'd never make it."

"Keep mouthing off and I'll shoot yer trap closed. I mean it, Vic."

His face contorted into one of barely contained rage and the gun began to shake a bit in his hand. Mikey always hated it when people questioned his manhood.

"Fallen angels? Really, Mikey? Let those things loose and what will your patron, Lucifer, do? Everything here will belong to them?"

"That's your problem, Vic. All muscle and no brains. Think about it. When the Lord of Light makes his move to reclaim his spot in Heaven, don't you think having two hundred pissed off fallen angels in your debt would be a good thing? Earth is only the first battlefield. Heaven is next. And when the war comes, the two hundred will be itching for a little payback for having all their children drowned like rats."

"So you're willing to kill everyone on the planet to get what you want?" I knew Mikey was evil, knew him to be certifiably nuts. But this far? "Mikey, you go down with everyone else. You realize that, don't you?"

"Like I said, all muscle and no brains. You keep thinking in this life. I'm working for a better position with the winning side in the next life."

"Always have a back-up plan, right Mikey?" Mikey used his other hand to make a pretend gun and pretended to shoot me. "How did you find them?"

"I didn't. Some poor college schmucks found them. One of them had a cave on a family farm down in Edmonson County and took some chick cave diving and got more than they bargained for. They possessed the girl and ate the guy. Guess the only one of them not shackled down was damn hungry. Then when they made it to the surface, the Lord of Light became aware of their presence and I made contact and we struck a deal."

"Which is why you needed Tommy Spenoza. You plan on digging them out, don't you? I figured as much. Well, plus you wanted that parchment. Sorry about that."

He waved it off. "Don't sweat it. I have others. I was never sure which one would work anyways. So, I tried to collect them all. All you did was slow me down. Was it you who whacked him?"

"I was. One less child molester in the world."

Mikey began to calm down, the usual sneer back in place. He always loved to run his mouth, so I let him.

"What about mom?" I asked. "You let these things out and she's as good as dead."

"Nah. You worry too much. I made a deal with the Watchers. A handful of people get to live. I mean, they will need people to help run things until their new children grow up. I'll see to it mom makes it. You have my word. I'll make you another promise, Vic—even though you don't deserve it. When I tell mom about your death, I'll tell her you died a hero, trying to save someone. I'll make up something good."

I let out a short bark of a laugh. "Thanks. You're still a prick, Mikey."

His smile, large and full, was sincere. "Yes. Yes, I am. Ain't it grand?"

"Where's the lap dog, Preston? I thought you two were best buds?"

"He's on loan to Cyrus Tyler in Washington, D.C. Changes are coming, Vic. Too bad you won't be around to see it happen. I wish I could say I'll miss you, brother, but you know how it is."

I shook my head. "Goodbye, Mikey."

His smile vanished. "Goodbye, Vic."

Pointing the gun at my head, he pulled the trigger. Then he pulled it again and again. In one swift motion, I stood, snagged the gun from him with one hand, and seized him by the neck with the other, forcing him back and onto his desk.

"Mikey, Mikey, Mikey. You think I'm going to come into your place and not look for weapons? I found the gun and removed the striker, then put the gun back. You should have thought about it, Mikey. You think I'd sit here and wait for you to blow me away? You know me better than that. Always have a back-up plan, right?"

I tossed the gun to the floor and started using both hands to choke the life out of my only brother. He clawed at my hands, but his fingernails couldn't do much damage to my already battered skin. His face began to turn a deep, purplish red.

"This is for Dominic Montoya, for the people you've allowed to be murdered in the name of the sick son of a bitch you follow. In a few seconds, you're going to be delivered to Hell. I've been given a taste of what awaits you. You are so royally screwed."

I tried keeping my emotions out of this, but I couldn't. I flashed back to when we were kids, fighting in the backyard, and I yelled to Mikey, "I'm going to kill you!" I didn't mean it then, but that was my intent now. The last three months set the two of us on this collision course with my hands around his throat. And in a few minutes it would be over. Eternal torment waited.

"And I won't tell mom you died a hero. I'll tell her you were on the run from the law, that you were caught up in some type of scam you couldn't get yourself out of and were on the lamb. There will be no fond memories of you, Mikey."

His eyes bulged and his hands slapped at my arms to make me stop. After a few moments, his useless efforts at fighting me slowed. And finally, all movement ceased, my brother's body sprawled across the beautiful antique desk, lifeless. I kept the grip tight a little while longer to be sure he was truly gone. Then I let go, walked back to the chair I was sitting in earlier and thought about the last time we were in the cabin with my dad. I thought about all the laughter we shared when our innocence was still intact. Now it was all consumed by the flames of Hell.

I swallowed hard a couple of times, staring at my brother's still body, then I put my head in my hands and wept.

CHAPTER TWENTY-NINE

I wiped down the few places I touched when I entered the house, threw Mikey's body over my shoulder, and headed across the mountain to my car. On the way there, I stopped at a deep sinkhole, tossed Mikey's body over the side, and watched it disappear into the darkness. I knew the sinkhole didn't go all the way to Hell, but at least it was now a bit closer. I said a short prayer for Mikey's soul, though I knew it was pointless. Mikey would spend the rest of eternity paying for his Satan-financed reign of terror.

I drove back to Louisville and thought about the story of Cain and Abel, one of the first lessons I learned when I was a kid. Now, as an adult, it seemed I was living my own version. The original Cain killed his brother and was condemned by God. I killed mine because I was told to do so, but by a higher authority. What did this mean for my own soul? One of the Ten Commandments is "thou shall not kill" yet that was practically my job description.

My brain bordered on exploding trying to reconcile the incongruity. There's no doubt God spent plenty of time punishing the wicked. The Watchers were directly responsible for God drowning every person who walked on the Earth not on Noah's boat. It was my job to track down and eliminate the worst evil the human mind could ever conjure into existence.

But this one, well, it differed from all the rest. It was my only brother. I had no clue how I would be able to sleep at night without Mikey's bulging eyes haunting my dreams. Mikey deserved his fate as Cain deserved his. But it didn't make it any easier to deal with. When Brother Joshua put me on the path to killing Mikey it had been an abstract kind of thing. Sure, I can do it. But actually choking the life out of him? Different matter.

I would like to say I would miss him. But we grew up to be very different people and were never very close. The best I can do now was try to remember the Mikey from my childhood and not the cold-blooded killer he became at the end of his life. The person I truly ached for was my mother. She would never know what happened to her first-born, that he was killed by his brother. I would never be able to offer her closure without confessing my own role in his death.

I decided to spend the rest of the night at a motel in Lexington. After paying the clerk, I walked slowly to my room. Once inside I locked and chained the door and then put a chair under the doorknob. I took a long hot shower and lay down naked on the bed and, to my surprise, fell into a deep and dreamless sleep.

I awoke refreshed the next morning and at peace. Mikey's fate—and and mine—were intertwined. Only my death would answer the question of whether or not I'd join him in Hell or with my dad in Heaven.

The temperature climbed into the mid-thirties and the snow was starting to melt. It felt as if the world surrounding me was beginning to cleanse itself after a long cold spell steeped in near total darkness.

Time to get back to hunting fallen angels.

I called ahead and was greeted by Rob McGeorge. He shook my hand and invited me in. "Evelyn is at the market picking up a few things. Do you have any news for me?"

"I do. The individual responsible for what happened to your son will no longer be able to hurt anyone else, ever again."

McGeorge closed his eyes and gave a small shake of his head. When he opened them again, the fierceness and intensity of the man showed through.

"Thank you. I'm sorry it wasn't me who did it, but that it's been done will have to do." He seemed truly relieved. "You said you have a question for Mal? Then come on upstairs."

I found Mal McGeorge still in his bed, but looking better. He sat leaning against his headboard with ear buds in his ears and an iPod on his lap. His father called his name, he pulled the ear buds out and pressed pause on his player.

"What's on your playlist?" I asked.

"I'm listening to an audio version of the Holy Bible. Makes my mom happy and I have some catching up to do. I never paid much attention back when I went to Sunday school. So, you know, there's a lot I don't know," he replied. "Dad said you have a question for me?"

"Yes, I do. Did Ruth Anne ever mention anything about a cave? I'm thinking she must have been in one recently."

"You know, she did. She was really hot for this guy at U of K. Jason something or other. His family has a farm with one on it and she was invited to go with him. You think that's where they first made contact with these guys? Father Colton told me they were imprisoned somewhere deep underground."

"I think you can guarantee it. And I think I know which Jason, too."

The P.I's report included the name of Jason Mueller. He was the only one of the missing students not to show any credit card activity. "Thanks, Mal. That really helps."

"Sure. Whatever. Happy to help." He put the ear buds back in and hit play on his iPod. Robert McGeorge and I left the room and he showed me to the front door.

"Do you really believe in this fallen angel stuff? I mean, I know Mal does and so does my wife, but do you?" he asked. I could read the skepticism on his face and couldn't blame him. To say it out loud sounded fantastical.

"Mr. McGeorge, yes, I do. They are very much real and before this is all over, I'm going to send them all to Hell. Just like the one who did this to your son."

I left him there, considering the existence of fallen angels, and returned to my car. If he didn't believe me, I couldn't blame him. Tell a man his son is the victim of a fallen angel and what would you expect? Our world is one of science, the real and the proved. Fallen angels were the stuff of legends. If I couldn't keep my promise to send them all to Hell, then everyone would soon learn how real they are.

Before I pulled out of the McGeorge's house, my phone rang. It was Winston. "We just landed at Louisville International a few minutes ago. Think you can come pick us up?"

"Sure. We? You bring Kurt back with you?" The fact Kurt survived his ordeal in Hawaii removed a huge drag on my emotional well-being.

"Him and the girl, too. Ruth Anne Gardner." Winston lowered his voice. "And man, you should see these two. They're all over each other." I could hear the laughter in Winston's voice.

"Really? Wow. So it took a girl possessed by a fallen angel to get Kurt a girlfriend? Why am I not surprised? See you in a few."

I drove up to the curbside pick up area and found the three of them waiting under the Delta sign, but I could tell something was wrong. Winston had a grim look on his face, while Kurt held Ruth Anne. The girl gripped him tightly, crying hard into his shoulder. I didn't have to be a rocket scientist to figure out what happened. She must have been contacted by the cops about her mother and brother.

I opened up the trunk and tossed in their luggage, while Kurt and Ruth Anne got into the back seat. The girl was a real looker, but the real shock was the look on Kurt's face. The man had always been, for a better word, soft. Not now. His eyes had a hard look and his jaw set with steely determination. Getting into the car with Ruth Anne, he gave me a tight, small nod in greeting. I expected him to start spitting out nails any minute, that's how tough Kurt looked. And Kurt *never* looked tough.

I walked up to Winston before he got in and asked, "She got the call, didn't she?"

"Yeah. She'd been trying to reach her mother. When she couldn't, she called a family friend and they told her. All of a sudden, her closest family is all gone. Doesn't help that they were done-in by the same group who hijacked her mind. Man, she's going to have a tough row to hoe, know what I mean?"

I did.

"Mikey's dead," I said. I worked to keep my emotions off my face, but there was no fooling Winston. He opened his arms and gave me a hug. I could feel myself tear up, but managed to keep the flood from springing forth.

"Lord's will be done. Ashes to ashes, and dust to dust. Your brother made his deal and now he's paid in full. I'm sorry for you, but you did the right thing."

"Yeah. I know. It's still hard." I glanced around to make sure no one was close by and then asked, "What about the P.I.? How did you handle it?"

"Wasn't easy. The first night Kurt and I took turns digging him up. I used my rental to dump the body in the middle of a thick wooded area. I don't think the body will be found anytime soon. Then we broke up the coffins and threw them in a dumpster behind a shopping center. When the next renters move in they'll be able to tell there was digging in the back yard, but not what for. Then we wiped down the entire house and checked out. She was paid up until the end of the month, in cash. So we're safe for a bit, at least."

"Good job. I understand the exorcism took most of the night before the fallen angel was kicked out. Did you guys get a name?"

"Yeah. Kokabiel. Where do they get all these silly ass names, anyway?"

"I have no clue. How did she seem when it was all over? Charlie had a real tough time adjusting to life once the freeloader was kicked out and dealing with the fact his body had been used to commit murder. How about Ruth Anne?" I asked.

"She kind of blew it off. Mainly because she never saw the guy die. She was forced to pour fire ants down a tube and could hear the guy's screams, but she never saw anything."

"Got it. Let's get these lovebirds back to the mission. I think I have a line on where the Watchers were hidden and she's the key. Time to devise a game plan."

Ruth Anne cried the whole drive and I didn't blame her a bit. Death had touched everyone in the car, one way or the other. When we got to the mission, Samantha waited inside the door, pacing back and forth. She hugged Winston first, then grabbed Kurt and held him for a very long time, whispering something softly in his ear. And, amazingly, Kurt hugged her back and kissed her lightly on the lips.

Wow. The old Kurt would've been frozen like a deer in the headlights. The events of Hawaii really had changed the computer geek. Samantha introduced herself to Ruth Anne, and then finally turned her attention to me. I took her in my arms and told her Mikey was dead and did my best not to cry. She kissed me, then told me to hold on a moment. She ran back to her room and returned with her winter coat.

"Let's go for a ride. I need some fresh air." She took me by the arm and tried to lead me out the door, but I didn't budge.

"I can't, Samantha. There's some things I need to talk over with Joshua. It's really important." I tried not to look her in the eyes, staring down at my feet, but she lifted my chin so we were eye to eye, my blues to her green.

"He can wait. Let's go," she insisted.

I didn't have any resistance left in me. I told Winston to fill in Joshua and to ask him to get Ruth Anne squared away and that I'd be back later. With that, Samantha and I walked out the front door of the mission and over to my car. I opened the door for her and then got in on my side.

"Where to?" With red hair framing a face to die for, I would have driven her through Hell itself if she asked me to. But she made it easy for me.

"Know of any good sword shops? I think it's time I get myself back in the game. But take the long way. We need to talk."

I did know of a sword shop over off Frankfort Avenue, where I previously bought one for a birthday gift. I pointed the Ford towards Market Street, then turned right, taking the side streets through town over to Frankfort Avenue.

She reached out and took my right hand in her left, lacing our fingers together, and covering it with her other.

"Tell me about Mikey," she said.

And so I did. About figuring out where he was holed up, about waiting for him, and about choking him to death. I told the story as if it happened to someone else. I told her about the weekend we spent at the cabin with my dad. And how I didn't know what I'd say to our mother, if anything. She listened to me without interrupting, squeezing my hand tightly between hers.

When I ran out of words, she said, in a very small voice, "John raped me down in Florida. More than once. I tried to fight him off, but he was so much stronger than I was that I couldn't stop him."

Tears of her own started falling from her beautiful green eyes. I pulled the car over, undid my seat buckle and this time it was my turn to hold her.

Over and over, she kept repeating, "I'm so sorry, I'm so sorry," as if what happened to her was her fault.

"You have nothing to be sorry for. I'm to blame. If I'd stopped them at the warehouse, then they would never have taken you to begin with."

She shook her head violently back and forth, "No, no, no. You did the best you could. I don't blame you for what happened."

I wasn't sure I believed her. Samantha's anger when I rescued her down south was very real. She was pissed as hell at me. I could still remember the left cross to the jaw.

"Look, we are two flawed human beings," I said. "Neither of us has lead a perfect life. How about from this point forward we do the best we can. Together."

I felt her nod into my chest. "It may take some time before I'm ready for intimacy. I hope you understand."

"I've waited my whole life to meet a woman like you. I'll wait as long as you need. And when the wait is over, I'll be here for you."

I kissed the top of her head, got back behind the wheel, snapped on my seatbelt and took us to the medieval weapons store. The woman knew her blades, and quizzed the guy behind the counter, as she picked out a new katana and carrying case. I damaged her old one when I took down a hellhound, so I paid for the new one. Seemed like a romantic gesture.

We returned to the mission.

"You go talk to Joshua. I want to go to my room and practice.," she said.

"No worries. But you're safe here. You won't have much need for it."

Some of the fire I remembered returned as anger and flashed in her eyes.

"Look, I won't be staying here much longer. I'm owed some payback of my own and I plan to collect."

I thought about telling her no, that she was going to stay put and be safe. I couldn't stand the thought of losing her again, but I didn't. For the last three months Samantha was kept imprisoned by her dad. She was raped, emotionally battered, and no telling what else. If I tried to make her stay here, how was I any different than those who hurt her?

"Don't cut yourself practicing."

She gave me one of her patented Spock raised eyebrows, turned on her heels and strode off, a purpose in her step. Heaven help the person on the receiving end of her katana. Eamon tried taking her on when she held one in her hand and it sent him packing back to Hell. My guess is a few more would be doing the same before long.

CHAPTER THIRTY

Buck Wilson was having one hell of a bad day. He continued to stare at the production schedules scattered across his desk, but no matter how he tried, he couldn't make them work. That meant the bonus he deserved for finishing the new bypass out in Shelbyville wasn't going to be his. The damn snow and cold kept his guys off their equipment and the dollars out of his pocket.

He and his top supervisor, Wendell Peters, were in the office doing their best to make the complicated schedules, and profit numbers, balance out. Perhaps they needed to hire another work crew or two? But that would eat into the profits. But no extra crews meant no bonus and no profits at all. So he asked Peters to work the phones trying to find warm bodies they could hire in case they got lucky and the weather broke.

He stopped what he was doing when he heard a truck pull up outside the doublewide work trailer. Glancing out the window he saw his cousin Bill get out and head towards the door packing his Dakota rifle. Hell, it wasn't hunting season, so what in the Sam Hill was he doin' lugging that thing around?

He didn't have to wonder long. The door opened and Bill came in, stamping the snow off his feet.

"Howdy, cuz. You doing alright?" Bill said.

"You know how it is, Bill. Could be worse, could be better. What the hell you doing out here?"

"I need you to do me a favor, Buck. I need you to give me some of that dynamite you keep in your storage shed, along with some blasting caps."

Buck laughed, a bit nervously. He looked over at Wendell who put the phone down, licked his lips and his face paled.

"Come on Bill, you know I can't just give away that kind of thing. You have to have permits to carry it and the state regulates that stuff. You come up missing even one blasting cap and your ass is grass. Whatcha need dynamite for, anyways?"

"Buck, if I told you, you wouldn't believe me. But I do need it, ya hear? So get your sorry ass up out of that chair, get your coat and get on out to the shed and get it for me," Bill insisted.

Wendell picked up the phone and began dialing. Bill turned to him, raised the Dakota to his shoulder and put a bullet right through Wendell's breast pocket, knocking him out of his chair—the phone still in his hands. Bill took a few steps and put another one in Wendell just for good measure. Buck peed his pants. He saw Wendell's feet twitch a couple of times, then stopped.

Bill turned his attention back to his cousin.

"Like I said, Buck. I need you to get up and get me what I need. Now, if you would be so kind."

Buck got unsteadily to his feet, and slipped on his old Army jacket, snatched the keys off his desk and eased by Bill out into the cold winter air and over to the metal storage shed. It took him a few tries to get the key into the padlock, what with how bad his hands were shaking, but he got it and slipped the lock off the door. He pulled it open and flipped on the single bulb light.

"How much do you need?" Buck asked.

Smiling, he replied, "All of it. Just pick it up and put it in the bed of my truck. Go on now, get moving. The daylight's a wastin'.'"

Several trips later, Buck leaned against the truck and said, "That's all of it, dynamite and caps. Tell you what, Bill. I'll just tell the Staties I had a break in. I won't tell no one it was you who stole the stuff."

Buck could feel the pain begin in his chest, his breath coming in wheezes. His doc had been on him about his weight for a couple of years and he knew he was having a heart attack.

He fell to one knee and looked at Bill. "Heart. Heart attack. Help me. Please."

"Be happy to, cuz. I wouldn't want ya to suffer." He raised the Dakota up and took aim down the barrel, the muzzle a few inches from Buck's nose. The last thing Buck thought before he died was, "That's not the kinda help I meant."

~*~

I entered J's office and found Kurt seated and typing away on his laptop he had balanced on his knees while Winston was leaned back in a chair, his feet propped up on J's garbage can that he pulled up in front of him. Since there were only two chairs in the room, I closed the door and leaned against the wall.

"Winston told me about Michael. I know it can't be easy for you. I'm sorry for your loss," Brother Joshua said.

"I don't really want to talk about it. Let's move on. Mikey did run off at the mouth a bit before the end and he told me the first contact with the Watchers happened in a cave between two college kids. I stopped and talked to Mal McGeorge and he said Ruth Anne knew a guy who had a cave on his family farm, which means Ruth Anne knows where they are. She's first contact."

Joshua picked up his phone and punched a couple of buttons. "Lisa, would you bring Ruth Anne to the office, please? Thank you." He hung up the phone and we waited.

When Ruth Anne entered the office, Kurt closed his laptop, stood and offered his chair. I'll be damned, I thought. I began to wonder if Kurt had been possessed and replaced by a tough but chivalrous fallen angel, but knew it was impossible. Kurt's faith in God was strong—stronger than mine, truth be told. Don't get me wrong. I know God exists, but faith? That's another matter and the events of the last few months were going a long way in testing mine. Still for Kurt, what a change. If a pretty woman walked into his presence like this before Hawaii, the hives would have already started.

I said to Ruth Anne, "You went with another student, Jason Mueller, to a cave on some property his family owns, right?"

A shudder shook her entire frame. "Yes. They have a farm down near Mammoth Cave. He invited me to go spelunking." Her eyes filled with tears and her bottom lip started trembling. "The guy we found down there," she hesitated, "ate him. Just ripped him to pieces and then . . . well, you get the picture. I don't have to go back there, do I?" She squeezed her hands between her knees and started to rock back and forth in the chair.

Before I could answer Kurt stepped beside her, bent over, and put his arms around her.

"Of course not," Kurt said. "We'll take care of it. Do you know the address?" When she shook her head no, he said, "Not to worry. I can find it." He sat his laptop on top of a file cabinet, flipped up the lid and started his search.

"We'll take care of it? You're not a field guy, Kurt," I reminded him. "Winston and I will handle it."

"No way, dude. I'm in. They tried to kill me and I won't let them get away with it. And after what they've done to Ruth Anne, I want in. Besides, you're going to need everyone you can get. Sounds like they're down four of them, but that leaves no telling how many more of them out there. You and Winston won't be enough if you go out to the farm and find them all there waiting on you."

"The man's got a point," Winston replied. "Especially if you plan on trying to take them out without killing them. If you want to sneak up on them and shoot'em all in the head, that's one thing. But otherwise, man, they're a little hard to bring down. I've got the stitches to prove it. And that one down in Florida nearly drowned your ass," he reminded me.

They were both right. But it didn't mean I had to like it. Kurt's only brush with danger prior to Hawaii was driving the van the night we sprung Samantha from the Church of the Light Reclaimed on a farm in the middle of nowhere. To put him in harm's way where the bad guys would like nothing more than to gut him and put his head on a spike would not be wise. I would have to try and find a way to convince him to sit this one out.

"Found it," Kurt said. "They own a farm in Edmonson County."

He got a post-it note from J's desk, wrote down the address, and then handed me the paper. I folded it and slipped it into my pants pocket.

"The person I met the other night, is he available to help out with this?" I asked Brother Joshua.

"He is not. He is not allowed to take a proactive role in what happens."

Winston and Kurt shot questioning looks my way, but I ignored them.

"How'd I know you were going say that?" I pushed off the wall.

"Alright then, here's what we do first. Winston and I will drive down to this farm and take a look around, and survey the place. Kurt, while we're gone, you pull up a map of it and any details you can about the topography, so we can make a battle plan. And Winston, do you think your uncle can get his hands on some tranquilizer guns?"

Winston scratched his side and said, "I doubt it. He deals in military grade stuff. Not much need for militias when it comes to tranquilizer guns. When the government comes to take all the guns away, they'll be shootin' to kill, not shootin' to snooze."

"Huh. Worth the thought." I turned to J. "We can try and use tasers, but when push comes to shove, we might not have any choice but to shoot them. I don't see how we can afford to let them get loose. The needs of the many over the needs of the few, or the one." I raised my left hand in a Vulcan V, but Brother Joshua ignored me. Again.

Brother Joshua replied, "Agreed. You do the best you can and—"

I interrupted, "Lord's will be done. Yeah, I know. I think I'll get that tattooed on my forehead."

"Now that'd be an improvement," Winston said.

I thought to myself, it might be the Lord's will, but it's my ass that will end up done.

CHAPTER THIRTY-ONE

I plugged in the address into the GPS and before long Winston and I were on I-65 heading south. We drove in silence for a bit then I asked him, "Do you ever have any trouble sleeping at night with what we're doing?"

He shook his head. "Nah, man. I sleep just fine. Why? You tossing and turning? I would have thought this wouldn't bother you. Hell, how many guys did you burn overseas?"

"Dozens, I'm guessing. It's not the killing that bothers me, it's that we don't seem to be getting ahead. I mean, here we stop the Church from killing a bunch of kids and their teachers, and I'm thinking it doesn't get much worse than that, only to be faced with a bunch of former angels who would like to kill everyone drawing a breath. And if we stop them, then what's next? I thought I saw the darker side of man as a bounty hunter." He paused. "I really had no clue."

"Vic, bad guys have been around since the beginning of mankind. There will be bad guys after the Rapture comes. You have to keep plugging along and do the best you can. They didn't choose just anyone to be the Hand of God. They chose you for a reason. Seems to me you're doing a damn good job."

I drove the next few miles in silence. I bet if someone asked Rose Mary and her son Tim, they wouldn't agree with Winston. I should have been quicker clueing into the danger the Watchers posed to the parents of the kids who were taken. I knew hindsight was twenty-twenty vision, but I had to wonder if the stress of the job was starting to affect my judgment. If I wasn't careful, Winston and Kurt, and everyone else close to me could get killed.

My thoughts turned to Samantha. The words of her father stuck in my craw. If Samantha stayed with me she would always be a target. I remembered watching one of the Spider-man movies where Peter Parker told Mary Jane he doesn't love her, driving her off to try to protect her for her own good. I always thought it was a cop-out, but now I wasn't so sure. I loved Samantha and it ate me up inside when she was taken. Now, learning she was raped, it made me feel even more guilty. What if something happened to her again?

Winston shoved me in the shoulder. "Snap out of it, man. You look like someone kicked your dog and then shot it. It'll work out."

I laughed. Winston's sunny outlook on life was as constant as the smile on his face. With a faith damn near unshakeable, he made a good counterpoint to my increasing disillusionment. "Yeah, whatever. Let's talk about the farm. When we get off at the exit and start heading into the countryside, I'll find a spot where you and I can load up. I want you to have an MP5 locked and loaded. If things start to head south, shoot anything that moves."

"You won't have to tell me twice. I'm not really up to having a toe-to-toe with another one of those guys if I can avoid it. The guy I fought at the reservoir put up a damn good fight. With as much trouble as these guys are to take out, you may need to increase my insurance policy."

An hour and a half later, we left the interstate behind and followed the directions down a lonely country road. I eased off to the side of the road and the two of us went to the rear of the Ford and accessed the hidden compartment. Winston carried an MP5 with several magazines up to the passenger seat. I got into my weapons bag and attached a taser to my belt under my coat. I snagged one for Winston and passed it over when I got in. He sat it on the floorboard.

"Time to go up and ring the doorbell. Maybe we'll get to clip a few angel wings before the day is done."

"Wings, hell. You shoot for the wings if you want. If I need to pull the trigger, I'm hittin' center mass."

We found the driveway for the farm and after a quick weapons check, I nosed the Ford onto the gravel drive. The snow was packed down into a couple of wide ruts by more than one vehicle coming and going; several of the tread marks were wider than the driveway. We rounded a curve and the house appeared. It was an old but well cared for white vinyl-siding farmhouse with a wide front porch which wrapped around one side. A Dodge Ram pickup sat in front. I unsnapped my holster, pulled out my nine, and slipped it into my coat pocket.

Short of the house, the larger tire tracks split off and disappeared around a huge weathered dairy barn and into a wooded area some distance from the house.

"You hang here in the car, locked and loaded," I said. "If you think it's going down, terminate with extreme prejudice."

"You got it. I'd tell you to watch your ass, but yours is so big, you can't miss it."

"Baby's got back," I replied.

I parked so Winston's door faced the porch and he rolled his window down. I opened my door and slipped out into a beautiful midwinter's day. The temp was around the mid-thirties and the sun shown down from a bright blue sky. I started towards the house and hadn't taken more than a couple of steps when the front door opened. A man stepped out wearing camouflage hunting clothes and matching hat with a large U of K emblem on the front of it. A feeling of wrongness hit me. Damn. Found one right off the bat. I wondered if they felt the same thing when I showed up.

"Go Big Blue,." I said.

The man, who appeared to be around fifty years old, smiled and replied, "Go Cats. What can I do for ya, mister?"

I stopped a few feet short of him, my hands in my pockets, one around the grip of my nine and my finger on the trigger. The buzzards had done a number on my bomber jacket, but the fact I didn't want to shoot a hole in one of the pockets didn't mean I wouldn't do it. I'd rather have a hole in the jacket than in me.

"I've been hired to look into the disappearance of the Mueller's son, Jason. You haven't seen him, by any chance, have you?"

I watched the man slip his own hands into the pockets of his hunting jacket. I wasn't sure, but I thought I detected a bulge in the right one.

"Can't say that I have. The Mueller's called me a few weeks ago, in case Jason went down to the old cave on the far side of the property, but no one's been here in weeks. It'd been snowin' the day he went missing, and the drive was covered in unbroken snow and his car wasn't here. So," he shook his head, "I don't think he was out here. I went and checked the cave, just in case, but same thing. No one's been in or out of the cave, unless they found a way to walk in the snow without leaving a trace."

I glanced over at the tracks disappearing into the distance and nodded at them with my chin, keeping my hands in my pockets.

"The cave out near where those tracks are going, you mean?"

The man followed my gaze and said, "Yep. Same direction, but not to the cave. We had some trees fall out that way and loggers came in and cut'em up and hauled'em out. That's one of the ways the Mueller's make money off the farm, ya see, is by sellin' some of the old growth trees."

"Huh. Go figure. Would you mind if I went out to the cave and took my own look?"

I sensed movement in one of the upstairs windows and could see the face of a young lady looking down at me. I got the same sense of wrongness when I looked at her as I did the man.

"Actually, I would. I need permission from the Mueller's to let you wander on the property. If you really are working for'em, have them call me and I'll be happy to give you free range out here. Otherwise, I can't let a stranger roam around on the farm. Sorry."

Something we both knew wasn't going to happen. Rusty said a car with Fayette license plates was one of the cars found in the barn out in Crestwood which meant they were buzzard food and wouldn't be talking to anyone this side of a séance.

"I'll do that. I'm sure you'll be seeing me again. And soon. Who do I have them call?"

"The name's Bill. I look forward to it. Be sure and tell the Mueller's I said howdy, because I'm sure you'll be seeing them—soon." He nodded goodbye.

Veiled threat. Well, not so veiled. Then again, neither was mine. I don't know if he knew who I was, but I really didn't give a rat's ass. Direct confrontation was something I was good at handling. Truth is, I loved it. With all the things I dealt with, having someone to pound on made me feel good. And Bill, or whichever fallen angel was playing around in his head, had thrown down the gauntlet. I planned on picking it up and smacking him around the farm with it.

I went back to my car, walking backwards and keeping the man where I could see him. I offered him a short wave with my left hand, got into the car, put it in reverse and headed down the driveway. The man stayed on the porch and watched until I was out of site.

Winston rolled up his window and said, "Did you see the chick in the upstairs window?"

I gave him an "oh, please" look and he laughed.

"I just wanted to make sure you did. You and the farmer were having a pissing contest I wanted to make sure you didn't miss it."

"Yeah. And she's one of the missing teens. I think her name is Rexena. Looks like one of them traded up to an older model. I can't picture Bill hanging with a bunch of teens unless one of them is his and I don't remember any parent named Bill."

Winston shook his head. "You saying this Bill-guy is one of them?"

"Yep. When I'm around one of the fallen angels I get this weird feeling. Kind of like having a Spidey sense. You don't feel anything?"

"Nope, not a thing," Winston laughed again. "Guess there were more perks with the job than you thought. I wonder if it works with Vamps as well?"

"No clue. But the next time I run into one I'll let you know. Let's get back to the mission and decide on how we're going to hit this place. I think there's no doubt we've found ground zero."

By the next morning, with any luck, the Watchers would be planted firmly back into their cage. If not, I would know if I'd done enough to demand a few answers of God or would now keep Mikey company. If I was a betting man? Toss up.

CHAPTER THIRTY-TWO

There wasn't enough room in J's office for the entire Scooby Gang, so we moved the meeting to the cafeteria, now empty with the evening meal finished. Everyone joined in: Brother Joshua, Winston, Kurt, Samantha, Father Colton, and Ruth Anne. The meeting started off with some somber news.

"Charlie Sutton decided to turn himself in and face the charges against him," Father Colton said. "While you and Winston were on your reconnaissance trip, the local news went with a story he was a person of interest in a murder at the farm. The police are keeping a tight lid on what went down out there, but they're on to Charlie. He said he would tell them the truth. That voices in his head made him do what he did. I told him we could find a new life for him, if he chose, but he declined. He said he would keep Victor and my involvement out of it."

"*Jiminy Cricket*, you guys should have done more to convince him not to do that! His life is over. The best he can hope for is life without parole, but we still have the death penalty in this state and you can bet to high holy Heaven he will get the needle," I replied. I was so frustrated, I wanted to break something.

"As in all things, the choice was his and his alone," Brother Joshua reminded me. "We did offer him a new life and he refused. There was nothing more we could do." Changing the subject, he glanced between Winston and I and asked, "What did you find out at the farm?"

I shook my head in disgust, but moved on. It's the place we're looking for. There are at least two fallen angels there and my guess is there are more. Kurt, did you pull up the maps of the farm?"

"Come on, dude. Easy-peasy." Kurt passed around several color print outs of the farm and the surrounding area. "The farm itself is several hundred acres. They mostly have cornfields and timber. Another farm backs up to this one and the house is down a really long driveway. We can start up that drive and then cut across the first field we come to. If we go late enough at night the people living at that place will never know we're there."

"Good work." I studied the maps for a bit and continued, "Even better, the second farm is nearer to where the cave is located. We can check it out before we hit the house. O.K. Here's what we'll do. We'll split into two groups. Kurt and Samantha will go with me. Winston you'll have Father Colton with you. If we encounter an unfriendly then we'll take them down with tasers, if possible, with lead if not. We can try and wound them, but that's really hard to do. If you need to shoot, unless you're really close, shoot them center mass. Everyone but Father Colton goes armed. Kurt, you ever shoot a gun before?"

"Paintball with my bro's, but how hard can it be? Point the thing at something and pull the trigger." Kurt pantomimed pointing a gun at me and pretended to shoot me, mouthing the word "pow."

"It's a lot harder than that, especially since you've never killed anyone before. If you hesitate, you're dead. And I've seen you cut up your food. Hell, you close your eyes if your steak even bleeds a little red. You close your eyes when you shoot tonight, they will close them permanently." I hated to be so harsh, but this was my friend, so I continued. "There's no shame in saying you'd rather stay here. You have nothing to prove to me or anyone else."

"Dude, they tried to kill me. They killed Ruth Anne's family. And if they aren't stopped, they will kill everyone on the planet anyway. So fight them now, or fight them later if you fail. I'd rather kick some angel butt now. Don't worry about me. I won't let you down."

I knew the man meant well, but all I could see in my head was Kurt going down with a bullet in his brain. But he was right. The choice was his. If someone tried to kill me I'd sure as hell want to take a piece of their hide. So be it.

I looked at Samantha and before I could say a word, she said, "Stuff it. I'm going."

I stared at the top of my shoes and chewed on my lower lip. I could do like her father and lock her in the basement to keep her from harm's way. After losing her twice before and considering what happened to her down in Florida, I had every right to try to protect her. But it would also be wrong. Like Kurt, Samantha needed to get some payback. She was not the "hide in the basement" kind of woman at any rate. I looked up and into eyes full of strength and determination. If only the two of us could have met under different circumstances because the two of us made one hell of a fierce team. Yet the longer we stayed together the greater the chances she would never see her thirtieth birthday and I wasn't sure I could live with myself if she died. But I couldn't tell her no.

"I wouldn't dream of it, honey. But this time, the only the way they get to take you is over my dead body."

She blew me an air kiss. "That's why I'm going, to make sure your body stays upright. They say behind every great man is a greater woman dragging his ass around."

The group laughed at that one, even J. "Whatever helps you sleep at night, sister. It's 9 p.m. I want everyone to get a few hours rest and we'll leave around 1 a.m. We'll hit them around three. Even angels have to sleep. At least their bodies do."

"I'm sorry I'm not going. I wish I could, but the thought of going anywhere near that cave again makes me want to throw up," Ruth Anne said.

I gave her my best high wattage smile, "No worries, little lady. You've done enough already. Right, Kurt?"

Enough of the old Kurt remained to send his face flushing red, but he said, "Damn straight. You've been through enough." Our little Kurt was growing up.

I looked from person to person and felt a great measure of pride in my friends. Despite knowing they were about to do something which could end in their deaths, they were going anyway, to help me. It didn't remove my concern for Kurt and Samantha, as they were stepping out of their element. But it was their choice. Brother Joshua always preached that our lives are about the choices we make and the good and bad consequences from those decisions. At least all of them knew the score and they chose to go anyway.

"Alright. Go get as much rest as you can. I will need you sharp, not bleary-eyed."

"I'm sleeping here tonight," Kurt said. "I'll just walk Ruth Anne to her side of the building then hit the hay." He helped Ruth Anne to her feet and the two of them left the office, hand in hand.

"Same for me. I'll be ready at the appointed time. See you guys in the morning," Father Colton said, and he also made his exit, leaving just Samantha, Winston, Joshua and me.

I asked Winston, "Think your uncle will mind us purchasing two more flak jackets? We have an extra out in the Ford, which Father Colton can use, since the two of you are about the same size. But we also need one for Kurt and Samantha. And I think we only have four com links, so we're going to need at least one more of them. Might want to get a couple more, just in case one or two don't work. And a couple more night vision goggles."

"Got it. I know he won't mind. I'll head his direction and call him on the way. I'll bunk down at his place and see you guys back here at one." He pushed himself up and out of his chair, kissed Samantha on the cheek, and left.

When he was gone, Samantha asked J, "Are you going with us?"

"No. I'm not. That's not the role I play." He folded his hands on top of the table and looked back at her calmly, knowing her well enough in their short time together to know what was coming.

"Another king sitting on his throne, asking others to do what he won't because either he can't or he doesn't have the balls to get involved." She looked at me. "Doesn't this bother you?"

Yes, it did actually. Having the archangel Uriel beside us walking into battle would be much better for our continued existence. But I also knew it wasn't going to happen, so bitching about it was useless. Trying to figure out why the Almighty did things the way He did was turning out to be more than my poor brain could handle.

"Doesn't matter if I do or I don't. He's out. It's my job to prevent them from getting loose and ending life as we know it. I'm guessing Moses, or Noah or Jesus, for that matter, didn't have all the answers either. We do what we are asked to do. Besides, with you watching my back, what could happen?"

She gave me a sad smile, stood, took me by the hand, and we left the room. She never looked back at Brother Joshua.

We made it down the hallway, but instead of crossing the lobby to the dorm area she pushed open the front door and led me out into the cold night air and down the block, where our breath mingled and made little clouds. She stopped and turned into my arms, kissing me, then wrapped her arms around me as far as they would go and buried her face into my chest. I squeezed her tight, pulling her close to me. We stood this way for several long minutes, neither of us talking, merely living in the moment.

Eventually she looked up at me and asked, "Do you think we will live to see the morning?"

I shrugged. "I honestly don't know. Most times, I know what I'm up against. the goals are clear and the objectives easy to figure out. This time, I'm supposed to kill the bad guys without killing the bad guys, stop them from taking over the world without knowing if it's even possible. There's a lot about this which is unknown."

I paused for a bit and glanced around at the other buildings surrounding the mission, the hustle and bustle of daytime activity given way to a quiet peacefulness. Most windows were now dark and silent.

"But, I'm good at these types of operations," I said, trying to reassure her. "Winging it is a strength. See what the bad guys do, react and then punch them in the mouth as hard as possible. The next few hours will decide not only our futures, but perhaps the future of mankind. And the fate of the world will come down to two bounty hunters, a computer geek, a priest and the most beautiful woman I've ever known. Maybe the angels will take one look at you and stand still watching you long enough for us to take them out."

She slugged me hard, but the smile which made my heart soar had returned. "Lord knows it won't be *your* good looks they'll be watching. You need a shave."

I rubbed my chin, feeling the several days' growth of a beard. "I've been thinking of growing a big beard. Maybe it will give me a more ferocious look."

"I've seen you in action. I don't think you need anything else to make you look ferocious. You probably scare women and children by just walking down the street."

Funny thing was? That thought made me feel happy. I offered her my arm, she slipped hers around mine, and we returned to the mission. I didn't know what would happen a few hours from now in the darkest part of the night. But for right now, for this moment, I found joy walking with the woman I loved. It sure would be nice to be alive the next night to do it again.

CHAPTER THIRTY-THREE

When the alarm went off at 12:30 a.m., I awakened and felt surprisingly rested. I wasn't sure if I'd be able to nap, with Samantha on my mind, but years of military training had taken over and I went right to sleep. As for dreams, if I had any, I couldn't remember a single one.

I padded down the hallway to the bathroom, hopped into the shower, turned the hot water up and let the water pound any residual soreness from my muscles. I used a towel to wipe the steam from the mirror and examined the face staring at mc. The beard and mustache were coming in a dark black and my hair was growing long. I looked a lot like the Viking down in Florida. I picked up my razor, twirled it in my fingers and then set it down on the sink. I kind of liked the look and decided to keep it another day. If I lived long enough to take another shower then I might shave it off. Then again, I might not.

In my room, I put on a T-shirt and jeans, slipped on my flak jacket and finally a long sleeve shirt. Sitting on the edge of the bed, I tugged on my old Army boots, laced them up tight and pulled my jeans down over them. Picking up my beat-all-to-hell bomber jacket I held it up to the light. Fashion statement it was not. When this was all over, I decided I needed a new one. This one had been to Hell and back, almost literally, and was way too beat up to keep wearing. Bummer.

I slipped my wallet and keys into my pockets, my holster and Glock onto my belt and left my room for what I hoped would not be the last time. I'd grown fond of living like a monk. Not.

I found the others waiting in the cafeteria. Kurt was next to Ruth Anne, arms entwined, while Joshua, Winston and Father Colton talked in low tones. Samantha stood by herself, looking out the window at the night, her sword case leaning against the wall next to her. Three flak jackets were sitting on one of the tables.

"About time you got up," Winston said. "I thought we might have to come getcha moving."

"Yeah, yeah, yeah. You that anxious to start killing people?"

I aimed for light banter, but the words caused everyone to stop and look at me. I asked, "What?" When no one answered me, I continued, "Samantha, Kurt and I will ride in the Ford. Winston, you and Father Colton will follow in the van."

They all nodded. I walked over to the flak jackets and handed one to Father Colton, one to Kurt and one to Samantha. "You three put these on when we get in the car. They're not all that comfortable, but they may just save your life."

Kurt lifted his up and down a couple of times. "Man, these things are kind of heavy."

"Tough. You don't put it on you ain't going. Simple as that."

"Dude, quit busting my balls. Never said I wouldn't wear it." Ruth Anne looked at Kurt, then reached up and patted him on the cheek, smiling.

"Good. There's an all night convenience store right off the exit. We can stop there for some coffee and a late night snack. They have a parking lot around back with no camera. Winston and I checked on the way back. We will arm up there. Let's get after it."

Samantha picked up her sword case and walked to me, slipping her hand into mine. Kurt hugged and kissed Ruth Anne goodbye right in front of us. I was guessing all those blow up dolls in his apartment would have to go before she came over for the first time.

Kurt, Samantha and I hopped into the Ford while Father Colton joined Winston in the church van, an older model white panel van. I lead our two-car convoy out of the parking lot to I-65 and then up to cruising speed. I asked Kurt, "You and Ruth Anne seem to have hit it off. Are you sure that's wise? I mean, she did try and drown your ass."

"No, that wasn't her. That was Kobiashi, whatever his name is. Dude was all messed up. She said even though she didn't have anything to do with her body when the fallen angel tried to seduce me, that at least I was hot and she really dug me. When you consider what we've both been through, at least we can talk to each other about it."

Well, that was true.

"I think the two of you make a cute couple. I'm happy for you, Kurt," Samantha said.

"Thanks, gorgeous." They blew each other kisses. I wasn't sure I would be able to take the new confident Kurt.

I reached over and clasped Samantha's hand in mine. It felt warm and comforting, a lifeline in a sea of chaos. We drove on through the night, the three of us lost in our own thoughts, staying silent until we were off the interstate and into the parking lot of the convenience store. The store closed at midnight and with nothing else around for miles we could arm up with little chance of interruption.

I told Kurt and Samantha to stay in the car, went and opened the rear hatch, pulled up the rubber mat and punched in the digital code to unlock the secret compartment. Winston got out of the van and joined me with a bag of his own. We took a few minutes to sync up the com links, then divvied up the weaponry.

Winston selected an MP5, night goggles and a couple of concussion grenades.

"You know, Father Colton doesn't want a gun, but maybe you can talk him into keeping a couple of concussion grenades with him. If he accidently gets himself in the fight, he can at least stun the bad guys, too," I said.

Winston nodded. "We were talking about that on the way up. He really doesn't want to hurt anyone, but he gets that he might not have a choice when it comes right down to it."

I got an MP5 for both Kurt and myself, and a Glock 21 for Samantha as well as the two last concussion grenades and my own pair of night goggles. I closed the gun safe and heard it relock. I put the mat in place and shut the door.

Opening Kurt's door, I handed him the MP5s and his com link, showing him how it worked. "Here's where the safety is located. Don't even play with it until we're at the farm and out of the car. I don't want you shooting me in the back on accident."

"Yeah, right. Dude, I got this. I've watched all the *Rambo* movies. I'm good."

Huh, I thought to myself. I tried to decide if he was joking or telling the truth. I gave up and closed the door then opened Samantha's handing her the Glock.

"Don't worry. I know how to use one of these. I'll have my sword, too," she said.

I smiled. "You know how sexy that sounds? Beautiful woman with a sword in one hand and a nine in the other?"

She kissed me and said, "I always wondered how you pictured me when you dream of me. Now I know."

I kissed her back and shut the door. Then I climbed in on my side, started up the car and we returned to the road. Kurt's maps showed the driveway we needed to be on was about three quarters of a mile past the Mueller's farm and I found it easily enough. The driveway snaked through a wooded area and I stopped well short of the house with the van pulling up behind me.

We both turned off the engines and sat there for a few minutes. I used my com link to contact Winston. "Let's sit here and see if anyone pays us any attention. Use the night goggles."

"Roger that."

I slipped on the goggles, pulling the harness over my head, and looked towards the Mueller's farm. The night transformed from a deep black to a ghostly green through the goggles viewer.

I saw three deer walking slowly through the woods between us and the entrance of the cave, but saw nothing else.

I pushed my com link and said, "Clear. Agreed?"

"Unless you think them angels are running around as Bambi, we're good." Winston replied.

"Alright, let's get this show on the road."

I slipped off the goggles and Kurt said, "Where's my pair? I want one of those."

"Hold your horses. Look in my bag and get out a pair for you and for Samantha. The power switch is on the side. If we use a concussion grenade, don't have your eyes open if you have the goggles on. Your eyes won't like you very much if you do."

I spent the next minute watching Samantha get her harness adjusted, watching the way her brows pulled down in concentration, the movement of her long, nimble fingers. She must have felt me watching because she glanced my way, her eyes shining in the dashboard lights with a heat which bore deep into my soul. She stretched out her hand, brushing the stubble on my cheek with the back of her hand. I snagged it and pressed her hand to my lips.

Over the com Winston said, "We're ready to go. How about you, old man?"

Kurt snickered and I turned to glare at him, but he had his goggles on, the one central eye staring back at which made me laugh. I pushed the button on my com and said, "Yeah, yeah. We're ready. Remember to turn off your dome light."

I switched my dome lights off, then got out of the car quietly, making sure Samantha and Kurt did the same thing. The moon, what was left of it, stayed hidden behind a thick covering of clouds. The weather gurus at the local news stations said we could get a couple more inches of snow. Or none. I was betting on snow.

I pulled the goggles into place, slid the safety on my MP5 to the off position and motioned the gang to come in close.

"We will need to spread out about ten yards between each of us in a staggered line," I said softly. "No chatter on the com's unless it's unavoidable. Sound carries a long way at night and we don't want them to know we're coming until we put the barrel of a gun next to their heads. Everyone understand?"

Each person nodded, their breath mingling as we huddled together. I stuck my hand out and each of them placed theirs on top of mine. I raised my fist in the air and then lead my little band of heroes across a field covered in a blanket of white to begin the hunt.

Before we left I memorized the map of the area and knew about where the cave was located. I took point with Kurt to my left and Samantha to my right. Winston and Father Colton fanned out further to the other side of Samantha.

I could feel the excitement level in me rising. This was what I was built for, to hunt down and deliver justice to my fellow man, sometimes killing them. And I was damn good at it. Winston was right. They picked me for a reason to be the Hand of God, just as they picked Dominic Montoya before me: killers who did what was needed with no remorse, no regrets.

I always wondered why I didn't feel at least some remorse when I found someone in my sights and pulled the trigger. In Iraq and Afghanistan, I killed people who asked for it. You take a swing at Uncle Sam and you better damn well know we're going to put a boot up your ass for the trouble. I knew every man I killed over there would have slit my throat in my sleep if given the chance. On one mission I shot and killed almost a dozen insurgents and that night I slept the sleep of the righteous.

In my fight with Satan and his minions, I was responsible for the deaths of over a dozen people and never lost one iota of sleep, no self-recriminations. Like the Taliban, they declared war on the world and I was happy to bring the fires of Hell right to their door.

Tonight, I didn't know if I would kill anyone or not. But I knew if called to do so, I'd pull the trigger and start looking for the next target. Which begged the question, how did stone cold killers like me ever make the trip up instead of down? In moments like this, I not only didn't know, but I didn't care.

Off to our left, the trees were thinned out and I could see construction equipment lined up around a mound of dirt. I got the attention of the others, raising my hand for them to stay put, then ran low to the edge of the dirt. I belly crawled the rest of the way up the mound and slowly looked over the top.

All the trees in the area before me were gone, with a large section of dirt removed and pushed to the side, creating a semi-circle of dirt, open at one end for trucks and equipment to move in and out. All that remained in the middle was the hard surface of a rock shelf.

Sitting upon the rock like two alien insects ready to pounce were two Furukawa hammer drills. I'd seen them over the years used by road crews building new highways in the rockier part of the state. They'd already begun to make little rocks out of big rocks with a pile waiting to be hauled away by the trucks. Now I knew what the fallen angels were up to, via a host of hijacked bodies, and that was digging a hole down deep enough to allow them to escape.

I was turning to crawl back down when I saw movement in the cab of one of the dump trucks and I froze. Colored by the green lens of my goggles, a face searched the night through the front windshield of the truck and I saw Maxwell Neunen, a foreign exchange student from Belgium who came to this country seeking a degree in engineering only to now find himself huddled in the front seat of a dump truck in the middle of B.F.E. with a fallen angel riding around shotgun in his head.

I surveyed the area and the equipment, but found no one else. Looks like Maxwell drew the short end of the stick and got the graveyard shift.

I eased my way down the hill, gathered everyone close, and explained the situation in a hushed tone. When I finished with the recap, I said, "Winston and I will circle the wagons and close on the truck." I pointed to Kurt, Samantha and Father Colton. "I want the three of you to do as I did, slowly crawl up the hill and watch us. If you see anything, use the coms to warn Winston and me. The MP5 has a night scope in case you need to let loose with it. Got it?"

Once again everyone nodded. I said to Winston, "You come up on the passenger side of the truck and I'll come up on the driver side. He's in the front truck. When I click the com, we hit him from both sides using tasers."

He gave me a thumbs up and we trotted off into the night, with me circling around the pit to the right as Winston went left. We made it around to the back of the dump truck without anything-untoward happening. I could pick out the rest of the group watching from the top of the hill.

I clicked my com and said, "Go," then raced for the driver's side door, taser in one hand, my MP5 on a sling around my chest.

I jumped on the door runner and yanked the door open. Winston did the same on the other side. The cab between us was empty except for a small cooler and a McDonald's bag wadded up next to it.

"Well, this sucks," I said.

Before I could turn around, Samantha's hissed in my ear, "Vic, behind you!" Her warning wasn't needed. The feeling of wrongness hit me like a mental whip.

I spun on the truck running board as Maxwell and another man sprinted from the hammer drill, his mouth drawn in an angry scowl. The new guy held a machete and Max held a knife long enough to be just this side of a short sword in his hand, raised to plunge as deep in me as he could shove it. I, of course, took exception to this, and dove into the cab, pulling my legs up with inches to spare. The knife whistled by my foot, struck the side of the seat, and ripped a long tear in the fabric. The other guy came sliding to a stop when I pulled the door half-closed and blocked him from getting a swipe at me.

Max readied his weapon for another swing when I aimed the taser at his face and pressed the button. I'm guessing they didn't have anything like tasers during their day. I did feel a bit guilty hitting him in the face and neck, but he wore a heavy winter coat and I went for exposed skin, not wanting to take a chance the layers would lessen the jolt. His body jerked in a spasm and he began to fall. I kicked the truck door all the way open, and he clipped the other guy squarely in the chin with the edge of the door, knocking him over.

I followed Max's body down, holding onto the taser—as the body, fallen angel and all—convulsed on the ground. I put a boot on his wrist, and kept the voltage going. Then I aimed the MP5 at the machete-wielding wild man's direction when I heard a quick three shot tap of a machine gun and watched him as he did a weird stilted dance as the shots hit their mark and he fell to the ground, landing flat on his back.

I quickly looked to the dirt hill and saw Samantha, eye to the night scope of Kurt's MP5, scanning for other targets.

Winston joined me and I let off the trigger of the taser. Max twitched a few more times and then was still. Winston unwrapped the stunned man's fingers from the knife handle, picked it up and tossed it into the darkness. We rolled Maxwell over and cuffed him.

I could see a walkie-talkie in his pocket and it was on. Pulling it out, I slipped it into my coat. I used the com and said, "Kurt and Samantha, stay in position and keep scanning in the direction of the house. Nice shooting, Samantha, but I had him. Father Colton, meet us at the dump truck, if you please."

"Maybe you did, maybe you didn't, but I didn't want to take a chance. I did promise to keep you upright," Samantha said.

"Roger that."

Winston and I picked up Maxwell, lifted him into the cab of the truck, and cuffed him to the steering wheel. I stood on the driver side door runner until Father Colton climbed into the cab on the other side. Winston did a quick check of the other equipment to make sure we didn't have any other surprises waiting.

Colton took a few items out of the bag he brought with him and prepared to do an exorcism on the spot. "Any idea who the dying man is?"

I glanced over my shoulder at the man bleeding out on the ground, his blood mixing with the snow and dirt.

"I think it's Bernard Rollins. He went to school with Charlie."

Rest in peace, Bernie, I said silently to myself.

I shook my head, saddened by his death, wondering which way he went, to Heaven or Hell. The poor guy went from worrying about finals to dead in a field nowhere near family and friends.

Father Colton crossed himself. It took a few minutes to bring Maxwell around. When he came to, he pulled hard on the steering wheel and only stopped when I put the muzzle of the MP5 to his head. "Settle down or I'll send you to the abyss faster than you can say, 'Ah, Hell.' Comprende?"

He started shouting things in a language I never heard of until Father Colton raised the cross in his hand and started the ritual which would kick out whomever was using Maxwell for a roaming Motel 6. The walkie-talkie in my pocket chirped. I jumped down from the cab and pulled it out.

"Armaros, what's going on? I heard gunshots. Answer, please," a voice said.

There were several ways to play things out. I could stay quiet and let them stew about what was transpiring out by the cave or I could engage the target in conversation. If I stayed quiet there was a chance the rest of them could load up and head out before we got there. Then again, he already knew we were here and one thing I learned in my brief encounters is these guys took arrogance to a new level. What the hell.

"Hey there, Bill. Hate to break it to you, but you're down a few more brothers in wings. They now know the answer to the eternal question of just how dry it is in Hell's desert. How's your night going so far?"

There was the briefest of pauses, then Bill replied, "The Spear of Uriel. I knew you would come sooner or later. Seems you picked sooner. Why don't you come on up to the house and stay awhile?"

"First off, dipshit, I'm the Hand of God. When are you guys ever going to get that part right? I know it's hard to teach an old angel new tricks, but get real. Secondly, we'll be there in a bit bringing the wrath of Heaven which will rain down upon you with the finality of Judgment Day." I delivered the last line with the cadence of a soapbox preacher. Father Colton never faltered in his exorcism, but he did shoot me a quick glance. I smiled and shrugged my shoulders.

I waited for another reply, but none was forthcoming. I added the "we" to give him something else to worry about. He had no idea if it was me or several hundred guys coming down on his helmet, but why make it easy for him?

Winston came jogging into view from behind one of the rock breakers and waved me over. After making sure Colton was O.K., I followed Winston to one of the hammer drills where he had the lid of a storage locker open. He nodded for me to take a look. Inside, stacked neatly in a large pile, was stick after stick of dynamite taped in groupings of five. Holy crap. My skin began to itch being this close to that much TNT.

He shut the lid on the locker and we rejoined Colton at the dump truck, Winston on one side and me on the other. We guarded our friend until, at last he called for me to join them in the cab of the truck. The feeling of wrongness had vanished, so I slipped a knife out of my pocket and cut the young man free from the cuffs. He rubbed his neck and face where the taser darts struck him and I could see fear on his face.

"What's going to happen to me?" he asked. "I didn't mean to attack you. The demon made me do it. I swear it."

"Relax, kid. Don't sweat it. We know you didn't have a choice. But you do now. Did Father Colton explain to you why you were possessed and how it can happen again?"

"Yeah, he did. Aw, man, I mean, I've never believed in all that Jesus crap, but now? Man, I don't know."

"Hey, up to you. But if you don't believe it, the fallen angel will return. And this time he'll bring friends. And each one will be worse than him. What can you tell me about the rest of them? How many are at the house?"

Max was shivering, despite wearing a coat, and kept rubbing his hands for warmth. "There are four more at the house, not including the leader. His name is Samyaza."

"Any idea how they plan to defend themselves?" I thought about the bulge I'd seen in Bill's pocket. "Any of them using guns?"

He pursed his lips. "Only Samyaza has guns. He's forcing the others to use knives and machetes. He seems to think only he should have the power to use guns. He's one warped asshole."

Colton said, "This is not really surprising. They didn't have guns when they were imprisoned and Samyaza, being their leader, would want the most power. Back in their day, the sword and spear were the weapons of choice and I'm guessing the ones they feel the most comfortable with using."

Max said, "Something else. I see you guys have night vision goggles.

These guys don't need them. They can see in the dark. That's how my guy was able to see you coming."

I let out a string of expletives. I was hoping the night vision goggles gave us a tactical advantage. Now I find out not only didn't they give an edge, they were no better than breaking even.

I motioned Max to get out of the truck and I helped him down. Pointing back the way we came, "Head that direction and you run into our cars. Wait there until we're done. If we don't return by morning, make your way up to the other farm and call the cops. Understand?"

He nodded. "Yeah. Sure. Good luck. Whatever you do, don't let these guys in your head. It really sucks." With that, he lumbered off into the night. I could only imagine what it would be like to have some whacked out fallen angel rolling around in my head. Then again, as I glanced at Bernard's body on the ground and his sightless eyes staring up into a starless sky. There were worse things that could happen to you.

I waved for Samantha and Kurt to join us. I knew of a few more fallen angels who needed to be introduced to Mr. Worse.

CHAPTER THIRTY-FOUR

My band of fallen angel hunters and I crept along the edge of the woods with no issues—other than Kurt tripping on the roots of two different trees. With no crops in the field during winter, there was little in the way to mask our approach as we silently moved forward.

Gazing towards the farmhouse, I could see the back of an old dairy barn between us and the house. And to the right there was nothing else but wide-open spaces. There was no way to sneak up on the house: with or without individuals possessed by divine beings with great night vision. Damn.

All the lights were off in the house. The *Night Before Christmas* verse kept running through my head, *and not a creature was stirring, not even a mouse.* Things were looking very quiet as Winston and I spent several minutes watching for movement. I started to worry they'd packed up and flown the coop when Bill appeared in an upstairs window, smiling a night vision green tinged smile and motioned for us to come on over.

I promised not to kill any of the possessed unless I absolutely had to. I understood the people the fallen angels took over were just innocent bystanders, not much more than kids in most cases. But if I got a clear shot at ol' Bill, I told myself, I would shoot the son of a bitch and wipe that grin off of his face without giving it a second thought.

I pushed my goggles up onto the top of my head, raised the MP5 to my shoulder and took aim at Bill through the night scope. As soon as I did, he ducked down out of view. I lowered the gun and moved my goggles into place.

"You see all that?" I asked Winston.

"Yeah. Seems he wants us to come out and play." His head swiveled towards the barn. "How much you wanna bet there's a few of them bad angels waiting in the barn?"

"No bet," I said. Figures it'd be a barn. Things didn't go so well for me the last time I got into it with bad guys on a farm. My mind did a quick rewind on my torching several members of the Church of the Light Reclaimed the night I met Samantha using Molotov Cocktails and hay

Tony Acree

soaked in gasoline. I'd be rotting somewhere in the woods, most likely, if not for being bailed out by Dominic Montoya, the last Hand of God.

"I hate barns." I mumbled.

"O.K. Here's what we'll do. Winston and I will hit the barn and make sure there are no hostiles inside. We'll slip through the rear door. Kurt, you take one corner, Samantha, the other. If anyone comes down either side, don't ask questions, just shoot'em. Father Colton, you stay between them and do whatever you think needs to be done. Everyone got it?"

They all nodded yes and I lead our small force to the other side of the barn where Samantha and Kurt took up their positions watching our flank. After Father Colton flattened himself against the barn, Winston and I pulled doors apart just far enough for us to slip in.

The barn was two stories tall. The ground floor had a main aisle flanked with old dairy cow stocks. The farmer put hay down in the troughs on one side of the stocks and as soon as the cows stuck their heads through the slats to get the hay, the farmer would squeeze the two sides of the stocks together, keeping the cows in place. Then milking equipment would be fastened to the udders of each cow with the milk flowing up to and then down a pipe to a collection tank in the front of the barn.

The equipment appeared ancient and rusted from disuse. It was obvious this farm hadn't seen a dairy cow in quite some time, but it still smelled of old hay, manure and dust. I took the left side and Winston the right and we moved silently down the main aisle. I scanned the ceiling as I moved. The second floor was normally where the hay was stored and could be accessed from the main floor. I saw a ladder leading to the above floor at the far end of the barn.

Winston raised a fist, bringing me to a halt. He stood still, looking through one of the stocks at something on the ground. Slowly he squeezed through the opening, gun first, barely fitting, and squatted down out of sight.

From the com in my ear, I heard Winston say, "There's a body here. Young girl, beat all to hell. I'm checking her now."

I heard Winston grunt and then nothing. I called his name and when he didn't respond, I started in his direction. I took a step, but heard a sound above and behind me. I glanced over my shoulder in time to see a trap door open, the kind farmers used to drop hay from the top floor down to the first, and a figure hurtling through it.

A man landed on top of me, planting two feet smack dab in the middle of my back, and we tumbled to the ground. I tried to roll into the fall, but didn't quite make it and instead slammed my head into the stocks. My goggles smashed on impact, twisting and breaking, and for a moment the

339

world moved in and out of focus from the force of the blow.

I started to push my way to my feet, but a length of twine, the kind used to hold hay bales together, looped around my neck and was pulled tight. The rough material bit into my neck and began to cut off blood flow to my carotid artery. The man pulled savagely, trying to keep it taut. My fogged brain reminded my body I had about ten seconds to do something about the situation, but my gun was trapped beneath me.

He leaned forward and said into my ear, in a voice more suited to a horror film soundtrack, "Time to die, Spear of Uriel."

I reached quickly behind me, using all the brute force of my six foot six inch frame, and seized the man's head in my hands. I pressed my thumbs hard into his eye sockets and squeezed his head in an attempt to crush it with my bare hands. He tried jerking his head free, but I held on as if my life depended on it. And it did.

With a howl of pain and rage, he let go of the twine, grasping my wrists and tried to pull them apart. Good luck with that, asshole. The twine loosened enough for the blood to flow freely and my anger to flow with it. I yanked hard, trying to pull his head from his neck, and the man flew forward as I drove his head into the same wooden beam I'd hit my own head. I heard a loud crack and wood splintering. Blood began to trickle down where I must have split his head open on the beam.

I heard another set of feet land behind me. I flung my first attacker off and rolled to the side as something slammed into the ground where I'd been laying. Without my goggles things were now cloaked in a deep darkness and they had the advantage. They could see just fine, but I couldn't. Before the new attacker raised his weapon again, I reached out and wrapped one of my big paws around the handle of what might have been a pitchfork or shovel, held it in place and struck out with my foot, smashing it into the side of the next attacker's leg. I could feel it buckle and he fell to the ground near me.

As he landed, I lashed out again with my foot, trying to kick the crap out of him, but his reflexes were good and I missed. With my head pounding from both my fall and the garrote, I needed some help. I wondered what had happened to Winston when the mystery was solved, as a woman screamed at me from where Winston had disappeared.

Sensing movement, I raised the MP5, using the side of the gun to block off her attack, and took the blow of something heavy that jolted my arms down to the elbow, then rolled over several times, putting distance between me and my attackers.

I hated to shoot them, but since I didn't plan on dying any time in the near future, I didn't know what else to do. If I started shooting wildly into the darkness, I was just as likely to hit Winston or another from my team standing outside the barn with one of the rounds as I was one of the fallen angels. Then I felt like an idiot. My night scope.

I managed to get to my feet, raised the rifle to my shoulder, and I sighted down the scope. The view was limited, unlike the wide-angle view of the goggles, but it worked. I swung the gun around just in time to see a woman, her face a mass of bruises, one eye nearly swollen shut, and her lips pulled back in an expression of pure rage, swinging a sap at the side of my head.

Ducking, I heard the sap wiz by, brushing the hair on the top of my head. I lowered my shoulder and lunged forward, swinging the stock of the gun at her midsection and felt the blow connect. She howled in pain. I followed the blow with another quick strike to her kidney and she fell to her knees. I hustled back a few steps in case it was a ruse, but a glance through the scope showed her writhing in pain on the ground.

Before I could decide what to do next, I heard duel battle cries from both Samantha and Kurt. Using the scope, I watched Samantha rain blows down on the man who tried to strangle me driving him back to the ground. Blood flowed from the wound on his head and there was no way a normal human being could have continued the fight after the blow I'd given him, but he was trying.

A multiple black belt in Tae Kwon Do, I'd seen Samantha use her sword and her martial arts fighting skills. Both beautiful and deadly, she followed one strike after another until the man was knocked unconscious.

Kurt had his hands full with the pitchfork attacker. Wielding a two-by-four he found somewhere in the barn, he slugged away on the other guy who was hobbled from where I slammed his leg. It took a moment for Kurt to be victorious, but in a spin move Samantha and I would be proud of, he feinted left, then spun around quickly in the other direction and clubbed the man on the head. The attacker fell to the ground as if someone had reached inside him and hit the off switch.

When all three fallen angels were cuffed, Kurt started shouting, "I'm the man, I'm the man!" at the top of his lungs, and in an imitation of Samantha's fighting style, kicked a nearby post. Unfortunately for Kurt, it dislodged a loose board from overhead which crashed down and hit him on top of the head.

Kurt sagged to the ground. I walked over, reached down and removed the goggles from his head and put them on.

"Taken out by an inanimate object. Great goin', Kurt. Samantha, keep a look out, I need to check on Winston."

I looked on the other side of the stocks and saw Winston sitting up with his back against the wall, cradling his own head in both hands. He had a nasty welt running down one side of his face.

"She sucker punched you, didn't she?" I asked.

He moaned as he got to his feet and picked up his MP5. "Damn. I have to remember just because they're women don't mean they ain't dangerous. Man, when I saw her on the ground, all beat up and shit, I thought she was out. I went to roll her over and bam, she pops me upside the head with a sap. Sorry. It won't happen again."

"Don't sweat it. I took my own beating out here. Nearly got myself strangled to death and aired out with a pitchfork. Come on."

I cleared the rest of the barn, leaving Samantha to guard Kurt and the captured fallen angels. I went to the rear door of the barn and motioned for Father Colton to follow me. We managed to capture all three without killing them, although the one with the split head would be hurting once his divine host was forced to flee.

"There ya go Father, three of them. The guy with the split head is Julio Railoa, the other guy Michael Peko and the girl is Angie Newman. Three more college students who had gone missing. Can you do the exorcisms here in the barn? And can you do all three of them at once?"

"I can try here, but I can only do one at a time. Exorcism is a personal thing. Casting out one is difficult enough. Three would be impossible to do at the same time."

"O.K. Do what you can." I reached into my jacket, pulling out a small flashlight. Kurt was coming around and rubbing his head where he got thwacked. I tossed the flashlight to him and he caught it after fumbling it a couple of times.

"Kurt, you and Samantha stay here and guard the good Father. Winston, you and I need to take the house. You feeling up to it?"

He gave me a quick smile and said, "Even after the beating I've taken, I can still kick more ass than you can." He took a couple of steps and then went down to one knee.

When he tried to get back up, I pushed him down to the ground and he didn't resist. I pulled away his coat and saw a trail of blood down his side. The knife wound must have split back open.

"Damn. Man, you're not going anywhere. Here, let me help you over to Kurt. You can help guard the fallen until I get back."

I got him settled and he said, "Vic, you can't take the house by yourself. You're going to need someone to go with you."

Samantha stepped next to me. "He won't be alone." She reached up and pushed my goggles back up on my head, did the same to hers, and kissed me long and deep.

I wrapped my arms around her, squeezing her as tight as I could. After a moment I said, "I love you, but you're not going into the house with me."

She tried pushing me away, but I held her tight. The fact I didn't have my goggles on and couldn't see her face gave me the courage to continue.

"I can't worry about you while I'm inside. I'm trained on urban assaults and you aren't. I can keep you updated via the comlink."

"But—" She tried to object, but I cut her off, adding some steel to my voice.

"No buts, Samantha. Besides, I'm not cutting you completely out. If I don't take down the two fallen angels inside, and they make a break for it, I need someone to take them down. I need you to do this for me. Stand at the barn door and if anyone but me leaves that house then cut them in half. Do you understand me?"

It took her a moment to respond, but she finally responded, "Fine."

Her body remained rigid and after a minute I broke our embrace.

I slid my goggles into place and said to the others, "I'll be back before you know it. Winston, if you or Kurt so much as see a nose, shoot it. There are at least two more so don't take any chances."

"Then you better make sure and let us know before you stick your nose back in here. As dizzy as I feel, I might get confused and blow your ass away," Winston replied.

Something told me that was the least of my troubles. Time to go cut the head off the snake.

CHAPTER THIRTY-FIVE

Samantha and I moved to the front of the barn. "You ready?" I asked her. I couldn't read her expression with the goggles on, but she seemed calm.

"I've been dreaming of getting revenge on these sons of bitches ever since . . . since . . . well, you know. Doesn't matter. I should be going in with you, but I get it. How do you want to do this?"

I took a quick glance through the crack in the two barn doors. Before I could answer her, a shot rang out, blasting the wood next to my head, sending splinters into my cheek. "Shit!" I pulled back and removed a sliver of wood nearly an inch long from the side of my face. I was starting to get really pissed at Bill. "I'm going to throw this door open then you're going to unload on that house with everything you've got while I cross to the house. Ready?"

She gave me a quick nod and raised the gun up to firing position. I kicked the door all the way open and tore outside. Samantha rocked the MP5 laying down a line of fire for me. There was only one brief shot from the upstairs window which missed, thank the good Lord, as the glass and wood of the window exploded and Bill was forced to dive for cover.

Miraculously, I made it to the porch without any extra holes in my body. I reached out and tried the knob on the front door and was surprised to find it unlocked. I reached into one of my coat pockets and took out a flash bang grenade. If they had superior eyesight, and perhaps hearing, then a flash bang might have even more of an effect.

I pressed my comlink and said, "I'm going to use a flash bang. When you see me open the door, close your eyes for a moment. Understand?"

"Yes. Be careful, please." I could hear the worry in her voice and I didn't blame her. Taking on someone on their turf is never optimal, but I didn't have much of a choice. Time to get moving.

I swung the door open and tossed in the grenade. I turned my head to the side and closed my eyes. A moment later a loud explosion rocked the night. I entered right behind the explosion into a living room. A long couch stretched out before me and I darted behind it, seeking what little cover it offered.

Plaster fell from the ceiling, but otherwise, there was no movement. The room had two open exits: one leading to a room off to the right, the other to a hallway. I duck-walked over to the room and took a quick look. The room looked like what my grandmother would have called a sitting room with all the furniture covered in plastic. No one was in it.

I then moved across the room to the hallway. Glancing in, I saw a kitchen off in one direction and stairs going up to where Bill was shooting in the other. I edged my way towards the kitchen to make sure no one was coming up behind me while at the same time I kept an eye on the stairs. I took another two-steps when someone began taking pot shots through the ceiling above me, trying to put one through the top of my head.

I dove into the kitchen and landed on my stomach next to a freestanding island in the middle of the room. The shooting stopped and I resisted the urge to return fire, not wanting to give away my position just yet. I laid there listening, reaching out with all my senses, my MP5 pointed towards the stairs. I thought I heard footsteps above me. I wondered if their hearing was good enough to hear my breathing through the floor between us. Screw it, time to take the fight to them.

I started to push myself to my feet when, with a yell, Rexena hurtled the island and tackled me, stabbing down with one long ass knife. I managed to roll onto my side, deflecting the strike from my chest, but the knife still sliced through my coat and shirt biting into my shoulder.

Gritting my teeth against the pain, I reversed my block, and slammed my fist into the side of her head, banging it off the kitchen island. She started screaming at me in the same ancient language the other fallen angels used.

She raised her knife to strike again, but I seized her wrist in my hand, stopping the blade a few inches short of my nose.

"Didn't your mother ever teach you not to play with knives?"

I managed to get my other hand around her throat and tried pushing her off me, but she was stronger than any woman had a right to be. Seems having a fallen angel inside you was better than any fitness workout program.

She started clawing at my eyes with her free hand. I turned my head to the side and her fingernails clawed my cheek, drawing blood. I used every ounce of strength I could find to sit up straight and threw her off of me and across the room into the door of the refrigerator hard enough to release a torrent of ice from the icemaker.

Good thing, too. Just then Bill appeared at the bottom of the stairs and aimed his gun in my direction. I dove to the side and tried to put Rexena between the two of us. I raised my gun and let loose a few shots in his direction as he did the same. Parts of the kitchen counter exploded around me, but I went unscathed. I, on the other hand, hit pay dirt when Bill howled in pain.

Rexena, who was gathering for a new assault, her knife raised in both hands, froze and her eyes widened when she heard Bill cry out. Bill began shouting in the same alien language I heard before. Rexena quickly turned and ran to Bill. He dropped his rifle and blood flowed from his now shattered elbow. Lucky shot, or perhaps divine intervention. When she reached him he put his other trembling hand on top of her head and closed his eyes.

It took every ounce of control I possessed not to let loose with a hail of bullets, killing both of them. It's what I wanted to do, to end it here. I'd killed dozens of people in my life. If I lived long enough as the Hand of God, I would kill more. But killing the two fallen angels meant killing two innocent people and consigning both of them to Hell. I wanted to scream out in frustration.

Getting a hold of my blood lust, I got to my feet and raised the MP5 to my shoulder. "Move and you both die," I shouted.

Bill cried out again, but this time it was different. The sound he made was more human and he tried to shove Rexena away from him.

Rexena took off up the stairs, leaving Bill behind. Bill let loose a string of curses and then shouted up the stairs, "So help me God, I will hunt you down and kill you for what you've done to me! Do you hear me, you son-of-a-bitch. I will gut you and watch you bleed out when I get my hands on you!"

He lay back on the stairs, moaning in pain. I moved quickly down the hallway, my gun trained on the wounded man, but when I reached him, I knew the fallen angel had fled. The feeling I had when I was around the fallen was no longer present in him.

"What did he just do?" I asked.

Bill, eyes filled with pain, growled, "He moved from me to her. They're both in the girl now. We *have* to kill that bastard."

He started to get up, but I pushed him down to remain on the steps. "I'm on it. You're badly wounded. Stay here. Try and get your belt off and use it to make a tourniquet. I'll go after them. Anyone else up there?"

He shook his head. "No. Just her. Or them. Christ, this hurts," he said, holding his shattered elbow. He continued, "Don't hold back. He wants you dead in the worst kind of way. Shoot the fucker. If you don't, I will." And I knew he meant it.

"I would rather take her down without killing her, then kick them out of her body. After all, if I followed your advice, you'd already be dead." I said.

"Damn straight. But they would be, too. You should've taken the shot."

"Rock and a hard place, man. Rock and a hard place." I patted him on the shoulder and started slowly up the steps, my MP5 raised and ready. I reached the top of the steps when I heard a crash, the sound of glass breaking, and a thump on the porch roof. Then I heard footsteps of someone moving fast. Damn. Rexena was attempting to escape the house.

I ran back down the steps, sliding past Bill, and headed to the front door. Suddenly I heard the bark of a machine gun, then Samantha yelling, "Get down!" At least this time she did as I'd asked her.

Making it to the door, I saw Rexena turn and face Samantha, a contemptuous smile on her face. Samantha, the MP5 in one hand, her sword in the other, screamed, "On your knees, bitch, or so help me, I'll blow your face off."

Rexena did as she was told, going down to both knees in the snow. Holding the gun in one hand and her sword rose in the other, Samantha closed the distance between them and hit the kneeling woman in the face with the hilt of her sword, knocking her to the ground.

"Samantha, no!" I shouted, running towards the women.

But Samantha ignored me, stuck the sword in the ground, grabbed a handful of hair, and yanked the young woman back up, blood running from a gash on her forehead. Samantha then placed the muzzle of her gun against the side of the woman's head.

"I should kill you now," Samantha said.

Rexena took hold of Samantha's wrist and tried to break free, but Samantha's grip was too tight. Finally, Samantha let go and shoved her to the ground and took a step back.

Before I could yell anything else, Samantha pulled the trigger. The round took Rexena in the chest, blood blooming a deep crimson across and down the front of her shirt. She collapsed onto her side, her life drained away.

I was stunned. I stopped a few feet away, shocked beyond belief. "Samantha, why in heaven's name did you kill her? We could've *saved* her!"

Samantha turned on me and said, "I told you, if given the chance, I would kill the bastard who caused all this to happen. And I did. The demon inside her didn't deserve to live another second."

Father Colton appeared in the barn door and began jogging our way.

I closed my eyes and said a silent prayer for Rexena. When I opened them again, I looked at the woman I loved and said, "No, Samantha. You just sent an innocent young woman to Hell. What you did was wrong."

"Whatever. You know why I did it. I won't lose any sleep over it. You shouldn't either," Samantha replied.

We both watched as Father Colton reached the dying woman and began saying last rites. Then Samantha pulled her sword from the ground and started walking towards the barn.

When she passed behind me, my world fell away, and the blood froze in my veins. The feeling I got when around the fallen moved with her. I pulled my Glock out of its holster and pointed it at Samantha.

"Samyaza, stop," I said, my throat choked with emotion.

Samantha turned to me with a look of confusion. Then the same sneer and contempt I had seen before on those possessed by the fallen now appeared on Samantha's face. Father Colton stood and I could see realization in his eyes.

Samyaza spoke, "Ah. You must be able to sense us. Is that it?"

When I didn't answer, he continued, "I should have considered such a thing. In the past, before we were chained in the darkness, one had but to look at us to know we were of the divine. That the Spear of Uriel would know us, no matter the form, should be of no surprise." The alien sounding voice, coming from Samantha, made the whole scene seem like a bad dream.

"I'm called the Hand of God now, asshole. And before long, I'm going to send you to the pit of Hell."

Samyaza raised one of Samantha's eyebrows. "You mean by exorcism? I don't think so." And with a casual move of her hand, the MP5 rang out and Father Colton danced backwards a few steps before collapsing to the ground, dead.

"Oops. Scratch one priest. They sure don't make them like they used to." Samantha/Samyaza laughed and dropped the gun to her side.

I howled in anger, closing the distance between us, putting both hands on my Glock because with one, it was shaking too much. "Raise that gun again and I'll kill you where you stand."

A porch light blazed to life and Bill came out onto the front porch, the Dakota rifle held in his left hand, his belt strapped around his arm to stop the bleeding. Winston slowly came out of the barn, his own weapon up, taking in the scene. I shoved my night vision goggles off my head.

"You won't shoot me. I'm controlling the love of your life. When I take possession of a body, I instantly know what they know. And I can feel her love for you as well as how much she believes you love her. Dangerous thing, loving the Spear of Uriel. But there is a way out. Here's what we're going to do. You're going to let me go. In a few days, I will find a new host and I will let your lover go. You have my word on it. You should know, when one of the divine gives their word, they must honor their promise. She will be unharmed. But you *will* let me go."

Standing there, all the emotion left my body. It was as if all feeling, the anger, the frustration, the hate, rushed down a well buried so deep inside me it would never resurface, leaving a vast emptiness inside me.

"She can hear me, right? She's aware of what's going on?" I asked.

"Of course. She is aware of all that happens." She smiled at me, and I knew it wasn't her, but the demon.

"Then Samantha, I'm sorry. I'm so very sorry. It should never have come to this."

I could feel tears stinging my eyes as I lowered the gun a few inches and fired.

CHAPTER THIRTY-SIX

I recalled Deveraux and Samantha in the warehouse, his gun pointed at her head. I thought about how, after rescuing her in Florida, she said, "How could you let them take me?" And here I was again, with one evil son-of-a-bitch planning to do it once again, to steal her away from me. And I wasn't going to let that happen.

The bullet struck Samantha in the right hip. I knew where the Kevlar vest ended and where I needed to hit her. She spun around, dropping her sword, took one-step and fell to the ground. I crossed the distance between us and trapped her MP5 on the ground with my foot as Samyaza tried to roll over and blow me away. The demon howled in pain and frustration.

I bent over, yanking the gun out of her hand, and tossed it away. Bill and Winston both ran up as I turned her over. Samyaza continued to scream with pain. I planted the muzzle of my Glock on Samantha's forehead.

"Move and it's over." I asked Bill, "Are there any animals on this farm?"

He looked at me bewildered for a moment, not answering. So I shouted at him, "Are there any animals on this farm?"

He snapped out of it.

"Yeah," he said. "On the other side of the house, there's a small pig pen. There's a sow with a couple of piglets. I keep 'em fed and make sure they have warm bedding through the winter. The owner loves country ham, so he raises his own."

I looked at Winston, "Go get one of the piglets and bring it here. Bill, you show him where they are."

The two men left and I looked back into the eyes of the woman I loved. In the porch light I could see stars falling through iris darker than the night surrounding us. We waited this way, as the blood continued to flow from the wound I'd inflicted on the woman I wanted to spend the rest of my life with.

It seemed like hours, but it was only a few minutes when Bill and Winston returned, a piglet under Winston's arm. He knelt on the ground next to me, holding the squirming pig still.

I said to Samyaza, "New deal. If you transfer into the pig, I will let you go free. I will give you one week to try and find someone else to transfer into. After one week, I will hunt you down and plant you so deep into the ground no one will ever find you again. You have the word of the Hand of God."

He snarled, "I will not. You won't kill her. You won't." I could hear the desperation in his voice. And the fear.

"Look deep into my eyes. I love her. But I won't let you take her from here. It's this deal, or no deal. If you don't take the offer, when she bleeds out you will spend eternity wandering in Hell."

He swallowed hard a few times and let out another scream.

"You swear that you and your friends will let me go?" he asked.

"As God is my witness, neither I nor my friends will do anything to harm or stop you. For one week you will have your freedom. But both you and the other fallen angel inside her must leave. If I feel either of you still there, she dies and Hell is your new home."

The fear in her eyes was replaced with hate. Seeing such hatred coming from Samantha, even though I knew it wasn't her, chilled me. She reached out a hand, placing it on the piglet's side, and closed her eyes.

A moment later the piglet squealed and Samantha opened her eyes, as pain, unfiltered by a fallen angel, racked her body. She gasped in a deep breath and began to moan in pain. I pulled the gun away from her and stood up. I motioned for Winston to move away from her with the pig, and the feeling went with the pig. It had left Samantha. She was now free from the evil residing inside her.

I nodded at Winston and he let the piglet go and it took off. Before it ran more than a few feet, however, a shot rang out in the night, the piglet squealed, rolled over, convulsing on the ground a few seconds, and died.

I turned quickly, bringing my gun up. Bill lowered the Dakota.

"I told you I'd kill that son-of-a-bitch," he said.

"What have you done? I promised none of us would hurt him. You broke my promise. You don't realize what you've done!"

"Like hell I did. I was listening. You said neither you or any of your friends would hurt him. Mister, I'm not yer friend. I don't know you. So I'm not covered by yer promise. If he was too damn stupid to know that, then screw him."

I didn't have time to argue and hell, he could be right. I went back to Samantha.

"We have to get her to a hospital. *Now!*" I shrugged out of my coat, pulled my shirt off and pressed it to her wounded hip. Her eyes were starting to glaze over with pain, but was aware of what was going on around her.

She gripped my hand and gasped, "Thank you." And then her eyes closed and she slipped into unconsciousness.

Bill stuck his good hand into his jeans pocket and pulled out a set of truck keys. Nodding to his truck at the side of the house, he said, "That's my truck. We can take it."

I slipped my coat on, then I bent over and picked up Samantha as gently as I could and carried her to the truck while Bill unlocked the doors and opened the back door to the dual cab. I laid Samantha on the seat, ran to the other side and got in. I lifted her head and rested it on my lap.

"You sure you won't pass out on the way to the hospital?" I asked Bill.

"I'm a lot tougher than ya think. It won't be a problem."

Bill fired up the truck and I rolled the window down.

"Winston, what about the fallen angels in the barn?"

"Colton was able to exorcise the one with the busted leg. I left Kurt and him to watch over the other two. They're tied down and won't be a problem. I'll go get our cars and the other guy and we'll drive our vehicles back here. We'll wait until you return or we hear from you."

There wasn't time for more conversation as Bill took off, tearing out down the farm's gravel drive. I hit the speed dial button for Brother Joshua and he answered on the first ring.

"Samantha's been shot," I said, trying to stay calm. "We're on our way to a hospital. I *need* you. I need Uriel. You have to help her."

"I'm sorry, Victor. But it doesn't work like that. Uriel is not 'on call.' I will say prayers for her. Which hospital are you going to?" All said as if we were discussing what place to go to dinner. I nearly crushed the phone in my hand.

"Didn't you hear me? Samantha's been shot. She's lost a lot of blood. She needs you. I need you. You can't let her die." I said, infuriated.

"I will pray for her Victor. That's what I can do. The other thing I can do is have help waiting when you get to the hospital, but I need to know which one."

I stared down at Samantha, brushing the hair from her forehead, her breathing shallow and rapid.

"Please, Joshua. Please," I was desperate. I knew Uriel had made it clear how much involvement he was willing to provide, but watching Samantha cling to life, I just couldn't lose her again—I *really* needed him.

"Victor. I will do what I can. But I need to know the hospital."

I asked Bill what hospital was closest, and relayed that information to Joshua. He once again said he would do what he could and hung up. I didn't even tell him about Father Colton. I thought about calling him back, but decided, "screw it."

I don't remember much about the rest of the trip to the hospital. I zoned out, watching Samantha take each breath, afraid each would be her last. I prayed with all my might, trying to will the next breath to come.

We roared up to the hospital emergency room door. There was a team of medics waiting. Bill gave them some story about someone trying to carjack his truck when a gunfight ensued which injured Samantha and him.

True to his word, Joshua alerted the hospital we were coming in and they hustled Samantha onto a gurney and rushed her into emergency surgery. They took Bill, who by this time, was starting to fade in and out, into a different surgical room.

I sat in the waiting room, hoping to hear news soon, but I realized it could be hours. I wasn't there long when two cops showed up to talk to me about the shootings.

I began reciting the story about the carjacking, keeping it simple. I told them the men had worn ski masks and there wasn't much in a way of a description I could give them. I talked with my head in my hands, not looking them in the eye. They kept asking questions, but I told them I couldn't add any more and left it at that. They weren't very convinced and told me not to leave town.

A few hours later, a doctor came out and told me Bill would be fine, but would need to stay the night for observation. When I asked about Samantha, all he could tell me is she was still in surgery.

A few minutes later, Brother Joshua walked into the waiting room and sat down next to me. He laid a hand on my shoulder and asked, "How are you holding up?"

I stared at him for a moment before answering. "Great. Just frickin' great."

"You do what you have to do, Victor," Brother Joshua said. "She went with you willingly." He paused, then continued, "Tell me what happened."

And I did. It all came pouring out, slowly at first, and then faster, as I remembered all of the events of the late night mission of my team at the farm. When I told him about the death of Father Colton, he didn't seem surprised.

"She's lying in there, near death, because of me."

"No," he replied, "She's in there fighting for her life because of you. If Samyaza had been able to leave with her, there's no telling what would have happened, but I can promise you it would not have been good."

"I can't believe he was able to possess her. I know she thought God was dead, but I thought I'd been able to change her mind about that, you know? But I failed her there, too."

Before he could answer, a very tired-looking doctor came out. He greeted Father Joshua by name, then turned to me. "It was close. But I think she'll be O.K. She will have to go through a lot of physical therapy following her recovery, and even then, I'm not sure how well her hip will function. The bullet did a lot of damage, but the surgery went well and I'm very hopeful for a full recovery."

I nearly wept at the news. I thanked him and asked how soon before I could see her.

"It will be some time. She's lost a lot of blood and will be in I.C.U. for the foreseeable future. I suggest you go home and get some rest and come see her in the morning."

I nodded my thanks and the doctor left us. I turned to Joshua and said, "We have unfinished business at the farm," I continued. "We need someone to finish the exorcisms. Care to help out?"

He agreed and we drove to the farm where we found Winston, Kurt, Neunen and Peko still watching over the other two fallen angels. They stepped aside to allow Brother Joshua to finish the job started by Father Colton. Newman and Railoa would need medical attention. Brother Joshua said he would take them to a clinic in Louisville where no questions would be asked.

"What do we do about Father Colton?" I asked.

"Bring his body back to the mission. I will handle things when I return from the clinic. We need to think about how to handle where the Watchers are buried."

"I already have a plan for how to deal with that. Let me make a few phone calls."

"Good. I will see you and Winston later. Get some rest."

Winston, Neunen and I helped him get the wounded college students into his car. Neunen said he would go with them, and I watched as they drove away.

"Man, being an operations guy instead of just a tech guy is rough." Kurt said.

I glanced at him and asked, "Ready to hang up your spurs there, Kurt?"

"Not a chance, big guy. I kind of like mixing it up in the trenches. Really gets the blood flowing."

Yeah, I thought. The problem is too often it's our blood.

~*~

I must have been more tired from our mission than I realized. Once Kurt and Winston were settled into spare rooms, I collapsed into my own bed and was sure I'd never be able to sleep with visions of Samantha and the way her hip exploded burned into my retinas. But within minutes of hitting my bunk, I was asleep and stayed that way until late into the morning of the next day.

I woke up, took a quick shower and went in search of Joshua, finding him in his office, naturally.

He waved me in and I took a seat across from him. "I'm going to head down to check on Samantha. Do you want to come along?"

"She isn't there." He stared at me serenely, hands folded in front of him.

"What? She's been moved to a different hospital? Where?" I felt my heart beat jump, my anxiety racing. "Is she O.K.? What's happened?"

"She's fine. But as for where she's at now I'm afraid I can't tell you."

"Why the hell not? That's insane. I have to see her." I didn't realize it, but I was no longer sitting. I was standing, my fists clenched at my sides. I forced myself to relax, breathe, and slow my racing heart.

If Joshua was upset by my body language he didn't show it.

"She's been moved to a private rehab facility at my request. As for you not seeing her, she requested I not share where she is."

"*Her* request? I don't understand. Doesn't she want to see me?" My chest felt as if a giant was holding me down and slowly squeezing me. "J, I have to see her!"

"I'm sorry, Victor. But it's for the best. She will get in touch with you when she's ready."

I couldn't breathe. Didn't want to see me? I paced back and forth in Joshua's small office, my mind racing through all the reasons. Who could blame her? I promised to protect her, to take care of her and what did I do? Not only did I not protect her from some of the worst evil the planet had ever known, but I shot her. My idea of saving her came down to me pointing a gun at her, the woman I loved, and pulling the trigger.

How many times had I thought, now that I'm the Hand of God, we can never be together, our relationship can never work, it's too dangerous for Samantha to be near me. And now that she didn't want to see me, why was I surprised?

I sat down, deflated. "Will she be O.K.? I mean, will she recover from where I shot her?"

He nodded. "All indications are, she will, at least physically. I will certainly pray that is the case. She will have a harder time coming to grips with what she did while possessed."

"You mean Samyaza shooting Father Colton. It wasn't her fault. She couldn't help it."

"All true. But the same could be said about you and the fact you had to shoot Samantha. Does the fact you had no choice make it any easier for you?"

Touché, Brother Joshua. I had no reply. I knew I'd never forgive myself for shooting Samantha. I can only imagine what she was feeling after shooting Colton.

"What about Father Colton? Will there be a funeral?"

"There will be a private service for him back in California. He served his faith well, Victor. He has moved on to a much better place."

I wondered, again, if I would make the same trip. I had my doubts.

"You said you had some ideas on what to do about the resting place of the Watchers. What did you have in mind?" he asked.

"I still need to make a few phone calls, but I have a plan."

I told him what I needed and Brother Joshua smiled.

CHAPTER THIRTY-SEVEN

Paulie, the Viking and I watched as the old man walked out of the cave. He stopped, looking up at the sky, stretched his back, and then walked over to us.

"Won't be a problem," he said. "You have enough TnT to close up this cave so that no one will ever climb down there again. The cost will be about what I thought it would be. You got the cash?"

"In the Ford. I added a bit for a tip. I appreciate you coming up and taking care of this personally for me."

The three of them drove up the day before. Winston's uncle was kind enough to put me in contact with the bombers. They'd been able to use the Florida action in a beneficial way and were happy to lend a hand—for a fee, of course.

"I'll get to it," the old man said. He glanced back at the mouth of the cave. "Damndest thing," he continued. "While I was looking around I could swear I heard somebody whispering. Made the hair rise up on the back of my neck."

"The cave has strange acoustics. Probably picking up our talking out here."

"We weren't doing no talking out here," the Viking guy said.

The old man gave me a long look, but said nothing more. I left them to their work and walked back to the farmhouse. Bill, Winston and Kurt sat around the kitchen table talking like three old women at teatime. Their drink preference was a bit stronger, though, than tea, something Bill called a Fire Pepper: Diet Dr. Pepper with a large portion of Fireball Whiskey mixed in for good measure.

"They going to blow the joint up?" Kurt asked, taking another swig of the cinnamon flavored whiskey.

I was still getting used to the "new" Kurt, the one infused with a gallon of testosterone. He insisted on coming along to meet with the bombers and I let him. After all, he'd done his part the night of the raid, so he earned it.

"Yeah. They're setting up the explosives now. In a couple of hours, the cave will be no more and the only way to get down to the fallen will be through solid bedrock. And that will take time. Not like you can do that in just a few days. They're hosed."

"Are you really going to buy the farm?" Bill asked.

He'd filled us in on Samyaza's plans, about the murder of his uncle, and the theft of the dynamite.

"Yes. The family had it for sale, quietly, before they were murdered and the estate is anxious to sell. I've hired a real estate lawyer to handle the purchase. In the next month or so this will belong to me. Then I'm going to donate it to the mission and we will build some type of retreat out here for kids. There will be no way to drill down to the fallen angels. Not any time soon."

"Too bad you're tearing down the barn, though," Bill said, with a hint of disgust in his voice.

"Bill, I really don't like barns. And this place won't miss it."

Winston laughed, but then turned somber, sipping his Fire Pepper, he asked, "Still nothing on Samantha?"

I shook my head in the negative. The more I thought about what Brother Joshua told me, the more I came to realize it was for the best. It didn't hurt any less, with Samantha not wanting to see me, but it didn't change the facts: the longer she was around me, the more likely she was going to get hurt even worse, or wind up dead.

Reading my thoughts, Winston said, "On a different subject, seems we got all the fallen angels, but one. Bill was telling us one of them had a huge knock down drag out with Samyaza."

"Ain't no doubt about it," Bill said. "And Samyaza was pissed to all get out. His name is Gadriel and I can tell you this much, Samyaza was afraid of this guy. When Samyaza told Gadriel his plans, Gadriel called him an idiot and said he wouldn't help. When Samyaza threatened to fight him over it, Gadriel spread his hands out to his sides and said, 'Give it your best shot.' Well, not in those words, but you get the message. It's one of the reasons he wouldn't let the others have guns. He didn't truly trust the other angels with them."

"What happened?" Kurt asked. He drained his drink, and motioned for Bill to fix him another round.

He handed Kurt a Fire Pepper and said, "Keep drinkin' these, it'll put hair on yer chest."

Kurt looked down his shirt at his still smooth chest. "Hmm."

"As fer Samyaza and Gadriel? Bill continued. "Not a damn thing. Samyaza backed down and the next day, Gadriel was outta here. Ain't heard from him since. So you still got one out there. And be careful. This one seemed smarter than the rest of them. He told Samyaza his problem was he was still thinking old school and wasn't keeping up with the times. Gadriel insisted on having a gun, but Samyaza forbid it. Gadriel just laughed. When this guy shows up, he'll be packing."

"Great," I said. "A gun-toting fallen angel with brains. Can't wait to meet him. You O.K. hanging out here until we can get a more permanent presence?"

"Shoot, since my old lady kicked me out, I need a place to stay anyways. Works for me. And with the salary you're offering, why the hell not?"

"Thanks, Bill. And sorry about the elbow. Hope it heals up alright."

He waved it off with his other hand. "Don't sweat it. Once you've had a prick angel in your head, everything else is a piece of cake."

I picked up the bottle of Fireball Whiskey and poured several fingers into a glass I found on the table. I leaned against the counter and downed half of the glass in one shot while I thought about Samantha and the badass angels she had in her head. I thought about a lot of things. I chugged the rest of the whisky, the cinnamon flavor adding a nice burn on the way down. And I thought about the future. At least I could now do the things I needed knowing she was safe from harm, wherever she was. For now, that was enough.

EPILOGUE

Elsa, the reigning Sports Illustrated Cover Super Model, followed Alex Dabney as he jogged up the steps of his private jet. She heard him leave strict instructions for the crew to take off as soon as they were ready—but under no circumstances, short of the plane about to crash, should they disturb him once in the air.

They made their way to the private cabin. He slipped off his sports coat and undid his tie, tossing them across a seat. Elsa walked to the wet bar and poured them both some Glenfiddich Janet Sheed Roberts Reserve 1955. He said the stuff cost him nearly a hundred thousand a bottle. But as one of the Fortune 500 richest men, he didn't care.

He told her after taking over his father's manufacturing company and turning it into one of the world's foremost weapons makers, he could afford just about anything, or anyone, he wanted.

She sauntered over with the drinks and handed him one. He sat down, then she sat on his lap and began nibbling on his ear. Life was very good. When she moved to kiss his lips, she hesitated for moment. Gazing into his eyes she swore she saw stars falling.

Nightmare

Short Story

Nightmare

I should've seen it coming, but I didn't. And that really pissed me off.

My name is Victor McCain and I'm the Hand of God, God's bounty hunter. My job is to track down and kill the truly evil things that walk, crawl and creep around in the darkest shadows of man's existence. I got the job because I was directly responsible for the death of the previous Hand of God, losing my soul in the process. Now I'm working to try and earn a ticket up when I die, instead of down. And trust me, you don't want to be on the escalator down when you die and end up a guest in Hell for eternity. I've met Satan and party animal he is not.

The main thorn in my side these days is the Church of the Light Reclaimed, a bunch of demented Satan worshipers who believe one day their savior will be Lucifer. Nothing like hopping on the wrong bandwagon while it's on fire and then riding off with it over a cliff. But hey, they're idiots, so who should be surprised?

The latest piece of scum who needed removing was one of the biggest fish in the Chicago Mafia: one Jessie "The Nightmare" Scotto. Scotto started out hustling counterfeit merchandise around Navy Pier. He moved up the ladder of underworld success by grabbing the ankle of the man above him, yanking him off and then stomping him to death.

One of his favorite ways to kill his enemies was to force them to take a drug named Bromo-DragonFLY (BDF, for short), which causes hallucinations similar to LSD—but it lasts for days, not hours. Then he drops his victims in a pit filled with rats and leaves them there to die. If being eaten by rats wasn't bad enough, the three days on BDF makes it like a trip to Hell, thus the nickname "The Nightmare."

Normally, I wouldn't give a rat's ass (pun intended) about mobsters killing other mobsters. But recently Scotto began sending out enforcers to dissuade community action groups from putting a dent in the drug trade on some of Chicago's more dangerous streets. He made it onto my radar when he used his "nightmare" treatment and killed a minister who was making a real difference here on the mean streets of the Windy City. Then I found out he was a major backer when it comes to funds for the Church of the Light Reclaimed. Every organization needs money to keep their operations afloat, and Scotto donated huge sums to the Church.

The time had come for the Hand of God to do what Scotto's rivals and the Chicago Police Department could not: end the Nightmare. The problem was getting anywhere near Scotto. He rarely left his penthouse apartment, and it seemed it would be easier to break into Fort Knox than busting my way inside past his heavily armed soldiers and alarm systems. When he did show up in the outside world, no one knew how he moved about, appearing to materialize out of thin air from one location to another.

I spent a couple of weeks staking out the penthouse building, but never saw him coming or going. Sitting outside in my Chevelle I sat, watching, only to find out he was at some benefit or dinner several blocks away. Theories from people in the know ranged from underground tunnels to heavy makeup and disguises, but I couldn't find anyone with a frickin' clue as to how he did it.

I liked hunting people down, but not the waiting. I decided the best option to get to Scotto was to flush him into the open. That's where Rory Stinson came into play. After weeks of pounding low-lifes down the food chain of the Mafia Don's operation, I latched on to him when I found out Stinson ran the gambling side of Scotto's business interests. From illegal poker games to sports betting, Stinson kept the chips turning and the profits coming in the door. What made him interesting to me was he and Scotto often got together on a regular basis to discuss business over dinner.

Stinson ran his part of the operation from a bar he owned on Chicago's Southside called *Fast Bobby's Good Time Emporium* and tonight I stopped by to pay him a visit. The time had come to push some buttons and make things happen. I'm great at pushing buttons. Ask any girl I ever dated. Ever.

The bar, a tall single story structure squeezed between a dry cleaners and a smoke shop, was a Chicago hot spot. Built in the 1880's it spent time during prohibition as a speakeasy, with the front boarded up to make the joint look vacant, while the nightclub rocked behind closed doors. The things you can learn on Google.

I shouldered the door open and stepped inside where my senses were assaulted with all the familiar bar sounds and smells, with a band playing loudly on a stage in the middle of the floor. The place was packed and I forced my way to the bar and bought a double Fireball Whiskey, neat, which the bartender poured into a heavy crystal glass. Ice was for wussies. Sipping my drink, I slowly eased through the crowd to the back of the bar.

I followed a hallway to the restrooms and then hung a right at the back door and found Stinson's office at the end of another short hallway. A man stood guard outside the door, his hands clasped in front of him.

A few inches shorter than my six foot six, but nearly as massive in the weight department, he stretched the fabric of his sports coat to near seam-busting proportions. He took one large step forward and said, "The men's room is around the corner, asshole."

I downed the rest of my Fireball. "Asshole? And here we've just met. What, are you psychic or something? Or maybe you've been talking to my ex?"

"I'll tell you what I know and that's if you don't turn around I'll rip you a new assho—" He never got the chance to finish the threat as I smashed him between the eyes with the glass. The unexpected attack rocked him backwards, the heavy crystal ripping a gash across his forehead. I kneed him in the groin, grabbed a handful of hair and brought his head down hard onto my knee. He'd be singing soprano for weeks through a busted nose, but that's part of the downside to being a rent-a-thug.

The man started a slow slide down the wall and onto the floor, but I slipped an arm around his waist, pushed him against the wall and held him up while I searched him. I found his piece tucked into the waistband of his slacks. I removed it and slid the gun carefully into the front of my own jeans. Then I spun him around, took hold of the knob and opened the door.

Stepping inside the office, I dumped the hired muscle onto the floor in front of a large green metal desk strewn with newspapers, Styrofoam cups, receipts and an over-full ashtray. I kicked the door closed, keeping my eyes on the guy sitting behind the desk, a cellphone pressed to his ear.

Rail thin with a long hooked nose, Stinson had the look of a predatory bird. Hard eyes glanced at the bodyguard on the floor, then back at me. "Hey, let me call you back. I've got a situation here needs handling."

He pushed a button on his phone, ending the call, and placed it carefully on his desk. "You've made a huge mistake, friend. Barging in like this, attacking the help. Not good for your long-term health."

"You should see my healthcare plan. This Obamacare stuff is unreal." I slipped out my new found gun, then pulled the only extra chair in the room to one side where I could keep an eye on both the door and Stinson, and sat down. Resting the gun on my thigh, I continued, "I didn't come here to discuss my health, Rory, but yours."

He spread his hands out to the side. "My health is fine. Doc says with my cholesterol levels, I could live to be a hundred. You, on the other hand, won't make it to your next birthday. I got connections. You do anything to me, and they will hunt you down. You have no clue what's comin' your way."

"You mean Scotto and the rats? Nah, he won't be an issue for me. Not once I put a bullet in his brain."

Rory's jaw dropped a few inches, his face incredulous. "What? Are you fucking nuts? You don't mess with Scotto. The man's a phantom. A ghost. He will pull your goddamm spleen out with his bare hands. You don't want nothin' to do with Scotto."

"Well, I do want him and you're going to help me get him, or I will kill you and move on to the next guy. You want to keep breathing more than a few more minutes, you will do what I tell you to do."

"And that's what, exactly?" He kept licking his lips while staring at the gun. I knew he was running the odds in his head, trying to figure a way out. But I wasn't going to give him one. Unlike the mob games which were rigged in their favor, I held the cards on this one.

"How does Scotto move around the city without being seen?"

"How the hell should I know? He tells me where to be and I show up first. He always comes later. I know better than to ask how he does it."

"In that case, I want you to pick up your phone and call Scotto. Tell him you have a problem with the books only he can help solve. Invite him for a visit. I hear Scotto is Johnny-on-the-spot when trouble pops up in his organization."

"Kiss my ass. I won't do it."

I stood, crossed the room and placed the barrel of the gun against his temple. "Up to you. But I'm going to count to five in my head. If you haven't picked up the phone and dialed, I'm going to pull the trigger and move on."

He chewed on his lower lip for a second, thinking hard. "I do this and I'm gonna need protection. How do I know you can provide it? Who the hell are you? You with the cops? The Feds? Who?"

I ignored his questions and pressed the gun hard against his head. "Time to dial a friend, Rory. Now."

His hand shook a bit while he punched the buttons, but he made the call. He said, "Let me speak to Mr. Scotto." After a moment's pause, he continued, "It's me. Look, there's a problem with the inventory here at the bar and I could use your advice about what to do about it."

There was a pause while the person on the other end responded. "Yeah. Tonight. Tonight is good. Ring when you get here and I'll buzz the backdoor open."

He ended the call. "You've signed both our death warrants, ya know that, right?"

I smiled, moving back to my seat to watch and wait. "I like to walk on the wild side. What was all that about inventory? And you should know, if anyone but Scotto walks through that door, you go first, Rory."

He waved off the threat. "We always assume the Feds are listening in on our conversations. The inventory is code for the books. I ain't worried about you shooting me. Scotto will come up with a lot more creative way to off me than puttin' a bullet in me."

The hired goon started to come around and he rolled over on his back. He started to sit up, then saw me holding his gun. "Lay back down, on your stomach, your hands out to the side and don't move." He did as I asked, collapsing onto his stomach.

"Rory, you must keep some sort of books on the gambling operation. Where are they?" Hatred filled his eyes, but he jerked a thumb towards a personal wet bar he kept in the corner of the room.

"Really? Get them out, please. And Rory? If you pull out anything but books, you're gonna find out if I can miss from about six feet away."

Stinson walked to the wet bar, slid open a door and took out a decanter of what I assumed was wine. He tipped the bottle up and removed a small cover in the thick base, taking out a small USB stick. Replacing the cover, he put the decanter back in the wet bar and slid the door closed.

"Pretty sly, Rory. Toss it here."

He did so and walked back to his chair, sitting down heavily. I put the USB stick into my jeans pocket, and we waited.

Time dragged on and sweat began to roll down his forehead, running to the tip of his nose. He brushed it away with his hand. I noticed his hand was shaking.

"What kind of name is *Fast Bobby's*, anyway? I asked.

"Guy who owned the bar before me was Fast Bobby Fulks. Made his bones with the Outfit during the 60's. People got used to comin' here, so when I bought the joint I never bothered changing nothin'."

I was about to make a snide comment when the door to the office opened halfway. I brought the gun up and waited, but no one came inside. I moved quietly to the door and yanked it the rest of the way open, but the hallway outside was empty.

My Spidey senses were tingling, but seeing nothing, I shut the door and sat down again. "You got some kind of draft around here, Stinson. I know your bar's old, but you need to get your door latches fixed."

Stinson swallowed hard a couple of times, appearing even more nervous. "We ain't got no drafts. That's never happened before. Look, mister, I don't think I'm gonna be able to help you. In fact—I—I know I can't. I need to get outta here."

"You aren't going anywhere, Rory. We have guests on the way."

He started to reply, but before he could respond his head was yanked backwards and a knife, appearing from nowhere and floating in mid-air, cut deeply from one ear to the other, slitting the man's throat. Blood sprayed the room, while Stinson's hands flew to his throat and tried to cover the wound to stop the blood flow, but he was a dead man.

And as quickly as the knife appeared, it disappeared. What the hell? I stood and backed into the corner by the door. As the Hand of God, I'd come up against hellhounds and the undead, but never anything like this. For the first time in my life, I froze, not sure what or where to shoot.

The thug on the floor started to scream and began to push himself up, when the knife appeared again, as if by magic, and jabbed down quickly into the base of his skull, quick and lethal. Then, just as quickly, it was gone. Holy crap. Two down, one to go. I wondered how long before it was my turn.

Turns out I didn't have long to think about it. The knife reappeared in front of me and slashed hard at my stomach. I got to see it up close and personal, a tactical knife, doubled edge. The knife ripped open my shirt like it was parting tissue paper, but my flack jacket stopped it from reaching my skin. Thank God it did a slash and not a jab, as my vest was not designed to stop a direct knife attack. Whoever, or whatever, held the knife just tried to gut me like trout headed to the frying pan.

I aimed above where the person holding the knife would be, if this was the real world, and pulled the trigger. The gun erupted, the sound huge in the small office. The bullet passed through the air and smashed into the far wall, hitting nothing else as the knife once again disappeared.

I could feel panic rising within me, but pushed it back down, forcing myself to think. One thing about being as tall as I am, I have a long reach. I clasped the gun with both hands, holding it out in front of me, then swung my arms hard, first in one direction and then in the other. On the backswing I felt my arms connect with someone sneaking up on me from the left.

I heard a grunt and then something crashing into the door, rattling the frame. I fired off another shot, splintering the door jam. The knob turned seemingly on its own and the door flung open and I could hear—but not see —someone running down the hallway.

I looked over my shoulder at Stinson, collapsed over his desk. The bright red of his blood covered the night's receipts and began to drip down the side of the desk, pooling on the ground, and mixed with that of the bodyguard. Being them really sucked. I started slowly down the hallway after the invisible assassin, gun up and ready.

The assassin must have stepped in some of the blood in the office, as there were partial footprints in red for the first few feet, then they petered out. It at least confirmed I was looking for a bad guy of the two-legged variety. I reached the back door and glanced into the main room, but with the band playing at full volume, no one seemed to have heard the gun shot. The crowd stood shoulder to shoulder making it difficult to pass through. The assassin likely would not have chosen this way to escape, so I pushed the back door open and exited the bar.

An alley ran the length of the block, illuminated by one lonely bulb over the door. I kept the gun up and ready, but nothing attacked me. I glanced at the ground, but couldn't find any more bloody footprints. I tried the door behind me but it locked when it closed, which meant whoever entered to kill Stinson did so with either a key or was let in, which meant there could be more than one person involved.

I was pissed. My only connection to Scotto was now spending eternity in Hell and of no further use to me. Weeks of work down the drain. When I told Stinson I would shoot him and move on to the next guy, I had no next guy.

And I was more than a little freaked out. How could someone move around invisible? I'd read H. G. Wells *The Invisible Man* when I was a kid and watched the *Predator* movies, but that was pure fiction. I needed to figure it out in the here and now.

But first, I had to get moving. The bodies would be discovered sooner, rather than later. I shuffled down the alley, trying my best to keep my back pressed to the wall and trying to watch every way at once.

I was almost to the end of the alley when the assassin attacked. I turned my head to look into the street at the end of the alley when I felt a sharp explosion of pain in my left leg. I stifled a scream and squeezed off a couple of rounds with my gun hand, while the other pulled out the end of a broken Bud Light beer bottle stuck in my upper thigh.

From somewhere in the alley, someone yelled, "You're a dead man. It's only a matter of time."

I spun around, gun raised in one hand, the beer bottle in the other, but nothing else happened. And that bothered me more than another attack. "Tell you what, asshole. Why don't you give it another shot and see what happens."

Silence. I waited a few more heartbeats, and hobbled out of the alley. I hustled to my red 67 Chevelle I'd left parked a couple of blocks away, blood streaming down my leg. Two very long blocks. I made it to the car, jumped in, fired up the engine and tore out, leaving the bar and the macabre scene behind.

I leaned over, yanked open the glove box, and felt around until I found some napkins I kept there. I pressed them onto the wound with one hand, steering with the other. I'm used to eruptions of violence. Hell, I planned on airing out at least one man, if not several, before I left the bar. Tonight, however, got to me.

I drove for a while through the city of Chicago, taking in the normal night scenes, while my thigh throbbed. People went about their business, all the while unaware of the grizzly things which go bump in the night. It's my job to face the evil, to punch it hard in the mouth and take it down. But how do you fight what you can't see?

It's years of evolution which teaches us to fear what's lurking in the dark. Ever been deep in a cave on a tour when the guides turn out the lights? You can imagine all sorts of things sneaking up on you in the dark. Is that a small breeze blowing through the cave or a spider on your neck? Or have you ever been paddling on a surfboard in the ocean when you think you see something in the water beneath you, but when you stare down you can't see anything? Is there a Great White waiting to snap you in half? If that doesn't make you paddle faster, nothing will.

I pulled over onto a quiet residential street and checked out the stab wound. The blood flow had stopped and the pain settled into a dull ache. I put it out of my mind and pulled out my cell, thumbed through some notes and called Scotto's number.

After a few rings, a voice answered, "Hello? How may I help you?"

"Is the boss around?"

"I'm sorry, sir, but no one is available. May I take a message?"

"Yeah. You can give him a message. Tell him he may have gotten Stinson, but I got his books. Tell him I will call this number back at 2 p.m. tomorrow. Tell him to answer the phone himself, or the books will be dropped off downtown at F.B.I. headquarters. You got all that?"

"And you are?"

I laughed. "His worst nightmare." I hung up and tossed the phone out the window in case they had some way to track the GPS in the phone. I would buy another burner phone in the morning.

After some time wandering down one street after another, I eventually made it to the rental house I booked for the month, not far from Wrigley Field. It was a single story clapboard house on a block with dozens of others just like it. I'd rented the house under an assumed name, Melvin Purvis, the F.B.I. agent who took out mobsters like Dillinger and "Baby Face" Nelson. I pulled around to the back and parked. Grabbing my weapons duffle bag out of the backseat, I got out and took a long deep breath of almost, but not quite, fresh city air.

I let myself in the back door, and stepped into the kitchen, locking the door behind me. I tossed the bloody napkins into the garbage can, then walked over and pulled open the oven and laid the USB stick onto a broiling pan on the top rack. There was no danger of me forgetting and turning on the oven and burning it to a crisp: if it couldn't be microwaved, I didn't eat it. The house came fully stocked with food, but I chose to eat most of my meals out.

With the mob books now properly hidden, I made my way to the bedroom, and tossed my duffle on the bed. I dropped the goon's gun inside the duffle, trading it for my own Glock, silencer attached. I laid the gun on my nightstand, stripped off the flack jacket and my clothes, then picked up the gun and headed to the bathroom. I turned on the water as hot as I could stand it and allowed myself a long hot shower while I cleaned up the wound. I thought about what happened and how someone could make themselves invisible.

I'd read somewhere the British had worked out a way to make tanks invisible to infrared sensors by using thousands of small metal panels which adjust their own heat signatures to match that of the area around them, thus hiding the heat signature of the tank's engines. But the concept did not extend to visible light.

The B-2 bombers used by the good 'ole U.S. of A. used materials which help absorb radio waves, making them nearly invisible to radar. But again, the concept did not extend to visible light.

When it came to the visible spectrum, it became more of an issue of bending light around an object. I had no clue as to how it could be done. But someone had. I'd seen it—or rather had not seen it—as the case may be, in action.

I finished my shower, toweled off, picked up my robe from where I'd dropped it this morning and shrugged into it. I retrieved a medical kit from my duffle and dressed the wound, covering it with a large bandage. I limped back to the kitchen and got a bottle of Fireball out of the cabinet along with a glass. I poured a couple of fingers, sipping while I carried it back to my bedroom and thought about what I'd say to Scotto when I called him the next day.

I was just about to climb into bed when I heard the sound of glass shattering outside. I turned off the light in my bedroom and looked out the window. The moon was half-full and gave off enough light that I could see my Chevelle in the driveway. The driver's side window was busted out.

I picked up the gun from my nightstand, made my way to the backdoor, and started to head outside when I stopped—my hand still on the door knob. I'd left nothing on the front seats which would encourage a smash and grab. The only things of value were the radio or the car itself, but looking out the window, there was no one near the car or in it. I could feel a tingle go up my spine. Maybe I was paranoid. But what if the breaking of the glass was designed to bring me outside, into the open? I watched my car for a few minutes longer from the small window in the back door, but nothing further happened. Nada.

I let go of the knob and quickly searched the kitchen, finding what I needed. I unlocked the door, then headed to my bedroom. I shut the door and made some preparations, one of which was to close the heavy curtains on my bedroom window to block the moonlight, plunging the room into total darkness. I arranged the pillows under the bed covers to give the illusion of someone sleeping, then crouched down behind the bed and waited. If I was wrong, then nothing would happen. But if I was right?

I strained to hear any and all night sounds. I thought I heard the floor in the hallway outside my bedroom creak. Was someone there? Or was it merely an old house settling in a Windy City breeze?

The minutes moved agonizingly slow and I almost convinced myself it was all my imagination and the car break-in was just one of the dozens which happened in any big city every night when my bedroom door began to slowly open. Someone had taken the bait.

I waited to a count of four, turned on the light, took careful aim and pulled back on the trigger twice, the sound still loud despite the silencer. I heard a thud as something heavy hit the floor and watched as blood began to flow about a foot and a half in the air, then spread in a widening circle and then cascade to the floor.

A second later, someone lifted a blood stained hand into the air. It looked like one of those hands kids make when they dip their hands in red paint and then press them down on white paper. The palm and the fingers were all that were visible. The hand moved, gripped something higher up and pulled. Instantly, a man became visible, as the hood he'd been wearing came off. Several wires dangled from the hood, while several others remained connected and disappeared into the suit which Jesse "The Nightmare" Scotto wore.

I approached carefully and could see the knife he'd used to kill Stinson and his guard laying a few feet away where he'd dropped it when I shot him in the abdomen. I kicked it to the other side of the room, then squatted next to Scotto. Scotto filled out the suit nicely. Jet black in color, he wore it skin tight, like a would-be super hero costume—or a super villain, in this case. Scotto belonged to a new breed of mobster who kept in shape. It showed.

"How'd you see me? You're not supposed to be able to see me." His face contorted in intense pain and he spoke through gritted teeth.

I drug a finger across the floor, then showed it to him, my index finger covered in white. "Baking flour. I got the idea when I saw the bloody footprints you left fleeing Stinson's office. I spread it on the floor. When I turned the light on, you froze. I shot several feet above where the last set of footprints stopped.

He let out a bitter laugh. "A multi-million dollar fuckin' suit, stopped by a five dollar bag of flour." He stopped laughing and gripped his gut with both hands now. "Jesus Christ. Call an ambulance."

"Cool suit, Jesse. Where'd you get it?" I made no move to call anyone. Not yet.

"Listen. You gotta help me out here." He rolled back and forth for a moment, the pain intense.

"I need some information first, Jesse, before we talk about me calling anybody. Where'd you get the suit and what is it?"

He groaned. "Dabney Industrial Tech. Stealth suit they're developing for black ops stuff." His body spasmed, rocked by more intense pain. "Please. You gotta make the call now."

Dabney Industrial Tech made high-tech military grade equipment for the U.S. military. We'd used some of their gear over in Afghanistan when I was with Special Forces. "And why would Dabney Industrial give something like this to you?"

"Because I learned their CEO Alex Dabney was doing things he shouldn't be doing. We worked out a deal. I kept what I knew to myself, and he helped me get a leg up on the competition while I tested his stuff out."

"So that's how you move around the city without being seen. And use it to listen in on the people who work for you. Pretty slick."

"Yeah. I like to get out, but it's dangerous. Everyone wants a piece of me. I was headed to Stinson's tonight anyways, when he called with the message. I should've waited until he left for the night, but when I saw you in there, I figured I needed to shut him up. Should've done you first."

"Yep. You should've. And the suit, how does it make you invisible?" I could tell Scotto was fading, his hands loosening their hold on his stomach. I slapped him a couple of times in the face. "Scotto, stay with me. How does it make you invisible?"

He came back around. "Nano technology. They found a way to make meta-material with nano wires, or some such shit. The suit has a built-in super processing chip, helps to manage the wires. I don't really understand how it works. Don't care. Now will you make the call?" he pleaded.

"One more question. How'd you find me? I made sure you guys weren't following me."

"Then you did a piss poor job of it. Hell, we've known where you lived for a few days. Followed you a few nights back. We didn't want to take you out 'til we knew who you were." He looked down at his bloody stomach. "Please, now will you make the call?"

I stood up and stared at him for a moment longer. "Nope," I answered. "And I've seen a few rats around here. Maybe they'll stop by for a visit before you die."

I got dressed while Jessie Scotto bled out on my bedroom floor, cursing me with his dying breath. I packed and got all my stuff together, then removed the suit from Scotto and stuffed it in a garbage bag I found in the kitchen pantry. I was way too big to wear the damn thing, even if I could figure out how to make it work. But there was no way I was going to leave it behind. After loading up my gear, and his suit, I went back inside and wiped the place clean.

I drove out of town and stopped at an all night truck stop on I-65 and bought a new burner phone. Then I called the Chicago F.B.I. office and told them where they could find Scotto and his books. When they asked who I was, I hung up and tossed that phone out the window while cruising down the highway back to Louisville. Either they would follow up, or they wouldn't. I didn't really give a damn. As for the suit, I'd give it to some super high tech guys I know, and see if they can reverse engineer the thing—not likely, but you never know.

As for me? I'd done what I set out to do: end the Nightmare.

The Speaker

Book Three

CHAPTER ONE

Eduardo kept watch out the front window while Congressman Owen Grenville committed suicide. True, the congressman was not doing so willingly, but in the end it would be suicide, nonetheless.

Outside all was quiet in this upscale section of Georgetown, not far from the university. A row of town homes crouched on each side of the street, occasionally illuminated by the light from a wan street lamp. It was a bit before ten p.m. at the end of July, the night warm and pleasant. Activity was starting to wind down, the sidewalks now mostly empty as residents settled in for the night.

Eduardo turned from the Norman Rockwell view out the window to take in the macabre scene inside this particular town house: Congressman Grenville stood on a dining room chair, a hangman's noose fit snuggly around his neck with the other end tied to the wooden balcony railing above his head, while tears cut a path down the wrinkled folds of his aging cheeks.

Standing in front of him was a woman holding in one hand an iPad, turned in such a way the congressman could watch what was on the screen, and in the other hand she held a gun down at her side. About five and a half feet tall, with a ballerina's build and long black hair cascading down to the small of her back, the woman was the picture of beauty.

Deadly beauty, Eduardo thought. For six years they were partners in death, hired assassins known for pulling off the perfect murders, the ones people never suspected were murderers at all. They charged exorbitant amounts of money for their services, but those in need paid. There was no one better than them.

He called her Donut because they could not pass a Krispy Kreme donut shop without stopping to buy a dozen for her to eat. It was her one and only vice, as far he knew. How she managed to keep her slim figure Eduardo had no clue, but she did. From time to time, they spent evenings in bed together and he knew her body was flawless.

She was the one who gave him the name Eduardo, saying his olive complexion reminded her of a Latin lover from her past she was forced to kill after he became too clingy. Neither knew the other's real name, nor likely ever would.

His reverie was broken when he heard the congressman plead, "Please, don't do this. You can't do this to me. You can't."

A pudgy man with only a hint of hair circling a bald head covered in sweat, the congressman cut a pitiful figure as he begged for his life. Known as a party firebrand, he would stand for hours in the well of the House of Representatives, taking on any and all who stood in his way as he climbed the ladder of the party hierarchy.

Eduardo was sure he never pictured in his wildest dreams his life ending in anything but personal glory and power. Life could really be a kick in the teeth.

"Congressman, you've seen what both my partner and I look like," Donut said, "and either way, in the next five minutes, you will be dead. The only question is will your wife and daughter join you."

The congressman's eyes darted back to the iPad where a video feed showed a view of his wife and teenaged daughter sitting on a couch watching television. The camera had a clear shot through a patio door in their suburban South Carolina home.

"The man operating the camera also has a high-powered rifle. It's five minutes to ten and if I haven't called to tell him to stand down by ten o'clock, he will put a bullet through the head of your daughter first, and then your wife. Kick the chair out of the way, congressman, and your wife and daughter live. Don't, and they die and we kill you another way. It's all up to you."

Donut turned the iPad off and tossed it onto a nearby couch, waiting. Eduardo knew from experience she hoped the congressman missed the ten p.m. deadline. Donut loved killing people. She got off on the mayhem and destruction it caused in the lives of the victim's families.

As for himself, he was in it for the money. And the challenge. Killing people in ways which went undetected was an incredible high for Eduardo. He considered the two of them artists. They didn't paint on a canvass like Da Vinci or work with marble like Michelangelo to make beautiful statues. Their art came in the form of murders which required great creativity and precision. Tonight, a suicide was preferable, but the client wanted him dead, in whatever way they wanted.

The congressman swallowed hard a couple of times, his Adam's apple bobbing against the tightness of the noose. "I'm in line to become the next Speaker of the House. I have very powerful friends. If you do this, there is no place you will be able to hide."

"And you have very powerful enemies, it seems, hence why we are here. Tick-tock, tick-tock." She pulled a phone from her pocket and waved it at the congressman.

His shoulders slumped in defeat. "You swear you will let them live?"

"I swear it," said Donut. She glanced at the phone's screen and said, "Three minutes, congressman."

The Congressman straightened and hate filled his gaze. Eduardo had to hand it to the little man, he finally looked like the man who struck fear into the hearts of his rivals in the House. "I'll see you in Hell, bitch."

And with a kick of his foot, he knocked the chair backwards to the ground. The fall was only a few feet, but gravity did the rest, with the congressman's feet kicking back and forth mere inches from the ground as the noose strangled him to death. Fingers scrabbled for purchase, as he tried to loosen the rope, but without success.

Donut smiled, waved the phone at Grenville, and then slipped it back into her pocket. Grenville reached out towards her in what might have been a pleading gesture, but Eduardo couldn't be sure.

Soon his efforts grew feeble, then stopped all together as the noose cut off the blood flow to his carotid artery. Eduardo knew it would take another ten to twenty minutes for the congressman to die and they would wait until they knew for sure the job was completed.

Donut picked up the iPad from the couch, walked over to stand next to him, dropping the iPad into a bag on the floor near the window, her disgust evident. "O.K. You win the bet. I thought for sure he wouldn't kill himself to save his family."

Eduardo laughed. "No biggie. I had a fifty-fifty shot at winning. But it does mean you get to do the driving tonight. The dumb-ass died not even knowing the iPad video was shot two nights ago. The power of suggestion. That was cruel, though, waving the phone at him."

"Perception is reality," she agreed. "I didn't like him. He was the one who lead the effort to kill the Equal Pay bill for women in the last Congress. Besides, he earned those last few minutes of torture when he called me a bitch."

When they were sure Grenville was dead, Eduardo pulled out a phone, took a picture of the congressman to send to their client later that night, assuring the rest of their fee would be placed into an offshore account for them the next morning.

He picked up the bag and they left the congressman's town home, leaving no trace of their visit behind. They quickly walked the three blocks to their car, with Donut sliding in behind the wheel, while he tossed the bag in the seat behind him, hopped in the passenger seat and hit the recline button.

She pulled slowly down the darkened street, while he closed his eyes and tried to get some sleep. They would be on the road for many hours as they drove to their next job and he wanted to be well-rested so he could watch the news coverage the next day.

The suicide of Congressman Grenville would be national news. And while the next murder wouldn't be as newsworthy, in the end, it would be the one to bring a nation to its knees.

CHAPTER TWO

God, I hate running. Especially when it's for my life. When you're six and a half feet tall and weigh nearly two-hundred and eighty pounds, running is right up there with water torture and being forced to watch a *Bachelor* rerun marathon.

Yet here I was, sprinting through the woods in the mountains of North Carolina, faster than I'd ever run before. Then again, I'd never gone running while being chased by a monster. If I had, I would have lost a lot more weight.

I resisted the urge to look over my shoulder and concentrated on making sure I didn't trip on a rock or tree root and fall on my face, which would be fatal if a nightmare pounced on my back.

The plan nearly worked to perfection, right up until the moment it didn't. A few weeks earlier, I learned about a man in these mountains raising hellhounds. Seems he found out it was more profitable to create monsters for Satanists than it was to create moonshine from several stills for the locals.

Down at the end of a deep holler, Thornton Hopper built special dog runs made of thick steel beams, strong enough to hold the hounds. Think of St. Bernard's, then double the size and replace the lovable face with a snarling mass of razor sharp teeth and you get the picture.

Thornton kept three hellhounds at any one time. A male and female for breeding and one pup. When hellhounds give birth, they usually did so four at a time, but then one of the pups will kill the other three in an ultimate battle of the fittest. The three losers become the winner's first meal.

In the current training cycle, the pup was nearly a year old. I'd faced one like him the year before in the Bluegrass state and was lucky to still be alive to talk about it. Taking on three of them at close range was not something I cared to do.

But as the Hand of God, God's bounty hunter on earth, ridding the planet of creatures like the hellhounds came with the job description. The ones who came before me, I'm sure, had no choice but to get up close and personal and then do what was needed. Me? I came up with a plan using modern technology more likely to ensure I'd live another day or two.

After watching a *60 Minutes* episode about personal drones, I envisioned many ways I could put them to use. I did some research and then ordered one at a cost of about thirty thousand dollars, mere chump change when you consider I stole thirty-million dollars from the Church of the Light Reclaimed, a bunch of Satan-loving idiots. This one came equipped with a high resolution camera which allowed me to do some aerial surveillance with little danger to myself.

I spent several days in the hot July heat on the ridge overlooking the holler, with my drone hovering high over the kennels using it to watch Hopper care for and train the hounds. With him, they were incredibly docile and obedient. With others? Not so much. On the second day of my stakeout, Hopper and two friends set loose five pit bulls into the cage with the young hellhound. The men then sat in folding lawn chairs, relaxing and drinking Budweiser to watch the show.

In less time than you can say, "Holy crap" the five pit bulls were dead. The young hellhound moved with an agility and speed only a supernatural creature could possess.

And while Junior destroyed his lesser rivals, mom and pop hellhound sat peacefully watching and waiting. When the carnage was over, their son picked up a dead pit bull and dropped one near the bars of his parents' cages, offering each a share of the spoils of battle.

Hopper and his friends high-fived each other, clearly enjoying the massacre. My guess is they also cheered when someone stole candy from a baby. Watching the slaughter, even from a distance, turned my stomach.

I kept tabs at night and learned the area around Hopper's double-wide trailer was surrounded by light sensors, bathing the area in bright light any time someone or something came near the cages, which was a rare event. Even the animals of the holler gave the hellhounds a wide berth.

I felt I could get close enough to take out Hopper and then kill the hounds in their cages, despite his precautions, but I wanted to try something else and this gave me the opportunity to use the drone for something other than surveillance.

I drove back to Louisville for a day and spent the time modifying the drone. The drone was made to handle a load of up to five pounds and came with clamps to hold several items.

In each clamp I put a dummy grenade and then pulled the pins. The pressure from the clamps proved strong enough to keep the grenade spools from flying off.

I then flew my drone up about sixty feet and hit the release control for each clamp. The grenades dropped quickly to the ground, and the spools came off the moment the grenade cleared the clamps. I had the option of releasing them all at once or one at a time.

With a weight of fourteen ounces each, I could drop four grenades at a time with the use of the drone, taking out targets from a discreet distance, much like the U.S. military does. Modern technology sure does make our lives a lot easier. It also opens up scary doors warped minds can step through to create havoc on those they choose to target...warped minds like mine.

With my machine of destruction tested and ready to go, I returned to North Carolina. Early in the morning, I climbed the ridge above Hopper's house, getting into position as the sun climbed slowly over the mountains.

I enjoyed the fresh air and slightly cooler temperatures at this elevation. I pulled a flask from my pocket and took a deep swig of Fireball Whiskey, feeling the burn down my throat.

I put the flask away and used the remote controls to lift the drone to head height, reached into my duffle and carefully took out four M67 grenades. The uncle of one of my cohorts in hunting down the forces of evil, fellow bounty hunter, Winston Reynolds, is associated with many of the militias around a good portion of the country. If you're looking for black market military grade equipment, he's your go-to man. Procuring several M67 grenades proved to be no problem.

I set each grenade in place, tapped a few buttons and closed the clamps. I then pulled the pins and managed not to blow myself up in the process. Score one for the good guys. The grenades hung suspended below the drone, dangerous fruit waiting for their drop of destruction.

I sent the drone flying high into the air, then down the ridge to hover over the cages of the hellhounds. When the little drone closed in on the first of the three cages, the hounds looked up, then came to their feet.

The drone came with a camera only and no microphone, so I couldn't hear their reaction, but I could see it. Teeth pulled back into snarls letting me know they didn't care for the drone's approach.

When I judged the drone was about thirty feet overhead, I punched the control to drop the first grenade. I watched as the grenade spool came off, the grenade bouncing off one of the metal bars, before landing in the cage with Junior.

The hound pounced, snapping up the grenade in its massive jaws right as the Composition B explosives lit, sending out the metal casing of the grenade in thousands of pieces and destroying Junior's head.

I quickly moved the drone over mom's cage and repeated the process. Instead of attacking the grenade, she tried to move away into a far part of her cage. Seems these nightmares were smarter than your average hound and she was trying to avoid baby boy's fate.

But she couldn't move far enough and when the grenade exploded, so did a huge portion of one of her back legs. She howled in rage and I could hear her easily from my position on the ridge.

She drug herself into a corner of the cage trying to get away from my flying machine of death. I nosed the drone over to where she lay and dropped the third of my four grenades. When the dust cleared from the detonation, mom lay twitching in death.

Before I could position the drone to take out dad hellhound, Hopper came running out of his double-wide in his underwear, shotgun to his shoulder. I saw him take aim at my drone and before I could move it or drop the next grenade, he blew it out of the sky, and the camera screen went dark.

Crap.

I threw the controller into my duffle, yanked the bag over my shoulder and took off at a quick shuffle down the ridge. When I hit level ground, I broke into a run, back where I'd parked my car. I could hear the one hellhound let out a howl which sent a chill down my spine because I could tell he was on the move.

I could only imagine what the other people living in the area thought hearing his battle cry echoing through the holler. I'm sure there would be stories for generations about the monsters of Jackson County, North Carolina.

Sweat beaded out on my forehead as I tried to release my inner Usain Bolt. I heard the hellhound crash up the ridge, plowing through underbrush to my former position. He must have picked up my scent as he began moving down the ridge, his bellows of rage getting closer as he battered down the side of the mountain like a deadly boulder.

I broke into a clearing and hit it at a full out sprint. My car, a Ford Flex, was parked behind an abandoned church. I guess the parishioners found other churches and left this one to rot away. Perhaps they sensed the evil lurking in the area. Who knows?

The hellhound burst into the clearing and I looked over my shoulder, knowing I shouldn't. The hound was huge and chewing up the distance between us. I tore my gaze away from my quickly approaching doom and focused on trying to keep from becoming a late morning snack.

With extra motivation, my feet flew over the ground and with a final jump, I dove through the open front doors of the church, turning onto my back, gun in my hand, sending a stream of lead at the hellhound as he crashed into the side of the church, rattling the entire building. Not that bullets would do much damage. I knew this from past experience. It's like shooting an elephant with a pellet gun. All I managed to do was piss it off even more.

There are very few perks to being the Hand of God. One of them, however, was as long as I'm in a church, I can't be touched by creatures spawned from the depths of hell. I am safe from harm and no hellhound can touch me, as long as I don't step back outside.

That didn't stop him, however, from pacing back and forth in the area in front of the door, his yellow eyes fixed on where I escaped within. Good thing I left the doors open when I left for the morning's mission. I could hear his deep growling and smell his foul stench from behind the church doors.

I moved out of site of the hound and started to put on the rest of my gear. Outside, I heard the roar of an ATV and glanced out a dirty window, watching as Hopper rolled up, coming to a stop a bit behind the hellhound.

The man's gut arrived a few minutes before he did. Stepping off the ATV the machine's shocks let out a sigh of relief. I know I shouldn't throw stones at glass houses, but this man's stomach was frickin' huge.

He held the shotgun loosely in his hand, walking up and scratching the hellhound behind one huge floppy ear. He'd gotten dressed in a hurry, his boot laces untied and his hair sticking up in all directions with a bad case of bed head.

"I don't know who y'all are or where yer from. But if y'all come out now then I'll be sure to blow yer damn head off before I let Biggin' here get atcha."

I continued to make my preparations and wondered if Hopper was under the same restrictions about entering a church as the hound. I was still new at this whole divine retribution gig and wasn't sure of all the ins and outs.

It's all on-the-job-training, with death being the ultimate penalty if you fail. I got the job when the previous Hand of God, Dominic Montoya, died at the hands of my brother, Mikey. Losing my own soul in the process, I'd been working every day since to punch my own ticket to the pearly gates. The jury was still out on if I'm going to make it or not.

"Y'all hear me? Hey, asshole. Who do ya think you are coming out to my neck of the woods and attackin' what's mine? Y'all got no right to be doin' such."

"I have every right," I yelled back. "I'm with animal control and it seems you failed to get tags for your hounds and the county found you in violation of county ordinance BR549. You were sent several warning notices and your failure to comply moved the ball into my court."

"What the hell you been smokin'? I ain't never seen no notices. And ole' Robbie Crabtree is the damn dog catcher and he spends all his days drunker than a skunk, so yer fulla shit."

"You're not the first person to tell me that, surprisingly enough. But I do know something you might be interested in."

"Oh? And what the hell might that be?"

"Do you know what hellhounds fear more than anything on earth?"

Hopper snorted long and loud. "Mr., hellhounds ain't afraid of anythin' or any one."

"You're wrong," I said, stepping into the open doorway. "They're afraid of fire."

I bet Thornton Hopper never thought he'd see a flamethrower and the look on his face before I pulled the trigger was priceless. In quick succession I saw confusion, realization and then fear.

Flamethrowers first came into use during World War I to clear trenches in up close and personal fighting in Europe. By the end of World War II they were being mounted to armored vehicles, which is a lot safer than having all the fuel strapped to your back. More than a few men died when the flamethrower would take a bullet to the tank and explode.

I was wearing a modified version of the M9 used during Vietnam. There were three tanks, two for the petroleum gel, and one for compressed air. When you squeeze the back trigger, compressed air mixes with the gel, forcing the mixture through the hose. Pulling the front trigger sets off the igniter and when the gel passes over it, you get a steady stream of fire in a bloom large enough to cover a Mac truck.

I learned over the last few months creatures spawned from the depths of Hell, feared fire more than anything. Satan once gave me a glimpse of what an eternity would be like in Hell, with my body nailed to the wall as flames engulfed me. A mirror was across from me so I could watch the whole thing happen. My body literally melted away. From time to time, I still wake up in the middle of the night, my bed sheets soaked in sweat, dreaming about it.

With safety goggles protecting my eyes and the memory of my brief trip to Hell in my mind, I pulled both triggers and fire roared out of the hose. Hopper yelled something and started to raise his gun, but never made it. The fire raced over the hellhound and engulfed them both, Hopper's screams mixed with the howls of the hellhound.

Hopper took a couple of steps, turning in a circle and fell face first to the ground. The hellhound tried moving away, but I kept pace, never letting up on the trigger and soon he also lay still on the ground. I didn't stop until the last spurt of flame died away, the fuel tank empty.

I reached over my shoulder and cranked open the pressure valve, letting out the last of the compressed air, then hit the quick release buttons on the harness and slid the flamethrower off my shoulders.

The entire area in front of the church was charred black from my attack but the surrounding trees remained untouched and I said a silent prayer the rest of the holler wasn't on fire.

I went inside, snatched up my duffle, unlocked the Ford and tossed it in the trunk. I decided to change later when I stopped for the night. I waited until the flamethrower nozzle cooled enough for me to pack it away, and then hopped into the Ford and slowly drove down the dirt path to the main drag.

The smell of burnt flesh road heavy on the air and I swore I could still smell it even after I was long gone from the torched remains of Hopper and the hellhound.

I wondered if I would have trouble sleeping when I stopped for the night. I knew I would, but not because of the image of Hopper and the hound burning to death in the fire, but because of a woman with bonfire red hair.

CHAPTER THREE

I called it quits south of Knoxville, Tennessee and checked myself into a two-bit motel next to an even seedier dive bar named The Mason Jar. After paying for my room, I didn't bother to take my stuff inside and headed straight for the bar.

I shouldered open the door and stepped inside. The smell of beer and cigarette smoke assaulted my senses, accompanied by the murmur of quiet conversations which all stopped the moment I made my entrance.

The room was thin and long, a shotgun design with an old wood-style bar down one side and booths down the other. The back of the room featured a pool table and dart board, but neither was being used. To say the lighting was dim would be an understatement.

I ignored the stares and made my way to the bar. A bartender so thin he could use a food sponsor, with the requisite dirty towel thrown over his shoulder, walked over to greet me.

He rested his hands on the bar, his face a mixture of boredom and weariness. "What'll you have, Mr.?"

"Moonshine. Lots of it."

"What flavor?"

"What flavor? Moonshine. You know, White Lightning. Rotgut, Hooch. I want the real stuff."

Back when I was younger, one of my great uncles used to make his own moonshine and always gave dad a couple of gallons of the stuff. One day I asked my dad to borrow twenty dollars and he said he'd make me a deal. He poured about an inch of clear liquid into a glass and said, "Drink this in one shot and you won't have to pay me back."

Snickering, I picked up the glass and downed it in one swallow. "That wasn't so—" and before I could say another word, the moonshine hit bottom and set fire to my insides. I turned on the water faucet, sticking my mouth under it trying to gulp down enough water to put out the wildfire raging in my gut.

My father, laughing, said, "That's the hardest twenty dollars you will ever earn." And he was right.

"We have all kinds of flavors: blackberry, peach, apple, cinnamon, cherry. All kinds."

"What the hell? Is this a Starbucks? Just give me a damn glass of moonshine. I don't care what flavor it is," I snarled. I could feel anger boiling its way to the surface. This had been happening more often in recent months. I knew the bartender was only doing his job, but I didn't give a rat's ass.

Raising his hands in surrender, the man turned and pulled a bottle from under the counter, set out a glass and poured several fingers. The label named it Old Smokey. When he started to put the bottle away, I grabbed his wrist, took the bottle from him and filled the glass three quarters of the way up, then handed it back.

"I'll run a tab. I'll need more when this is done." Without waiting for his reply, I snatched my drink, turned and made my way to a booth in the corner and away from the other patrons.

I heard some angry mumbles, but ignored them and began to take long pulls of the moonshine. From the taste, the bartender chose cinnamon. Considering my newly acquired taste for Fireball Cinnamon Whiskey, it fit. I began to wonder if my whole life would be full of fire. My mind thought about Thornton Hopper's blackened body, the smoke rising lazily into the air. But not for long.

The moonshine did what it was supposed to do and hit my system like a hard jab to the mid-section. I'd found myself drinking more and more lately, trying to get the memories to go away.

When I wasn't killing monsters in real life, I tried to slay others from my memories. Despite my best efforts, my mind always drifted to her. I played, over and over, the scene when I pulled out a gun and shot Samantha Tyler, the only woman I've ever truly loved.

My love life was very complicated.

I shot her in order to save her life....and to drive out the demon lodged in her head. But it didn't make it any easier to pull the trigger or live with the fallout afterwards.

After the shooting, I managed to get her to a hospital, but she nearly died. The morning after her surgery, she was moved to a rehab facility. When I plugged her, I shot her in the hip, doing a ton of damage and her rehab was still on-going.

Now months have passed since the shooting and I've heard nothing from her. Nada. Nothing. Not a peep.

Brother Joshua, the man who tells me where to go and who to kill, coordinated Samantha's care. When I asked to see her, Joshua told me she "needed time to sort things out" and would contact me when she was ready.

But now it's been nearly five months and she hasn't picked up the phone and tried to contact me and it was eating me up inside. More than this moonshine ever could.

The TV over the bar was tuned to Fox News and I could read the headline: **Congressman Commits Suicide.** I squinted trying to read the man's name and suffered a moment of disappointment when the name was not Cyrus Tyler, Samantha's dad. I went back to my drink, thinking of the old joke, "What do you call a hundred politicians at the bottom of the ocean? A good start."

Music played in the background and I finally caught the lyrics, realizing the song playing was *The Devil Went Down to Georgia* by Charlie Daniels. The song took on a whole new meaning for me and I knew the Johnny of this song was an idiot.

According to the song, Satan offered Johnny a fiddle of gold if he won a fiddling contest, but Satan got his soul if he lost. If you know Satan is real, why take the chance? Arrogance, that's why. The same thing which doomed me. I believed I could save my brother's soul, despite all the evidence showing my brother was going to Hell no matter what I did. Risking your soul for gold proved Johnny was a frickin' idiot. Trying to save Mikey proved I was one.

I downed the last of the fiery liquid and it rocked me like a speeding train. I slammed the glass down on the table much harder than I planned, shattering it. I became light-headed and plopped my arms down onto the shards of broken glass, ignoring the pain, then rested my head on my arms for a moment.

The bartender began yelling at me, but I ignored him and welcomed the sweet feeling of oblivion, finding it hard to think about Samantha or anything else. The only thought pushing through the haze? Get another drink.

I don't know how long I stayed light headed, but when I raised my head to contemplate walking over to the bar and put action to the thought, I noticed I was no longer alone.

A woman just this side of pretty stared back at me. Hair, black and cut to shoulder length, framed a thin face and eyes the color of arctic ice. I blinked several times to make sure she was not a figment of my imagination. Yep. Still there.

"You are bleeding."

I have an ear for accents and the lilt in her voice suggested a European origin. It took a moment for her words to hit home. I looked down at my hand and saw there was a slash along the bottom of my palm, blood dripping over the table and across the broken glass.

The stranger pulled a couple of napkins out of a holder, turned my hand over and placed them against the wound, holding my hand between hers, pressing down, trying to stop the bleeding.

Her touch was warm and in my head, the way she held my hand felt intimate, familiar. Like the touch of an old lover. Despite being dead ass drunk, I knew we'd never met. Her eyes were not the kind you would ever forget. A mixture of intelligence and humor danced together in their depths.

I rolled my tongue, trying to lose the cotton mouth. When I could finally get a word out, I glanced over at the bartender. "I need some more Old Smokey."

The woman shook her head. "Coffee. Black. Nothing else."

I yanked my hand from between hers, the bloody napkins stuck to my hand. "Look, Lady. I don't need you to babysit me. I'm not in the mood for coffee. Thanks for your help. But you can move your ass somewhere else."

The words came out harsh, but I didn't really give a flyin' flip. I didn't need female companionship. At least not hers, no matter how pretty.

She got up and went to the bar, talking to the bartender in a tone low enough where I couldn't hear what she said. I watched her and admitted to the red-blooded American male inside me the part of her I couldn't see before looked pretty damn good.

She wore a purple skirt down to mid-thigh and black knee high boots. The dress hung around a figure which began to get a response from the part of my body south of the border.

With week after week passing with no word from Samantha, my friends suggested I should move on. Let my hair down, have some fun. I'd resisted the idea, sure Samantha would come around. This woman made me wonder if I should take their advice. I tore my gaze away, working hard to get the carnal thoughts out of my head.

A few moments later, the woman returned, carrying a tray with a cup and a steaming pot of black coffee. She slid the tray in front of me, and sat down.

"Lady, when I tell you to leave me the hell alone, I mean leave me the hell alone. Can't you take a hint?"

She didn't answer right away. Instead, she picked up the pot, poured the coffee into a cup and placed it in front of me with the pot beside it. She then took a few more napkins out of the holder and brushed the broken glass onto the tray. Once finished, she sat the tray next to her on the seat.

The aroma from the coffee made it to my nose, but I resisted the urge to pick it up and take a drink. I peeled the bloody napkins off my hand, the blood flow now stopped. I wadded up the napkins and tossed them onto the table.

Looking into the eyes of this woman, "This is the last time I'm going to tell you. Leave. Now." I tried to put as much malice as possible into my words, wanting to drive her away. Even the biggest bad asses tended to leave me alone when I got angry, but this woman seemed unaffected by my growing irritation.

After a moment, she replied, "I think there is something you should know, before I do."

"Oh? And what pearls of wisdom do you wish to share? Do you know the cure for cancer? The secret to ending world hunger? Maybe you know if Paul McCartney really was the Walrus?"

She laughed and damn if it didn't sound beautiful. "No. What I know is more immediate and pertains only to you."

"Then speak your piece and move on." I grumbled. My brain wanted her to leave. My body wanted her to stay and I wasn't sure which would win if she hung around much longer.

"In a few minutes three men will come in here and kill you." She smiled sweetly and waited to see what my reaction would be.

I thought for a moment or two. Then I picked up the coffee and began to drink.

CHAPTER FOUR

I downed the first cup, the hot coffee burn bringing my senses back to life. I picked up the pot, my hand shaking slightly and poured another, this time drinking in steady sips.

"Why should I believe you? Who are you, anyway?"

She pursed her lips. "I am the woman they hire to come inside to seduce you and to get you drunk. You already beat me to the whole 'getting drunk' part."

"And what about the seduction? Still planning to give it a try? And why didn't you call them in when you found me passed out on the table?"

She tilted her head to the side, seeming to examine me like someone seeing a strange creature for the first time and trying to figure out what it might be. Or if she should kill it.

"Maybe I like you," she shrugged.

I laughed. "Lady, you don't know me. And very few who do know me like me. Try again. Why not?" I polished off the coffee and poured one more, the caffeine racing into my blood stream, battling the moonshine for domination.

"Maybe I not like them. Does it really matter? Having said that, I'm going back outside and tell them you are in here, drunk. Perhaps they will still kill you. They have good chance."

I smiled, but there was no warmth. "You do, do you? Care to make a wager?"

She stood up and looked down at me. "If you die, there is no way for you to pay. Not much of a bet when one cannot pay. I can only lose."

"Fair enough. I guess I will have to satisfy myself with your shock and surprise when I walk out the door. I do have another question for you. How did they know I was here? I didn't even know I was going to stop here."

"They follow you here from North Carolina. When you killed the trainer, they knew who they were looking for and there are only so many ways out of the mountains. They have been following you for hours, waiting for you to stop."

She turned and headed for the exit. Before she got there, I shouted,

"What's your name?"

She paused, one hand on the door. "Elizabeth." She pushed her way outside and disappeared from view, the door swinging closed behind her.

I briefly considered checking for the rear exit and making a run for it. But only briefly. Running from hellhounds was one thing. Running from two legged attackers, however, wasn't an option. With the dark mood I was in, I wanted someone to pound on and it seemed fate would provide several in short order.

I slumped back over the table, resting my head on my arms. This time keeping a watch on the front door. I didn't have to wait long as three men entered the bar, sized up things and headed straight to my table.

I picked up my head, swaying a bit. "Hey, bartender. I need more moonshine over here. Chop, chop. Let's get moving."

The bartender didn't move an inch, watching as the men approached me. The men were all on the large size. Two were in decent shape, the other evidently loved mamma's cooking a bit too much.

They stopped next to my booth, blocking my view of the bartender. "Hey, fellas. Mind moving your asses out of the way? I'm trying to get another drink."

The one who loved the home cooking said, "You've been cut off. That was our sister you just tried to put the moves on and we ain't happy about it. I think we need to teach you a lesson about being a gentleman. Ain't that right boys?"

The other two nodded and began to clench and unclench their fists, anxious to get it on.

"You are one lyin' son of a bitch. There's no way she was your sister. Too good looking. If you had a sister, she would have to be one butt ugly woman if she was related to you. You're so ugly when you were a kid I bet you ran through the ugly forest and hit every tree." Oldie but a goody.

I guess I pissed him off. He snarled something and reached for me. I grabbed the coffee pot and threw the half-full pot into his face, the still hot liquid scalding his eyes.

He screamed, his fingers clawing his face and I turned sideways in the booth and kicked him hard in the crotch, adding injury to insult. His two buddies moved him out the way and tried to jump me as I slid out of the booth.

Wielding the pot as a weapon I swung it hard right into the side of the head of one of them. His knees shook for a moment, then buckled and he collapsed to the floor.

The only one left didn't back down, catching me with a good right to the chin. I slipped with the blow and dropped the coffee pot to try and catch my fall on the edge of the pool table.

Then the unexpected happened. A couple of the locals, evidently not caring for my earlier behavior, joined in the fight. If I'd only needed to face one more attacker, I would have made short work of the fight and strolled out into the night a happy man.

Now three more joined in and the four of them forced me back and onto the pool table, pressing my face into the red felt, blows raining down around my head and my mid-section. I bellowed like a cornered bull and fought back. I found a loose pool ball, wrapped one large paw around it and then used it to pound one of my attackers in the head, over and over. It only took a few seconds and then there were three.

I tried sitting up, but one of the locals broke a pool cue across my shoulders, the pain nearly sending me down for the count. One thing I learned from my father, don't fight fair when your life is on the line. I managed to get a fist full of his hair with the other hand and pulled the man's face close to me. I bit down savagely onto the man's nose, twisting my face back and forth like an angry dog.

The man screamed and tried to push himself away. I let go and shoved him hard. Now there were two. I spit part of the man's nose into the face of my original attacker and managed to throw him and the other guy off me. I rolled backwards across and then off the pool table, slamming into the dart board.

I grabbed a couple of darts out of the board, then ripped the board off the wall and threw it at the two men who circled the pool table, looking for their next chance to attack.

When the men ducked, I put a dart in each hand, the sharp end sticking out through my knuckles, holding them like they teach women to hold their car keys in self-defense classes.

The local yokel decided discretion would be the better part of valor and turned and ran for the door. The remaining man, one of the three who planned to kill me, slid a switch blade out of his pocket and snicked it open.

With a yell he charged me, stabbing low, surprising me. I expected a more measured approach, not a kamikaze attack. I danced sideways, but the move worked better in my head than in practice, with my reflexes slowed by the remnants of the moonshine and the knife connected.

The blade pushed deep and I could feel it scrape a rib, the pain roaring across my nervous system. The analytical part of my brain admonished me for being sloppy, for taking my opponent for granted. The animal part of my brain demanded a reaction.

I brought my fists together hard on each side of the man's head, right behind each ear and buried the sharp point of the darts into his skull, then lifted up, taking the man off the ground.

The man let go of the knife, still stuck into my side and grabbed my wrists, but after a moment his fingers went slack and I let him slide to the ground. I watched him for a moment, then tossed both darts into his chest, each sticking in about a quarter inch from each other. Triple twenties.

I yanked the knife out of my side and nearly collapsed, a wave of nausea hitting me hard. I leaned on the pool table for a moment, waiting for the feeling to pass and scanned the room for more threats, but the battle was over. The two men who came in with the dead man, were still laying on the floor. Everyone else exited the bar, running for cover.

The bartender held a phone to his head, but did not appear to be talking to anyone. If he called the police, I needed to hit the road, and quickly.

I tossed the knife onto the pool table, took a couple of steps and nearly fainted, but gathered myself and headed for the door. I pushed it open and stepped into the warm, muggy night air. I fumbled in my pockets for my keys and could feel my shirt sticking to my side as the blood flowed from the wound.

When I finally managed to pull the keys out, I dropped them on the ground. Cursing, I bent over to pick them up, but kept on going, finding myself lying on the ground. I rolled over, staring up at the stars, becoming incredibly tired.

The last thing I thought, before darkness overtook me, was "well, this sucks."

CHAPTER FIVE

Eduardo watched doctor Alfred Michaels dive into one end of his Olympic length swimming pool, neatly cutting the water. He dove deep, then surfaced and started what would be the first of fifty laps. The pool lights lit the water from above and below, the warm Pennsylvania air making it a perfect night for a swim. The house, a four bedroom colonial, sat off U.S. 30, a few blocks off the Main Line in the western suburbs of Philadelphia.

Michaels put himself through med school at Dartmouth on a swimming scholarship where he graduated top of his class from the Geisel School of Medicine. While in school he medaled in the World Championships and briefly flirted with trying out for the Summer Olympics. A specialist in the hundred meter free style, he decided the extra hours it would take to make the Olympics would put too much stress on his school work.

After completing six laps, he stopped and took a long drink from the glass of scotch sitting at the edge of the pool, then flipped back into the water, heading for the other end.

Eduardo knew this to be his regular routine, having watched the good doctor over the last few nights hit the pool after long hours at the Hospital of the University of Pennsylvania. The doc loved swimming and loved his scotch and found a way to combine the two of them. Twice divorced with no kids, swimming and a good scotch whiskey were his only passions.

Eduardo also knew something else. Doctor Michaels suffered from anxiety and kept a stash of Valium at home in case of attacks. An illegal stash, not that Eduardo was judging him. A man's gotta do what a man's gotta do to feel normal.

Donut found the plastic baggie full of pills in the bottom of a dresser drawer, underneath the neatly folded pairs of argyle socks in his bedroom during a reconnaissance mission inside the house. She climbed a tree overhanging the back of his house, then moved, hand over hand, down a branch until dropping onto the roof and entered through an unlocked upstairs window.

Michaels kept a detailed diary about cases and his own battle with anxiety. He lived in fear of his colleagues finding out about his mental issues, which only added to the anxiety. Recently, he needed to take Valium to get through a speech at a conference on the latest innovations in joint replacements.

Eduardo gave Michaels another lap, then stepped from his hiding place in the shrubs, moving quickly to the glass of scotch, emptying three crushed Valiums from the doc's stash into the cut crystal and stirred it quickly with a latex gloved finger. He was back in his hiding spot before Michaels made the turn and kick to return.

He watched and when Michaels finished lap twelve, he stopped and took a large drink of the whiskey, flipped and was gone. He did the same on laps eighteen and twenty-four, draining the last of the scotch, his movements becoming slow and clumsy.

He fell back into the water, but this time he did not turn for the other end, instead, tried to tread water. Eduardo left his concealment and walked to the pool. Doctor Michaels went under and then resurfaced, reaching for the rail of the ladder to climb out.

He made it about half way up when Eduardo put a hand on his head and pushed him back into the pool, Michaels landing with a large splash. Michaels broke the surface one last time, shouting to Eduardo for help, only to slip below again. He watched as Michaels floundered below the surface of the water, clearly disoriented, until the last of the air bubbles raced for the surface. A few minutes later, his body floated up and joined them.

Eduardo picked up the glass by the rim, went inside to the kitchen, washed the inside of the glass completely and then poured a few splashes, enough to cover the bottom of the glass, from a bottle of Bowmore Devil's Cask setting on the wet bar in his living room. Eduardo was a Glenlivet man himself, but again, who was he to judge?

He walked to the pool and put the glass down in the same spot he picked it up, then pulled out his phone, snapped a photo of the floating form of Michaels and left.

~*~

Brad Stiles pulled the Lincoln Town Car over to the side of the road when the phone in his pocket beeped. He slid the phone out of his sports coat pocket, and glanced at the texted photo of a man floating in a pool. Putting the phone away, he put on his car's signal, and merged back into the Belt Line traffic. Later he would delete the text and then smash the phone to bits, discarding the pieces into different trash cans around Washington D.C.

He glanced in the rearview mirror at the man sitting in the seat behind him. Dark brown hair going gray at the temples, Congressman Cyrus Tyler looked more fit than most men half his sixty years. Dressed in a blue blazer and khakis, they were on their way to a private dinner at the home of a well-connected lobbyist. Fundraising for members of the House took place twenty-four hours a day, seven days a week.

A former Marine, Brad kept himself in even better shape than the congressman. His hair shaved in the classic jarhead style, flat top with the hair on the sides and back cut short, sat on a head which seemed not to be connected to any neck, and appeared to rest upon his shoulders. He needed to have his suits custom made to be able feel comfortable as the congressman's occasional driver and fixer, and to hide the gun in the holster under his left arm.

Tyler met his gaze and Brad nodded slightly.

~*~

Tyler smiled and then returned to reading a draft of an immigration bill his party hoped to push through following the August recess. In his current position as the Majority Leader of the U.S. House of Representatives, it was his job to schedule when pieces of legislation would, if ever, get brought before the House for a vote. The latest draft of his party's immigration bill would piss off a lot of people on the other side of the aisle, which suited him just fine. Tyler knew the bill would never get beyond the Democratic controlled Senate, but he didn't want it to pass, being in favor of the status quo. The longer the country raged over the immigration debate, the more chaos would reign.

Tyler found it hard to concentrate on the bill, however, and after a moment tossed it into his suitcase on the seat beside him, closing the lid. With the doctor's death, another part of the puzzle snapped into place and he spent the remainder of the trip to the fundraiser thinking about what would happen in the next few days. All his planning would come down to a simple lunch, already scheduled. Then it would be time to move on to phase two.

Tyler knew a secret few others knew: the Speaker of the House of Representatives would soon be dead. Diagnosed with stage four colon cancer, the disease had already progressed to his lungs and liver and the Speaker had declined further treatments which would prolong his life. The only people who knew were the Speaker, his wife and Tyler.

A news conference was planned for the next day. The Speaker

planned to announce his immediate retirement at the news conference. Following his resignation, the Republicans in the House would meet in caucus to elect a new Speaker and Tyler knew it would be him, with his only competition having committed suicide a few nights earlier. Decades of slapping backs, gathering favors and more than a little dirt on his fellow members of congress, assured him of the votes. By the end of the week, he would be the new Speaker.

Some men waited for Providence to land in their laps. Tyler created his own Providence, with help from the Lord of Light, Satan. A battle would soon arrive, with those who followed the Lord of Light helping him reclaim his rightful place in Heaven.

In his position as leader of the Church of the Light Reclaimed, he directed the battle on Earth. His goal? To create as much chaos in the world as possible. Chaos bred opportunity to turn people away from God. When he became the Speaker of the House of Representatives, he would become the second most powerful man in the country.

But Tyler did not plan to stop there, with another rung of the ladder to climb: to become President of the United States. Gazing out the window, he could see the White House in the distance, the front lit by a host of flood lights. Before long he planned to be the one sitting in the Oval Office, the most powerful man on the planet. And when he was, he would set the world on fire.

CHAPTER SIX

Samantha nibbled on my ear and I struggled to wake up. I felt her hand move down my stomach, and then lower, and I began to respond. I slid my hand slowly down the curve of her back, caressing her with the tips of my fingers. I tried to turn my head and find her lips with mine, but it felt as if the messages from my brain to my body traveled around the world before registering.

I pulled her tight and breathed out, "I love you, Samantha."

"Who is this Samantha?"

My eyes snapped open and staring down at me was not Samantha, but the woman from the bar. It took a moment, but I remembered her name. "Elizabeth?" I said hoarsely.

She sat up on the edge of the bed, naked with only the sheet pulled around her lap. I tried to sit up, but she pushed me down easily and I didn't have the strength to resist.

"Yes," she said. "I will ask again. Who is this Samantha?"

I felt lightheaded and found it hard to focus on what she was saying. Then another fact battered its way through the fog in my brain: I was also naked under the sheet.

I tried to roll over but could not, as my left arm was strapped to the side of the bed with my own belt. "Hey. What the hell is going on?"

I reached for her with my free hand, but Elizabeth stood and walked over to a chair, picked up a robe and slipped it on, tying it in the front. I was forced to admit to myself I missed the view and liked her better with it off.

"You move around too much and I needed you to be still for the IV."

I glanced down at my arm and could see several strips of tape holding the IV needle in place. A funnel with a long tube hung above my head, running down to the needle. I could see the tube was coated with something dark and red. I tried to remember where I was, but the last thing I could remember was going to my car outside the bar and then collapsing on the pavement. I tried to undo the belt, my fingers fumbling at the buckle, and I fell back on the bed, weak beyond anything I'd ever felt.

"IV? What have you been giving me? And how did I get here? And where are my clothes?" I could feel panic rising and I tried to shove it aside, to concentrate on what was happening to me.

She put her hands on her hips. "You needed blood. You nearly die and go into shock. You got here because I bring you here. I throw away your clothes. They were soaked with blood. Very bad. Who is Samantha?" she demanded to know.

"Blood? You don't know my blood type. You could have killed me. Why didn't you take me to a hospital?"

She rolled her eyes and spoke slowly, like talking to a child. "You kill two men at the bar. If I had taken you to a hospital, then they would have taken you to jail, no? I brought you to my cabin, but you need the blood. So I get you some. It is O negative, so you are alright. Nothing to worry about. Why won't you tell me who this woman is?"

"She's a friend. What were you doing just now? With me, in bed?"

She flashed a grin so wicked it almost made me blush.

Almost.

"You know what we were doing. You like it."

She flipped around the end of the tie on her robe and moved her hips seductively.

"You like it very much, no?"

"Don't flatter yourself, lady. You caught me at a weak moment." I licked my lips. "Water. Could I please have some water?"

She pouted for a few seconds, but then she left the bedroom and I could hear her in another room, running water. I took the moment to assess my situation. I lifted the sheet and stared at a strip of gauze over the left side of my stomach. I lifted an edge of the gauze and could see the knife wound, now stitched up, ugly and red. Hells, bells.

I let my head sink back into the pillow. I lay on what felt like a feather bed in a small bedroom. The walls were made of logs and through the two windows in the room all I could see were trees. I wondered how she could have gotten me from the parking lot to this bed. It should have taken several good-size men to carry me this far.

She came back into the room, carrying a blue Solo cup. "Drink this. You will feel better."

She put the cup to my lips and I drank deeply. The water tasted off, somehow, but I drank it all, my mouth being so dry. "How long have I been here? And who sewed me up? You?"

"So many questions. Every time with the questions. Yes. I am the one who closed the wound. You bleed very much. But I have some experience with battle dressing wounds. It will be ok. And you have been here...hmm...three days now."

"Three days? Holy crap. Where's my phone. I need to call someone."
She shook her head.

"No good. There is no cell signal here. You cannot make call. And there are no phones in the cabin. We are," she paused, struggling to find the right words. "How do you say? Off the grid?"

I swore under my breath. I tried once again to sit up, but my body felt heavy and weak. I felt like I'd drank a whole gallon of moonshine at once. I looked at the cup in her hand.

"What was in the water? You drugged me?"

She didn't say a word. She just stood there and watched me until my eyes closed and the world went black.

~*~

She set the cup on the nightstand next to the bed and watched him for a few more minutes to make sure he was sound asleep.

She pulled the sheet down and removed the gauze covering the wound and made a clucking sound. The wound was red and she worried infection might be setting in. She would have to find some antibiotics.

With the amount of sleeping pills she gave him, he would sleep for many hours. She would have time. But first, she needed a bath.

She went to the bathroom and glanced at the woman hanging above the tub by her ankles, the rope tied off to a hook she'd screwed into the side of one of the cabin logs.

The woman stared at her with pleading eyes and tried talking despite the duct tape placed across her mouth. She ignored her and began to run water for her bath.

They'd met at a different bar, following the fight at The Mason Jar. It took her hours to find a woman with just the right blood type. She claimed to be doing a study on drinking and whether there was a relationship between it and a person's blood type to get people to voluntarily provide their information.

The woman had been sitting at the bar alone and when it was almost closing time, they left together. She pretended to be parked close the woman's car and walked along with her. Luck was on her side with the parking lot nearly empty. She slipped the TASER out of her purse, pressed it to the woman's side as she was unlocking her car, and squeezed the trigger.

As the TASER discharged, the woman began to fall to the ground, confused and immobile. She caught her easily, opened the woman's driver-side door and shoved her onto the seat. Then she moved her over to the passenger side, climbed in, removed the keys from the woman's still clenched hand, started the car and drove off. No one saw her. She knew how to move quickly.

She turned off the water, the bath now nearly three quarters full. She reached out and took hold of the woman's hands, also duct taped at the wrist. In one arm, the end of an IV line hung loose, clamped at the end. She pulled the arms over the tub and then loosened the clamp.

Blood began to flow out in a steady stream, turning the steaming water a burgundy red. The woman began to scream, but they were muffled by the tape. After a moment, she closed the clamp, cutting off the blood flow. Tears flowed from the woman's eyes, dropping and mixing with the blood.

She stirred the water with her foot, mixing the water and blood, and then shrugged out of the robe and sat in the water, sinking down to her neck and closed her eyes.

In the past, she would have killed the woman and been done with her. But she was trying to do things...differently. She would not kill the woman if she could avoid it. She breathed deeply and let the water relax her.

When the time came, if the woman still lived when it was OK to move the Hand of God, then she would let the woman go. It would be up to her to survive the wilderness and find help. It wouldn't be her problem.

She smiled to herself. Things were going even better than she could hope. Before long, the Hand of God would be hers.

CHAPTER SEVEN

"You know that bill will never see the light of day in the Senate, Cyrus. You guys continue to waste the time of the American people."

Tyler wiped his mouth with his napkin and dropped it in his lap. From the terrace of Charlie Palmer Steak House right off the National Mall, Tyler and Senator Hedley Stafford enjoyed the finest cut of steak in the city while enjoying a great view of the Capital.

"And your bill will never see a vote in the House. You need to move those socialists in the far Left of your party more to the center. We can't get anything done until you do."

"Socialists? Is that any way for the new Speaker of the House to talk?"

Hedley Stafford, a black man in his mid-sixties, had been the Senate Majority Leader for almost six years. They'd known each other for the better part of thirty years, with both of them being from Philadelphia.

Stafford's parents had been teachers. Early on, Hedley followed in their footsteps, first teaching at Philadelphia public schools and then a professor of ethics at Temple University.

Driven into politics by what he saw as a failing education system, he ran for Congress, winning a close election in his first race, then serving four more terms in Congress before running for the Senate, and winning.

Adept at party politics, he moved up the political food chain, landing in the top spot when the Democrats regained control of the Senate in a landslide mid-term election.

A quiet man when away from the microphones, Stafford preferred to listen and watch, missing nothing. Stafford bucked the modern political trend and sported a full beard, now mostly gray.

Tyler raised his hands in mock surrender. "Fine. I will tone it down." He sliced off another piece of steak and popped it into his mouth, chewing thoughtfully. "Changing the subject, I was sorry to hear about Dr. Michaels. He was your knee doc, right?"

"He was. Damn shame. Really screws me up. I need to have my knee replaced when the August recess starts next week and he was going to do the surgery. Now I'll have to find a new doctor, which will take time. I'd like to put it off, but it keeps me up at night and I don't want to take meds to help me sleep. You know how it is. Men in our position have to be alert and ready for anything."

Tyler nodded knowingly. "I think I can help you out. You and I go way back and despite you being a card-carrying Communist, I know who you need to talk to. And she's in the same practice."

Stafford raised an eyebrow. "We communists don't carry cards anymore. Just like you fascists don't wear swastikas. Who are we talking about?"

"Dr. Teresa Collins. She operated on my knee a year ago when I tore my meniscus and it's done really well. With her being in the same practice, you won't have to have all your records transferred. And the A.M.A. rates her higher than Michaels, so it will be a step up."

"Most of these specialists stay booked. It might be hard to get in."

Tyler held up a finger, pulled out his phone, searched for a moment and then selected a number and dialed. Tyler placed the call on speaker and a moment later a woman answered. "Well, hello Cyrus. You having more knee problems?"

"Not me. A friend of mine." Tyler explained the situation. "I was hoping you might be able to work him in. He's right here with me. You're on speaker."

"Senator Stafford, when were you scheduled to have your surgery?"

"A week from this Friday. How soon could you get me in?"

There was a pause while she checked her schedule. "I tell you what. Considering your circumstances, I will move some things around and we can do the surgery as you currently have it scheduled. Dr. Michaels was a good friend of mine and I know he would want you taken care of right away."

"Thank you, doctor. I can't tell you how much I appreciate you doing this for me. Anything I need to do?"

"I will have my assistant contact you. Have you already had your pre-op blood work completed?"

"Scheduled to do the blood work this coming Monday."

"Then come on in as scheduled. I will have some additional paperwork for you to fill out, but I'll make sure the transition is a smooth one. We'll have you up and back on your feet in no time."

"Thanks, doc. I'll see you next week."

They said their goodbyes and Tyler hung up and put the phone away. "See. How's that for bipartisan cooperation?"

Stafford laughed. "Step in the right direction, Cyrus. Step in the right direction."

CHAPTER EIGHT

I awoke in the middle of the night to find myself still in bed, still naked, with Elizabeth snuggled close, her head on my shoulder and her arm draped across my chest. She was sound asleep and also wasn't wearing anything. I loved the feel of her skin against mine.

I took a moment to take stock of how I felt. Physically, the wound in my side had gone from a sharp pain to a dull ache. My left arm was no longer strapped to the bed and attached to an IV. A Band-Aid covered the needle hole in the crook of my elbow. I ran my fingers gingerly over the gauze over my knife wound, and while it was sore, it wasn't more than I could handle.

With the drugs she gave me to sleep having run their course, my brain felt clearer. I'm guessing it had been for my own good, but I'm not sure I liked being drugged up by a stranger.

Then again, the only reason I was alive and not either dead or in jail was evidently because of her. Moonlight streamed through one of the bedroom windows and I watched her for a moment. She was worth the look.

Which lead to the other self-assessment, the mental one. Being in bed with this woman made me wonder about Samantha and the life I dreamed we would share together. Lying in bed with Elizabeth felt like cheating, but was it? If my relationship with Samantha was totally one-sided, was I like a high school boy pining for the prom queen he would never have?

Right here, right now, a beautiful woman who had saved my life, lay next to me. I was torn. I closed my eyes and thought about my life. Screwed up would be a good description. I knew the work I was doing was the right thing. The evil I removed from the world made everyone safer. I also knew it was the only way I could save my own soul.

Yet I spent all the time I wasn't kicking bad guy ass by thinking and obsessing over Samantha. I didn't know how much longer I would be alive on this planet, but, at best, it would likely only be years, not decades. The bar fight proved how quickly my life could be snuffed out. If not for Elizabeth, I might have died bleeding out in a parking lot in some backwater Tennessee town, far from home.

In the time remaining to me, shouldn't I do my best to enjoy the world around me? Experience the few shots at happiness life offered? Introspection was not one of my strong suits. I'm the kind of guy who rips off the rearview mirror and plunges straight ahead, never looking back. Kurt, a computer geek I use in my fight with the Church of the Light Reclaimed, even suggested I see a therapist.

Can you imagine the therapy sessions? "Yes, I kill people for God and love a woman who is the daughter of Satan's pope, who won't talk to me anymore because I shot her to force a demon to leave her body. What do you think my issues are?"

My guess is there would be a phone call to bring in the guys in the white uniforms and straight jacket. I laughed to myself over the weirdness of it all.

I opened my eyes to find Elizabeth staring at me, the moonlight turning her eyes luminous. She shifted and moved on top of me, careful not to put too much weight on my injury.

"So. Dreaming of this Samantha?"

"As far as I can remember, I didn't dream at all." I paused a moment, then continued. "Thanks for saving my life."

She smiled, leaned forward and kissed me, her hair falling around my face. My hands slid down her back and across her bottom. Responding to my touch she lifted and guided me inside her and we spent the next hour making love and not talking.

When we were finished I sank back into the feather bed, exhausted. The Toby Keith song, *As Good Once As I Once Was* played in my head. Elizabeth put her head back on my shoulder and made small circles with her fingers on my chest while lying next to me.

"Before we go any further, we need to get back to those questions you don't seem to like."

She didn't answer but flipped her hand in a "go ahead" gesture. "Since they sent you into the bar to get me drunk before they came in to kill me, you have an association with them. What is it?"

"I'm a mercenary. Freelance gun for hire. They brought me on board to do this thing in the bar. But they were pigs. If I know this before, I not have worked with them," she said.

"You double-crossed them. Won't they want revenge?"

She laughed. "I did what they ask. You were drunk when I went into bar. They could not handle you. That is their problem. It was three on one. Incompetent pigs."

"Yeah, but they almost succeeded. Would have, without you. These guys are not the kind of people to forget what you've done when they find out I'm still alive and kicking."

She raised up and looked at me, one eyebrow arching high in a way which reminded me of Samantha and I felt a pang of guilt deep inside. "They will not want to mess with me. This I promise you. But there is more you don't know."

"Sister, you could fill the Grand Canyon with what I don't know. Feel free to enlighten me."

"These men, they were excited. Not just because they kill you, but because they have something big in the works. But not them, I think. They are not very important men, these men sent to kill you. The man they worked for, he knows more. For this thing, they needed you dead before something happen in Philadelphia. You must be someone very important."

I grunted in a noncommittal way. "Part of my job description is to screw these guys over any way I can. Philadelphia, huh?"

"Yes. Philadelphia. This means something to you?"

"Oh, yeah, it means something." I thought to myself, "Cyrus Tyler is what it means."

She started kissing my neck, then nibbled my ear. "What will you do?"

"To them, or to you?" I rolled over on top of her, my fingers in her hair.

A wicked smile on her face, she said, "I much rather know about me."

"How about I show you, instead?" And I did.

CHAPTER NINE

The next morning I awoke, famished and feeling ready to rejoin the world. Elizabeth fixed breakfast while I spent time in the bathroom taking a long shower, the hot water working out cramped muscles from spending the last four days in bed.

The face staring back at me from the mirror looked tired despite the days spent recovering. I could see bags under my eyes and my beard and mustache were in need of a serious trim, not to mention my hair, which dove down below my ears. I looked like a wild mountain man.

I stepped out of the bathroom to the smell of bacon, eggs and fresh coffee. It was all I could do to not run to the kitchen. I settled for walking quickly back to the bedroom where Elizabeth put my bag with my clothes. The night she rescued me from the parking lot, she managed to get me into my own car and drove away. Good thing. I would have hated to lose all my gear.

I re-dressed the wound with gauze she left for me on the dresser, then slipped into a black T-shirt, jeans and my steel toed shit kicker boots and made my way to the kitchen where Elizabeth put down a full plate and mug of coffee on a small table in the breakfast nook. A bay window gave a breathtaking view down the mountain, but I spent my time watching Elizabeth, who wore a tight fitting beige top, black leggings and knee high black boots.

I took my seat and she bent to give me a kiss, then I dug in. She poured herself a cup of coffee and took the seat across from me. She sipped from the cup while I devoured my breakfast, both of us quiet while I ate.

When I sopped up the last of the egg yolks with a piece of toast and wolfed it down, I put my fork and knife on my plate and stretched contentedly. "Damn, but that was good."

She dipped her head in a nod of thanks. "I have many talents, as you will find out. How do you feel today?"

"All things considered, not too bad. My side is sore and stiff, but I'll manage. Just getting up and moving is helping. And this breakfast? Wow.

410

Thank you. Aren't you going to have any?"

"I ate before you got up. I don't sleep much. Never have. What will you do now?"

I scratched at my beard, thinking. "First thing is to return to civilization. I need to check in with some people who are probably freaking out with me being gone for so long. Then I want you to tell me about this man who hired you. I think he and I need to have a talk. Where's my phone?"

"It is out in your car, in the glove box. You should be able to make calls when we get to the bottom of the mountain. This man will not want to talk to you. You know this."

"He will, whether he wants too or not. Cooperation is not optional. Tell me where I can find this guy."

She shook her head. "No. I will take you to him. I will help you in this."

"Not a chance. Listen, I appreciate what you've done for me. I really do. But I prefer to work alone when it comes to matters like this."

"Too bad," she countered. "Because I will not tell you unless I go with you. You need me. I watch your back."

"I have people to do that for me, if needed. Please, just give me his name and where I can find him. Then I'll be happy to drop you off wherever you want."

She leaned back in her chair, crossed her legs and said, "No." Then smiled at me.

I grounded my teeth for a moment, but then sighed. "Fine. You can come. But you have to let me handle things. Kapeesh?"

"I let you handle. Then I clean up when you screw up. Like last time," and smiled again.

"It ain't happening again. I can promise you that much. You packed?" I was getting ticked off.

"Yes. My things are already in the car. I guessed you would want to leave right away."

I got up, taking my dishes to the sink. I washed them and set them in the rack to dry, then went to get my gear from the bedroom and the two of us walked out to my car. I threw my things in the trunk, next to the flame thrower and then glanced into the front and back seats.

"I don't see any blood. You clean that up, too?"

"I tell you. Many talents. Besides, you have leather seats and floor mats. Make things easy."

We both got in and fired up the car, punched up "home" on the GPS and started down the mountain. The device told me we were in the Great

Smokey Mountain National Park. The day was pleasant at this elevation so we rolled the windows down. We were a bit under five hours to Louisville.

"This man I need to talk to, do you know his name?"

"Yes. Of course. Before I tell you, I must have your word I will get to go with you. You make this promise?"

"Do I have a frickin' choice?"

No. You do not have a frickin' choice. Only my choice. You promise?"

I growled out agreement and she patted my cheek in response. "You are smart man. His name is Preston Deveraux. He is also a pig. But he pays well and is very handsome. You know this man?"

I felt my blood freeze over at the mention of the name. The last time I'd seen Preston Deveraux, he held a gun to Samantha's head, promising to shoot her if I so much as twitched a finger. Moments before, he'd shot and killed Dominic Montoya, the previous Hand of God, while I looked on, helpless to stop him.

Deveraux had movie star good looks and an incredibly evil world outlook. Over the past ten months, I'd kept my ears open, hoping to catch wind of where he was hiding out. Seems he'd once again tried to have me bumped off.

I tried to keep from ripping the steering wheel off in my hands. "Yeah. I know this man," I said, trying to contain my growing rage within. "Where can I find him?"

"I know not where he is now, but I can arrange a meeting, between him and me. This is how you find him."

I drove for nearly twenty miles, thinking as the world passed by barely noticed. If Deveraux was out to punch my ticket, then they must have something really big planned. Considering their last two efforts included infecting children with a genetically altered form of bird flu and releasing the Watchers, badass fallen angels buried for several millennia who were looking for some major payback against mankind, I hated to think what they had planned next.

I had to hand it to the Church of the Light Reclaimed: they went for the home run. And I'd proven to be quite the thorn in their side and knew I was public enemy number one. There was some thought whether it was better to watch me rather than kill me, since with my death a new Hand of God would be tapped to continue the good fight and they wouldn't know who it would be until he (or she) made their presence known.

Bumping me off would give them a short window to pull off something big with a chance a new Hand would not yet be in place.

Something to think about.

"Here's what I want to do. Let me get back to Louisville and see if my crew knows anything about what's going on. Then you can call Deveraux and try to set up a meeting. I'm gonna kick his ass from there to Sunday and back before I kill him."

"Sounds like plan. It would be a shame to spoil such good looks, but if we must we must."

I opened the console, picked up my phone, thumbed in the passcode and accessed my contacts list. I found the listing for "Big Honcho" and pressed call.

A few moments later the dulcet tones of Brother Joshua, the minister in charge of the Derby City Mission, picked up.

"Victor?" A man of many words, is Brother J.

"Yeah. It's me. Returned to the land of the living." I gave him a brief description of what transpired both in North Carolina and in Tennessee. "I'll be back at the mission around mid- afternoon and I'll fill you in completely."

"This woman, is she with you now?"

"Yep. She saved my life, J. Without her help, you'd be ringing up another poor soul to run around and whack the bad guys."

"Can you trust her?"

I glanced at Elizabeth as she stared out the window. "Not a chance." I hung up and slipped the phone into my jeans pocket. She looked my way and I leaned over and we kissed. "My friends can't wait to meet you."

She snorted in a very un-lady like manner. "I listened to what you told him. You did not go into any detail about my being part of the team sent to kill you."

I shrugged. "But you didn't. You did the opposite. Puts you on the side of the righteous."

She wagged a finger at me. "All the same, when we get to Louisville, I prefer you drop me off at a hotel. I would rather we proceed slowly. I do not know your friends or how they would react to me. One must be cautious in my business."

"You said you were a mercenary. You're for hire? Then I would like to hire you. How much?"

She turned in her seat and ran a hand down the inside of my thigh. "For you? I think of discount plan. I think you will like it."

"I'm sure I will. You can go with me to the meeting with Brother Joshua. I can vouch for your safety."

She pulled her hand back and sat in her seat, crossing her hands in her lap. "I say no. I mean no. I not want to meet this man. If you can't do as I ask, then you can pull over and let me out here. Find this Deveraux on your own."

"How do I know you won't bolt on me the moment I drop you off at the hotel?"

"You have my word. That will have to be good enough."

She was right. Forcing her to come with me wasn't my style and I don't think she would have cracked even if I did. I would play things out her way and see what happened.

"Alright. Your way. The Galt House is right downtown. You can stay there while I meet Joshua and see what's what. Good enough?"

"They have room service with cute waiters?"

"Room service, yes. Cute waiters? I have no idea." I shook my head in mock disgust. "Women."

"Ehh, can't live with us, can't shoot us," she responded.

"Don't count on it," I thought.

CHAPTER TEN

After getting Elizabeth squared away at the Galt House, I drove over to the Derby City Mission, parking out front. I carried my gear to my room, a monkish ten by ten space down past the maintenance room. My digs were quite a bit away from the homeless men and women who stayed at the mission. Seems I made most of them nervous. Go figure.

I strolled down the hall to J's office and knocked on the door frame before stepping inside. Brother Joshua, a middle-aged black man, hair cut short with streaks of gray at the temples and black framed reading glasses on his nose, sat behind his desk going through some papers.

I plopped down in one of the two seats facing his desk, and waited. If J was curious about my absence over the last few days, he sure as hell wasn't in a hurry to ask me about it.

He finished perusing the last sheet and set it to the side. Then he pushed his glasses on top of his head and steepled his fingers, resting his elbows on his desk.

We stared at each other for a few minutes, neither of us speaking. I used to play this game in elementary school and usually I won. Today, I lost.

"I met a girl."

He continued to stare at me for a moment longer before joining the conversation. "I'm sure you meet lots of women. Tell me about this one."

And I did. From how she gave me the heads up about the men planning to kill me to how she saved my ass.

"Lift up your shirt. Let me see how she sewed you up."

I stood and pulled up my shirt. J leaned closer, and then evidently satisfied, sat back. "Her work is first rate. There are battlefield doctors who might not have closed you up any better. What do you know about her?"

"Not a damn thing, other than she says she was hired by Deveraux to help the men plant me six feet under. She claims she became a turn coat because the men were pigs."

"And you believe her?"

"Hell no. She's playing her own games. I'll play my part long enough to learn what she's up to. No one who has any brains would double-cross Deveraux and from everything I can tell, she's smarter than your average merck. So she's playing an angle, but I haven't a clue what. What I do know is I'd be trying on wings and picking out a harp if not for her."

"Don't count your harp strings before they're plucked. Why didn't you have Winston with you on this job? Sounds like you could have used him."

Winston Reynolds is a former bounty hunter and now my top warrior in the battle with Satan and his lackeys. Winston was a former All Big East linebacker for the Louisville Cardinals. After a brief stint in the NFL, he went to work for bounty hunter J.B. Booker. That's how he and I met, following J.B.'s murder by the Church of the Light Reclaimed, Winston joined up with me for some sweet payback. Now he was my go-to backup when I needed the help. At six foot two and nearly two-hundred and forty pounds, he packed quite a punch.

"Winston and Kurt are taking care of some loose ends from the crap that went down in Hawaii. I expect them back by the end of the week."

Brother Joshua moved the glasses back into place, picking up another stack of papers. "Do I want to know?"

"I could tell you, but then I'd have to kill you."

He sat the papers down and stared at me. I got up and left. Some people have no sense of humor.

~*~

Kurt closed his eyes, squeezing the grip of the gun hard enough he feared it would go off without him even touching the trigger.

He sat in the dark in an off-campus apartment near the University of Wisconsin, a stone's throw from Camp Randall Stadium. He set the gun on the small coffee table next to his chair and rubbed his hands on his jeans. Despite the latex gloves, it felt like his hands were still sweating.

He thought about the events which brought him to this place to kill a man. Following the big throw down with the Church of the Light Reclaimed, he'd left Vic and Winston to hide out in Hawaii. He worked hard to hide his tracks, but somehow, the Church still found him.

They sent a fallen angel by the name of Kokabiel, to first seduce him, having possessed the body of a beautiful woman, and ultimately to kill him. Kokabiel, or Ruth Anne as he knew her, buried Kurt in a coffin with a pipe coming to the surface. The fallen angel threatened to drop fire ants, scorpions or rattle snakes into the coffin with him unless he gave up where to find the money Vic stole from the Church of the Light Reclaimed.

When they learned it would take both Kurt and Vic to retrieve the money, Kokabiel opted to fill up the coffin with water and leave him to drown. If not for Winston saving the day at the last moment, they would have succeeded.

True, once they kicked Kokabiel out of the body of Ruth Anne Gardner, he and Ruth Anne fell deeply in love, which means he did get a girlfriend out of the deal. But it took him nearly dying for that to happen.

What always bugged him was how they found him in Hawaii. Kurt had been very careful hiding his tracks. He was terrified the Church would one day come after him and went to great lengths to make sure they never did. But never say never, right?

When the Watchers were finally defeated and sent to whatever hell it is they go to when forced out of a body, Kurt began the process of finding how the Church tracked him down.

Kurt belonged to a collection of hackers much in the vain of Anonymous, the famous hackers known for wearing Guy Fawkes masks and taking on corporate and government stooges.

Kurt enlisted the hackers he knew to take on the Church of the Light Reclaimed and they laid siege to every facet of their operation, from the money supply chain to discovering who made up their membership. It was a tip from one of the hackers which led to the rescue of Samantha from captivity down in Naples, Florida.

It took him several months, but in the end he found out one of his own hacking buddies sold him out to the Church. All it took was a grand and a new laptop. Kurt thought he would be worth more money. He was worth two grand if he was worth a dime.

The hacker's online name was the Silver Ghost. His real name was Sarka Buranak, an exchange student from Romania, majoring in computer science at U.W.

Sarka was a Black Hat. They considered themselves the outlaws of the hacking world and at one point he found out the Church put a bounty on Kurt's head and he claimed it. Like the bounty hunters of the Old Wild West, they didn't care who put out the bounty, only getting paid when they claimed it.

Kurt didn't know if Silver Ghost knew it would mean Kurt would die a horrible, excruciating death, but after making his way into Buranak's system, it didn't matter. The Romanian Black Hat now worked for the Church, trying his best to track down and drop polymorphic viruses into any computer Victor or Winston may have access. His goal? Find the money Victor stole from the Church. Nearly thirty million dollars. It is why they travelled to Hawaii to begin with. Follow the money. They offered Buranak a ten percent cut of any money recovered.

And when they had the money, they wanted him to help plan an ambush of anyone associated with the Hand of God. This included another run at Kurt. Seemed Buranak put key logger and logic bombs in the computers at the Derby City Mission. Kurt went in behind Buranak and removed them, despite the fact he doubted the mission possessed any information they would find useful.

After talking it over with Victor and Winston, the decision was made to remove Sarka from the board. Permanently. With Vic out in North Carolina dealing with hellhounds, it fell to Winston and Kurt. They spent a few days following Buranak and formulated their plan to eliminate him.

Winston was happy to be the one to pull the trigger, but Kurt felt it important to be the one to take out Buranak. After all, it was personal. Buranak was in bed with the most evil of evil people. It was up to Kurt to avenge Ruth Anne's mother and brother, killed at the hands of another demented fallen angel. And as far as Kurt was concerned, Buranak was as responsible for him being buried six feet under as the fallen angel hiding out in Ruth Anne's body.

But now the time was here and Kurt found the thought of killing another person unpleasant. Winston and Victor told him they were at war and in a war people die. And they were right. The "new" Kurt wanted to be a part of the war, taking on the bad guys on the frontline.

And here he was, as far forward on the frontline as a man could get. Yet now that he was here, he wasn't sure he deserved the chance. Winston waited in a car down the street and Kurt wondered if there was time to call him and switch places.

Before he could text Winston and ask, the front door opened, and then closed. A person was whistling, and Kurt heard what he assumed were keys dropped into a bowl.

A few moments later, the door to the room where Kurt waited opened and a young man walked in and dropped into a swivel chair in front of a bank of computer screens. He pushed a few buttons and a moment later his fingers began to fly over the keyboard.

Buranak was of average height with wild, spiked blonde hair. Kurt almost busted out laughing when he realized the song Buranak was whistling was the theme to Gilligan's Island. Kurt picked up the gun, stood and walked silently until he was right behind Buranak. He pointed the gun at the man's head. "This is for—"

Before he could get the words out, Buranak whirled around in the chair, knocking Kurt backwards. The gun went off, the bullet striking one of the monitors, punching a small hole in the glass and blowing out a large hole in the back.

Buranak hurled himself out of his chair and onto Kurt, the two of them crashing to the ground, fighting for control of the gun.

Buranak shouted at him in what Kurt assumed was Romanian, but was too busy trying not to die to point out he didn't understand what was being said.

Buranak kneed him hard in the groin and Kurt almost lost his grip on the gun, but managed to hold on. Barely. The other man held onto his wrist with both hands, trying to turn the gun towards Kurt's face.

The hacker began to grin, as inch by inch, the gun began to point at Kurt's nose, yelling out, "Yes, yes, yes."

"No, no, no," Kurt thought. Kurt tried to think of what Vic would do in a situation like this and it came to him, he knew what Vic would do.

Instead of resisting Buranak's efforts, he used his anger and fear for a burst of strength and pulled the gun up and over his head. Then he rolled slightly to the side and drove his forehead into Buranak's nose.

Pain exploded as it felt like his head would tear apart from the attack and his eyes began to water, but they weren't tears, he told himself. Buranak seemed to be in an equal amount of pain, letting go of the gun and falling onto his back, holding his nose as blood poured between his fingers.

Kurt got to his knees, shaking his head back and forth, trying to clear the cobwebs from his brain. He needed to think, but all he could think about was the pain.

"You broke my nose, you asshole," screamed Buranak in English, and he lunged for the gun, trying to pull it from Kurt's hand.

The gun barked once and a look of surprise crossed Buranak's face, his hands going to his chest, blood welling out between his fingers. "You shot me."

"Well, yeah. That was kind of the point. I'm Kurt Pervis. This is payback for what you did to me."

"Who?"

Before Kurt could explain, Buranak fell back onto the carpeted floor, dead.

Kurt stared for a moment at the blood pooling on the carpet, mesmerized by what he'd done. The largest thing he had ever killed in his entire life was the occasional bug, and even then he usually picked them up with a tissue and then let them loose outside.

He forced himself to get moving, doing everything he could to avoid looking at the dead man on the floor. He gathered up Buranak's three laptops, and dropped the computers into the duffle bag next the chair where he'd waited for the hacker to come home. He felt a surge of excitement about getting the computers home and learning all of Buranak's secrets. Kurt knew he might even learn more about what the Church of the Light Reclaimed planned for future attacks.

When he was sure he had left nothing of importance behind, he again averted his eyes from the dead body and went to the front door. He cracked it open, and not seeing anyone, slipped the gun into his jacket pocket, left and quickly walked down the hallway, leaving the building by a side stairwell.

He forced himself to walk slowly down the block to Winston's car. He admonished himself: next time no monologue. The one doing the monologue always ends up catching the bullet. Kurt was lucky his desire to let Buranak know who was killing him had not ended up with his own death.

He reached the car, opened the door and slid into the passenger seat, pulling the door closed. Winston put the car in drive and they left, ghosts in the night.

Kurt glanced at his hands in his lap, amazed they were not shaking. In truth, he found his breathing to be easy, his pulse rate normal. Surprise, surprise.

"Everything go O.K? I saw the dude go inside and wondered what was taking you so long. I almost came to check on you."

Kurt looked at Winston, and with a slow grin spreading across his face, said, "Just like we planned."

CHAPTER ELEVEN

The next morning I picked up Elizabeth at the Galt House, half-surprised she was actually there, and drove out to Wild Eggs on Dutchmans Lane for breakfast.

I chose the omelet with every known form of protein tossed in with green peppers, onions and tomatoes, while she chose strawberry pancakes. Both of us drank our coffee leaded.

"How did you sleep?" I asked. She sat across from me wearing a yellow sundress and flats to match. Her perfume smelled like an early spring rain.

She forked a generous amount of pancakes into her mouth, chewed for a moment, and then flipped her hand back and forth.

"Yeah. Same here." We avoided the small talk for the next few minutes while we both demolished our breakfast, Elizabeth keeping up with me forkful for forkful.

I took a sip of coffee and spent a moment watching her. The longer I did, the more beautiful she seemed. Her pale blue eyes haunted my dreams the night before. For the first time since meeting Samantha, I couldn't remember a single dream about her, which bothered me.

She paused, her fork half-way to her mouth, and said, "What? Why do you stare?"

I shook myself out of my private thoughts. "You have some strawberry on the corner of your mouth."

She wiped the corner of her mouth with her napkin, but seeing nothing on it, looked dubious, but shrugged and went back to eating.

"When we are finished, I want you to place the call to Deveraux and set up the meeting."

"What, no small talk? Right to business? No 'you look beautiful,' Elizabeth? No, 'the dress is pretty,' Elizabeth?"

Laughing, I shook my head. "You're gorgeous and the dress is lovely. Happy?"

"No. Elizabeth is not happy." She gave me a fake pout, then kicked my shin under the table. "Next time, tell me nice things without me having to ask you. Women like to hear compliments." She shook her head. "Men can be very stupid sometimes." Her accent seemed particularly thick when irritated.

"You won't get any argument from me. I have no doubts the person who wrote *Everything There is to Know about Women* isn't a man."

"This is probably why this Samantha left you. Because you can be a pig, too."

The dig hit me deep down in my soul. I worked to control the anger which blossomed at her comments. In a voice barely above a whisper, I said, "You don't know what you're talking about and I would take care in how you use her name."

She was quiet for a moment, drinking coffee and watching me. She put the cup down. "I am sorry. The comment was meant to be a joke, but it did not come out right. Forgive me. Sometimes I talk before I think. Do you want to talk about this woman?"

"No. Not now. Not ever. Let's call Deveraux and get this train rolling."

She sighed, but reached into her purse and got her phone and made a call. She listened and then mouthed, "Voice mail."

When the message was over she said, "This is Elizabeth. The man is still alive and I know where he is. I tell you where, but I want more for the efforts I make. You send stupid men. Do the right thing this time and pay me and I will bring you his head."

She hung up and smiled at me. "Satisfied?"

I rubbed my neck. "I kind of like my head where it is. You sounded convincing. Almost too convincing."

She stuck her tongue out at me. "If I wanted you dead, I could have let you die in the parking lot. I could have killed you many times while you slept. Instead I sew you up, get you blood, make you better. And still you doubt me?"

"Trust but verify. Why don't you tell me about yourself?"

"I only tell small amount. I am from Hungary, but I move around a lot. I worked with *Terrorelhárítási Központ,* the anti-terrorism force. But they don't use me well and I leave. Now I hire out to those who can afford me. Deveraux asked me to come to America and do work for him. But when I meet men in Tennessee, they spend more time trying to get in my pants than planning to attack you." She shook her head, disgusted, and after a moment continued. "Then I learn they have big plans. They hint it will lead to many deaths, so I make decision to warn you about their plans to kill you, see what you can do. When you take them out even though you were so drunk, I like.

When you fall down in parking lot, I make instant decision. Help you, hurt them."

It sounded good. Sounded believable. The question was how to separate the truth from the bull shit, because I knew what she was telling me wasn't the whole truth.

"Is Elizabeth your real name?"

She snorted. "I work intelligence for my home country, and now for others. I have many names. But this one is all you will know. I chose it because I see dancer with this name I like. Now I am Elizabeth."

Before I could respond her phone rang. Looking at the screen, she moved to sit next to me, putting the phone next to her ear, but tilting it so I could hear.

"Hello?"

"What happened in Tennessee? You were supposed to kill Victor McCain for me."

Preston Deveraux even sounded smooth on the phone. If I could jump through the phone and wrap my hands around his throat, I would do it in a heartbeat.

"What happened is you sent idiot boys to do real man's job. But you are wrong. You did not hire me to kill this man, but to be bait. I was bait and he was there for your men to kill. They screw this up, no? This time, I do the job for you. He will be killed. I want five-hundred thousand. You do this?"

"Where is he?"

"He is back in Louisville, but I know where he will be in three days and I will kill him for you. But I must have money before then. Cash."

"I can do that, but if you double-cross me, you will regret it. Do I make myself clear?"

"Do not insult me. I always do what I say I do. Where your men failed, I will not. Do we have a deal?"

"Yes. We do. Where would you like me to wire the money?"

"No good. I just tell you, I work in cash. You tell me where to meet you and I will be there. And I want it from you. I not trust anyone else. You do this, and I will kill this man."

"I will be in Columbus, Ohio tomorrow. Meet me at the Dublin Cemetery tomorrow night, eight p.m. Drive through the main entrance and bear to the right when the road forks. There's a huge tree on the left. I will meet you there."

He hung up and Elizabeth put her phone away. I could not help but groan. "A cemetery? Nothing ever good happens in a cemetery. Doesn't he know he is perpetuating the Satanist stereotype?"

"Satanist? This man is a Satanist? There are really such people?" She rested her hand on my leg, casually massaging the inside of my thigh.

I cleared my throat. "Yes he is and yes there are. Do you know anything about me?"

"I know you are supposed to be a man who is hard to kill, who they want to kill very badly. But no, I don't know about you. What is there to know?"

I gave her a brief rundown about being the Hand of God, what the job entails and who the hell Preston Deveraux is and who he worked for.

She laughed long and loud. "You kill people for God? And you believe this? Do you have visions or do you have a phone to call for your assignments?"

"Mind keeping your voice down, please?" I glanced around the restaurant, but no one seemed to be paying us any attention.

I have to admit, her laughter was a blow to my ego. The only people who I ever talked to about my job were Winston, Kurt, Samantha and Brother Joshua. Elizabeth was the first person outside of our group with whom I shared my situation and her disbelief bothered me.

"How I get my jobs is not something we will be talking about. Whether you believe me or not, Preston Deveraux does. If you think I'm some nut, forget it. I will go to Columbus on my own and take this son of a bitch out."

She wrapped her arms around my neck and pulled me to her, and kissed me. I resisted at first, but then gave in. She was a better than average kisser.

Breaking the kiss, she said, "I am sorry." The amusement in her eyes said otherwise. "But I do believe you. More importantly, I know this Preston believes it. I will go with you to meet him. If he do not see me, he may not show."

She had a point. Deveraux was expecting to meet Elizabeth and if he got a whiff of Vic being there then things were likely to go very badly. Deveraux was a smart guy. They would need to get there early and scope things out.

"We will need to get there way ahead of them and take a look around. How about we check you out of the Galt House and hit the road?"

"I am afraid I cannot. I have other business, unrelated to this, and must take care of it first. We can leave at first light in the morning."

"Other business? Like what?"

"Other business which is not your business. I am a mercenary. I must make a living and I have an interview with a prospective client tonight. It cannot be helped. We leave in the morning."

I did not like this development one bit. I didn't trust Elizabeth any further than I could throw her, though I could likely throw her a pretty good distance.

"You are one frustrating woman, you know that?"

"Yes, but lovable. I need to rent a car later today. For now, I would like you to take me back to hotel."

"And what is back at the hotel?"

She slid her hand higher up my inner thigh. "My bed, which you have yet to see. I thought I might show you how firm is the mattress. Does this work for you?"

I snagged the waitress walking by. "Check, please."

CHAPTER TWELVE

Hedley Stafford sat on the edge of the examining room table, his legs hanging off the side. Dr. Collins sat on a rolling stool and explained the process.

"I know Dr. Michaels told you about how the surgery would take place, but I wanted to go over it with you again to make sure you understood what would happen."

"Doctor, being overly prepared when you plan to saw my leg in half is not a problem for me."

"Not your leg, Senator, just the bone. We are doing a total knee replacement, due to extensive arthritis in the joint. I will start by making a ten inch incision from here to here." She ran her finger from a spot above his kneecap to a few inches below it.

"Once I do this, I will have access to the knee. I start by resurfacing your femur and attaching the metal component of your new joint to the end of the bone. I will then do the same thing with the tibia. In between there will be a plastic component for flexibility. Once I am happy the joint is properly sized and bending properly, then I will close the incision. I use staples to keep the skin closed."

Stafford nodded. "How long do you expect me to be laid up?"

"We will put your knee to work following your surgery. Once you are back in your room, you will be attached to a continuous passive motion machine, or CPM. You will use this during the first night. We will have you on your feet the following morning, if you're doing well enough. You will be home in three days. We will have a regiment of pain medication we will want you to adhere to so we can stay ahead of the pain. During the surgery, I will be inserting a pain block which will keep the pain at bay for twenty-four to forty-eight hours. Following surgery, I will want you to take the Hydrocodone at the prescribed intervals. Then we will move you to Tylenol."

"Good enough. How soon before I will be able to return to work?"

"That is up to you and how well you do with your physical therapy. Most people do their physical therapy at home for the first one to two weeks, then they are well enough to continue with physical therapy at a nearby facility. Because of your unique position, I understand Dr. Michaels arranged for you to have your physical therapy at the Capital. I see no reason why you can't still do this, again, based on how well you do the first week you are home."

"Most excellent. I can't thank you enough, doctor, for keeping my surgery on schedule. This will allow me to be fairly full strength when the August recess is over. We have many events leading up to the election and I want to participate as fully as possible."

She stood and Stafford did the same. "We will have a list of do's and don'ts for you. It is almost as important to not do what we tell you not to do, as it is to do what we tell you to do. You are a very healthy man and you have a reputation for being a workaholic. If you feel you must stay very active, there's no shame in using a wheelchair to get around the Capital."

"You can count on me to behave, doctor." He extended his hand and she took it. Stafford was pleased to note her grip was firm and steady. He hoped it would be the same when she held the scalpel.

"Then I will see you next Monday at six a.m."

They said their goodbyes and Collins watched the Senate Majority Leader leave. She then went to her office, closing the door. She sat behind her desk, opened her briefcase and pulled out the burner phone which arrived in the mail. She pushed a button for speed dial. A moment later a man answered.

"Yes?"

"We are on schedule. Stafford just left. The surgery is next Monday. You will need to make sure I get the product this weekend."

"It's all been arranged. I will meet with you Sunday at the hotel. You're sure you can make the switch with no issues?"

"Yes. The entire surgical team are my people, from the anesthesiologist to the nurses. There won't be a problem."

"Good. See you Sunday, doc."

The man ended the call and Collins put the phone back into her briefcase and shut the lid softly. She closed her eyes and took deep, steadying breaths. Soon it would all be over. Until then, she needed to continue to act like she did not have a care in the world. No matter how hard it would be.

~*~

Brad Stiles walked to the large oak door, knocking twice before opening it and stepping inside, closing the door behind him. Tyler sat behind his desk, feet propped on the edge, the phone to his ear, gesturing with his hands while he talked.

"Look, Bob, I'm not going to barter with you. I'm the fucking Speaker of the House of Representatives. When I tell you how I want you to vote, that's how you're going to vote. Being the chairman of the Agricultural Committee helps to bring a lot of donations into your campaign coffers. Screw with me over this vote and I promise you when the next session of Congress starts in January you will be lucky to be chairman of your son's Boy Scout troop."

He slammed the phone down, dropped his feet on the floor and broke into a Cheshire Cat grin. "I do love this job. Whatcha got for me?"

"Everything is a go for Monday. I will need to be gone for a day or so, to get things ready."

"No worries. I'll get Randy to do the driving. Let Brenda know when you go back out and she'll take care of it."

Stiles nodded and left. He did as he was asked and informed Brenda, Tyler's scheduling secretary, he would be gone for a few days and to have the other driver, Randy, handle things while he was gone.

He left the Capital, found his car in the security lot and made his way out of the city. He stopped to gas up on the Beltway and punched an address in the GPS. The machine found the proper mapping and he saw it was a bit over thirty minutes.

He stopped briefly in a strip mall, parking in the back long enough to remove a stolen license plate and switched it for his government plate. Once finished, he pulled out and resumed his trip.

He turned on the satellite radio and found the MLB channel. The Nationals were having a hell of a season and he wanted to hear about the previous night's game.

Traffic was heavier than normal, even for D.C., and it took him nearly forty-five minutes to make it to his destination, a non-descript building at the end of a row of warehouses. The sign over the door read Bio-Enhanced Robotics.

Only one other car, a Toyota Prius, was parked out front and he pulled his Navigator in beside the smaller car and got out. He could pick up the Prius and put it in the back of his car.

Glancing around and seeing no one else nearby, he removed a handkerchief from his suit pocket and held it in his hand while he turned the knob and opened the door. He knew from previous reconnaissance trips there were no obvious security cameras to worry about.

Inside, he used the handkerchief to softly close the door. He found himself in a classic corporate waiting area. A receptionist's desk sat in one corner, empty. Several comfortable chairs lined one wall with an end table supporting a lamp and a smattering of different magazines.

Stiles crossed the room to the only door, and once again using the handkerchief, opened it and stepped through, closing it behind him. A hallway ran straight ahead, three doors on the left side, two on the right. He knew the two doors on the right ran to advanced development laboratories.

B.E.R. was involved on the frontlines of creating prosthetics which combined cutting edge technology and the latest in surgical techniques. The company was the brainchild of Isaac Peck. Peck double-majored in engineering and computers at M.I.T.

When a close family friend was injured fighting in Afghanistan, Peck went to work developing new arms and legs which were inching closer and closer to the stuff of science fiction. The latest success was the development of a prosthetic leg which worked exactly like a human leg, even to the point of being controlled by the unconscious thoughts of the recipient.

Peck's office was the last door on the left and Stiles could hear music through the closed door. Holding the handkerchief, Stiles checked the labs and the other two rooms to make sure they were the only two people in the building.

Satisfied they were alone, he turned the knob and opened Peck's door an inch, putting the handkerchief away, then pushed the rest of the way open with the toe of his shoe.

Peck, thin and balding and in his late twenties, sat bent over a drafting table, his left knee pumping up and down in continuous motion. The music came from a computer on his desk, hip-hop turned up to ear splitting levels. A box the size of a bread box sat on the desk next to the computer.

When Stiles kicked the door shut, Peck jumped out of his chair, his hand flying to chest. "Jesus. You scared the crap out of me, man. What the hell?"

Brad sat down in one of two chairs in the room, crossing one leg over the other and resting his hands in his lap and stared at the other man, saying nothing. Peck went to his desk, tapped a few keys and the music stopped. Sitting back down, his knee pumped double time, while Peck gripped the arms of his chair like a man who believed it would rocket into outer space at any moment.

Nodding at the package on the desk, Stiles asked, "Is that for me?"'

"Yeah. Just like you ordered. Man, this was a fun project. Never ever considered using quantum computing this way. Some of my buds at M.I.T. would shit their pants if they knew this kind of technology existed. This is way beyond anything Farhi, Goldstone and Harrow are working on. Any chance I could get a look at the research white papers? This is science fiction-type stuff. Really cool."

"I don't think so. Anyone else here, Isaac?"

"Nah, man, I gave everyone a half-day off, like you asked. They loved it, with it being Friday and all. So this is our little secret. Did all the work myself. What's this going to be used for?"

"You take notes on this, Isaac? I find out you wrote anything down, took notes, I won't be very happy."

Peck raised his hands. "Hey, man. No. Nothing. When I make a deal, I keep it. Besides, we don't want a paper trail, do we? Am I right?"

Brad stood, pulled a pair of gloves out of his inner suit pocket and slipped on first one, then the other.

"Isaac, when you're right. You're right. We don't want a paper trail. Or a people trail."

Stiles reached under his suit coat, slid the gun out of its holster and shot Peck twice in the chest and once in the head. Putting away the gun, he spent the next ten minutes going through Peck's desk and briefcase, looking for anything related to the job. Finding nothing, he picked up the package and left the way he entered.

Back at his car, he opened the rear hatch and sat the package down carefully and shut the door. Climbing back behind the wheel, he entered another address from memory, this one to a hotel in Philadelphia. With any luck he would be there early enough to catch the last part of the Nationals game with the L.A. Dodgers.

A Nationals win would make it the perfect ending to a good day.

CHAPTER THIRTEEN

After spending the better part of the morning in bed, we made our way to an Avis store, where she picked out a Mercedes. I guess being a mercenary pays better than average. She promised to call me later and then tore out of the parking lot, cutting off two other people in the process, the sound of horns showing their displeasure.

I was still hungry and found my way over to Molly Malone's Irish Pub. I sat in my usual booth where I could watch all three doors. Being a regular helped as my server placed the Guinness in front of me moments after I sat down and let me know my order was already entered.

I thanked her, picked up the glass and drained about half of it in one pull. I couldn't ever remember being this conflicted about anything in my life. Not hearing from Samantha made me want to find someone right this very moment and pound the ever lovin' daylights out of them. And this thing with Elizabeth wasn't helping. The sex was beyond fantastic, but when it was over, I felt like I was cheating on Samantha. But how can you cheat on someone who is not a part of your life?

I polished off the Guinness and motioned for another one. When my meal arrived, that glass was nearly empty as well and I told her I wanted one more. I dug into the shepherd's pie, but ate without really tasting it.

Near the end of my meal, Winston walked up to the booth and sat opposite me. The server asked if he wanted anything and he shook his head no, then stared at me.

I forked the last bite of food into my mouth and finished off the second glass of Guinness, set it to the side and picked up the new one.

"How many have you had?" he asked.

I held up three fingers and he shook his head. "Man, it's only one in the afternoon. Hitting it pretty hard, aren't you?"

"Listen, if you plan on being my mother, you need to put on a dress. Hell, I know my limit and I'm not there yet. I can handle it."

"I'd put on a dress, if it would help. But I'm not shaving my legs for you. And, yeah, you can handle it. Just like you handled North Carolina.

Brother Joshua filled me in on how it went. Hear you got sliced and diced. Lucky to be alive. What if they come for you again, when you leave here, with you all liquored up?"

"Then I'll kick their ass, like I always do."

A long belch slipped out and Winston waved a hand in front of his face.

"Dude, you need to ease up. You want to die, that's fine. But do it the right way. All you're doing is making it easy for them. You need to stay sharp. These are bad MoFos you're after."

"Whatever." I didn't appreciate the lecture. Winston and I were now good friends, but he had no clue what I was going through, what I was dealing with. It didn't help I knew he was right. The drinking nearly cost me my life. True, I wasn't expecting an ambush in Tennessee, but I should have considered the possibility.

He was also right I didn't care anymore. It was more than not hearing from Samantha, although her silence played a huge part. I was getting tired of the fight. Even the time spent in bed with Elizabeth, while enjoyable in the moment, did nothing for me when it was over.

I found myself taking more and more chances and sooner or later it would catch up with me. Maybe not today, but soon. I began wondering what the point was. I take out bad guy number one and move on to bad guy number two. Once I wipe his ass off the face of the planet, the next one steps up.

I knew I needed to keep working as the Hand of God, for as long as possible, to win back the soul I lost when I caused the death of Dominic Montoya. But even if I did this another ten years or more, there was still no guarantee I would win back my soul.

I took a deep breath and, for the moment, crushed my personal pity party. "How did things go up in Cheese Land?"

"Well enough. He almost blew it when it came time to pulling the trigger. He didn't know I put a mini-camera in the dude's room and I was watching it all go down from out in the hallway. I thought for a moment I would need to bust in and help, but he got it done. He's back at the mission working on the laptops the guy was using."

"How was he after? Did he seem to be handling it O.K.?" I kept thinking about the Clint Eastwood movie. *Unforgiven.* There's a line in there where Clint's character says, 'It's a hell of a thing, killin' a man. Take away all he's got, and all he's ever gonna have.' Some people can do it and never lose a second of sleep. I worried about how it would affect Kurt.

"Too early to tell. He did talk ninety-miles an hour on the way home, but then again, he talks a lot anyways. Dude never shuts up."

"That's Kurt."

"What's up next for you? You and your new lady friend have big plans?"

I filled him on the plan to drive to Columbus and meet with Preston Deveraux.

"You know this is a trap, right?" he asked.

I nodded, draining the last of my beer. "Yep. Only question is for whom? Her or me? Deveraux agreed way too quickly for the meet. No negotiations on price. No pressing for details."

We both got up and I dropped some cash on the table to cover my meal and drinks, plus a healthy tip, and we made our way outside.

"You want me to ride up with you guys? Help back you up?"

"No. I don't. She won't allow it. She says it has to be the two of us because she doesn't trust you guys yet."

"That's bullshit."

Before he could get going on a full rant, I held up my hands. "Hang on, hang on. You're not going up with us because you're going up first. I want you to leave as soon as you can get ready and scout the place. You can bet they picked this meeting place for a reason. Get up there early and find a spot to hang out, watch who comes and goes. Then let me know what I'm walking into."

"Now that's more like it. I can be on the road inside of an hour. If I hit the road by two, I can get in Columbus by six. What time are you guys supposed to meet with him?"

"Eight tomorrow night, just before dark. I've looked at a Google map view of the cemetery and there are a couple of large trees and several large monuments near where they want to meet. I'll need a good threat assessment."

"You got it, man. Late on a Saturday night, I can't imagine there'll be many people in the cemetery so they should be easy enough to pick out. And watch your ass, Vic. They may not wait until tomorrow night to take a shot at you. Which does raise one other question. Why now?"

"No clue. But I plan to find out. Right after I put a bullet between the eyes of Preston. He thinks Satan will send him right back here. Time go give him the chance to find out."

CHAPTER FOURTEEN

I parked my car in the Galt House parking garage and made my way to the lobby. The day started out hotter than Hades and promised to climb even higher before the day was through. In Columbus, the temperature was predicted to hit a high of ninety-eight with a heat index near one-hundred and three.

Carrying my duffle it didn't take long for me to break out in a sweat, even in the short walk to the lobby. I dropped my gear next to the concierge desk, gave the man behind the counter her room number and asked him to let her know I was here.

He picked up a white phone, punched a few numbers and a moment later passed along my message. I thanked him, picked up the duffle and found one of the chairs in the lobby and had a seat.

A half hour later I watched Elizabeth as she rode down the elevator, the back half of which was all glass. She wore a white T-shirt tucked into blue jeans, and black running shoes. The strap of her purse was slung over one shoulder. When she walked from the elevator over to where I sat, the eyes of every man followed her. Including mine. I had to admit, she moved with the kind of grace most of us dream of, but sadly never achieve.

I stood and we embraced and shared a long, slow kiss. If public displays of affection bothered her, she didn't show it. She took my hand and we walked out the front doors. She pulled a slip out of her pocket and handed it to the valet and a few minutes later, her Mercedes stopped in front of us.

She glanced at me, expectantly, and I fished a five out of my wallet and tipped the valet. He smiled a thank you and handed me the keys. I used the fob to unlock all the doors and opened the passenger side for Elizabeth. She got in and I shut the door. I made my way to the driver side, stopping long enough to toss my duffle into the back seat, then got in behind the wheel.

It took me a moment, but I finally figured out the built-in GPS and entered the address for the cemetery in Columbus. It could be an easy drive up I-71 for most of the trip, passing through Cincinnati on the way, with a total drive time of a bit over three hours.

I got an early morning call from Winston and there was both good and bad news. The good news was there was no one already in the cemetery waiting. I figured if we were going to get there early, then the bad guys were likely to do the same. Winston would keep watch on the cemetery to let us know if someone showed up early to set up.

The bad news was there were many houses nearby and if they had access to any of them, then any person in the cemetery would be an easy shot with a rifle. Not much we could do about it, so there was no real point in worrying about it.

"Mind if I roll down my window?" I asked.

"No. I like the breeze."

I hit the buttons and rolled down all the windows, but left the air conditioner on high, getting the best of both worlds. The Mercedes, an E class coupe, purred down the highway. Not exactly the kind of car which blends in, but Elizabeth was anything but normal.

"So what did you do with the rest of the day?"

"I needed time to take care of some business. Then I found a place where I could be pampered. I took a long bath, with a few extra perks. Why? You worry I spend time with another man?"

I laughed.

"No. I really couldn't care less. You're a big girl, you can do what you like."

She shot me the bird and started flipping through the dial on the satellite radio. I thought about what she asked me and wondered if I did care. I wasn't sure one way or the other. To say I was conflicted would be an understatement. What I did know, it made me realize I needed to get past my current rut where Samantha was concerned. There was no way to know how many more days I would have on this planet. How many of them could I spend pining away like a love sick puppy?

Traffic was light with only a minor delay going through Cincy because of a jack-knifed big rig. Dublin Cemetery was on the north-west outskirts of Columbus, so we took I-270 around the city and got off on US 33 East. From there it was less than a mile to the cemetery.

I raised the car windows and we drove past the front entrance and then circled the block, checking out the area from all sides. The Mercedes windows were fully tinted and I wasn't worried about someone seeing me. I'd made sure on the way up we weren't followed and I kept an eye in the rearview mirror to make sure we didn't pick one up while we were here.

I pulled into the parking lot of a middle school across the street from the cemetery where we would have a full view of the entrance and texted Winston to let him know we were on the scene and he could take a break and grab some lunch. When Elizabeth looked at me questioningly, I told her I'd texted my team to let them know I'd arrived on the scene. She seemed satisfied and began to search the radio for a different station.

I got a "thumbs up" picture in text response and Elizabeth and I settled in for our turn keeping watch. I used the power button on the side of the seat to lower the seat until my head was barely above the bottom of the window, trying to keep a low profile. Elizabeth matched me and we let the car run for a bit, keeping the interior nice and cool.

"How do you want to handle this when it comes time for the meet?" I asked.

"I have looked at a map of the area. I will meet them as they have asked. I will drive in with the car. There is a park to the west and I think it best you enter this way, no?"

"Monterey Park. I saw it on the map as well. Good entrance point. There is a tree line I can use to make my approach and get some cover. Looks to be a fair-sized mausoleum near the end of the circle. I will work my way as close as possible using it for extra cover. Are you sure you want to do this?"

"But of course. I am on your side now. I like you. And I don't like them. I will help you with this Preston Deveraux."

"And after? What's next for you?"

She shrugged a shoulder. "I always have offers. I may go back to Europe. Many things happening. Many opportunities for intelligence work. And the pay is good. Very good. Will you miss me?"

I smiled, saying nothing. We spent the next hour sitting and watching, neither of us speaking, until my phone beeped with Winston saying he was back on the job. I raised my seat upright, Elizabeth following suit and I was impressed. I never saw Winston leave or return. I was tempted to ask him where he was holed up, but didn't.

I pulled out of the school parking lot and we drove into downtown Columbus, killing time. Elizabeth wanted to see the Franklin Park Conservatory and Botanical Gardens, saying the gardens reminded her of where she grew up. To me, they were a bunch of flowers and my only thought was how much weeding would need to be done.

When it got closer to dinner time we made our way back to Dublin, hung a right at the Convention Visitors Bureau and pulled into the Dublin Village Tavern. I was hungry and you have to eat when you can.

The tavern, an Irish pub with a Victorian feel, suited the bill just fine.

I ordered the Irish Kettle dinner, simmered corned beef, Irish bangers and vegetables, while Elizabeth got the meatloaf. We both ordered Guinness to wash it down.

We made small talk until the waiter brought us our food and we tore into it. The corned beef was excellent and Elizabeth devoured her meatloaf. Lord, I do love a woman who likes to eat. I can't tell you how many times I'd take a girl to dinner and I would finish off half a cow in the time it would take them to eat a small salad. Elizabeth ate like it would be her last meal.

And I did the same. For all I knew it would be. When we finished we got back in the car, crossed the Scioto River and found a park on the other side, pulling up near the river's edge. We got out and wandered down to the river bank and spent the next hour stretched out, watching the sun sink lower in the west. The river wandered slowly by, the current in no hurry to get to where ever the ultimate journey would be.

The day was hot, the woman next to me hotter and for a bit it was easy to forget why we were there: to kill a man, perhaps several, depending on who Deveraux brought with him.

My phone beeped, a new text from Winston. The only activity in the cemetery during the afternoon was a backhoe digging a new grave in the area where they wanted us to meet. He added several people came in and out to pay respects at one grave site or another, but no one stayed overly long.

An hour before the meeting time, we left the location next to the river and drove to Monterey Park. I snagged the duffle from the back seat and she got out, moving behind the wheel. She pulled out, planning on driving a few blocks down, waiting for the appointed time. I watched her go and I felt a pang of worry. I tried hard not to be a chauvinist pig, but the last two times Samantha went with me on a job, she ended up in the hands of Satan's minions—the last time with a demon buried so deep in her brain, the only way to get him out was to shoot her.

I knew Elizabeth was different, having been trained to be on the front lines. Hell, she was paid to be on the front lines. But my track record with women wasn't great. Lord's will be done, right?

I crossed the tennis courts and waited behind a stand of trees where I could see, barely, the place where she was to meet with Deveraux. I wondered if he would really show. I wondered if he would be surprised to see me. I hoped so.

The next fifty minutes went by slowly and I could feel my adrenaline ramp up. These are the moments I live for: brief moments of intense violence. Me against them, with the ultimate prize on the line: my life.

I knew Winston could be counted on to back me up. We'd seen

enough action together and the man worked well under pressure. Nothing seemed to faze him. Elizabeth was the wild card. We knew nothing about her, how she would hold up if and when the bullets started flying. She talked a good game and she exuded the kind of confidence you can't fake, but I couldn't be sure until the moment came. I only hoped it wouldn't be her last.

I also needed to keep in mind she could be leading me into a trap. True, she could have killed me several times over, as she herself pointed out. It would make no sense to keep me alive only to bring me here to die. But I'd seen many strange things over the last nine months.

Time would tell. And it would tell soon. Through the leaves I watched as the Mercedes eased down the cemetery's main drag, pulled into the circle and came to a stop. She parked so the driver's side window faced me, rolling down both windows and turning off the car waiting. But not for long. A Lincoln Town Car made its way into the cemetery and into the circle, coming around the opposite way from the Mercedes, parking so the cars were nose to nose.

Elizabeth pushed her door open and stepped out, leaving the door open and standing behind it, keeping her hands low and out of sight. I could see the butt of a hand gun tucked into the jeans in the small of her back. A moment later, the doors of the town car opened and four men got out. One of them was Preston Deveraux.

Show time.

CHAPTER FIFTEEN

The sun dropped nearly to the horizon and it was behind me as I crossed the street into the tree line bordering the cemetery. Other than the two cars and the five people near them, the place was empty. Well, of live people. It was full of dead people. And one way or the other, the total of dead would be going up.

I unzipped the duffle and pulled out my Heckler and Koch UMP, the gun of choice for shooting a lot of rounds quickly and accurately. It was a change from my usual H and K MP5, but the UMP used larger cartridges and sometimes I have to shoot very large things which don't always want to stay down. I slipped an extra magazine into the back pocket of my jeans.

I needed to be careful. A residential area surrounded the cemetery and I didn't want a stray round to miss and find its way into someone's home. Collateral damage was not an option.

I took out one of my coms, hung it around my ear and switched it on. I texted Winston to do the same. A moment later I heard a quick series of three clicks in my ear to let me know he was plugged in and ready to go.

I stashed the duffle behind a large oak and slowly eased my way up to the mausoleum which would put me about forty yards from the two cars and with only the newly dug grave between us. The backhoe remained parked a few feet away, ready to push the dirt pile back into place.

I passed several headstones, some with kind words for the dead. "Loving Husband, Father and Son" and so on. It made me wonder about what would be on my tombstone when I died. If I even got a tombstone. I could end up dying in some backwoods place and buried where no one would ever find me.

Even if I got the full funeral, American flag and all, what would go on mine? My mother dreamed of grandkids, but the dream became less likely the day I became the Hand of God. With Mikey dead, my mother was likely to die with no grandchildren.

I shook off the thoughts and tried to get my head back into the game. I could hear Deveraux and Elizabeth talking, but not quite what was being said. I reached the mausoleum without issue, got onto my stomach and belly-crawled my way around the corner, keeping low behind a hedge row which lined both sides of the mausoleum.

A flower pot capped off the end of the hedge, a bronze colored pot holding some type of blue lily. The pot and hedge left enough room for me to see what was going on and I was now close enough to hear the conversation, but it wasn't going well.

Deveraux's men spread out, one starting to walk down the other side of the Mercedes, the other two took up positions on both sides of Deveraux's car, trying to see the whole cemetery at once. No one had guns out. Yet. Deveraux stayed behind his own door, much like Elizabeth, his hands crossed and resting on the door frame.

Elizabeth motioned with her head in the direction of the man moving to flank her and said, "If your man moves another foot, I will kill him."

The man froze and looked to Deveraux, who motioned for him to stop. The man did so, but squared up, with the car between him and Elizabeth.

Deveraux held his hands out to his sides, a smile on his face, but not in his eyes. "I thought we were all friends here, Elizabeth," he replied.

"What was it one of your presidents say? Trust but verify? Me? I trust no one. Especially a man who says he will bring me money for information but who gets out of his car empty-handed. Where is the money?"

Deveraux shrugged and slipped his hands into the pants pockets of what I assumed was an Italian tailor-made suit. "About that. I don't think I will be paying you anything. Will I, Elizabeth?"

I could see Elizabeth stiffen and I could tell she expected trouble.

"If you think you can cheat me, then you know nothing," she hissed.

"Thanks to the Lord of Light, I know everything there is to know about you. You've been a very naughty girl and he is very upset with you. You have not been doing what you promised him you would do. He sent me here to ask you why not?"

Holy crap. The Lord of Light meant Satan to these dumb asses. I knew making promises to Satan usually came with some pretty stiff eternal strings attached. Ask my brother how it turned out for him. Eternal damnation was his normal choice of payment. Was Elizabeth another lost soul? Or had she made him a different promise. Like to deliver my head on a platter?

Elizabeth relaxed visibly, the tension in her stance melting away. "Why not? Because I chose not. You should have brought my money. Time for you to leave now."

Deveraux lost the smile. "You're right. It is time for me to leave. And you're coming with me. Now. You can ride with me. One of my men will follow in your car."

"I think not." And then things happened very fast.

When I was a kid, I was fascinated with who history thought was the fastest gunman in the Wild, Wild, West. Many thought it was Wild Bill Hickok. Others claimed it was Johnny Ringo, who took on Wyatt Earp and died under mysterious circumstances.

I would practice facing my bedroom mirror, over and over, wearing a huge white Stetson hat my dad got me for my birthday one year, along with pearl-handled fake six shooters. I would draw, fire and then blow the pretend smoke from the end of the gun. I got to where I was fast. It has paid off many times over my career.

She was faster than I ever could have been. Her hand flew to the gun tucked into the back of her jeans, then her arm straightened, pointed through the car window and she pulled the trigger, shooting Deveraux's thug in the stomach before he could so much as take a breath. Her hand was a blur I could barely follow. Damn.

The gun's sound was large in the quiet of the night. I could almost picture the entire neighborhood stopping whatever they were doing and trying to decide if what they heard was a gun shot or a car backfire.

In a moment they would have no doubts. I rose to a shooting position, watching as Deveraux's two men pulled guns from shoulder holsters, and started to draw a bead on Elizabeth.

Using the car door for cover, she crouched and headed to the back of the car, while Deveraux dove inside his, pulling the door closed behind him. I squeezed off a quick three shot burst from the UMP, taking one of the men down. From somewhere off to my right, I heard another shot and the second man was down for the count, neither having fired a shot. Score one for Winston.

I moved from my covered position and closed in on the Town car, with plans to air out the backseat where Deveraux was hiding. The car's driver must have dropped the car into reverse as the rear wheels spun gravel, dragging the car backwards and away.

I pushed the switch on my UMP to full auto and squeezed the trigger. Bullets hammered the front windshield, six-hundred rounds a minute, but all they did was spider the glass. Bullet proof glass. To stop the kind of rounds I was firing, I knew the windows must be made from two inches of a polycarbonate and lead glass layers.

Elizabeth moved into view, firing her own shots at Deveraux, but doing no more damage than I did. The car did a swerving three point turn, tires churning up the grass and knocking down a tombstone, and floored it down the cemetery drive.

I emptied the thirty round clip, dropped the magazine and pulled the spare from my back pocket, then slapped it in and got off a few more rounds before the Town car made it to the street. The tires squealed as it swerved into traffic and disappeared from view. The body of the car was punctured with dozens of bullet holes, but my guess is the people inside were protected by bullet proof plating.

I dropped my gun to my side, frustrated and pissed. I turned to Elizabeth, my mind flooding with questions, when her eyes went wide, and she grabbed me by the front of my shirt, lifted me off my feet and threw me into the newly dug grave as easily as I would push a small child to the ground.

A fraction of a second later, a bullet passed through the space she tossed me out of, and struck her in the chest, causing her to stagger. A clean shot, center mass. Laying on my back in the grave, I could see her face travel from shock, to anger. Yet she did not fall to the ground dead.

Winston's voice shouted in my ear, "Mausoleum to your right."

I stood, my head barely clearing the top of the hole, facing the mausoleum, and let loose, with Winston doing the same. The gunman who had snuck up behind me, followed the same path I had moments before. He danced in place as each bullet struck him, then fell to the ground dead.

I quickly scanned the area for another shooter, but found none and turned to face to Elizabeth. She stood there for a moment, then raised her shirt and looked at the wound. A black hole showed where the bullet entered, slightly below and between her breasts. She let the shirt fall back into place and then she sprinted past me to the dead shooter and began kicking and stomping him, over and over.

I was stunned. She should be dead. In my ear, Winston asked, "How is she still alive? Man, she was shot. I saw her take the bullet for you. How's she still breathing?"

I pulled myself out of my would-be grave, walked over to her, my gun raised and pointed at her head, my blood frozen in my veins. I knew how. The strength to throw me around like a rag doll, the incredible speed drawing her gun, taking a rifle shot and living to talk about it? A deal made with Satan?

She was a vampire.

442

CHAPTER SIXTEEN

A vampire.

I'd been sleeping, eating and driving around with a vampire. Elizabeth stopped stomping the man on the ground, took a step back, her breathing still hard. The man's body was barely recognizable, with every bone from the neck up crushed flat, blood and gore spreading on the ground where his head used to be and spattered over her black shoes.

She watched me for a moment, her face expressionless. Then she slowly tucked her gun back into her jeans at the small of her back, her movements exaggerated, my guess in hopes of keeping me calm.

Satan allowed twelve people, twelve truly evil people, to have a second chance at life on earth. His versions of the twelve disciples. When they died the second time, they were stuck in Hell forever. But while back on earth, they were directed to do Satan's bidding and cause as much chaos as humanly possible.

I'd fought one once before by the name of Eamon. A demented little prick who died the first time during the potato famine in Ireland back in the 1800's. He'd nearly beaten me to a pulp before Samantha took his head off with a sword. Samantha told me they'd been the inspiration for the vampire legends from centuries ago.

There are several ways to kill them. You can burn them, grind them up, or cut off their heads. I did have a short sword, but it was in my duffle behind the oak tree.

"A frickin' vampire? Really?"

She shot me a dirty look. "We hate the name vampire. We are not vampires. Can we help it if humans can't understand us, so they make up things?"

"But you don't deny it?" I'd pressed the button on my com so Winston could hear the conversation. I could only imagine what he thought.

"No, I don't deny it. I am one of the *Infernus Domini*. But I wish to no longer be so. I wish to…change."

"Change? You wish to change? A vampire wants to change. Sure. And I want to be a jockey in the Kentucky Derby, but that ain't happenin' either."

She tilted her head, like a dog does when it hears a dog whistle. "We must go. The police are on the way. I can hear the sirens."

I could not, but then again I didn't have super human hearing. "We need to go? Sister, I'm not going anywhere else with you."

"If you wish to stop what this Deveraux has planned, then you and I must work together to stop him. It is the only way."

I could now faintly hear the sirens. She moved by me, walking to the Mercedes. "What will it be, Hand of God? Without me and my contacts, you will have rough time stopping this man."

I stood still for a moment, then made my decision. "Wait one second."

I jogged back to the oak, grabbed my duffle, ran to the Mercedes and threw my gear in the back. The vamp got in behind the wheel and I hopped into the passenger seat.

"What are you doing," Winston practically yelled in my ear.

"Following my instincts. Get away from here. I will call you later."

I turned off the com-link, reached behind me and tossed it into my duffle bag.

The vamp floored the Mercedes and it jumped forward, her natural reflexes matching the response of the car effortlessly. We came out of the cemetery, turned left and hit the ramp for I-270. Looking over my shoulder I could see the cops coming around the corner and then heading into the cemetery. Won't they have fun?

She eased the car into traffic and punched the cruise button. She reached over and turned on the radio, and I quickly turned it back off.

"What, we talk now?" she asked.

"Hell yes, we talk now. Why are you really doing this? What's you game plan?"

She didn't answer at first. Then in a quiet voice said, "You have never been to Hell. If you had, you would know why."

She was right. I'd never been to Hell. But Satan gave me a taste of what Hell would be like for my brother, the day he visited me in my office. The vision lasted less than a minute. The memory would haunt my nightmares for as long as I lived.

"But why now? How old are you?" It was weird. When Satan gave the people he chose a second time at bat, they came returned in the same condition they were when they died. Elizabeth must have died young. She was nearly flawless.

"I am sorry. But I am not permitted to discuss such things. I am older than you, which is all you need know."

"What did you do to deserve another chance among the living?" There were only twelve of them at any one time. Satan did not send back low level evil people. Only the crème de la crème of the most wicked people to have ever lived got the call.

"Many bad things. More bad things than we have time to discuss. What does it matter? I am one of the damned. I would like not to be."

"*Infernus Domini*. My Latin is a bit rusty. Inferno Master?"

"Inferno Lords. Lords of the Inferno. I wish to no longer be such." She paused for a few beats. "You know what I am. Yet you come with me. I am surprised at this."

"Like you said earlier, you could have killed me any one of a number of times, but didn't. I still don't trust you, but I am curious. I am trying to understand what you want from me."

"The final battle for who will sit in Heaven is drawing closer. From all I see, I am on the losing team. When we lose the last battle, then I will be back in Hell. Maybe it is not possible to be redeemed. But I think so. So I will do what I can to help you."

There is no doubt not going back to Hell would be incentive enough for anyone. It wasn't exactly Club Med, even for those who were high in the good graces of the Lord of Evil.

On the other hand, I don't think a tiger can change its stripes even if she wanted to do so. Mikey sold his soul to Satan and it was clear he could not be saved. True, he wasn't trying to be saved, so I guess he didn't work as a blueprint.

If I was a betting man, switching sides because you wanted to live in a better home in the end was not reason enough to be saved. Not like I was the man to make the decision. One thing I did know, it was my job to kill the person sitting in the driver's seat.

"And if you can't be saved? What then?"

"There is no way to know if I can or can't. I can only do what I can. I must. But I am afraid. For maybe the first time in my life, I am afraid."

Good call on that one. "I'm not sure how I'm even supposed to respond to what you're saying."

"Will you help me? To find redemption?"

"I can't help you find what doesn't exist. I can talk to some people. See what they think. But this is a longshot, you know this, right?"

"What else can I do, Victor? You tell me?"

A single tear tracked down her cheek. It did make her appear more human. Yet for all I knew, this was part of her shtick. She claimed she was good at intelligence work and playing different rolls would come easy to someone in her line of work. Was she playing me? Certainly. Was the tear genuine? Perhaps.

All I could do was run out the string and see what happened. And be ready for anything. At least I now knew what I was dealing with. Hells bells, riding with one of Satan's top killers. It felt like riding down the highway with a sleeping cobra. When it woke up, what would happen next? If nothing else, it did give me a chance to learn a few things.

"A few other questions. When you got shot, did it hurt?"

"Not like it would have before my rebirth." She raised her T-shirt and I could see the bullet wound was no longer there, the blackened hole now a slight smudge on her skin. "It is more like discomfort. But I heal again, quickly."

"Can Satan track where you are? Does he have like a spiritual connection?"

"No. We are independent. Once we are sent back, we have free will. But rebellion against the Lord of Light by one of the Inferno Lords has never happened. I am the first. It means when I die, if I go back to Hell, then my punishment will be worse than you or I can ever imagine. I have risked all for a chance to be redeemed."

"Do you keep in touch with the other eleven Inferno Lords? Do you guys have like a clubhouse? Membership dues?"

"You are a silly man. There are no dues. Once a year we must meet, all in the same place, with the Lord of Light. If we cannot make it, we must get word to Lord of Light."

"Let me make a suggestion. If you do wish to ever get to Heaven, then I suggest you stop calling Lucy the Lord of Light. Just sayin'. When is the next group meeting?" Lucy was the pet name Dominic Montoya had for Lucifer. I kept up the tradition.

"It is always the same night. The last night of October."

"You can't be serious? Halloween?" These guys were trying hard to meet every stereotype.

"Once again, people take what they don't understand, and create something they can deal with. It was not uncommon for the Lords to leave the meeting and terrorize whatever country we were in for the rest of the night."

"Where will the next meeting take place?"

"We never know. w. The month before I will have a dream which will tell me where to be. It is up to me to show. I will not be there this year, no matter what happens. Refusing to join this Deveraux to meet with the

Lord—, my former master, declares my rebellion. I am now on a path with no return."

Sucks to be you, I thought. But if I could find out where they were meeting and the exact time, perhaps I could find a way to wipe out all twelve at one time.

But as soon as I started to think "what if" in my head, I just as quickly thought "why bother?" Even if I managed to kill all of them, Lucifer would tap twelve more on the shoulder and send them back to torture and torment all over again.

Lord, I needed a drink. I remembered my uncle used to carry a flask around of "tea." The only thing the contents of the flask and tea, however, had in common was the color, as it was normally filled with a cheap Irish whiskey. Right now? I would have given just about anything to have a flask in my duffle. My North Carolina flask sat on the end table in my room at the mission.

My phone beeped and I pulled it out, expecting to find a text from Winston berating me for losing my mind. Instead, it was Kurt. He found something in the hacker's computers and needed to talk to me right away. I texted him indicating I would call him in a minute.

"Is that the person you had at the cemetery? I asked you not to bring anyone else with us."

"What was it you said before? Trust but verify? I wanted to make sure I had someone there watching my back. If you were on my side, he was watching yours, too."

She pouted for a moment, then put her hand on my thigh, running it to my crotch. "I forgive you."

I took her hand in mine and moved it over to her side of the car. "I think under the circumstances, I would like to keep the hand of an Inferno Lord away from Mr. Happy. Nothin' personal."

She once again stuck her tongue out at me. "Your loss," she replied.

Losing a part of me was exactly what I wanted to avoid.

CHAPTER SEVENTEEN

Kurt answered my call on the first ring.

"Hey, big guy. How did things go up in Columbus? Did you get him?"

"No. I don't think so." I filled him in on what happened, leaving out the part about the woman next to me being a vampire.

"Well, that sucks. We'll get him. Just a matter of time. And I may have a clue to what they have planned. You said they wanted you dead now because they have something in the works and I think you're right. I've been making headway into cracking the files on Benedict Arnold's computer. I've gotten into his emails and one thing they asked him to do was to keep track of what this dude is doing in Alexandria, Virginia. They told him it's a high priority that he must keep a cyber-watch on the guy's computers."

"Alexandria, Virginia? Any idea what he's doing for them? What's his name?"

A fraction of a second passed before both Kurt and the vamp said the name at the same time, "Isaac Peck."

I stared for a moment at the vamp, while Kurt said, "Not sure exactly what he's doing for them. I'll try to hack into Peck's system later tonight. Ruth Anne and I are going to see *The Rocky Horror Picture Show.* I'll hit it hard when we return from the movie. Well, once Ruth Anne goes to bed. Sometimes she wants to, well, you know," he stammered.

"No. She sometimes wants to...what?" I liked yanking Kurt's chain. He may now be the "new" Kurt, but there was still a lot of the "old" Kurt left in him. I could practically see the blush coming through the phone.

"Dude, I'm not telling you details. I don't tell war stories. That's between us. Sheesh." He hung up on me and I put the phone away.

"How did you know who my friend was going to name?"

She drove for another mile, the darkness crowding around us, before she answered. I watched her closely in the glow of the dashboard lights.

"Because that is the name of a man they pay me to get close to in Alexandria. I was the first contact. This could not be coincidence."

"Did they tell you why?"

"No. They did not share the why. But they want him for a project they were working on."

"Why you? What did they tell you?"

"They want me to get him to fall in love with me. To get him to do what I ask. I do this. He is very needy. I don't think he spend much time with a woman. It was easy."

"So you slept with him. Is this why you slept with me? To get me to do what you wanted?"

"Of course I slept with him. He is what is called...a genius. But he think more with what is in his pants than his brain when it comes to beautiful women," she stated in serious tone. "And no, I do not sleep with you to get you to do what I want. I sleep with you because it is what I want."

I'm not sure I believed her when it came to her motives for sleeping with me, but I didn't make an issue of it. "What type of genius? What does he do?"

"Again. Not sure. He make robots or something. When I had him wrapped around my finger, I asked him to work with this one guy. Told him it would make me happy. He agreed. Then later they pulled me away from him to come meet you."

"You were supposed to get me to fall in love with you, too?"

"Yes. They bring me to Louisville, but then you showed up in North Carolina killing one of their men, and they had me change plans to meet them in Tennessee. But they were pigs and I not like them. Then I meet you, and I made a decision to help you instead and here we are."

Once again, I'm sure there was a grain of truth in what she was telling me, but how much? "You said you introduced Peck to a man. What's the guy's name?"

She shook her head. "I don't know. But I do have his picture. I take it the night I introduce him to Isaac. I not tell him I do this."

She slipped her phone out of her front pocket, thumbed to her photos app and pulled up the picture, showing it to me. "You know this man?"

I took a long look at the picture and searched my memory. "Yeah. I know him." The name came to me. "Brad. His name is Brad. Does that sound familiar?"

"I never know his name. He met Isaac and me one night out at dinner. He sat down and I left. I told Isaac he must do what this man say, if he and I were to stay lovers. Isaac would have killed his own mother, if I'd asked him to do so. Who is this man?"

"The last time I saw him, he was driving for Congressman Cyrus

Tyler." In Elizabeth's photo he was still sporting his flat top haircut. I remember he mentioned he was ex-Marine. "My guess is he does a lot more than drive. If this is the man who was meeting with your Isaac, then you can bet Tyler is mixed up in this. You know about Tyler, right?"

"We have never met. But yes, I know of this man. He is one of the main followers of my former master. I understand he is also big in your government. I spend most of my time in Europe. They brought me to this country for Isaac. Then you."

"Gee, thanks. Let me see what I can find out about Isaac Peck."

I tapped my screen until I found the Google app, typed in Peck's name and hit the search button. A second later, several entries popped up, including the top heading under news. The headline? "Young Entrepreneur Murdered at Work."

I pulled up the article from the *Washington Post*, dated this morning indicating he was shot three times. There was no forced entry and nothing stolen, as far as anyone could tell. He was the owner of a company called Bio-Enhanced Robotics. The cops had yet to develop any leads. They found it curious he had given the staff Friday afternoon off, having never done so in the past, fueling speculation he was meeting with someone.

The rest of the article was dedicated to his background and his philanthropic endeavors. I closed the app and turned off my phone.

"Seems your former boyfriend is dead. Someone shot him yesterday." I gave her the run down on the newspaper article.

"This cannot be coincidence. We must go there."

"We are not going anywhere. If I decide to check it out, I will go on my own. I haven't decided what to do about you yet."

"You will take me with you. This I know." She smiled and I didn't like it.

"Look, Elizabeth. You saved my life and I thank you. You say you want to redeem your soul. I wish you luck. But when I say you won't be going with me, I mean it. I can't trust you as far as I can throw you." I didn't add in the thought I would also likely kill her, sooner rather than later.

"You will take me because I know something else you don't know," she paused and looked at me. "About Isaac."

"And what, pray tell, would that be?"

"Isaac was scared of this Brad, and who he worked for. They tell him not to keep any records of what he do for them. But he did. He called it his CYA file. You know what this mean?"

"Yeah. Cover Your Ass. Where did he keep it? Surely the cops have already found it."

She shook her head no. "They will not have. He hid the file where only he would find it. And one night he told me. I know where this file is and how to get it."

"O.K...Where and how?"

She wagged a finger at me. "I will not tell you. I will show you. You must take me with you."

"And if I refuse?"

"Then you will need much luck. If they kill Isaac, and try and kill you, then they are close to putting into action what they have planned. Perhaps you can find out what and stop them without the file. Perhaps not. Are you willing to run the risk?"

She had me over a barrel and she knew it. I needed to get a look at that file. No matter what Cy Tyler and his crew planned, I knew it was something horrific. I needed every edge possible and the things Peck hid in this file might give me one. But if it meant working with an Inferno Lord, was it worth it?

Would the ends justify the means? While I couldn't be sure, I was fairly certain working with one of Satan's twelve super villains would not be something Joshua would want me to do. But if I didn't, and this was another plan to murder thousands of innocent children? Or release another plague on the world like the Watchers? Or worse?

When I was nothing more than a bounty hunter, I often worked with people who were only shades better than the ones I was hunting. Was this situation any different? Well. Yeah. Elizabeth was more than your average scum ball.

I would have to think carefully about what I did next. Another thought occurred to me. What if the goal had not been to kill me, but to keep me occupied chasing phantoms which had nothing to do with the real objective? If so, Elizabeth could be leading me around by the nose, keeping me busy until it was too late.

We drove on through the night, neither of us talking, both lost in our own thoughts. When we got close to Louisville, I said, "Fine. You can go with me. I will need to make some plans and talk to my crew. If you do go, you will do what I tell you to do, when I tell you to do it. Understood?"

She blew me a kiss. "Of course, Victor. I will be an angel for you."

Wrong choice of words, lady, I thought. Your chance of being an angel ended a long time ago.

CHAPTER EIGHTEEN

It was after 1 a.m. when she pulled up to the Galt House drop off area. I was worn out, the adrenaline of the fight had worn off a long time ago. I started to get out of the car, but she put her hand over mine, stopping me.

She opened the car's console, took out a pen and then turned my hand over, writing a phone number on my palm. "This is my new cell number. The phone will be off, with the battery removed, until eight tomorrow morning. I will turn it on so you can call me. I give you fifteen minutes. After that, the battery is back out. I will not stay here tonight. You call me in the morning and let me know what you plan to do."

I glanced at the number, then back into her ice blue eyes. "What, you don't trust me?"

"No further than I can throw you. Though, I throw you a long way," she replied.

Thinking about how easily she threw me into the open grave, I knew she wasn't bragging, but stating the cold hard truth. "Suit yourself."

I climbed out of the car, opened the rear door, snagging my duffle. I walked around to the driver side window, and she rolled it down.

"If you run on me, I will dedicate my life to tracking you down and breaking that pretty little neck."

"I will not run. I promise you I will help. And I will."

She rolled the window up and drove off, leaving me standing there, thinking hard. I'd threatened her, trying to push her buttons, to get a reaction. She claimed she wanted to change, to find a way to redeem her soul. But how in the hell could I know if she really meant it?

She hadn't jumped at the bait, threatened me back, or seemed pissed. She'd answered in a matter-of-fact way, and left. If I'd hoped to learn something, I didn't.

I dragged my ass to my car parked in the hotel garage and returned to the mission. I took the long way, changing directions and moving slowly through downtown, watching for tails. Nada.

I pulled into the parking lot, grabbed my stuff and locked the car. I pushed through the front door and could see Brother Joshua's light in his office down the hallway. I wondered whether he ever slept.

I thought about heading to his office and hashing out what happened tonight, what I'd learned about Elizabeth, but decided to hell with it. I was tired and all I wanted right then was to go to bed. And that's what I did. I went to my room, kicked off my boots and fell into bed, still dressed. I drifted off to thoughts of Elizabeth and how both of us wanted the same thing: redemption. And that both of us might not get it.

If I dreamed, I didn't remember them the next morning. I woke up around seven, stiff and sore. I wrote her number down on a notepad, then ambled to the shower, cranked up the hot water, and worked out the kinks. By the time I got dressed and headed to J's office, I felt almost human. Almost.

His door was open, so I knocked on the door jam and stuck my head in the door. J was sitting behind his desk, as usual, calm and composed. Good thing because, occasionally, he found himself hosting the essence of the archangel, Uriel. I could generally tell when Uriel was with us because the man oozed power when the angel made an appearance. When the Watchers claimed possession of someone's body against their will, Joshua allowed Uriel to take control. Freaky.

Today, J was his normal self. The woman sitting in the chair opposite him, however, was anything but normal. She was tall, her long blonde hair tied back in a ponytail. Dressed in a white shirt, brown leather vest and pants, with what I thought of as elf boots, she looked like a Tolkien wet dream. The sword laying across her lap didn't hurt the look.

She turned to face me, her features hard and unforgiving. She had high cheek bones, a prominent chin and hazel eyes which held as much warmth as an Icelandic glacier. She looked me over like she was trying to decide if I needed to be welcomed or dispatched. I thought her sword hand may have twitched, but that might have been my imagination. She would not be the first woman to react that way around me.

The sword was some type of katana, the handle worked in silver with what looked like a family crest on the pommel.

"Nice toothpick you're carrying around. Bet it drives all the boys crazy."

Her eyes narrowed. "You might want to watch your tongue before I cut it out."

I laughed and looked to J. "Who's this Xena warrior princess wannabe?"

She stood, the sword held tight against her thigh. "I will not warn you again to watch your tongue. I would choose your next words carefully."

"Whoa, slow down, princess. I'm guessing when you were born, you missed the line where God handed out a sense of humor."

Joshua stood. "Mirsada, please. Victor, show our guest more respect. She is, after all, a fellow Hand of God."

The statement hit me like a thunderbolt. "Hand of God? I'm the Hand of God. You mean, there's more than one?"

She pointed at me with the sword, as incredulous as I was about the revelation. "This is the man you were telling me about? This...this..." She was at a loss for words.

"Yes," Joshua said to the woman. "Victor is the Hand of God we were talking about." Then to me he continued, "And, Victor, surely you must have guessed there was more than one Hand of God. This is a very large planet, after all. Victor McCain, meet Mirsada Vesela."

"To be honest, J., I've been too busy trying to kill things that were usually trying to kill me to stop and give it much thought."

Lowering her sword, Mirsada relaxed, but only by a smidgen. "I am sorry. I expected something different."

"Yeah, most women tell me that." I glanced between the two of them. "Where do you call home?"

She sat back down and I took the chair next to hers. "I am from Bosnia, but was educated here in the States. I am tracking a woman I have reason to believe is here. And when I find her, I will then remove her head."

Bloody hell, I thought. Removing heads? Needing a sword? I knew the answer to my next question, but I asked it anyway. "This woman, does she have a name?"

"Yes. Elizabeth Bathory. The Countess of Blood. And a member of Satan's twelve demons let loose on Earth."

Hells bells, did I have to be right? Now I knew Elizabeth's last name, which tickled the back of my mind. I remembered reading about her when I was younger.

"Countess of Blood? I think I've heard of her. She's from your neck of the woods, right?"

Mirsada nodded. "Yes. She died the first time in the year 1614. She earned her name because of her torture and murder of nearly six-hundred and fifty young girls. She believed their blood could keep her young, taking baths filled with the blood of virgins. Following her death, she struck a deal with Satan to stay young forever, but this time instead of bathing in blood of young girls, she agreed to spill the blood of as many innocents as she can, no matter the age."

"Sounds like a real witch. I hope you catch up to her." I was stalling.

I didn't want to tip my hand to what I knew until I got the chance to talk it over with J. But his next question torpedoed my delay tactics.

He asked, "This woman you have met, you said she sounded like she was from Europe and claimed to have worked for Hungarian intelligence. This cannot be a coincidence. Do you think this woman is Bathory?"

"I would like the chance to talk to you about what I think, in private." I looked at Mirsada. "No offense."

She practically seethed. "Of course you mean offense. If you know where this woman is, you must tell me. Now."

"Hold your horses, sister. This isn't your home base, it's mine. You have no right to come here and make demands."

"Enough," Joshua said. "Victor, we don't keep secrets from other Hands. If the woman you have met is Elizabeth Bathory, then share what you know."

"Starting with where she is," said Mirsada.

"I don't know where she is. And that's the truth." Only barely, as I had not called her yet this morning. I needed to be careful. I wanted time to think things through, but lying to Joshua would not be good for my eternal soul. "I suspect this woman is who you claim. Yet she saved my life and has information about the plans of Cyrus Tyler. They targeted me because they have something major in the works. She has offered to help me. As hard as it is to believe, she claims she wants to redeem her soul."

Mirsada laughed. "She is playing you. Like so many others in the past. Let me guess. She took you to bed? Am I right?"

It was all I could do to not blush. I didn't answer.

"This is what she does. She seduces men to get what she wants. Then she kills them."

"If she wanted me dead, then she could have killed me several times by now."

"Which means," Mirsada continued, "she has yet to get from you what she wants. The knife in the back is coming. You are too stupid to realize it."

"Stupid? Why do I get the feeling you don't play well with others. But what if you're wrong, and what she wants from me is to help her soul to go to Heaven? What then?" I looked to Brother Joshua. "Is such a thing possible?"

He steepled his fingers under his chin, thinking. "I don't know. It would be unprecedented. None of the Twelve has ever sought redemption before."

"But it's possible?"

"Yes," he replied. "I would think it possible."

"No, it is not," said Mirsada. "She cannot change. Will not. She is working for Satan and it will mean your death to trust her."

"And if I have no choice? If she holds the only key to stop Tyler? What then? What if killing her now means the death of thousands? Millions? The first time I ran into these wackos they planned to kill thousands of children. I stopped them, but barely. Until we know more, killing her is a risk."

For a long moment, Mirsada was silent. "She cannot be trusted." And that's all she would say.

"Hell, lady. I don't trust her. It's as much my job to kill her as it is yours. But I've seen what these guys are capable of doing. No matter what Tyler has planned, he needs to be stopped. She might be the key to bringing him down."

"And if it means your death?" she asked.

"Lord's will be done. What do you think, J?"

"It is not for me to tell you what to do. You are both the Hand of God. You must make your own choices and live with the consequences."

"You know, J, there are times you frustrate the hell out of me, you know that? You could tell me, but you won't."

"It comes down to—"

"Yeah, yeah, yeah. Free will. I know. But you have a direct pipeline to the Big Guy upstairs and could make this really simple for me." He started to say something, but I waved him off. "Never mind."

I stood and started for the door. Mirsada also stood and began to follow me. "Where do you think you're going?" I asked.

"You say she wants to help you. Which means she will contact you again. When she does I will be there as well. Where you go, I will also go."

"And if I tell you to kiss my ass? What then?"

"I have tracked her here. Do you really think you can lose me? I will be with you, no matter what you wish."

I appealed to Brother Joshua. "Dude. Really?"

He said, "One Hand of God has always extended cooperation to another Hand of God. In her own way, Mirsada is asking for your help. But again, the choice is yours."

"Great. Thanks a lot." I turned to face Mirsada. "If I allow you to come with me, you do as I say. My house, my rules. If you can't agree, then you're on your own. And I *will* lose you if you say no. Want to risk it? This isn't exactly my first rodeo. And I've already killed a vamp. How about you?"

She shot a look at Joshua. "This is true?" He nodded it was and her attitude softened. The way a mountain loses a few pebbles when a hard rain hits it.

"Your house, your rules. Unless the game changes. Then I use my rules."

"And no killing Elizabeth until I say so. I want your word as the Hand of God you won't make her a head shorter until I say so. This is a deal breaker."

She walked to the door and picked up a small pack next to it, along with a sheath for her sword. She slid the katana home, the pommel still visible. "For now, I give you my word. I hope you will not be the death of both of us."

"That makes two of us," I thought.

CHAPTER NINETEEN

We stepped out into the steamy morning, the temperature already soaring. I glanced at Mirsada's outfit. "Doesn't the leather get a bit hot?"

"I am used to the feeling. I wear leather because it is stronger than regular cloth, better protection during a fight. The heat is but a minor inconvenience."

"Whatever floats your boat. Does Elizabeth know you are after her?"

"Yes. She does. It's one of the reasons she left Europe. I got close to finding her on two occasions. I made sure to burn her bridges behind her, trying to force her into the open. Her old contacts were no longer willing to protect her."

"Great. This should be a real joy." It was now eight a.m. straight up. I took out my phone, along with the note with Elizabeth's number and called her.

She answered, "You are punctual. Rare for most men."

"Yeah, right. Whatever. Everyone's a comedian. Are you ready to hit the road?"

"Yes. I will drive."

"Not this time. I get to drive. And we will have someone with us."

She paused, before asking, "Your friend who was at the cemetery?"

"Not exactly. An old friend of yours from back home. Woman who dresses in all leather, looks like an elf? Ring any bells?"

Mirsada narrowed her eyes and tightened the grip on her sword, but otherwise remained quiet.

I could hear Elizabeth hiss. "Mirsada. She is there? With you?"

"Yes. She is. And she is coming with us to Alexandria."

"I cannot allow this. I will not travel with this woman. She wants me dead."

"Then I guess you didn't mean it, when you said you wanted to find redemption. She's going with me to Alexandria and she has given me her word she will not try and kill you, without my O.K. When a Hand of God gives their word, they are bound to keep it. Time to prove you meant what you told me, Elizabeth."

For the longest time, she did not say anything. I raised my face to the sky, letting the sun bake my skin, but it did little to warm the cold I felt deep inside.

"This woman. She will kill me. No matter what she promises. She will kill me. You know this, right?"

"Elizabeth, she won't. You have to trust me. As long as you play it straight, she won't lay a hand on you. She will have to go through me first. But understand, you betray us, all bets are off and we both come for you. Time to decide if you want that chance at redemption. You have to trust me."

"You ask much, Victor McCain. She has told you who I really am? My past?"

"Yes. She told me who you are. You are Elizabeth Bathory, the Countess of Blood."

"And yet you say you will protect me? Why?"

Good question. Was I trying to save my brother all over again? Did I not learn anything from what happened with Mikey? The last time I trusted one of the damned, it lead to Dominic Montoya being murdered, setting me on the path I now traveled. This time it could be me taking a bullet, moving over to the ever-after. Yet Brother Joshua didn't say she couldn't be saved. Only that it had never happened.

"Elizabeth, you say you want to help me. I believe you. I'm not sure why, but I do. I will protect you, as long as you keep you word. In return you have my word, as the Hand of God. The decision is yours."

"Then I will trust you, Victor McCain. With my immortal soul. Bring this woman. My life is now in your hands."

"Where do you want us to pick you up?"

"I am here." The phone disconnected and Elizabeth stepped out of the doorway of the building across the street. She stood on the sidewalk, waiting. She once again wore jeans, a white T-shirt and boots, a small travel bag slung over one shoulder.

Mirsada saw her and drew her sword faster than I could have pulled my gun, the bright sunlight glinting off the slender blade. She took a step in Elizabeth's direction, but pulled up short when I moved in front of her.

"Out of my way, Hand. It is time for me to end this."

"You gave me your word, Mirsada. Put the sword away or I will take it from you. To kill her, you will have to kill me first."

Mirsada flicked the sword up, the point digging into the skin under my chin. She moved in close, her face inches from mine. "She is a monster. She will kill us both, given the chance. Join me, Hand of God, and together we can take her before she can leave."

"No. By all that's holy, no. Your word, Mirsada. Does it mean nothing?"

Her lips pulled back from her teeth, a look both feral and fearsome at the same time, and for a moment I thought she would ram the tip of her sword straight up through my chin and out the top of my head. But instead, she dropped it and re-sheathed the blade.

I ran my finger to where the sword had been and came away with a drop of blood. Close. I glanced over at Elizabeth, but she had not moved. With her improved hearing, I knew she'd heard every word. She had a brief chance to escape, to run for it, but she never moved. Trust in me? Maybe.

I unlocked the car and stowed my gear in the rear of the Ford. I held out my hand for Mirsada's bag. She gave it to me and I tossed it in with mine. She held on to the sword.

I got behind the wheel while Mirsada got into the back seat. I looked into the rearview mirror. "No backseat stabbing, O.K.?"

I got no response other than her hard stare. I started the car and pulled up to the curb in front of Elizabeth. She stared for a moment at Mirsada in the back seat holding her sword, then got into the front passenger seat. She did her best to ignore the woman sitting behind her with the deadly weapon.

I asked Elizabeth if she had an address in Alexandria.

"Yes. We go to the Jones Point Lighthouse. It is on the Potomac River, in Alexandria."

She gave me an address and I programmed the GPS for the trip. It did its calculations and told me the trip would take about nine and a half hours to reach our destination, putting us there late in the evening. Nine and a half hours in a car with two pissed off women: one carrying a sword, the other imbued with hellish abilities sitting just inches from me.

The road trip from Hell. Almost literally. Heaven must love me.

CHAPTER TWENTY

Brad Stiles turned into the parking garage of the Double Tree by Hilton on South Broad Street in Philadelphia and made his way to the back corner of the first level. He pulled into a spot next to a black BMW 3 series and turned off his car.

An attractive woman in her late fifties got out of the Beamer, pushed a button on her key fob, and popped open her trunk. Stiles got out of his car, doing the same thing. Walking around to the back, he picked up the wrapped box and carried it over to her vehicle and placed the box carefully into her trunk. Closing the door gently, he faced Dr. Teresa Collins.

"You're almost home, Doc. Perform the surgery tomorrow, as scheduled, and your part is finished."

She glanced around nervously, wringing her hands. "My daughter. When will I get my daughter?"

"For obvious reasons, we will need to hold on to her for a few weeks."

"I promise, I won't tell a soul what I did. I swear it. Please bring my baby home to me."

Dr. Collins' baby, Stiles knew, was thirty years old and a meth head. After getting hooked on prescription drugs, her daughter, Misty, started turning tricks to help support her habit, transitioning from crack to meth. She found her way onto the radar of the Church of the Light Reclaimed and Stiles arranged to have her picked up and admitted into a rehabilitation clinic. After several months, she came out the other side, clean and sober.

The Church found her a good paying job working as an admin for a local law firm, the owner of which was a long time member of the Church.

Dr. Collins at first, was over-joyed at her daughter's transformation. Then came the day they approached the good doctor with their plans and she had balked. Pressure needed to be applied.

Misty went on a business trip with the law firm, but never returned. The Church let Dr. Collins know they had her daughter and the only way she would return, alive and in one piece, was if she did what they wanted. Misty was Collins' only child and they knew she would come around. Eventually she relented and the plan moved forward.

Stiles said, "I tell you what, Doc, when the surgery is over, why don't you take some time off? Use whatever excuse you want. When you get the time off, I will take you to your daughter and you two can hang out until this all blows over."

A single tear tracked down her cheek. "You plan to kill us both, don't you?"

"Doc, that's not how we work. We make you a deal, you take it and we keep our end of the bargain. We already have the money we promised you in the numbered account in the bank in the Caymans. You and your daughter can live out your lives wealthy and well. By this time tomorrow, your part will be done. The surgery is scheduled for seven tomorrow morning, right?"

She nodded. "Yes. We asked him to arrive at 5:45 a.m. for registration. Surgery takes about an hour and a half." She hugged herself. "This means my career is over. All I've worked for will be gone."

"Look, Doc, we've gone to great lengths to see to it that you're not implicated. When the investigation into what happened cranks up, we've created a paper trail that will lead them to a white supremacist group in Georgia. They've been calling for someone to kill the Senator for years. Everything will point to them, not you. You will be completely in the clear. You have my word."

She walked back to her car and opened the door. Before getting in she said, "Your word? I only want my daughter. I do have some time coming to me. I can clear my schedule by Friday. I would greatly love to see my daughter."

She got in, closed the door and started the car. Backing out of the spot, Stiles watched her drive away. When she was gone, he pulled out a burner phone and dialed a number from memory.

A man answered and Stiles told him what he wanted and when.

"The charge will be twice the cost of the first doctor. There are two of them, after all," the man said.

"Not a problem. I will have the timing lined out by the end of the week. Go ahead and move into position."

The man hung up without saying another word and Stiles did the same. He got back into his car and a few moments later was pulling out of the garage and heading to D.C. The Nats lost the night before and he hoped they could turn things around today. He looked at his watch. If the traffic was good, he could even make it to the park and watch the game live.

Whistling *Take Me Out to the Ball Game* he decided a dog and beer at the park would make the day complete.

~*~

I remember one long distance trip my family took to Gulf Shores, Alabama. I must have been around ten years old and the entire trip, Mikey and I fought in the back seat of dad's Oldsmobile. Even dad's threats of a major belt whipping couldn't stop us. Both of us were even afraid to fall asleep for fear of what the other brother might do to them. My mother still calls that vacation the "trip from hell."

Well mom, you ain't seen nothing until you take a long distance trip with a vamp and a Hand of God who want to kill each other. For long stretches of highway, the two would sit quietly, Elizabeth looking out the window, Mirsada staring at the back of her head. Then the same argument would begin again. Like the one which had been going on for the last few miles.

"Why don't you admit your plans to betray us, witch," Mirsada said to Elizabeth. "If you do, I promise your death will be quick. You have my word."

Elizabeth snorted. "Quick death? That can be arranged for you, too, bitch."

I did my best to listen to the music on the radio, pretending I was on my way to Disney World and this would all be over soon, but the problem was I wasn't traveling with Mickey and Goofy.

Mirsada opened her mouth to say something else, but before she could say a word, Elizabeth's hand came out of her bag, holding a Beretta Nano 9 mm, and she pointed it at Mirsada's nose.

"We must come to an agreement, you and I. You do not like me? I understand why. You want to kill me? I understand why. For what I did, in my past, perhaps I even deserve to die. But I make promise to Victor, to help him in any way I can to stop this Tyler. But I grow tired of your constant yapping, like some little dog. Yes, you have big sword, can take off my head. You are good, yes? But I can also kill you. Even easier than you can kill me, I think. Until such time as we find out if you really can be faster with the sword than I with my gun, may we please stop this fight? Let's help Victor. I may even let you kill me, when this is done. I grow tired of this life."

She pulled the gun back and slipped into her purse, and I let out the breath I'd been holding. For her part, Mirsada, who'd pulled her katana partially out, slipped it into the sheath.

I looked out my window at the car passing next to us and a woman stared at me, her mouth hanging open and her eyes wide. I smiled weakly and shrugged. Elizabeth leaned forward, locked eyes with the woman and mimicked shooting her with her finger. The other car sped off in front of us.

I glanced up and watched Mirsada in the rearview mirror and I could see her fighting for control of her anger, the battle playing out across her face. I could understand such anger. It filled me more often than it should or was even good for me. Towering anger, wanting to strike out at anyone or anything.

I didn't doubt she thought less of me for working with a vamp. Hell, I couldn't blame her either. When you become a Hand of God, there are things that go bump in the night and it's our job to slam them back into the deep dark pits they crawled out of and into oblivion.

Working with one, no matter what Elizabeth claimed, was a risky business. Often I went with my gut when it came to decisions and I was not often wrong. And my gut told me Elizabeth was sincere in trying to find her way to heaven. That didn't mean she wouldn't revert to her previous ways when things got tough. Mirsada's anger was understandable.

Mirsada didn't respond to Elizabeth's pistol-backed plea, but she did stop the haranguing, choosing to continue to watch the back of the vamp's head. One didn't need to be a mind reader to tell what she was thinking. Kill.

I wondered at her story. I'd become the Hand of God because of my vanity in thinking I could save my brother's soul proved incorrect, one time my gut had been wrong. I'd allowed Dominic Montoya to be murdered while trying to protect Mikey, even though I knew him to be evil personified. Montoya became the Hand trying to atone for years serving as a hit man for a Mexican drug cartel. One does not come to the job as the Hand of God from being a gentle keeper of souls. The job called for someone to be able to perform incredible acts of violence and to punish those chosen with extreme prejudice.

Mirsada brushed back a stray lock of hair behind one ear, and I could see her hand was scarred and rough, nails at the end of long fingers, cut short and devoid of nail polish. Fighter's hands.

She wore no makeup. Hell, it would be like putting makeup on a wildcat. If you were to stand her in a lineup with other women, you would take one look at her and say "warrior."

The contrast between her and Elizabeth was stark. Now that I knew Elizabeth's past, you could see the regal bearing in her movements, even after all these centuries. She was used to giving orders and confident in every fiber of her hellish being they would be obeyed. I had to guess being given near super human powers only made her feel even more the noble compared to the rest of us.

Mirsada, on the other hand, seemed to be wound tight, her intensity switched on, unable to ever turn it off. I wondered if she was comfortable in her own skin. Hour after hour, she never relaxed, her gaze staying almost strictly on Elizabeth, like two heat-seeking missiles.

Now that no one died in the exchange, I was very happy Elizabeth took steps to end the bickering. If she hadn't, I might have pulled my own gun out and used it on myself.

We stopped for a quick lunch at Wendy's and I learned something else I didn't know about Infernal Lords. While they don't have to eat, some of them still enjoy eating food. In Elizabeth's case, she loved greasy cheeseburgers. Between the sex and her culinary tastes, she could almost be the perfect girl. Other than the whole "most evil woman who ever lived" thing.

Mirsada chose to eat a salad and drink water. I bet she also ran ten miles a day, did five-hundred set ups without breaking a sweat, and saved puppies in her spare time.

I gave myself a mental slap. I needed to cut Mirsada some slack. She was here to kill a woman who, by her own admission, was evil. Or had been. And is there really a difference? Sure, Mirsada was incredibly intense. But I would bet that's what kept her alive. I'd nearly died several times over since taking the job and I was twice her size. Though size wasn't everything. She managed to get the point of her katana under my chin faster than I could blink.

After lunch, we returned to the highway and this time the tension seemed to have been cranked down a few notches. Perhaps breaking bread helped the two women come to some unspoken agreement.

Mile after mile drifted into the rearview mirror as we cruised down I-64 through the mountains of West Virginia, then headed north on I-81 through Virginia. It gave me time to think, especially about Samantha and what the future might hold.

And I didn't think it held much. Deep down inside, I knew a final confrontation was coming with her father and it likely would end with one or the other of us dead. Cyrus was the only family Samantha had left in the world, with her mother dying when she was very young.

What would it mean for the two of us if I ended up putting a bullet between his eyes? Most men, when they worried about a potential father-in-law, wondered how things would go at family gatherings or how protective they would be over their little girls. Here I was worried we might be taking each other out, with the victor burying the body in an unmarked grave. The irony made me laugh out loud, with both women in the car shooting me strange looks.

Samantha knew her father was rotten to the core, yet she loved him, much as I had my brother. While in her heart she might appreciate why I needed to whack her dad, forgiving me for doing so would be another matter.

I could picture the family Christmas parties, all of us standing in front of the fireplace for the family photo, with both Cy Tyler and I pointing guns at each other behind the backs of the rest of the family.

It was hard to imagine. Yet here I was in a car with a vamp on my way to try and ruin yet another one of the congressman's plans. I was willing to bet a vamp and Hand of God, let alone two Hands of God, had never worked together. Strange times.

Night had descended on Alexandria when we came to a stop not far from the Jones Point Lighthouse park front gate. I rolled down the windows and turned off the car, listening to the sounds of the world calling it quits for the day.

The lighthouse surprised me. I pictured a tall lighthouse like I'd seen on the coast of Massachusetts, stretching up into the night sky, but the Jones Point Lighthouse was not. This lighthouse was a two story clapboard building perched on the edge of the shore. The lighthouse tower sat in the middle of the roof, flanked on either end by a chimney. It looked like there was a smaller outbuilding off to one side.

During lunch I'd looked up the history of the lighthouse and park. The Jones Point Lighthouse was the only surviving lighthouse left on the Potomac. Built in 1855, it continued to be used until 1926. Its main use was to keep boats from slamming into the Washington Navy Yard. It switched hands several times in the decades since and the main building was now boarded up to keep out looters and vandals.

The lighthouse was part of a federal park and a large sign said the park would be open until ten p.m. It was now twenty after ten and a large gate closed off the parking lot from traffic, so this was as close as we were going to get by car. I turned slightly in my seat and looked at Elizabeth. "O.K. We're here. What next?"

"I'll show you." She opened her door and got out. I reached up, turned off the interior lights and then Mirsada and I both joined her. I told Elizabeth to wait a second, walked to the back of the Ford, lifted the hatch and accessed my hidden weapons locker. I opened a side flap and got Mirsada a Glock like mine and another clip.

I handed them to her. "I noticed you weren't carrying. Figured you might want one." She took the gun and clip and slipped them inside her leather vest, sliding neatly into a hidden pocket.

"My thanks. Your TSA does not take kindly to foreigners bringing in guns. Getting in my sword was hard enough."

I nodded my sympathy. I tucked mine into the back of my jeans, pulling my shirt down over the gun to cover it, then I got a Maglite flashlight and offered it to Elizabeth.

"I do not need it. I see fine in the dark." I would have sworn she sounded smug, but it could have been my imagination.

"Of course you do. How silly of me." I motioned for her to lead the way. She walked near the front gate, turning right and followed it around and into the woods nearby, I followed her and Mirsada followed me. The heat, barely reduced despite the hour, caused my shirt to stick to my chest. I slapped occasionally at mosquitoes who seemed to view every bare section of skin as their personal banquet. Damn bugs.

Walking deeper into the darkness, it became harder to see and I brought out the Maglite, turning it on for Mirsada and myself. Through gaps in the trees we could see the bay and lights shining on the other side of the Potomac River and hear the traffic from behind us on the Capital Beltway. A bit further down the river, I could see fog rolling in, devouring lights as it drifted in our direction.

Elizabeth stopped between two large oaks while her eyes scanned the brush nearby. Finding what she was looking for, she strode up to a large hedge of wild blueberries and reached deeply into the bush. When her hand re-emerged, she held a small satchel.

"Isaac loved to come to the park to relax and think. He always carried his backpack with him," Elizabeth said. "A couple of days before he was murdered, he called me to say if something happened to him, to come to our favorite spot, and reach past the dessert. That was code, in case someone was listening. We found this spot during one our visits. Isaac loved the blueberries and would eat a couple of handfuls every time we came here. This was the first spot where we..."

She trailed off. Mirsada finished the thought. "Where you had sex with him. Little did he know he was sleeping with the enemy."

Elizabeth bristled. "I was *not* his enemy. Despite what you may think, I actually liked Isaac. You know not of what you speak, bitch. Keep it up and I may forget my promise to Victor."

Before things could get out of hand, I stepped between them, both hands up. "Ladies, ladies. Instead of fighting each other, how 'bout we open up the bag and see what he left for us to find."

They stood and glared at one another in the glow of my Maglite, but Elizabeth broke eye contact first and practically ripped open the satchel. I shined my light into the bag, showing its contents.

The first thing I pulled out of it was a label. I tipped it towards the light so I could read the writing. It was from Dabney Industrial Tech and it listed a serial number. Nothing else. I knew from my time in the military that Dabney was a weapons manufacturer, but they also owned many other companies. I showed it to both women and they both shrugged. I tucked the label into my pocket. I would have Kurt track down what Dabney made which used this type of label.

Next out was a small pamphlet. In the glow of the Maglite I could tell I was holding a copy of the U.S. Constitution. I flipped quickly through the pamphlet, but there were no notes or markings inside. I shook my head in frustration.

The last thing in the bag was a single folded sheet of paper. I opened it all the way, and began reading what to me was gobbledygook. There was a diagram of what appeared to be an electric circuit, but beyond that I had no clue what the rest entailed.

The two women crowded in, one on each side, and they had no more clue about the paper than I did. "What the hell?" I asked. "I was a history major, not electrical engineering."

"Isaac was very smart. It is what made him attractive to the Church. That and his cocaine habit. They kept him supplied and on their leash."

"I'll have to check with a few people, see if they can figure out what this is all about." I refolded the paper and shoved it into my pocket with the label. "If he was so smart, why didn't he leave something more useful? You know, like a taped video of what the hell they were up to instead of all this Da Vinci Code crap?"

Elizabeth was about to answer when she stiffened, her eyes darting around. She hissed, "Turn off your light, now."

I did so and strained to hear what might have spooked her, but I couldn't hear anything. The fog began to ease between the trees, causing our path to the car to disappear with the lights in the parking lot.

"What's going—" I didn't get anything else out as she covered my mouth with her hand. I could hear Mirsada behind me draw her sword from its sheath, the blade whispering as it cleared the leather. I yanked my gun from my jeans and held it down by the side of my leg.

Then I heard it. Laughter. But not "ha-ha, funny" kind of laughter, but crazy as a loon kind of laughter. And it was getting closer.

"Muramasa. It's Muramasa," whispered Elizabeth, the closest thing resembling fear I'd ever heard in her voice.

"And that would be?" Mirsada asked.

"Muramasa Sengo. Former swordsmith to generations of samurai warriors. One of the greatest swordsmiths to have ever lived. He went mad before he died and it is believed all of his blades possess some of that madness. And now, he is an Infernal Lord."

A sword wielding samurai madman vampire, in a fog, at night. What could go wrong?

CHAPTER TWENTY-ONE

The laughter was coming from the direction of the lighthouse. "Can you guys see through fog?" I asked Elizabeth, my voice pitched softly enough for only her and Mirsada to hear. So I thought.

"No. But we don't have to. Our improved hearing will guide him in our direction. There is no need to whisper. Speak normally or not at all."

I turned my light back on. "Then there is no need for us to go around in the dark." I flicked the light around, but there was not much to see as the fog engulfed us. "Can you take him?"

She glanced around looking for the best way out. "On an open field, with clear vision, we would be nearly even. But I cannot say. Now that I've made my intentions clear, I think he is here for me, not you. There is little which frightens an Infernal Lord more than a sword in the hands of a Master."

"Then let him come," Mirsada said. "I've trained my whole life in the use of the sword. He will find me no coward."

"Then you are an idiot. You will not be facing any average swordsman. But one of the greatest the world has ever known. He has spent the last few centuries getting even better. You will be like a child to him. But please, why do you not see if you are better, while Victor and I try and return to the car?"

"Damn it, will you two give it a rest? Elizabeth, try and lead us back to the car and let us know if you think he is close. I have something in the car which might slow his ass down."

Elizabeth started out, Mirsada right behind her and I brought up the rear. We could only see about five feet in any direction. Trees seemed to spring out of nothing to block our way, and branches slapped against my face and arms.

By my guess we were about half-way to the car when Elizabeth first froze, then dove to the ground, doing a quick somersault and landing in a crouch as Muramasa stepped forward, his sword whistling through the air where she had stood only seconds before. Without the dive, Elizabeth would be a head shorter.

I raised my gun to take a few shots but stopped short as Mirsada slid forward, her sword snaking out to take the ancient Samurai in the side.

He pivoted with ease, his own sword sweeping sideways, deflecting her strike while never taking his eyes off of Elizabeth. A man of average height, he wore a black silk kimono, tied at the waist with a red sash. A blood red sword sheath was tucked into the sash. His katana gleamed when my flashlight beam struck it. The handle, also blood red, was covered in several symbols I assumed was Japanese, but hell, it could have been Greek for all I knew. The disturbing thing was his Kabuki mask. It was designed from some type of metal, with a large grin showing pointed teeth and two devil horns adorning the top. Unlike most Kabuki masks, this one covered the back of his head as well.

He backed up a step and bowed slightly to Elizabeth. "I did not believe it possible, but it is true. You work with our enemy." He wagged a finger at her. "The Lord of Light will see you suffer for your treason, once I kill you."

Mirsada circled one direction and I the other, as we tried to make him fight multiple fronts.

He gestured in our direction. "Run now. You get head start. I kill her quick. Then come for you. Kill you quick, too. Run now."

Elizabeth picked up a large log about six feet long that I would have struggled to lift, let alone wield as a club. She didn't even break a sweat. "I don't think even your sword can slice through this much wood, Muramasa. Come near me and I will flatten you with this toothpick."

"To hell with this," I thought. I took aim and fired several rounds, popping him in the side of the head. The bullets ricocheted off the mask, and other than rocking his head back and forth, appeared to do no damage. Now I understood why he wore the mask. Protection. I knew shooting him anywhere else would have little to no affect. He would heal quickly, like Elizabeth did in the cemetery. Punching holes in his body wouldn't stop him.

He turned his head slowly in my direction. The only thing not covered by his mask was his eyes, and they were the eyes of a full-fledged nut-bag. "I change my mind. I kill you slowly now."

I glanced at both Elizabeth and Mirsada. "Well, just remember what ol'Vic McCain says at a time like this. Ol'Vic always says...WHAT THE HELL!" And I attacked.

Even knowing it wouldn't hurt him, I shot him in the head twice more, while I rushed towards him. Ringing his bell might not hurt him, but perhaps it would disorient him for a few seconds. Mirsada shot in behind him, forcing Muramasa to spin her direction, while Elizabeth swung her improvised club in an overhead arc, trying her best to drive the swordsmith into the ground like a tent peg.

But Muramasa was fast. Incredibly fast. Elizabeth missed him by inches, her log splintering in half as it crashed into the ground.

Mirsada and Muramasa traded a flurry of blows and I pulled up short, worried I would hit Mirsada instead of the samurai. Elizabeth did the same, watching for an opening.

Mirsada's sword blurred, her movements flowing from one form to another with a skill I'd never seen before. Her footwork made it seem as if she floated above the ground, effortless. I'd seen Samantha wield a sword and had been impressed, but Mirsada was on a whole other level. She was good. Damn good. But he was better.

Muramasa barely seemed to move, a statue in the midst of the storm. His blade countered all her attacks, his wrist unbending. Then he went on the attack and one of his thrusts got past her guard and nicked her shoulder, causing a grunt of pain. But to her credit, it didn't slow her down. Her life depended on it.

She pressed another attack and their two swords slid down together, until they caught on each other's hilt guard. He laughed again and shouted, "It is time to end this dance."

"I agree," I said. His head might be protected by a large metal helmet, but his hands weren't. I stepped forward, putting myself inside his sword's reach and prayed I calculated correctly. I pulled the trigger and half his right hand exploded, taking his thumb with it. I don't care if you are an Infernal Lord, or vampire, or whatever you wanted to call him, you can't hold a sword with half a hand and no thumb.

The next two seconds saw more action than most battles do in an hour. Muramasa howled in fury and shot a foot out in a side kick which sent me flying backwards onto the ground. I kept the flashlight on him and watched him drop the sword with his right hand and snatch it in mid-air with his left. But the fraction of a second cost him.

Mirsada spun in a tight circle and her sword flashed in a feint towards his head, only to alter the arch when he raised his own sword in defense. Her sword met dead flesh and passed through his shoulder with his right arm hacked off at the joint.

She ducked and rolled past the infuriated sword master when he counter attacked. She started to stand when Elizabeth shouted, "Duck, child." Mirsada did as commanded and crouched low, while Elizabeth swung her club sideways, whistling inches above Mirsada's head, but catching Muramasa high in the chest with a large thump. He flew backwards into the fog, howling once again, crashing through trees and underbrush, disappearing from view. It was a swing to make Babe Ruth proud.

She said, "We run now." She took off into the night, with Mirsada and I right behind her, the light from my flashlight trying to cut the fog, but having little affect. I bounced off several trees in our flight to freedom, my face scratched from limbs that slapped me in the face.

I heard several accompanying grunts from Mirsada taking her own punishment from the trees. We broke out of the tree line and the fog thinned a bit. I could make out the Ford in the haze and we hit an all-out sprint.

Only a few seconds behind us our silver helmeted foe emerged in pursuit. I glanced over my shoulder and felt a moment of Deja Vu, reliving the chase by the hellhound.

I shouted to the two women, "Try and keep him busy for as long as you can. I need about sixty seconds."

I didn't even watch what they did, but pulled the key fob out my pocket and hit the unlock button, ran to the trunk of my car and lifted the hatch. I threw the blanket off the flame thrower, and quickly unscrewed the propane canister from the back of the rig, and replaced it with one of two spares I kept in the car. Another example of how far I'd slipped. I should have replaced it while in North Carolina, a blunder I hoped didn't cost me or either woman their lives.

I didn't bother to put the damn thing on, but carried it tucked under my arm, the nozzle extended in my other hand. And just in time. Mirsada was only barely able to keep Muramasa off her, with Elizabeth swinging but missing the other vamp with her log, while he countered with blows in her direction. He may have been fighting one handed, but the man remained incredibly dangerous. Her shirt showed several spots where the sword ripped through to her torso, but seemingly doing little damage. If he managed to connect with her neck, that would be a different story.

"To me," I yelled. Both of them retreated in my direction and they gained a moment when Elizabeth scored another hit with the log, staggering the samurai backwards. Mirsada sprinted behind me and then, for a second, both vamps were in my sight. I could have ended two Infernal Lords at once. Mirsada screamed at me to pull the trigger.

But I hesitated. I'd given Elizabeth my word. The Hand of God was put on Earth to destroy people like her. She, by her own admission, had tortured and killed hundreds, if not thousands, of people. A death by fire was what she deserved. I knew that to be true. But I'd also given my word. I told myself I still needed her, to see this through. But now that I had Isaac's stash, did I really?

I might find out, to my eternal ruin that Elizabeth was beyond redemption. Like my brother, she had chosen a path of evil and the only end for her would be suffering in the fires of Hell. But if it were true, then what would that mean? How evil was too evil to right the ship and sail in the other direction?

My finger tightened on the trigger, but still, I did not pull it all the way. "What are you waiting for? End them. Now!" Mirsada shouted as she grabbed my arm.

And then the moment was lost. Elizabeth tossed her log at Muramasa's feet, forcing him to dance in the air, while she ran behind me. With her now safe, I let loose with a steady stream of fire, advancing on the samurai. He both screamed and laughed, almost at the same time. His body engulfed in flames, he staggered towards me, waving his sword as if trying to slice the flames in half.

I back-peddled up a few steps keeping my finger on the trigger and the flames roared, but then he closed the gap with a rush and with a final lunge, he stabbed with his sword, trying to spill my guts across the ground. I was shocked he could move at all, let alone attack. Thankfully, he was slowed by the damage from the flames and I parried the thrust with the backpack. Just. I dropped the nozzle and swung the flamethrower backpack with everything I had and caught him across the side of the head, staggering him.

He fell to his knees and the sword slipped from blackened fingers onto the ground. I guess even Infernal Lords have their breaking point. I kicked him in the chest, sending him onto his back, steam rising from the eye holes of his mask. I snatched his dropped sword from the ground, singeing my fingers in the process, and with a quick strike, severed his head from the rest of his body. I may not be as graceful as Mirsada, but I make up for it with brute strength.

A moment later, his body turned to brimstone, black in color with red streaks running across his entire body. I kicked him hard and the whole thing disintegrated into dust, with the mask the only thing left. A small sulfur cloud hovered in the air and I stepped away.

Anger contorted Mirsada's face, her fury barely kept in check. I am sure if there was a way to remove me as the Hand of God, short of killing me, she would have found a way to do it.

Elizabeth watched me, her face expressionless, impassive. She knew I could have taken her out as well, but didn't. If she were grateful, she didn't show it. Perhaps the former Countess in her took it for granted people would do what she wanted. Hell if I knew.

I walked past both of them and tossed what was left of the flamethrower back in the car, covering it and laid Muramasa's katana behind our bags. "There will be people who heard the shots I fired back in the woods. We better get out of here, even if there isn't a body to be found."

I drove several miles from the lighthouse and turned into a school parking lot, made my way into the darker shadows under a line of trees, parked and turned off the engine.

"Everyone out."

I didn't wait on them and got out and went to the rear of my car, once again accessing my weapons locker. The two women exited the car and watched while I walked around the car holding a small electronic device.

"What are you doing," asked Mirsada.

"Checking for bugs. I once had one planted under my car and that's how the bad guys kept track of me. We were the only ones who knew we were going to Alexandria. So how did Muramasa find us?"

Mirsada turned a thumb in Elizabeth's direction, causing Elizabeth to sigh heavily.

"No, she didn't. The man was there for her, not us. He made that clear." I finished my sweep of the car, but found nothing. I opened the rear hatch and checked out the bags, but they were also clear.

I walked over to both women. Mirsada stood still while I ran the device up and around her body. Nada. Then I started on Elizabeth and the thing went nuts: right where she'd been shot during the shootout with Deveraux. She took hold of a rip in her shirt from one of Muramasa's sword cuts and widened it. The signal finder redlined at the spot.

"Bloody hell. I thought the bullet made a funny sound when it hit you, but lying in the bottom of that grave I thought it was my imagination."

"What do you mean? What are you talking about?" Elizabeth asked.

"Tracking bullet. Cops use them to shoot the back of cars so they can fall back and track criminals instead of engaging in high speed chases. The guy who shot you had to know a regular bullet would have no real effect on you. I mean, why bother? But shooting you with a tracking bullet would allow them to follow your movements."

Elizabeth said some things in Hungarian which I assumed to be swear words. She then turned to Mirsada. "Cut me open. Right here, please."

Mirsada drew her katana, her knuckles white on the handle. Elizabeth held her hands out to her sides and waited. With a low growl, Mirsada thrust the tip of her katana at the spot indicated and gave her wrist a twist, opening up a good sized wound. She yanked the sword out, pulled a small towel from an inside vest pocket and wiped the blade clean.

Elizabeth reached into her own chest, her fingers searching around, until she found the bullet. She pulled it out and held it up, examining it. She held it out to me and I ran the scanner over the bullet and the little machine lit up like a Christmas tree.

Elizabeth turned and threw the bullet into the darkness. She then went to the car, got out her bag and changed shirts.

I tossed the bug sweeper back into my locker and removed a first aid kit. I walked over to Mirsada and examined the cut she'd received from Muramasa. It wasn't very deep and I didn't think it would need stiches. I put some hydrogen peroxide on a cloth and cleaned the wound, then applied a pressure bandage.

"You are an idiot and it will get you killed," she said.

"I have no doubt you're right. But I keep my word. Remember that."

I finished and Mirsada stalked to her side of the car and got back inside. Newly clothed, Elizabeth did the same. I breathed easier with the mystery of how they found us resolved.

In Alexandria, we found what we'd come for, not that I knew much more than I did before the trip. At least we now had clues.

And the world was down an Infernal Lord. Rumble, rumble, scratch one bad guy.

CHAPTER TWENTY-TWO

Senator Stafford watched on as the attending nurse swabbed his elbow with antiseptic and inserted the I.V. needle. Wearing the backless gown all patients hate and covered with a blanket to the waist, he rested his head back onto a pillow and tried to relax.

Giving up control to anyone, even an operating team, was hard for Stafford. Truth be told, he felt a sense of foreboding about the surgery. His mother, following surgery to remove a gallbladder, found it difficult to come out of anesthesia, and spent nearly a day on a respirator. While he never experienced the same thing, he always worried the next time would be when it would happen to him.

His thoughts were interrupted when Dr. Collins pulled back the curtain surrounding his bed and moved to stand next to him, pulling the curtain closed behind her.

"Good morning, Senator. How did you sleep last night?" she asked.

"I didn't. I stayed up most of the night taking care of last minute Senate business. We may be on our August break, but that doesn't mean things stop. Besides, the more tired I am, the easier this will be. When you give me the Valium I will be out long before you give me the gas."

Dr. Collins laughed, but to Stafford it sounded forced. She pulled down the blanket, took a marker out of her pocket and wrote on the left knee THIS ONE. On the right knee she wrote NOT THIS ONE.

"We wouldn't want to take out your good one, would we?" Again she smiled, but briefly.

Stafford rose to power by being able to read people and watching the body language of Dr. Collins, she seemed tense. "Everything O.K, doc? How did you sleep last night?"

She pulled the blanket back up to his waist, avoiding eye contact. "I slept like a baby. You're in good hands, Senator." She watched the nurse put a needle in the I.V. and push down on the plunger, administering the Valium. Finally, she looked him in the eyes and he wasn't sure what he saw there. Apprehension? Worry? Maybe his own feelings were coloring his perceptions.

He would have asked more questions, but the Valium hit him quickly and with the lack of sleep he started to drift off. While he did, in his mind's eye, the doctor's face grew larger, her eyes huge. Then her face contorted and changed, becoming the head of a dragon. Her mouth opened wide and fire erupted from her throat. He tried to raise his hands, to protect himself, but his body would not respond, and he screamed.

When he awoke hours later, following the surgery, he would not remember the dream.

~*~

Stafford opened his eyes slowly, blinked several times and woke up to find his wife Delores sitting in a chair reading a book. When she noticed he was no longer asleep, she put her book aside, stood next to his bed and kissed him.

"Could you give me some water, please," his voice just above a whisper.

She picked up a Styrofoam cup with a straw and let him take a sip. He swished the water around his mouth for a moment, then swallowed. He thanked his wife and then let his head fall back onto the pillow.

A nurse came in a few minutes later and greeted him, then went about checking his temperature and blood pressure. Shortly afterwards, they brought in a Continuous Passive Motion Machine. They removed his knee brace, gently lifted his knee into the device and it began to slowly work his knee back and forth.

Near the end of his first CPM session, House Speaker Cyrus Tyler knocked on the door and came into the room carrying flowers and a gift wrapped box. He waited until the nurse left the room and said, "The flowers are for your lovely wife for putting up with you. As for you, I brought Kentucky bourbon. I know the kind that will bring you more enjoyment."

Tyler kissed Delores on the cheek and handed her the flowers. She sat the flowers on the windowsill and Tyler set the bourbon on a table near his bed. He glanced at the knee moving back and forth with the steady hum of the CPM. "Things go well?" he asked.

"I guess so. I don't really feel anything at the moment, thanks to the pain block and meds. They want to get me up and walking around later this afternoon. Let's see how it does then."

"I'll let you boys have a few minutes. I need to call some more family members and let them know how you're doing." Delores grabbed her purse and left the room.

Tyler watched her go, then pulled up a chair next to the bed. "How long will you be here?"

"Three days. Once I get home, I'll hit the therapy hard. I have a good friend who went through a knee replacement and he's never been able to bend it all the way. That's not going to happen to me."

"Nor would I expect it. Hard work has never been your issue. Taking this country into the crapper because of your liberal politics is the issue."

Both men laughed. "You know what, Cyrus? You coming in here and giving me shit lets me know everything is going to be just fine". He turned serious. "Thanks for arranging for Dr. Collins to get this done during the break. I appreciate it. I can't tell you how much."

"Don't say that where people can hear you. There were some in my party who were saddened by the death of your doctor, but were hoping you would have to have the surgery during the fall, taking you off the fundraiser trail."

"True, that. We have several big events planned and I likely would have had to miss some of them. Now things can keep on schedule. And that includes our legislative slate. There have to be things you, me and the President can find common ground on and move some bills forward. Cyrus, the country needs to see we can work together."

"Don't worry, Hedley. There will be a lot getting done this fall."

"Too bad you won't be around to see it," thought Tyler.

CHAPTER TWENTY-THREE

Elizabeth, Mirsada and I spent the night at a Comfort Suites off the Capital Beltway. I made sure both women were in their rooms before I went to mine. Elizabeth offered to join me in my room, but I politely said, "No." Not only did Mirsada not offer to join me, but she hadn't said a word to me since we left the school parking lot and slammed her door closed.

Once I got to my room, I used my phone to take a picture of the Dabney Industrial Tech label and the circuit schematic. I texted them to Kurt and asked for details on both as soon as possible.

I then stripped out of my clothes, headed to the bathroom and took a long, hot shower. I let the water wash over my head, deep in thought about the label, the schematic and the U.S. Constitution, hoping to have an epiphany. Sadly, I didn't.

I toweled off and made my way to my bed, exhausted beyond measure. The aftermath of the fight with Muramasa had been exhausting enough. But dealing with Elizabeth and Mirsada wore me down mentally.

I checked out the mini bar in my room, found a couple of small bottles of Jack Daniels, opened them and poured their contents into a hotel room plastic cup. I sat on the edge of the bed and started to sip the whiskey, but changed my mind and tossed it down in one shot. I felt the burn in my throat and wanted more, but all that was left in the mini bar was vodka and gin, so I passed.

I did wonder if I had a drinking problem, with Winston's admonition bouncing around in my head. I came from a long line of professional drinkers, but it was never an issue for me in the past. I could go down to Molly's and tie one on with the best of them and then not have another drink for months. Recently, however, you were more likely than not to find a drink in my hand. Something to consider. I only wished I could consider it with another belt of bourbon.

I turned off the lights and crashed onto my bed, my arms out to my sides, and tried to will sleep to overtake me. I thought I would be asleep in minutes. Unfortunately, my body failed to cooperate and the rest I desperately needed alluded me.

Tony Acree

An hour later, I was still awake. An hour after that, no change. I'd hoped the whiskey would help turn my brain off, but it didn't. I found it hard to keep my thoughts in one place, racing from one thought to the next. I thought about what we'd learned, trying to put the pieces of the puzzle together, but no dice. Then my mind switched to thoughts of Samantha, with feelings of anger, sadness and shame tagging along for the ride.

And as quickly as thoughts of Samantha would come, they were replaced by thoughts of Elizabeth and what I was going to do about her. Had our nights in the sack tainted my judgment as Mirsada claimed? I didn't believe that was true, but hell, how could I be sure?

I started humming an old country song I'd heard years ago, about a preacher who held sermons while handling snakes, only to be bitten by one and dying. Is that what could happen to me with Elizabeth? Was I trying to prove if she could regain her soul and redemption that I could do the same thing, only to die because my hope turned around and bit me in the ass?

Then I spent a few minutes thinking about my brother. Was he proof positive Elizabeth was damned beyond saving? Elizabeth, at least, claimed she wanted salvation. Mikey didn't. He embraced his role being the point man for chaos and mayhem for Satan. Not only did Mikey not want to be saved, he believed Satan would be the one holding all the cards during the final showdown with God and he would be made a king among men. He now had the rest of eternity to find out how wrong he turned out to be.

My random thoughts were finally interrupted when my cell phone dinged indicating the arrival of a text message. I sighed, picked up the phone to find a text from Kurt asking me to call him when I got up. I thumbed to his number and hit dial.

He answered with a hushed request for me to hang on. A moment later he said, "Dude, I didn't expect you to call me back in the middle of the night. You almost woke up Ruth Anne. What are you doing up?"

I explained my inability to find some shut eye and he commiserated. "I know what you mean. Ruth Anne likes to keep at it until late. I didn't get to do your research until after midnight. Best time for hacking anyways."

"What'd you find out?"

"I got good news and bad news. The good news is I found out what the label belongs to, but you aren't going to like it."

"Do I ever? Let me have it."

"Looks like Dabney Industrial Tech has invented a new form of plastic explosive. Do you know how C-4 works?"

"Yeah. We used it all the time when I was Special Forces. It uses RDX mixed with a bunch of other crap. Very stable. You have to have heat

481

and a shockwave to detonate. You telling me this is a C-4 label?"

"Kind of. They've developed a newer nastier version. They worked out a new type of nitroamine, whatever the hell that is, and you only need a quarter of a brick of their version to get the same explosive power as a full brick of C-4. It also takes less heat and a smaller shockwave. That makes it a bit more unstable, but, man, what a blast."

Dabney Industrial seemed to always be on the cutting edge of the technology used to kill people. Good thing they were on our side, though some claimed a lot of their weapons seemed to end up on battlefields far from any American soldier.

"How about the schematic? What'd you find out about it?"

"That's the bad news. What I can tell you is it's some kind of switch. But, dude, there is a ton of quantum mechanics shit and I don't have a clue what it does or how it works. You don't happen to know any quantum physicists do you?"

"Turns out, I do. Thanks, Kurt. I will let you know what I find out."

"Any clue what's going on, Big Guy?"

"Only that they plan on blowing something up. What that is, I don't know yet. But I will. Thanks again."

I hung up and lay back in bed, this time more relaxed than I'd been before. The puzzle was becoming clearer and I knew I was close to figuring it all out. And when I did? I would be the one lowering the boom.

~*~

The next morning I met Elizabeth and Mirsada down in the hotel dining room for breakfast about 8 a.m. The eggs were likely instant, the sausages greasy and the juice glasses incredibly small, but I ate like a man who won the lottery. While we had yet to uncover what Tyler and his underlings were up to, we were closing in and I could feel the itch. I got it when the back of my brain began figuring things out and I knew it wouldn't be long before we knew it all and we could take steps to stop things.

Both women avoided talking to each other and only barely spoke to me. At 8:30 I took out my phone, scrolled through my contacts and made a call.

On the second ring, a woman answered. "Well I'll be damned, if it's not the soldier of fortune himself."

I laughed. "Hello Bethany. How's life? Keeping busy down at the U?"

Bethany Dezaro was born in California and educated at Cal

Berkeley, majoring in molecular biology. Now she taught the same subject at Temple University in Philadelphia. It's where she met Joseph Dezaro, a good friend of mine back from my army days and the reason I called her.

"Classes pick back up in a couple of weeks so right now I've got some free time." She paused briefly before continuing. "If you're looking for Joey, he's not here. Sorry, Vic."

"Let me guess, he's out throwing around grown men for money."

Joseph Dezaro, known to the wrestling public as Joey Image, served with me in Afghanistan and Iraq. Joey was one of the more interesting people I'd ever met. He got his degree in physics from Harvard, his doctorate in quantum mechanics from M.I.T. and then decided to join the Army for shits and giggles.

Reaching the rank of Staff Sergeant, Joey was the top noncom in my unit. He kept the enlisted men in line and could kill the enemy in about three dozen different ways. Five-nine and built like a bull dog, the man could go all day and all night and seem to never tire. Despite being almost a foot taller, even I found it hard to take him off his feet when we would wrestle for the hell of it during our down times.

When we got back to the states, he took a series of jobs with start-up companies looking to cash in on the exploding frontier of quantum physics. With several patents under his belt and a large increase in his bank account, he'd jumped off the corporate gravy train to accept a research fellowship at Temple, met Bethany and settled down.

In his spare time, Joey got involved with independent wrestling outfits in the Northeast and developed a following under the name Joey Image. Most weekends you could find him pinning people to the mat.

"He's at a fundraiser in Houston, Texas. He's helping raise money for an autism group down there."

"And let me guess? Still no cell phone?" Joey worried what the cell phones were doing to his brain. At the quantum level, of course.

"Like he ever will. He'll be back later in the week. I can have him call you when he gets back, if you like."

"It can't wait that long, Bethany. What's the name of the event? I'll fly down there and talk to him."

"*Bustin' for Autism.* It's being held downtown. Is everything O.K., Vic?"

"Yeah, things are fine. I've run across something in an investigation I'm involved in and it involves me needing to talk to Dr. Dezaro not Joey Image."

I thanked her and hung up, then filled in Elizabeth and Mirsada.

"Looks like I need to fly down to Houston for a day or two. Why don't the two of you hang out here until I get back? I bet whatever's going on is happening somewhere near here. Can you two manage not to kill each other while I'm gone?"

"They have a very nice pool here. I can manage," Elizabeth said.

"I make no promises on not killing people. It depends on her," Mirsada said, pointing a thumb at Elizabeth.

"Great. What more could a guy ask for?"

CHAPTER TWENTY-FOUR

I caught a flight out of Reagan National late in the morning, transferred through Atlanta and arrived at Hobby Airport around 5:30 p.m. I rented a convertible Mercedes because...why the hell not? The Church of the Light Reclaimed paid the bill.

I dropped by Joey's hotel only to find out the whole group had gone to Longhorn Steakhouse for dinner. *Bustin' for Autism* raised money to send special needs children to camp. They brought in celebrities, mainly pro wrestlers, as well as cos players (the ones who dress up like super hero characters) along with writers and other local celebrities.

I made the short drive to Longhorn Steakhouse, parked and walked in the door. At the far end of the dining room they had shoved several tables together for the large dinner party. And when I say large, I mean large. Wrestling royalty sat around the table. Sgt. Slaughter, Hacksaw Jim Duggan, Honkey Tonk Man, the Real Rikishi and Gene Snitsky. It's not often I go out and find men my size, but hell, the whole table came close.

Joey sat near the end of the table with a beer in one hand, laughing and trading tales with Snitsky. He was decked out in a black t-shirt which matched his dark hair and beard, and had a bandana wrapped around his head. The man remained just as ripped as his younger days.

I walked to his end of the table and punched him hard in the shoulder. Joey, showing the kind of reflexes you normally see on big cats, went from drinking and laughing to having me thrown to my stomach with my arm cranked behind my back.

"Good to see you, too, Joey," I said through gritted teeth.

"Victor McCain? Jesus man, hitting me from behind is a good way to earn a trip to the hospital."

He helped me to my feet and hugged me in a fierce bear hug, while I rubbed my arm, trying to make the pain go away. "I had to see if you still had it. Seems like playing around in the ring hasn't hurt you any."

He introduced me to the guys and gals at the table who raised their glasses in ceremonial greeting, then he grabbed his beer and the two of us found a booth in a corner away from everyone else.

"How ya been, Joey?"

"Life as an independent wrestler is tough, but I love it. I was injured a few weeks ago, but feel great now and will be back in the ring soon."

We spent some time catching up, talking about women, fighting and Fireball Whiskey.

After the waitress brought me another beer, he said, "I'm guessing you didn't fly down here from Louisville to share a few beers. Am I right, or am I right?"

"Flew here from Virginia. But you're right. I need you to take off the bandana for a moment and put your doctorate hat on for a bit." I took out a folded copy of the schematic I'd printed at the hotel and slid it across the table to him.

He took another drink of Coors Light while he looked over the paper. His brows furrowed and he sat the beer down, bending closer to the paper. I watched his eyes read the paper from top to bottom, then do it again.

Finally he met my eyes. Very quietly he asked, "Where did you get this?"

"From a dead man. Ever heard of Isaac Peck?"

"Yeah, man. Most in the field have. Died in a bad drug deal last week, right?"

"Dead, yes. Bad drug deal?" I shook my head no. "He left this to be found in case he turned up dead. So what is it?"

"Armageddon, Vic. Armageddon."

~*~

We said our goodnights to the *Bustin' for Autism* crowd and went back to his room at the hotel, with the two of us now in chairs staring at the screen of one seriously large laptop computer. Joey spent a few minutes checking some of the computations listed on the print out.

"Vic, tell me what you know about quantum entanglement."

"Not much. From what I gather when two particles are entangled, whatever happens to one particle happens to the other."

He nodded agreement. "Simplistic, but that's basically it. Entangled particles have no set state until they are measured. But when you do measure one the observed state will be the same in the other entangled members, but opposite."

I must have shown my confusion because he stopped talking like a doctor and more like a sergeant. "Look, if one particle is spinning to the right, the other spins to the left. If you change the spin of the first particle to spin to the left, then the other will start spinning to the right. And the change is instantaneous. Faster than the speed of light. But the measurement always adds up to zero."

"O.K. So?"

"So, the big advantage is, the distance is irrelevant. The big goal for a lot of researchers is using this property to create a quantum computer or a new form of encryption." Holding up the paper he said, "What you have here is the creation of a quantum switch. It appears someone managed to do what others have dreamed about doing."

"A switch? You mean like a light switch?"

"Sure. Or a computer switch. With this switch you can be sitting in a room on Mars, press the switch and the light comes on in a room on Venus. Instantaneously, without the signal having to travel the traditional route between the two places."

"You said this was Armageddon. Isn't this type of technology a great thing?"

"Sure. But think about it, Vic. There are a lot of things you can turn on with a switch. And not all of them good."

And then I got it. What Tyler and his goons planned. "You mean like a bomb? Holy crap." I told Joey about the other items I found in the bag. "One of the problems with setting off a bomb is the trigger. You can set a timer, but you may not know when the target will be there. You can use a cell phone, but if the target can turn off the cell phone towers in the area then your bomb is a paper weight. And you can use an RF transmitter, but there is an issue with the range. You're telling me with one of these you can set off a bomb in New York and be sitting in a bunker in North Korea, right?"

"You got it. Design the switch so that when the particle spins to the left, the device is off and when it spins to the right, it turns on. This switch is designed to do just that."

"How do you stop it? There has to be a way."

"There are only two. Find the bomb and remove the detonator. Or find the person who has the switch and take it away from them. Those are your only options. You can't jam this type of signal, Vic. Once the bomb is in place, there would be no way to stop it from being detonated. None."

We sat there in silence for a few moments then Joey asked, "Let me guess, from the way you look, the guys who have this aren't the good guys."

"Joey, they are as evil as it gets."

I thought about telling him about what was going on, about me being the Hand of God, but decided I was better off leaving him in the dark. I didn't like the thought of Joey thinking I was a nut bag if he didn't believe me.

"Well, one thing I can tell you is I doubt Isaac did this all on his own. The type of testing this would require would be really expensive. We're talking large company or world power."

"Do you think Dabney Industrial Tech could pull it off?"

Joey stared at the ceiling, his hands behind his head. "Yeah. I do. They are involved in all kinds of stuff involving new technology. They are into a lot of nano technology stuff, too. Anything to get an edge. So yeah, I can see them involved in this."

"Sounds like I need to get deeper into those guys. I think I have a bigger problem on my hands than I expected."

"How do you think the Constitution fits in to all of this?"

"Hell, I'm not sure. Perhaps they plan to target government institutions. Look, Joey, thanks. But at this point, the less you know about what is going on, is probably a good thing. Plausible deniability."

We both stood and hugged each other again. "Listen, Vic, you need me, you call. I don't mind getting my hands dirty."

"Thanks, Joey. I mean it, thanks. Hug Bethany for me."

I made my way back into the cool night air and to my car. I sat behind the wheel for a few minutes before I started the engine and headed to the airport.

The sons of bitches were going to blow up something or someone and I didn't have a clue how to stop them. Dealing with the supernatural is a hard enough proposition. But when the bad guys start using quantum physics and cutting edge military tech, it had a way of sucking all the fun out of my job.

One on one, I believe I can handle any single opponent and come out on top. But spooky bombs?

Yowza.

CHAPTER TWENTY-FIVE

I spent the night at a Holiday Inn near the airport, sleeping like the dead for once, turned in my car the next morning, and hopped the first return flight to Alexandria.

I got back to the Comfort Suites around mid-afternoon and true to her word, I found Elizabeth doing laps in the pool, while Mirsada sat under an umbrella watching her. Mirsada still wore the leather outfit, but traded the white shirt for a tan one. Such a fashion diva.

I asked them to meet me in the dining room in a half hour and went to my room to do some research on Dabney Industrial Tech.

Behind only Lockheed Martin and Boeing when it comes to defense contractors, the past year saw nearly thirty billion in total arms sales bringing in a profit of almost three billion, with a B, dollars. Owned and run by Alex Dabney, the grandson of the company founder, Levi Dabney, their reach now extended to dozens of complimentary companies around the globe. They invested heavy in Russia, China and Brazil.

Their R & D department made up a large portion of the company. If a new technology needed to be created, then D.I.T. got it done. They also contributed heavily to political campaigns on both sides of the aisle, but the person they contributed the most to, for the last five years running? The newly minted Speaker of the House Cyrus Tyler.

That in and of itself, meant nothing. But knowing Tyler like I did, it couldn't be a good thing. I closed my laptop and went down to the hotel restaurant to meet with Elizabeth and Mirsada.

The women were already there, sitting at a corner table near the end of the bar, well away from the other patrons eating a late lunch. The TV over the bar, tuned to Fox News, showed talking heads speaking about Majority Leader Hedley Stafford.

I filled them in on what I'd learned down in Houston, about the new type of C-4, the quantum switch and my thought Dabney Industrial Technologies somehow figured into a plot to blow something up.

"There is no doubt Isaac could have helped to design such a thing," said Elizabeth. "I know money was not an issue. He asked and they would provide. That is how it worked."

I started to say something else when Elizabeth pointed up to the TV. "Isn't that your House Speaker?"

I turned around in my seat and glanced at the screen and sure enough, Senator Stafford was at a podium talking with Tyler and a few other senators and congressmen standing behind him.

"Hey, barkeep. Mind turning it up a bit?" I asked.

The bartender picked up a remote and jacked the volume up enough for us to hear Stafford speak.

"I want everyone to know my recovery is going very well. I want to thank Dr. Collins and her team for taking such good care of me. She might even have a future in politics, since she's operated on both myself and Speaker Tyler. The Speaker went to great lengths to make sure she could step in once my doctor suffered his unfortunate accident. Now we have some common ground where we can both agree. Do we not, Mr. Speaker?"

Tyler laughed and nodded an enthusiastic yes. Stafford started talking again, but I was no longer listening. A cold chill ran down my spine and I turned back to Elizabeth. "Isaac worked on creating new and improved joints, legs and arms for people who suffered crippling injuries, right?"

"Yes. He make men walk again. Women who lost arms to hold their babies again. Very talented."

"Knee replacements?"

"Of course, knee—" She stopped, and with wide eyes, stared at the TV screen. "Oh, no. Isaac, what did you do?"

Mirsada scowled. "Please, would you two explain?"

"Holy hell. I know where they put the bomb. The bottom of a knee replacement is plastic. If you used the C-4, especially the new stuff, there would be enough explosives to take out a good sized house."

The three of us watched the end of the press conference but learned nothing more. "What did he say his doctor's name was?" I asked.

"Collins, I think," said Mirsada. Elizabeth nodded in agreement. "But surely, there would be no way this Senator would agree to have his knee replaced with such a bomb."

I agreed. "He wouldn't. But what if he didn't know? We need to talk to that doctor. I can't see a way this could happen without her being in on the plans. If nothing else, we can try and find out where they get their knee joints. If they ordered them from Isaac's company that would almost be like a real clue."

I got out my iPhone and did a search on Dr. Collins and Senator Stafford. I found quite a few news articles about the good doctor and the surgery she performed on Senator Stafford at the Hospital of the University of Pennsylvania. I found her office phone number and dialed.

I got the office receptionist and told her I was a reporter with a paper in Harrisburg and wanted to know if Dr. Collins could answer a few questions, only to find out she was out of the office for the next week, taking some overdue vacation time with her daughter. Citing HIPAA regulations, they also wouldn't tell me where they buy their artificial knees.

I thanked her, hung up and called Kurt.

"Yo, dude. What's up?"

"Dr. Teresa Collins, I need you to track her down. She performed the operation on Senator Stafford. I need you to see if you can get a cell number for me. Can you do that?"

He made a very inappropriate sound and hung up. About ten minutes later, he texted me her number. I sent back a "You da man" text and dialed her number, but it went straight to voice mail. I hung up without leaving a message and called Kurt back.

"Listen, she didn't answer. Any chance you can use the GPS in her phone and get me a current location?"

"Any reason you keep insulting me? Geez, man."

Once again he hung up and the three of us ate our lunch while occasionally discussing Stafford. I stuffed the last bite of my dessert in my mouth, a better than expected piece of carrot cake, when Kurt called me back.

"Hey, dude. Her phone is currently at an address near Seaside Heights, New Jersey. There's a couple of beach houses south of town. That's where she is. I'll text you her address. She also drives a black BMW. I'll shoot you the license plate as well."

"Thanks, man. One last thing. Can you research her practice and see where they order their artificial joints? I have a theory and want to see if it pans out."

"Dude, the only thing you may need replaced is your head. Winston told me you were on a road trip with a demon and a Hand of God babe. Well, that they were both babes, but one was evil, one not, that you had sex with one of them but might want to—"

I hung up the phone when I saw Elizabeth look at me, eyes narrowed, knowing she likely could hear the whole conversation. My phone beeping bailed me out.

"Time to check out, ladies. We have a lead. Time to head to the beach." I pulled up Google Maps and checked the drive time, finding out we could be there in about 4 hours, less with good traffic.

We checked out of the hotel and hit the road. This time, I felt much better than the last time the three of us went on a long trip. For one thing, they fought less than before. It seems they finally found a way to work together until this whole thing was over—not that Mirsada looked any happier, but the constant nagging at Elizabeth had stopped.

For her part, Elizabeth continued to ignore Mirsada, while carrying on about her love of the beach, young men and good food. When I pointed out virtually every man on the planet was younger than her, she very sweetly offered to turn me into a eunuch.

Seaside Heights sat on the Barnegat Peninsula and was a popular resort destination during the summer months. Their latest claim to fame was the reality TV series *Jersey Shore* was filmed there. Maybe I would get to meet Snooky while we were tracking bad guys. My luck, I'd get *The Situation* instead.

This time of year, the traffic was packed in the main part of town and it added a good forty minutes to our trip. Finally, free of the strip, we headed south down Shore Road. The houses became less common and further apart.

I finally found our address near the south end of the peninsula. We drove by at a slow but steady pace. The house looked to be a small villa nestled in the trees, with a view of the beach. A black Beamer took up one of the two spots in front of the house, the other a Jeep Cherokee. A petite woman with long black hair tied back in a ponytail, got out of the Jeep carrying a Krispy Kreme donut box and headed towards the front door.

She glanced our way but we were soon out of sight. Not far up the road, I nosed my Ford into a parking lot for those who were headed to the beach. A dozen or so cars filled the parking lot and I could see people scattered up and down the beach.

I parked the car and cranked up the air conditioning with the sun beating down through a cloudless sky. I turned in my seat so I could talk to both women at once without breaking my neck.

"I'm sure both of you noticed two cars in the driveway and the young woman carrying the donuts. Must be her daughter."

Mirsada snorted. "How can you be so sure they were donuts?"

"Sister, I'd recognize a Krispy Kreme donut box from almost a mile away. My favorites are the chocolate ice with cream filling. Love 'em."

They stared back, not saying anything verbally but saying it all with their looks. "Anyways. Here's what I think we should do. I will go to the door pretending to be a federal investigator. I have a fake badge I can flash. I will put the screws to her and see what I can shake loose."

"And what will the other Hand of God and I be doing while you play cop? I can go with you. We make a good team, you and I. We can do, what you call it? Good cop, bad cop. I would love to be bad cop."

"Hold your horses, Natasha Fatale. I'm not playing Boris. I'm not playing anything. You two can wait in the car until I find out what's what."

"I do not like this idea. What if something happens?"

"An orthopedic doc and her daughter? What's the worst that can happen?"

~*~

I went to the back of the Ford and got my fake badge out of my supply locker and tucked it into my pocket. I got a belt holster and secured my gun on my hip, then got back into the car and returned to the villa.

The tires crunched on the gravel driveway and I parked in such a way as to block both cars from being able to leave until I moved my car, parked and got out, leaving the car running so the gals would have some cool air, with the temperature already above the ninety degree mark.

The license plate matched the info Kurt sent me. It amazed me how easy modern technology made tracking down someone who didn't want to be found.

I walked to the door and both rang the doorbell and knocked hard on the front door. Listening, I couldn't hear anything inside, no TV, no sound or movement. I waited a few heartbeats and then repeated the process, knocking loud enough to wake up Rip Van Winkle himself, but still no response.

I glanced through the window closest to the door, but nothing. I stepped off the small porch and started around the house. Elizabeth and Mirsada opened the car door and got out.

"Watch the front door. With the cars blocked in, it ain't like they're going anywhere," I said.

They nodded their agreement and I circled around to the back of the house, where I found a back door and a fantastic view of the Atlantic Ocean. This particular villa came with a small dock which extended out a ways into the ocean. Tied up to the docks I could see a speedboat with a man behind the wheel. The girl I'd seen carrying the donut box was on the dock tossing down some luggage and then the donuts.

I made my way down the docks and they saw me coming. The man, dressed in a sleeveless T, cargo shorts and hiking sandals, smiled and offered a short wave. His olive complexion made me think South America, but I couldn't be sure. I would put him somewhere in his thirties.

The girl, gorgeous in a petite baby doll kind of way, wore a bikini top and shorts with no shoes. She gave me a million dollar smile when I stopped next to her, looking down a short ladder to the man below.

I removed the badge. "Hi. I'm Charles Winstead, U.S. Marshall's office. I wonder if I could ask you two a few questions about Dr. Teresa Collins." I used the name Charles Winstead, the man credited with shooting and killing John Dillinger. Another man who removed the bad guys from the land of the living.

The man glanced up at the woman, a confused expression on his face. "I don't know any Teresa Collins. Do you pumpkin?"

She picked up one of the last two bags on the docks and tossed it down to him, which he snagged out of the air. "Can't say that I do. I'm sorry Marshall, but I think you've made a mistake."

"That's funny. That's her car parked back in the driveway. May I ask who you are, please?"

The man started to answer when the girl, picking up the last bag, swung it around hard, catching me behind the knees, causing them to buckle and for me to fall backwards onto the dock.

Crashing down, I went for the gun on my hip when I felt a stinging sensation in my neck, like being stung by a hornet. I reached up in time to catch the girl's wrist and twisted upwards, making her drop the syringe she'd used to stab me. I noticed the plunger was pressed all the way down.

She twisted back and did a flip over me, wrenching free of my grasp and then scuttled down the ladder to the boat. I stood up, finally getting my gun free of the holster and yelled down to the two of them. "Make another move and so help me God, I will blow your asses out of that boat."

The two of them stood still, watching me, smiling. I started to ask them what the hell they thought was so funny, when the world started to spin.

I could hear them talking, but it seemed like from a long ways away.

"Do you think he will fall into the boat or back on the dock," he asked.

"I'm betting the boat. Loser drives next?"

"You're on."

My tongue grew thick and this time, my knees buckled all on their own and I felt a falling sensation. The last thing I heard, just before my face hit the floor of the boat was the man saying, "Looks like you win."

CHAPTER TWENTY-SIX

Damn my head hurt. It felt like someone had been using it to drive fence posts into the ground and not being gentle about the process. I tried to grab my face in my hands, but they stopped a good two feet short on either side. I finally managed to open my eyes and what I saw didn't give me the warm and fuzzies.

Both wrists were shackled, each connected to a long chain made of huge steel links, threaded over a large pipe above my head. I stood in the middle of a long tunnel, lit every ten feet or so with a weak lightbulb, giving off the effect of rings of light alternating with rings of darkness. I tried to find a life metaphor in the image, but gave it up. My wrists were sore from taking the weight of holding me upright while I was out.

Dirt and grime covered every inch of the tunnel, including the floor, suggesting little, if any, use. It was about ten feet wide and about the same in height. To my left, the tunnel ended about a hundred yards away in a large door. To my right, it sloped up and out of view. The air smelled of mold and decay.

A bulb to my left gave me enough light to see by and I glanced at the wall behind me, seeing several dark stains and what seemed to be spatter patterns. My imagination told me the stains were blood. My brain said "good call."

Oh, goody.

Physically, other than the head, I felt relatively okay. I could also feel a pain in my neck and the last few minutes of consciousness came back to me. For the second time in as many weeks, I'd underestimated an opponent. Most of my focus had been on the man instead of the woman. I didn't anticipate the attack and never saw a syringe. This time, the lesson could end up being permanent. At least it seemed tracking down Dr. Collins had been the right call. But it did make me wonder about the good doctor's health.

I no longer wore a shirt or my bullet proof vest and my skin prickled in the cool air. I could see no vents anywhere near me, which made me think I was somewhere underground considering how hot the day turned out to be. Which brought up another question: how long were my eyes closed? No clue.

It could be the same day or several, and I would have no way to tell from my surroundings.

I tested the chains and manacles from here to Sunday, but found no weakness or give. I gave it up and tried to relax and conserve my energy for whatever came next. A few moments later I heard a sound and saw a rat inching his way down the tunnel in my direction. He got within about three feet of me when I gave a loud shout, causing the rat to scamper away.

I've always considered myself to be high on the bravery scale, but if someone were to turn out the lights, leaving me in the dark with a tunnel full of rats? I'm not sure how long my sanity would hang around.

In what could have been minutes, but seemed like hours, the doors at the far end of the tunnel opened and a man walked in my direction and a few minutes later stood in front of me, staying near the far wall, and trying hard not to smirk. He did it anyway.

"I'll be damned. If it isn't the Jarhead. Brad Stiles, right? Congressman Tyler's lackey."

"Good memory, asshole. But that would be Speaker of the House Cyrus Tyler. He's been promoted. You need to get with the times."

"And the world is far worse off for the change. Funny, I ran off one rat only to have him replaced by a bigger one."

"Yeah. Keep on cracking the jokes, McCain. See how that works out for you." He took out a piece of gum and popped it in his mouth. He offered me a piece, but I declined.

"Suit yourself. You're lucky you're still alive. The hired help wanted to head about ten miles out into the Atlantic and drop you overboard. Not to mention the shot they gave you would have killed most men, but I reckon you're leading a charmed life."

"If you're an example of how charmed my life is, then I need to try something new. Maybe it's time to try Feng Shui. What was in the shot?"

"A derivative of propofol. The stuff that offed Michael Jackson. My operatives said they didn't have time to measure it and gave you the whole load. I bet you have a whale of a headache."

"I've had worse, but some Tylenol would be nice."

"Sorry. Left the bottle in my other pants pocket. How about you and I get down to business? How much do you know? You're going to tell me, one way or another. I'd as soon not have to get all bloody. And I'm sure you would rather be all in one piece when your body turns up."

"Torture? Really? And you think that will work with me?"

He smiled. "I was rather hoping it wouldn't. I'm not a pain-inducing kind of guy, but I have people for that type stuff. And they love it."

I'd hoped the guy would get closer and within range of my legs, but he didn't. Smart. I can do a lot of damage with my feet, but he wasn't taking any chances.

"Sure. Why not. What I know is you used Dr. Collins to plant a bomb in the knee of Senator Hedley Stafford. How am I doing so far?"

"Not bad. But I don't think you know much else."

"I know about the quantum switch and how you plan on using it to detonate the bomb."

He tried hard to hide the surprise and the expression on his face was brief, but it told me I'd hit home. "That's what you needed Isaac Peck to do, work the quantum switch into the knee replacement. Who has the detonator? You or Tyler?" It was a shot in the dark, but turned out to be a good guess on my part.

Stiles slipped a hand into his suit coat pocket and pulled out something which looked like a calculator and held it up. "Power it up, put in the code and BOOM. I've never seen anything like it."

"What about Dr. Collins, did she know what she was doing?"

"She did. At least some of it. We had her daughter and it was either help us or her daughter died. She chose her daughter over Stafford."

Not like I could blame the lady. I would have made the same choice when it came to Mikey. And there could be little doubt she would pay some type of terrible price, like I had.

"What else," he asked. He stood with his hands in his pockets, rocking back and forth on his heels, blowing and popping bubbles. Not a care in the world.

"That's about it. When do you plan on setting off the bomb?"

"Sorry. Need to know. And you don't need to know."

"You Satanists need to learn to share. It's like all you guys have trust issues." I shook my chains. "Where am I going anyway? You can tell me. It will be our little secret."

"I'm not a Satanist. I'm more of a raging agnostic. What I am, though, is a merc who likes to get paid. Tyler pays me well and I get things done in return. Like taking care of you."

"You know he's planned to kill women and children, and will do so again. You know this, right?"

He started to leave, but said over his shoulder. "We all die, McCain. Women, children. Men. And especially the Hand of God. It's what we do with that life while we're here that's important." He turned around, walking backwards for a few steps, so he could see me. "I plan on making as much money and having as much fun as I can before I go over the rainbow to see

Dorothy and Toto."

When he got back to the doors, he opened them and waved to someone. A moment later, a man wearing a leather apron and carrying a large toolbox walked passed him and started my way. I could feel my breathing pick up and a queasy feeling explode in my gut.

I shouted, "I thought you didn't want this to get bloody?"

"I lied," he shouted back, and left, closing the door behind him.

I watched my torturer make his way towards me. He walked very slowly, no doubt trying to give me as much time as he could to agonize over what was coming. When I served in Special Forces, we trained for these type of situations, but no amount of training can prepare you for the moment torture begins.

The man stopped in front of me, but also out of kicking range. He opened the toolbox, took out a plastic faceguard and slipped it onto his head. Next were a pair of rubber gloves.

"Worried I might have something contagious? Don't worry, I've had all my shots."

"One can't be too careful these days. Why take the risk? Besides, the facemask is as much to make sure you don't spit in my face. I hate it when they spit in my face. It really pisses me off."

He reached back into his bag and came out with a Taser. "Now, I've been warned about you. I think I need to make sure you will be nice and behave for me. It's nothing personal."

"Oh. This is very personal. When this is over, I *will* kill you. You know that, right?"

"I kind of doubt it." He pointed the Taser at me and pulled the trigger. The darts flew across the tunnel and embedded in my chest while fifty-thousand volts of electricity shot through my body.

The last thing I thought of before darkness crashed into my brain was that I doubted it, too.

CHAPTER TWENTY-SEVEN

When I could once again move, I found myself spread- eagled, my ankles tied by rope to bolts in the floor on either side of me, keeping me from being able to attack with my feet. He'd also covered my mouth with duct tape. I worked hard to get my breathing under control, forcing myself relax.

Leather Apron leaned against the far wall drinking from a bottle of Jim Beam, waiting for me to get back up to full speed. When he saw me staring back at him, he put the cap on the bottle, set it down next to his toolbox, and lowered his faceguard into place.

He walked right up to me, inches from my face. "Welcome back. I guess you've been having a bad day. Well, it's going to get worse."

I could smell the whiskey on his breath despite the facemask and decided it was time for him to know this would not be a one-way street if I had anything to say about it.

I turned my head away, crinkling my nose at the smell, then accelerated forward. I used my forehead as a battering ram and slammed it into his faceguard, right above the bridge of his nose, flattening the plastic and smashing it into his face.

It knocked him backwards and he yanked the faceguard off, both hands trying to stem the flow of blood from his nose. He cursed a blue streak for a few minutes while I laughed at him.

He used some paper towel from his toolbox and held it up to his nose while he glared at me. When I winked at him I thought he would kill me on the spot, which, all things considered, would be a good thing for me.

But he stood there, one hand holding the paper towel to his nose, the other hand at his side, his fist clenching and unclenching. When the blood stopped flowing, he tossed the towel down into his box, exchanging it for what my grandmother called a pruning knife. The blade was short with a wicked hook on the end. She used hers around the garden. A quick glance up and down the tunnel showed no plants needing a trim, so I figured it was meant for me.

"They told me to keep you alive for a few days and I said I would. But now I'm really going to enjoy making you scream. I may keep you alive for a few weeks. If you move so much as an inch this next time, then I'll start on the lower half of your body first."

He put his facemask back on, then carefully used the hook on the end of the blade to cut a horizontal line about two inches long below my left shoulder blade, then two vertical lines on each side, blood welling up from the cuts. He peeled back the skin, leaving a small flap. Next he reached into a pocket to get a pair of plyers and used them to slowly yank the piece of skin down.

I stifled the scream I felt rising form my throat, my body on fire from the wound. Leather Apron got great enjoyment from his work, an expression of almost ecstasy on his face. I tried to stand still, knowing his threat to turn me into a eunuch would come to pass if I didn't.

"See, they want me to flay you alive. I was going to do your chest and arms today. Then your back tomorrow. Then your legs the next night, leaving your face and neck for last. Now, I think I may do only a little each day, make this last four or five days. Every day when you see me coming down the tunnel, you will beg me to kill you. But I won't. I'll even take a few pictures on my smartphone so you can see what you look like. And don't even think about closing your eyes, or I'll cut your eyelids off.

"The real trick will be to keep you from dying due to shock. I've gotten pretty good at keeping people from bleeding to death, but shock is the tricky part. You never know when the body will decide to quit and shut down. But you're supposed to be a real bad ass. Guess my nose proves that, eh? So I have high hopes for you."

He went back to the bottle of Jim Beam for a couple of more swigs while he let what he said sink in. I knew what a flayed body looked like. One of the guys in my unit disappeared while on patrol in Iraq. His body showed up in the middle of the town square two days later, all the skin flayed from his body. I could feel the bile rise up my throat, but forced it back down.

Leather Apron once again capped his whiskey and started back in my direction when the far doors opened and a woman stepped into view. Leather Apron froze, his knife paused in midair, but only for a moment. He quickly went back to his toolbox and got a Glock, switching the knife to his other hand. My Glock. Son of a bitch.

When the woman got closer, I nearly cried. Elizabeth. She wore a white T-shirt, jeans and boots, her hips swaying while she sang a song, sauntering our way. I could swear she was singing *I Feel Pretty* from *Westside Story.*

I watched Leather Apron and he licked his lips, watching her move, his eyes following the movement of her hips. When she got about twenty feet away, he said, "Stop right there. Who are you?"

"I'm your bonus. Didn't they tell you?" It would be impossible for a woman to be more smoking hot than she looked at that very moment. I made a mental note to ask her later if being an Infernal Lord gave you some type of sway over a man's libido. She bit her bottom lip and smiled in a way that would make gay men switch teams.

I watched Leather Apron swallow hard a couple of times, before he managed to find his voice. "Nah. They didn't tell me nothing about a bonus. You got a name?"

"Uh-huh. I do. Death. Mirsada?"

And the lights went out. Leather Apron fired his gun and in the muzzle flash I saw Elizabeth standing beside Leather Apron, having closed the distance insanely fast. In the darkness, I heard a slight gurgling sound, then Elizabeth shouted out to Mirsada once again.

When the lights came back on, Leather Apron stood facing me, a long red slash under his neck, running from ear to ear, where Elizabeth used his pruning knife to slit his throat. He dropped to his knees, then onto his face, landing at my feet.

"Miss me?" she asked. She used the knife to cut my ropes free, then rummaged in the toolbox until she found the keys to the manacles, unlocking them. I nearly dropped to my knees from exhaustion, but she caught me and held me steady.

I hugged her fiercely, holding her tight against my body. She laughed and it sounded like angels singing. Mirsada came through the doors and jogged down to join us. She took in the scene, the wound on my chest and the dead body at my feet.

"Good to see you still in one piece. Mostly."

I thanked her and broke off the hug with Elizabeth, feeling a bit self-conscious after Mirsada's claims I could not be trusted because of the time I'd spent in bed with Elizabeth. I hugged her, too, to prove I am an equal opportunity hugger. To my surprise, she actually hugged me back.

I bent over and removed my gun from the dead man's hand, slipping it into the back of my jeans, then tried to shake the fatigue out of my arms. I walked over and grabbed the bottle of whisky, removed the cap and, after wiping the top of the bottle with my arm, took a long pull, the whiskey's burn a comfort.

"Thank you, both of you, for bailing my ass out. How did you find me?"

"When you didn't come back around the house, we went looking for you and saw the boat leaving the dock," Mirsada said. "A woman was doing her best to rearrange something in the bottom of the boat, and we saw her lift your arm. There was no way for us to follow the boat, so I called Brother Joshua. He, in turn, had a man, Winston Reynolds, call me. He said they had a way of tracking you and with his help, we got close. After that, it was a matter of searching 'til we found you."

"Thankfully this man," Elizabeth said, kicking the dead body of Leather Apron, "talks loudly. I could hear him from the other side of the wall. We found the breaker box next to the door and Mirsada and I worked out a plan to save your bacon."

"And none too soon, it would appear," said Mirsada, pointing to the wound on my chest. "Flaying is very painful. You are a lucky man we came when we did. How did Reynolds track you?"

"I have a tracking device in my belt, it allows the person with the right software to find me."

In truth, I'd had a chip inserted below the skin at the base of my skull. Only Winston and Kurt knew the right website, ID and password to find me. The three of us decided to take the plunge after Kurt got buried alive in Hawaii. All three of us carried one in the same place. I hated lying to them, especially after they saved my life, but I was only willing to trust them so far.

"When it comes to this guy, I had him right where I wanted him."

Both women snorted at the same time, then looked at one another, almost ashamed to have shared even a snort.

"Dr. Collins and her daughter, were they at the house?" I asked.

Mirsada nodded. "Yes. Unfortunately, both dead. They made it look like a murder suicide. They set it up to look like the daughter shot her mother, then overdosed on heroine. There was a suicide note on the table. How did they take you?"

I spent time bringing them up to speed on my humiliating take down and my conversation with Stiles. "Now we know we are on the right track. The question is, what to do next. First things first, I need get some Neosporin or something on this and a shirt," I said pointing to the spot on my chest where the skin had been removed. "Where are we?"

"This is a tunnel off the Spring Garden train station in Philadelphia. The station has been closed for decades, but there are several maintenance tunnels here and there and this is one of them. Seems over the years the area around it went downhill, drug dealers, high crime and, at one point, the city walled off the station," Mirsada said. "There are many openings which go who knows where. I get a very bad vibe down here. I think we should go."

"You get a bad vibe," Elizabeth said, "because you are children of the light. As a child of the darkness, this feels more like home." She said this while her fingers brushed lightly against the wall. "I wish it not to be so any longer. I wish to be a child of the light. Let us go."

Mirsada reached behind her back and slid out Muramasa's katana, balanced the blade on her palms, and offered it to me. "You need to keep this with you. If they sent one Infernal Lord after Elizabeth, they may send others. Be prepared, Hand of God."

I tossed the whiskey down and accepted the blade with a small bow, the hilt feeling good in my hand. She then handed me a leather sheath with a shoulder strap and I gently slid the katana home, then slung the strap around my neck, positioning the sword on my back where I could get to it quickly. "Thanks. Better safe than sorry."

The three of us walked down to the door at the end of the tunnel. It opened onto a set of railroad tracks with a small sidewalk on either side and a couple of feet higher than the tracks. There were lights out here as well, set further apart, but they still illuminated the tunnel enough for Mirsada and I to walk without tripping. Elizabeth turned to her right, leading the way. "We have about a mile to reach the access tunnel we used to get down here," she said.

The three of us remained silent while we walked, lost in our own thoughts. I'd once again come close to finding out what my fate would be once I died. Winston warned me at Molly's I'd started to slip, drinking too much and not worrying enough about what could happen if I didn't stay sharp. The woman who took me down on the pier once again proved his point valid. If my time as the Hand of God taught me anything, it was danger came in all kinds of packages, sizes and genders.

Another point to his credit was how bad I wanted to bring the whiskey with us and polish off the bottle. I felt a tremor in my hand and I couldn't tell if it was the rush of adrenaline from being rescued or the shakes from wanting another drink. Too often I turned to the bottle to deal with the stress of my life and I worried it now controlled me more than I controlled it.

Hell, next thing you know my troubles would be dramatized as a Lifetime movie of the week. I was in a rut and the sides were too high for me to see a way out. But if I didn't find a way to change this around, I would get myself, and perhaps others, killed.

Maybe I needed a therapist, but the thought only made me laugh out loud, causing Elizabeth to look over her shoulder to make sure I was OK.

I started to say something but never got the chance. We'd come even with two dark openings on either side of the tracks, likely other long lost maintenance access points. From the one on our left I heard the unmistakable sound of a shotgun being pumped, a round being chambered.

The sound would likely make most people freeze, standing in place. The three of us, being far from normal, reacted instantly. Elizabeth and Mirsada, dove down next to the tracks, both women pulling guns in the same motion. I hit the sidewalk and rolled into the opening to my right, my own gun finding its way into my hand, only a slight fraction behind the women. The shotgun blast followed a fraction of a second later, the blast passing over where we'd just been standing. The sound of the blast seemed to fill the whole tunnel.

I let loose a few shots in the direction of the shot and then moved further down the side tunnel I was in, trying to disappear into the darkness. The women also returned fire, then spread out, so they could cover the opening from different angles.

I could hear nothing from the other opening, but then, in the distance, I heard something: a train. Mirsada and Elizabeth looked to the right and then jumped back onto the sidewalk, their backs to the wall on either side of where their attacker had waited.

"Victor, were you hit?" Elizabeth shouted the question.

"No. I'm good. Can you hear anything?"

I knew her hearing put to shame anything Mirsada or I could hear, but she shouted a no. I watched her say something to Mirsada and the other woman nod back. A second later Elizabeth, gun extended, flew into the other opening, Mirsada right behind her. I started to follow them when the train, sounding like an enraged dragon, barreled by me, blocking my path.

I could see people through the train windows, reading, listening to iPods, or staring into space, unaware of the battle taking place outside their windows, ordinary people leading ordinary lives.

I took a few steps back, forced to wait until I could move, when I sensed something behind me. I turned quickly, my gun held out in front of me, all my senses on high alert. I about chalked it up to my imagination, when I saw a soft glow coming towards me.

I moved in the glow's direction, slowly, turning all my senses up to high alert. After a few feet, the glow got stronger and I saw a man standing in the middle of the passageway. The glow got stronger still and I could see the man's face.

I froze and I felt my world turned upside down, my gun nearly slipping from my fingers. It couldn't be. Can't be. Not possible. But there he stood, his arms out wide, beckoning me.

Son.

Bloody hell. It was my father.

CHAPTER TWENTY-EIGHT

Vincent Donal McCain died at the age of sixty-two from a heart attack, following nearly forty years working the line for Ford Motor Company, building pickup trucks. He'd been dead almost six years now, so all things considered, he looked pretty good.

My father topped my six foot six by two inches and weighed nearly three hundred pounds at death. The men picked to be his pallbearers were all strapping young men, not a lightweight among them.

He looked much like he did the last day I'd seen him alive: a full mane of grey hair which looked in need of a brushing, topped a face which showed the results of decades of consuming Irish whiskey and smoking unfiltered cigarettes. His nose was large, red and covered in drinker's veins.

Dressed in dark blue coveralls he wore every day to work, he looked as I remembered him. I felt my heart stop and break. I loved my dad and we were incredibly close. When he died, I refused to believe he was really gone. There could be no way this mountain of a man could ever die. And now that he stood in front of me, there could be no way he was alive.

I steadied the grip on my gun, keeping it pointed center mass of the man standing in front of me. "I don't know who or what you are, but you're NOT my father. My dad's dead."

My father shook his head in agreement.

I've been granted a few minutes to talk to you, son. Allowances have been made for me to do this. You are in grave danger and you will be dead before nightfall if you don't listen to what I have to say.

Could this be true? I'd seen a lot of weird things since taking over as the Hand of God. I've battled hellhounds, fallen angels, Infernal Lords. Hell, I almost bought the farm when I stopped to gaze at a frickin' cursed painting. I stood next to Uriel, an archangel, when he banished one of the Watchers back to oblivion, wielding the kind of power only surpassed by God.

"Fine. What do you have? Let's hear it."

He walked closer to me and I caught a whiff of Old Spice Aftershave, the kind he used to buy by the gallon. I almost burst into tears and I lowered my gun. He reached out, one big paw sliding around the back of my neck, and pulled me close, hugging me.

A sob escaped my chest and I hugged him back, experiencing something I thought lost forever. I wasn't home the day he died. I'd been halfway around the world in the mountains of Afghanistan, hunkered down behind some boulders waiting for a target to pass by on the trail below my unit. We were under radio silence and I didn't find out about his death until several days after the funeral. The last time I saw my dad alive was Christmas the previous year and I never got to say goodbye.

I have missed, you my son, and am very proud of you.

His words came to me in my mind, without him having to speak. Somewhere back in the deepest part of my brain, warning bells were trying to go off, but they were faint.

You have been fighting for too long, my son. It is time for you to rest. You are weary and you need your strength for what is to come.

His grip on me tightened and I felt a cold settle into my bones, and he was right. I was very tired. Tired of life, tired of the stress of never knowing when my time would come. Tired of worrying about my soul and what would happen when I did die. If I could only shut my eyes for a little while, I would be stronger, ready to face what came next. With my father watching over me, I would be safe.

Safe. Safe. Safe.

The word repeated over and over in my mind. I became distantly aware I was no longer holding my gun, it had fallen from my hand to the ground.

Safe. Safe. Safe.

And then I smelled it. Not the cologne my father always wore, but something else. Something rotten, a smell of decay and death. The smell wasn't strong, but it was there and the warning bells began to ring loudly, drowning out the feeling of peace and comfort that the words my father brought. The cold in my joints made it feel like each limb weighed more than I could lift.

When I tried to break the embrace, my father squeezed tighter and it became hard to breath. I fought for each breath like a man having run back-to-back marathons, my lungs burning from lack of oxygen.

Stop fighting me, son. I bring you the peace you need. Let me stop the pain of your existence.

And that's when the truth hit home like a hammer. Hell, my father never talked like this. Pain of your existence? My father came from Irish immigrants and cursed in ways that would make a sailor blush. My father would be more likely to say "stop your belly achin' and sit your ass down and kick back for a bit."

When I raised my head to look into the eyes of my father, the thing which held me knew the jig was up. The eyes turned from green to a bright red and his form changed. My father's face melted into one of nightmare, a walking corpse with most of its face rotted to nothing. It wore some type of cloak, black, dirty and torn in several places.

I felt fingernails dig deeply into my back and the coldness intensified. I knew if I didn't do something soon, I'd be a dead man. The thing gripped me so tightly I could barely move my arms. I tried breaking free, but no dice. Fine. Instead of trying to break free, I squeezed the thing with all the strength I had left and lifted it off its feet. While large, it didn't weigh as much as expected and I bent forward and ran the thing into the closest wall.

It screamed in my mind when I smashed it into the wall and I felt a jolt of intense pain when the creature retaliated and bit savagely into my shoulder. I screamed my own shout of defiance, turned and then drove the thing into the other wall, hearing bones crunch.

Its grip loosened and I shoved myself away, gaining a few feet of space.

You will die, human, and your soul will be mine.

Drawing Muramasa's katana, I said, "I think you're going to find out it sucks to be you." And I attacked.

I may lack the skill of an ancient samurai, or the grace of a well-trained swordsman like Mirsada, but I make up for it by being large and pissed off.

Tears streamed down my face, the thought of losing my father once again, fueling my rage. For a brief moment, I was able to hold my father and thought I would be given the chance to finally say goodbye, but instead I found something wicked this way comes and another slice of evil that wanted me dead.

I swung the sword with abandon, not trying for precision or skill, but to hack off as much of the thing in the quickest amount of time. Only later, when I relived the moment, did I realize I'd been yelling to my father while doing so.

The creature fought back, long finger nails scratching me across the chest and arms, but I paid the wounds no attention. Muramasa's blade, sharp beyond measure, passed through skin and bone, and with one last, mighty swing, I severed the creature at the waist, killing it and plunging the passageway back into darkness.

I dropped to my knees, breathing hard, my body covered in sweat and blood, and I spent the next several minutes, crying and praying to my father. I promised him I would make Cyrus Tyler, Preston Deveraux and any other follower of the prince of darkness I could find, pay for sullying his memory.

I searched in the darkness, found my gun and started back down towards the tracks. The train had long since disappeared into the night and I approached cautiously, listening.

From the other passageway, on the other side of the tracks, I heard someone sobbing and wailing. I practically hurdled the tracks to the other passageway. In the distance I could see the same kind of glow I noticed before my attack.

I picked up my pace and when I got close, I saw another creature like the one I'd encountered, holding Mirsada, her body stretched out in its arms at waist level.

"I tried to save you, I swear, I tried. Heaven help me, but I tried. Radomir, I'm sorry, but I tried."

Her skin, pale normally, seemed to be almost translucent, and I knew the thing was slowly killing her. When I got close enough I tucked the gun back into my jeans and moving quietly, got behind it before making my presence known.

"Hey, asshole. That's a friend of mine."

Flaming eyes turned my way, but too late. This time I aimed my strike, and I'll be damned if I didn't separate the creatures head from its body on the first try. The glow instantly vanished and I heard both bodies hit the concrete floor. I sheathed the sword, careful not to cut off a few of my own fingers in the process, searched until I found Mirsada, picked her up and headed back to the train tunnel and what light it provided.

I sat on the edge of the walkway, holding Mirsada. Her eyes were closed and her breathing ragged. I held her, rocking her like a child, and talked to her softly, telling her to come back.

I'm not sure how long we were there before her eyes opened, but finally, they did and when they met mine, they welled up with tears. She sat up shakily, looking around.

"Where is Radomir? He was here. I don't know how, but he was here."

"I'm sorry, Mirsada, but he wasn't."

I told her about my own battle and how the creature came to me in the form of my father. "Who is Radomir?" I asked.

She buried her face in her hands and cried more, before answering. "I grew up in Bosnia. My parents were Serbian and my father played a role during the ethnic cleansing which ravaged my country. Radomir and I were friends. Close friends. He and his family were Muslims and one night my father and a group of his friends were rounding up any Muslims they could find in our neighborhood. Radomir and his family went into hiding, but he told me where they would be so I would not worry," She choked down a few sobs, then continued.

"My father knew we were friends and when they could not find him and his family, my father came to me and asked me if I knew where they were hiding. I didn't want to tell him, but my father appealed to my nationalism. He told me it was my duty to tell him where they were hiding and I had to make a choice: my Muslim friends or my own family. I told him where Radomir's family were and they sent a mob over to the house, found them hiding in a hidden room in the basement, and drug the whole family into the street. They made Radomir rape his own sister, then shot them. I know all this because my father made me watch." Her whole body shook at the memory. "I begged him, to spare his life, to let him go. He ignored me and, in the end, I did nothing. Radomir *pleaded* to me to make them stop, and I did...nothing," Her voice trailed off, and a tear tracked down her cheek.

A minute passed, then she said, "When the peace came and the widespread ethnic cleansing stopped, my father and his friends? They continued to carry out attacks against Muslims and other non-Serbians, anyone not of pure Serbian bloodlines. I helped them," She shook her head in disgust. "I learned to fight and I was good. I felt numb to the suffering of others."

She stopped crying and held her hands in her lap. "For a time I no longer cared if I lived or died. But every night, Radomir came to me in my dreams, pleading for me to save him. And every night, I let him die. Finally, I met a woman who introduced me to the Faith and in time, I became the Hand of God. I work now, to atone for what happened to Radomir and his family, and all the other innocents we killed."

"The sins of the father are not the sins of the daughter. And, hell, you were only a kid. You did what you did because you didn't know any better."

"That's not true. I knew better. I could have lied and said I didn't know where they were and perhaps, if I'd done so, they would be alive today. But I have no regrets, Victor. I fight those who create such evil."

I nodded. My own story was not much different. I knew trying to save Mikey was wrong, but I did it anyways. I wondered if every Hand of God had a similar story. If we were all wayward people, adrift and trying to find our way back to shore.

I glanced around and then another wave of concern hit me. "Where's

Elizabeth?"

Mirsada turned and looked down the passageway. "She was in front of me when we started trying to find the shooter. She told me to hang back a bit because a gunshot would likely do little damage to her, compared to me. I did and then a glow appeared between us and I saw Radomir. Or, what I thought was Radomir. What do you think those things were?"

"I don't know, but I bet Brother Joshua will." I stood, went to the passageway and shouted for Elizabeth. Nothing. "You don't happen to have a flashlight, do you?"

Mirsada reached into an inner pocket of her vest and came out with a keychain with a small flashlight on the end. We searched the passageway until it ended in a supply closet, long since abandoned and a ladder leading up. Two bodies lay next to the ladder. I think they were both men, but one was stomped beyond recognition, so I couldn't be sure. The other must have been the shotgun shooter. I figured this to be the case as he had a shotgun sticking out of his chest, having been rammed through his body from behind. There could be little doubt Elizabeth came this way.

I climbed the ladder and lifted the door. It groaned, rusty hinges protesting, but with a last shove, it flopped open.

The warm night air greeted us and we both climbed out into an alley between what looked to be two warehouses. I lifted the door and dropped it shut. We could see a main thoroughfare at one end of the alley and we walked that way.

When we got to the end of it, we got our bearings and Mirsada lead the way back to my car. We got there with no problems and Mirsada handed me the keys and I opened the trunk, got a new shirt and more ammo for the Glock.

She took out the medical kit and our roles were reversed, with her now taking care of my wounds. There were scratches on my body I didn't even know about until she gently rubbed antiseptic covering each one. She did the same for the torture wound and then covered it with gauze, taping it into place.

While she worked, I asked, "Do you ever wonder what the hell we're really doing? If we're making a difference?"

She let out a small sigh. "Only every day. Every time we eliminate a threat, two more show up. It's one reason I've been on edge since arriving here in the States. I'd hoped it might be different here and it's not."

I smiled. "Suggesting I need to do better?"

"No. Suggesting no matter how good we are, we won't ever be good enough."

She tore off the last piece of tape, secured the gauze, and then put the kit away. I put my shirt on carefully, trying not to rub the wounds, but did it anyway.

"But there's one thing I know for sure," she said.

"And what's that?"

She stared off at the city lights. "That if you, I and the other Hand of God around the planet weren't doing what we do, things would be even worse. Every time we kill something evil, that's one more thing which can't hurt anyone."

I breathed in deeply and let it out slow. I knew she was right. That was always the argument, it could be worse. Without myself, Winston, Kurt, and others there would be hundreds, if not thousands of dead people from the foiled bird flu attack. And the Watchers would have laid waste to the entire planet, if set free. There could be no doubt we were making a difference. Only it was hard to tell if we were making a real difference or trying to empty the ocean one spoonful at a time.

"Do you think that's enough?"

It took a while, but she nodded slowly. "It has to be."

We got into the car and waited for two hours before we left, neither of us talking about the obvious. Elizabeth was gone and we didn't know why.

CHAPTER TWENTY-NINE

"Do you think she brought those creatures to kill us?" Mirsada finally asked.

"I've been wondering the same thing, but I doubt it. I mean, if she wanted me dead she could have let the guy flay me alive and then try to take you out. For all we know they were sent after her and we were collateral damage. She could have killed me several times over and hasn't. I will cut her some slack until we find out what happened. After all, another couple of minutes and people would be wondering the same about you and me."

We were holed up at a Waffle House in downtown Philly. I ordered the largest omelet on the menu, added hash browns, four slices of toast, butter milk gravy, and a side order of bacon, washed down with a gallon of coffee. Mirsada sat eating a bowl of oatmeal with chocolate milk. Wimp.

I could not ever remember being more tired than right at that very moment. Yet at the same time, I could not be more ready for a fight. I called J when we pulled into the parking lot with a backup burner phone I kept for emergencies and he told me we likely came up against a couple of wraiths and were lucky to be alive. Their main claim to fame came from their ability to, literally, suck the life out of you. They read your surface thoughts and then pretend to be someone you know, to draw you close. Then they drain your life force, thereby extending theirs.

J believed Lucifer and Tyler kept them in the area to act like spiders, capturing anyone who came too close to finding their kill spot in the abandoned train station. I didn't really give a damn one way or the other. They tried to use the memory of my father to kill me and it royally pissed me off. Fine. They want to play hardball, then fuck'em.

My resolve, which left a lot to be desired over the last few months, needed a good ass kicking to get it on track and the last twenty-four hours did the trick. And now they had not one, but two ticked off Hand of Gods to rain down fire and brimstone on their ass. Like me, she was angered to the core with the wraith using Radomir to try and kill her. Sons-a-bitches must pay.

"I'm surprised to hear myself say this, but I think you're right. It goes against every fiber of my body to believe her, but I do. I now think she does want to be redeemed. Do you think she died down there?"

"Anything is possible. But it's been my experience when you kill an Infernal Lord, they turn to brimstone and we didn't find her body or smell any sulfur. Maybe they've captured her, but it would take a small army to put that woman down."

She drank her chocolate milk and took another bite of her oatmeal, with half a bowl left, while my plate was two pieces of bacon short of being clean. "What do we do next?"

I wolfed down the bacon, set my plate to the side, took my laptop out of the carrying case and fired it up. "We know there's a bomb in Stafford's knee and they can set it off any time they want, so the question is when? Let's take a look at his upcoming schedule and see what he has planned."

I spent the next ten minutes checking out his calendar, that of the Senate and found several things which might be the target, but nothing jumped out at me. Then I found it.

I clicked over to the Google Machine and typed in Senator Stafford and schedule and hit enter. Three lines down, under the news tab, I found a short blurb about a fundraiser to be held here in Philadelphia, hosted by Stafford at his home. The guest list? No less than the President and Vice-President of the United States. Every big money donor and bundler would be there as well, not to mention anybody who was anybody.

"Holy hell." I flipped the laptop around so she could read the same blurb.

Her eyes widened. "The Constitution. The one Isaac put in his duffel. The order of succession here in the States. If both the President and Vice-President are killed, then—"

"Tyler becomes the next President of the United States. The last presidential election was last year, meaning, he would be president for three years before there's another election. Think of the chaos the man could cause between now and then."

"Hold on. If the President and Vice-President are both there, then security will be jacked up for their visit. They will have bomb sniffing dogs and electronic devices. Won't they find the bomb?"

"I doubt it. Stafford will already be there. Besides, the Majority Leader of the U.S. Senate won't be going through the same security checks anyone else will be that night. I'm guessing they won't. I'm sure Tyler will have someone on the inside, and the moment the three men are together, they will set the bomb off and this country will have its second President Tyler. Ironic. The first President Tyler also became president with the death of his predecessor, William Henry Harrison."

"How do we stop them? Is there someone we can call?"

"That's the problem with things like this. We ran into the same problem with the Church's plans to infect thousands of kids with a virus delivered by computers. It sounds like you've been sniffing glue when you say it out loud."

"Still, with the President and Vice-President on hand, they have to take any threat seriously. How could they ignore it?"

"I would normally agree with you. But again, say it out loud. 'Dear Mr. Secret Service agent, the President is in danger because the Speaker of the House arranged for a bomb to be planted into the knee joint of the Majority Leader of the Senate.' See the problem? We would get the same reaction going straight to Stafford. They'd lock us up on a seventy-two hour psych hold."

"Then we need to attack it from the other end. You said this man, Stiles, showed you the detonator, right? So we find him and take it away from him."

"Now you're talking. But we need a backup plan, just in case we can't find him or he doesn't have it any longer. How well can you cut a rug?"

Her spoon stopped half-way to her mouth. "Come again?"

"Dance. How well do you dance? I think you and I need to attend that fundraiser this weekend. Part of the event is a ball being held in the convention center next to the building where Stafford lives. It also means you will have to find something else to wear. I mean, I love the whole wood elf garb, but I'm not sure you should wear it to a black tie event."

She gave me the finger, but smiled doing it. "You really think you can get us in?"

"All it takes is a fifty grand donation to the Democratic Party. Piece of cake. Let me call Kurt and tell him what I need."

I got my hacker friend out of bed, gave him the details, and set him to work. I paid our bill and we left the Waffle House. When we started we had no clue what we were after. Now we had targets and a working plan. I worried about what Elizabeth's disappearance meant, but shoved it to the side. Forward momentum is what I needed. We now had it and I wanted to make sure we kept it.

First things first, I called and booked adjacent rooms at the Hotel Monaco. The hotel, rated the best in Philadelphia, sat right downtown, with Independence Hall and the Liberty Bell across the street. To stay there, we would both need a step up in wardrobe. I hit the Brooks Brothers in town to pick up slacks, shirts and new shoes, claiming lost luggage as my excuse. Right down the street, we found a boutique to suit Mirsada's European sensibilities. Between the two of us, we racked up a clothing bill of several thousand dollars, but we were now dressed to the nines.

We hid our weapons in the weapons locker of my car, though Mirsada was not happy parting with her sword. When I pointed out you can't walk into one of the country's premier hotels packing a katana, she relented. But not easily.

Our rooms were not overly large, but both had king size beds and a view of Independence Hall. We made arrangements to hook up mid-afternoon. I then went to my room, took a hot shower and then went to bed for a quick power nap, asking the desk to wake me at one p.m.

It seemed I'd barely closed my eyes when I got the phone call to get up and at 'em, but I got dressed, this time in slacks, loafers and a polo shirt and headed to the lobby to wait for Mirsada. She came down a few minutes later wearing an all-white tennis outfit, shirt and shorts, with white Nike shoes. She'd braided her hair into a French braid. All she needed to complete the ensemble was the racket.

The change in outfits made her into a completely different woman. The warrior now became every man's desire and more than one head turned to watch her walk from the elevators to join me.

I offered her my arm and she slipped her hand around my elbow and we walked outside into the shimmering heat. Stafford's town home was only a few blocks down the street and we took our time getting there, window shopping and acting like a happy couple.

Stafford lived in the Founders Building, situated on Washington Square, a six acre park in downtown Center City. We strolled down paths winding in and out of the trees, while watching the comings and goings from the Founders Building. The Secret Service undoubtedly were already engaged in pre-visit planning and I wouldn't be surprised if someone was keeping track of us while we walked around. We sat on a bench for a bit on the other side of the park, Founders partially visible through the trees.

My phone chirped, I pulled it out of my pocket and answered. Mirsada crossed one long leg over the other, bouncing her foot and I tried hard not to stare.

"I'm on the scene," Winston said. "Kurt will be here on the next flight. I'll work to find our missing friend and let you know when I can track him down."

I'd asked Kurt to get a hold of Winston and set him on the trail of Stiles. Kurt did some digging and found a man with that name and general age owning a small home on the outskirts of D.C. Winston and Kurt would set up surveillance and see if it was our guy, while Mirsada and I would watch for him here in Philadelphia. I had to think he knew I had made it out of the train station by now, skin intact, thank the dear Lord, and would be coming for him. I hoped I saw him coming before he saw me.

"Good. Call me as soon as you know anything."

"Any word on Elizabeth?" Winston asked.

"Nothing, man. It has me worried. But all we can do is what we're doing. Happy hunting."

"Yeah. You, too. Try and stay alive."

We both hung up and I put my phone away, then filled in Mirsada on the part she couldn't hear. "Now we wait. With any luck, Winston and Kurt will be able to track down Stiles and then we can move on him."

"And what do you and I do?"

"Pray for divine intervention."

"Does that work for you very often?"

I laughed. "Almost never."

And then it did. Across the park I saw a man I knew, walking past the Founders Building. a man I would never forget. Preston Deveraux strode down the sidewalk like a man without a care in the world.

Time for Fate to give Preston something to care about. And I was the man for the job.

CHAPTER THIRTY

It's hard for me to blend in with the crowd, considering I'm a good foot taller than anyone else and almost twice as wide. This meant letting Mirsada take the lead in following Deveraux, while I hung back even further and followed her. We were on the opposite side of the street and it gave me a chance to watch her at work, not to mention to admire her figure and the way she walked and moved through the crowd.

I'd never given any thought to there being other people who were the Hand of God. And if I had, I would never have considered one being a woman. That's not a sexist comment—at least I don't think it is. There have been times when the only reason I survived an encounter with a big ole' nasty was because I was bigger and stronger than the whack job I was up against.

For Mirsada to do what I do, day in and day out, that made her one tough lady. She didn't have my size to help out, which meant she needed to compensate for it in other ways. I thought back to her fighting Muramasa and how she did so with no fear, no doubt. She expected to kick his ass and gave it a good run.

I'd asked her earlier how many years she'd served as the Hand of God and she told me she'd been doing this for going on four years, a lot longer than me. The years gave her a hard look and I could only imagine how I would look after a few more years of doing this job, if I managed to stay alive. I remembered once seeing the before and after pictures of presidents and how the job aged them. I now understood how they felt.

And yet, the woman was beautiful in her own way. You would not call any one feature gorgeous, but the collection made her the kind of woman most men turned and gave a second glance. More than one man whistled while she strolled down the sidewalk. One of them pushed things a bit far and it was hard for Mirsada to ignore him, but she did to keep up with Preston. When I went by the asshole I pretended to stumble and slammed him into a light pole, giving him a little extra shoulder for good measure. Jerk.

Mirsada stopped at an ice cream shop and placed an order. When I finally caught up she gave me a cup filled with a double scoop of strawberry and a spoon, her cup filled with chocolate. We found an empty table in front of the shop and sat down, tearing into the ice cream, my back to where Preston had been walking.

"He met a woman in front of the coffee shop on the next block. I couldn't see her face because she wore a hoodie and kept her face hidden. The two shook hands and then walked inside together. Deveraux was smiling. It seemed like they knew each other well."

I ate my strawberry ice cream and considered what I wanted to do. My preference was to walk into the coffee shop, grab a handful of hair and then slam his face into a table a half dozen times. Not a good call in a busy city in the middle of the day, but that's what I felt like doing.

"He doesn't know me," Mirsada said. "Why don't I go inside and maybe I can even get a table close enough to them to listen in on their conversation."

"You only assume he doesn't know you." I glanced around, seeing a bookstore a little ways up the block. "Let's find a spot inside the bookstore where we can see the coffee shop."

She finished her ice cream, tossed the cup into a trash can and walked inside the bookstore with me right behind her. I found a magazine rack near the front window and browsed through a copy of the *Economist* while watching for Deveraux. I learned the Iranian revolution was over, politicians were moving to the center, which was utter bullshit, and European banks were looking for stress relief. Aren't we all?

A half hour later, Deveraux walked out and headed in our direction. But he was not alone. The woman he had met with came out on his arm, and the two of them were laughing like old friends. She tilted her face in my direction, and despite the hoody, I could clearly see Elizabeth's face. I nearly ripped the magazine in half, watching as they walked past the bookstore and up the street. A clerk shot me a dirty look and I smoothed out the magazine, returning it to the shelf slightly more wrinkled than when I picked it up.

Mirsada appeared beside me, her anger barely in check. "Did you see who he was with? You don't get to keep me from killing her this time. Swear it."

I didn't answer, but watched until they were nearly a block ahead and left the store, Mirsada fuming at my heels.

I didn't know what to think about what Elizabeth was doing. There could be no doubt she found a way to get in Deveraux's good graces, but I didn't have a clue what the end game could be. In Columbus, they tried to kill her. Or had they? In the end, the most they did was shoot her with a tracer bullet. Did they do all that for my benefit? I couldn't see how it helped. Now my head really did hurt.

They turned left and walked down to another hotel, going into the lobby. When I got to the door, I waited a few beats and then went inside in time to see the door close on an elevator with the two of them inside, starting to kiss as the door closed.

I watched the numbers go up over the elevator, finally stopping on the ninth floor, staying there. I walked over and punched the button harder than normal and waited for my ride up. I don't know why her kissing Deveraux bothered me, but it did. Mirsada stood there, arms crossed, and the two of us looked like ticked off lovers.

It made me think of the first time Samantha kissed me in a small dive bar in Louisville, not out of love, but to cause a distraction hoping an Infernal Lord would not notice her. And Elizabeth first plying me with sex to get me to do what she wanted. It was a new world and I felt like I was walking in quicksand a lot of the time.

The elevator dinged, the doors opened and we got on and rode up to the ninth floor. It opened onto a quiet, red carpeted hallway, rooms stretching off in both directions. We stepped out and the doors closed behind us and we tried to decide which way to go. Then my phone chirped and I got a text from a number I didn't recognize which said "room 914."

A sign on the wall pointed me in the direction I needed to go and made my way to the right room. At the far end of the hall, I noticed a door leading to the stairway was closing. I stood to the left of room 914, and Mirsada stood on the other side. We listened for a moment, but heard nothing. The door was cracked open with a drink coaster.

I almost charged into the room, but made myself walk normal, trying to stay calm. I know most martial arts teachers will tell you to be an effective fighter, you must keep your emotions in check, the spiritual and the physical working in harmony. I've found, for me, the angrier I am, the more emotional I am, the more carnage I can create. I feed off the turmoil and it brings clarity to what I need to do. Weird, huh?

The room was large with a king size bed, full sofa, two armed chairs and a desk. I stopped by the bed, and looked around but did not see Deveraux. His suit coat and tie were folded on one of the chairs, but that was the only evidence he'd been in the room.

Mirsada shut the door behind me and said, "In the bathroom?"

I walked over to the bathroom door and opened it, finding Deveraux in the combination shower and tub, trussed up with what looked to be a phone cord, a wash rag stuffed into his mouth. His normally perfectly quaffed hair now stood on end. The man, at least, had put up a fight. But lost. He stared at me a moment, his eyes dazed, but then they focused and I could see intelligence return. And hatred.

I grabbed him by the shirt and lifted him out of the tub and sat him down hard on the toilet. "I'm going to remove the rag. If you start screaming I will put it back and then do things to you which might not help me get to heaven, but will make me feel a whole lot better. How the next few minutes go, is up to you. Understand?"

He nodded his agreement and I removed the gag. He spat out threads for a few moments, while he regained his composure. I could see a nice welt popping up on his forehead where Elizabeth clocked him with something, a nasty bruise marring those George Clooney good looks.

"Well, well, well. Victor McCain stooping so low he needs to have a woman do his dirty work for him. Oh, how the mighty have fallen. First you use Samantha Tyler, then Elizabeth Bathory." He leered at Mirsada, "and now this gorgeous creature. Hiding behind skirts. Maybe you should be called the Wimp of God."

"So says the man tied up like a Thanksgiving turkey because he thought with the wrong head. But you're wrong, Preston. This woman is not an empty skirt. She's also a Hand of God. Where's Elizabeth?"

"Then my apologies, my dear. You must be Mirsada Versela, since you don't look Asian. I've read about you, but never seen a picture, much to my sorrow. We knew there were two female members of your little club, one European and one Asian."

"Preston, I asked you where's Elizabeth? Don't make me ask you again."

"Obviously, not here and where she is now, I have no clue. She betrayed me, tied me up and tossed me in the tub, then left."

I let that go for the moment, because he was right. If she left him for me, he likely didn't know where she was going.

"How did she get to you? A few days ago you wanted to kill her. You sent Muramasa to cut her to pieces. Why the meet and greet?"

"She contacted me, said she wanted to turn you over. She told me you knew about the bomb and she wanted to be forgiven by the Lord of Light. She also told me if I tried to double-cross her again she would rip my throat out and eat it. I believed her. She suggested we meet in a public place, one with a lot of people, just the two of us. I agreed and you see how it turned out for me. You would have thought an ex-lover would treat me better."

"What the hell are you talking about?" The cold, dark anger which seemed to be a large part of my existence these days, began to fight for control of my brain. I didn't want to hear what the man had to say, but knew I would beat him to death if he didn't talk.

"Elizabeth recruited me when I was a young man, showed me the pleasures I could enjoy if I agreed to follow the Lord of Light. She is greatly responsible for making me the man I am today. I owed it to her to at least listen. In Columbus, we weren't trying to kill her so much as punish her and kill you."

I looked at Mirsada and I could see doubt in her eyes. I didn't know what to believe myself. If Elizabeth and Deveraux had been lovers, it would explain the kiss in the elevator. Considering she murdered women and children to bathe in their blood, the fact she slept with Deveraux shouldn't make one bit of difference to me, but it did. I could feel my cheeks burning with Mirsada standing next to me, once again being proven right that the Infernal Lord used sex to get what she wanted. Did that include me? I liked to think when it came to me, it wasn't all about the sex. Idiot? Wishful thinking?

More immediately, if she was still on my team, then why didn't she wait for Mirsada and me at the hotel room? She must have seen us in the bookstore, since she sent me a text to tell me the room number. But why run and not wait for us? The closing stairwell door must have been her. It appeared Elizabeth was running her own game now and, for whatever reason, cut Mirsada and me out.

I shoved my anger and hurt down and tried to focus on the matter at hand. I needed to know what Deveraux knew.

"Time to cut this short, Preston. I need to ask you a few questions about what Cyrus Tyler has planned. When will he set off the bomb?"

"No clue. Not to change the subject, but I am curious. Have you ever wondered how your life would have been different if you'd killed me in that kitchen in Louisville, like I advised you to do? Not killing me lead directly to the death of Dominic Montoya, the capture of Samantha Tyler, and many other things you have no knowledge of, all because you didn't have the guts to do what needed to be done. You lost your soul because you were too weak to do what needed to be done. No wonder you have women doing your work for you now. I think—"

I grabbed him by the throat, cutting him off. "You know what, Preston? You're right. I should have killed you when I had the chance. That's a mistake I won't make this time."

I lifted him off the toilet, raised the lid and forced Deveraux onto his knees. "I hope you find this a fitting way to die, Preston, because this is what your whole life means in the grand scheme of things."

I shoved his face into the water, pressing down as hard as I possibly could. I thought he would fight me, try and raise his head out of the water, but he didn't. Not at first. His body remained calm, almost relaxed, with the occasional air bubbles floating to the surface. Back on that night long ago he told me he didn't fear death because Satan promised him another shot at the big time and he would come back stronger and more powerful than ever. What kind of man wants to die bad enough so he can go to Hell, and then come back? Whack job.

Facing death bravely in thought, is one thing. Doing it is something else altogether. When the last of his air was gone, he started trying to fight his way free, his body's need for air overpowering his desire to die his way. His feet drummed the floor and he tried to twist out of my grasp, but I had strength and leverage on my side, and kept his face planted inside his porcelain grave. In the end, his struggles didn't make any difference. I held him down until I was sure he was gone.

I stood, breathing harder than I should have been. I could cross killing Deveraux off my bucket list, yet it didn't make me feel any better. And that surprised me. I finally had revenge for Dominic Montoya, a man I knew only for a few days, but for whom I felt great empathy. And for Samantha, who spent a brutal three months being ravaged by a fallen angel, thanks to this man.

In the end, his death meant very little in the grand scheme of things. None of our lives did, when it gets right down to it. But in the here and now, they were all we had. Hell, when did I become so maudlin?

Mirsada laid a hand on my arm. "We should be going, don't you think?"

"Yeah. We should. Let's toss the place first."

We did, but found nothing useful. We agreed to leave separately then meet up at the Hotel Monaco. She left first. I sat on the edge of the bed and stared at Preston through the bathroom door. I wondered if Satan would grant his request to return as an Infernal Lord. Wouldn't that be a kick in the teeth? Not for the first time I wondered how I'd die. One thing I promised myself: death by toilet would not be allowed to happen.

I gave myself a mental bitch slap to snap out of it, saluted the other man's dead body and left the room. Mikey and Deveraux were together again, maybe even nailed to the same wall. Sucks to be them.

Now it was time to add Cyrus Tyler to their growing old boys club in Hell.

CHAPTER THIRTY-ONE

Mirsada and I laid low for the remainder of the day, hanging out at the hotel and rested. She joined me for dinner in my room and then retired early to get some sleep. She didn't bring up what Deveraux told us about being recruited by Elizabeth, never said I told you so, and didn't rub it in my face. For that I was eternally grateful.

I almost asked her to stay with me for the night, but resisted the temptation. If I didn't reign in my libido, I would need to change my theme song to *I Get Around*. Perhaps I wanted to put Elizabeth and Samantha out of my mind. Who the hell knows? I think what bothered me more than anything else was Elizabeth not telling me about her past with Deveraux. We all keep secrets and I could intellectualize why she wouldn't tell me, but it didn't help.

I checked in with Winston and Kurt, but no sign of Stiles. Kurt did his best to find the man via cyber space, but Stiles lived off the grid. I suggested he used an alias for most things and we weren't likely to find anything, but for them to keep after him.

Several times while lying in bed, I picked up my phone and started to call Samantha, only to put the phone down each time. I needed to move on, but found it hard doing so. I wondered if it would be too late for me to join a monastery and live out my life reading esoteric texts and chanting Latin songs at sunset. Yeah, I think that ship sailed a long time ago.

The next morning, I thought for sure the death of Preston Deveraux would make the morning paper and the local stations, but there was no mention of him. Nor later that night on the evening news shows.

That was not the case for Dr. Collins and her daughter. Their deaths were all over the news for several days. Senator Stafford issued a statement of sympathy for her family and promising to do something in the next session of congress to increase funding for drug treatment programs. If he only knew. The Speaker of the House, Cyrus Tyler, said this proved we had to get tougher on crime and to put an end to the movement to make illegal drugs legal.

What a sanctimonious son of a bitch. I almost threw the remote control though the TV set, it made me so angry. The man made the usual politician seem like an angel in comparison.

My phone shouted at me and a glance at the screen told me Winston was calling.

"What's up brother from another mother?"

"Man, we're bringing the circus to you,' he said.

"Tyler is coming to Philadelphia? Damn."

"Yeah, to a place called Washington Square. I've never been there, but with a name like that, I'm guessing it's not far from where you're holed up?"

"Very close. Stafford's fundraiser is being held at a building right off the square. Why's Tyler coming?"

"He's called for all good Republicans to show up in the park and protest the fact the President is holding a fundraiser while the country is having problems abroad and at home. They hope to get a couple thousand Tea Party members to show, make the news. Same old bull shit. You think he wants to be nearby when things happen?"

"Stride right into the rubble and take charge? With a bank of cameras and microphones already there? I think you can bet on it."

"Well, we are on our way. Save us a spot at the party. Still no sign of Stiles. He's gotta be there someplace."

He hung up and I went back to wanting to throw things. Over the next few days Mirsada and I kept up our tour of the city in our down time. We visited Independence Hall, took in the Liberty Bell and ate our dinners at different restaurants around town. I got fitted for a tux for the fundraising dinner and ball on Saturday. Mirsada picked out a stunning blue Donna Karan dress. I only knew the name because she told me. I knew it to be fancy by the price tag. Ouch.

I called a car company to arrange to pick us up at the appointed time and then we settled in to wait. Winston shadowed Tyler to a couple of different events, but found no signs of Stiles. Kurt sat in a van near the man's house, same result. Nada. Both Winston and Kurt would drive to Philly Friday night, then join the Tea Party crew with Tyler in Washington Square.

Time seemed to drag by until Saturday. Mirsada and I ate a large lunch at an outdoor café. One thing I can say about the woman, is she's not afraid to eat. We both took naps late in the afternoon, not knowing when we would get the next chance.

While asleep, I dreamed about Samantha, Elizabeth and Mirsada. They kept saying I overlooked something about Tyler's plan. They berated me for not seeing it and I pleaded with them to tell me what I'd missed. I tossed and turned, but when I woke up, I knew what they were talking about.

I got my phone and sat heavily in one of the chairs and called Kurt. When he answered I said, "Kurt, I need you to look at who works for Senator Stafford, the President and Vice-President, but I'm thinking you need to zero in on Stafford."

"I can do that, dude, but what am I looking for?"

"If they plan to set the bomb off tonight, then they need to do it when the three men are together. How will they know when that is unless someone tells them? They need a bird-dog to alert them to the right moment. Otherwise, the plan fails. Have your hacking buddies hit this hard. We've only got a couple of hours left."

"You got it, man." He hung up and I tossed the phone on the end table and took one of the longest showers of my life, trying hard not to think of anything, but thinking about everything.

An hour and a half before the event, we got dressed and met in my room for a last strategy pow wow before the car came to pick us up. Mirsada dazzled in the Donna Karan, her hair once again in a French braid, with a blue clutch purse to complete the ensemble.

She helped me with my bow tie. God how I hate ties. Suits and I rarely ever made an acquaintance and I hadn't worn a tux since my senior prom. I apologized for not getting her a corsage, making her laugh.

Once we were both properly dressed, we sat down on the bed to discuss the evening. I told her about my thoughts on the spotter, but admitted I didn't have anything else.

"I wish I could tell you what I had planned, but I don't have a clue. With any luck, we will see Stiles and can take him down. Or Kurt comes through and we find out who they have on the inside. If not, we need to try and get to Stafford. I still think if we tell him there's a bomb in his knee, one he won't believe us, and two, I can't afford to be that much in the spotlight. But we might not have any other play. Do you have any last minute insights?"

"I spend most of my time improvising when I am in situations like this, so I think we go, see what's what and then react the best we can."

"I'm beginning to think you are the female me. Besides, if you're like me, you work better when you're winging it."

We went downstairs and a man stood in the lobby holding a sign which read "Clay." Clay is one of my favorite undercover names and tonight Mirsada and I were Wilson and Audrey Clay, of the Kentucky Clay's. Henry Clay is surpassed by only Abraham Lincoln, when it comes to politicians born in Kentucky. Kurt created a good back story and documents for me some months back, for when I needed an alias. It didn't take much for him to do the same for Mirsada.

We introduced ourselves to our driver, and then followed him out to the car, a Cadillac limo. We got in and the driver started on the short drive to the Founders Building. The evening was warm, with a bright full moon hanging over the city. Things slowed when we turned right by Washington Square, with the traffic backed up due to people being dropped off for the event.

To my left, I could see the protestors in full swing in Washington Square. I could make out several protest signs, one saying "stop shredding our Constitution." Another said "English is our language, no excetions, learn it" with exceptions misspelled. Glorious.

In the distance I could see a stage and guessed that was where Cy Tyler and the other pols would be speaking. I texted Winston and asked if he was in position, getting a smiley face in response. Cute.

Our car made it to the curb at the Founders Building, and we got out. The driver gave me his card and told me to call when we were ready to be picked up. I thanked him and offered Mirsada my arm. She accepted and we walked inside.

We were required to first meet a hostess where my ID was checked, confirmed, and signed in. Then we passed through a security check. Despite my nervousness, we got through with no issues. People shot glances at us constantly. I am sure it was due to Mirsada looking so lovely and not because she walked with a man twice the size of everyone else there.

The ballroom at the Founders was huge and decorated in Early American, what else, with a nod towards modern sensibilities. Yeah, whatever. The main thing was a band played at one end, there was a spot for dancing and off to either side of the room, there was a large bar. I steered Mirsada to one of these and ordered a Fireball Whisky neat, while she asked for a Riesling.

When our drinks were served, we made our way to a table off to one side, allowing us to people watch. The President, Vice-President and Majority Leader would not make an appearance until much later in the evening. My watch showed seven p.m. and I knew from the email we received in response to my donation, the President and VP would show around eight, giving us an hour to figure something out.

About half way through my whisky, my phone vibrated in my tux pocket. A quick glance showed me it was Kurt.

"Tell me you got something," I said.

Tony Acree

"Janet Marx. She's an assistant to Stafford's chief of staff, the one who makes sure things run on time and acts as the go-getter when anyone needs anything. One of the things we got from the Black Hat's computer was a list of Church members who could prove useful. Her name is on the list. She has be your girl."

He texted me her DMV photo and I thanked him and hung up. I put my lips near Mirsada's ear and whispered, "We have a name. Janet Marx. Aide to Stafford. We need to find her. Now."

I pulled up the picture and showed it to Mirsada and we both stood, leaving our drinks behind. At several spots around the room, there were volunteers wearing blue Democratic National Committee jackets. A young man wearing one of the jackets walked through the room near us, so I intercepted him.

I stuck out my hand. "Hi. I'm Wilson Clay, this is my wife Audrey. I was wondering if you could help us. I was told by a good friend of mine, once I got here I should speak to Janet Marx, an aide to Senator Stafford. Can you tell me where I can find her?"

"I'm not sure. One second, let me call someone and ask." He pulled out a phone of his own and punched in a number. While he did this, I glanced around the room and my eyes landed on a man across the room and I was rocked by a feeling of wrongness strong enough to make me take a step back.

Mirsada tightened her grip on my arm and hissed, "What's wrong?"

For a moment I couldn't answer. But I'd felt this feeling before. Several times. When coming face to face with a fallen angel. The man looked familiar, but I couldn't place him.

I raised a finger, asking Mirsada for a moment. The man locked eyes with me and even from this distance, I could see his eyes, for a brief moment, changed, and I knew there would be stars falling in them.

The young man put his phone away and smiled. "Ms. Marx will meet you at the north ballroom entrance." He pointed to double doors in the far corner of the room.

"Thank you. One more thing. Can you tell me who the man is over there, the one with the woman in the red dress?"

The young man turned to see who I meant. "Oh. That's Alex Dabney. He's the owner and CEO of Dabney Industrial Tech."

Holy hell. When I fought with and kicked the ass of the Watchers, one of them had already flown the coop, going rogue. None of the others knew where he'd gone. Now I knew. Gadriel had taken up residence in the mind of one of America's largest weapons makers. No real surprise there. I'd done some research on him in the months following my take down of

Samyaza and the others. Gadriel was the angel who taught man how to make and use weapons, before his banishment until Judgment Day. I could only imagine what type of horror Gadriel could bring about in Dabney's body.

I thanked the volunteer and started towards Dabney. Mirsada said, "Victor, when I look at Dabney, I get a bad feeling."

"Yeah. Me, too. It's because he has a fallen angel in his head. Be ready, this could get nasty quick."

I also recognized the woman on his arm. She'd been on the cover of this year's *Sports Illustrated* swimsuit issue. Guess being a fallen angel had its perks.

When Dabney and I were face to face, the other people around us gave us some space. I'm not sure what type of vibe regular people got around one of these things, but the tension between the two of us could be felt, the air practically full of electricity. Mirsada stepped a few paces to the side, putting some distance between us and seeing to it if an attack happened, Gadriel would need to fight two fronts. Elsa, the super model, also moved back and away from the two of us. A supermodel with a brain.

I didn't offer him my hand. I wanted to keep them free in case he decided to attack here and now.

"Gadriel. We finally meet. Seems you found a fun place to call home."

Gadriel/Dabney set his drink down, freeing up his own hands. "And not one, but two Hands of Gods. I feel honored. How did you find out about me?"

"Luck. We're here on another matter. But I'll make time for you. After taking out the other eleven fallen angels, being able to say I'd kicked the ass of a dozen fallen angels would be sweet. Kind of like collecting the whole set."

He glanced around the room. "You mean to take me on here? In front of all these people? I don't think so," he shook his head. "And if you did, what about the real reason you are here? Think you would still be able to stop what is coming if you were fighting me? I don't think so."

He was right and it pissed me off. Fighting an angel, even a fallen one, could get ugly. And people would get hurt. Regular human beings are nothing more than cattle to the Devine. He would kill everyone in the room without shedding a single tear.

I leaned in close, our noses almost touching. "You'd better find another body because when I'm done here, I'm going to hunt you down and rip you to pieces with my bare hands. I will send you to share oblivion with Samyaza and the rest of your old buddies."

He rubbed his chin with one hand for a second, then smiled. "I don't think so. I like this one. And Alex wants me to stay. He's found my knowledge to be...invaluable. The two of us can create weapons never dreamed of by common man. The two of us have grand plans. I think the one who needs to be careful is you, Victor McCain." He glanced at Mirsada. "And I'll know everything there is to know about you before the night is over. You'll be next."

"You are fallen for a reason," she responded. "And I will wipe the floor with your entrails before you could lay a hand on me."

Yep. No doubt, the female me. I reached out and adjusted Gadriel/Dabney's bow tie, then smoothed out his lapels. "When I put you in the ground for good, I'm going out to the farm where your body is buried and take a leak over the spot. I'm sure it will get down to you eventually. Enjoy what little time you have left."

He made no attempt to hold back the hate he felt, his mouth pulling back in a snarl. I gave him a wink, once again offered Mirsada my arm, and we left in search of Ms. Marx.

"Life keeps getting better and better," I said.

"Do you think he will jump bodies?"

"While I don't know for sure, I doubt it. Dabney is as close to perfect as a fallen angel can get. Rich, weapons making bachelor? Hell, he's Tony Stark without the Iron Man suit. I wouldn't want to change if I were him. Plus he has the resources to make my life difficult. So, no. I think he will come after us first. Better watch your ass when this is done."

She nodded agreement and we made our way to the north entrance. I can't begin to tell you how hard that was with a deadly fallen angel behind you, but we managed.

We only had to wait a few minutes, when the door opened and a woman matching Marx's photo ID walked out. Wearing a cream colored dress which stopped a few inches above the knees, and a string of what looked to be very expensive pearls, she smiled at us and offered her hand.

"Hi. I'm Janet Marx, and you are the Clay's?"

She had a firm handshake and a pretty smile. "Yes. Is there a place we can speak with a little less crowd noise? I would like to discuss contributing more to the DNC, but I have a few questions about how the money will be spent."

"By all means, follow me."

She turned, held the door open for us, and then led us down a long hallway to a conference room with a long table and a dozen chairs. She waved us to a seat. I took the chair at the head of the table, with Mirsada sitting on one side of me, Marx on the other. I got up and closed the door. Marx didn't seem to mind.

"What type of questions can I answer for you?" she asked after I returned to my seat.

"I'm afraid we got you here under false pretenses, Ms. Marx. We're not democratic donors. Truth be told, I could care less about politics. And my friend is not even from this country. She doesn't get to vote here."

She furrowed her brow, looking from Mirsada to me. "But you donated fifty-thousand dollars to attend this dinner. If you don't care for politics, then why—"

"To meet you, actually. We know you're the one who will tip off Cyrus Tyler when it's time to set off the bomb. We want you to tell us how you plan to do it. Phone call? Text? How?"

Her face went pale and her eyes fluttered so badly, I thought she might pass out.

"I don't have a clue what you're talking about. I would never—"

I slammed my hand down on the table, cutting her off and making her jump in her chair. "We know it's you, Janet. There's no use denying it. You have a choice: you can tell me what you know, or we can kill you here and now and end the threat. Up to you."

Her hand flew to her throat. "If you kill me, they will blow up the bomb anyway. It gains you nothing."

At least she was no longer denying her role in the plan. "We'd rather not kill you," Mirsada said. "But we will and take our chances. Answer the question."

Her eyes darted to the door, but Mirsada moved, blocking her way. Marx looked like a deer in the headlights, afraid to talk to us, afraid we'd kill her if she didn't.

Finally, she gave in. "I have a phone. I'm supposed to text "happy birthday" when Senator Stafford sits down with his guests."

"Are the President and Vice-President here yet?"

She shook her head. "They're running behind. They won't get here until closer to nine." Tears streamed down her face. "Are you going to kill me?"

I ignored the question. "Where's the phone?"

"In my purse, back in Stafford's spare bedroom."

"Here's what you're going to do. You're going to take us there and hand over the phone. If you so much as point a finger in our direction, then you are a dead woman. No matter what happens to us, we know who you are and we have people who will take you out. Do you understand?"

Again she nodded, ringing her hands. Mirsada opened her clutch and removed a tissue. She handed it to Marx. "Get yourself together, woman. You best introduce us as the huge donors we are pretending to be. And you'd best look the part. Stop crying, it's making your eyes look puffy."

Marx blew her nose in the tissue and steadied her breathing. She stood and I stood with her. She offered a wan smile, walked to the door and opened it when Mirsada stepped aside. We followed her out and she led us away from the ballroom, the fallen angel, and the other guests.

In a few minutes, I would be in the same room with a bomb big enough to blow up us and half the building. Nothing like ending the evening with a bang.

CHAPTER THIRTY-TWO

We stopped at a bank of elevators, with a security guard keeping watch. Marx told him we were with her and he used a key to open one of the elevators and we stepped inside. Marx pushed the button for the top floor and the doors shut with a whoosh.

Marx looked everywhere but at us while we rode to the top. I could only imagine what was going through her mind. Mirsada, for her part, seemed relaxed, almost happy. I think, like me, she loved the action, the adrenaline of getting it on with the bad guys. I knew the feeling.

The elevator came to a stop and the door slid open: open upon a scene from Hell. Marx started to scream, but I put a hand over her mouth, cutting it short. On the floor in front of us was another guard. He wore the same uniform the guard wore downstairs except his black uniform looked mostly red, smeared with his own blood. Someone had ripped out his throat. I knew this because it lay on the floor next to him. Blood covered one wall, where I could see the handprints of someone wiping off the blood from their hands.

The elevator door started to close and I blocked it open with my foot. The elevator opened onto a short hallway leading to a polished oak door. From here, I could see blood on the doorknob.

Mirsada quickly searched the dead man, finding his gun still in its holster. Whoever attacked him, caught him off-guard and killed him before he got the chance to react.

I turned to Marx and asked, "How many were up here when you left?"

Unable to speak, she lifted her hand and held up the number three, her hand shaking so bad I had to ask her to make sure. I snagged the leg of the dead guard and pulled him across the elevator threshold to block it open. I didn't want to hit the emergency button and set off the alarm.

I took Marx by the arm and stepped over the dead man, dragging her with me. She pulled back, trying to break my grip. Mirsada stepped up and clipped her hard on the chin, and the woman crumpled to the ground, dazed.

"We don't have time for this," she whispered. "Problem solved. Let's get moving."

She took the lead towards the door and I nearly laughed. I could get to really like this woman. I fell into step behind her and when we reached the door, she reached out and turned the knob, pushing the door open with her foot, gun at the ready. She had to be the best dressed shooter walking the planet. Donna Karen dress and a 9 millimeter. Quite the pairing.

The door opened onto a small entryway, with a coat closet on one side and a mirror on the other wall. We moved into the apartment and hadn't gone far when we found a man on the floor, his head bleeding from a blow to the back of the head. I knelt and felt a pulse, but a weak one.

We could hear a voice coming from up ahead and to the left. The entryway gave way to a living room, with a kitchen and dining room on one side and two other doors on the other. One door was open and I could see a huge bedroom, but the lights were off. I could hear sounds behind the other door and we quickly crossed the living room. I was about to open it when I heard a man's muffled scream.

I turned the knob and threw the door open. On the bed lay Senator Stafford, a strip of duct tape across his mouth, dressed only in an Oxford button down shirt and underwear, his hands tied to the head board, his feet tied to the baseboard. Well, one foot tied to the head board. The problem was that the other leg was no longer attached to the rest of his body, having been severed a few inches above the knee.

Elizabeth stood with a meat cleaver in her hand, blood dripping from the blade, wearing a black cocktail dress. She looked like a scene out of *American Psycho*. I could tell from the end of the Senator's leg, it had taken several hacks to cut it off.

Elizabeth tossed the cleaver onto the bed, dropped the leg into a carry bag on the floor, then picked up a belt and strapped it around the stump, pulling it tight, using it as a tourniquet. The senator shook back and forth, his muffled screams continuing.

"Bloody hell, Elizabeth, what have you done?"

"Do you always ask such obvious questions? This man had a bomb planted in his body. I removed it. I would think you would be happy, no?" She picked up the bag and wrapped the leg in plastic, then zipped the bag closed.

Mirsada entered the room, moving off to one side, the gun pointed squarely at Elizabeth. "This is a monster's solution. Not that of a normal person. Victor, if I get off a couple of quick shots, I might be able to blow her head off."

Elizabeth rolled her eyes. "Oh, please, child. If we do nothing, the man blows to pieces. Now, he may live. I pulled the belt tight, stop the bleeding. Better than what was going to happen. We must get moving before they use code and blow up the bomb. Besides, if you try and shoot me, I will have to kill you, too. And I don't want to do that. I've grown quite fond of you."

"You left us. Why? We were supposed to be a team."

"Victor, if I'd told you what I plan to do, remove this man's leg, would you have agreed? I think not. I knew what needed to be done."

"And the wraiths," Mirsada asked, "you left us behind with those creatures?"

"What are you talking about? What wraiths?"

The look of confusion seemed genuine, but at this point it was irrelevant. She was right about one thing, we could not stay here. "Ah, hell. Let's go. We will sort this out when we are away from here."

The last thing I needed was Mirsada and Elizabeth going toe-to-toe. With my luck, the moment they did, the bomb would go off, killing all three of us.

I covered the Senator with a blanket, hoping he didn't fall into shock and die, then we left the room. Mirsada went into the other bedroom, found Marx's purse, and came back with two phones, and we left the apartment. I lifted Marx to her feet and rubbed her cheeks until she came around long enough to tell me which phone she was to use to send the text. She pointed to an iPhone in a green case.

I turned the phone on and went to the text messages.

"Which one?"

Marx pointed to the third one down, a number with the Philly area code. She got a text saying "it's my birthday".

And all you do is type in "happy birthday"? That's it?"

She nodded yes, and I turned the phone off and slipped it into my pocket. "We need to call an ambulance for Stafford. Despite your poor man's tourniquet, the man will die if not treated soon." I turned to Marx. "Do you know this building well?"

"Yes. We spend a lot of time here, especially since the surgery." She finally noticed the bag Elizabeth carried. "What's in the bag?"

"A leg of Senator," Elizabeth said. "Not quite a leg of lamb, but what can you do?"

Her attempt at humor only made Marx slump against the wall, but I held her up by one arm. "Get yourself together. We need to get out of here, but not by the main floor. Which way?"

She led us to the elevator and nearly screamed again looking at the dead security guard. I dragged the body into the hallway and we got in the elevator. Marx frantically punched the button for the fifth floor.

The door closed, leaving the dead guard behind. I tried to keep my temper in check, but it was hard. "Did you have to kill the security guard? He was only doing his job."

Elizabeth pouted for a moment, but answered me. "He started to pull his gun. I reacted on instinct. It's hard to break centuries of bad habits overnight. I am sorry for his death."

I wasn't sure I believed her, but what could I do? The elevator opened on the fifth floor and we got out, Marx in the lead. This floor featured business offices, all darkened on a Saturday night.

"This floor connects with the building next door. There are guards at the other end, but I know them, so getting out won't be a problem."

We made it to the other doors and then through to stairways going up and down, but there was no guard. "That's strange," Marx said. "There's always a guard here."

"Always?" I asked. My spidey senses went off full blast and I shoved Elizabeth and Mirsada back inside. I was too late to save Marx, as a man wearing black fatigues leaned over the top railing and shot her with a quick burst from an automatic weapon, maybe a Heckler and Koch, but I didn't watch long enough to find out. The poor woman bounced against the stairwell, then fell down the next flight of stairs, dead before the first bounce.

"Gun!" I shouted to Mirsada, my hand outstretched. She tossed me the handgun, and I rolled next to the door in time to shoot the man coming down the steps. He fell next to the door, with two more guys right behind him. I fired off a couple of rounds, driving them to cover, reached over, snagged the dead guy and managed to drag him into the hallway with us. Bullets slammed into the door frame, shredding it in a matter of seconds.

Mirsada unslung the machine gun from around the guy's neck, while Elizabeth searched him for other weapons. When the shooting paused, I stuck my hand around the corner and emptied the clip. Mirsada then traded places with me and we waited. A moment later I heard the sound of metal hitting the ground and looked around the corner in time to see a grenade thrown in our direction. I didn't even think, but caught it and flung it back up and over the railing.

I started to shout grenade, but it was too late. I'd managed to turn my head when the grenade went off, but the flash was intense, the sound even louder in the enclosed space. I could hear Elizabeth scream. With hearing as fine-tuned as hers, I could only imagine how much pain it caused her. My own ears rang and you could have shouted in my ear from a foot away and I wouldn't have heard a thing.

Most flash bangs are set to a bit over a second. The fact I still had all ten fingers thrilled me to no end. Mirsada had dropped her weapon and lay on the ground, hands over her ears, curled up in a little ball.

I picked up the Heckler and Koch and bounded up the steps. One of the two men started to get up and I shot him with a quick three shot burst, sending him back down. I didn't bother on the other one. When I tossed the grenade over the railing, it must have gone off right in front of his face, ripping off his nose and turning the rest of his face to pulp. Uggh.

I hurried back to Mirsada and Elizabeth, got them on their feet and headed down the steps, saying a quick prayer for Marx. All the gunfire and the blast would bring people running soon enough and we needed to be far away when they did.

When we got to the last landing, I laid the guns on the floor and we hit the bottom at a fast walk, Elizabeth still carrying the bag. The stairwell emptied into a parking garage. We made our way quickly to the other side, then out onto the sidewalk full of people staring up the street.

There were blue lights galore in front of the Founders Building. Guess we didn't need to make a call about the Senator. The three of us crossed the street and into the park where even the Tea Party folks were no longer screaming and waving signs, but watching the unfolding scene across the street.

I texted Winston, asking where our friends were. He responded with "still on the stage." I asked him to meet us at the Tomb of the Unknown Revolutionary War Soldier. Five minutes later, Winston, Elizabeth, Mirsada and I were huddled together and I made the round of introductions and filled Winston in on what happened, including Gadriel running around in Alex Dabney's body. Kurt and his laptop were holed up in a car a few blocks away, keeping track of things in cyber space.

"Damn. This is one screwed up evening." Looking at Elizabeth and her bag, Winston asked, "And you have what I think you have in that thing? If so, we need to get rid of it and soon. What if they decide to set the bomb off?"

We all agreed, but before we could decide what to do, a man on the stage shouted into a microphone, asking for everyone's attention.

"Tonight, there has been an attack on Senator Stafford." Half the crowd cheered and the man shouted them down. "Stop that! We don't condone violence of any kind. Senator Stafford has been rushed to the hospital and we all pray for his steady recovery."

Amen to that brother. I turned to say something to Elizabeth, but she was gone. I searched the crowd, but didn't see her.

Bloody hell. She'd taken the bomb with her.

CHAPTER THIRTY-THREE

Cyrus Tyler made sure to keep a look of great concern on his face, while at the same being filled with rage on the inside. Months of careful planning blown. With any luck, the President and VP would visit Stafford in the hospital and he could still pull it off, but he knew that was a pipe dream. Word reached him that Deloris came back to the room to find Stafford had been assaulted, but that's all he knew.

Tyler walked off the stage and over to a younger man waiting for him. "Randy, let's get out of here. I want to get to the airport and back to D.C. as soon as possible."

"Yes, sir."

The two men walked to a VIP lot and waited for the valet to bring his car around. When the car pulled up, Randy opened the door and Tyler got into the backseat. Before he could close the door, a woman stepped up to the car, stopping him from closing the door.

She stuck her head in the door. "Congressman Tyler, Preston Deveraux said if anything happened to him, I should find you."

Tyler thought for a second. "It's o.k. Randy. She can join me."

"Are you headed to the airport?" she asked.

"Yes. And you?"

"The same. Thanks." She tossed her bag to Randy. "Mind putting that in the trunk?"

Randy stepped out of the way and the woman slid onto the seat opposite him. Randy popped the trunk, tossed her bag in next to Tyler's bags, slammed the lid shut, got back behind the wheel and eased the town car out of the parking lot and onto south Sixth Street.

The woman wore a black dress which showed off her body to the max. When she crossed her legs, one foot brushed against his calf, lingering a second longer than would be normal. Twenty years ago, her flirting might have paid off dividends. Not now.

"Alright, young lady. You have my attention. Why did Preston Deveraux send you to me? Do you know who murdered him?"

"I do. It was Victor McCain. You may have heard of him. I warned

Preston McCain was in town, but he didn't take the proper precautions and it got him killed. McCain will come for you next."

"Sweetheart, McCain is in over his head. He should have died the other night, but he was rescued by—"

The woman smiled at him, waiting, and for the first time in years, Tyler felt fear. Real fear. He looked at the woman more closely, noticing a hint of red on the inside of her wrist. Blood.

She followed his gaze and when she saw the blood, she brought her wrist to her mouth and licked the blood away.

"Sorry. Seems I missed a spot."

"Elizabeth Bathory, I presume? Do you plan to kill me?"

"Heavens, no." She waved a hand, dismissing the thought. "Why would I want to kill you when you do such a great job of creating chaos in the world? I feed off chaos."

"We'd been told you were off the reservation, trying to switch to the other side."

"That's what I wanted people to think, so I could get in close to them, learn what they were thinking. I went undercover, something I did often for my former employers in Hungary."

Tyler sat thinking. If anyone else told him such a story, he would dismiss it out of hand and arrange for such a person to die a slow agonizing death. But when it came to an Infernal Lord, he was not always told what they were doing.

He needed more information.

"Stafford. Do you know what happened?"

"From what I can understand, when McCain showed up at the fundraiser, he found out Alex Dabney was possessed by a fallen angel. The two nearly came to blows in the middle of the ballroom and when McCain and another woman went to see Stafford, Dabney sent men after them, trying to take them out. Stafford was injured during the confrontation."

"And McCain? What happened to him and the woman?"

"I honestly don't know. I tried to get upstairs to see if I could take out McCain myself, but they were involved in a firefight, so I left, waiting in the park. I saw you and here we are."

Tyler relaxed a bit. He didn't feel any immediate threat from Bathory and he felt confident in his ability to read people.

"I want a full debriefing. I want you to tell me everything you learned in your time spent with McCain, his weaknesses, strengths, anything you can which will help me kill him once and for all."

Bathory stared out the window for a moment, then tapped on the glass between the passenger compartment and the driver. He rolled the window down. "Yes ma'am?"

"Would you pull over, please?"

He did as she asked, pulling to the curb a block before the entrance to the interstate. She then motioned for him to raise the glass back up, and he complied.

Tyler, back on edge, asked, "What's the meaning of this? I thought you said you were going to the airport?"

"The more I think about it, the more I think I don't want to be around you at the moment. McCain and his forces are going to come for you and I don't want to be near you when they do. If you survive the next few days, I will be in touch and tell you what you want to know. The Lord of Light will be very displeased your plan to blow up the President and VP failed. I think I will wait to see what happens."

She opened the door and stepped out of the car, but leaned in for a last word. "There are times when we all think we are indestructible. And we all find out we are wrong. Be careful, Cyrus Tyler, or you will find this out yourself, sooner than you think."

She shut the door and tapped on the passenger window. When Randy rolled it down, she asked him to pop the trunk so she could get her bag. He complied and the woman walked to the trunk, taking out her bag, then closing the lid.

She stepped to the curb, holding the bag and Randy merged into traffic, then onto I-95 to the airport. Tyler stared out the window watching the city flash by, but not really seeing, his thoughts turned inward, thinking about what Bathory had to say.

They were half way to the airport when his blood ran cold. The bag. He pressed the intercom button. "Randy! Pull over! Pull—"

~*~

Elizabeth removed the green iPhone she stole from Victor, flipped over to text messages, selected the third one down and typed in "happy birthday."

She tossed the phone and empty bag into a garbage can and walked down the sidewalk singing *I Feel Pretty,* until she disappeared into the night.

~*~

I sent Winston to hook up with Kurt, while Mirsada, and I left the park. I called the driver, telling him we wouldn't need him as we'd walk to the hotel. We were almost there when a huge explosion rocked the night. A fireball rose high into the air, but because of the buildings surrounding us, we couldn't see where it came from.

Mirsada turned to me. "Oh my God. Victor. The phone!" I frantically checked my pockets, but the phone was gone. I looked at her and shook my head.

"It has to be her. Has to be. But where did she set it off?"

We hustled to our room and turned on the TV, horrified at what we saw. A large section of an I-95 overpass simply ceased to exist when a car bomb went off, turning the road to rubble. At least half a dozen cars were on fire or completely destroyed, having fallen into the street below. The TV talking heads were calling it an act of terrorism.

They said the attacks on Stafford and now the car bomb had to be related and authorities were treating them as such. I said aloud to myself, "No shit, Sherlock."

They reported Stafford was in surgery, after suffering a major attack in his own home. At least six were dead at the Founders Building and adjacent property. Unnamed sources were reporting several para-military soldiers among the dead as well as a member of Stafford's staff, last seen giving a tour to a pair of wealthy donors who were also missing.

When we saw this, the two of us quickly packed, went down to the valet, got the car and left. We called Winston and Kurt and arranged to meet them outside of Harrisburg, Pennsylvania. If the authorities tracked down our IDs they would find them to be bogus. Kurt said he would take care of changing the photos attached to the IDs to keep our pictures off the TV.

We kept the car radio on the news channels on XM radio, trying to learn what the main target had been. We'd been on the road about a half hour when word came the car may have been that of Speaker of the House Cyrus Tyler. The Speaker left the park not long before the explosion and had not been heard from since. Shortly thereafter, a smartphone video surfaced of Tyler getting into his car with a woman. Mirsada went to CNN.com and checked out the video. It was Elizabeth. It also showed a young man putting a bag into the trunk, then getting into the car and driving off. Elizabeth's bag.

Speculation was rampant as to the identity of the woman leaving with the Speaker of the House, but to this point she was a mystery.

"Victor, do you think she blew herself up? Would she do such a thing?"

"I have no clue. From what I could tell, she was very self-absorbed. I find it hard to believe she would commit suicide. But maybe she thought this would get her into Heaven, taking out the top leadership of the Church."

Before I could say anything else, my phone rang. I didn't recognize the number, but assumed it was Elizabeth. I answered and my world fell away.

"Vic. This is Samantha. Where are you? My father, did you kill my father? Please tell me this wasn't you."

Samantha Tyler practically yelled her questions into the phone. Having lost her mother at a young age, Cy Tyler was the only family she had left in the world. The fact he was a scumbag murdering son of a bitch, made little difference. Samantha held out hope she could one day change her father's path. We both knew it was a false hope. But now that chance was forever gone.

"Samantha, you have to listen to me. Your father—"

"Don't you dare. Don't you even dare. You did it, didn't you? You're in Philly. And don't lie to me. You owe me the truth." The pain in her voice cut me to the core. And she was right. I did owe her the truth.

"Not directly. No. But I've been working with the person who did. The person who did this did so without my knowledge, but Samantha, he deserved it. He created the instrument of his own death. I wish I could tell you I was sorry, but I'm not. You don't know what your father had planned."

"It wasn't for you to judge." I could hear her crying.

"It is for me to judge. Your father chose his path, just like Mikey. Now he will live in Hell with the consequences for the rest of eternity."

She didn't say anything else. Not a word. The phone line went dead. I stared at it for a moment, then called Winston, telling him we needed to scrub it, and hung up. I rolled down my window and threw the phone out into the darkness. He would be doing the same thing. We wouldn't take any chances the government could filter our phone messages and find us. With an attack on the Speaker of the House, the Feds would be cranked up and while I was supposed to be immune to prosecution, I didn't want to push it.

Mirsada laid a hand on my shoulder. "Do you want to talk about it?"

I didn't. I really didn't. But over the next hour and a half, I talked about Samantha, how much I loved her and why we would never work out. I'd hurt her too much, allowed others to hurt her. I rambled on and Mirsada let me. She never interrupted, or belittled what I said.

When we approached the Harrisburg exit, she took my hand in hers and squeezed. "You are a good man, Victor McCain, but I have no words of comfort. You and I lead a hard life. One which will end in violence for both of us. We cannot make everything right, but we can make a difference. Honor her with how you live your life."

I got off at our exit and I found a dark spot and changed the license plate on my car. The hotel would have made a note of the old one and I kept several in the hidden compartment for such emergencies.

We met Winston and Kurt at a Holiday Inn Express and we checked in. We agreed to meet for breakfast the next morning before getting back on the road to Louisville. They went up to their rooms and I started to follow them, but paused to glance into the bar. I'd never needed a drink more than right at that very moment. It called out to me, whispering my name. A line from a Robert Frost poem came to mind:

The woods are lovely dark and deep,
But I have promises to keep,
And miles to go before I sleep,
And mile to go before I sleep.

I did have promises to keep. And I wouldn't be able to do them if I turned to a bottle every time life punched me in the face, since that seemed to be a near daily occurrence. I sighed, took the elevator up to my floor, found my room and collapsed on the bed, asleep in minutes. And like the night I murdered my brother, I did not dream.

CHAPTER THIRTY-FOUR

Breakfast was a solemn affair. Death totals for the bomb damage sat at nine, including four members of the same family whose minivan had been in the lane next to that of Speaker Tyler at the moment of the explosion. Injuries counted in the dozens. Elizabeth Bathory may have killed the deadliest man in the world, but she also robbed many innocent people of all they would ever be. If she was alive, she had not contacted me and the authorities said it could take weeks before DNA analysis could prove if she was still in the car when the bomb went off.

The ride to Louisville passed in a haze. Mirsada and I hardly spoke. I think she knew I needed time to think about what had happened. It took us nearly nine hours to get home and I couldn't tell you one thing about the trip. One moment we were on the road, the next we were at the Derby Mission.

Winston and Kurt went home while Mirsada and I went straight to J's office. Mirsada and I took turns filling in J on the events in Philadelphia. He listened, only interrupting to ask questions clarifying something we said. When we were through he steepled his fingers, pressing them against this lips and we waited for him to speak.

"It shouldn't take them long to find out if Bathory was in the car. There is no point on speculating any further until we hear one way or the other. As for Cyrus Tyler, he is now paying the ultimate price for selling his soul. With his death, along with that of Deveraux and your brother, Victor, this will leave a power vacuum at the top. I am curious to see how this affects the Satanist church. One school of thought is cut off the head of a snake and kill the snake. But this is more of a hydra than a snake. Cut off one, and perhaps several more grow in its place."

"Aren't you a ray of sunshine? Thanks, J. What a real pick me up this conversation is turning out to be."

To Mirsada, I asked, "You came to this country to hunt down and kill Elizabeth Bathory. Will you hang around until you find out if she's really dead?"

She shook her head. "I don't think so. I can always return. I think there is no doubt she tried to do the right thing, but being the creature that she is, she could not find it in herself to do it the right way. She murdered those other people when she set off the bomb. I am torn about what to do where she is concerned, and for people like you and me, such indecision leads to an early grave. The way I see it, as long as she stays in America, she is your problem."

"And the gifts keep on coming." I managed a smile. "Thank you, Mirsada, for all you've done. I wish you the best of luck back home."

"They need me there. We have evil much older than what you normally deal with here in the States." She stood and we embraced. At least this time she didn't threaten to run me through with a sword like our last meeting in this room.

She asked, "You're sure you don't need me to help with the fallen angel?"

We discussed it briefly on the trip home and she'd offered to stay. "Nah. Besides, keeping the two of us in the same place makes it easier to take us both out at the same time. I'll rest up a day or two and then come up with a plan to take him out."

"Then be well, Victor McCain. Good hunting."

She left to go to her room at the mission and to arrange her flight home. Lisa, J's assistant, would then take her to the airport.

"Samantha called me to get your cell phone number," J. said. "I assume she called?"

"Yeah, and as you can imagine, it didn't go well. She blames me for her father's death. I don't know if I will ever hear from her again."

Deep in my heart, I knew this to be true, but saying it out loud drove the dagger home. I did my best to push the thoughts of Samantha into a dark corner, and lock them away. Time would tell if they would stay there.

I left the office, went out to my car and drove to Molly Malone's. I found my regular table and the waitress brought me a Guinness. I spun the bottle around a few times, took a sip and set it to the side. I would nurse it through dinner. Time to institute a one drink minimum.

I was watching the news about the bombing on a TV over the bar when the door opened and Brad Stiles walked in, glanced around until he found me, then walked in my direction.

I reached behind me and found the grip of my gun, pulled it out and held it on the seat next to me.

He approached my table, hands out, showing me he didn't have anything in his hands. I motioned for him to lift his jacket. He did and turned around, lifting it up in the back, showing me he was unarmed.

I motioned for him sit on the other side of the booth and he sat down heavily, keeping both hands on the table where I could see them. I waved to the waitress and she brought him a Guinness as well. He thanked her, took a long pull on the beer, then set the bottle down.

"You used me to kill Tyler, didn't you?"

"What? No small talk? No foreplay? You cut right to the chase? You're no fun."

"Well, it's been a rough last twenty-four hours. My gravy train is now in a million different pieces. Kind of kills the mood, pun intended."

"I know what you mean. But to answer your question: no. It wasn't me."

He nodded. "The woman getting into the car with Tyler was Elizabeth Bathory, wasn't it?"

I tipped my bottle in his direction, taking another sip of mine. The man seemed to have aged ten years and his suit looked as if he'd slept in it overnight. Good bet he had.

"Will they come after you?" I asked.

"I doubt it. The only one, as far as I know, who knew I was involved, was Tyler. You know, I warned them, Tyler and Deveraux, Bathory would be a problem when she found out about Isaac. She really had a thing for the guy. Out of all the men she ever met over the last few hundred years, she falls for a braniac. Go figure."

The last thing I wanted to discuss was Elizabeth's love life. "Why are you here, Stiles? Nothing personal, but the last time you and I talked, you'd hired a guy to peel the skin from my body. Doesn't make you one of my favorite people."

"You and I both know that was just business. They hired me to do a job, and I did it. That's one of the reasons I came here. I wanted to make sure you and I were square. I don't want to spend the rest of my life looking over my shoulder wondering when you're going to show up. Thought we could come to an agreement. A truce. I agree to never come after you, you agree to never come after me."

"I'm not sure I can make that promise. You work for some pretty bad dudes. You stay on their payroll, then I'll have to take you down."

He lifted his hands in defense. "No worries on that score. I think it's time for me to retire from the merc business. I have a buddy in D.C. who's offered me a job with a security company. I told him I'd take the job, asked for a week before I started. I wanted to see you first."

I thought about it for a moment, then did what I always do: trusted my gut. I stuck out my hand and he took it. He drained the last of his Guinness, set the bottle back on the table and stood.

"You said make sure we were square was one of the reasons you came. There's another?"

"Yes. I wanted to tell you, there's a contract out on you. I got the word from an associate. Wanted to know if I'd be interested in accepting the job. I told him no, I wouldn't."

"How much money?"

"Ten million dollars. Cash."

I whistled. "Wow. Thanks for the heads up, but as the Hand of God, there is no shortage of people who want me dead."

"Yeah, but for that kind of money, it will bring out the weirdoes and professionals alike. You need to watch your ass."

"My thanks. Anything else?"

He took a card out of his inner suit pocket and tossed it on the table. "As a gesture of good faith, I thought you might want to visit this address this coming weekend. A man and woman will be there on vacation. I hear they took you on a boat ride. Thought you might want to pay them a visit."

"Payback's a bitch. If I find out you're setting me up..."

"No, no. You'll find out I'm not. Take friends. These two are worse than a den of rattlers."

He offered a small wave, then left. I pulled the card to me, and read the address, a street somewhere around Lake Tahoe.

The waitress brought over my shepherd's pie and while I ate, I thought to myself, "Road trip."

CHAPTER THIRTY-FIVE

Eduardo drove the convertible down the winding road above Lake Tahoe. With the convertible top lowered, they watched the sun dip behind the mountains while taking in the fresh evening air.

Donut removed the scrunchie keeping her pony tail together, allowing her long black hair to blow in the wind. They were enjoying a bit of down time while trying to decide what job to take next.

Like everyone else, they were shocked at the level of destruction which took place in Philadelphia and were glad to be well removed from the East Coast.

Tonight, they ate at a little hole in the wall Italian place in town, then saw a movie. Even assassins needed time to recharge their batteries. Donut changed CDs, punched a button or two, and then they were listening to the new Darius Rucker album. Donut was on a country kick and Eduardo knew to go with the flow.

They rounded a curve and Eduardo locked up the Mercedes, skidding to a stop, and trying to keep from crashing into two other cars stopped in the middle of the road. He saw two men arguing with each other and could hear bits and pieces of the conversation, with one blaming the accident on the other.

Donut rolled her eyes and muttered under her breath. Eduardo got out of the car, making his way over to the two men.

"You guys need any help? If you don't get these cars out of the way, you're going to get someone killed."

One of the men, a large black man, said, "This MoFo done dented my ride, man. He can't drive for shit."

The other man, with sandy brown hair and a nice California tan, said, "Dude. You're the one who crossed the line and hit me."

Eduardo stepped past them, looking at the two cars. "I don't see any damage. What's the big—" He never got out another word. The black man jabbed the syringe into his neck, pressing the plunger down. Eduardo reacted instantly, launching into an attack, but it only took a second for him to feel his knees buckle and then pitch forward onto the blacktop.

548

Donut, who'd been watching the sun reflect on the lake as it set when they attacked Eduardo, started to slide over into the driver's seat when a man stepped up beside the car and pressed a gun barrel to the back of her head.

"I would place both hands on the steering wheel. Now, if you please."

She did as the man asked. "You're the man from the boat. The one they had us take to Philadelphia, aren't you?"

"That would be me. I hope you don't mind, but I'm going to take the donuts you have in the back seat. I do love me some Krispy Kremes."

She thought furiously about what to do, then felt a needle stick her in the side of the neck. The man said, "I thought I would return the favor. This is for Dr. Collins and her daughter."

Her last thought, before blackness overcame her, was "I hope they got the dosage right."

She was dead before she finished the thought.

EPILOGUE

I got home from Tahoe feeling better than I'd felt since becoming the Hand of God. Maybe it was the fresh air of Lake Tahoe. Perhaps it was avenging the deaths of Dr. Collins and her daughter. I had no clue. Maybe I had begun to come to grips with the emotional state of my love life, or lack thereof. Who knows?

While we were gone the investigation into the bombing continued in Philadelphia. Forensics found DNA of three people in Tyler's car: his, his driver and Senator Hedley Stafford, but not the woman seen on the video getting into the car.

This meshed with the story Stafford told authorities following his brush with death. The EMTs got him to the hospital in time to save his life—though he died twice on the table before being stabilized. He told the police a woman knocked on his door, assaulted one of his staffers, and then forced him into the bedroom where she tied him up and then cut off his leg.

She told him his knee replacement contained a bomb and she intended to save his life. He thought she was nuts until the news about his DNA was found in the bomb debris. He also confirmed the bag she was seen walking to Tyler's car with was similar to the one she brought with her to his apartment.

The explosives used in the attack were traced to Dabney Industrial Technologies. They'd reported a theft of explosives to the A.T.F. some weeks prior to the events in Philadelphia. Alex Dabney promised to cooperate fully with the investigation and offered a twenty-million dollar reward to anyone who helped to identify the people involved.

A white supremacist group in Alabama claimed responsibility for the attack on Stafford, but nothing could be proven at this time.

I knew the truth, of course. I was happy Elizabeth hadn't died when the bomb went off, but I wasn't sure I should be. Being an Infernal Lord still meant it would be tough for her to make it to Heaven, but I believed she deserved the chance.

I got a cab from the airport and rolled into the Derby Mission in the early afternoon. I dropped my gear in my room and contemplated where I wanted to have lunch when the phone rang.

I picked it up and offered a very upbeat, "Hello."

"Victor, this is your mother. I need you to come over here, right now."

Her voice dripped with tension. "What's wrong mom? Are you feeling alright?"

My mom was closing in on her mid-sixties and, all in all, was in good health. But I worried about her living alone with dad gone.

"I'm fine. Victor, there are some police detectives here. They want to talk to you. Can you come now? Please?"

"Sure mom, I'm on my way."

I sat the phone back on the charger and thought for a moment. Brother Joshua told me the police wouldn't bother me for as long as I was the Hand of God. Why would they want to talk to me?

I went out to the car, hopped in and drove to mom's house. She lived in a small home in Anchorage, about a twenty minute drive from downtown Louisville.

I pulled into the driveway and parked next to a Ford Crown Vic. It seemed every police department in the world used Crown Vics.

I went inside and found my mother on the couch in the living room with a man and woman sitting on a love seat across from her. They both wore suits, and hers fit better than his. They stood up and the woman did the introductions.

"Victor McCain? I'm Detective Linda Coffey. This is my partner, Detective Sam Wallace. We'd like to ask you a few questions about your brother, Michael McCain."

Coffey, a woman of average height, with brown hair cut short and brown eyes, offered her hand and I shook it. Wallace didn't offer, and I guessed he must be bad cop, with a Marine buzz cut with white wall sides, and a gut which strained the buttons of his shirt. He opted for the cop glare.

My mother, a petite woman with hair gone gray, and smile lines around her eyes, gave me a hug and a kiss when I sat down next to her. She'd placed a tray of cookies on the table between her and the cops. They'd not partaken of any of them, but I grabbed two and started munching.

Around a mouthful of cookies, I asked, "What's this about Mikey?" I wondered if someone had found his body. I thought this unlikely, since I tossed it down a sinkhole in Eastern Kentucky.

"When was the last time you saw your brother," asked Detective Coffey.

"Hell, I haven't seen Mikey since last November, when his warehouse burned to the ground. Why are you asking? What's he done?"

Detective Wallace said, "If you know where he is and don't tell us, you know that's obstruction of justice, right? We can have your bounty hunter's license yanked."

"Well, golly gee Officer Krumpke, I ain't seen nothin'. I swear."

My mother slapped me on the arm. "Victor Riley McCain, you behave. Show Detective Wallace some respect."

I started to point out to my mother that Wallace started it, but Detective Coffey jumped in. "We're not accusing you of anything. We just need to find your brother and would appreciate your help."

"You still haven't told me why?"

"Do you recognize the names Ron Fisher and Gloria Small?"

I thought for a moment. I didn't recognize the last names, but I did the first. "I'm not sure. My brother employed two security guards at his warehouse who were named Ron and Gloria. Are you talking about them?"

"Yes. We are. Did you know them at all?"

"No. I only met them once when Mikey gave me a tour of the warehouse. What about them?"

"They're dead. Murdered," Wallace said.

"I'm sorry," I said, confused. "You think Mikey killed them? When were they killed?"

"Three days ago," Coffey replied

"How were they killed?"

"He broke both their necks. Each were found at home, with their necks nearly snapped in two," Wallace said.

My mother covered her mouth with her hands, and I put my arm around her. "Look, Detectives, there's no way my brother did this."

"Oh, and why not?" asked Wallace.

I wanted to say because I killed him and dumped his body nearly a year ago. But I decided that wasn't a good response.

"Detectives, there are Smurf's bigger than my brother. Hell, there are Yorkshire Terriers bigger than my brother. My brother couldn't snap a cannoli in half, let alone someone's neck. You're barking up the wrong tree here. Sorry, but you have to be wrong."

"I'm afraid not," said Coffey. "He left fingerprints on their necks from where he squeezed them to death."

I sat, stunned. This couldn't be. Mikey was dead. I killed him. I watched the light fade from his eyes. There was no way he was alive. Unless...

"Are you o.k., Mr. McCain?" asked Detective Coffey.

"He's o.k. Linda, he's finally realizing his brother is a murderer," sneered Wallace.

I got control of my emotions and resisted the urge to grab Wallace by the side of the head and drive my knee through his face.

I stood and so did they. "I'm sorry detectives, but neither my mother nor I know where Mikey is hiding out. We haven't seen him or spoken to him since last November."

Detective Coffey took out a business card and gave it to me. "If you hear from him, call us right away. It's best for him if we bring him in peacefully. We don't want him to get hurt."

I showed them to the door, then shut it behind them. I watched from a front window until I was sure they were gone.

Mom joined me and I hugged her.

"Do you think Mikey really killed those people, Victor?" She spoke quietly, afraid to hear my answer.

"I don't know mom. But I will find out."

I kissed her on the forehead, then left. I called Winston, who came in on the flight before mine.

"Listen, I need you to take a trip with me. Do you have any climbing gear?" I asked.

"Yeah. I do. We going climbing? I've had enough mountains after Tahoe."

"Just get the gear ready. I'm on my way over to pick you up."

I nearly flew to Winston's house and he was waiting in the driveway. When I pulled in, he tossed the gear in the back and got in on the passenger side.

I told him what the cops said and he listened, then reached the same conclusion I did.

"You don't think—"

"That's what you and I are going to find out."

We drove to the mountains of Eastern Kentucky. I parked in the same spot I'd parked in the previous year when I hiked over the mountain to kill my brother. The two of us followed the same trail until we came to the sinkhole, out in the middle of nowhere.

Winston tied off a long length of rope, knotted every three feet, to a large maple tree, and then tossed the loose end down and into the sinkhole.

"You want me to go down?" he asked.

"No. I have to see for myself."

I strapped on a miner's hat, and turned on the light. I grabbed hold of the rope, then started over the side, going down hand over hand. The sinkhole ended up being about thirty feet deep. When I got to the bottom, it didn't take long to look around. No Mikey. The bottom, covered in piles of leaves, broken sticks and the bodies of a few dead animals, showed signs of someone having walked around.

I used the light from my helmet to check around the walls. On one of them, I could see deep gouges where someone had dug deep into the dirt, finding hand holds and toe holds. They went straight up to the top of the sinkhole.

I could feel my breathing coming in quick, short breaths and my head swam with the consequences of what I was seeing, or in this case, not seeing.

Winston looked down from up above. "Is he down there?"

It took a moment before I could reply. "No. He's gone."

I took hold of the rope and struggled to the top. Winston offered me his hand, and helped pull me up the last few feet.

We stood for a moment, staring at each other.

"You know what this means, right?" he asked.

I nodded, but was unable to find my voice.

Bloody hell. My brother was an Infernal Lord. Killing Muramasa opened up a spot and Satan gave it to my brother. Mikey was back and he finally had what he'd always dreamed of: power, strength and immortality.

And I knew what he would want next.

Payback.

I looked for the last time down into the sinkhole where my brother should have stayed until his bones turned to dust, my light only penetrating so far into the darkness. By murdering the two guards in such a blatant fashion, he knew I would find out. Mikey was sending me a message.

The McCain boys were going to have a reunion. And this time, he planned to be the one tossing bodies down a sinkhole.

It was Cain and Abel all over again. More like the Brothers Grimm. At the end of this story, only one McCain brother would be left standing. The question being, which one?

On the drive back to Louisville, a quote I once read by Marlon Brando popped into my head. "If we are not our brother's keeper, at least let us not be his executioner."

Too late, Marlon. I killed him once and I would do it again. This time, permanently.

About the Author

Tony Acree was born in La Grange, Kentucky in January 1963. His short story fiction has appeared in *Kentucky Monthly Magazine*. He has written articles about his time as a stay at home dad for a women's magazine as well as sports and information articles. His work has also appeared in *The Cumberland*, the Kentucky state wide newspaper outlet of the Sierra Club. He is a member of the Green River Writers as well as The Bluegrass Writers Edge, a creative writers group in Goshen, Kentucky, where he lives with his wife and twin daughters. Visit his website at Tonyacree.com. You can find him on Twitter and Facebook. You can email him at Tonyacree@Gmail.com.

www.ingramcontent.com/pod-product-compliance
Lightning Source LLC
Chambersburg PA
CBHW051054030726
47504CB00006B/1629